Rys Rising

by

Tracy Falbe

Rys Rising: Book I
Copyright Tracy Falbe, all rights reserved
First published 2011 by Brave Luck Books ™ an imprint and
trademark of Falbe Publishing.
ISBN 978-0-9762235-7-3

To contact Tracy Falbe, please visit her website at www.braveluck.com.

Cover image copyright Mates Laurentiu, Lead Artist, Deific Design.

Dedication

This one is for me.

Other fantasy novels by Tracy Falbe

Rys Rising series
Rys Rising: Book I
Savage Storm: Book II
New Religion: Book III
Love Lost: Book IV

The Rys Chronicles series
Union of Renegades: Book I
The Goddess Queen: Book II
Judgment Rising: Book III
The Borderlands of Power: Book IV

Find all novels in multiple formats at www.braveluck.com.

Map of Gyhwen

Nufal

Tracy Falbe

Eastern Pass

Jingten

Lake Nin

Gamuvet Glacier

Jingten Valley

The Rysamand Mts.

Jingten Pass

Lin Tohs Domain

Hekanau Domain

Tutter-Shen River

Dajendarli

Patharki Domain

Dengar Nor

Hjin Lam River

Eferzen Springs

Sady River

Temulanka Domain

Do Jempur

Kelsur River

Nurati Domain

Telop

Tacolucus Domain

Daler's Hill

Chadenedra

Sabar'Uto River

Sabar'Uto Domain

Kelsur Wilds

Lake Elyn

N

Map of Nufal

Tracy Falbe

Drathatarlane

Kvelnjeran

Alicharaf

Lake Kwellstan

Kwellstan

Ring Road

Tabren Mts.

Smet River

Budjip

Kahtep

Bigalia

Hedenar

Upella

NUFAL

Willow Spring

Eastern Pass

Jingten

Galnuvet Glacier

Lake Nin

Jingten Valley

The Rysamand Mts.

Jingten Pass

N

"When I'm near you I feel that I own the world," he whispered. His words chilled her with excitement. To know that she could inspire such passion encouraged her greatly.

Table of Contents

1. Mountain Daughter

The strong are strong for a reason, usually not a good one. ~ saying of the Patharki Tribe

Gendahl laughed as Hin Lol teased Medu about riding into a low tree branch and falling off his horse during the boar hunt. Medu was taking the teasing well, even knowing that his blunder would be exaggerated when retold at that night's banquet.

The dangerous boar had led them all on a merry hunt. Gendahl and his dear companions had tracked it through the Espen Forest for three days, beneath the leafy canopy of patch-worked greens that crowned the ancient trees. After hitting many dead ends, they had joked that the hefty boar had magic with which to elude them. Then, late yesterday afternoon, Gendahl and his warriors had cornered the boar in a canyon, and the tasty animal had ceased to possess the craft to avoid their spears. Gendahl and Hin Lol had thrust the killing blows, skewering the beast from both sides. They had slain the boar beside a dead oak tree, whose bulky skeleton stood with its bare gray branches spreading against a bright blue sky. Tiny green sproutlings and saplings populated the sunlit circle around the dead tree, and, from a perch in the brittle treetop, a gold-feathered eagle had watched the boar die with an interested gaze.

Gendahl looked forward to celebrating that night with his fellow hunters who were as close to him as the brothers he had never had. These warriors were his Infoh, sworn bodyguards to the Lord of the Lin Tohs Tribe. They came from families that had served Lin Tohs leaders for the eight generations since Gendahl's illustrious forefather, Axerpen, had founded the tribe.

It would be tomorrow before the roasting fires transformed the boar into a splendid main course. Then Gendahl would feast with his entire household, indulging in the joys of hearth and home. There would be meat and drink, his baby son to brag about, and his fine wife to bed as he pleased. When these luxuries grew boring, he and his Infoh would arrange another amusing adventure in their remote realm.

Gendahl switched the reins of his mount back and forth in his hands as he shrugged out of his leather jacket. This was the first year that the blue-dyed bull skin jacket had fit him with perfect comfort. Three years ago his late father had given him the jacket as a present for his manhood year, and it had taken that long for the leather to mold itself over Gendahl's well-muscled shoulders and firm chest that had all the lean strength of youth without the bulk of later manhood.

Gendahl handed the jacket to his nearest servant, who spread it carefully across his lap as he rode. Gendahl shook out his loosely woven red linen shirt that was clinging to his sweaty bronze skin. He had emerged from the forest into the outlying pastures of his domain, and the noon-time summer sun pressed down bright and hot.

Riding at the fore of his sprawling hunting party, Gendahl was the first to see the horizon scarred by columns of smoke. An unconscious tug on the reins slowed his horse.

"No," Gendahl whispered like a little prayer to Jayshem that he knew could not be answered. The smoke came from exactly where his fortress, Do Tohsall, stood.

His Infoh began to shout. "My Lord!" "Lord Gendahl." "Curse them. It must be the Patharki!"

Gendahl grasped the hilt of his sword and called for his armor. His body servants jumped from their mounts and ran to the pack horses to grab his helmet and body armor.

Medu and Hin Lol stopped their horses alongside Gendahl. Almost in unison, each man drew his copper-trimmed bronze helmet over his head.

Hin Lol said, "My Lord, Den will be holding the walls. We can strike our attackers at their backs."

Medu added, "We can rouse villagers to the defense between here and Do Tohsall."

Their voices came to Gendahl's ears like the whispers of concerned relatives talking in the next room about his incurable disease. Already he felt as if his heart had been ripped from his chest and icy water poured in the hole. The rising smoke came from big fires -- fires that had been burning while he had been frolicking deep in the Espen. Fires of victory.

His wife and small son were at Do Tohsall. Had a grim fate already claimed them while they had no man to protect them?

The irresistible despair that assailed Gendahl surprised him with its strength. He had never expected to feel so deprived of hope and courage when a dark day came to test him. Gendahl only found his resolve because his loyal men looked to him for leadership. He must fight and show his good men the hope that had already been stripped from him like an avalanche wiping clear a stand of pines.

Gendahl dismounted so that two servants could swiftly outfit him for combat. He donned again his blue leather jacket. A helmet settled over his head. The metal cap gave him strength as the padded interior gripped his skull and the lapis lazuli beads rattled on the fringe. Next, a heavy net of small diamond-shaped bronze plates joined by chain links was pulled over his shoulders and torso and bound tightly around him with strong cords of braided leather. The servants adjusted the side slit in the flexible armor so that Gendahl could grasp the handle of his sword strapped to his hip.

He did just that, and drew out his blade made of the new metal, the iron that the forge masters made hard and sharp. Gendahl thought of how Axerpen had carved a noble name for himself and his descendants. Now Gendahl meant to defend that legacy, his family….

He looked at the bleary horizon where a sweet summer breeze smeared the dark smoky bars of the dungeon door closing in on him. This smoke was born of burning buildings where many things burned, like furniture, rugs, linens, foods, oils, animals…people.

Gendahl whispered the names of his wife and son. His dread pained him. All of his youthful confidence seemed already to be burning on the fires of Do Tohsall. He felt too young. His small experiences in battle now inadequate. His prowess at sport, at riding, at loving, at speaking was now useless.

Armored and mounting up, his Infoh were ready. Their weapons rattled and the squealing horses reflected their anxiety. Gendahl shouted orders. He designated a group of six warriors to ride for the nearest villages and rouse the peasants to the fight while he and the rest of the Infoh raced straight to Do Tohsall.

But instead of hearing them shout with desire for battle, Gendahl heard curses and watched horror goad their ugly rage. He pivoted in his saddle and saw what they saw: armed warriors pouring through the gaps in the closest hedgerow. Men in black cloaks and smooth round helms, polished and bright in the sunshine, rode hard toward Gendahl and his Infoh. After the riders galloped through the hedgerow, they regrouped into a daunting charge line, prickly with spears and swords. Long thin red banners with white symbols and fringe streamed over grim warriors and marked them as Patharki.

Ginjor Rib, the Patharki King, had harried the Lin Tohs for several years because he coveted the developing farmlands and ore mines in the foothills that Gendahl controlled. At last the desire of Ginjor Rib had matured into outright invasion. Gendahl had hoped to cure this threat one day with marriage treaties, but Ginjor Rib had decided to rape him instead. The Patharki had grown too big and greedy to dicker with the modest forces of the Lin Tohs.

"Fight!" Gendahl shouted. "Fight!"

Gendahl raised his sword and turned toward the charge. More warriors came through the hedgerows, darkening the pasture like flies over a dead bird. Ginjor Rib had sent a surplus of warriors to hunt down and destroy the Lord of the Lin Tohs who had so inconveniently been absent from the destruction of his stronghold. Gendahl saw little chance of hacking his way to escape, but then he met with his first foe, and his thoughts were reduced to the next swing of the blade.

A Patharki warrior died swiftly on Gendahl's sword, and the screaming spray of blood urged Gendahl to greater fury. He blocked blows. He killed and rushed on to confront the next warrior. For an unknown time, Gendahl existed in battle ecstasy that let him dream of winning, but his warriors were falling around him and his enemies were pressing hard. Gendahl's brief offensive collapsed as he whirled his horse and deflected weapons from all sides. Without any thought of his pride, Gendahl retreated.

The Patharki chased him and his scattered knots of Infoh into the shady edge of the Espen. The servants who had attended the warriors on the hunt were run down and killed as the fight swept over them.

It was cooler and quieter beneath the old trees. The thud of hooves and the grunts of fighting men were softened by the forest into the subdued beat of a funeral drum.

Gendahl knew the Espen well, and he and his Infoh gained a lead from their pursuers. The surviving Infoh reunited with their lord, and they sought a rougher trail that looped to the east and then out of the forest. Gendahl's goal remained to reach his stronghold and join with his people who still gave battle, if any did.

The noise of warriors rushing through the forest warned Gendahl that the Patharki were close again. Their numbers allowed them to spread through the trees and throw a wide net to find the Lin Tohs.

The Lin Tohs warriors urged their tiring mounts eastward. Each man knew how to get to the trail. As they fled with the Patharki bashing through the forest behind them, the Lin Tohs had a sad moment in which to notice those comrades who did not ride beside them any more. Already half of them were dead or dying in the trampled pasture.

The Patharki ranks thickened and cut Gendahl off before he could reach the hidden trail. The Patharki had known that their quarry would know the forest well and sufficient numbers had been dispatched to ensure the capture of the Lin Tohs lord.

When the black-cloaked riders appeared in front of Gendahl, he cursed them. They popped up amid the trees like mushrooms after a week of rain. Horns brayed all around as the Patharki signaled that they had found their victims. Patharki warriors abandoned the dragnet and rushed toward the wailing horns.

Medu came to Gendahl's side. Blood seeped from wounds on both arms of the loyal bodyguard, and his fun spirit had been extinguished from his twinkling brown eyes.

"My Lord, keep going. We will cover your escape. Alone, you can elude these dishonorable dogs," Medu said.

"I will fight with you," Gendahl declared.

Two more of his Infoh urged him to heed Medu. They were drawing arrows from their quivers. Iridescent green feathers fletched the pale wooden arrows that were being set to bows. Both men insisted that it was their duty and privilege to fight while he made it away from danger.

"It's why we are here, my Lord," Medu insisted. "It's your duty to live and find vengeance for our tribe."

"You are bold to tell your lord his duty," Gendahl scolded.

The two Infoh beside him shot arrows at two advancing Patharki. True shots both, and the riders fell from their mounts.

"Go now while you can, dear Lord Gendahl," Medu pleaded.

More Infoh were firing arrows, keeping the Patharki back as long as possible before they degenerated into hand-to-hand combat with the overwhelming force.

Gendahl looked into Medu's eyes, knowing suddenly with awful certainty that he would never look upon that face living again. Such a short time ago they had ridden on a path toward merriment, roast pork, and the arms of warm sweet wives. But that path was gone, washed away by flooding fates.

With the sorrow of their final parting twisting his face, Medu said, "My dear Lord, let us not fight and die and not have you escape. An Infoh could know no greater cruelty."

Gendahl wanted to say goodbye to them, to praise their courage and express his love, but words were now meaningless and time was everything. He yelled to his horse and slapped the reins. He galloped by the freshly dead warriors with arrows protruding from throat and chest. Forest litter sprayed from the hooves of his horse. Infoh rushed through the trees at his flanks, confronting Patharki with arrows, spears, and swords. The fighting pressed closer, and he heard the shouts of great effort, failure, and death bash through the trees.

Utterly alone, Gendahl spurred his horse up the slope toward the trail on the ridge. The steed labored upward, but in his desperate haste he had chosen a poor spot to ascend, and the animal lost its footing in the loose leafy litter over the rocky soil. The horse fell, and then rolled sideways as it tried to regain its feet on the treacherous slope. When the horse started to roll over, Gendahl grabbed a sapling and pulled himself from the saddle as the horse rolled away. It crashed through underbrush before righting itself amid flapping leaves. Battered and panicked, the horse skittered down the slope.

Gendahl swore at the animal. Through a few gaps in the foliage, he saw Patharki warriors advancing on him. Then three Infoh overtook the Patharki, rushing like angered merchants chasing down a shoplifter in the market square. Two of them were mounted and one was on foot. When Gendahl heard their battle cries and watched them engage their enemies with furious metal, he rushed unthinking to give them aid. His booted feet took long strides down the slope, leaving long gashes in the carpet of leaves and exposing moist soil.

He recognized the Infoh warrior on foot as Temdi, who confronted his mounted foe with the strength of a granite cliff. In an extraordinary move he chopped off the rider's hand that held his sword, and then Temdi hacked at the rider's torso and knocked him from the saddle. He tried to grab the horse's bridle and claim the mount, but more Patharki attacked and he had to dodge behind trees.

Expecting to see another attacker, Temdi whirled when he heard someone behind him. Surprise flashed on his face and he halted his bloody blade.

"My Lord!" he cried. "Go away from us."

Just then a man cried out as a mortal blow fell upon him, and one of the mounted Infoh slumped across his horse's neck. His blood gushed into the animal's amber mane, darkening it with wet gore.

Dismayed by his gathering defeat, Gendahl was drained of the will to go on. He desired only to die fighting with his Infoh, who were better than kin. But Temdi was driven by a different duty. He grabbed Gendahl and started pulling his lord up the rough slope with great speed. Gendahl ran with him. Fleeing with a companion felt better.

They reached the trail that threaded its way along a wooded ridge. The narrow path gripped by tree roots disappeared in both directions into pleasant secretive shade. They started east but were soon confronted by riders on the trail. Their helmets sparkled in the green-dappled sunlight and their black cloaks joined with the forest shadows. Some men whacked leafy branches out of their way, whetting their blades' appetite for noble blood on the sap of Lin Tohs wood.

Temdi grabbed his lord again and led him in the opposite direction, deeper into the Espen forest. They ran for their lives, and for a while their armor was light on their bodies, but eventually it taxed their stamina, and both men puffed and sweated with mounting exhaustion. Riders thudded and clanked behind them.

Gendahl and Temdi realized that they could not stay on the trail. Beckoned by the comparative safety of the forest, they dashed into the trees. They ran farther up the slope and grabbed small trees, roots, and branches to haul themselves up. They reached the top of the ridge, and

Gendahl stopped to catch his breath. He leaned against a gnarled old maple with his sword drooping in his hand.

Temdi needed the break too, and he reluctantly stopped beside his lord. Perhaps it was best to gather the last of his strength for the final fight. Although the treetops masked the riders below them on the trail, Gendahl could hear them slowing and talking. They would see where their victims had left the trail. Gendahl and Temdi had blundered up the slope without any craft, and a half-blind old man born of the town could have tracked them.

The Patharki tongue was not so different from the dialect of the Lin Tohs, and Temdi and Gendahl heard the shouted orders for warriors to dismount and pursue them up the slope.

"We must go on," Temdi said.

Gendahl nodded, but he paused to survey the land from his vantage point. The ancient stretches of the Espen forest unfolded around him and climbed gradually into the foothills of the Tymelo Mountains. The mountains were tall, massive, behemoths of blue stone that guarded the sky with their icy peaks. So much older than men. So much more beautiful than women. Gendahl admired the landscape and saw its beauty as only a man about to die can see such things.

Then he was running again, following Temdi along the ridge, weaving among the trees. He had no shame in fleeing now. Patharki warriors were swarming up the slope. When the first four Patharki warriors reached Gendahl and Temdi, they fought with the ferocity of cornered beasts. They killed the four warriors and felt the joy of giving pain to their enemies. Lord Gendahl of the Lin Tohs had bid up the price of killing him.

Although their brief battle had been victorious, it had slowed them, and now dozens of Patharki warriors had overtaken them. Gendahl and Temdi swerved down the opposite side of the ridge. Two Patharki engaged Temdi, and he whirled to fight them. Gendahl tried to stop and help his Infoh in this final struggle but the slope was too steep. He skidded and tripped. He flailed his arms, seeking balance, but the slope turned into a cliff and he fell. Trees branches and trunks blurred by him and then he hit the ground. Bones snapped and he shrieked with pain. He rolled down another small slope and came to rest on a sun-warmed slab of rock beside water. Pain sickened him, and he groaned and writhed.

In great contrast to his agony, he had landed in a lovely spot. A waterfall rained over a cliff and the waters collected in a deep pool. Not far away a burbling creek quickened as it flowed away from the pool. Old trees and smooth rock embraced the pool that reflected fluffy white clouds.

A wonderful place to die. I can accept this, Gendahl thought.

His pain spiked and he grabbed at his thighs. His weapon fell from his grasp, forgotten and useless anyway. He knew that he could not even attempt to stand. The pain made it hard enough to breathe.

He heard a scream through the trees and then the metallic crash of an armored body rolling over the cliff and down the slope just as he had. Gendahl saw Temdi flop and then stop in the crook of a tree root. Temdi was dead, bloody from a dozen wounds, and an arrow was broken off in his hip.

Seeking a way down the cliff, the Patharki shouted different suggestions to each other until someone finally decided to use a rope to descend the cliff and confirm the death of Gendahl, as Ginjor Rib had commanded.

Tormented by waves of swelling pain, Gendahl awaited them. They were taking forever to reach him. He expected that he was too miserably injured for them to bother hauling him out of the forest for prolonged torturing. They would give him the killing blow and rightly punish him for being such a failure. He had lost what his family had created over eight generations. For a time, he would be remembered as the man who let the Lin Tohs be destroyed, and then no one would even remember that the Lin Tohs had ever existed.

Gendahl tried to unstrap his helmet. To feel a bit of the cool breeze through his sweaty hair would be a final mercy. But his gloved fingers lacked any dexterity, and he gave up after a feeble attempt. Groaning, he clawed at the stone. He tried to move his legs, but flexing his muscles smacked him with terrible pain.

"Come get me. I'm here," he called, thinking that he was shouting, but his voice was really only a hoarse mumble.

Water dripped on his face, and he opened his eyes lazily.

Over him stood a vision of some spirit daughter of Gyhwen. Long black hair, shiny like spider web strands of spun volcanic glass, hung wet around her face. Water dripped from the spiraling ends of her hair and splashed onto him like sweet rain. Her eyes were black and seemed as if they could see all the secrets that darkness had ever hidden. Her skin was blue, like the sky, no…. like the mountains. She was a spirit daughter of the Tymelo Mountains that had looked over the world of men since their beginning and would be there to watch their end. Her body exemplified feminine beauty. Her perfect shoulders, her breasts, muscled stomach, curving hips and thighs possessed no flaw, and droplets of water sprinkled her skin like dew on morning glories.

Indigo blue cloth woven of fantastically thin fibers bound her breasts. The fabric was so fine and wet it did nothing to hide her nipples. Her short pants were made of the same fabric and the clinging thin pants mocked the concept of modesty. The thick leather belt at her waist only accentuated her lack of clothing and gear.

She looked deeply into his eyes. Gendahl realized that he could not blink, nor did he want to. Her curious penetrating gaze pulled the pain out of him. Gendahl sighed with relief and relaxed. Pale blue fire began to burn in her eyes, blazing brighter the longer Gendahl stared at her. He felt like he looked at the sun but was not blinded.

Somehow he heard the stomp of booted feet and rattle of gear as Patharki warriors scrambled down the cliff, and he remembered that he was a broken man lying on the world of Gyhwen. Gendahl finally looked away from her and saw four men standing around Temdi's body. He glanced back up at the blue female, wondering what her reaction would be, but she had not shifted the focus of her glowing eyes and showed no awareness of the warriors.

One of the Patharki squatted next to Temdi and shook his head. He spoke, but Gendahl did not catch his words. The others warriors were looking around. Two men broke off from the group to search under trees, and a third walked out onto the slab of stone where Gendahl lay at the feet of the mountain daughter. The warrior apparently had no awareness that his quarry was only two steps away. Dark blotches of drying blood were visible on the shiny studs of his gauntlets. His sword was sheathed. The leather binding on its handle was faded and worn smooth. Veteran warriors had been sent to hunt down the Lord of the Lin Tohs.

Rage suddenly boiled inside Gendahl, forcing away the queer peace that he had found in the eyes of the blue female. Pain returned to him as well when he looked on the flat brown face of his enemy, whose comrades were no doubt mopping up the destruction of Do Tohsall.

Gendahl was about to yell an insult, but a strong will stifled his words.

"Speak not, human man." The command echoed in his mind. He let the female voice soothe him and his pain receded into only a warm fever.

The closest Patharki warrior walked by Gendahl and his mysterious guardian. The warrior walked along the water's edge and looked into the clear pool. He moved up and down the bank and passed Gendahl several times. Each time that Gendahl glimpsed the warrior's face, it bore an increasingly troubled expression.

He cannot see me, Gendahl thought although it was difficult to believe. He started to wonder if he had already died and all this was a confused vision misinterpreted by his soul.

Gendahl watched the warriors assemble beside Temdi. They all shook their heads and gestured with frustration.

"We have to find him!" declared the warrior who had walked by Gendahl.

The warriors searched again. This time going farther through the trees and even wading into the pool to check whether the clear water had played tricks and hidden the body of Lord Gendahl.

A fifth warrior eventually appeared, huffing from his descent of the cliff. Gendahl noticed red tassels on the warrior's cloak and belt, which marked him as a captain. He glanced at Temdi's body with irritation and then stepped onto the sunlit stone bank. He shouted for the other warriors and waited with his hands on his hips for them to come to him. He scanned the waterfall and let his eyes follow the flowing water.

As the four warriors returned from their fruitless searching, he listened to their reports with a deepening frown. The body of Gendahl could not be found.

"I saw him go over that cliff myself," the captain insisted.

"We have looked all around, even in the water," a warrior insisted and then suggested that the current may have carried away the body of the vanquished lord.

The hypothesis did not seem to impress the captain. Gesturing at Temdi, he asked if they were certain that this body was not Gendahl.

"His is an Infoh," a warrior said. "See, he wears the bodyguard badge around his neck."

The captain squatted and tore the amulet on its silver chain from Temdi's neck and threw it into the water. "Fools," he chided, standing up. "His bodyguards would have sought to mislead us. Gendahl switched gear with this bodyguard so we would not know who was who during the fight. Take this man's head and be done with it. I want out of this forest before dark."

"We should check his hands," a warrior suggested, but the captain narrowed his eyes at him menacingly. His men had no place discussing things with him. The captain kicked one of the gloved hands and grunted that the Lin Tohs were probably too ignorant to mark their leader with proper tattoos.

The gathered warriors considered what their captain had said, which seemed reasonable. It did explain why they could not find Lord Gendahl's body, but it would be perilous to risk a mistake with Ginjor Rib.

Gently, another warrior said to his captain. "Sir, I believe that you have undone this riddle, but our Lord might know the face of Gendahl from the descriptions of our spies. Are you sure this is the head that we should take to him?"

The captain gave the questioning warrior a sour look. For an answer he raised his foot and smashed twice with his heel at Temdi's face. For good measure, he gouged a dead eye with his spur.

"Take his head," the captain ordered. "And let us be done with this task. The Lin Tohs are no more."

Obediently, a warrior lifted his blade and, after taking aim, hacked the head from the body. Stabbed with grief to witness the defiling of Temdi's body, Gendahl growled wordlessly. Abruptly, the Patharki captain and two of his men turned their heads toward the sound.

"Sssshhhh."

Becalmed by the female voice in his head, Gendahl stayed silent. The eyes of the Patharki roved the area, but still they did not see. The waterfall tumbled and splashed, and the wind chattered in the trees.

Gendahl watched a warrior lift Temdi's dripping head. Even if it was not the head of the Lord of the Lin Tohs, Gendahl still saw his own death in the ruined face of Temdi.

The Patharki warriors departed with the head, and only one of them looked back wonderingly before disappearing amid the gloomy trees.

With the Patharki gone, Gendahl suddenly felt as if he had left the world entirely. His domain was surely conquered, and he sprawled helpless at the feet of a mysterious creature. She now kneeled beside him, willing to claim that which cruel fate had chewed but spit back.

"How did they not see us?" he asked her.

The water had dried from her hair and a few lovelocks fluttered in the breeze. Her hair looked soft and inviting, and Gendahl wanted to touch it. At first, he did not think that she understood his language, but eventually she replied. Her voice was as lovely as the burbling creek but possessed a timbre that suggested it could speak with the force of the waterfalls.

"Because I did not want them to see us, human man," she said.

She released the strap of his helmet and slid it off his head. The helmet clanked against the stone and rolled a half turn closer to the water. She ran her hands over his thighs, examining his injuries.

"Who are you?" Gendahl asked.

She looked straight into him with her magical eyes. Sparks of blue fire pulsed in her pupils. "Onja," she said.

2. Lord-Born No More

Gendahl dreamed often of his wife and baby son. Their smiling faces and warm touches delighted him more than he remembered. But disaster always consumed the blissful dreams. A dark storm sickened the sky and angry winds hurled destruction upon them. A roof collapsed on them, or a falling tree crushed them. Once a flood grabbed them tight in its drowning embrace.

Between these unbearable dreams his physical pain tormented him. Then the beautiful female came and eased his discomfort. Her powerful aura enveloped him. She was his protector now. He was a babe in the arms of a new mother. His smashed soul accepted rebirth into her world.

When Gendahl became lucid, he was alone. Bright sunshine warmed the air. He heard the waterfalls and smelled the good water. A flowering bush arched over his head, dappling him with shade, and a butterfly sipped on a blue flower. Its yellow and black wings opened and closed lazily.

Then memories of his desperate battle, the death of his Infoh, and the smoke over his home poured over his heart like a mudslide gobbling a building. Moaning, he touched his aching thighs and found that they were bound in mud casts from crotch to shin. Except for his red shirt, he was naked. Beside him his armor, blue leather jacket, boots, sword, and other items of clothing and gear were neatly stacked.

Gendahl stroked his face, trying to judge from the stubble of his thin beard how much time had passed. His sprouting mustache seemed to indicate a week. Aching and hungry, he awkwardly rolled over and dragged himself to a tree. He pushed his torso up with his arms. His weakness was distressing and he was puffing by the time he had lifted his butt into the air. He pushed himself off the ground and quickly grabbed the tree trunk. Placing more weight on his feet added to his pain, but he pulled himself straight and tenderly stood up.

Gripping the tree, he circled to its other side and urinated, taking care not to hit his casts. His life had been reduced to counting a piss as an achievement.

He called for Onja. His voice mixed with the mellow rumble of the falling waters. The trees stood watch silently with their green leafy limbs reflected in the water. Birds flapped and sang in the branches.

His legs were hurting more, but he did not want to get back down until he was ready to stay down for a while. The cool pool beckoned his thirst. When he was ready, he let go of the tree and bent over. Gradually he shifted his weight forward until he fell onto his hands and he hand-walked until he was flat on the ground again. Gendahl soon found that dragging himself naked out onto the stone shore was unpleasant. He grabbed his leather jacket and spread it on the ground. Then he shifted his midsection onto the leather, which would serve as a protective sled.

As he slid across the flat rock, the stone was hot beneath his hands. The sun beating down on his back soothed his muscles, and when he dipped his hands into the pool, the cool water was refreshing to drink. After quenching his thirst, he washed his face and rolled onto his side. He stared at the peaks of the Tymelo beyond the waterfalls and thought about how the water that he had just drunk had journeyed from the snowy crown of Gyhwen.

Hungry and miserable, he wondered if the graceful blue spirit daughter had abandoned him. Fear gripped him as he contemplated not having her help any more.

I deserve no help, Gendahl thought darkly. After losing his domain and family, he should be left to die slowly.

Mired in self-loathing, Gendahl stared at the waterfalls and lost his mind in the ceaseless flow. The sparkling light upon the falls grew brighter until Gendahl finally blinked. Onja had appeared.

Hope sprouted in his heart like a new embryo of life. She stepped out of the waterfalls and dropped into the swirling frothing waters. When her feet touched bottom, she walked toward him through the water, ascending the gradual bank and rising from the pool with water spilling off her perfect body and glistening like frost on her blue skin. She came to him on the ledge of sun-warm rock and pulled herself out of the water.

"You should not be moving about, Gendahl," she said.

"I was thirsty," he explained. "I called for you but could not wait."

"I heard you," she said, and then after a pause, added an apology, "But I do not always realize how time can pass. I must be more mindful of that."

She spoke his language beautifully and without flaw, but Gendahl knew that it could not possibly be her native tongue.

"Are you from the mountains, Onja?" Gendahl asked.

She nodded.

"I have heard that spirit creatures live in a valley surrounded completely by the high snows. They say it is a paradise where none grow old. Take me to your fair home and let me dwell in forgetfulness of my sorrow," Gendahl said.

Onja sensed the grief that clawed at the human man who had fallen into her care. His belief that her homeland would save him from his pain made her experience pity for the first time. It was an intriguing feeling.

Perhaps pity is why I show him such kindness, she thought, but she knew it was more than that.

"My home is not as you would imagine it, Gendahl," she said with sadness.

Her statement disappointed him. There was no escape from the life with which fate had saddled him.

"I do not remember telling you my name," he muttered.

"I do not need to be told that which I want to know," Onja said. "Speaking your name helped to soothe you as I tended your legs."

He touched one of the casts. His legs were becoming hot inside the mud casts. With a fearful whisper he asked Onja if he would walk again although he was not sure why he cared.

"Yes, I have mended your broken bones with my power, but some spells only time can cast. You must stay still for a few more days while the bones become strong again," she explained.

Gendahl remembered the ugly snap and explosion of pain when he had fallen over the cliff. For certain both legs had been broken. Such an injury should keep a man down for months, if not forever, but Onja spoke of his recovery being only a few days off.

"You are magic?" he said although the truth of it was plain.

"That would be your word for it," she said. "But it is normal for my kind. Do you think of yourself as magic because you can start and control fire? But then, I suppose a squirrel looks at you cooking food and forging metals and sees magic."

"Do you see a squirrel when you look at me?" he asked, more resigned to the fact than offended.

"I see a human. I know that you are more than a squirrel, and I am more than a human," Onja answered.

"What are you, Onja?" he asked.

"I am rys," she said, drawing herself up proudly.

"So it is true," he whispered. "The magic land of the mountains is real."

"Jingten," she said, giving him its name. "A fair valley with vital forests and a great deep lake nourished from the womb of the Rysamand Mountains. But it is a troubled place."

"They say that none who go into the Tymelo Mountains ever comes back," Gendahl said.

Onja smiled. "Then how is it that you have heard of my magic land?"

Rethinking the drama of the fairy stories told to him as a boy, he conceded that perhaps the mountains were not as perilous as reported.

"A human must never discount the peril of the Rysamand," Onja said. "But going there and returning are not impossible. People of your land must have ventured in and out of my homeland, perhaps before I was born. I know that humans from the east come and go from Jingten."

"From the east? East of the Tymelo?" Gendahl asked with surprise.

"Call the mountains of my home the Rysamand," Onja corrected. "Someday the humans of the west shall all call my home by its proper name."

"Rysamand," he said to show her that he would use the name from now on. "And there are more men east of the Rysamand?"

Onja answered that it was so and then asked him why he thought that there would not be more world beyond the mountains.

"Because the mountains are the roof of Gyhwen," he answered quickly.

"A roof with one wall?" she chuckled and made him see the smallness of his thoughts.

"There is much I do not know, and of what I did know, I showed no intelligence," he muttered and dipped back into his sorrow. He had been a worthless leader. Too young and optimistic without a chance to absorb lessons or heed counsel before his enemy had struck. No doubt Ginjor Rib had acted so quickly after Gendahl had become Lord of the Lin Tohs to take advantage of a young leader's foolish first years spent in sport instead of preparation for the worst.

"You hunger," Onja observed, trying to distract him from his depression. "I shall feed you."

"I want no food," he said.

Onja bent over him and placed her hands in his armpits. Tingling energy wrapped him and he suddenly felt light. He floated more than she lifted him. Onja embraced him and carried him upright with his feet gently dragging. She was tall, and Gendahl eased his head onto her shoulder, giving himself over to her care.

Onja returned him to the bed of leaves and dried grass that she had prepared for him. She moved her hand over his eyes and he dozed off, and this time no dreams bothered him.

When he awoke, the sun was a bright glare at the top of the ridge and the treetops shimmered gold over darkening green. A faint rainbow clung to the vapor rising around the falls. The fatty scent of roasting rabbit nudged his despondent appetite.

Close by, Onja tended a tidy fire with a rabbit on a spit. Gendahl watched her remove the rabbit from the fire. With deft fingers she tore the small tasty animal into two portions and set it on a smooth flat rock that she had found in the water.

"You shall eat," she said and set the stone within his reach.

For a moment, he appraised the meat with sullen disinterest, but the splotches of juice on the stone and the tender strings of meat hanging on the bone called to his animal desire to live. He reached for the meat and, after each bite, he ate with increasing gusto.

Onja ate as well. As he observed her straight teeth biting the flesh and the grease smearing her finger tips, he could believe that she was something beyond a spirit daughter. She was flesh and blood, but her magic powers could not be denied. Under different circumstances, Gendahl suspected that he would be afraid of her.

When his meat was gone, he sighed. The full warmth inside his stomach felt good now that he had done it.

"Why do you help me?" he asked.

Onja licked her fingers carefully and seemed to be overanalyzing the taste of the rabbit. When she was satisfied that her fingers were clean, she turned her intense black eyes onto him. "You were hurt," she replied simply.

Even if he hated being alive, Gendahl thanked her. Courtesy toward Onja seemed appropriate.

Onja had never been thanked before. To receive gratitude touched her with unexpected force, and she rewarded him with a better explanation. "I have never had a human friend before. This seemed a good opportunity for making one," she said.

"I fear you have made a poor choice," he said.

She cocked her head, increasingly intrigued by his growing self-hate. "You blame yourself for being attacked?" she said.

"I blame myself for not preparing my domain properly to defend itself. I was playing at games in the forest when I should have been at home…" he stopped speaking as grief clamped his throat. Images of his wife and son pierced his mind with sharp regret. He wrung his hands, rubbing his fingers over his knuckles and contemplating the blue tattoos. The tattoos wrapped his wrists in blue stags and sunbursts, marking him as a lord-born.

Lord no more, he thought.

"Could you have done something to prevent the killing and destruction that I have seen in the settlements near here?" Onja asked, curious to learn more about how the humans interacted, attacked, and defended. For what did they struggle?

"You have seen what was done?" Gendahl said, agonized by the report.

"I can see near and far," Onja said and explained that the sudden death of so many people nearby had captured her attention and she had watched the progress of the attack. The gates and walls of the stronghold had been stormed. Villages torched. People dragged from their homes and slain or cut down whether fighting or fleeing. Those who had attacked had seemed to want to eradicate the residents and make the land vacant for their own purposes.

Gendahl clutched his face as ragged sobs escaped him. After finally wrestling and pinning his emotions, he explained in a strained whisper that he had been the leader of that small but growing tribe.

"My family," he moaned without any hope that they had been spared by Ginjor Rib.

"Family," Onja echoed him thoughtfully.

"Yes, my family. Do you know what that is?" Gendahl demanded, lashing out in his grief.

The set of her jaw hardened and she looked toward the Rysamand Mountains. Anger twisted her beautiful face for a moment, but then she softened and turned back toward Gendahl.

"I did not know those who bore me," she said. "I was fostered by many rys over the years, but never truly did I have any to call my own. I have lived alone of late. I am different."

She seemed to Gendahl almost forlorn now. "I am sorry that I yelled at you," he said.

Onja shrugged. No hasty words from a human could hurt her feelings. "You wanted me to understand you. To have sympathy," she said. "I shall try, Gendahl."

Gendahl shut his eyes and reclined onto his grassy bed. "I thank you again for your kindness, but it has been a waste of your talent," he said. "When I am able, I will go back to my domain. To see what I can do."

Tears pooled in his eyes. What could he expect to do? He could not even fantasize about finding his family alive. His wife and child had probably been dead by the time he emerged from the Espen Forest and saw the smoke. The best he could do was go back and get himself killed, which seemed the right thing to do. He should have died fighting in the forest, refusing to be taken alive, but instead he had fallen over a cliff.

More days passed and Gendahl lay on his bed of leaves and contemplated his bleak future. The exercise was frustrating. Even before the tragedy, he had never given much thought to his future. It had simply been something set before him. He was his father's heir. His life would go by much as his father's had.

Onja continued to bring him food. Usually fish, sometimes rabbit or duck. About half the time, he lacked an appetite, but he ate anyway because he did not want to be rude to her. Grudgingly he healed. During the day, he watched the sun travel the sky and the rainbow sprays around the waterfalls shift from one side of the pool to the other side. Each night he watched the horned moon grow and fell asleep staring at its silvery reflection on the night-black waters.

By the time the moon was half full, Onja declared that his casts could be removed. She came to him in the morning with a round rock in her hands. She gripped the rock tightly and blue light flashed between her fingers. When she opened her hands, the cracked rock fell away in two pieces that had sharp serrated edges that she used to saw away his casts of mud and tree bark.

Although his time healing had been abnormally brief, already his muscles had begun to wither. His skin was dry and flaky, and his knees looked big and knobby.

"Move them," Onja commanded, wondering at his reluctance.

Gendahl had to make a conscious effort to control his muscles. Painfully he bent his creaking knees. Stiff muscles and ligaments groaned, but the striking pain of broken bones was gone. He bent and straightened his legs until they ached. Sweat dotted his forehead from the strain.

"Get up now," Onja said. She stood and swiftly grabbed him under the armpits and hoisted him to his feet.

Gendahl bit his lip, fearing to test his wobbly legs, but Onja gave him his weight gently, and the legs held him up. The bones were knit, set straight and properly. Such an injury should have crippled him. Even a skilled healer would have been challenged to right the bones of both legs, but Onja had fixed him with swift perfection.

As if he were a baby learning to walk, Onja stood behind him and held his hands as he took hesitant shuffling steps. She guided him to the water, and it was a sweet relief to his crying muscles to get into the pool. Onja joined him in the water and they spent the rest of the morning walking in the water until he was exhausted and begged to rest.

Onja helped him out of the water but then, without a word, she jumped back into the pool and swam toward the waterfalls. She disappeared behind the curtain of water.

After resting and drying in the sun, Gendahl struggled to his feet and put on his pants. To be dressed again felt good after flopping about half naked.

Sitting next to his gear, he drew his sword. He turned the blade and examined its sheen in the sun. The weapon that had once given him such a thrill to hold now seemed puny and useless. A man needed much more than a sword to keep him safe. He needed to know what was going on around him, where his enemies were and when they might strike. But too late the lesson had come. The joys of lordship coupled with the pleasures of a new wife and family had distracted him. His sense of security and power had dulled the counsel of wiser Lin Tohs who had feared the greed of Ginjor Rib. Diplomacy had been boring. There was so much more to amuse a young lord and he did not want to worry. The Lin Tohs had always been able to deal with Patharki raiders and common bandits before. Nothing beyond the dithering of balding warriors, fat from years lounging in their lord's good house, was going to happen.

Foolish boy! Gendahl fumed at himself, suddenly as wise as the hills.

Gendahl raised his left arm and set the blade along the arteries of his wrist. His guilty conscience demanded that he make the blood flow, yet the pride of his manhood cried for vengeance.

"Vengeance," he whispered derisively. What hope could he have for vengeance?

He heaved a sigh and sheathed the sword. To kill what Onja had saved seemed too rude, and Gendahl escaped his depression in sleep. Free of the chafing casts and itches that he could not reach, he slept well for once.

Over the next five days, he continued his therapeutic water walks. Aches and pains went away. He saw little of Onja, who, as far as he could tell, stayed behind the waterfalls. Gendahl thought of swimming into the foaming waters and seeking her lair, but he decided not to disturb her.

He finally dared to approach the spot where Temdi had died, but there was no headless body. A blackened patch of ground attested to a cremation likely performed by Onja's magic. Gendahl touched the ashes and groaned at the grief grinding his heart before slinking away.

Through these lonely days of punishing sadness, he did not draw his sword from its scabbard again, but sometimes he sat with the covered blade across his knees and contemplated returning to his domain. Could he seek out scattered warriors and rally them to attack? But such thoughts stirred no hope. He doubted that he could find any surviving Lin Tohs warriors. Ginjor Rib had apparently attacked with overwhelming force. Any surviving Lin Tohs warriors would have believed their lord to be dead and had most likely fled the area.

Still I must go back, Gendahl thought. He had been the lord of his tribe, and he deserved to look upon his failings.

Gendahl prepared to leave. He washed his clothes and cleaned his armor. When he assessed his possessions, he saw that he was woefully lacking in gear and food. The bare minimum he had—a knife and tinder kit with flint, although he was not accustomed to starting his own fires.

And he was hungry. Onja had not served any meat for days, and Gendahl found that he missed the meals because sorrow was not stemming his appetite so much when food was not at hand. Plucking greens and foraging for berries was not going to sustain him. Gendahl fashioned a fishing spear with his knife and a stick. He moved quietly to a shady section of the pool and spied some trout. Anticipating their flavorful flesh, Gendahl thrust for a fish impatiently and missed.

He waited for the fish to return but he finally had to find another fishy corner of the pool. As he circled the shore, scanning the water, he saw a shining strand in the stony silt. Gendahl paused for a long time before he pulled out the silver chain. A hawk carved from amber dangled from the chain. It was Temdi's Infoh amulet, and Gendahl shut his eyes with deep respectful grief.

The chain was broken. Gendahl tucked the amulet into a pouch and resumed fishing with a fresh crack in his aching heart.

After four artless attempts at spearing fish Gendahl concluded that it was hopeless for him right now. His legs were not yet strong enough to keep him steady so that he could make a true throw.

Hungry and sore, Gendahl returned to his campsite. After repeated effort, he managed to get a fire going right at dusk.

He crouched over his little fire. Once he had settled with his tribesmen beside comforting fires. Now loneliness and bitter shame comprised his retinue of loyal followers. Thinking of what had likely happened to his wife and son tore at him.

Perhaps they are still alive. Hostages or trophies, he thought, but he quickly kicked that possibility to the side of his mind like a dog rejected from the pack. It was impossible that his son would have been left alive, and his wife, even if taken as a hostage, would surely have killed herself at the soonest opportunity.

In the darkness he heard Onja's beautiful hard body sliding into the water like one lovely note struck in the quiet forest. Dripping water pattered on the stone after she got out of the pool. When the firelight revealed her, she made a striking figure. Powerful, confident…superior.

The sight of her immediately comforted him. The destruction of his small life did not mean the world lacked majesty.

"I missed you, Onja," Gendahl admitted.

She squatted by the fire and offered him the fish in her hand. He never saw Onja fish. She simply came out of the water with a fish. And it was always a big one.

They sat together in silence while Gendahl cleaned and fileted the fish. He arranged the filets on some grilling sticks over the fire.

Onja sat down and crossed her legs. Petting her black hair over her shoulders, she said, "You are going to leave."

"I can't stay here forever," he said.

"Nor shall I," she said, although she sounded sad at the prospect of both of them abandoning their little watery haven.

"Why are you here, Onja?" Gendahl asked. "What do you do behind the waterfalls?"
Onja considered his questions, trying to decide if she could even explain. How could a rys tell a human of rys things?

"I think about my powers. The waters have come down from the Rysamand, and this is a special place. With the waters of my homeland flowing over me, I can think on the greatness of the world. I can learn. There is power in the moving water," she said.

Gendahl grasped slightly what she was trying to say. He understood that forces existed within Nature. Mountains, moving waters, winds, fire. There were many powers beyond the control of man, but perhaps not beyond Onja.

"When will you leave this place?" he asked.

"I shall go home when the snows begin to fall in the Rysamand," Onja replied. "It is good to be home in the winter."

Gendahl said, "I think that I'll go soon. I must see what has happened to my domain."

Onja frowned. She was uncertain why he would want to further torment himself by viewing the destruction of his home. "I have told you what you will find there," she reminded him.

He flinched with anger and dumped the fish in the fire. He cried out with frustration. His supper was going to be incinerated, but Onja swiftly thrust her hand into the flames and grabbed the filets. Without suffering any burns, she handed them back to him. Blue sparks snapped in her eyes, and Gendahl knew that she had used her power to protect her flesh from the heat.

When the fish was sufficiently cooked, he offered her some, but she was not hungry. As Gendahl flaked the food into his mouth, he told Onja that he had no where else to go except back to his domain.

"What will you do there?" she asked.

"I don't know," he snapped. "Try to find out what happened to my family." His voice cracked when he said "family." He shoved the rest of the fish in his mouth, eager to be done with the chore of eating. Surly, he stretched out. "I must sleep. I will go tomorrow. I am well enough."

Onja watched him roll over and put his back to her. Having nothing to say, she left him.

Eventually Gendahl wiped his eyes and tried to think more rationally. Onja was right to ask him what he might do. Simply wandering around whatever horrors he was sure to find was going to accomplish nothing and probably get him killed when the Patharki discovered him.

There was a path open to warriors whose lives were ruined for one reason or another. Those who had murdered, stolen, or committed adultery and could no longer live within decent tribal society. Those whose lands had been lost or overrun. Or, those whose lords had been vanquished. Such warriors could take the bandit path. Some lived as pure criminals, menaces to all, but others lived in enclaves of semi-criminals and mercenaries, who lived by their own laws and sold their loyalties at their convenience, if at all. Most infamous among them were the Kez.

But Gendahl was lord-born. His tattoos marked him as such. They were traced into his skin in childhood to forever place him above the lesser segments of society. Hiding his identity would be hard. The evidence of his high birth would draw attention, and it probably would not take other criminals too long to figure out who he was. His Lin Tohs accent would always be strong in his speech, and someone would eventually get the idea of hauling him to Ginjor Rib and asking for a bounty.

Gendahl was surprised that the option of turning bandit did not disgust him like a mouthful of vomit. Before the Patharki attack, he, like any man of any tribe, had viewed the outlaws as scum. The bandit folk were the grime that made decent society shine that much brighter.

But now Gendahl could not imagine a fate better suited to his disgraced existence. Best that he let Gendahl, Lord of the Lin Tohs, stay dead in the minds of all who might care. His foolish inadequacy as a leader rightly decreed that he should slink from society in shame. A lord-born without lands or retainers was worse than dead. The only place he could go was to the criminal underworld.

He wrung his hands against his tattoos. The indigo stains in his skin had once been such a source of pride, but now they were shameful and dangerous.

Gendahl squirmed fitfully for most of the night. A thousand fears assailed him. Since falling from the cliff, his life had become a surreal mystery that sheltered him from the full impact of his grief. His strange circumstances kept the crushing loss of his family and tribe at a distance. Tomorrow when he walked out of the Espen Forest, he would be rushing into the burning building of his ruined life.

Gendahl wanted to sever himself from the hideous feelings. He wanted to be spared dreams of his family that was surely lost. He wanted no more to think of Temdi's head being carried away in place of his own. Gendahl must cease to exist.

******

When morning came, Gendahl's scream roused Onja from her watery lair. She burst through the waterfalls, swam across the pool like an excited otter, and sprang onto the shore. She marched purposefully to Gendahl's camp. His back was to her, and she grabbed his shoulder and flung him back from the fire. He writhed on the ground, holding his hands out and shaking. His wrists and palms were red and black, charred by the fire, where he had been holding them against the coals and flames with all of his will.

"What are you doing?!" Onja yelled, astounded by his action.

Tears streamed from Gendahl's eyes and he could only gasp in pain. The skin split on his fingers and a rugged spasm of shock wracked his body.

Onja exhaled sharply with exasperation and understood the futility of questioning him at this moment. She knelt beside him and seized his forearms. He had rolled up his sleeves, showing more concern for his shirt than his flesh.

Blue light rose in Onja's eyes until they brightened her whole face. Wispy blue fire radiated from her hands over Gendahl's wrists and then his hands. His pain stopped entirely as her magic soaked into the charred skin and he relaxed against the ground.

Onja pressed on with her magic until blisters receded and fresh pink skin glowed with health. When she was done, she brushed ashes from his hands. His burns were gone, replaced by tender new skin that was pale next to his brown skin. Only scattered remnants of his tattoos remained. They looked like the shards of a painted vase broken on a floor.

"You are a wonder, Onja," Gendahl murmured, not ungratefully.

"I do not understand this," she said.

"The tattoos," he said. "I must get rid of them."

Onja leaned away from him and put her hands on her hips. Angered, she demanded if he had counted on her healing him.

"That was and remains your choice, Onja. I only knew that the tattoos had to go," Gendahl explained. "If you are upset with me, you can stay to watch me suffer for I must burn away what remains of them."

"Foolish human," she scolded. "Why did you not ask me to rid you of your marks? I could have done it without causing you so much pain."

He answered, "I have never asked anything of you."

"No, Gendahl, you have not," Onja agreed. "But you may ask. I have much that I could give."

His dark brown eyes glistened with curiosity, perhaps even temptation. Onja had frequently analyzed his thoughts about vengeance, and she wondered if he would ask her for the power to pursue his enemies.

With polite humility, he asked her only to remove the remainder of his tattoos. He said nothing as Onja worked on his skin. Gendahl paid attention to the sensation of having her magic touch him. She was blocking the pain as she burned the pigments bit by bit from his flesh, and then healed the skin as she went. The stags with their blue antlers gradually disappeared, and Gendahl forced himself to accept the end of his old life. It was the only way he could even attempt to go on. Gendahl could not be forgiven.

A breeze stirred and it was cool against his sweaty skin. He stared at his hands. The absence of his tattoos made him feel different. When his skin was tattooed, he had been only a small boy, and the painful task was one of his earliest memories.

This is my earliest memory of my new life, he thought.

With Onja's firm slender fingers massaging his hands, Gendahl wondered if it had been the will of Jayshem, the God and creator of Gyhwen, that he experience a life other than being Lord of the Lin Tohs.

"Does it comfort you to think that your God willed your suffering and loss?" she asked.

Taken aback by her knowledge of his thoughts, Gendahl pulled his hands away. "What else can I think?" he asked back.

She lifted her eyebrows thoughtfully. The slight stretching of her eyelids sharpened the beauty of her features. His answer intrigued her greatly.

To change the subject, Gendahl examined his hands and thanked her. "I could not go on with my lord-born markings. I am lord-born no more," he announced.

"You are still what you were, Gendahl," Onja contradicted. "Tattoos did not make you a lord."

"But they showed others what I was. I am something new now, but I know not what," he said.

"You are Gendahl, my friend," Onja said, and she smiled.

Her smile seemed to reveal a vulnerability that he would not have expected from her. She was alone as well.

"Your friend," he said although he had no smile to give. "But call me Gendahl no more. I am Amar."

"Amar," she said and liked the name.

"I must go," he said. He scanned the trees, rocks, waters, and mountains around him. Onja's presence enchanted the landscape and made it more beautiful. It was a good place to die and to be born. "Back to the world of men," he added.

Onja nodded with understanding. The time would come when she would go back to her kind as well. "If you want my help before I go back to Jingten, I will be here until the day equals the night," she said, still hoping that he would make a request of her.

"Thank you, Onja," he said and stood up.

Onja reached into his pile of gear and pulled forth his weapon. Proffering it, she said, "Your sword, Amar."

Receiving the weapon from her opened a door in his mind, but he did not yet dare to look inside. He was not ready to receive any knowledge from this awesome being. As he took the sword from Onja and strapped it over his shoulder, he looked into her eyes that sparkled with powers to which no man could aspire. He would miss her.

Amar said, "I start a new life today. It is not a life I want, but perhaps if I keep living, the path to vengeance will present itself." He decided that he needed this goal to keep going. He would view his smashed domain and take to the bandit life, and he would look for a way someday to hurt the Patharki and Ginjor Rib.

He parted from Onja without any more words. Planning to follow the stream through the hills, Amar walked away along the bank. When he turned back, Onja lifted a hand in farewell and he waved back to her. Onja sensed among his many harsh emotions, his sadness at leaving her. It was good to have a friend.

You shall have your vengeance, she thought.

3. Volatile Spells

The road to Jingten was familiar to Breymer, but the destination disturbed him. His caravan stopped at a great tower beside a lake in the isolated valley. He stepped out of his coach and inhaled deeply of the pure pine air. The alpine landscape was lush and enthusiastically green at the height of its short summer. Even four centuries after the Kwellstan Sect had founded this colony, the place still seduced him a little. He exhaled and reflected upon how the profound perfection of the landscape had inspired his colleagues to pry open the toolbox of creation and tinker.

In this stimulating land the tabre priests of the Kwellstan Sect had sought to expand their powers and improve their race. Breymer had been among those bold tabre. He had been a Master Priest then and had enjoyed the ecstatic glories of the work. Now he was the Daykash of the Kwellstan Sect, second only to the Grand Lumin, and his mission concerned the results born of those daring experiments.

Breymer looked across the dark blue waters that warned of a frighteningly deep lake. He knew that this water-filled gap in the land reached into the colossal forces within the living body of Ektren. Minds such as his were sensitive to this power and could tap into it and work high magic. This place felt so different from the lowlands of Nufal. Here the elements were raw and treacherous. Pleasure surged inside him as he stood again in this potent place after long years of absence. But he squashed his feelings, except for regret.

By tapping into the forces emanating from the Rysamand Mountains, the tabre had expected to bring forth a more powerful and enlightened generation. The magic of the Kwellstan Sect had already been uplifting the tabre race for thousands of years, and its ambitious priests had anticipated success, but they had spawned a new race instead. The offspring in Jingten were always rys, and the tabre shrank from their kinship with their visions wrought in flesh and blood.

The rys were abominations, and they were breeding. The Kwellstan Sect could no longer ignore its looming problem of what to do with them.

One rys in particular was aspiring to inclusion in tabre society. Daykash Breymer felt the mind of this one watching him from the tower. Hope normally excited Breymer when he tested a worthy student, but this time he dreaded what his tests might reveal. The power of the mind spying on him was disquieting.

Turning away from the lake, he looked up the stark stone walls of the tower. Only the surrounding vista of blue stone mountains subdued the otherwise grandiose structure. The shadow of the tower was upon the Daykash, and a chilly foreboding prickled his sensitive dark skin. He pulled his formal outer robe over his shoulders and buttoned it across his chest. The dense red fabric was slick against his fingers. Talented weavers cast spells to tighten the threads during its crafting, which made the fabric impermeable to liquid and fire resistant.

The Daykash's attending priests dismounted their horses and clustered behind him. Resident tabre were assembled at the tower doors to receive him, but he ignored them and continued to study the tower. Enchantments flowing from the stone blocks stroked his senses. He had been among the tabre who had built the tower. They had strengthened it to last the ages with the secret spells of the Kwellstan Sect.

"Daykash Breymer, I welcome you," announced a tabre who stepped forward. He wore a red and black robe that marked him as a Master Priest.

"Thank you, Master Halor," Breymer said tersely.

"Jingten is honored by your visit," Halor added.

Breymer's smooth face twitched as if he smelled something bad. Halor ushered the Daykash toward the tall doors. The other tabre bowed as their Daykash passed, and their black hair fell across their dark faces.

"How was your journey?" Halor inquired.

The Daykash recalled the open undulating grasslands he had crossed to reach the mountains and then the twisting ascent up the pass into the Jingten Valley made possible by the excellent road built by the Kwellstan Sect. "Uneventful," he responded. Nothing ever happened on the Nufalese frontier.

A wide hallway led into the heart of the tower and terminated at its grand reception hall that was open all the way to the tower's roof. Sunlight streamed down from skylights on the soaring observatory level. A platform of white and black marble filled the back of the chamber, creating a broad threshold for an ornately framed doorway that was dark within.

The priests and acolytes that had come with the Daykash filed in behind their leader. The resident acolytes and priests escorted them into the dark doorway where they levitated upward two by two. Halor and Breymer were left alone in the magnificent space. The Daykash stepped onto the platform. The polished stone reflected his image as if he stood on perfectly still water. His magic lit his eyes and his senses searched out the one he had come to see.

Nervousness eroded Halor's patience and he asked, "Daykash, shall I show you to your quarters?"

Daykash Breymer blinked and came back to himself. "Do you expect your student to pass my test?" he said.

Halor hesitated before answering yes. He knew it was not what the Daykash wanted to hear.

"Bring Dacian to me now," the Daykash said.

Halor bowed and hurried into the levitation shaft to fetch his student.

******

A crucial rite of passage was upon Dacian. The Daykash had come. Amazingly Dacian was not as nervous as he had expected to be. He had been ready for this moment for years.

At last his extraordinary talents had earned him the right to be tested. After passing the test he would advance to studying at the Atocha in Kwellstan, where he would ultimately become a full Nebakarz priest of the Kwellstan Sect. He had dreamed of this achievement, but not just for his satisfaction. He wanted to show that rys were as good as tabre. Dacian wondered if he would look back on this day as the time when the tabre began accepting rys as their equal kin. For decades that hope had sustained him.

The Daykash seemed to share in Dacian's eagerness because Halor soon darkened the door to Dacian's chamber. Dacian noted how his master rubbed his pinkies against his thumbs. This sign of Halor's fluster amused Dacian. Usually Halor was calm and controlled. He set an example of order as he taught Dacian the value of it. Power required control, Halor always said. Without it, power became chaos. Even the storming heavens focused its greatest energy into lightning instead of exploding the sky.

"The Daykash summons you," Halor said.

Dacian rose from a glossy stone window seat, smoothed the front of his long shirt, and petted the white fur collar that ringed his blue neck. The soft fur was calming. He took a slow deep breath and observed the morning light that glowed through the stained glass window. Twenty-nine triangles of different sizes made up the design. Dacian had counted them decades ago when Halor had first assigned him this room. Only shades of purple, a difficult color even for a rys glassmaker to imbue into glass, were used in the design, and the purples turned the warm sunlight cold to match the snowy mountains beyond the window. The sight of Dacian's native Rysamand Mountains encouraged him. All things seemed possible when looking upon them.

Dacian inhaled the destiny that he had imagined for himself like the aroma of bread baking in an oven. The arrival of the Daykash proved to Dacian that he would become a Nebakarz priest. The Daykash only tested those who qualified for further training. And, after his ultimate success, Dacian knew that he would inspire more rys to do great things, and then Nufal would be greater for it.

"I am ready, Master Halor," Dacian said.

Halor stopped rubbing his pinkies. "I know," he said, somewhat wistfully.

Dacian followed Halor into the curving hall. Their soft suede boots padded gently on the tile floor and the glowing crystals set in the walls grew brighter as they passed them. The bronze-bound wooden doors of other modest chambers were all closed. Most of them were unoccupied. Dacian had few neighbors in the Jingten Tower. A few rys worked as servants in the tower, but they lived in quarters on lower levels. Dacian was privileged to live in the middle levels reserved for Halor's few acolytes. Nebakarz priests who worked as bureaucrats in the Jingten Colony lived in the levels above the student levels.

Halor surprised Dacian when he stopped at the stairwell instead of the levitation shaft. The crystal glow from the hallway revealed only a few steps, and darkness quickly consumed the steps beyond the entrance.

"The stairs, Master?" Dacian asked, looking down his nose at the steps used only by servants.

"A lesson in humility, Dacian," Halor said firmly.

Dacian comforted himself with the belief that surely Halor's lesson had value. "As you say, Master," he said.

"I will be waiting below," Halor said.

Dacian shyly entered the stairwell. It was unlit, but the darkness hardly hindered him. His mind could sense and map every surface, crack, and angle of the stairs. He descended quickly. Blocks of light came in at the entrances of each level. At the bottom, bright light blasted in from the reception hall.

Dacian exited the stairwell, and the awesome grandeur of the Jingten Tower consumed him. On the uppermost levels, balconies clung to the inner edge of the tower's hollow center, but most levels of the tower were closed off from the inspiring space.

Halor and the Daykash were cross legged and floating about three guli above the marble platform.

Halor had instructed Dacian that he would be expected to kneel. Dacian approached the platform, and with sincere respect went to his knees at the edge of the thick marble.

"Daykash Breymer, meet Dacian, my finest student," Halor said.

Dacian shivered with pride. For his tabre Master to praise him in front of the Daykash meant a great deal to him. No rys had ever been blessed with such an honor.

"Come closer, Dacian," Daykash Breymer invited. Nearly ten centuries of life had eroded the sweetness of spring from the Daykash's voice, leaving it gravelly and with little emotion.

Dacian stepped onto the enchanted marble platform. He pushed himself into the air with one springy step, folded his legs beneath him, and levitated forward. He came to a gentle stop before the Daykash. Blue light glittered in Dacian's eyes, the tint of which was in contrast to the pure white fires that burned in the magical eyes of Halor and Daykash Breymer.

"You honor me and my Master by your visit, Daykash Breymer," Dacian said.

"I am pleased to be here," Daykash Breymer said.

Dacian sensed insincerity in the voice of the Daykash, but he quickly admonished himself for analyzing his superiors. It was enough that Daykash Breymer had said that he was pleased, whether he meant it or not.

Halor spoke. "Daykash Breymer has accepted your request to be tested, Dacian."

A happy aura flared around Dacian. "I am blessed by your consideration, Daykash," he said.

Breymer said. "Many tabre aspire to the priesthood, but few are worthy of acceptance into training, and even fewer graduate."

Dacian dipped his head respectfully, uncertain of what he should say.

"Dacian, the Daykash's time is precious," Halor said. "Follow his instructions without hesitation. Complete each task as it is set before you. Ask no questions."

"Yes, Master Halor," Dacian said.

Without delay, the white fires within the eyes of Daykash Breymer intensified, and the smooth features of his dark gray face were obscured in the brightness. His voice sounded inside Dacian's mind. "Create two warding crystals. One is to be a basic spell blocker and the second is to be a basic mind blocker."

Dacian obediently descended into trance. The details of the fabric of existence sharpened in his mind. The weave of energy and matter and lifeforces and the omnipresent elemental forces of the world were clear to

Dacian. He could see the interconnected lines and manipulate the forces with his natural magic. His ideas could become spells, and his spells could become real forces that acted upon the world.

Tabre often concentrated their spells into warding crystals as a means of preserving the magic for repeated use. The crystals made for handy containers for their magic, and their spherical shape cast the enchantment in all directions equally. Dacian had been able to make them since his fifth decade of life, which was tremendously precocious because tabre and rys were not considered mature until age one hundred. His first efforts at making warding crystals had been toddling devices of limited enchantment, but now at age one hundred eighty his warding crystals were potent.

Although Dacian had the magic blocker spell memorized, he modified it a bit to make it unique. He altered slightly the enchantment of each warding crystal that he made because it challenged him to do so and it left no clear signature upon his work. He liked being difficult to identify.

When the magic blocker spell became clear in his mind, Dacian clasped his hands and focused the energy into matter and began organizing the structure of the crystal. Within his palms, intense heat blazed harmlessly against his skin where he formed a smooth crystalline orb. Finishing, he released the crystal orb from his hands and it floated outward and stopped between him and Daykash Breymer. The crystal pulsed faintly with blue light.

Without pausing, Dacian created the mind blocker crystal, which soon drifted out from his blue hands to bob in the air near the first one. Although his assignment was complete, Dacian scrambled together another spell and released a third crystal from his hands in a hot flash. This one he let spin over his left palm.

"A mind and magic blocker," he announced as the bubble of double warding enveloped him. He felt the minds of Halor and Breymer press against the warding as they tested his claim. Their initial effort could not penetrate the invisible barrier of magic that shielded him.

"Enough, Dacian!" Halor said impatiently. "This is not a game. Stand in submission."

Dacian had expected his teacher to be pleased by such a wondrous display from his student. But, shamed by Halor's chastisement, Dacian lowered all the warding crystals to the marble floor and eased his feet down. His power receded into his lifeforce, and he stood before his superiors naked of magic.

Daykash Breymer eyed him with great seriousness. He reached out with his right hand and the third crystal that Dacian had made flew into his grasp. While examining the warding crystal, the Daykash complimented his work. The crystal's quality was high and its creation speedy.

"Thank you, Daykash. Do you have another test?" Dacian asked.

A sharp look from Halor made Dacian drop his gaze. He should not impatiently goad the Daykash for tests as if they were trifling riddles meant for amusement.

The Daykash said, "The path to Nebakarz priesthood is made of tests. Your testing will never truly be finished, not even a full priest ceases to be tested."

"Of course, Daykash, my question was stupid," Dacian said.

Talent is often eager to show off, the Daykash thought. "Your work is good, Dacian," he said.

The praise relieved Dacian, who had been worried by his Master's severe reaction. Dacian realized he had been cocky making the third crystal, but he desperately wanted to amaze the Daykash. Dacian had studied his whole life to get his chance with the elite of the Kwellstan Sect. If he could prove his value, then the status of all rys would be lifted. Dacian struggled to calm his needy emotions. He must not let the high stakes muddle his discipline at this crucial time.

The Daykash released the warding crystal from his hand and targeted it with his magic as it floated away. Dacian had to squint against the bright white light that vaporized his crystal. A strange burning odor wafted toward him.

"I see you hope to impress me with little things," the Daykash said. "But to be a Nebakarz is to have a strong mind. How strong is your mind, Dacian?"

The tabre spoke the rys's name like the crack of a whip, and an egg-shaped aura of pure white enveloped the Daykash's floating body. He hurled his immense mental bulk at Dacian's undefended soul.

Dacian stepped back and clutched his head. Caught off guard, he reeled as he tried to cope with the stampede of outside thoughts violating his mind.

The Daykash badgered him with questions. "Can you defend your thoughts? Can you maintain your independence? Can you resist my will?"

Dacian's vision blurred as his mental faculties were slapped around by the intrusive lifeforce.

"Go away. You're not worthy to be Nebakarz!" commanded the Daykash and Dacian felt his feet move back.

"No!" Dacian gasped and reclaimed control of his limbs. The Daykash was trying to control him through his own mind! This realization horrified Dacian. And resisting was so hard. He respected the Daykash and the Kwellstan Sect. Respect and obedience were pillars of Dacian's existence. He believed in the glory of the Kwellstan Sect and wanted to add to it. But to be bullied by the will of another was abusive. And to be rejected was intolerable. Was the true test one of resistance? The Daykash had asked how strong his mind was, and Dacian decided he would prove his strength.

He rallied his mental discipline and summoned his magic. He grappled mentally with the Daykash, who persisted in trying to control his body and physically make him leave. Dacian asserted his will and blocked his tormentor, but the Daykash assaulted Dacian's mental integrity from various angles. Driven by defensive instincts, Dacian sought to seize the energy of the Daykash's lifeforce. Dacian had never attempted such a thing before, and Dacian could not trap the invasive mind. Seizing control of his opponent's will was like trying to catch a fish with his bare hands while not being able to look in the water.

Dacian pitted his youth and raw talent against a thousand years of experience and blundered into a prolonged stalemate. Time disappeared from his perception as he began to thrive upon the pure challenge of the difficult test. After achieving a full defense of his physical body and consciousness, Dacian continued to pluck the thorns of the Daykash's mind from his own even if the task seemed futile. The Daykash battered him mentally without pause as if he truly wanted to inflict crushing defeat. Indeed, Dacian began to sense that the Daykash was frustrated that his assault had been even partially repelled.

As this battle of wills dragged on, the Daykash added a psychological attack. Intruding upon Dacian's mind had given him insight into this rys's motivations.

"Stop. You're not doing the test right," the Daykash announced inside Dacian's mind.

Dacian almost faltered, appalled that he might have made a costly mistake, but he realized this might be a trick. The Daykash's test was supposed to be intense. No one, not even Halor, had been willing to describe what this intimate entrance exam would be like, and Dacian decided to persevere.

Reclaiming his confidence, he forced his own words inside the mind of the Daykash. "Have I shown my strength yet?" he dared to demand. An incoherent burst of indignation erupted from the Daykash's thoughts, and Dacian pushed back even harder. The invisible fingers of the Daykash slipped from his mind, and a surge of fresh power reinvigorated Dacian and his magic flowed unhindered. He thrust his will against the lifeforce of the Daykash while casting a new levitation spell. The tabre and the rys pushed so hard against each other with their thoughts that the opposing forces set their floating bodies in motion. They orbited each other with magical light blazing from their eyes.

At last Dacian sensed a crumpling of the will of the Daykash, and he tried again to pin the lifeforce of the illustrious tabre leader, but it was a trap. The weakness of the skilled Daykash had been a feint, and he seized Dacian's mind. Startled, Dacian was suddenly sundered from his thoughts, and blackness consumed his powerful perception. The effect was fleeting, but when he flared back to consciousness, he was on the cold marble floor and the Daykash was levitating over him.

"Enough," the Daykash declared and settled onto his feet. His white aura receded.

With the crisis passing, fear and regret replaced Dacian's confidence. He moved onto his knees and said, "Daykash, forgive me if I have given offense. It seemed you wanted me to defend myself."

The Daykash stared at him with an inscrutable face. At length he said, "Leave the tower."

Dacian slowly got to his feet. An exhaustion never before experienced dragged at his body and mind. He glanced at Halor who hung nervously in the background. His Master gave him a clipped but reassuring nod, and Dacian felt better. After studying under Halor for eight decades, he could tell when his Master indicated success.

Dacian bowed his head and thanked the Daykash for the privilege of being tested.

"Privilege indeed," the Daykash said and resisted adding the derogatory words "for a rys."

Dacian understood that they wanted privacy so they could discuss his performance. Being asked to leave was actually a good sign because it showed that they acknowledged his mental abilities. They assumed they needed the heavy enchantments wrapping the Jingten Tower to block his perception. Once Dacian turned away from them, he smiled. After decades living in the tower, all the secrets of its layers of enchantments had been peeled by his mind like brushing sediments aside to reveal a fossil long locked in total secrecy. Even Halor did not suspect how much Dacian understood the advanced Nebakarz magic insulating the tower.

Although capable of spying on the Daykash and Halor, Dacian resolved not to do it. Halor and the Daykash would likely sense his mental presence if he listened in, and Dacian did not want to anger them. He believed that he must have tested well. How could any acolyte have done better? Surely he had shown that rys were just as good as tabre. The Daykash had needed to expend considerable power to best him. Dacian had not even realized a tabre could act with such force. Now that the possibilities had been revealed, he now wondered just how much force he could exert with his magic.

The entrance of the tower stood open. High doors built of timbers harvested from the local forest were bound by bands of metal that gleamed like gold but were as strong as iron. The alloy was a Nebakarz secret. As Dacian passed through the doors, he felt the push of Halor's spell that closed them behind him.

After the timbered doors shut with a ponderous thud, Halor set his feet on the platform and straightened his robes.

"He has grown powerful, Master Halor," Breymer said.

Staring at the doors that presumably insulated him from the perception of his greatest student, Halor said with some affection, "Dacian is extraordinary."

Breymer sighed and rubbed his temple. The gray skin of his hand was darker, almost black, when seen against his lighter face.

"The Grand Lumin will not like what I must report to him. I've never had a tabre resist so well. Only his naiveté made it possible to beat him down," Breymer said.

Responsibility settled onto Halor's shoulders with visible weight. "Perhaps this does not have to be treated with such negativity. Dacian proves our case for colonizing the Rysamand. Expansion across Ektren has expanded the powers of our race. A greater footprint upon Ektren made us grow in spirit and intellect."

"A grand idea that in reality did not fit the vision," Breymer said with regret, but then, with a firmer voice, he declared, "Your Dacian is not tabre, Master Halor. None of those rys are. They are abominations."

"Daykash, they were born of us," Halor reminded, but his meek posture drained his opinion of power.

"Born of us, but not of Nufal. These mountains make their own creatures. The tabre should not have come here. We were wrong. Great Divinity, the Drathatarlane Sect was right to warn us not to come here," the Daykash said, referring to their rivals who considered tabre expansion to be heresy. He added, "The current Grand Lumin accepts what his predecessor refused to see. No more tabre will settle in Jingten. None wish to. Indeed you must acknowledge that almost all tabre settlers have moved back to the homeland already."

Halor agreed sorrowfully. He knew that no more tabre wished to risk producing rys offspring. It had begun as soon as tabre had settled in the Jingten Valley. Their tablings had been born with blue skin instead of the dark gray skin of their Nufalese parents. The tabre had been horrified. They had adjusted their spells to correct the situation, but all reproduction produced the same result: a breed apart. Those tabre with harsher hearts had even abandoned their offspring.

Strolling around the marble platform, Breymer looked up the center of the tower. "A pity this building is here. It really is some of our best work," he commented.

"Yet again our theory is proven," Halor murmured, persisting in his defense of the Jingten Colony.

Breymer was not angered by Halor's lingering enthusiasm for Jingten. "Sometimes it is not such a good thing to be right," the Daykash reminded.

"But is it not good to show that we have power greater than the Drathatarlane Sect?" Halor rejoined.

Breymer smiled in agreement. His contempt for the Drathatarlane was innate. Although the Kwellstan Sect had become distressed by the unexpected developments in the colony, it remained rewarding to see the Drathatarlane Sect nervous. Something new, potentially radical, had resulted from the experimental colonization of the Rysamand Mountains. The onset of rysness from tabre stock disturbed the tabre, but this new thing belonged to the Kwellstan Sect and not the Drathatarlane.

"Halor, I can see that you have some sympathy for these rys, but as the deputy of the Grand Lumin, I am here to remind you that you must maintain control. There could be others like this Dacian, perhaps just reaching maturity. They all must be kept in submission to the Kwellstan Sect," Breymer said.

"I am aware of my purpose, Daykash," Halor said defensively. "Surely you see how well I have done with Dacian."

Grudgingly the Daykash agreed, "Yes, Master Halor, you deserve praise. I see the respect you have instilled in Dacian. He is obedient. His juvenile eagerness to join the Nebakarz was easy to sense. He is naive and therefore controllable, but I do not want you to become lax because of your success. Dacian is young, and youth and power cast volatile spells."

"I will not become lax with him, Daykash," Halor vowed. "I know more than anyone the power he possesses. I have used great care in guiding his attitude toward Nufal and the Kwellstan Sect."

Although Daykash Breymer agreed, he still seemed dissatisfied, and Halor continued, "Once Dacian is accepted into the priesthood, his potential for ambition can be distracted by serving our society. He values the order and greatness of Nufalese society."

Growing stern, Breymer said, "He will not be allowed to enter the Nebakarz priesthood."

The statement stunned Halor. How was he supposed to deflect Dacian from his life's dream? Why would the priesthood spurn such talent?

Breymer said, "We will have no rys. The Grand Lumin has said so himself. This place must wither and we will salvage what we can. The rys must always believe that they are beneath the tabre because they are not born of the homeland. This is our official policy now, but it only makes clear the truth in our hearts."

Halor said nothing as he absorbed the knowledge of how much the tabre had come to dislike what had happened in Jingten. The grand experiment of expanding the tabre range had resulted in a subspecies, and the impurity was not going to be tolerated. Having lived and worked so closely with the emerging rys population over the last four centuries, Halor felt much more comfortable around the rys than his associates in Nufal, but he now realized that, deep in his heart, he considered himself superior, cleaner, better than all of them.

The Daykash understood that he had placed Halor in a difficult position. In a supportive fraternal manner, Breymer said, "An excuse will eventually present itself that will allow us to deny Dacian a Nebakarz education and ordainment. I will strive to separate you from the ultimate disappointment of your brash pupil. Proceed, for now, as if Dacian is on course for the priesthood."

Halor felt a brief urge to argue on Dacian's behalf, but Halor knew not to contradict the Kwellstan leadership. He served his Sect faithfully and believed utterly in the authority of the Grand Lumin. Halor had his career to consider as well. The difficulty of his assignment in Jingten would be rewarded in due time.

"Such a pity," he murmured. "Dacian had much to contribute."

4. Kwellstan

When I could not move my body I begged my friends to kill me. How could I return to my family like this? They ignored my pleas and took me across the wild lands to the nearest temple. The tabre healers could only restore half my body. Am I grateful? Yes. I've watched my children grow and learned from watching my wife the true meaning of duty. ~ Journal of Zehn Chenomet, 2042 Kwellstan calendar

The final Bozee bout of the summer was about to begin. Spectator barges filled with tabre and humans converged on the watery arena in Lake Kwellstan. For centuries the competitions had been among the fighting guilds of the Kwellstan Sect, but in recent years a pair of Bozee champions from the rival Drathatarlane Sect had claimed all glories. Their extraordinary skills kept them undefeated, and the crowds swelled more every summer when they fought. The Kwellstan Sect organizers had begun limiting spaces for human spectators, but the big event still put the whole city in a festive state.

Cruce Chenomet was excited to have obtained a place on a spectator barge. Because of high demand for the available spots, the Kwellstan Sect issued barge passes through a lottery to members of the estate and trader classes. Cruce's sister had won two passes. She would have preferred the company of her favorite suitor, Radello, but Cruce had blackmailed her for the extra pass by threatening to tell their father about her escapades with her lover.

"Radello should be seeing the twins and not you," she complained.

"Forgive me, Dayd," Cruce said without a hint of regret.

Dayd moped over the glassy smooth wooden rail of the barge. Her bare arms glowed like warm ivory in the sunshine. A thick bracelet of jasper beads clustered around her left wrist, and her lacey white dress fluttered in the breeze. Her blue eyes matched the lake splendidly, but her long golden hair that she had so painstakingly curled that morning was going limp in the humidity.

Before she had become a woman, and a bold one at that, Cruce and his older sister had spent their childhoods together in fun and sport. It was nice to have some time with her again.

"At least you get to see the twins fight," Cruce offered.

Dayd straightened from the rail and fussed with her hair. "You should be embarrassed to be seen out with your sister. Can't you find a girl to spend time with you?"

Cruce answered, "If you're so concerned about my love life, you should have given me your pass too so I could have invited a girl."

Dayd shot back that it made just as much sense that she should be there with Radello.

Anticipating his little victory, Cruce said slyly, "Your love life doesn't need any help now does it?"

Dayd smirked. She supposed there was no point in spoiling the day to spite him. "I hope they are as marvelous as I have heard," she said. Twins among the tabre had never occurred before. The twins, Tempet and Alloi, were the pride of the Drathatarlane Sect, and their powers were the envy of the Kwellstan Sect. For ten years, the twins had made Kwellstan their summer home in an unprecedented display of Drathatarlane diplomacy. The more cynical among the Kwellstan residents, both tabre and humans, insisted that the twins only summered in Kwellstan so they could show off their supposed Drathatarlane superiority. A friendly spirit of competition could not have been the sole motivation for the twins to end their seclusion in Drathatarlane, as was expected of adherents of that Sect.

A final thump was struck on the drum and the rowers brought in their oars. The barge slowed and anchors were cast off each side. Cruce moved closer to his sister as the observation deck became more crowded. Other barges were anchoring in a semi-circle on both sides of their vessel, and slender skiffs were slicing toward a cluster of tiny islets that sprouted from the shallow north shore of the otherwise deep lake. Banners flew from poles at the back of the skiffs where sculpted tabre warriors paddled vigorously. Male-female fighter duos occupied each skiff. There were seven teams. Four from Kwellstan, two from Kahtep, and the twins from Drathatarlane. All the colors of the major Bozee guilds flapped over the waters that dazzled in the noon sun. The Kahtep guilds flew crimson or green and beige. The orange and blue stripes of the top Kwellstan pair were in the lead skiff ahead of the white and gold stripes of its sister guild. Kwellstan fighters had the advantage in water fighting because their city bordered the lake, but the battle skills of the Drathatarlane twins had usurped the glory of the traditional champions.

The twins approached at a leisurely pace. Their confidence was total and they had no use for haste. The male, Tempet, precisely plied the water with his paddle. Water hardly dripped from the paddle when he raised it, and, when he plunged the paddle into the lake, he pulled hard and efficiently. His arm muscles rippled and his lower body was steady inside the skiff. His skin was darker than most tabre. His black hair was cropped short, which drew attention to his sharp symmetrical face and full lips. White enameled armor encased his torso and his white pants met the straps of his white sandals just below his knees.

His sister, Alloi, stood behind him with the black and white flag of Drathatarlane rippling behind her. Her hair was long, and its onyx shine was striking against her white tunic.

The crowd around Cruce and Dayd murmured with excited observations as the twins cruised by their barge. Tempet did not deign to look upon his admirers but Alloi raised a hand to them. Her eyes twinkled with her rising powers, and, as she passed by, every man and woman on the barge felt that she had looked at each of them individually.

"Ah, if only Kwellstan could have two such as that," Cruce lamented quietly.

"Are you going to cheer for Drathatarlane?" Dayd asked.

Cruce glanced over his shoulder. Everyone on the top deck still tracked the twins with their eyes. "I want any team from Kwellstan to win, especially Tavo Guild," he said.

"Oh," Dayd said, uncertain of his sincerity, but it did not matter. It was appropriate for Cruce to speak his support for the Kwellstan Sect, which contracted with their family for food, horses, copper, iron, precious metals, and other supplies.

Once the skiffs had passed the spectator barges, they fanned out among the islets. Cruce and Dayd watched Alloi hop lightly from her skiff and climb to the top of one of the chimney-like islets. The female partners of the other warriors were doing the same. The lone males paddled vigorously back to open water. The people on the barge jittered with anticipation, and those near Cruce and Dayd pressed closer, coveting their good spots by the rail.

The males formed a ring with their skiffs. The combat had few rules. Nothing prevented teams from negotiating deals ahead of time to gang up on other pairs. A team was finished once either fighter was knocked into the water although a fighter could enter the water voluntarily as long as he or she was not forced by an opponent.

The male fighters set down their paddles, and their skiffs bobbed gently. Each picked up the single weapon that he had selected for the battle. Four carried simple staves, one a flail, and two had whips, including Tempet.

"He's not used the whip before." Cruce overheard a man behind him say. Cruce assumed he spoke about Tempet.

The nearest barge to the competitors bore the Nebakarz priests who presided over the event. Only members from the Kwellstan Sect were present because Drathatarlane priests rarely left their sacred city in the mountains. The tabre priests in their red and black robes began chanting in their temple language that the humans did not understand. The low pulse of their voices came across the water.

"I can feel it happening," Dayd breathed excitedly. She had been told that people could feel the rise of magic when the bout began. She felt it start inside her and swell like the thrill of waiting to hear the winner of an award.

The sensation peaked and then the fighters erupted into action. Four tabre sprang from their skiffs, buoyed by levitation spells, and jumped onto the skiffs of opponents. Two landed on Tempet's craft, obviously trying to knock him out fast and early. One fighter swung at Tempet with his flail. Tempet ducked low. His whip remained coiled in his hand and he fought with his magic. He appeared to the humans as only a blurred ball of white light and then he was gone. The two fighters on Tempet's skiff looked around frantically, seeking to spy him under the water. He had slipped into the lake before they could touch him. Tempet pushed his skiff out of the water with an explosion of magic. The fighter from Kahtep was dumped into the lake, the first loser of the day. The other fighter from the local

Tavo Guild bounced himself off the surface of the lake with a fast levitation spell and landed back onto the small deck of the skiff.

Tempet grabbed the edge of his craft and pushed himself quickly out of the water. Steam rose from his skin and armor that were hot from his magic. He landed in a crouch on his skiff and met the descending staff of his opponent with a bare hand. He grabbed the staff, twisted the fighter off his feet, and then shoved him into the lake with a fierce attack spell that caused a cloud of steam to explode from the water and even left part of the skiff smoldering.

"So much for Tavo," Cruce muttered, glad that he had not placed any bets on the fights.

The other skiffs moved toward Tempet, except for one who started paddling toward Alloi on her mount of rock. A cheer rose from the Kwellstan spectators as they saw their Bozee fighters continue to press the Drathatarlane pair.

Three skiffs came alongside Tempet, and he put his whip into action. The lash coiled around the pointed prow of the closest skiff and, with a mighty pull, Tempet upended the craft. The tabre fighter hovered a moment with his magic, seeking purchase with his feet on the flipped boat. Tempet raised his hand and a flash of attack magic flew from his fingers. It struck the armored chest of the fighter and sent him into the water.

Just as two tabre attacked Tempet, he jumped onto the upturned boat and shook loose his whip. Attack spells crackled around him, but he kept his balance on the rocking boat. One tabre leaped onto to Tempet's empty skiff, and Tempet jumped back onto his boat to confront the opponent. He punched the Kwellstan Sect tabre, whose face twisted aside from the impact. Tempet kicked the tabre's legs out from under him and grabbed him with a levitation spell and made him slide into the water.

The remaining tabre confronting Tempet struck. He used a whip also. The harsh leather braid laced with threads of enchanted metal coiled around Tempet's waist. He braced himself with one foot against the side of his skiff and resisted the pull of his opponent. They were stalemated physically, so Tempet cast an attack spell. But the Kwellstan fighter was protected by the magic of his female partner. They had combined their shield spells into a double layer of magical resistance to fend off the powerful Drathatarlane fighter.

Alloi wanted to the assist her partner, but the two remaining female fighters were hitting her with attack spells, and the male fighter who had broken off to come to her was now climbing her rocky perch. The worthy challenge of three attackers excited her and added to her power and confidence. Dividing her mind among the trio, she kept the attack spells of the females at bay with her shield magic, and then created another spell in her mind. The stone islet beneath her feet grew hot and started to crack. She shoved her mind into the fracturing stone, guiding the cleavage. The rock crumbled and cracked beneath the hands and feet of the male fighter climbing the islet. He scrambled to gain new purchase and grabbed the hot broken edge of the islet and started to pull himself up, but Alloi exploded more rock and flung him back. With chunks of rock pelting him on the way down, he landed hard on the water, back first. Stunned, he sank until struggling weakly back to the surface.

When Alloi defeated the advancing male fighter, his female partner was obligated to break off her attack, defeated as well. Harried now by only one attack spell, Alloi threw back the other female's magic and bested her with an attack spell that sprawled her across her rocky mount. Rattled, she clung to the rock, trying to unscramble her mind and cast another spell.

Tempet finished the contest. Because his opponent was no longer assisted by his partner, Tempet crushed his shield spell as if he squeezed a rotten tomato in his hands. Then his whip grabbed the fighter about the neck and pulled him down. The tabre fell hard on the edge of his skiff. Tempet let go his whip and jumped into the rocking boat. He reached down and grabbed the fighter by his armor and tossed him in the lake. Breathing hard, he raised his arms to exult in his victory.

Defeated fighters slowly pulled themselves back onto their skiffs as the Kwellstan priests in the barge looked on with palpable disappointment. Being bested again by the Drathatarlane fighters stung, especially in front of a home audience.

The human spectators on the barges clapped and cheered. Although their local champions had not won, the fighting talent of the twins had been amazing to see.

Cruce leaned into his sister's ear. "It took longer to cross the lake than to watch the combat," he said, almost complaining.

Dayd continued to clap. "Do not tell me you are disappointed after ruining Radello's day," she warned playfully.

"I'm not disappointed," he said and admired the Drathatarlane twins as Tempet paddled toward the islet to retrieve Alloi.

Alloi descended onto her skiff in the glow of a levitation spell. After she landed on the deck, she took the flag into her hands and lifted it higher. The black flag showed a white tree inside a comet. Tempet paddled the skiff in a victory lap around the spectator barges.

Cruce watched the twins cruise by. They were beautiful and powerful, and Cruce was thankful that tabre Sects no longer fought in real combat. Bouts such as these were only ceremonial remnants of the actual battles once waged long ago among tabre factions. In the old days, the tabre of Drathatarlane had sought dominance over the other tabre settlements, at least as the story was taught in Kwellstan, but the separate tabre groups had finally allied and fought Drathatarlane to a stalemate that eventually created a society of peaceful coexistence.

Cruce appreciated the course that history had taken. His ancestors had found civilization among the tabre in their land of Nufal, and they had been welcome in the tabre cities with the exception of Drathatarlane. Humans were not allowed in the secluded mountain city where the twins had been born.

Although humans were a part of Kwellstan-ruled Nufal, no one had any illusions of equality between humans and tabre. Many tabre enjoyed humans for company, made friends, and respect was often given, but tabre were superior and the Nebakarz were supreme. Officially, humans were to look to them as the agents of the Great Divinity. The Nebakarz reached out to the divine for the benefit of the world and they offered the humans spiritual guidance and morality as well. The Nebakarz were typically disinterested in the economic and petty concerns of the human society in their midst. Wealth was the birthright of tabre for fine homes and jewels and all the bounty of Ektren were theirs to have. Their magic made all things easy and they had never known want. They could survive such hardships as bad winters and failed crops much more easily than tender humans whose mouths always needed to be filled.

As the crew of the barge weighed anchor and the rowers extended their oars, Cruce watched the twins finish their victory lap and paddle to the Nebakarz barge. The Bozee pairs that had lost lined their skiffs up and saluted the victors when they reached the priests' barge.

The crowd loosened up on the spectator barge as people moved away from the rails. Cruce turned his back to the lake and lounged with his elbows on the rail. His blue shirt with black trim was open across his chest, where a few hairs curled upon his lean but maturing chest. His brown hair was thick and short.

Fidgeting with the black horn handle of his dagger in his silver studded belt of blue leather, Cruce remarked to his sister that he was glad that the tabre had no cause to fight for real.

Dayd chuckled at the silly concept. "They are too civilized for that. All men would do well to follow their example," she said.

"Truly," Cruce agreed. Although Kwellstan in the heartland of Nufal knew only peace, Nufalese militias defended frontier settlements beyond Kahtep from marauding savages.

The plodding thump of the rowers' drum started again and the barge swung ponderously back toward the city. Dayd slipped away from her brother to mingle in the crowd. She was young and lovely, and not quite officially unavailable, and she enjoyed a good flirting session.

Cruce scanned the crowd. He had not actually needed a second pass to invite a young woman who interested him because she was already in attendance, but Cruce had not roused his nerve to insert himself into her company yet. He would have to do it soon or lose his chance.

"Cruce Chenomet?" a man said.

Cruce tore his focus from scanning females and saw a man he did not immediately recognize. By his nice clothing and the fact that he was on the barge, he had to be estate class or trader class, and Cruce thought that he should know the man who looked a few years older than himself. He had tan skin, gray eyes, and wavy light brown hair. Over a white shirt, he wore a stiff vest of leather armor, beautifully tooled and dyed burgundy. Then Cruce noticed the blue and green patch on the man's sleeve that signified the Kwellstan Militia.

He was the commander of the Kwellstan Militia, and Cruce finally remembered his name. "Bradelvo?"

"Gehr Bradelvo," the commander said and lifted a hand. "What did you think of the bout?"

Cruce clasped Gehr's palm in the upright handshake that was standard between Kwellstan men. "It was a short show," Cruce said as he recalled that the Bradelvo family was a minor estate class family. Gehr was the son of his family's matriarch, who had never married. Their name was not on the Founding Tablets, but they did hold upland pasture lands between Alicharat and U'telmeran where they grazed sheep and therefore supplied a good portion of the wool market. But it was not a glamorous or exclusive commodity, which limited Bradelvo affluence and probably accounted for Gehr's militia career.

Gehr laughed, and his grin showed his appreciation for Cruce's willingness to criticize the season's most hyped event. "Maybe it does not go so quickly for tabre eyes," Gehr suggested.

Cruce shrugged, supposing that made sense but starting to wonder why this man had struck up a conversation.

Rolling his eyes toward the Nebakarz priests' barge, Gehr commented, "I'm sure our Divine Lords are just thrilled."

"Beating the twins does not seem possible," Cruce said. He was not happy with the Drathatarlane victory. Like any Nufalese, his faith was guided by the Kwellstan Sect, but there was no denying the Bozee skills of Tempet and Alloi.

Gehr said, "Fast as it was, it was still awesome to see. I've been trying to get a pass for the lake bout for three years. The Kahtep temple finally decided to reward militia commanders for once and I got one."

"You fight on the frontier?" Cruce said, realizing he wanted to hear about it.

The pleasant mood that lighted Gehr's face dimmed. "Yes, I fight the savages," he said. "If you want to hear about it, I'm having a party tonight. My friends and some other militiamen. I've got a place off Fisher Circle."

Like any eighteen-year-old, Cruce perked up at the mention of a party, especially an informal one not hosted by stodgy parents. "Thanks. Sounds fun," he said and then gestured to Gehr's leather armor and told him it was nice and asked him who had made it.

Gehr explained that a craftsman in Kahtep did the work and added, "It's just for show. I don't actually wear this when I'm on patrol."

A couple men near Cruce parted to make way for Dayd. She smiled to Gehr and welcomed him back to Kwellstan. "Enjoying your summer leave, Commander Bradelvo?" she inquired politely.

"More now, Lady Chenomet," he said and deftly plucked up her right hand and kissed her fingertips. "Please, call me Gehr," he insisted. Their eyes danced together. Dayd withdrew her hand, but her gaze remained engaged by Gehr's eyes that were disarmingly bright on his tan face.

Gehr continued, "I was just telling your brother about my party tonight. If you were to attend, I'd promise to be on my best behavior."

Dayd tried to avoid smiling with naughty interest. "Is Cruce going?" she asked and skewered her brother with a demanding look that warned him she was about to assign him a position in one of her games. Cruce considered a moment and then nodded. He wanted to go to the militia party. Gehr Bradelvo surely had many interesting experiences to recount and his easy confidence was the type that any young man wanted to be around.

But Dayd had Gehr's attention now, and Cruce was more interested in his own opportunity to flirt, which was quickly ending as the barge closed on the shore. He spotted a trio of young ladies, pleasing as flowers in their pastel summer dresses, climbing the steps to the upper deck.

Cruce slipped through the crowd like a snake through daisies and caught up to the women. He greeted them confidently then focused on the girl he admired. "It is good to see you, Ribeka," he said, enjoying the quickening pace of his heart.

Her hair was dark brown, like deeply polished hardwood, and her eyes were an intriguing hazel. Under the bright sun, they seemed to be all colors. Ribeka smiled to him reservedly with little uncertain curves at the edge of her exciting lips. At her side was her older sister, Chelma, who was not nearly so attractive. She had a plain face and dishwater hair, and was drifting toward plumpness. They were estate class like Cruce although their family, the Larka, was not nearly as prestigious as the Chenomet. Growing up in the same social class, Cruce had met the sisters superficially over the years, and he had recently decided to expand his relationship with Ribeka, if he could. The third girl, he presumed to be one of their friends.

"Cruce Chenomet," Chelma said like a challenge. She edged just a bit between him and her sister. "Are you having fun playing the little lordling?"

The derogatory question jostled his poise. How else would a young male heir comport himself? And Chelma was only one year his senior, which he hardly considered license to treat him like a child.

"I am not playing at anything," he said and cursed the hurt tone in his voice. After clearing his throat, he asked the women if they had enjoyed the show.

"Oh yes. Alloi is breathtaking. Oh, to have such power," sighed the girlfriend.

Cruce nodded stupidly, wishing Ribeka would say something.

"I saw your sister," Chelma commented.

"We came together," Cruce said and then thought how lame that sounded. The confidence that had taken him by the shoulders and marched him over to the women was stumbling.

"What are you doing when we get to shore?" Cruce asked, making sure not to direct the question to Chelma.

Ribeka actually responded. "Our parents have arranged a concert at our house," she answered.

Merciful magic, she spoke to me, Cruce thought. "That sounds nice, but, um, would you like to go to a party with me?" he said, relieved somewhat to have forced out the words, but now aching for acceptance.

Chelma presumed to answer. "We're expected at home," she insisted.

"Sorry. Maybe next time," Ribeka offered and Cruce rummaged out a smile for her despite his disappointment.

Chelma slid a hand around her sister's waist and moved past Cruce. "Have fun," she said with a triumphant air that annoyed Cruce. He even narrowed his eyes at her before he could help himself, but it only seemed to amuse Chelma. He could not imagine why she wanted to give him a hard time. At the age of eighteen and the Chenomet heir, he presumably was wildly appealing.

The ladies brushed past him although Ribeka did glance back. "Have a nice evening," Cruce said to her.

Ribeka turned away and Cruce stared at the laces on the back of her dress. He sighed with frustration. He had approached her with such confidence but had lacked any game plan for retaining her attention or sidestepping her bothersome sister. Tension squeezed his shoulders and he glowered at the scrubbed boards of the deck.

Discouraged, he returned to where his sister was still chatting with Gehr.

"Who were you talking to?" Dayd asked.

"The Larka sisters," Cruce said, trying to sound indifferent. He could see in her eyes that she knew about his growing crush on Ribeka, but she was kind enough not to tease him.

The Kwellstan docks grew closer. The tall, conical and segmented building that was the Nebakarz temple called the Altular loomed above the city. The polished granite temple seemed to absorb the sunshine and glisten with its never-diminishing power. With the exception of the four towers of the Atocha, the great school of the Kwellstan Nebakarz, the rest of the city seemed small beneath the temple, like kittens gathered around their mother cat. Most of the buildings were constructed of cut blocks of granite. The tabre dwellings were encased in polished marble or limestone. The human buildings were left as bare granite, but they were decorated with bright flags, glass windows, and red-painted trim. Great old trees thrived in the city that was carefully built into the ancient forest that filled the Valley of Nufal. The trees' crowns spread over the cobbled streets and slate roofs. Thick green flowering hedges grew in the boulevards that all met at the docks and dissected the city like the spokes of a wheel. East and the west of the docks artificial shores of enormous stone blocks framed waterfalls that poured into the lake. The famous springs of Kwellstan were organized by channels and collection pools throughout the city, and the waters exited through the falls.

With an elbow on the rail, Cruce watched the city draw closer. Dayd and Gehr joked with each other and talked about people who were a few years older than Cruce. A couple times, he wanted to join the conversation and ask Gehr a question about the militia, but he supposed he would hear enough about it at the party. Although bored, Cruce discarded the idea of seeking out Ribeka again. He figured bungling one attempt to speak with her was enough for one day. He made a mental note to try to run into her when Chelma was not around, if that ever happened.

The drum beat of the rowers slowed as they maneuvered into dock. The other spectator barges were lining up behind the barge in which Cruce rode. The docks were crowded with people. The tabre on shore would have already spread the word of who was the winner of the combat, and presumably people lingered for a glimpse of Tempet and Alloi when they returned. The barge with the Nebakarz priests and tabre fighters was still across the lake though.

Before being engulfed by the urban press, Cruce lifted his gaze and took in the vista around the lake. Kwellstan and its lake sat in the center of an oval valley that was surrounded on all sides by mountains except for a gap in the west that opened onto a prairie. Two cities were set above the valley on the lower slopes of the mountains, and Cruce could see them. U'telmeran in the east and, to the north across the lake, the buildings of Alicharat rose bright and white amid many green terraced fields. Only forest and open water surrounded Kwellstan. The woodlands had not been cleared for agriculture. Food was shipped in from the grain fields and pastures of the prairie towns or the terraced gardens and orchards of U'telmeran and Alicharat. Except for home gardens, Kwellstan did not undertake the mundane task of large-scale food production.

When the barge docked, Dayd took Cruce's hand and told Gehr that she would see him later, and Gehr melted appropriately into the crowd.

Radello was waiting for them on the docks. Dayd waved to him happily as she and Cruce waited in line to get off the barge. When they reached Radello, Dayd kissed him merrily on the cheek. Radello was shorter than Cruce and he kept his light brown hair long. He wore green trousers, leather sandals, and a sleeveless cream-colored linen tunic. Radello smiled to Dayd with genuine pleasure and then greeted Cruce curtly.

"You didn't miss much, Radello. It went quick," Cruce said. "I won't steal your place in the future."

"Nice," Radello grumbled, uninterested in Cruce's condolences. Putting an arm around Dayd, Radello led them through the crowd. He was stout and broad-shouldered and had little trouble making his path clear.

Cruce hung back, finding his own way off the dock. He noticed Gehr reuniting with a half dozen of his militia comrades. By his sweeping hand gestures, Gehr was presumably describing the action of the combat to them. Gehr noticed Cruce and waved to him invitingly.

A little surprised, Cruce hesitated but he did not want to be unfriendly so he joined the group of militiamen.

"Cruce, hello," Gehr said jovially. "Tell my fellows how fast Tempet is. He makes the other tabre look like turtles."

Cruce grinned and shared his observations about the fight. Gehr then told everyone that Cruce was coming to the party that night, and the other militiamen approved. When Cruce took his leave, Gehr ducked close and said, "Even if your lovely sister changes her mind, you still come."

Cruce moved on. It felt good when he reached the shade of the stately old maples that lined the meandering avenue to his family's home. His skin stung slightly from being in the sun on the open water half the day.

Ivy-coated stone walls encased the grounds of the Chenomet house that lounged long and low among ornamental trees whose red or purple leaves mingled with pale green willows that hunkered like shaggy cows in a flower garden. The gates were open. They were always open. As Cruce entered the yard, an orange cat stood on top of the wall, stretched, and then settled back down.

"Good afternoon, Slick," Cruce greeted the cat that was so named because supposedly not even a tabre could catch him. Tempet or Alloi could, he thought.

Blaker, the head gardener, was trimming shrubs near the front entrance. Snips of branch and leaf were speckling the ground around his worn leather sandals like dandruff. Blaker waved to Cruce with his wood-handled bronze clippers. "How was the show, Lord Cruce?" he inquired cheerfully.

"Quick, yet amazing," Cruce answered and continued down the lane.

The front doors to the house were painted red and had brass handles and hinges. Cruce pushed one open on its quiet oiled hinges. The foyer had a domed roof, and slender skylights let sunlight peek down unto the polished birch floor. Cruce crossed the golden floor and headed down the left-hand hall to the informal chambers of his family. The right-hand wing of the house was for formal gatherings and the central wing was for the kitchens, workshops and servant quarters.

The walls of the hall Cruce walked down alternated between stained wood panels and paintings of Chenomet ancestors in various settings. Women and men dressed in the fashions of their times watched Cruce go by. Some of them looked strikingly similar to Cruce, while others did not. The older portraits had been preserved with costly tabre spells to delay decay.

Because it was summer, the windows of the home were open, and lightweight linen drapes with delicately embroidered edges fluttered in the languid afternoon breeze. Tiny chimes hanging in the windows tittered happily.

Cruce entered his family's private water chamber. The burbling water fountains and pools made the marble-paved room cool, and gauzy curtains across the ceiling filtered the sun through the skylights. Here he found his father, Zhen.

Zhen bathed in a deep pool. Beside him on a stool sat a tabre small in stature with large eyes and thin silvery hair. Steam rose from the pool that had been heated by a tabre spell. The steam mingled with the therapeutic vapor drifting from the simmering pots of herbs, also heated by the tabre.

"Father," Cruce said and bowed his head respectfully. "Artor," he added in greeting to the tabre.

"Greetings," Artor said pleasantly. He liked Cruce as most tabre did. They found him more interesting and worthy than most humans, although he could not guess why.

"Cruce, I did not expect you so early," Zhen said.

Cruce explained that the combat had been quick.

"Tempet and Alloi the victors?" Artor said as if resigned to the fact.

Cruce nodded. "I am sorry, Artor, they are much better than our Kwellstan champions. I must admit it."

"Drathatarlane pride will run like rivers in spring," Artor muttered.

Zhen chuckled. "We don't envy them on their bleak mountain, do we? Kwellstan is beautiful, and we are luckiest. Cruce, get me that robe."

Cruce picked up the cream colored robe draped on a bench and stepped closer to the pool. As he held the robe open for his father, Artor lifted his hands like he was feeling his way in the dark. White light snapped in his eyes. Slowly, Zhen rose from the water. The skin on his soft skinny body was pink from the heat and his withered legs were wrinkled from the soaking. Cruce held the robe out so that his levitating father could put his arms through the sleeves. Zhen tied the robe closed and Cruce slipped his arms beneath his father's armpits and embraced him from behind. As the levitation spell ended, Cruce bore the weight of his father and took him to his nearby wheelchair. Zhen relaxed into the chair that had conveyed his body for over a decade. Artor inhaled deeply to recover from his exertion.

Zhen thanked his tabre physician. "That bath was most soothing," he said.

Cruce moved behind the wheelchair to push it, but his father waved him off and grabbed the wheels himself. His muscles bulged in his thin arms and the chair started to move, slowly. Fine crafting and maintenance kept the tabre-engineered chair in good operating condition and allowed Zhen some mobility in his crippled state.

Zhen told the tabre that he would see him tomorrow.

"What of your treatment?" Artor inquired gently.

Cruce knew that Artor referred to the regular pain treatments the tabre applied with his magic healing powers. Since Zhen Chenomet's horse riding accident while hunting, his body had been broken and left in chronic pain.

"The bath will suffice," Zhen said, and Cruce was heartened to hear that his father was presumably having a good day. Pain ruined many of his days. Since the effects of drugs had weakened over the years, Zhen had needed to seek tabre healing more often.

"As you say," Artor said, although he did not sound convinced.

Artor set the stool against a wall and then held open the curtains of a doorway for Zhen. Cruce followed his father out of the water chamber and Artor took another way out.

Cruce walked slowly beside his father. Although he wanted to push his straining father, Cruce admired how his father labored with the wheels.

Moving his wheelchair had not always been so difficult, but Zhen's strength ebbed a little more each year.

When they reached another door, Cruce opened it and Zhen rolled down a ramp that had been installed since his accident so that he could access an inner courtyard. The sun was bright and hot. Sweat sprouted on Zhen Chenomet's balding head by the time he managed to reach the shade of a dogwood tree's spreading braches. Groupings of roses grew throughout the courtyard, and the perfume of their full blossoms weighed upon the air like an invitation to dream.

Cruce sat on a bench in the shade next to his father.

"Is my son troubled?" Zhen prompted.

Cruce shrugged. "No."

Zhen raised his eyebrows, showing his doubts, but he accepted the answer. A son new to manhood did not always need or want to take his father into his confidence about everything.

"Did your sister come home with you?" Zhen asked.

"I think Dayd is on her way," Cruce said.

Zhen chuckled and told his son that he was a loyal brother.

"I am supposed to go out with her this evening," Cruce said.

"Not as her chaperone, I am sure," Zhen remarked.

"Father, she is twenty one," Cruce said, trying to prove he had no way to be responsible for her.

"I know, Cruce. And she's a fine daughter. I am not worried by her," Zhen said and he meant it. A Chenomet woman was supposed to be bold. He then urged his son to describe the combat. It had been many years since Zhen had watched one. He stayed home mostly, receiving visitors and conducting his business in private. Although he had accepted his infirmity, he remained reluctant to face the public. Competition among the estate class families for Nebakarz contracts, land, and markets was an omnipresent reality, and he did not want to project weakness.

As Cruce described the combat to his father, he recalled Tempet's unconventional tactics and the precision of his fighting moves. Surely such a warrior had not been born since the dim ages of the Sect War.

Listening to his son speak, Zehn admired how well his son had grown up. Cruce was everything that Zehn had once been: vital and strong, handsome and swift. Seeing that the future of the Chenomet family was secure comforted Zhen more than tabre spells. He believed that Cruce was ready to accept the reins of family leadership. The maintenance of Chenomet political power needed youth and energy instead of the tinkering of a recluse. Zehn could not delay transferring these burdens to his son much longer.

5. Lords of Opportunity

After slinking away from his ruined domain, Amar lost himself in lawlessness.

"Be quiet, woman!" snarled the thief who Amar knew only as Smart Grab. The thief was short with shoulders and arms so thick that they made his greasy-haired head look small.

The woman, draped in simple cream-colored garments, travel stained at the hem, pleaded for the thieves to stop tormenting her husband, who was face down in the road. Another thief named Huan ground his boot between the man's shoulder blades. Smart Grab struck the increasingly shrill woman across the side of her covered face and sent her crashing into the side of her donkey cart.

Amar watched the abuse from atop his stolen horse. Part of him lurched inside as the woman cowered, finally silent after the blow from Smart Grab. Her headdress was askew and she struggled with shaking hands to straighten it and uncover her eyes.

Harshly, Amar pushed back his feelings. They belonged in Gendahl's grave where he now stored his many griefs. Better to be this animal that had no compassion or responsibility.

Huan stomped the squirming man. He shook the confiscated purse containing only a few copper rings over the man's head and demanded to be told where the rest of their market coin was.

"I know you have more than this," Huan said. "Your carts are empty. I know you sold goods in town."

The dust of the road made mud on the man's bloody, tear-streaked face. The man insisted that he had given them everything. He begged to be left alone and then offered his donkey and cart. The desperate generosity irritated Huan immensely. He kicked the man in the ribs and spat at him.

Amar turned his horse that he had stolen five weeks earlier from Patharki warriors and surveyed the area. A tall field of sorghum, green with brown crowns of grain, hid their activities from the direction of the nearest village, and the cut hay fields on the other side of the road were empty. The hay was curing in the hot sun, and its sweet grassy scent wafted over the bitter drama unfolding on the road.

"There's only one place left to look," Smart Grab decided and reached for the woman. He jerked her harshly to her feet and tore at her voluminous garments. She fought him frantically, wailing for help. Her husband, despite his cracked ribs, tried to rise, but Huan hit him in the face with his confiscated purse and then, with frightening speed, cut his throat in a dagger flash.

Amar heard the unmistakable gurgle of blood in the throat and watched the progress of his two loathsome companions.

Huan put his dagger away and assisted Smart Grab in pinning the woman to the road in the shade of the cart. The donkey, heedless of it masters' suffering, blinked patiently at flies. Perhaps the donkey had been worked too hard to care about the fate of its owners who had burdened it for years.

Once the woman's clothes were half torn away, Smart Grab shouted with victory as he lifted out the fatter purse, heavy with coins from her time at market. Huan laughed at the silliness of men who expected the bodies of women to hide their coins when they could protect neither. Huan pushed off her headdress. Her begging for mercy was sobbing gibberish. With her husband's blood soaking the dusty road in the late summer heat, she knew that she would not escape more suffering.

Amar saw her wild white eyes and silver hairs streaking her black braids that had been loosened in the scuffle.

Smart Grab moved quickly to dishonor her. Huan, still laughing, got up and bounced the purse in his bloodied hand.

"I told you they would be easy pickings, Amar," Huan said amiably and walked over to him.

"I had only said that they were hardly worth the trouble," Amar said defensively.

"I know," Huan recalled and peeked inside the purse. "But even wolves hunt mice."

Amar did not comment. He still was not quite sure how to talk to a man who would murder for the pittance paid a peasant's produce.

The moans of the woman decreased as she diminished into silent horror, waiting for her attacker to finish.

Huan gathered the reins of his skinny horse and then swung into the saddle. "You want to have a go at her?" he asked Amar.

Amar narrowed his eyes contemptuously and still said nothing. He had found that his silence tended to elicit respect from rogues.

"I know. She's too old for a young vulture like you," Huan said. "Come on, Smart Grab, I've seen this show before and it's not entertaining."

Vulture. That's apt, Amar thought. Many carrion birds had wheeled over the lost domain of the Lin Tohs.

Smart Grab left the woman crying and drooling in the dirt. He pulled up his pants and tied them closed and then proceeded to unharness the donkey from the cart. After scratching its face with an innocent friendliness that defied the nearby evidence of his viciousness, he swatted the animal playfully on the back and shooed it away. The donkey trotted into the hay field and began to eat.

Amar glanced questioningly at Huan, who shrugged. "He always sets donkeys free," he explained.

Amar had not expected to discover a trait in Smart Grab so benign. Once Smart Grab was back on his horse, they rode away quickly. Although Amar tried not to look at the poor woman, he glanced down at her as he rode by. They had left her alive, but it was no mercy. A rape victim was expected to commit suicide. The shame would be too much for her family.

Agony exploded inside Amar as thoughts of his lost wife barged into his mind. Had she had a chance to kill herself when the Patharki broke through the defenses? Or had she been violated and then killed?

A sick chill swept through his soul. He kicked the ribs of his horse and galloped ahead of his companions. Emotions clawed at him like starving senshals quarreling over a rabbit. He had learned to block his tears, but memories of what he had seen in his devastated homeland could still break loose.

Images stampeded through his mind. He saw again the charred heap of fallen stones that remained of his stronghold at Do Tohsall, where once he had been lord. Thick timbers stuck out of the debris, blackened and crumbling. All the villages had been burned, except for a few houses here and there that had escaped the flames by only chance or laziness. The ashen remains of pyres accompanied each settlement where the bodies of people and animals had been burned. Bodies hanging from trees, bird-pecked and rotting, swayed in his mind. By their defiled clothing, Amar knew that they had been warriors in his service.

The demons of his memories were inescapable. The bitter punishment of it all smashed Amar's heart upon a rock over and over. But he deserved his suffering, and it was far better retribution for his failings than quietly killing himself in the forest. He had no family left to shame.

Amar urged his horse to go faster and he veered off the road, cut across the last hay field and entered the forest. He wove between the trees, heedless of where he was going. He let the horse choose the path if only the animal would go fast. Wind rushing in his ears and the slapping of low branches helped to distract the mad rages in his head.

Eventually his mount tired of the pointless course and stopped by a stream to drink water. Amar dismounted. He stared at the flowing water. Vaguely he was thirsty, but he did not have the ambition to bend and scoop the water into his hands. He sank to the mossy bank and let his memories spill over him, surrendering to the current of his horror.

He recalled staggering from burnt village to burnt village in his former domain, weeping often and collapsing with grief. Only when he had been completely parched had he sought a creek from which to drink because he dare not draw any water from the wells.

As Gendahl's tormented shade, he had wandered his old domain. This land that had always been his home had become entirely foreign to him. If the Gods of Gyhwen had not killed him here, then it was his place no longer.

He had resolved to leave. He would cast himself upon the world and fall into whatever crack opened for the ruined and damned. But before he went, he had traveled the roads of his domain again and cut down the bodies of his warriors. Digging them graves was too difficult but he had managed to pile crude cairns upon them. The effort had been exhausting and prompted him to seek food. From abandoned orchards he had found ripening fruit, and the occasional root cellar had been unmolested and given up vegetables for him to roast. The first time he had tried to eat, he had retched it up. The stench of death had permeated the land as well as his mind, but on subsequent tries, he had kept down some food.

Without Onja to provide for him and coax his body toward health with her power, his ribs had become more prominent and his cheekbones had sharpened. Yet he had continued to prowl about the Lin Tohs Domain in his sad limbo and attend to the bodies of his warriors, who unlike the common folk, had been left to rot instead of being burned.

As far as he could tell, he had finished the grim task late on a particularly hot day when the grip of summer was strongest. While washing his hands in a pond, Amar had heard the rumbling of approaching riders. Instinctively he had crouched among the reeds and watched a dozen Patharki warriors pass the pond on the road to the nearby village. He had presumed the warriors were there to begin staking out their land claims, which would be their rewards for the extermination of the tiny Lin Tohs Tribe, up and coming as a people no more.

They had slowed and then stopped when they had passed a row of fresh cairns. Amar had been able to faintly hear them discuss the cairns, but distance and their dialect prevented him from understanding them.

Bending deeper among the reeds, Amar had waited for night to fall. After having spent so much time outdoors, the half moon gave him plenty of light to see by. The campfires of the Patharki had been bright, and Amar had crept close to the tethered horses with his sword drawn.

With silence and swift anger he had slain the sentry posted on the horses. The blade chopped through muscle and bone and the sagging head never issued a warning cry. Amar had gone to his knees as the body slid off his blade.

Killing after so much time spent in useless despair had made his blood run hot again with life. Perhaps a cruel world had bequeathed him only cruelty as pleasure.

Amar had wanted to rush into the camp and kill as many Patharki by surprise as he could before being overwhelmed. But a chilling rationality had consumed his mind as the Patharki warrior cooled on the ground.

Gendahl is gone. Let Amar be what Amar can be, he had thought.

Amar had then stripped the dead Patharki. He had taken a sword, a dagger, some silver coins, and various small tools useful to life in the saddle. He had selected a horse and led it quietly away. With enough of a head start, Amar had escaped whatever pursuit the warriors had launched after finding their dead comrade. Amar had ridden west from his lost domain, descending the rougher foothill country and entering the flatlands. In the dense forests between the tribal domains, Amar had encountered his new companions.

Smart Grab and Huan had of course tried to rob him. They had confronted him openly in daylight as he rode a lonely trail between the lands of the Tacolucus and the prominent domain of the Temulanka. From the outset, Smart Grab and Huan had been assessing him because they suspected that he was more rogue than foolish traveler. Amar had met their threatening presence without fear. After drawing his sword, he had rolled his shoulders to warm up his body for the fight.

Naturally, Huan had chuckled. "You must have many valuables to risk fighting us, young man," Huan had said.

"The Philosophers say that one's greatest value cannot be taken," Amar had said back.

"The Philosophers? What a high-born wanderer you must be," Huan had said.

"The prattle of the Philosophers is no secret to common men who do not favor ignorance," Amar had said. "Now move aside and let me pass or start this fight."

But there had not been a fight. Huan had exchanged a look with Smart Grab, and in the silent way of men who ride together and commit crime together, they had made a decision without discussion.

Huan had asked Amar where he was going, and Amar had said that his business was his own but had added, "And who are you to question travelers in this place? Would you be the lords of this land?"

"We are the lords of opportunity. We obey no laws and impose few," Huan had answered. "You, I'm thinking, are a citizen of our realm."

Amar had given them his name then and they had done the same. He had been riding and thieving with them since that day, and they had pried little into his origins, except to ask him about his burnt hands. Amar had told them that it had been an accident with an oil lamp, which was plausible enough. With a sly and suspicious look, Huan had asked Amar about one of his swords. Not the common warrior's sword taken from the Patharki, but the other blade that was smithed by a skilled man and crafted for a lord. The blade was of iron, not bronze. To maintain his aura of mystery, Amar had said that he did not recall where he had stolen it.

Amar supposed that soon enough he would lose track of what he had stolen or not stolen. With Smart Grab and Huan, he had robbed eight people and broken into three homes. He was not proud of it, but nor did he dislike it. There was a genuine thrill in living outside the confines of society and law. He could do what he wanted without regard to duty or family, past or future. He could forget himself.

Today had been especially violent though. Amar had no desire to be wanton with the employment of terror, but he had no right to judge his companions. They were vicious, and Smart Grab was arguably crazy, but they did not judge him and did not compel him to be overly violent if he had no urge to do so.

Amar blinked. The sunlight was dazzling on the jingling stream that he had been staring at for some time. He took a deep breath and emerged from his fog of memories. The pain remained, but his mind had regained a hold on the moment.

Suddenly, he realized he was not alone. He spun around and drew his sword. Panic slapped him for being oblivious to his surroundings.

Huan and Smart Grab stood among the trees just beyond the bank of the stream. They had chosen their ground well. The shadows of the trees fell across them, making it easy for the eye to pass over them if they did not move.

Amar lowered his sword warily.

Smart Grab moved through the foliage that crowded the bank. The sunlight over the stream was shiny on his oily hair. "What are you doing, Amar?" he said.

Amar did not answer.

Huan followed Smart Grab into the light. "If you meant to steal the loot and run off, you forgot to rob us," he joked.

"I wanted to be alone," Amar said grudgingly.

"Are you done?" Huan asked.

Amar nodded and splashed down the stream to retrieve his horse that had wandered down the bank. Huan called after him that they needed to ride all night.

Returning with his horse, Amar asked why.

"Summer's end has a Thievesmeet," Huan replied.

Amar wrinkled his forehead questioningly. It made him look young and naive.

Smart Grab chuckled. "He knows nothing."

"That's why he's got to be introduced around," Huan said.

Annoyed to be spoken of in the third person, Amar demanded to know what they were talking about.

"The weaklings who hide behind their lords' laws have their faires and festivals. We have ours," Smart Grab said and clearly he thought that Amar was hopelessly green.

With sudden seriousness, Huan said, "Amar, I see that you suffer. This is the life for men who have lost their place in the other world. You have nothing left to lose. That is why you are with Smart Grab and me. I know this."

Amar had not expected such analysis from Huan. He had expected even less for Huan to care anything about him, but he seemed to be reaching out to him. Huan, and perhaps even Smart Grab, had shown him the concern of genuine companions. The bandits and rogues who roved the gaps between the tribal towns and cities were men as much as monsters. Amar realized that there was a culture in which he could live. At the very least, he supposed he needed a community where he could survive the winter.

"I lost my family," he whispered. Harshly he chastised himself for sharing the detail. Exposing the vulnerability of his emotions was risky but the words were spoken.

Huan nodded and seemed to be on the verge of saying something meaningful, but he reverted to his lighter side and said, "Maybe you'll have another someday."

No, Amar thought without any doubt.

They traveled north. Smart Grab apparently knew every deer trail between the Temulanka Domain and the northern Kelsur frontier. They kept to the forests and did not use the roads, which was surely to the benefit of travelers.

After three days, they met another group of four men, who appeared even rougher and more dangerous than Huan and Smart Grab. They wore armor, much of it scuffed, dented and mismatched, and they bristled with maces and shields in addition to swords and daggers. One carried a bow with a quiver of arrows fletched in black and iridescent blue. Two dead ducks hung from his backpack. The men wore no tribal insignia that Amar recognized, but he saw how war had hardened these men. They were not just robbers and scoundrels. They were mercenaries.

Huan clasped his hands together and walked slowly toward the mercenaries. When Amar saw that Smart Grab was doing the same, he intertwined his fingers as well, but still hung back.

The mercenaries stared at the three thieves for a long uncomfortable moment, until the captain joined his hands in the same way and introduced himself as Rakir. Then the tension dissolved, and they all exchanged names. The other three mercenaries were Utuh, M'hen, and Daso, the archer.

Rakir and his fellows were traveling north to the Thievesmeet as well, which Amar surmised welcomed mercenaries as well. They all camped together that night, and Amar listened to Rakir share news of the larger world. Hearing about the intertribal goings-on interested Amar more than he had expected. Maybe he might be able to take an interest in the world again. Trying to function, even among the lawless, was better than blundering in his grief. But when Rakir started to speak of the destruction of the Lin Tohs, Amar's stomach strained queasily against his supper.

"No one saw how hard the Patharki were going to hit that little tribe," Rakir said. He paused to suck some meat off the leg bone of a duck.

I should have seen it, Amar thought, and Gendahl's shade stirred restlessly. Amar could try to stow away his grief, but he had only leaky jars to hold it.

Rakir continued, "Ginjor Rib, cheap bastard, didn't hire any mercenaries to keep it all quiet. But I'm thinking next year, we find some work with the Tacolucus or maybe even the snobby Temulanka. They'll be nervous from this boldness shown by Ginjor Rib. I'm thinking those tribes might want the Patharki annoyed and distracted on a regular basis." He tossed his bone aside. "We'll see."

"I heard the Patharki made a thorough ugly job of their attack," Daso said in a whispery voice reminiscent of an arrow hissing through the air.

Amar's guts coiled around themselves. Even with his appetite killed, he shoved the duck wing in his mouth and picked at it with his teeth as a way to keep his horror from showing on his face.

Daso said, "It is being said that the Lin Tohs are no more. Has anyone seen stray warriors escaped from the fight?"

"I heard some rumor of a few going south," Huan answered carelessly.

Amar wondered if there was any truth to Huan's statement. Then he noticed Smart Grab giving him a queer look across the campfire.

He knows, Amar thought, but what did it matter? As long as no one suspected that he was Gendahl, he was just another ruined warrior without a home.

Rakir said that he believed hardly any Lin Tohs escaped the carnage because of their remote home. The Patharki would have had much opportunity to cut them down before they could reach distant towns or cities into which they could disappear into anonymity. "Or, they have gone into the wild lands that surrounded their domain," Rakir suggested.

At the mention of the wild lands, Onja sprang into Amar's thoughts. Her beauty and power exploded brilliantly out of his memory, and he was comforted to know where she dwelled in the Espen Forest. With a sudden pang of regret, he wished that he had not left her.

Amar considered returning to her. He was not so close to these new companions that he needed to give any explanation or excuse about leaving. He could just ride away, but curiosity compelled him to stay. Amar wanted to see the Thievesmeet and learn more about the workings of the underworld.

I will look for Onja after I have done this, he thought and he liked the decision. He could discuss what he learned with Onja. He suspected that she would be interested.

The next morning, the thieves and mercenaries started early when the birds were just greeting the dawn with songs. They broke their fast on the trail, eating hard stale hunks of bread. Amar considered how they killed for money yet lived with no luxury. Perhaps it would be different at the Thievesmeet.

6. The Thievesmeet

Chatting seemed to interest everybody more than speed while traveling to the Thievesmeet. Because the mercenaries were on foot, Amar, Huan, and Smart Grab walked and led their horses. Heading north through hills and forests uncut by plows or parceled by fences, Amar listened to their conversations. Rakir and his fighters recounted many battles, especially from the notorious Temulanka-Sabar'Uto War that had ended six years ago after a decade of conflict. The mercenaries mixed their exploits from that big war with episodes from tiny interfamily and intertribal squabbles.

Amar remembered hearing about the Temulanka-Sabar'Uto war. Although distance had shielded the Lin Tohs from the violence, the scale of the conflict had been well known and the terrible stories of sacking, burning, raping, killing, abducting, and mutilating had been carried to all hearths in Gyhwen. Even as an adolescent, Amar, or rather Gendahl, had been sometimes shocked by the cruelty reportedly exchanged between the large tribal kingdoms. In retrospect, he should have become wary of such tactics instead of shocked. The brutality of the war had evidently given Ginjor Rib inspiration for cleansing one of his borders of inhabitants.

Huan shared many tales from his criminal history. Amar suspected that Huan often exaggerated the grandiose amounts of gold and silver he had stolen. By Huan's accounts, he should be a wealthy lord by now, and Amar could not imagine that one man could have spent it all on whores and strong drink.

The mercenaries accepted Huan's stories without criticism. Whether they believed him or not, Rakir and his fighters enjoyed the telling of the tales, which Huan had a skill for enlivening by changing his voice to perform the complaints of his victims and gesturing broadly to demonstrate his bold struggles.

Like Amar, Smart Grab was mainly quiet. Amar suspected that Smart Grab's stories would be unfit to share with even this rough lot.

On the sixth day of travel, they swung east into a rough piney forest and entered the foothills of the Tymelo Mountains.

The Rysamand, Amar reminded himself.

Great granite boulders dotted the land, like the discarded blocks of child gods. Buttes of gray and pink granite and hard facades of blue stone that matched the great mountains broke the landscape and created a giant shattered stairway on the threshold of the mountains. On secret trails that ascended through the broken places in the buttes, the men hiked until they came upon a wide wall of cliffs that jutted above the forest.

Amar smelled cooking fires. His stomach rumbled for something fresh and savory to eat. As they headed toward the cliffs, the land dipped and they emerged from the trees on the shore of a narrow lake below the cliffs. Many tents, people, and horses were clustered on the far shore, and the music of pipes, strings, and drums crossed the open water. The festive sound startled Amar's spirit that staggered in gloom.

A clear wide path circled the shore and many fresh footprints were pressed into the moist soil. As they walked around the lake, they encountered men and some boys. Some wore tattered clothes, but others were better dressed in newer clothes dyed red, blue, and yellow, and others had a more military appearance like Rakir and his mercenaries. All of them, even the younger ones, had watchful predatory eyes, but their faces bore smiles and they called out to Amar and his companions words of welcome in a variety of dialects.

Some campers recognized Rakir or Huan. Amar watched the reunions closely, marking those who called themselves friends of Rakir or Daso or Utuh or M'hen or Huan. No one rushed out to greet Smart Grab, which did not surprise Amar nor seem to bother Smart Grab.

Amar and his companions hastily claimed a little area for a camp, unpacked their few possessions, and staked the horses to graze on meadows beyond the reedy shallows of the lake shore. When Amar was reluctant to leave his things, the others laughed and insisted he had no need to fear for his possessions at the Thievesmeet. Although doubtful, Amar allowed himself to be ushered away.

When they entered the main camp, everyone shouted to the new arrivals. Drums beat out the message that more men had come. Within the camp, Amar noted the presence of women as well, some young, some old. Their heads were uncovered and knives jutted from their sashes. Several women rushed forth to greet the newcomers with horns of drink. A white-haired and toothless woman shoved a polished cow horn rimmed in copper into Amar's hand. She cackled happily, squeezed his cheek, and spoke to him in a language he did not know.

"Drink!" Smart Grab commanded and thumped Amar on the back in an unexpected burst of camaraderie. Smart Grab lifted his horn and drank deeply.

Amar nodded in thanks to the old woman, who trotted off to her campfire. When Amar looked at his horn of light brown liquid, he noted the snake and daisy design in the copper lip. The design was Temulanka.

Stolen, he thought and raised the horn to his lips. The drink was strong, burned his throat and warmed his chest. On the second sip, the sensation was more pleasant, and Amar was suddenly tempted by the sweet sanctuary of intoxication. But the desire was fleeting. Drink could not compare to the relieving embrace of Onja's magic, and Amar suspected that he would do best to keep his wits active in this throng of scoundrels.

Smart Grab drained his horn and traded it for another proffered by a dark woman. He grabbed her breasts as she handed him the horn, but she smacked him off with a scolding laugh. She whirled away and danced into the growing crowd.

Again Smart Grab told Amar to drink but he did not wait to see if his companion complied. With his horn lifted and chin dribbling, he stomped off.

Cautiously Amar nursed another sip and moved aside from the parading traffic. Rakir bumped up against him and encouraged Amar to have fun. "You are among friends here," he said.

An extraordinarily tall and burly man with shaggy black hair stood at the opening of a large tent of skins. He bellowed to Rakir, who yelled back and quickly rushed to greet his friend. The big man grabbed Rakir and pounded him on the back in an embrace that seemed more an attack than a greeting. Amar veered away from the tent and caught up to Huan, who was talking to an elderly man clutching a gnarled staff with both hands.

Huan greeted him happily. "Good thinking to stay close to me, Amar. A man can get pulled into many directions at his first Thievesmeet. You don't want to end up sharing furs with a murderess or sorceress, do you?" Huan asked playfully.

"No," Amar said with a wary glance at the drink-toting women in the crowd.

"That how I get this nasty son," the old man announced with a thick accent.

"Amar, meet my father, Gadoh," Huan introduced.

"Of the Kelsur Tribe," Gadoh added with a regal nod.

"I am pleased to meet you, Gadoh," Amar said, and the courtesy seemed to amuse the old man.

"Is this Kelsur territory?" Amar asked. He had heard of the Kelsur, a wild nomadic people whose exact numbers were unknown. Where and how far they ranged beyond the borders of the civilized tribal kingdoms he knew not.

"Any territory can be Kelsur territory," Gadoh said matter-of-factly.

More practically, Huan explained that the Kelsurs attended the Thievesmeet to trade goods, stories, and news.

"And women," Gadoh said. He smacked his son on the chest and added, "And boys dreaming of cities and foolish riches."

"And I have had both, Father," Huan responded.

Gadoh sighed. "I come every year to see if my son is ready to return to the free lands and be a proper Kelsur."

"He has been a proper friend to me," Amar said, groping for something polite to say.

"Hah! You must have nothing to steal then," Gadoh said.

"No, I have nothing to steal," Amar agreed.

"Except that nice sword," Huan noted with a greedy glance.

Amar placed his hand on the handle of his lord's sword and commented only with a reproachful look.

Huan tossed an arm around Amar, who could not help but tense a little. He had ridden for some time now with Huan but this closeness surprised him. The atmosphere of goodwill and fun at the Thievesmeet would be difficult to get used to, and Amar considered that he should not be too trusting of the friendliness all around him.

"We need to show Amar around," Huan said.

"I stay here," Gadoh said. "Trade minerals and balms."

"Trading," Huan huffed as if his father were hopelessly old fashioned.

Huan tugged Amar through the crowded camp toward the looming cliffs. Amar shrugged out of Huan's brotherly arm.

"I can drink with two hands if I must," Huan said and reached for a horn and cup carried by passing women.

One of the women stopped and offered a full horn of drink to Amar. She had a triangular face made more severe because her black hair was pulled back so tightly. She was thin, except for the round swell of pregnancy pushing at her dress, and her wiry brown arms showed through the slits in her sleeves. Amar declined the drink, and she moved on after giving him a puzzled look.

"I would eat if I could," Amar mentioned to Huan.

Wiping his chin after sloshing the horn to his mouth, Huan nodded and assured his friend that there was feasting to be had. Gesturing vaguely toward the cliffs, he led Amar across the camp.

Tiny waterfalls trickled down the cliff in many places. The water collected in small pools and then spilled in streams toward the lake. At the base of the cliff, Amar saw the wide mouths of deep caves overhung with ivy and dripping water. At the threshold of the caves, hunters had hung dozens of deer from trees and were cleaning and skinning the animals. Fires and roasting spits were being set up, and boys were scurrying to unload the wood that they had gathered.

"See, much food to come," Huan said.

Amar nodded approvingly and lifted his horn to actually take a drink, but a commotion of shouting behind him distracted him. Even as he turned to see what was happening, Huan pushed on his chest, spilling a little of his drink onto his armor and moving him aside.

The crowd of revelers was parting for a group of three dozen warriors that marched toward the largest cave entrance with ominous confidence. Their steps never slowed as they pressed forward because they knew that everyone would get out of their way. The sides of their heads were shaved, but the hair on top of their heads was long and sometimes braided into thick coils. Feathers stuck out from some of the braids, and bronze helmets bound with black leather cording hung down their backs from loosened straps. They carried warhammers and spears, and each man had at least two daggers sheathed at his waist along with a sword.

From the cave emerged a tall muscular man. His bare chest was sweaty in the heat, and he wore leather pants, dyed a deep red, with fringes of leather down the sides of the legs. As he came out of the shade of the cliffs and the sun hit him, jewels twinkled on his many necklaces and bracelets and his bare head gleamed from a fresh shaving. Black makeup surrounded his eyes, giving him a pantherish gaze. He awaited the approaching warriors.

Amar leaned close to Huan and asked if the man from the cave was a chieftain of some kind.

"Oh, yes," Huan answered. "He is Lax Ar Fu. Overlord of the Kez."

"The Kez," Amar repeated, startled. He knew the Kez were the elite among outlaws, ostensibly priests to Vu, the God of Contests. They were often hired to serve as guards at tribal negotiations because they would be loyal to neither tribe in a dispute. When tribes decided to meet in parley between battles, they both contributed to the pay of Kez to provide security at such meetings. The Kez fought as dreaded mercenaries too. They had made much profit during the Temulanka-Sabar'Uto war. Amar had not expected to see them here, and he said so.

Huan chuckled at his ignorance. "They are kings among rogues. They fight for the highest bidder, they steal, they meddle in the affairs of lords. They make trouble to amuse themselves. They will do anything. Even us thieves are cautious of them. They come here to hear news, rumors. They have an eye open for talent too. Be careful of them, Amar. That's the best advice I'll ever give you," Huan said.

Amar eyed Lax Ar Fu thoughtfully. "They will do anything," Huan had said, and the statement spawned possibilities in Amar's thoughts -- ambitions that he had not expected to feel.

Amar then took a deep drink that he hoped would help him dodge the dark cravings of his splintered soul.

The Kez warriors reached the black-eyed Lax Ar Fu, who raised his arms in a symbolic embrace of the warriors. The men thumped their chests with their right hands and then held out open palms to Lax Ar Fu to salute him.

Lax Ar Fu welcomed his Kez warriors. They shouted his name and the warriors dispersed into the crowd, except for two warriors who ascended the rocky threshold of the cave and joined Lax Ar Fu. Amar watched the three men go into the cave. He sipped from his horn and realized he disliked watching leaders from a distance, like a field mouse observing a coven of cats.

Losing everything had been horrible, and being nothing tore open stubborn wounds.

Huan pulled Amar away from his brooding. They wandered the festive sprawling camp. There were jugglers and singers and magic-workers, all of whom entertained Huan thoroughly. He picked up a woman on each arm and shook his head every time Amar declined the advance of female company.

Amar traded his drinking horn for a plate of crispy fried fish, fresh from the lake, delicious and spicy with an herb he did not recognize.

At summer's leisurely pace, the day dawdled into dusk. The setting sun blazed on the west-facing cliffs as it sank farther into a forested landscape vast and dotted by distant mesas. The heat diminished and a breeze off the lake carried a fresh coolness into the camp.

Huan was staggering drunk at this point and he shook off his female companions and took Amar by the arm. Without knowing what else to do, Amar guided his friend back to his father's campsite. Gadoh was sitting cross-legged with another man going over several small piles of colorful powders displayed on a skin. The elderly man rolled his eyes when he saw the condition of his son.

"Put him in my tent," Gadoh said.

The man with whom he was meeting took a pinch of orange powder from one of the piles, rubbed it between his thumb and finger, and sniffed at it.

Huan leaned heavily on Amar, who tried to slip past Gadoh and his customer, but Huan managed to trip over his father's staff and knock the stick into the displayed powders, smearing three piles into each other.

Gadoh barked in his own language, presumably cursing at his son. Amar rushed his companion toward the open tent flap and rolled him inside. He hurried back to pick up the staff and try to set things right, but Gadoh snatched the staff and shooed him away.

Amar decided to check on his horse. As he rushed away, he overheard Gadoh's customer dickering for a lower price on the contaminated samples.

To Amar's genuine surprise, his horse was staked where he had left it. Amar led the horse to the lake to drink and then staked it out in a fresh area to graze through the night.

Beyond the cliffs, the stars were coming, twinkling over the peaks of the Rysamand that looked tall even next to the heavens. Only a turquoise glow remained of the sun in the west. Music and laughter rumbled from the Thievesmeet. Amar paused to appreciate the stillness of his separation from the gathering. He patted the neck of his horse and hoped that the animal would be there in the morning.

I could always steal another, Amar thought, wondering why he bothered to worry. He lived free now. Anything that he could take could be his.

Mosquitoes that had been gathering over the lake were moving onto land, and Amar hurried back to the camp where the smoky commotion would help keep back the whining biters. While still on the lake shore path, he spotted hundreds of blazing orange torches atop the cliffs. Many blasting horn notes spilled over the cliffs onto the Thievesmeet.

Amar rushed back to Gadoh. The old man's customer was gone and his powders were put away. Huan's snores rattled from the small tent.

Gadoh stirred a pot of broth on his fire, and he greeted Amar with a smile. His teeth were good for an old man.

Amar apologized for his sloppy delivery of Huan earlier.

"Not your fault," Gadoh said.

Another bombast of horns sang from the cliffs, and Amar peered at the fluttering torches high in the night sky. There were at least a thousand now.

"Who are they?" Amar asked.

"The Kelsur," Gadoh answered with considerable pride.

Amar asked if the whole of Gadoh's tribe had come, but Gadoh only chuckled.

"How will they get down?" Amar wondered. The torches were clustering along the edge, lighting the landscape with a line of fire as if a giant floating field was being burned of chaff and stubble.

Gadoh hauled himself to his feet with his staff. He cleared his throat and said, "Only one way to get down a cliff alive, young man."

People were rushing to the base of the cliffs and coming out of the caves as well. Fresh fuel was thrown onto campfires and braziers, illuminating the lower cliffs with a milling mix of human shadows.

Dark lines streaked the cliffs, uncoiling and dangling like snakes held by their tails. Soon many ropes draped the cliffs, and Amar watched people swing off the edge onto the ropes even as the lines were falling. People poured over the cliff, rappelling rapidly with breathtaking confidence. Some even had torches stuck through their backpacks with the flames burning just above their heads as they descended.

Kelsurs scuttled down the cliff like hatching spiders, but the mass of torches atop the cliffs did not diminish. The Thievesmeet swelled from the arrival of several hundred people. Kelsurs spread through the camp like flooding waters, and Amar watched them walking by. Five of them, four men and a young woman, joined Gadoh, who promptly dug five bowls out of his pack and gave them to his guests and gestured to the hot broth. Amar watched them dip out the modest meal and sip from the bowls. They varied in appearance. Some taller than the others. Some with slender faces. Others had round broad faces. Four of the guests had black hair, but one of the men had lighter hair that was reddish brown. Amar had not seen hair that color before. They wore leathers and furs, and the woman was dressed much as the men were in breeches and a tightly laced vest trimmed with polished stones.

None of them gave Amar more than a passing glance. Gadoh chattered to them pleasantly in the Kelsur language, and after one of the men gestured toward the incapacitated Huan, they all shared a laugh.

Amar looked back to the cliff. Many thousands of Kelsurs still remained above, and he imagined their grand camp up there under the stars.

A deep long note sounded from yet another horn and the raucous Thievesmeet grew quiet. The five guests at Gadoh's fire set down their bowls and stood.

Gadoh came over to Amar and was excited to explain what was happening. "She is here. Loxane, our Shamaness," Gadoh said. He herded Amar forward with his staff. "Come. See her close. Make a path for an old man. You must see her, Amar. Your civilization blindfolds you. Hides many wonders, and Loxane is one of the greatest."

Willingly, Amar shouldered his way through the crowd, with Gadoh eagerly steering from behind. They made their way to the front of the crowd gathered at the threshold of Lax Ar Fu's cave.

Another horn note sounded, hanging in the air meaningfully before fading away. Torches were thrown down onto the threshold of the cave. They landed in a semi-circle, forcing the crowd back.

People started to cheer and Amar looked up and spotted three figures coming down on ropes. Two men rappelled alongside the third figure that was draped in a voluminous hooded cape. Torches burned on the backs of the men, and the firelight rippled on their well-muscled arms as they came down the ropes.

When they reached the top of the cave entrance, they had no more rock to rappel from and they climbed the rest of the way down with their hands and feet on the ropes. The men alighted on the smooth rock before the cave, and they drew their torches off their backs like they were drawing swords. More slowly, the cloaked figure came down the rope and touched the ground between the two men. Wrapped tightly in the cloak, the third person advanced with the two men into the semi-circle of torches. The crowd became hushed, and Amar found himself sharing in the excitement. The sensation of awe and anticipation surprised him, and he thought nothing of his sorrows for more than one heartbeat.

When the Shamaness Loxane threw off her cape, people cried out with reverence and joy. She was naked and her wonderful body, both strong and soft, glistened in the torchlight. Tattoos of green and blue adorned her body, bright upon her exceptionally light skin. Her hair was long and curly and the most amazing color that Amar had ever seen. Red it was, like copper made soft and inviting. The enticing locks flowed over her shoulders but did not cover her full breasts that displayed her femininity unabashedly.

A sunburst tattoo encircled her navel and tattooed eagles adorned her thighs and perched on her knees. Snake tattoos coiled around her arms and their heads were drawn onto the backs of her hands with forked tongues going down her middle fingers. When she turned, Amar saw an elk tattoo on her back. Its great rack of antlers spread over her shoulder blades and its snout reached to the small of her back. The animal had starbursts in place of eyes, and when Loxane began to sway her body, the elk looked to be shaking its head.

Loxane began to move more of her body, limb by limb. Her hands rotated and then her arms lifted and her shoulders circled. Her torso circled with ever-increasing exaggeration of movement and her pelvis gyrated. Her buttocks lifted and squatted, glorious in their curvaceous smoothness.

The Shamaness Loxane danced naked in front of the gathered rogues and lawless wanderers, and she had no shame. Amar watched every move of her body, only blinking when he consciously thought to do it. Never had he seen, nor imagined, a woman making such a display of herself. And never had he imagined that a woman could be so beautiful, so powerful, but so wicked.

People were playing drums for her. First one drummer, and then three, and then dozens pounded a beat that was all life and no judgment. Their rhythms guided her and coaxed her to move faster. Her body joined with the beating of the drums, until the drummers seemed to respond to her movement as much as she responded to them.

Loxane moved to the edge of the semi-circle of torches and began to dance around the edge. People reached out to her but did not touch. She arched and swayed just beneath the fingertips of her admirers.

The crowd pressed hard against Amar and Gadoh as Loxane came closer to their position. Like all the others, Amar had no intention of giving up his spot. He turned sideways so that two more men could squeeze in next to him. Behind him, Gadoh giggled.

Closer she came to Amar, and his breath quickened and his eyes widened. The absolute scandal of her brazen nudity and erotic dancing pounded against all that his culture had ingrained in him about the modesty of women. Far back in his mind, his sensibilities railed against her outrageousness. She was the worst of the worst, criminal beyond the most wanton whore, but Amar paid less attention to the dogma of his upbringing the closer she danced to him. Indeed, as Gadoh had said, Loxane was among the greatest of wonders.

Although enthralled by her provocative display, Amar did not reach out to her when she danced before him. The fellows alongside him spread out their hands toward her, just barely missing her skin, but Amar only looked. His eyes went up and down her body, and he was truly awed by her lovely strength that went past simple maddening sexuality. His eyes traveled up her naked body, pausing at her breasts that glistened with the sweat of her dance, and then he looked at her face. Loxane's eyes were half rolled back. The trance of her dance was deep upon her. Her lips hung open as if she would cry out with ecstasy at any moment.

Amar envied the oblivion on her face, doubting he could ever experience such inner peace.

Loxane's eyes snapped into focus. The men reaching for her withdrew their hands, each gasping as if the snakes on her arms had come to life with venomous anger. She stopped dancing and lowered her arms. Her chest heaved with hard breathing and she stared intently at Amar.

He looked into her eyes that were shockingly blue.

In the background, the drums continued to beat, loud and hard like the heartbeat thudding in Amar's ears. Just when the drums started to slow, she began to dance again, but this time with her eyes firmly on Amar. She took her gaze from him only when her dancing steps spun her around. She studied him and then step by step moved away. Amar watched her go. He could not have described his feelings. Desire, curiosity, perhaps even wariness confused him as he realized that she had shown him special attention.

Loxane finished her circuit and danced back toward the cave. Lax Ar Fu waited for her at the cave entrance.

She went to him. As if in a meeting of equals, they bowed to each other. They exchanged words but the drums covered what they said.

The crowd loosened around Amar as people started to dance. Loxane had enflamed their passions and people swayed, kissed, caressed, and invited pleasure into their bodies. At the heart of the thumping mass of dancers, Lax Ar Fu extended a hand to Loxane, and he took half a step toward the cave, apparently to guide her inside. She reached slowly for his hand, but then withdrew it and looked over her shoulder at Amar who had not moved from his place.

When Loxane stalked toward Amar, Gadoh cringed and clutched his staff close. The other people still near Amar moved back, leaving him exposed. Gadoh began to do the same, but Loxane speared him with her striking eyes and commanded him in the Kelsur language to stay.

Gadoh dipped his head respectfully to the Shamaness. "How may I serve she who dances with spirits?" he asked in the Kelsur language.

"I would speak with this stranger. He does not know our tongue, does he?" Loxane said.

"No. What would you say to him?" Gadoh asked.

Loxane made her statement and Gadoh pondered his interpretation.

When Gadoh turned to Amar, the old man looked at him in an entirely new light.

"What does she say of me?" Amar demanded.

"She says you spirit-touched," Gadoh said.

Amar frowned and looked at Loxane suspiciously. Onja, he realized. She knows that magic has touched my body.

He nodded. "Ask her if she has been to the Rysamand?" he told Gadoh.

"What?" Gadoh said.

"The Rysamand," Amar said louder, directly to Loxane.

She did not need the interpretation. She recognized the word.

"Have you been there?" Amar asked, but when Gadoh relayed the question, Loxane shook her head. She began speaking, and Amar awaited the translation impatiently.

Gadoh finally told him that Loxane said that her ancestors had come from a land beyond the mountains. She was of a special lineage, the blood of the sun it was called. Other Kelsurs did not possess the knowledge that was her heritage.

"What do you know of rys?" Amar said.

Loxane looked down wistfully and spoke in a tone of ripened sorrow. She explained that her grandmother had taught her about rys when she was a small girl. Her grandmother had been into the mountains, in the Valley of Powers as she called it, and she had encountered the rys and learned what she could of them.

By now, Gadoh had warmed to his role as interpreter because of the fascinating topic. He said, "Loxane asks where you saw rys?"

Amar withdrew physically from the question. The growing intimacy that had been quickly forming between him and Loxane receded, and he noticed again her wild nakedness. Her brazen body distracted him and added to the threat he felt at her question. Even though she had freely told him about herself, he had no desire to speak of his experience. His time with Onja was his, and not to be spoken of loosely.

"I have not seen these creatures," he replied, but looked at the dirt as he said it.

Loxane sneered at his lie.

"Elder Kelsur," Loxane said to Gadoh. "Tell this man born under a roof that rys command the powers of Nature. They perhaps even dip into the well of creation, but their hearts remain the hearts of animals. In their thoughts and deeds they are no better than man or woman. Beware them."

When Amar heard the translation, he spurned the warning of Loxane. He knew more of rys than her little girl bedtime stories that she sold as wisdom. Who is this woman who would call Onja an animal? he thought with much disdain. Onja's power is true. Not some trick from a shameless savage Shamaness who confuses sex with power.

Amar crossed his arms and indulged in one long good look up and down her truly luscious body. "Loxane of the Kelsur, you were kind to speak with me," Amar said with cool courtesy.

After Gadoh told her what he had said, words hesitated on Loxane's full lips until she decided to say nothing. She gave Amar one more quizzical look and then spun around. Her red hair, glinting in the torchlight, flipped off her shoulders and bounced and swished as she trotted toward the cave.

Amar watched her go until he noted the dark piercing eyes of Lax Ar Fu that were trained on him. Male jealousy seethed on the face of the Kez leader, but Amar did not flinch from the hostility. With neither fear nor anger, Amar met the look of Lax Ar Fu.

It was Lax Ar Fu who disengaged eye contact first when Loxane took his hand and they walked into the cave and were swallowed by the dark gash in the cliff. For the first time since his new and rotten life had begun, Amar felt alive. Fate had more plans for him than tramping about with Huan and Smart Grab. The cold twinkle in Lax Ar Fu's eyes had shown him as much.

7. The Brotherhood of Vu

Peace is death. Battle is life. Victory is everlasting heaven. ~ Incantation to Zatooluh, God of War

Amar needed relief from the dense crowd. He returned to his camp at the sprawling fringe of the Thievesmeet where Smart Grab was already sleeping contentedly, like a child who had played hard. Amar went to sleep as well, but he tossed with dreams of Loxane. Her flowing body saturated his sleep with her naked energy, and his mind ran laps around his encounter with her.

Eventually he escaped the dream and took deep slow breaths to try and clear his mind. He forced away the image of Loxane and eased himself back into sleep. This time Onja's face greeted him, and he welcomed her soothing beauty. Sparkling water drenched her head, flowing through her hair like liquid crystals and her eyes gathered the light of the dancing droplets and grew brighter. He slept more deeply. His flesh was renewed as his spirit snuggled with the memory of Onja.

Amar was as defenseless as a babe when two pairs of hands grabbed his arms and jerked him to his feet. Fright obliterated his sleep. Before he could even struggle, the two men were dragging him away.

Smart Grab awoke and protested. A wild look ignited his bleary face. He was half way to his feet when a third man kicked him in the chest and yelled at him. Apparently Smart Grab knew he could do nothing because

Tracy Falbe

71

he halted and only looked at Amar with anxious regret. The third man quickly frisked Amar and yanked his weapons off. Then the trio hauled Amar deeper into the encampment. When they broke from the tree cover onto the lake shore, Amar looked up at the cliffs looming over the mass of people. Smoke drifted from dying fires. The ropes of the Kelsurs hung down the cliffs like a great fringed shawl draped over the land.

Amar seized his senses and recognized his attackers as Kez. Their braids dangled over the shaved sides of their heads much like the ropes on the cliffs. The man twisting and yanking Amar's left arm had two cream and red hawk feathers sticking straight up in his hair.

A mass of people carpeted the ground between the lake and cave. The orgy of the night had collapsed in a stupor. Men lay with women and men lay with men. Discarded drinking vessels and clothing peppered the slumbering crowd, and the rising daylight cast no beauty upon the debaucherous debris. The Kez stepped over people as they marched Amar toward the cave of Lax Ar Fu. Forced to be hasty, Amar kicked some unfortunate sleepers.

He passed by the ropes dangling in front of the cave where Loxane and her attendants had descended. Stumbling over the rock where she had danced so wondrously, Amar resisted his urge to shout at his abductors. He would face this trial with what dignity he could snatch from the situation.

Inside the cave was cool and thick with the scent of burning incense. Beyond the yawning entrance, the cave ceiling reached even higher. The cliff was nearly hollow here and the ceiling was a frightening spearscape of hanging stalactites. Firelight flickered on gold, red, white, and purple mineral drippings.

The Kez hauled Amar deeper into the cave. Torches burned in sconces carved into the walls and on top of stalagmites. Teeth-like shadows snarled at the paintings on the mineral-streaked walls. Elk and bears painted in brown, black, and ocher dominated the scenes where eagles flew and speckled senshals prowled on large paws with their long tails curving. Kez lounged around fires. Their shields and weapons and other gear were stacked against the walls and stalagmites. Conversations died as Amar was noticed and the snores of those who were sleeping halted as they were roused to witness the encounter.

In the rear of the cave, Amar was shoved to his knees before steps carved into the rock. Four steps up, there was an altar-like platform lit with oil lamps and covered in furs. Chunks of incense smoldered on the steps and the smoke curled toward the dark ceiling. Lax Ar Fu rolled out of the altar furs and came to his feet two steps down. Except for his necklaces and bracelets, he was naked, still slick from his coupling with a woman. The black eye makeup had smeared onto his cheekbones and nose, making him look scorched. The obvious strength of his body was naturally intimidating. His sculpted biceps and pectorals advertised his power and his hard abdomen looked like a battle shield.

He came down the last two steps. Amar was released and looked up at Lax Ar Fu. He studied the Kez leader but felt no fear. The numbness that locked much of Amar's emotions protected him from caring about his safety. If he was to be tortured and killed, then that was no less than he deserved, and, if that did not happen, then he would learn from the encounter what he could.

"Who are you?" Lax Ar Fu demanded in a dialect understood among the civilized tribes.

Amar would not answer questions on his knees and he moved to get up, but one of the Kez slapped a spear against his thigh, warning him to stay down.

"Answer," Lax Ar Fu said.

Amar turned away from him and showed only his profile. With downcast shifting eyes he watched Lax Ar Fu and the warrior with a spear.

"If you continue to pursue the Shamaness, I will chop your legs off and feed them to you," Lax Ar Fu announced.

A smile cracked Amar's face that stiffly resisted the expression. "You have a great sense of possession over she who dances naked before so many," he commented and peeked slyly at Lax Ar Fu, inviting a response.

Lax Ar Fu took a swift terrible step forward and backhanded Amar to the rock floor. Amar groaned and breathed hard against the pain as he picked himself up. Sitting back onto his heels, he held the side of his face and looked directly at the Kez chieftain.

"I do not pursue her. She talked to me," Amar said.

Amar observed how his fearless calm intrigued Lax Ar Fu, who was used to taking the measure of men but was finding this prisoner hard to judge.

Does he see what Loxane saw? Amar wondered.

Almost at the thought of her, she emerged from the furs on the platform. Wrapped in a cloak of wolf hides, she came down the steps, nuzzling a fluffy gray tail on her shoulder. Covered now, her face and eyes were even more striking. She appeared amused by the situation. She stopped on the last step and Lax Ar Fu moved over to her.

She rubbed his shaved head and said in her language, "He is spirit-touched, Lax-a-fu. That is why I went to him."

"Spirit-touched?" Lax Ar Fu repeated, and Amar recognized the word that Gadoh had translated for him the night before.

Lax Ar Fu asked Loxane if she was certain, and she widened her eyes with indignation that he would doubt her judgment of such a thing.

"But none have been touched since your kin came through the mountains," Lax Ar Fu insisted and regarded Amar warily.

Brushing Loxane's caressing hands from his temple, Lax Ar Fu approached Amar again. Amar turned away slightly, disliking the proximity of the chieftain's genitalia.

"Who are you?" Lax Ar Fu demanded. "What's your tribe?"

Again Amar started to rise and this time when the spear came to restrain him, he grabbed it quick as a lizard and flung it to the floor. Embarrassed, the Kez warrior rushed forward, but Lax Ar Fu raised a hand and the warrior withdrew, abashed. Amar stood up and faced Lax Ar Fu. He was not quite as tall as the Kez leader, and he doubted that he matched the chieftain's strength but apparently being spirit-touched counted for something.

"I am Amar. I have no tribe," Amar answered.

Lax Ar Fu walked slowly around his captive, eyeing him suspiciously. He asked one of his warriors to show him the weapons taken from Amar. The well-crafted sword immediately got his attention. A dirty life in the wilds had barely diminished the precisely made sheath. Every leather stitch was still perfect and discs of jade carved with spirals adorned it. Lax Ar Fu pulled out the blade, iron instead of bronze. It glistened with oil and sharp edges. He asked Amar where he had gotten such a good weapon.

"I stole it. This is the Thievesmeet. How else do you think I came by it?" Amar said.

Lax Ar Fu pressed the sword behind Amar's ear and left the cold edge against the tender skin suggestively. "Of no tribe? I don't believe that," Lax Ar Fu said. "You do not have the speech of a whore's bastard. You're educated."

"Perhaps I am a very smart whore's bastard," Amar said.

Lax Ar Fu scoffed. He shoved the sword back into its sheath. "This is Lin Tohs," he said. "You're some leftover retainer from that sad massacre. You probably took this from your dead lord before fleeing for your life."

The unfeeling fortress that guarded the remnants of Amar's soul cracked. He sucked in his stomach and tried to keep the sudden spurt of his emotions from surfacing.

"If the Lord of the Kez knows so much why does he drag me from my sleep to question me?" Amar said, proud of his cocky tone. This interrogation by a powerful man excited Amar. The attention summoned ambition. The shell of his brittle soul cracked and the hungry beak of a raptor broke through.

Lax Ar Fu returned to Loxane. She pressed against him, covering half his nakedness with the fluff of her furs. He embraced her with one arm and fingered her red tresses with his free hand. Lifting a lock to his nose, he savored her smell a moment and then said, "Amar of no tribe, I brought you here to warn you against attracting the attention of the Shamaness. Her power is such that I cannot bear my jealousy. Leave here and do not come back."

Amar looked into Loxane's eyes. Her fascination for him remained, but she seemed unrepentant about getting him in trouble with her lover. Amar realized that perhaps the attention of Lax Ar Fu was not such a bad thing. When was he likely to have a meeting with a powerful man again?

Daring to reach beyond his defeated obscurity, Amar said, "Lax Ar Fu, Lord of the Kez, I was told that the Thievesmeet is a place where thieves and rogues are brothers. We who live outside the society of farmers and palaces suffer no judgment here."

"I make the exceptions," Lax Ar Fu said.

Amar bluntly asked what would happen to him if he did not leave.

"Pray to Vu that you don't find that out," Lax Ar Fu warned, but he studied the young outlaw more carefully.

Unimpressed with the vague threat, Amar said, "What would the Lord of the Kez do if I said that when I saw him and his fine Kez warriors yesterday that I decided right then that I would join your ranks? I would be one of these brothers who know no law or border."

Lax Ar Fu frowned. "A man does not just join the Kez. We recruit only. And you seem to have the brains to realize you are not being recruited," he said.

Again, Amar shifted his gaze to Loxane, flaunting his disregard for the Kez Lord's jealousy. "There must be something that you desire but cannot have. Name a thing that would make you recruit me, and I will see it done," he said.

Lax Ar Fu separated himself from Loxane and stalked up to Amar, who did not flinch. He could smell the body odor of the Kez Lord. Its thick masculine scent was charged with agitation.

"There must be something that would change your mind about me," Amar added.

Finally Lax Ar Fu's annoyance shifted to curiosity. Amar of no tribe, who according to Loxane was spirit-touched, was simply too strange to dispatch with thoughtless violence. Sometimes strange had its uses, and the Kez could value that.

Lax Ar Fu turned away from Amar and went up the steps to the platform where he had lain with Loxane. He retrieved a fur robe and clothed himself. When he came down the steps he ordered food and drink and invited Amar to sit at a fire with him. Loxane stirred the coals and added a few sticks of wood, and the fire brightened. The orange flames sparkled upon her wondrous hair like a sunset through amber beads. She settled down next to Lax Ar Fu and snuggled him affectionately like a cat. She draped her head against his broad shoulder and idly stroked the fine hair of his chest, but her blue eyes stayed on Amar.

A man gave Amar a cup of water and a plate of cold meat and fresh fruit. He ate while Lax Ar Fu told him what he desired.

"In the war between the Temulanka and the Sabar'Uto, I was cheated by a warrior chieftain named Wayndo. Both of us had been hired by the Temulanka to siege the town of Deko. I was not the Kez Overlord then. I was a lieutenant to my predecessor, Pepum, and great man that he was, he was often too quick to make a deal. He was bought by the Temulanka for the siege before he knew that Wayndo had been hired as well. Wayndo is a Temulanka, a noble's bastard, yet a bastard warlord with many tough warriors.

"Deko was a big job and we needed our combined forces. We torched the villages and plundered the land. We strangled that town. The people of Deko knew that their fellow Sabar'Uto could not come because their armies were bogged down in fighting with the army of the Temulanka king. Eight times the warriors of Deko came forth to drive us from their gates, and eight times we battled them until they buckled and we broke into their town and laid it waste. Before the smoke of the fires rose very high in the sky, Wayndo was riding to the Temulanka king to announce the victory and collect the payment for gutting the town.

"Wayndo never returned. His arrangement with the Temulanka king had been to earn estates and legitimate titles if he could destroy Deko. He kept the pay for the Kez for himself.

"My Lord Pepum never pursued him as he should have. I do not know what restrained the revenge he must have craved. If there was some influence within the Temulanka Tribe that made him forego revenge, I do not know. But I have not forgotten this insult. I have always wanted the Temulanka, and especially Wayndo, to learn that the Kez do not forget.

"I want revenge, but the Domain of the Temulanka has been full of its warriors since the end of the war, and it's been difficult to organize a proper hunt for Wayndo. Amar of no tribe, since you're so willing to impress me, you can act as my assassin. No one will suspect you of being my agent. Bring me the head and cock of Wayndo, and I will recruit you to the Kez and you can join the Brotherhood of Vu."

Amar ate the last two morsels off his plate, chewing thoughtfully on the tough meat. He doubted that Lax Ar Fu lacked assassins to send after Wayndo. It was most likely that Wayndo was a well-protected target and there was no profit beyond settling an old score in the killing. And Amar suspected that he was meant to get killed on the mission.

The option to refuse and walk away from the Thievesmeet remained, but Amar decided to take the offer he had so boldly gained from Lax Ar Fu. He had nothing else to do, and the life of common artless criminality that he had fallen into with Huan and Smart Grab had no appeal. Amar craved to be part of something larger, and he believed he would find opportunity instead of death on a mission against Wayndo.

Amar nodded and said, "His head and his cock."

Lax Ar Fun grinned for many reasons. "Good, Amar, good. I will even be generous with you and assign three fine Kez to accompany you. They will be watching to see that you undertake what you have agreed to do. A man does not make a deal with Lax Ar Fu and then not follow through."

"Yes, Lord of the Kez, I understand," Amar said. "I shall go today."

The three of them rose to their feet. Loxane let go of Lax Ar Fu and hugged her furs close. Amar noted that she looked tired now, having no doubt been up the whole night busy with her depravity.

Lax Ar Fu summoned three Kez to him and introduced them to Amar. Vame, Kym, and Cybar were their names, and each of them smirked skeptically when their lord described their assignment and Amar's mission.

Amar disregarded their attitude and told them where he was camped and that they should meet him at midday and be ready to leave.

Eager to leave the depths of the cave and feel the warm sun, Amar dipped his head to Lax Ar Fu after a courtly fashion. "I intend to serve you well, Lord of the Kez," he said. Then, he bowed to Loxane and said, "It has been a pleasure, Shamaness."

The parting comment visibly rankled Lax Ar Fu, but the deal had been made and he let Amar walk away.

Outside the cave, the hungover participants of the Thievesmeet groggily welcomed the day. Fires were stirring, and people were bathing in the lake. A few Kelsurs were even climbing the cliff; their packs already loaded with goods for which they had traded.

Not far from the cave, Amar encountered Smart Grab and Huan. An expression of happy surprise lighted Smart Grab's face, which startled Amar. He would not have expected such a look to cross Smart Grab's mean features.

"You live!" Smart Grab exclaimed and grabbed Amar by the shoulders and gave him a shake. He also looked Amar up and down as if checking to make sure all body parts were present.

Huan moaned, "Amar, I told you not to bother the Kez."

"They bothered me," Amar explained while he gestured to Smart Grab to back off. "But do not worry. I am going to join the Kez. It's all arranged."

Huan laughed and demanded to know what Amar had been drinking.

Amar walked with his comrades back to their camp and explained what had happened between him and Lax Ar Fu.

Smart Grab digested the news and then commented that only a fool would meddle with Wayndo.

Amar stopped. "You know of him?" he asked.

Smart Grab nodded and almost seemed a bit insulted that Amar was surprised that he knew something. "I worked for him seven summers ago. He is cruel and devious. So suspicious that he kills friends and allies before an enemy can even have the chance to get close to him," Smart Grab explained.

Amar asked Smart Grab what work he had done for Wayndo.

"Things," he replied with disturbing suggestiveness. "But too much work. I left. Better to thieve and have fun with no master."

"Yes, I see," Amar murmured. "What does Wayndo look like?"

Smart Grab told him that Wayndo was wiry with scarred arms, especially his right arm because it was his sword arm. He was a little shorter than most men, bald but what hair he had he kept long and in a single braid.

Amar thanked him for the information and declared that he would be a fool and seek Wayndo.

They reached his camp and Amar began to organize his few possessions that had been scattered during his scuffle with the Kez. Smart Grab and Huan watched him pack. Both of them were still clearly surprised by his sudden Kez mission.

"You shouldn't do this, Amar," Huan cautioned. "Even if you could get Wayndo and become a Kez, why would you? The Kez must serve their master and their god Vu always. You should live free like us."

Amar tied shut his pack and shook his head. "I want to be part of a big group," he said. "But I thank you for the companionship," he lied.

Smart Grab snorted with amusement. No one had ever said that to him before. He slapped Amar on the shoulder and then strode off toward the Thievesmeet, indifferent to Amar's departure.

Huan, however, was annoyed by the abandonment. "You are too green for this nonsense. Stick with me. I'll make a good thief out of you," he insisted.

"I am sure that you would, Huan," Amar agreed. "But I cannot get what I want wandering around with you and Smart Grab."

Huan frowned and asked what Amar wanted. In his mind there was little else to desire besides total freedom.

Amar did not answer. He wanted to hurt Ginjor Rib, and perhaps he would be a step closer to that goal after trying his hand at being an assassin. The idea suited him.

"The Kez interest me," he said simply.

Huan groaned dismissively and seemed very like his father in that moment. "Good luck to you, Amar," he said and left to catch up with Smart Grab.

Without watching Huan or Smart Grab go, Amar slipped his pack across his shoulders and adjusted his swords. He would not miss their company. He knew whose company he craved, and he would seek Onja before confronting Wayndo.

8. Primitive Sports

Until the breeding spells are perfected, I recommend that the rys be kept ignorant of their powers and trained to look up to native tabre as their superiors. ~ Daykash Fane, 1806 Kwellstan Calendar

The unfamiliar games of tabre acolytes sparring outside the tower distracted Dacian. Prodding his discipline, he tried to focus. Halor expected him to discuss Emjar's treatise on clairvoyance "Perceiving All" that afternoon, and Dacian had barely reached the middle of it.

Halor honored him by allowing him to study the treasured record that Emjar had written a thousand years ago. Only preservation spells were keeping the book's delicate binding and thin stone leaves together. Dacian enjoyed a rare privilege to actually touch the book that was on loan from the Atocha for the summer.

Dacian attempted to read again. The fine script was only faintly etched on the brittle stone wafers, and the letters blurred in his vision when another blast of raw magic shook his senses. Leaving the book open on his desk, he went to his window. The panes with their purple triangle designs were open, and a fresh pine breeze carried in the omnipresent chill of the nearby glaciers. Oblivious to the icy peaks, warm sun fell upon a green valley reveling in its furlough from hard winter. Flowering meadows and cold sparkling streams fed Lake Nin amid the primeval pines. Dacian saw the landscape. He smelled it. He heard it. He felt it, all the way from the drip of snow upon the mountainsides to the strained grinding of monstrous stone deep inside Ektren beneath the blue stone mountains.

The Rysamand, he thought lovingly.

Dacian transferred his sight into the farseeing senses of his mind. Perhaps Emjar's "Perceiving All" could teach him the finer points of clairvoyance, but his natural ability served quite well. Flying through the trees, fragrant with pitch, Dacian spied upon the tabre acolytes.

He saw two teams of three tabre males running among the trees north of the tower. They carried weapons and their eyes blazed with a diamond glow. One of them was sprawled upon the ground. Pine needles clung to his black hair and stuck to his wet lips when he rolled over. A tabre came down an outcropping of rock. Made nimble as a mountain goat with tiny levitation spells, the tabre descended the rock face where small pines grew in stubborn defiance of their poor luck in having sprouted in so hard a place.

The tabre laughed as he jumped onto the ground and trotted to his victim. Gloating, he prodded the tabre with his staff.

"I have bested you," the victorious tabre said. "You are out."

But his supremacy ended as quickly as he uttered the words. Spells latched onto him from two sources. He cried out indignantly and sheltered himself from the magical onslaught with a shield spell that encased him in a shimmering bubble of energy.

Two tabre came out from the cover of the trees near the rocky outcropping. They intensified their attack spells as they came closer. The tabre who had been knocked down got to his feet. Although still swaying, he picked up his staff and charged his opponent. The two tabre struggled until the one previously sure of victory was thrown down.

"Nooo!" he shouted angrily, but with the smooth walnut staff of his opponent shoved under his chin, he could not work himself free.

The two tabre who had saved their friend ran up to the struggling duo. While one of them scanned the area warily, the other insisted that the opponent yield. Pinned by physical force and magic, the tabre admitted his defeat with a sour grimace.

Dacian could see the two remaining teammates of the bested tabre. They were creeping around the outcropping of rock. They hid themselves with an interesting spell that apparently cloaked them from their opponents' perception. Although their spell wanted to deflect Dacian's senses and make him see nothing more than lichen, rock and trees, he still detected them. He studied the spell, fascinated by the concept. He wondered when the other tabre would detect the cloaked tabre.

The two cloaked tabre rushed forward. They were a blur in Dacian's mind. Too late the trio of tabre sensed their attackers. Before they could fully turn around, attack spells blazed across their backs and the two cloaked tabre leaped at them. One was struck with a high swinging kick to the head and another tabre suffered a blow from a staff between his shoulder blades. The attack dropped two of the tabre instantly. The third, who was still rattled from his near defeat, raised only a puny shield spell, and the two tabre fell upon him with swift blows. Raising his hands, he crumpled to his knees and cringed beneath the bashing staves of his opponents.

"My team is done," he cried and covered his head.

The surrender was accepted and the tabre lowered their weapons and grinned happily. One helped his third teammate up while the losing team dusted themselves off and rubbed their sore spots.

For half the morning, they had been rushing about the forest, hurling attack spells and trading blows like unruly hooligans. Now they talked as friends, recounting the better moments of the fighting game.

With the game over, Dacian realized how caught up he had been in their competition. Their violent struggles had been thrilling. Dacian wondered what it would feel like to flex his magical powers in such a contest.

He observed the tabre on their walk back to the tower, using their staves now as walking sticks. They continued to chatter about their game. Even from five elti away, Dacian felt their eagerness as they planned another match for the next morning.

"Dacian?"

The voice of Halor called Dacian's attention back to his body. His senses whirled, and the jagged treetops veered beneath his farseeing mind. A half dead pine, taller than the others around it, wore an eagle's nest crown. His mind flew by the lofty platform of sticks, and he noticed two fluffy white eagle chicks before his mind plummeted into the tower.

Dacian turned from the window and dipped his head to his master.

"You are supposed to be studying," Halor scolded and frowned at the abandoned book on the desk.

"I was, Master," Dacian responded. "But the fighting of the acolytes from Kahtep seized my interest."

"Rowdy fools," Halor muttered. He fidgeted with his collar. "They treat their visit here like a holiday instead of taking their tour of the realm seriously. I should tell Master Darjeir to mind them more closely."

Halor checked to see where Dacian had left off in the book. His student's progress was quite insufficient, and he said so. "Dacian, you should not let yourself be distracted. I came up here because I sensed your mind wandering all over," he said.

Still reluctant, Dacian left the window. He regarded "Perceiving All" with little enthusiasm and said, "Master Halor, I think that I will go join the sports tomorrow."

Halor stared at him. The presumptiveness of his student was nearly as surprising as his disinterest in his scolding. But, as usual, Halor softened and looked dotingly upon Dacian. Putting a hand on Dacian's shoulder, he gestured out the window and said, "Dacian, you should not waste your talent on such primitive sports. There are far better things than knocking each other about."

Dacian looked wistfully at Emjar's great work. Such studies had always been his passion, but today something new had aroused him.

"Master Halor, the acolytes were using spells that I do not know. Some of them could—"

"Dacian," Halor cut him off. "You surprise me. You are no brute. Did Daykash Breymer want to see how well you could hit someone with a stick?"

Dacian did not doubt that Halor was a wise and good teacher who gave him many scholarly opportunities, but it now occurred to him that perhaps not everything could be learned from one teacher. Apparently tabre acolytes in other Nufalese schools enjoyed learning more subjects.

Accepting that Halor had no interest in sports and perhaps had never thought to instruct him, Dacian said, "I will get back to my studies, Master Halor."

Halor smiled, and the curve of his fine lips accentuated the length of his nose. "Of course you will, Dacian," he said and wagged a finger at Emjar's book.

Dacian returned to his seat.

"I expect to discuss the first half this evening. No excuses, Dacian," Halor said.

Dacian nodded and Halor left. Taking a deep breath, Dacian lifted his eyes past the book and looked out the stained glass window again. The urge to observe the tabre acolytes persisted, but he did not dare. Halor was monitoring him.

Dutiful again, Dacian applied himself to the book and sensed Halor move off. Dacian's annoyance with his master started to pass. Dacian supposed that he did not need Halor's approval in every matter, and this realization comforted him.

That evening Dacian discussed his reading with Halor. Dacian stood in Halor's receiving chamber on the second highest level of the tower. The stone bricks of the floor were laid in a great spiral that radiated throughout the round room and Dacian stood at the vortex of the floor bricks while Halor sat in a high-backed chair upholstered in green leather. Halor questioned him on certain points and nodded with approval for some answers and corrected him on others.

As usual, Dacian received more approval from his master than correction. Halor seemed pleased with him again, but the satisfaction that these sessions normally provided Dacian eluded him this time.

"You have done well, Dacian. You are excused," Halor said.

"Thank you for the instruction, Master," Dacian said and bowed out of the room.

Standing now on a great balcony that encircled the hollow center of the tower, Dacian could see the rim of the topmost level where Nebakarz priests occasionally met for ceremonies. But, because the Jingten Tower had never been formally declared a Nebakarz temple, ceremonies were infrequent. The stars that he could see through the skylights complemented the glowing crystals set in the walls. The lighting offered a pleasing ambience, and Dacian studied the many spells that had been incorporated into the tower's construction. He admired them like a gardener notices an impressive flower bed.

He walked along the balcony until he reached the levitation shaft and gripped the focused line of energy as easily as a squirrel jumps and seizes a branch. He gave just enough of his weight over to gravity and rode the energy down to the third level that contained the common areas for the Nebakarz residents.

A great sprawling kitchen and dining area arced around half the tower. Pillars separated the kitchen and dining area. Cooking fires, racks of gleaming copper pots and pans, and shelves of food were visible beyond the tables. Chandeliers of glowing crystals hung over the dining tables that were made of hardwood imported from the forests of Nufal. The white light from the crystals lighted the faces of tabre gathered at the tables. A few rys, who were employed at the tower, sat in cliques separate from the iron-skinned Nebakarz acolytes and priests.

Most had finished eating. The rys chef, Exaton, sat at a table with his apron tossed over his shoulder. He looked up from his penarta game when Dacian walked in. He told Dacian some soup was keeping warm on the middle hearth and then he resumed his game with his two friends. He drew in one eyebrow as he concentrated on using his magic to move a cube-shaped piece across the penarta board.

Dacian thanked him but he was not hungry. He had come to see the acolytes from Kahtep. They lounged around their table talking. Their dinner plates and bowls were strewn before them. Dacian approached the table and stood there while the acolytes continued their discussion without looking up.

Eventually one of the tabre looked at Dacian when he realized that the rys was not going to clear the dishes. Dacian recognized him as one of the tabre who had been able to cast a cloaking spell.

Impervious to the tabre's haughty attitude, Dacian introduced himself.

One of the other acolytes chuckled. "So you are the rys being schooled in Nebakarz ways?" he said.

"Yes," Dacian said, ignoring the tabre's disdain. "I would be pleased to acquaint myself with the visitors from Kahtep. I hope that you are finding my homeland interesting."

The tabre who had initially acknowledged Dacian rose from the table. Leaning close to Dacian's face, he said, "Yes, this is indeed your homeland."

"May I join you?" Dacian asked.

Nonplussed, the tabre said nothing, and Dacian took it as an invitation to sit. He stepped into the bench at the table. The tabre slowly returned to his seat, bothered by Dacian's assertiveness.

Dacian looked around the table. The six tabre stared at him with various degrees of discomfort.

"Your name is Bagdoa," Dacian said to the tabre on his left. He then named the others at the table. "Athur, Teev, Mithel, Ensel, and Blaysh."

"How is it you know our names?" Bagdoa asked.

"I have heard you talking," Dacian said.

"It's rude to eavesdrop," Teev complained.

"Is it?" Dacian said, amused to be scolded for such a ridiculous thing. Tabre, rys included, all possessed varying degrees of clairvoyance. Without taking precautions for privacy, a tabre could expect that anyone might be hearing his words and seeing his actions. It was the way of things.

"What do you want?" Bagdoa said impatiently.

Dacian analyzed the feelings of the Kahtep acolytes. Their hostility wounded him.

Why do they think me so low? he thought, but said pleasantly, "I watched your game this afternoon. I am interested to know more about it."

"What about it?" Bagdoa prompted.

"Everything. May I join you in this game?" Dacian said.

The tabre acolytes relaxed, and they exchanged grins around the table.

Athur spoke. His smile showed off his big bright white teeth. "You lack the training to spar with us in Bozee bouts," Athur said.

"What know you of my training?" Dacian rejoined.

Teev and Mithel chuckled loudly, but it was their apparent ringleader, Bagdoa, who answered. "It is common knowledge that you study under Master Halor. He is not a teacher of the Bozee."

"He is a librarian," snickered Ensel.

Although there was nothing ignoble about being a librarian, the comment still stung Dacian. "I would still join you in a Bozee bout. I learn quickly," he said.

"He is not on my team," Blaysh declared and set his hands on the table.

Dacian looked at him sharply. He was becoming riled, and the sensation was strange to him. He had done nothing to provoke these arrogant acolytes, who were barely past their tablinghood.

Bagdoa chuckled. "For once, Blaysh, you are quicker than me. But there will be no teams. I would be happy to let Dacian study the Bozee in a one-on-one bout with me."

"Excellent," Dacian declared and looked Bagdoa in the eye. "I would be honored," he added, employing some sarcasm of his own. Dacian then let his power show in his eyes. Bagdoa flinched ever so slightly.

"Meet us in the forest tomorrow at dawn," Bagdoa said.

Dacian agreed. He excused himself from the table. The rys kitchen workers were looking at him with surprise, perhaps even respect. Dacian glanced into the eyes of the chef when he walked by his table. Dacian was not sure what he saw there, but his heart was beating with an excitement foreign to him.

******

Dacian went warily into the forest. Even in the summer, the pre-dawn hours were crisp in the Jingten Valley. The starscape above him was bordered by the tops of the pines, blacker than the dark sky. Each tree around him hummed with a lifeforce that he could feel, but Dacian worked to tune out the natural notes that always sang through his senses. He expected the Kahtepian acolytes who were capable of cloaking themselves to ambush him.

When the dawn whispered the first word of its bright spell, the night was banished. Blackness turned gray and cast the colors of the land in strange shades that were only visible in those short moments before the sun crested the eastern peaks.

Dacian stopped and scanned the area. As he had predicted, cloaked tabre were approaching his position. He spied Bagdoa, Athur, and Ensel all cloaked in their magic that they assumed would conceal them from his senses. Dacian decided to waste no time putting a stop to their tricks. He wanted his chance to spar with Bagdoa in a fair fight and learn properly.

Picking out Bagdoa from the trio of skulkers, Dacian jogged directly toward him. Bagdoa continued to come toward Dacian, moving from tree to tree. Sometimes his cloaking spell did filter him from Dacian's perception, but Dacian always quickly picked up his lifeforce again.

Close to Bagdoa now, Dacian ducked behind a tree and in his mind watched the tabre creep closer.

"I see you," Dacian announced into the forest. "I can see all of you."

The sun was just coming over the mountains and shining mauve light into the valley and glowing pink upon the snowy peaks. Bagdoa froze. The fresh morning light shimmered on the magical forces that enveloped his body. Dacian sensed Bagdoa's uncertainty.

The tabre did not stop his cloaking spell, so Dacian decided to demonstrate his sincerity. He nudged Bagdoa with his mind and said mentally, "You are not hidden from me."

Dacian left his hiding spot and continued to the meeting place where Teev, Mithel, and Blaysh waited. Dacian greeted the three tabre who stood leaning on their staves. After a silence that revealed their surprise at Dacian's arrival, Teev finally spoke a stale good morning.

Pleasant birdsong was filling the forest now, and finches and sparrows were flitting happily about the meadow where Dacian stood with the tabre. Dacian reached out his hand and a white butterfly flew jaggedly and landed in his palm. Dacian studied the insect casually and did not look up as Bagdoa, Athur, and Ensel entered the meadow from separate points.

"Are you ready for your lesson?" Bagdoa said.

With a smile, Dacian bounced the butterfly back into the air. He could see that Bagdoa was no longer so cocksure. Dacian asked if he could borrow someone's staff.

"You should have brought your own, rys," Athur said. He walked up to the group and closed the ring of tabre that surrounded Dacian.

Dacian was not immune to the stinging tone, and, for the first time, fear stirred in the pit of his stomach. Bagdoa smiled, and Dacian realized that the acolyte had liked his sudden disquiet.

"Give him your staff, Athur," Bagdoa commanded. "First level Bozee is fought with staves, and Dacian must have one if he is to learn."

Dacian accepted the staff from Athur that was grudgingly given. The wooden shaft had been enhanced with spells of strength, and Athur's magic felt foreign in Dacian's hands.

"Shall we?" Bagdoa said. He stepped back with one foot, assumed a fighter's stance, and held his staff defensively.

The other tabre moved back and formed a wide ring at the edges of the meadow. Mimicking Bagdoa, Dacian took up a similar position. He could not tame his pounding heart, and he was not used to his emotions interfering so wildly with his concentration.

This is a good thing to learn, Dacian realized. No matter what Bagdoa did to him this morning, he would be better for it.

To his surprise, Bagdoa began to give him a genuine lesson. He demonstrated a half dozen basic attack moves with his staff.

"Center thrust. Back hand. On the spin," he explained. "Overhead. Ankle sweep. Double strike." He repeated the moves and then began to methodically strike at Dacian with them but stopped short of hitting him. Bagdoa named the moves again and increased his speed with every demonstration. "Now imagine the countermoves. Do the countermoves," he instructed and came at Dacian with a real attack.

Dacian blocked awkwardly and caught part of the blow on his knuckles. He stumbled back, gasping at the pain. Bagdoa came again and this time Dacian failed to protect himself at all. Bagdoa schooled him with a painful double strike by cracking each end of his staff across Dacian's shins.

Dacian cried out and retreated farther.

"Pitiful!" Athur yelled. "You are not worth my stick."

"Clumsy rys," Blaysh said. He stood with his arms crossed, as if bored.

"A human could do better!" Mithel declared.

Their jeers rattled Dacian and he suffered more blows to his knees, his elbows, an ear, and finally across his jaw, which dropped him to the ground.

Grinning, Bagdoa relented. "Get up," he commanded.

Dacian gripped his staff tighter and saw his purple blood oozing from his bashed knuckles and dripping on the lush grass. Shocked by his patheticness, he commanded himself to do better. He had to concentrate. Watching a drop of his blood drip down a blade of grass, he connected to the land beneath him, the land of his birth.

My pain is nothing, he told himself and pushed himself quickly to his feet. He lashed out at Bagdoa and caught him off guard. Dacian hit him on the torso just above his hip. Bagdoa shouted in painful surprise but then laughed as he recovered and deflected Dacian's next swipe.

"Good. Good," he said. "We'll have a bout yet."

They continued through the morning, trading blows without rest. Dacian began to imagine the countermoves, and he performed them. He blocked. He attacked, and they sparred with increasing speed as Dacian's ability and confidence swelled.

When their staves were locked after a long flurry of exchanges, Bagdoa took one hand off his staff and cast a spell at Dacian's face.

"Attack spell," he said and a flash of white light dazzled Dacian.

Dacian yelled in dismay and Bagdoa hit him hard in his momentary blindness. Dacian buckled over and hugged his belly where he had been hit. Bagdoa struck him across the shoulders and forced him down to the trampled grass and flowers.

"That was not even a real attack spell, Dacian," Bagdoa said.

The other tabre were laughing. Dacian allowed himself two breaths to renew himself before springing back to his feet. He reminded himself that the fighters had been trading attack spells when he had watched them yesterday. The Bozee was much more than knocking together wooden sticks.

Pushing his sweaty black hair out of his face, Dacian began to unbutton his jacket. He slipped out of the fur-trimmed black brocade jacket and walked it to the edge of the meadow where he hung it on a pine branch. A mountain breeze fluttered across his sleeveless linen tunic and cooled his bare arms.

Returning to face Bagdoa, he gripped his staff anew and said, "Show me an attack spell."

Bagdoa raised an eyebrow. He thought Dacian foolish but was eager to give the lesson.

Dacian stood patiently, unafraid and ready to learn. He sensed how Bagdoa summoned the spell, and Dacian was gratified when Bagdoa briefly had trouble focusing. Dacian hoped that his confidence unsettled Bagdoa a little.

Bagdoa's spell exploded with hot fury all over Dacian's defenseless body. His skin blistered, even beneath his clothes, and his nerves were seared deeply with a pain he had not ever imagined. Even his scream was weakened by the instant agony. Dacian sagged and sweat glistened on his bubbling skin. He delved into an unexplored reservoir of strength and battled the pain.

Aghast, Bagdoa stared at him. He had thrown a heavy attack spell at Dacian, wanting to impress him with his power, but he had not expected that Dacian, ready for the blow, would not protect himself with a shield spell.

Bagdoa lowered his staff. He took a few steps forward but stopped short of offering help. He could see the hot ugly blisters on Dacian's arms and face, and he was startled by the damage. Bagdoa had not hurt someone so badly before.

"You were supposed to do a shield spell," Bagdoa whispered.

Dacian looked around him. The other tabre had tightened the circle, but no one dared come close enough to aid him. On their faces he saw a growing fear of what the consequences of his injury might be. They were all guilty of wanting to hurt him. They might ridicule Halor as a weakling scholar but they did not want to be punished for harming his best student.

But Dacian knew spells greater than their brutish magic.

His eyes glowed fiercely as he organized his magical power and enveloped himself in a healing spell. The clinging pain of the burns dissipated and fresh healthy skin replaced the angry blisters.

When he was finished, he smiled to Bagdoa. "I have learned your spell," he said and, raising his hand ominously, added, "Teach me a shield spell, Bagdoa."

The bold acolyte from Kahtep did not hesitate. Having seen Dacian's amazingly swift and thorough healing magic, he realized the power of his opponent. When Dacian cast his first attack spell, triumphant power flowed from his mind and through his fingertips. Bagdoa staggered within the blaze of blue energy that Dacian sustained as he advanced with his raised staff.

Bagdoa gave ground now, shielding himself with his magic and his staff. Dacian pounded at him with his weapon and repeated attack spells. Although his assault was heavy-handed and artless, he enjoyed watching the tabre, so supercilious at dawn, now learning that he could be hurt as the sun reached its zenith.

Smoke began to rise from the ends of Bagdoa's staff. Dacian heard the other acolytes yell for the bout to stop. Dacian was not about to stop and pride prevented Bagdoa's surrender.

Dacian was learning his opponent's shield spell, and he dismantled its energies a little more with each application of attack magic. One end of Bagdoa's staff actually caught fire and Dacian struck off the glowing coal and shortened the weapon. He cast another attack spell and bored through the shield magic like a plow cutting through turf.

Bagdoa screamed. Dacian felt his magic burning into the flesh of his opponent, whose lifeforce shuddered from the impact.

Bagdoa fell backward clutching his chest, and Dacian stopped his magic. Bagdoa's clothing was on fire and his exposed chest was scorched a horrible black and violet. Half of his face was badly burned as well, but he seemed not to know it yet. Teev and Ensel, who were closest to their fallen comrade, rushed forward and smacked out the flames on Bagdoa's clothes.

Flailing at his friends, Bagdoa screamed on.

The glorious joy of fighting and winning abandoned Dacian, leaving only concern for his victim. He rushed forward, but Bagdoa retreated madly. His feet dug into the turf and he flopped backward, shaking off the hands of his friends. He shrieked for Dacian to stay away from him.

His terror startled Dacian, who had never harmed anyone before. The stink of burned flesh tainted the clean air, and Dacian learned that violence was not a game.

He pushed past Teev and Ensel and, dropping to his knees, grabbed Bagdoa. Immediately Dacian poured his awareness into the tabre's body. Bagdoa's struggling became feeble. Dacian felt his heart fluttering in deepening shock.

Dacian's healing magic quenched the burns and then renewed Bagdoa's flesh as sod mends a bare spot in a lawn. When it was done, Dacian eased Bagdoa into a comfortable position. His clothes were tattered and blackened, but his skin was whole again and he rested, free of pain.

But fear remained in his dark eyes. Bagdoa set a hand on his chest that had been so grievously charred and he looked as if his body would never entirely be his own again.

Dacian did not know what to say.

The shadows of the other five tabre crisscrossed over Dacian and Bagdoa, and in the shadows, Dacian saw their heads turn. Only then did he hear the approach of riders, one of whom was Halor.

Dacian could feel the wrath of his master already. He stood, brushed off his pants, and walked to the pine tree to retrieve his jacket. He was pulling his arms through the sleeves when Halor and Master Darjeir from Kahtep galloped into the meadow. Their black and red robes flapped around their bodies and matched the dark moods cast upon their faces.

Master Darjeir went to his group of acolytes, and Halor confronted Dacian.

"What are you doing?" Halor demanded. He jumped from the saddle and stalked up to Dacian.

Dacian did not answer. He assumed that Halor had seen all or much of what had happened.

Silence was no defense. Halor hollered into Dacian's mind. "Raw impudence! What cause have you to disobey me?"

He thrust his rage down the length of Dacian's spine. Dacian cringed. He had not expected to evoke such anger from his master. He had only been curious.

"Curious!" Halor railed upon reading his mind. "Your power is not to be twisted in games. You hurt him!"

"I healed him, Master," Dacian defended.

"Bah! You know not what you have done, fool," Halor said.

The insult startled Dacian, but he remained convinced of his innocence "If I had known how to properly play at the Bozee. If I had been instructed—"

"Silence!" Halor commanded. "Get back to the tower."

Halor narrowed his eyes at Dacian and looked down his long nose. Disappointment highlighted his anger, and he shook his head slightly before getting back on his horse.

Halor rode over to the group of Kahtepians. By now Master Darjeir had helped Bagdoa to his feet. His acolytes were gathered close, each offering an explanation for what had happened.

"Master Darjeir," Halor said. "Is your pupil well?"

Master Darjeir patted Bagdoa affectionately on the shoulder and murmured for him to be quiet. Darjeir answered that his student had been properly healed. When he said this, he glanced at Dacian with a look that bore more suspicion than gratitude.

Halor said, "Good, yet I must admonish you to keep your reckless acolytes away from my special student. You are here to observe not rouse trouble where there is none."

Ever so slightly, Darjeir bristled at the upbraiding from one of his equals, but he did not argue. He knew he should have watched his acolytes more closely around the rys. In retrospect the whole trip to Jingten was probably ill conceived.

Dacian approached the tabre. They tensed at his presence, and Bagdoa slid half a step back. Dacian regretted the fear he had accidentally inspired.

"Bagdoa, I offer my apology," Dacian said. "I should have controlled my actions better. I did not know that excitement could be such a hindrance to caution."

The honestly spoken apology softened Bagdoa's fear. "I know," he whispered. "I apologize as well."

"Enough," Halor snapped. "Go."

Hurt by the incomprehensible harshness from his master, Dacian meekly turned away from the tabre. Confused by more things than he realized, Dacian walked back to the tower with Halor glowering down at him from the back of the horse.

When they reached the white gravel lane by the tower, Dacian heard each piece of grit grinding beneath the horse's shod hooves.

"I am forced to curtail your freedom for this," Halor announced.

Dacian looked up at his master. The degree of punishment moved him to boldness. "I was only exploring new activities. I think you are overreacting, Master," he said.

Halor said, "An acolyte does not re-think his master's decision."

"I am not a rysling. I deserve my freedom," Dacian insisted, unintimidated by Halor's scowl.

The word "deserve" riled Halor, but he bit back his angry response. Calming himself, he dismounted and came around the head of his horse to speak to Dacian on an equal level. He held the bridle and petted the white horse's soft black face while he spoke. "Dacian, my most prized student, I must make sure that you regret this recklessness. To be a Nebakarz is to learn far more about your power than a normal tabre. But you must be careful. I know you learned this today," he said, once again the kindly teacher.

Dacian resisted his natural need to accept the soothing tone of his master. "Will Bagdoa be punished?" he demanded. "He hurt me as well, and I had to heal myself. They were not going to help me. I doubt if they could," he added with sudden arrogance.

Showing exasperation again, Halor told his pupil that it was Master Darjeir's place to discipline Bagdoa.

Dacian refrained from making another outburst. He remained confused by the episode and needed time to sort out his feelings. He resigned himself to losing his freedom. He expected that Halor would grow lenient with him and restore his privileges in due time.

Halor smiled once he saw that Dacian's aggressive mood had relented. Gently, Halor reaffirmed the reasoning that had always fostered Dacian's conformity. "This reprimand will pass, and news of it will not reach Daykash Breymer, at least not from me. Remember to tread carefully in these coming years, Dacian. To be the first rys to enter the Nebakarz priesthood will be a great and good thing, but it will not be an easy thing," Halor advised. "With my help, you will teach the rest of the Nufalese to respect your fellow rys. You know that you are the one to do this, but it cannot be done without patience and obedience."

Dacian hung his head and rubbed the purple scabs on his knuckles, realizing that he had not healed all of his hurts yet. "Yes, Master," he muttered. He knew that it was not right to cause trouble in a peaceful land.

9. Three Pledges

Standing outside his parents' chamber, Cruce overheard his mother complaining good naturedly about having to polish his father's boots.

"You should have had Gulden polish these days ago," she scolded and slapped the sturdy leather boots.

Zhen rarely bothered with anything more than slippers, but today he would drag his old riding boots onto his withered feet. Every year Zhen acted as host to a private meeting of the Adarium so he could participate. He shunned the Council's public meetings because of his infirmity, but, coming from a family with its name upon the Founding Tablets, Zhen would always retain his seat on the Council.

"Where do you keep the cloth and polish, Zhen?" his wife asked him.

"Boot polish is the last thing I think about, Viv," Zhen said, a little wearily.

Viv grumbled something that Cruce did not quite hear and then she hustled into the antechamber. Shaking the boots at Cruce, she told him to find Gulden and have them polished.

She plunked the boots against her son's chest, and he reluctantly took them in his arms. Viv was about to rush back to her husband but stopped mid spin and gave Cruce her full attention. His unease had wiggled her intuition. "Cruce, is something wrong?" Viv asked quietly.

Cruce shook his head. He looked down and rubbed some dust from a boot. They had been sitting on a shelf untouched since last year's Adarium meeting. The leather was dry and stiff beneath his thumb.

By his non-verbal responses Viv guessed that something troubled her son. Hoping to encourage him, she straightened his collar and told him that he looked good.

Cruce forced a smile to reassure her. He was a head taller than his mother. His sister and he had inherited their father's bigger physique, or what had once been his physique. Viv Chenomet was daintily beautiful. Gray mingled freely with her strawberry blonde hair that she always kept in firm braids. Few lines surrounded her blue eyes despite the responsibilities she had taken on over the past decade, not the least of them being the maintenance of her husband's ego that had been shattered with his body.

Viv wore a conservative black dress with a lightweight black scarf tied around her neck. Emerald rings sparkled from three of her fingers and told of her wealth.

"Are you nervous?" Viv asked.

"I think so," Cruce admitted.

"Your father has looked forward to this day for a long time," she said and her eyes sparkled with proud happiness. Her son, her baby, was a man now and soon his status among all of Kwellstan society would be official.

Cruce chewed his lower lip and avoided her eyes. "I'll go find Gulden," he said and rushed off on his errand.

After delivering the boots to the valet, Cruce went to the foyer and greeted Councilors as they arrived. The annual meeting at the Chenomet home was the last big social event of the summer for the Kwellstan elite, and Councilors attended with their wives and children. The notorious Bendag Anglair, fat and bearded, dared to come with his mistress.

A banquet was planned for after the meeting. The meaty smells from the barbecues in the backyard were already drifting into the house. Extra servants had been hired for the week, and trays of the best Kwellstan spring water, doubly blessed by Nebakarz priests, were being circulated to the guests. Fine wines and spicy brews would be served later. The day was hot and humid. No doubt late summer thunderstorms were brewing out on the Nufalese plains but would hopefully stay out of the valley until the next day.

Dayd was at the front door, and she waved to Cruce. He took his place on the other side of the open pair of red doors and welcomed guests along with Dayd. She was lovely in a blue dress that was slit up the sides of her legs just a little farther than their mother would have liked. She wore silver bracelets on both wrists, and a headdress of topaz beads contained her golden hair. She had decided not to defy the humidity today and attempt to curl her hair, and it was braided in the same fashion as their mother's hair.

"Welcome, Elder Manderlini," Dayd declared as she gave her hand to the Adarium's Senior Councilor. He was bent and thin and his bald head was speckled with age, but a ribald gleam danced in his rheumy eyes as he grasped Dayd's hand.

"You know I'm available now, Maid Chenomet," Manderlini cackled. He had been a widower for the past year and apparently found consolation in advertising himself to young women.

"That gives me something to think about it," Dayd said cheerfully.

Manderlini kissed her knuckles and then gave her hand a more grandfatherly pat. "Has that Radello proposed to you yet?" he inquired.

"He has yet to decide if he has the courage to be my husband," Dayd replied and Manderlini laughed.

The old Councilor then turned to Cruce, and appraised the young man as they clasped hands. Cruce welcomed him warmly and offered the hospitality of his home.

"Thank you, Young Lord Chenomet," Manderlini said and then with a wink quietly added, "I look forward to seeing you at more meetings. I'm tired of all the old men I have to put up with."

"Yes, Elder," Cruce said and was glad when the old man continued into the house.

Cruce shared the greeting duties with Dayd through three more families. The Promentros entered, followed by the Bunzees, and then came the Hebenstens.

Peeking out at the guests still coming up the lane, Cruce quietly asked Dayd if the Larkas had arrived yet.

"You missed them coming in when you were still in the back," Dayd said sympathetically. "They are probably at the buffet. Their mother has no fear of food."

Cruce wanted to go greet the Larkas, particularly Ribeka, but time was short. He would just have to find her after the meeting.

"I have to get Father," he said.

"You're supposed to help me," she whispered with annoyance as the Enberns approached with their six children. By the gate of Lord Enbern, Dayd judged that he was already drunk.

"I am supposed to do many things," Cruce said mysteriously and abandoned her as the six unruly Enbern children streamed shrilly over the threshold. Dayd reached out to Lady Enbern with excessive enthusiasm so as to avoid the lingering sloppy embrace of her husband.

Cruce wove his way through the crowd in the large foyer. He nodded when spoken to, but did not stop to make conversation as he rushed with the urgency of an eighteen-year-old. It was a relief to break past the servants and enter the private wing of his home. He returned to his parents' rooms just as Viv wheeled Zhen out with his boots on. He looked thin and pale, even at summer's end, and the tailoring of his white shirt and burgundy vest had been done for a more robust man. A silver crescent pendant hung across his chest. It was the symbol of their family.

Zhen waved his wife off the handles of the chair. "Go on, Viv. We'll be right behind you. Thank you for your help," he said.

Cruce admired how his father, needy as he was and often distracted by pain, always remembered to thank his mother.

Viv bent and smoothed his wavy silver hair back from his cheek so that she could kiss it. On her way out, she smiled to Cruce with excitement.

"Am I fashionably late yet?" Zhen asked.

"Almost," Cruce replied. "I saw the Enberns coming in, and they are usually last to arrive."

Zhen chuckled and then began to wheel his chair toward the hall, obviously straining. Cruce rushed behind the chair and suggested that his father let him push. Before Zhen could protest, Cruce added, "It's muggy, Father. Let me push so you don't get sweaty."

"I suppose that is a good idea," Zhen admitted. "It's good that you are thinking about appearances. Push slowly. We should talk about a few things before the meeting. I had hoped to get a moment with you sooner, but you haven't seen fit to be home for days, except to eat and wash."

Instead of pushing slowly, Cruce did not push at all. He gripped the smooth handles of the wheelchair hard, then let them go and wrung his hands.

Zhen craned his neck and peered up at his son. "This is very slowly," he commented.

Cruce's heart was thumping and his chest was tight. Sweat burst out beneath his good clothes. "Father, you can't name me your proxy to the Council today," he said.

Zhen frowned, very puzzled by his son's statement. Being placed as a Proxy Councilor in his father's seat had been planned for some time now that Cruce was eighteen. Although Cruce was young, the proxy appointment to represent the Chenomet family was legal. Zhen had groomed his son for his role, knowing that Cruce would have to assume the responsibilities as head of the family while Zhen still lived. In essence, Cruce would inherit much of his rank while his father lived because of Zhen's disability.

Zhen tried to turn more completely around so he could confront his son, but twisting his body shot pain through him. With an angry gasp, he righted himself in the chair and pointed to the floor in front of him. "Get around here!" he barked.

Meekly, Cruce stepped around the wheelchair and even kneeled before his father. The humility took Zhen aback.

"What is this about?" asked the crippled patriarch.

"Father, I've joined the Kwellstan Militia," Cruce answered. The words had been weighing on him like a sinus headache, but saying them brought no relief.

Clearly Zhen Chenomet had never expected his son to say such a thing. Hesitantly he smiled, hoping he had reason to laugh. "What is this nonsense, Cruce?" he asked.

Cruce felt sick. He tried to answer but his mouth had gone dry and he had to clear his throat to get out words. "Father, I have decided to serve five years in the militia because, ah, because I want to do something on my own. See more of Nufal," he said. His reasons sounded so lame when he saw their effect on his father, whose face crinkled with rising dismay.

Zhen looked away at the wall, apparently seeking a better explanation from the relief sculptures of men on horses hunting buffalo and antelope upon the prairie. The carved and painted wood was as close to hunting as Zhen had gotten since his accident. Cruce was always amazed that his father had not had the décor stripped from his private chambers. It seemed to him that the artwork would be an unbearable of the accident.

Fighting back his anger, Zhen said hopefully, "Cruce, my son, why did you not say you want to do some traveling. Of course you can see more of Nufal. A man of your station should certainly tour our fine realm, maybe even go see this Jingten that has the Nebakarz so bothered." Zhen became happier now and continued, "You can still be named my proxy and have time to travel. Do not worry, Cruce."

Cruce tried to divert his father's fantasy and explain, but Zhen interrupted him sternly, "I shall have no more of this ridiculous talk, Cruce. The militia is not for a firstborn heir of your prestige. You have no place among those blockheads. Whatever you have said or promised to those rowdy militia boys you've been running around with all summer -- yes I know -- you can take back without shame. You will do this. I command it."

"Father, it is done. I gave my pledge three times at the Adlemont these past three nights. I must report for training by the equinox and I will be on frontier duty all winter protecting settlers from raiding savages," Cruce said.

The news shoved Zhen into the back of his chair. He stared at his son, appalled. A militia pledge had to go three nights in a row and swear his pledge three times at the temple run by the Nebakarz for humans. The three-night process gave a man a chance to reconsider, but the third pledge was binding. No one could be released from their duty after that, not even a Chenomet.

Zhen clutched his forehead, thinking over the horrible facts again and coming to the same conclusion. All that remained was his anger. He lashed out at his son with both hands, slapping him hard on both sides of the face. At first Cruce cringed like the child that he was, but then he defended himself. It was what a militiaman would do. He seized his father's wrists and stopped the beating. Cruce was so much stronger, and the eggshell frailty that he felt in his father was agony.

"Father, stop. You will hurt yourself," he said. Cruce replaced his father's arms to his sides and stood up.

Pain throbbed through Zehn's body. The exertion had punished what was left of his back. Then the pain hit the hopeless wall of paralyzed numbness in his lower body. He hated the places he could not feel the most.

"Why, Cruce, why?!" Zhen demanded, not caring if the servants heard his wail, or the guests.

Cruce glanced nervously into the hall. He should have been stronger and told his father earlier that morning or even in the middle of the night. Now, his stupid timing was going to create monstrous embarrassment for his family.

He asked his father not to yell. Shaking, Zhen leaned an elbow onto an armrest and let his forehead sink into his hand. "My son. My only son," he muttered sadly.

Cruce returned to his knees. Desperate to mend his father's misery, he tried to apologize, butZhen would not look at him.

Confessing more truly now his feelings, Cruce added, "Father, I am too young. I don't want to sit on the Adarium and listen to the bickering of old men. I want to ride upon the prairie and the mountains. To defend my homeland and people and become a man."

His father scoffed at his son's juvenile lust for danger. "You could get killed," he warned.

The notion confused Cruce's eighteen-year-old optimism. Cruce was not worried. Although the savages were devious and cruel, the militias were superior. "Deaths are rare," Cruce said dismissively.

"I will have to pay the Nebakarz to pray for you. Indeed I will," Zhen said. "If you come to harm it will be as a spear in your mother's heart. Did you think of that?"

Cruce resented having his mother's love thrown in his face. "A man must think of more than his mother," he said.

"A man!" Zhen sniped. "You think the militia will make you a man? A man is made by duty to his family not this militia foolishness. I needed you to be on the Council. True, we Chenomets are wealthy, but I too long have been broken. Our political and business relationships are decaying.

There are other more active families moving in on what was once ours. I needed you on the Council to give the Chenomets a voice again. A strong young voice that others would respect. Not my long wheezing death rattle. I thought you understood these things."

Cruce had never heard his father speak with such dark despair and describe himself with vile morbid terms. None of it was true, Cruce believed.

"You are respected, Father," he said simply.

"Bah! I have the respect of the dead. The estate class of Kwellstan gathers here just because I can still throw a good party," Zhen said.

Confronting his father's rising depression, Cruce tried to soothe him because it would only be five more years. He pleaded, "Father, please, announce to the Adarium that I have chosen to defend Nufal and then I will take your seat on the Adarium."

"Do it yourself!" Zhen declared and wheeled his chair backwards with a disgusted flourish. He steered around his son and headed for the door.

Cruce stood. He grabbed the wheelchair, intending to push it for his father, but Zhen ordered him to let go. "I'll see you in five years," Zhen said. "Till then, I might name Dayd to the Adarium. There's no legal precedent for it, but at least she understands her duty to those who bore her."

The rejection stung Cruce, and watching his father struggle down the hall with angry speed was a sad sight. For the first time, Cruce regretted giving his third pledge the night before.

When they assembled for the meeting, Zhen had to allow Cruce to hold onto his wheelchair as he led the Councilors into the amphitheater behind the house. Otherwise the wheelchair would have accelerated disastrously down the ramp that had been built over the steps. The Councilors filed slowly into the amphitheater behind their host.

The outer third of the theater was shaded by a high wooden trellis overgrown with grape vines. Being late summer, heavy bunches of fruit hung down from slack masses of leaves and vines. As the Councilors settled onto the stone seats that were thoughtfully padded with pillows, they plucked grapes from above.

At the center of the theater a cloth canopy in Chenomet red provided shade for the speakers over two padded benches. Cruce parked Zhen beneath the canopy and then took his place in the first row of seating. Zhen called the meeting to order.

He was joined beneath the canopy by Elder Manderlini and Temmer Mulet, the esteemed Lord Scribe of the Adarium. A servant accompanied Mulet with a small writing stand that he set up with a supply of writing cloths, inks and styluses. Manderlini shuffled toward his bench with much of his weight on his cane. He slowly lowered himself to his seat and then leaned over his cane with both hands on it. Mulet, much younger with a forest of light brown curls atop his head, bowed respectfully to the Senior Councilor and his host, Zhen, before taking his seat and dismissing the servant.

Beside Cruce, fat Bendag Anglair fanned himself with a broad hand and loosened the laces of his billowy cream-colored shirt. Perspiration dotted his florid face. He obviously would have loved to have taken off his long green vest.

"It's hot today," he grumbled to Cruce. "Let's hope this meeting is mercifully short."

Cruce politely agreed that it was hot. He felt feverish from distress and his shirt clung to his back beneath his red jacket. He could not even focus on the opening blessing that Manderlini delivered in his rasping old man's voice as he praised the Kwellstan Sect for its guidance in the ways of the Great Divinity. Then Mulet began to read from the Adarium record.

Resisting the urge to squirm, Cruce tried to make eye contact with his father, but Zhen stared past his son into the assembled men of the Kwellstan estate class. Desperate desire to appease his father raved inside Cruce. Indulging his own interests in the militia now seemed so reckless after the lecture from Zhen about his familial duties.

Are we really in a needy state? Cruce wondered. Do our relationships really decay?

The disappointment and despair of his father battered Cruce. Although his father had been emphasizing his need to takeover Adarium duties, Cruce had not imagined that the need was dire and could not wait a few years.

Even Mulet, a normally engaging speaker, had started to drone as he plowed through the notes of Adarium business and reported the status of current projects. The tedium bored Cruce and affirmed a little bit his decision to pledge to the militia. It would be good to leave this dirge of the city fathers and ride free upon the frontiers with men near his age. Gehr Bradelvo had been right about that.

Attending the party at Gehr's house after the Bozee bout had led to a summer of good times drinking with the militia commander and his buddies and soaking up their tales of dangerous adventures. Life seemed so sweet to the militiamen, and the chance to earn a reputation instead of inheriting one had enamored Cruce.

Miserable, Cruce longed to make himself and his father content. His mind raced still trying to come up with a solution that would match all of his duties.

Mulet finally finished his opening report and moved onto current business. Bendag Anglair sighed tiredly, and Cruce reflected that not even the older men seemed to enjoy this process.

"Our first item of business," Mulet said and then with a friendly gesture toward Zhen added, "And certainly happy business for our esteemed host Councilor Chenomet is the appointment of his son, Cruce, who has achieved the age of manhood, to act as his proxy at regular meetings of the Adarium."

Cruce suddenly felt nauseous and Zhen still refused to look at him. Applause arose from the Adarium, and a few men gave Zhen supportive cheers.

After the congratulatory noise stopped, Zhen cleared his throat. He was still able to project his voice somewhat, but he surprised his peers with his bitter tone.

"Strike that from the agenda, Lord Scribe," he announced.

Mulet blinked with surprise. Shocked muttering swept through the theater, like a big gust of wind hitting a pile of leaves. Anglair puffed and turned to look at Cruce although he seemed actually happy that something interesting had happened. Cruce felt everyone's eyes on the back of his head. He did not know what to do.

Zhen stared at the smooth paving stones of the amphitheater with a profound frown.

Elder Manderlini was the first to remark openly. He tapped his cane three times, which brought a little order, and leaned toward Zhen. "You surprise us with this order, Councilor Chenomet," Manderlini said. "Your son is young, but I know I can speak for the Adarium and say that his appointment will be accepted without protest."

"My son has other plans," Zhen said. "Let my announcement be stricken. I have nothing to say. Let us move on with our important business."

The brusque dismissal of the subject flustered Manderlini. He knew how Zhen had been looking forward to the proxy appointment of his son. The old man squinted at Cruce and wondered what had happened between father and son. Employing the wisdom of his years, Manderlini decided that the issue was probably best not aired in open meeting. That was the least he could do to show respect to his Chenomet colleague.

Manderlini turned toward Mulet and started to tell him to strike the agenda item, but Cruce interrupted the Senior Councilor. He was on his feet and speaking before he had fully realized what he was doing. "My esteemed Estate Lords of Kwellstan," Cruce said. "Allow me to clarify the intentions of the Chenomet family. My appointment as proxy must be delayed for I have pledged to the Kwellstan Militia for the next five years."

Bendag Anglair erupted with laughter. His girth lent his guffaw much force, and Cruce gaped at him. He had not expected such rudeness, but it made him finally realize how inappropriate his joining the militia was. It made him look foolish. Cruce was an heir, not a lesser son or bastard.

Yet, confused as he was, Cruce latched onto his anger at Anglair's laughter.

"You would do well not to laugh at a Chenomet in his own home," Cruce declared, and Bendag Anglair was taken aback by the young man's forthright defense. Anglair removed his smile.

"Order!" Manderlini said firmly. "Order!" He thumped his cane insistently. "You have been given no leave to speak, Young Lord."

Cruce hastily bowed to the Senior Councilor. He asked forgiveness and permission to continue.

Manderlini granted it because he was truly curious.

Cruce looked at his father, who was actually looking back at him with an expression that combined anger, surprise, and genuine interest.

Cruce stepped away from his seat and positioned himself tentatively within his father's sphere. He continued, "I have chosen to serve Nufal in the militia and defend the good people of our civilization. I ask to attend regular meetings of the Adarium, when my militia duties allow. This, I would, um, appreciate…if…" He began to flounder, uncertain of what else to say, or if he should just conclude. Cruce glanced pleadingly to his father, wanting help.

Zhen gave his chair wheels a half turn and moved a little closer to his son. He was undecided whether his son had been hopelessly stupid or rather deft. The Bunzees and Hebenstens had founded new estates on the frontier, and Cruce's participation in the defense of those ambitious families' holdings was a good show of Chenomet strength now that Zehn considered it. And, despite his wrath, Zhen could not resist the pride he felt from Cruce speaking so boldly. Perhaps in five years, all would be well, except of course for his withering body.

Zhen addressed his peers. "The added commitments Young Lord Cruce has taken on will prevent him from regularly attending the Adarium. I would, however, ask the Adarium to permit his attendance on behalf of my family when he is available."

The attending lords began to discuss the proposition among themselves, and Manderlini fingered his cane thoughtfully. The Senior Councilor locked eyes with Zhen, who conveyed a desire for Manderlini's support. The request was an inconvenience to the Adarium. At best, Cruce would only attend a third of the meetings, but it was progress considering that Zehn attended none of the public meetings.

Once the collected conversations began to die down, Manderlini gestured with his cane for Cruce to come before him.

"Young Lord Chenomet, are you serious about juggling your responsibilities between the militia and Adarium?" Manderlini asked.

"Of course, Lord Elder. No effort would be too great in the service of Nufal and Kwellstan," Cruce replied earnestly.

Manderlini arched his shaggy eyebrows. "And have your militia superiors approved of your desire to serve in the Adarium as well?" he said.

Uncertainty blazed in Cruce's eyes. He had not thought of this. He had pledged to serve Militia Master Bellastan Carver. He had not asked for accommodations for civilian commitments. He had not even met Bellastan Carver yet.

"I shall obtain the approval from the Militia Master," Cruce said.

Manderlini gave him a knowing look, doubtful that Cruce would get permission. But for the sake of Zhen, Manderlini declared that the Adarium would vote during that day's session to approve or deny the Chenomet request.

Zhen openly expressed his gratitude. Cruce returned to his seat and expected Mulet to move to the next item of business, but Lord Syman Bunzee rose to his feet and requested to speak, which was granted. Zhen tensed in his chair. The Bunzees were the most bold about seeking the lucrative contracts the Chenomets held with the Kwellstan Sect. Rumors hinted that the Bunzees planned to bid openly next spring, which would be a terrible act of disrespect to the Chenomets but also a clear sign of the family's eroded influence.

Bunzee said, "My Esteemed Estate Lords, allow me to propose a condition upon the Chenomet request. Because Young Lord Chenomet has yet to get permission from the Militia Master, let it be set that his acceptance to the Adarium relies upon this permission as well as our vote."

Zhen grated his teeth, but otherwise hid his displeasure. The closest ally of Bunzee, Lord Esseil Hebensten quickly voiced his support for the proposed condition, and it was added to the Chenomet request upon which the Adarium would vote. With the soft scratching of his inky stylus, Mulet noted down the perilous condition that Zhen knew was meant to keep Cruce out of the Adarium.

That day the Adarium voted to allow Cruce to join the Adarium meetings when his duties allowed, provided that he obtained permission from the Militia Master. Cruce was happy as the meeting concluded. His youthful confidence allowed him no doubt, and he believed that he had found a solution that would eventually please him and his father.

As Cruce went to push his father out of the amphitheater, Zhen grumbled that he had made a fine mess of things. Cruce glanced at Manderlini and Mulet to see if they had heard, but Manderlini's aged hearing had most likely missed the comment, and Mulet did not look up.

Cruce wheeled his father up the ramp and the Councilors followed them out. The crowd of guests in the large backyard of the estate clamored happily now that the banquet could begin. A warm dusk gathered over the valley and servants lit torches to control mosquitoes and lanterns were strung over tables now laden with food. Cooks were carving beef and pork over the fires and dishing up dripping platters. The bounty of summer's vegetables and fruits cluttered the tables with a variety of salads and side dishes, and servants carried pitchers of water and wine on both shoulders and attended to the cups of the guests.

As the Councilors dispersed among their families, the hot news of Cruce's pledging to the militia circulated quickly.

Viv intercepted Zhen and Cruce as they arrived at the head of the main banquet table. The news had yet to hit her ears, and she received her husband and son with happy flutters. Viv embraced Cruce and kissed him on the cheek. Her eyes beamed with teary happiness. She loved her son, was proud of him, and knew how much his success meant to Zhen.

"Tell your mother," Zhen commanded grumpily and wheeled himself up to the table and snatched a silver goblet of wine.

Dayd, who stood nearby with Radello, perked up with curiosity as she instantly sensed that her sibling had somehow offended.

"What?" Viv asked, giving her husband a curious look.

Cruce wet his lips and took hold of his mother's hand.

Sweet Mother, I will make you proud. Do not fear for me, Cruce thought wistfully and then told her.

Viv jerked away from him, startled by the impossible news.

Zhen drained his wine cup and gestured impatiently to the nearest servant. "Our son has gone idiot," he declared.

As the servant refilled his cup, Zhen looked up to Dayd and said, "I shall have to rely on you more, dear daughter."

Dayd blinked with confusion, wondering what her father could mean.

Other guests were seating themselves at the tables and everyone was speaking about Cruce's surprising news. Many of the Councilors openly asked Cruce questions. Some politely, some with mocking mirth. Cruce weathered all of their comments and questions, unashamed of what he had done.

Viv sat beside her husband in shocked silence. She alternated between giving her daughter helpless looks and watching her husband drink. Zhen was often given to consuming drink and other pain medications, but not to excess in front of guests. But judging from the pace he was setting today, Viv planned to make sure he retired early from his party. She and the children could entertain the guests without him.

Predictably, Cruce ate hastily and fled his father's side to mingle. He filled a tray with desserts and headed for the Larka table. Ribeka rewarded him with a quick smile. He respectfully greeted her parents. Her father, Tekar Larka, immediately expressed his surprise about Cruce's militia choice.

"I felt it was time a Chenomet tried something new," Cruce said brightly, ignoring the veiled disapproval in Tekar Larka's voice.

Quickly, Cruce distracted the family with the dessert tray. Tekar's wife was immediately appeased and took two plates. Chelma gave him a hostile look but took a dessert all the same. Tekar declined, and Cruce gladly set the tray near Ribeka and asked if he could sit.

Tekar waved a permissive hand. "Go ahead. Last we'll see of you for a while," he said.

Cruce thanked him and tried to contain his excitement as he sat down next to Ribeka. Her dark hair was pulled up and then divided into a dozen small braids contained by a wreath of lavender flowers. She smelled good and today her hazel eyes matched the soft gray-green leaves intermingled with the flowers in her hair. Her white dress was modestly cut, but still flattered her maiden's figure much to Cruce's approval.

He pointed out the dessert to her that he considered the best. It was the Chenomet chef's specialty.

"Oh, I don't know if I have room," Ribeka declared and held her flat stomach protectively.

"I'm full too. Would you like to dance?" Cruce asked, but then worried that he was acting too quickly to separate her from her family.

Ribeka seemed eager and asked for permission. Her mother hardly glanced up from her second dessert as she reached for a small pitcher of golden cream. Tekar Larka frowned but said that he would not deny Ribeka the famous Chenomet hospitality.

They excused themselves from the table and quickly moved off to the section of the yard where the younger people were gathering. Musicians were just coming back from their break and setting up to play for dancing. Cruce was glad to have Ribeka's attention, and when she slipped her soft hand into his, his heart beat with hot excitement.

It was good to escape the adult pressures that had gripped him all day. The scrutiny of the Adarium and his looming service in the militia receded, and Cruce welcomed the unjudging presence of his peers. Ribeka introduced him to her friends as they mingled among the dancers, and Cruce did the same when they encountered his friends. Ribeka often commented about how exciting it was that Cruce was going to get out of Kwellstan and do something daring.

Cruce and Ribeka danced until their feet hurt. Holding her was a pleasure and he knew the memory of it would keep him awake many nights with desire. Cruce enjoyed avoiding his family as well. He did not even investigate when he saw his father retire from the party. He judged it best to keep his distance. Zehn's opinions would not have improved after hours of drinking.

Cruce eventually persuaded Ribeka to escape the warm press of revelers around the tireless musicians. Cruce led her deeper into the sprawling Chenomet gardens. They crossed a wide lawn and entered a grove of old trees, preserved from the ancient forest from which Kwellstan had been thoughtfully carved. A couple night birds sang among the drowsy dark limbs of oak and maple.

They did not talk. It was easy in the darkness for them to twine their arms around their torsos and begin kissing. At first, Cruce kissed her tentatively, fearful that she might rebuff him, but when her soft unschooled lips clung to him with growing excitement, he kissed her harder and deeper. His hands moved down her body. Her buttocks arched into his hands and he pulled her against his body. The hot thrill of her body that fit against him in the most sensual fashion injected him with passion. His body burned to continue and he kissed her neck and started without thinking to pull up her dress into his greedy hands.

Then she pushed him away. "Cruce," Ribeka said breathlessly. "Cruce. I'm…I'm not ready. No."

He kissed her a few more times, wanting, needing to ignore her, but she spoke again her denial and Cruce loosened his hold. Her skirt slipped back down her legs and she stumbled away from him. Ribeka leaned against a tree. She touched her flushed cheeks and then wiped her lips.

Cruce wanted to persuade her to continue, but he silently forced himself to honor her wish.

"I should get back," Ribeka said.

Cruce kindly took her hand and led her back toward the lights and noise of the party. It was hard to leave the dark private grove of his desire, but perhaps he had been too optimistic to hope that he could have everything now. She was a fine sweet woman and deserved his patience.

"Ribeka, may I visit you next time I am in Kwellstan?" Cruce asked.

"Yes, Cruce. Please," Ribeka answered and kissed him once more before they emerged into the lights of polite society.

10. Followers

Uncomfortable silence hung like a bad odor between Amar and his new Kez companions as they rode away from the Thievesmeet. Amar endured their critical gazes as they measured him up. Kym, with his widely set brown eyes, watched Amar the most.

The similarity in hair and dress among the three Kez automatically made Amar feel vulnerable because he was not like them. His hair was getting long and it hung loose and shaggy, unlike the shaved sides of the Kez warriors' heads that guarded their tightly braided black hair like a moat around a fort. The Kez must have had a dozen knives among them too, sticking out of their belts and calf sheaths. Each man had a good sword too.

In the heat of the day, the Kez threw off their black cloaks. Sweat glistened on their bare arms and chests, revealing bodies that possessed strength and little softness. Because they were moving through the empty back country, the Kez felt no need to wear their helmets that were tied to their saddles along with pans, water skins, and various small tools.

Amar hid his discomfort despite feeling conscious of his shabby appearance and poor gear. He often rode in front of his Kez keepers, putting his back to them in an audacious display of confidence. Despite his brave front, Amar slept little, allowing himself only reluctant dozes late each worrisome night.

For three days they traveled, sharing few words. Without asking for their opinion, Amar set their course south and kept to the rugged foothills of the Rysamand Mountains that his companions still called the Tymelo. Amar recalled vaguely from his limited study of maps that the Domain of the Temulanka was to the southwest, but he meant to return first to what had been the lands of the Lin Tohs.

At the end of the fourth day when they were making camp, Amar was exhausted and fuzzy-headed as he hobbled his horse in a meadow where the dusky lavender and pink sunset cast long tree shadows. Kym snuck up on Amar and seized his throat with two hands clad in worn leather gloves. Amar shoved at Kym. The horse neighed and reared in its hobbles. Amar threw himself forward and knocked Kym off his feet. They landed together on the ground but Kym's hands were still at his neck.

Through spotty vision, Amar saw Kym's determined face. Knowing he had to do something now to save his life, Amar forced his knee between Kym's legs and smashed him in the scrotum. With a deep groaning cry, Kym let go and Amar kneed him in the groin two more times before lurching back to his feet. Gasping raggedly and swaying on his feet, Amar pulled his good sword off his back and looked around.

Vame and Cybar were crossing the meadow with their weapons out. The Kez stopped alongside their battered comrade, and everyone eyed each other.

"What are you doing?" Amar demanded.

Kym rolled over onto all fours. He retched a little, still trying to recover from the shock of pain. Vame offered the big man a hand up. Kym got to his feet and pulled in a deep breath.

"Testing you, Amar," Kym finally answered.

Amar narrowed his eyes, silently demanding a better explanation. The brief struggle had banished his fatigue. It was a relief to finally be attacked.

Kym spat to clear the nastiness from his mouth and said, "If you were supposed to be dead, I'd slit your throat in your sleep."

Cybar spoke up now. "If you want to be Kez, you have to prove yourself to the brothers too, not just Lax Ar Fu."

Amar surveyed his companions, trying to judge if they were about to rush at him and kill him. But no one attacked, and Amar supposed what Cybar had said could be true. If the Kez were a brotherhood, it made sense that other warriors would want to determine his worth. Amar drew upon the strength of his hardened heart and looked at them without fear.

"Enough of this nonsense. If you want to test me, Kym. Test me," Amar said. He stepped forward and held his sword as if ready to begin a duel.

Kym ignored the invitation to fight and said, "You passed, Amar. I've grabbed a lot of outlaws in my day and only the best can escape me." He approached Amar, albeit with a tender gait, and extended his hand as if to congratulate him.

Amar looked at the gloved hand that had so recently been hot and hard against his neck that still hurt. He wanted to swipe down with his sword and see the hand fly bloody into the grass. His dark eyes glittered with his perilous thoughts.

"If you want to keep your hand, apologize for attacking me," Amar said.

Kym withdrew his hand. "A Kez warrior does not apologize or answer to anyone outside the brotherhood," he said.

With a baleful expression, Amar slowly sheathed his sword, and gradually Vame and Cybar replaced their arms as well. But tension still clung to the group and no one moved. The hobbled horse moved across the meadow to stay clear of the agitated men and returned to grazing.

"What now, Kym?" Amar demanded. "How are we to travel in peace after this?"

"I said you passed the test. I wanted to feel your strength in a fight. It's my right to judge such a thing," Kym explained.

Amar asked if this meant he had the Kez's word that he would not touch him again or otherwise bring him harm.

"I can't give you such a pledge. You are not our brother," Kym answered. "If you would be Kez, you will just have to show your bravery and worth and continue traveling with us."

"I see," Amar murmured and seemed resigned to the precarious situation. He started to walk toward their camp and bowled through the trio of Kez. Surprised by his confidence, Cybar and Vame stepped aside. Kym, of course, did not budge but that was as Amar planned.

With a deep aquifer of rage to draw upon, Amar summoned the sick viciousness that had been growing inside him since the massacre of his family and tribe. He punched Kym in the neck. They spun onto the ground as intense as fighting cats.

Vame and Cybar did not react. Kym had been the one to start the fight with Amar, and even his Kez brothers seemed inclined to let Amar continue it.

Although Amar had gotten a good surprise strike in at Kym, he was soon hard pressed to maintain an advantage. Kym was strong and skilled in combat. Gone was the cool gaze of a man performing a test. He fought now with personal fury.

Kym rolled away from Amar and sprang to his feet. Before Amar could rise, Kym landed a kick to his hip. Amar cried out, but he managed to seize Kym's foot when he kicked him again. Amar yanked Kim back to the ground and flung himself at Kym, trying to get on top of him. Kym pulled a knife and stabbed at Amar, who deflected the blade with his bare right hand and grabbed Kym's knife-wielding hand by the wrist with his left hand. Holding the knife back, Amar planted a knee on Kym's chest and started beating his face with his bleeding right hand. Soon Amar's blood flowed across Kym's bleeding face.

After three fast punches to the face, Kym began to weaken. He blinked at the blood pooling in his eyes.

"Apologize, damn you!" Amar yelled, punctuating his words with his striking fist. "I will be a Kez, and as far as you're concerned, I am!"

Kym swung up a leg hard and tried to knock Amar off him. Amar sprawled across his opponent and switched from punching to strangling him with his free hand while he still held back the knife with his other. He squeezed Kym's throat until he saw fear and regret bulge in his eyes. He dug his nails into the flesh and was going to crush the windpipe in a final hateful squeeze, but Vame and Cybar grabbed him by the shoulders and flung him away.

Amar snarled rabidly and almost lunged at Vame, but he was hurt and could not fight all three Kez.

Breathing hard with sweat dripping down his face, Amar got drunkenly to his feet and retreated a few steps. Blood was pouring from his right hand that was badly slashed, and he clamped a hand over the cut.

As the boiling pressure of his battle rage released, he realized how sweet the thrill of the brutal contest had been. While fighting for his life with a strong foe, Amar had briefly been free of his self-hate and grief. It had not been his usual refuge of numbness either. The passion of the violence had sheltered him with an exciting urgency. There was pleasure in such a contest that could not be found in the pathetic harvesting of weaklings that he had joined in with Huan and Smart Grab.

Amar staggered toward Kym, who Cybar was helping up again. "We are done with this, Kym," Amar announced. "Let us travel as brothers or not at all."

Kym held his bloody mouth. Amar could see the dark half moon cuts left by his nails on Kym's blood-streaked neck. One of his eyes was already swelling. Painfully, Kym nodded and there seemed to be the beginning of respect shining from his good eye.

"I give my apology, Amar. I will not start a fight with you again," Kym said.

"Good," Amar said but did not reciprocate the pledge. He then looked at Cybar and Vame and demanded to know if they had any intentions of testing him. Both men gaped, too startled by Amar's venom to reply.

Kym spoke for them. "We all are assessing you," he explained. "But, as their brother, my pledge can include them. We will start no more fights so long as you pursue your mission. And now, tell me where you are going. This is not the way to the Temulanka Domain."

Amar disliked the amended apology, but it remained a small victory. "We go to the Espen Forest," he answered.

Kym sucked blood off his teeth and spat it out before asking why Amar was going there.

"Because that is where I must begin my mission," Amar said cryptically.

In unison, the faces of the Kez scowled with skepticism. Kym placed an arm around Cybar's shoulders, but, before letting his comrade help him away, he reminded Amar that they would make sure that he performed his assignment.

"But you are not here to tell me how to do it," Amar said.

The trio of Kez moved off and settled into the camp. After a pause, Amar followed them, squeezing the dripping wound on his hand. Reluctantly, he accepted that he should ask for help.

When he joined them, Cybar was blowing on some smoking tinder he had just sparked with his fire stone. Kym stretched beside him and started wetting a cloth from his water skin so he could wash away the blood and soothe his swelling eye.

"Can someone help me?" Amar asked, but avoided sounding contrite.

Vame came to him. Vame was the quietest of the three and close to Amar in age. He had a unique look with a narrow face and sleepy eyes, making his tribal origin hard for Amar to place. Vame pursed his lips thoughtfully as he examined the deep cut on Amar's hand and then started digging through his pack. He retrieved a small copper mending needle and a coil of fine fiber. He told Amar to wash the cut while he sharpened the needle with a stone.

The blood from the cut soaked two rags red before Vame started stitching. His sutures helped, but the wound continued to soak blood into the bandage that Vame made with Amar's last scrap of clean cloth.

Amar thanked Vame when he was done.

Vame glanced up at him shyly. The dusk had deepened and night was embracing the land. "I would have you do the same for me if I was hurt," he said.

Amar nodded, wanting more than ever to belong to this brotherhood of rogues.

"Why do you go to this forest you call the Espen?" Vame asked.

When Amar thought of Onja, the pain in his hand dimmed, but he would not speak of her, at least not yet. "I cannot explain right now," he murmured as he imagined seeing her again. His longing filled him with impatience.

Vame frowned at the answer, but his patient nature prevented him from pressing Amar on the subject.

There was no conversation around the campfire that evening, but their mood was silently transformed. Introspection replaced suspicion. Insects sang in the cooling evening of late summer, and an owl announced its flight with a screech somewhere among the dark trees.

Gradually the four men fell asleep. A watch was not set. Out in the wilds and with most ruffians still at the Thievesmeet, there seemed to be little concern.

When the group resumed their journey in the morning, no one spoke of the fight the day before. Amar continued to ride in front to show the Kez that he still did not fear them.

As their journey continued, Amar spoke little. After five more days, they emerged from the wilds into cultivated lands sprinkled with villages. Men and women worked the fields. Scythes cut the grain and the women gathered it and bundled the shocks. The women in their head-to-toe clothing looked like bags with straw hats perched on top of them. In contrast to the fully covered women, the men labored with their shirts off.

When Amar and his group rode out of the bush and into a field full of harvesters, the people moved quickly into a group. Although the men held their scythes low, their weapon potential was clearly advertised.

"We will stay at the village tonight," Kym decided.

At dusk, they reached a large village called He San at a crossroads. It was the agricultural center of the Hekanau Tribe's heartland, and the place was dusty and quiet. Most of the residents were still laboring in the fields and would not trudge back to their homes until the night forced their urgent work to stop. Only the tavern street was busy because grain buyers from the cities were starting to arrive.

Kym chose the only establishment in the village with red curtains in the upstairs windows, which meant that more appetites than hunger and thirst were satisfied there.

The merchants looked up from their drinks when the three Kez and Amar crossed the threshold. The bell over the door rang like a tiny song bird twittering a warning. One of the prostitutes, her head and shoulders conspicuously uncovered, got up from the lap of a paunchy man with a long thin black mustache. Red ribbons were braided into her thick coil of black hair that snaked over one shoulder. She was thin and looked not to have much softness left in her body or spirit. She walked over to the arriving men and casually sized them up. She smiled to the Kez but spoke to Amar.

"You are a sweet young pup to run with these big wolves," she commented. Her eyes were inviting.

Without a word, Amar walked by her and approached the bar. The tavern keeper was just coming out of the kitchen and his eyes lit up with excitement, interest, and a bit of worry when he noticed his new guests. His dingy apron had grease stains, and the wisps of hair remaining on his bald head were slicked back. Amar listened behind him to the jingling of the Kez warriors' spurs as they walked across the room and claimed a big table.

"What do you need, traveler?" the tavern keeper inquired.

While tucking his gloves in his belt next to his bronze sword, Amar said, "Lodging and food for four men, plus stabling and fodder for our horses."

The tavern keeper's uncertainty about whether he really wanted them to spend the night flickered across his face. He cleared his throat and began to figure out what everything would cost. Amar gave him a harsh look just before he stated the price. The surprising lack of youthful naiveté in Amar's gaze warned him not to overcharge.

After a thoughtful pause, the tavern keeper quoted him a fair price. Amar dug through his pouch and slapped coins from three different regions on the wood of the bar that was smooth except where someone had scrawled their name symbol with a knife. The tavern keeper had no doubts about the origins of the coins, and he gathered them with downcast eyes.

Amar joined his companions at their table. The prostitute who had spoken to him was now being led upstairs by the paunchy man.

"She wanted you, Amar," Kym noted.

"I have no need for such as her," Amar said contemptuously.

Kym laughed agreeably. "You're right. Give me a good young woman married off to an old man any day," he said.

The comment puzzled Amar, who asked Kym why he had wanted to come here. Kym swung his feet onto the table as the tavern keeper's servant delivered food and drink.

"I don't have to live every day outdoors, and it is good to see women," he explained.

The servant distributed bread and greens alongside meat stewed with vegetables. On his second trip, the servant set down a pitcher of water and a jug of strong fruit liquor. Vame curled his nose up when he sniffed at the liquor and complained about the Hekanau's taste in drink. He poured himself a shot anyway. Amar filled his cup with only water.

The Kez did not share Amar's taste for sobriety and they downed three shots of liquor in quick succession. Flushed and happy, they relaxed into eating their food.

Amar picked at his food even though it tasted good. He was eager to be back on the road. He hungered for nourishment of a different sort.

Three more prostitutes entered the main room after the Kez had settled into their drink and food. Kym paid two of the girls to dance. The third woman fetched her bedecka, a nine-stringed instrument played with a bow, and started to play. The dancers shook their bracelet bells as they danced. Their swaying jingling steps pleased all who occupied the room, and more visitors began to come in from the street. Lanterns were lit throughout the main room as night fell, and men watched the women dance with hungry eyes.

In the warm lantern light, Amar watched the women dance. They stirred no desire in him but their movements induced a somewhat pleasant trance in him. He recalled the sensual body of Loxane naked before all the Thievesmeet.

He did not notice right away when a dozen local warriors came into the tavern. The crowd parted for them, and the women stopped dancing when they saw the agents of Lord Tepter, who enforced tribal law throughout the farming villages of that province. The warriors wore leather armor, stained blue, upon their torsos and bracers on their forearms. Their clothing was soft yellow and their bronze helmets were polished brightly.

Kym still had his feet up on the table, and he remained in his relaxed position as the Hekanau warriors stopped at the table. They did not concern him. They would not dare offend the servants of Vu.

But Amar had no notorious brotherhood to protect him from a disapproving society.

"Who are you?" the lead warrior demanded of Amar directly. He spoke with the tone of someone who was accustomed to being obeyed.

Amar crossed his arms. "Who are you?" he asked back.

The leader blinked with surprise at the rogue's audacity, but then recovered his stern countenance. "Don't be insolent. You are a thief," he said pointing at Amar. "People saw you come out of the wilds. Be gone from He San. This is a decent town and Hekanaus don't want scum like you around. Go."

"A decent town you say? Then why are your whores so popular?" Amar remarked.

The leader stepped forward, incensed, and grabbed his sword. Kym swung his feet down from the table and told the Hekanau warrior that Amar was with him.

The Hekanau shot Kym a bold look, but he needed to assess the reason for the Kez's presence in his town before acting further. "Are you bound for the Patharki Domain? I'm told Lord Tepter is setting up a negotiation to settle disputes with them. The Patharki have been aggressive this year," he said.

"You seem to have things figured out," Kym said. He had no intention of describing his business for anyone outside the Kez, but he would let the Hekanau believe what he wanted.

Amar stood up. "I am not scum," he stated.

The Hekanau shot his eyes back to Amar, genuinely shocked by the young thief who seemed to have no sense.

"Are you here to charge me with a crime?" Amar said. He could see that the manner of his speech prompted the Hekanau to question his assumptions. Perhaps, the apparent rogue traveling with the Kez was an important person in disguise, an agent of some tribal leader.

Amar continued, "I'll be on my way in the morning with my companions. I prefer you leave us in peace or I just may commit a crime."

The Hekanau bristled at the challenge, but despite having the squad of men behind him, he decided not to act. "I'll expect to see you leaving in the morning," he said. He whipped around and pointed for his men to head for the doors.

Speaking with an imperious tone, Amar advised, "The Hekanau best give their attention to the Patharki and not concern themselves with common thieves."

The Hekanau warrior paused before deciding that he was already sufficiently embarrassed by his encounter with the Kez and their mysterious companion. He knew it was best not to meddle in the affairs of the Kez and he regretted even trying.

As the warriors filed out the doors, the prostitute resumed playing her bedecka. Kym signaled for the other two women to dance again and they went back to the pleasing task.

Kym poured himself another shot of liquor. "Amar of no tribe," he chuckled knowingly and drank down the shot.

After that evening, Amar and his companions returned to traveling the back country and did not visit villages. They left the Hekanau Domain behind and approached the former frontiers of the Lin Tohs Tribe. Amar adeptly avoided the roads when they entered his homeland. Sometimes from vantage points in the hills, he would look into the untended farmlands and see people on the road. Patharki warriors along with peasant work crews were scavenging the land for produce and livestock. Amar also saw a burnt out village that had been mostly knocked down and cleaned up. Nearby trees had been felled and were being milled into timbers for new buildings.

The Patharki were wasting no time occupying the land, making it their own, and erasing the Lin Tohs.

The spirit of Gendahl stirred like an old blind dog that could bite out of frightened confusion. Amar struggled to quell the misery inside him.

Onja, please still be here, he thought and clung to the joy that she would give him.

His despair increased when they approached the Espen Forest. Crossing the hedge-rowed fields at the edge of the woodland, Amar resisted the urge to peer into the tall grasses where the corpses of fallen Lin Tohs likely lay.

When he entered the Espen Forest, the shaded hush of the place seemed respectful of his tragedy. Amar saw no fresh tracks on the path. The Patharki had probably not defiled this place since that terrible day when Gendahl died in spirit if not in flesh.

Then he saw the bodies. Beneath the old mossy trees there were no tall grasses to hide the warriors and servants. Of course, animals had been at the remains, from small insects to large prowling cats, wolves and bears. Little was left. Clothing was withering over bones, and vines and mosses were spreading over the unfortunate scraps of the unburied. When the leaves fell in the autumn, these dead Lin Tohs would finally know the peaceful embrace of Gyhwen.

Amar stopped his horse and looked down. His face was hot and he struggled against the urge to scream.

Kym came alongside him. "What is this place?" he demanded. His eyes scanned the ranks of old growth trees, whose leaves were silent in the stillness of the midday heat.

Cybar, showing his agitation more than Kym, also asked why Amar had brought them to this haunted place.

Amar wet his lips and turned his horse so that he could face his companions. He decided to tell them the truth. "Loxane, Shamaness of the Kelsur, said I was spirit-touched. This is the place where it happened. I come here to find again the rys that saved me from dying in the battle that happened here," he said.

The revelation disturbed the three Kez. Vame glanced about nervously, as if expecting the rys to strike him instantly. Cybar whispered a warding phrase in his native dialect.

"A rys?" Kym asked. "Here?"

Amar nodded, and the thought of Onja gladdened his broken heart.

Kym exchanged a look with his comrades. None of them had ever seen a rys, but they believed in the existence of the mountain spirit creatures that inspired folk tales.

Amar found new resolve after speaking of his purpose. "Follow me if you dare to see what I have seen," he said. He continued into the forest, and the Kez followed warily.

Amar eventually left the hunting trail and ascended the rough ridge that had brought him to the waterfalls. He moved back and forth along the ridge. Sometimes he had to dismount and lead his horse through the thicker brush. Failing to find the route to the waterfalls, he began to question if he had gone far enough or perhaps too far.

The Kez straggled after him without complaint until dusk when roaming a forested cliff became obviously unwise. Kym ordered that they camp, and Amar, although anxious to find the waterfalls, did not argue. Around the campfire that night he brooded on the patch of stars that showed through a break in the tree canopy. Amar forgot to eat.

Kym pulled out a small leather canteen and offered it to Amar. The three red tassels hanging from the canteen's strap made it look to Amar like it was dripping blood in the firelight. He shook his head once. He knew the canteen held Kym's supply of liquor, and he wanted none.

Kym shrugged and took a pull of the strong drink and passed it to Vame. The Kez leader sighed as the liquor eased his aches from travel. "Amar," he said. "What were you among the Lin Tohs?"

The question visibly bothered Amar, but he glanced around his companions and saw how curious they were for his answer.

Looking down, he said that he had been a bodyguard to his young lord Gendahl. He took out the amber hawk amulet on a broken chain and explained what it was. "Why Jayshem thought to spare me I do not know," Amar added.

Cybar remarked that Jayshem tended not to be thorough, unlike Vu, an honest God. The others, except for Amar, chuckled. Thorough enough, Amar thought.

Cybar took his turn with the liquor and passed it back to Kym, who took a final drink before tucking it away. Everyone was tired and they spread bedrolls. Kym decided to set a watch and told Vame to take the first shift.

Amar did not attempt to sleep. He leaned against a tree that clung to the edge of the cliff. His vigil over the canyon was silent and patient.

Vame checked on the horses and then quietly came to stand by Amar. The nocturnal noise of bugs and distant frogs advertised the secret activities of the dark land. A breeze picked up along the cliff, and the tree leaves rustled happily. The cool was good after the hot day. During a lull in the wind when the trees quieted, Amar finally heard the flowing water.

"Do you hear it?" he asked excitedly.

"What?" Vame said. He had no idea which night noise Amar referred to.

"The waterfalls," Amar said and he sighed with relief. "Wait here."

Vame stopped him with a tentative hand on his shoulder. The Kez did not hear any waterfalls and he warned Amar that it was dangerous to wander in the night along the cliff.

"I will be fine," Amar assured him and left.

Vame considered following him, but feared how easy it would be to tumble over the cliff.

Despite Amar's confidence, he had no desire to cast himself over the cliff again. He groped carefully along the land, reaching blindly for tree trunks and vines. He knew there was a way down.

He crept through the trees all night, heedless of the sting of insects. The hum of falling water sang in his ears and beckoned him. Amar did not rest until he slipped on a patch of rotted leaves and slid down a dark slope. With his hands flailing about, he managed to grab a sapling and halt his descent. Once he was certain that he would not fall, he released the bent sapling and stayed still. His heart thudded with great panic as he relived his fall over the cliff and the breaking of his legs.

Amar waited for the dawn before continuing. Once the birds above him in the trees started their joyous songs, he got up and brushed himself off. He saw that the way down was right in front of him. A deer trail broke the underbrush and wound into the canyon. He hurried into the canyon as if he had known the trail his whole life. Deer tracks marked the soft places where rainwater puddled on the lower land.

The waterfalls hummed close by and the moisture tickled his nostrils. Amar ran out onto the flat expanse of rock. The bright sun hit his face and he squinted at the dazzling waterfalls.

"Onja!" he cried. "Onja!"

The deep wide pool churned on one end where the falls hit, calmed in the middle, and then hurried away into the stream. The waters were lower than when he had been there before.

Calling out for Onja again, he splashed into the pool. He pleaded to the waterfalls for her to come out.

"Amar."

He whirled and she was standing on the rock shore that he had just left. Breathing hard, he rushed out of the water with big steps. She helped him out of the pool. Climbing onto the rock, he stayed on his knees. It was a blessing to hold her hand and he pressed the smooth blue fingers to his cheek.

"Onja," he murmured.

"I am glad to see you again, Amar," she said, gently easing her fingers out of his affectionate grip.

Amar stood up. He cared nothing about the water in his boots. The water streaming off his wet pants puddled on the rock.

"You have come to ask for my help," Onja surmised.

Confused and ashamed, Amar looked down and nodded.

"And you have friends now," Onja added.

Amar frowned thoughtfully. "I don't know what they are," he said.

"They follow you and that is good," Onja said. She stepped around Amar, eyeing him like a concerned aunt. "You are thin, Amar. You should give more thought to the strength of your body," she admonished.

Amar ran a hand over his stomach. His armored net of diamond-shaped plates hung looser than it used to, and he knew that his clothing covered ribs that pressed against his skin.

Onja guided him into the shade beneath the trees where she had healed his legs.

"What would you ask of me?" she said in a kindly way.

Amar explained his encounter with Lax Ar Fu and the mission that he had accepted. He told her everything about Loxane as well and expressed his desire to become a member of the Kez.

"And you want me to help you kill this Wayndo," Onja determined.

"I want you to help me find him," Amar clarified.

Onja became pensive and watched an osprey swoop over the pool and pluck a fish from the water. The bird cried triumphantly as it flapped toward its nest in a tall dead tree. Then Onja smiled and said, "Of course I will help you find him."

11. Rising Will

Amar approached the Kez stealthily through the steep hillside undergrowth. He could hear them complaining about his absence. Kym was on the verge of hunting him down. Vame and Cybar were agreeing because they had expected Amar to be a deceiver to their Overlord.

Amar was pained to overhear their low opinion of him. He missed having respect. Even that fool man-child Gendahl had been respected by his people.

The vine that Amar held cracked off the dead branch it was clinging to. The noise put the Kez on their feet with weapons drawn. Amar scrambled out of the foliage, sweaty, scratched, and dusty. He nodded amicably to the Kez despite their hostile attitude. Slowly they put away their blades as Amar pulled off his helmet and drank deeply from his water skin.

"Did you find what you were looking for?" Kym asked skeptically.

Amar poured some water over his head and shook his black dripping hair that had not been cut since the demise of the Lin Tohs.

"Yes," Amar replied happily and looked around.

Onja appeared next to the tethered horses, and she sauntered out where all the men could see her. She had perhaps been standing there for some time without being noticed.

"Great Vu!" Cybar shouted.

Kym whispered, "It is true." Neither he nor the others seemed capable of doing more than stare at her alien beauty. Her strong long limbs, perfect bosom, and curving hips triggered a natural awe of her feminine perfection. She studied them with her mysterious dark eyes as if she was a rare animal that had never seen men.

Her presence filled Amar with confidence. "This is Onja," he said and walked to her side. "She is a rys and desires to travel with us."

Cybar's hand flopped to an inside pocket of the loose vest that he wore over his tough leather armor. He brought out a stone female statuette and held it toward her in a warding fashion.

"Beware the spirits of the mountains!" he declared. He took a few steps toward her, trying to fend her off with his charm. She only cocked her head and regarded him with bemused curiosity.

"Begone! Evil trickster. Begone!" he cried.

His negative view of Onja angered Amar. He stalked up to Cybar and batted the statuette from his hands with such force that it flew against a tree and nicked away some bark. The little stone woman landed face down on the ground and did not stir with the supposed powers that Cybar attributed to her.

"Stupid peasant!" Amar shouted and cuffed Cybar and then kicked him.

Stricken with his fear of Onja, Cybar scrambled backward.

"Do not call Onja evil," Amar declared. "She is only curious about the peoples who border her homeland. You will not be rude to her!"

Kym pulled Cybar closer to reassure his Kez brother. Glancing from Amar and then to Onja, Kym was in awe of the relationship between the man and the rys. He could not guess what it could mean, except that he now knew with certainty that he would not want to cross Amar in anything. This rys companion was a wonder and not to be provoked with simple superstition. This was the power that the Shamaness Loxane must have sensed in Amar. Quietly, Kym admonished Cybar to control himself.

Onja came closer and set a restraining hand on Amar's shoulder. His seething anger at the insult given her had shot through her body like a strong liquor hitting an empty stomach. His rage on her behalf was a sweet thrill that she would want to feel again.

But her words were kind. "Forgive me for frightening you, human man," Onja said. "And forgive Amar. His temper, it would seem, is swift."

Onja extended a hand toward the three Kez men. They tensed but were otherwise too stunned to react. Blue light snapped on her fingertips and the cut on Cybar's lip where Amar had hit him stopped bleeding.

Now he is spirit-touched as well, Amar thought with a pang of jealousy, but he also saw opportunity in Onja's act because it gave him and Cybar a shared experience.

Cybar touched his lip and marveled at the sudden cessation of pain. His brothers were also amazed by the healing.

Onja said, "I have come to learn and ask to travel with you in these human lands."

Cybar and Vame looked to Kym who nodded dumbly.

Onja walked over to Cybar's woman statuette and picked it up. She brushed some dirt from it and contemplated it as if it were the strangest thing she had ever seen. With her thumb she stroked its tiny rock breasts and then returned it to Cybar. Reverently, he plucked it from her fingers and put it back in his pocket.

Amar introduced the men. Onja repeated their names as she was told them. Alone with a group of humans admittedly made her nervous because she had yet to learn how to predict their behavior.

It will come, she assured herself. Have not all the other animals been easy to master?

Noting the similar dress and hair among the Kez, she asked them about their relationship.

Kym explained that they were servants of Vu, God of Contests. They provided security or fought where their lord deemed it the most useful or profitable, and they had other talents that people sometimes hired them to perform.

Vame added, "We are brothers in our service to Vu. Amar seeks to join us, but has yet to prove himself."

"I have yet to complete my mission," Amar corrected.

The challenging statement almost provoked Vame, who narrowed his sleepy eyes menacingly until he realized that Amar had just struck one of his brothers and he had not even thought to retaliate, nor had Kym. Amar's sudden dominance disturbed Vame, but he was uncertain about resisting him. His mysterious intensity seemed to build a crossroads where insignificance met greatness. Vame suspected his brothers sensed the same thing. As the Kez said, Vu revealed leaders.

With the awkward introduction done, Amar was anxious to move away from his extinct domain. "Let us go to the Temulanka Domain and seek Wayndo," he announced. "But we must settle something first. Kym, Vame, and Cybar, I would have you accept me now as your Kez brother."

His aggressive demand unsettled the Kez, but their usual arrogance was subdued and no one scoffed at his audacity.

Constantly glancing at Onja, Kym said, "It is by the authority of our Overlord that a brother is declared and initiated. We cannot just make you a Kez, but I will admit, Amar, that I do not oppose having you join the brotherhood."

"Let your wish become the authority," Amar proposed. He stepped a little closer to the trio of Kez. "It is time that I began to be instructed in your ways."

Onja observed how Amar asserted his desire upon the men. She realized that her influence added to Amar's natural confidence, and his striking boldness was making the other men respect and fear him, and these men did not easily fear another man.

The presence of Onja made it difficult for the Kez to refuse Amar's direction. The rys female was obviously allied with him. What might Amar ask her to do?

Amar quickly became impatient with the hesitation of the Kez. He wanted to extract their loyalty before proceeding against Wayndo. Amar needed again the feeling of men in his service.

He said, "If the vengeance against Wayndo is so important to the Kez, how could you allow someone not of your brotherhood to be the instrument of it?"

Cybar answered him. "Amar, the mission is impossible. Lax Ar Fu sent us to watch you give up and then kill you. I am sorry."

Kym jabbed his comrade with a disgruntled look, but Cybar did not regret telling Amar the truth.

"I appreciate your honesty, Cybar, but I had guessed as much," Amar said. "Even so, I still intend to perform my mission and join the Kez. I am an outlaw. I have no other future, yet I wish to be part of something. I promise you that I will not fail. Onja will advise me on how best to reach Wayndo. Now, I would have you accept me as your Kez brother before we proceed. If not, then I will ignore my pledge to Lax Ar Fu and then you can try to carry out the orders he has given you."

Observing closely, Onja tried to pierce the reasoning of Amar's mind. Did he expect her to defend him? Or was he simply hoping to win on a gamble? She suspected the latter because Amar was wildly unthinking of his safety. His grief begged for death, yet he was corralling his craziness and transforming it into power, or at least trying to. His reckless experimentation was intriguing to watch.

Kym moved a little closer to Onja to study her. Summoning his courage, he asked her if she would use her magic to defend Amar.

"Amar does not need me to defend him," she replied.

"I must speak with my brothers," Kym announced and walked a short distance away to confer privately with Cybar and Vame.

As the Kez murmured in the shade of vine-laden trees, Amar looked to Onja for approval.

"Are you trying to amuse me, Amar?" she said and smiled.

"When I'm near you I feel that I own the world," he whispered.

His words chilled her with excitement. To know that she could inspire such passion encouraged her greatly.

The Kez glanced at Amar frequently during their quiet meeting before they finally called him over.

I am not afraid, Amar told himself. He approached the Kez. Vame, Kym, and Cybar stood in a semi-circle waiting for him. In their eyes Amar could see that they were killers of both the guilty and the innocent.

"We have agreed that we can share with you the pledge of brothers, but we cannot fully initiate you as a Kez. That is a special process done in a special place." Kym said.

Amar nodded. "Very well. We will share the pledge of brothers," he said.

"First, you must let us cut your hair," Kym said.

Cybar and Vame stepped forward suddenly and grabbed his arms. Amar squashed his urge to resist and submitted. Their strong hands gripped him hard and forced him to his knees.

Kym untied a worn animal skin sack from his belt and removed a small segment of carved bone that had a fine bronze blade about three fingers across set in its edge. Kym gave the thin blade a few careful scrapes on a sharpening stone and then pushed the hair back from Amar's face. He began to cut and shave away the lower half of Amar's black hair from his temples past his ears and around the back of his neck. The long hair was left only on the top of his head. Amar watched the locks of black hair drop to the ground. In Kym's skilled hand, the blade almost caressed his skin. After completing one side, Kym sharpened the blade again and then finished.

Amar was eager to run his hands across the liberated portions of his head, but Vame and Cybar tightened their holds. Kym seized him roughly by the back of the neck and pulled him close. He pressed the blade against the thick artery on Amar's neck.

"A Kez would give his life for any of his brothers," Kym said.

Amar felt his pulse push against the little blade that was biting into skin. If Kym pushed just a little harder, Amar's life would gush away like a butchered animal.

Kym added, "I have your life right now."

Amar met his gaze. "And I gave it to you freely, did I not?" he said.

Kym nodded. He rolled back off his knees onto his heels, but, as he let go of Amar, he gave Amar's neck a stinging slash.

Cybar and Vame let him go. Amar reached for his neck that was slick with blood. The cut hurt but it was not mortal. He looked over his shoulder at Onja, who observed but showed no distress. Amar turned back to his new comrades. "What else must I do?" he asked.

Kym answered that for now he needed to give his pledge to be their brother. That their secrets were not to be shared. That he was not to work against the interests of his brothers. That he would share the danger of battle with them and the rewards of victory. That he would let no woman or property interfere with his loyalty to his fellow Kez.

Easily Amar promised these things and then Kym, Vame, and Cybar joined him on their knees and made the same pledges back to him. For a beautiful moment, Amar felt renewed. He belonged to a group. He no longer had to wander in madness like a ghost bound to Gyhwen by tragedy. But the comfort was only a dreamy flicker. This was not his tribe born again and welcoming him back. This was the Brotherhood of the Kez, and with them, he would do little that was good.

The men rose together and congratulated Amar. No one seemed to regret accepting him. Vame commented that he had seen better haircuts. In his defense, Kym said that Amar had not held still. "He was nervous," he teased although he knew it was not true. Kym had judged many a man in uncomfortable circumstances, and he had seen that Amar had not really cared if he cut his throat.

To be fearless is to be dangerous. He is a true Kez, Kym thought admiringly. He then warned Amar that there was more to becoming a Kez than this simple ceremony among brothers. He would have to declare himself loyal to Lax Ar Fu and pass more tests. And of course he must pledge himself to the service and glory of Vu, their God.

The men started packing up their small camp. As they were set to leave, Amar offered his horse to Onja, but she declined and said that it was no trouble for her to walk. The thought of her walking while he rode bothered Amar, but Onja told him to ride his horse and so he did.

Amar's regret about Onja walking did not last. The next morning, a fine stallion appeared among their hobbled horses that had been grazing and dozing through the night. The horse was black, burnished by the summer sun to a coppery sheen, and his mane and tale were long and silky. One spot of white on the stallion's forehead marked him like a guiding star orients the heavens. Onja walked over to the stallion that bore no halter. The horse placed his soft nose in her hand and she petted him. From where the stallion had come she never said.

Onja mounted the horse without needing bridle or saddle, and the horse obeyed her without the slightest resistance.

When they set out that day to travel, Amar said that he wanted to avoid the roads. Running into any Patharki would anger him, and he did not want the distraction. The Kez were accustomed to cross country travel, and they soon learned that Onja, although unfamiliar with the land, could see ahead in her mind and discover paths through the forests without any trouble.

In order to aid Amar in his quest against Wayndo, Onja spent time in conversation with him. He told her what he knew of Wayndo's appearance from his conversation with Smart Grab. The Kez also added details about what they knew of the warlord. As the oldest man present, Kym had seen Wayndo several times during the Temulanka Sabar'Uto War although his sightings had only been at a distance. Even without a close image of the man in his memory, Onja gained much knowledge from him. Her continual questions caused him to think about the Temulanka warlord, and she could see him in Kym's mind.

Because the Kez were well-traveled, they were able to answer her questions about the Temulanka Domain. What were the towns and cities? Where were the fortresses or pleasure palaces? Where was Wayndo likely to be? Cybar was the most responsive, eager to help her. His fear of her was quickly turning to devotion.

Although Kym and Vame were still cautious in her presence, they were polite and gave her what information they could. Kym even asked her how she planned to use the information.

She did not respond right away. How did one explain such a thing to a human? Onja told him simply that she would seek Wayndo with her mind.

Over the next days, Amar began to condition his body before they spent the day traveling. At the first light of dawn he went for long runs. When he returned to camp, he ate quickly and then trained with weapons with Kym, Vame, and Cybar. Although Amar had been educated in fighting since boyhood, he had much to learn from these black-hearted servants of Vu. They knew many techniques and tricks and they drove him hard with their sparring. Sometimes Amar took a minor wound, and those lessons he learned from the most.

During the mock battles, Amar pushed himself with all his will and fought hard. In front of Onja, he did not waver or show his exhaustion, and daily he grew stronger.

After sparring, Amar grabbed a low tree branch and pulled himself up over and over, dozens of times, until his arms felt like they would rip, and then he focused beyond the pain and pulled up two more times.

Onja enjoyed watching Amar train, and she was especially pleased and inspired by his rising will. She remembered him broken and weak. If not for her power, he would be dead, and she was proud of what she was achieving with him.

12. Sky Temple

Oh, Preem, Judger of men, we save those most wicked for you. Take the flesh and soul of this condemned man whose offenses deserve your divine cruelty. ~ Nurati prayer of execution

After six days, Amar and his group approached the Temulanka Domain through its wild borderlands along the Nurati Domain. Subdued by the afternoon heat, the men were silent and daydreaming until Onja abruptly stopped her horse. She looked north across the landscape like a fox that has heard a mouse in the grass. She told them to follow.

Her course took them into rough land, and their horses sweated on an incline among thinning trees. They came out onto a windswept ridge that offered a wide view. Ahead rose a blocky weathered butte formed from the withered heart of a mountain exposed by eons of elements. Above it wheeled carrion birds.

Onja rushed them onward across a shallow brushy canyon. They splashed through a tiny stream, lazy in the late the summer. Flies hovered the water and bothered the men and horses.

When they reached the butte, Onja found man-made steps. She slid from the slick back of her horse and danced up three steps before noticing that the men had not moved. Amar and the others recognized now what the place must be. Kym was the first to protest.

"We must not go up there," he told her. "It is a sky temple to the God Preem, Judger of men. The birds are the eyes of Preem. We invite his judgment to approach."

From the base of the butte, the carrion birds could not be seen, but Onja saw them in her mind's eye. Fear of judgment from some human God troubled her not at all.

"Will you come, Amar?" she asked.

Inside he wavered, but Onja's request superseded his fear of the Gods. He dismounted and then looked questioningly to his new Kez brothers. They seemed much less intimidating now that he saw them cowed by superstition. Cybar then surprised him by getting off his horse. The memory of Onja's magic on his lip emboldened him.

Onja and the two men ascended the butte. On top seven old oaks grew in a wide circle. Juvenile trees and sproutlings were scattered in the shade of the gnarled giants. Within the ring of oaks, stood a ring of bluntly cut blocks of stone that, despite their colossal size, had obviously been erected by human hands. Onja recognized in the monoliths the blue stone of her mountains. She was mildly offended to see a portion of her homeland dragged by humans to this lonely spot.

Three vultures hunkered on standing stones and crows clattered in the trees. Amar and Cybar watched the birds warily as they entered the rings of trees and stones.

At the center of the sky temple, a horizontal altar stone was angled to the west so that the worst of the afternoon sun would beat down upon it. A wretched man was chained to the altar. He writhed weakly and tried to shoo away the crow perched on his thigh. The bird flapped and danced between his legs and chest. Exhausted, the man rested after his futile fit, and the crow settled on his stomach and continued to shred his ragged linen shirt. He moaned.

Onja stopped with her companions several paces back from the altar. Inside the ring, faces were carved into the stones. Their expressions alternated between laughing mirth and stern disappointment. Beyond the ring of stones, Onja took in the breathtaking view of wooded foothills with her beloved Rysamand rising over them. Benign white clouds cast their shadows across the forests as if the sky caressed the land. The grand landscape was beautiful and utterly heedless of the pathetic suffering figure dropped within it. The shadow of a circling vulture crossed his torso.

"Why has this been done?" Onja whispered to Amar.

He answered that he had heard of sky temples as a place for punishing criminals. Preem delivered judgment, usually with the carrion birds.

Transfixed by the suffering man, Cybar added, "Not every criminal is executed so ceremoniously. He must have given great offense to the Gods and his tribe."

Amar said, "I have heard that the Nurati Tribe honors Preem more than others. This elaborate sky temple seems to prove it. I think their capital is close to here."

The crow upon the harshly judged man tossed aside an unappetizing scrap of cloth and pecked at the man's abdomen. He screamed and flopped in his chains. The bird ripped a jagged bloody tear in the man's flesh. Blood oozed slowly from his dehydrated body. The other watchful birds cheered their brother, and two more crows flew over to the altar.

Amar drew his good sword and approached the altar. Onja followed him, captivated by everything she beheld. Cybar trailed them, stalling fearfully. Amar waved the birds away from the altar with his sword. The tormented man squinted into the sun. Amar, silhouetted by the brightness, was fuzzy to his bloodshot eyes. He tried to speak, but his dry thirsty throat barely made a sound better than the coarse crows.

Cybar called to Amar, "His life is for Preem. You must not interfere."

Amar studied the man on the altar. His brown skin glowed red from the burning sun. His lips were cracked and darkly clotted. His chin length black hair with a deep widow's peak was dirty and stringy, and blisters mottled his forehead, nose and cheeks. He had only been left clothed in a linen tunic and loin cloth and his bare legs showed the wounds of many probing pecks.

Upon hearing voices, the condemned tried again to speak. "Mercy," he groaned. "Mercy. I do not deserve this."

"Amar, we must go," Cybar insisted. "Do not give him swift death."

Amar had initially thought to end the man's suffering with a merciful blow, but now that he looked at him, he changed his mind.

"I would free him," he said.

"Preem will punish you," Cybar warned.

Amar dismissed the threat of Preem's ire. "I seek no forgiveness for anything that I have done. One more thing will not matter," he said and then looked to Onja, seeking her opinion.

She came beside the altar. "Free him," she concurred.

The bronze chains that draped the altar were old and corroded, but still firm enough to restrain a tortured man. Amar found a particularly weak link and smacked it with his sword. Three strokes and the link broke. Amar pried the link apart and then pulled the chains off the loop set into the stone.

The condemned man watched Amar with amazement. The young wanderer bore no resemblance to anyone he knew and he certainly lacked the appearance of a Nurati. With the chains loose from the rock, Amar looked at the manacles on the man's wrists and ankles.

"I can get those off him," Onja said.

The condemned man turned his head toward her lovely voice. "Sweet lady…." he started to say in a voice as rough as split logs but then he stopped. He did not understand what he saw. He fainted when her eyes began to glow with blue fire.

The bolts of the manacles softened as Onja precisely heated them. Amar pulled the manacles open and freed the man's limbs. Amar gathered the limp man into his arms. He was slight of build, and Amar was able to place him over a shoulder. The man smelled terribly, and Amar turned his face away from his wretched body.

Cybar had retreated outside the ring of stones. From the shade of an oak he watched Amar approach with the unconscious man. Cybar shook his head insistently. "Put him back," he advised urgently.

Onja tugged on Amar's sleeve to stop him. "He truly fears what you have done," she commented.

"He will get over it," Amar said, unconcerned about Cybar's opinion.

"The others truly fear this sky temple," she said.

"The Gods are to be feared, Onja," Amar replied matter-of-factly. "You are born. You die. The Gods are always there."

She contemplated his simple words and then asked, "But you do not fear your Gods, Amar?"

Amar would have shrugged if he had not been burdened with a stinking half-dead man. "I do not care," he said and continued toward Cybar.

Onja lingered in the sky temple and studied the faces carved in the stones. Their blank eyes now looked at her invitingly, welcoming her into their mysterious club.

So simple, she thought.

She set a hand on a monolith. The stone had been cut from the Rysamand and somehow the humans had dragged it up this butte. The effort that must have taken astounded her. So very strange that the humans would work so hard for something that benefited them not at all. Most of them lived in little huts and enjoyed no luxuries. Why did they not put their efforts toward making better shelters for everyone?

Onja looked at the men under the oak tree. Amar had set the man down in the shade and was dripping water onto the man's ragged lips. Cybar frowned over them with worry.

There is power in fear, Onja realized.

A crow flapped over her head and landed on the nearest monolith. He squawked at Onja irritably, apparently blaming her for the removal of the sacrifice. She looked up at the impertinent bird. He turned his head and regarded her closely with a perfect black eye that glistened with intelligence. Onja shifted her attention entirely to the sentience radiating from the shiny black bird. Her wondrous mind that knew no bounds connected with the bird's alien awareness.

"Yes, I took your prize. Forgive me this once, and I will make it up to you," she told him mentally.

Utterly surprised by the communication, the crow tucked his dark beak against his feathery chest and peeked at her shyly. Onja lifted a blue hand and invited him gently with a twitch of her white-nailed fingers.

The crow looked back at his mates that were strutting across the altar stone, complaining among each other. Tentatively the crow on the monolith opened his wings, and, after one more encouraging gesture from Onja, flapped down to her hand. His feet dug into her skin but did not pierce her flesh. She stroked his neck and purred to him lovingly.

"You shall have to tell me your name someday," she told him.

He squawked and took to the air. He landed in the oak tree over the men tending the victim plucked from Preem's justice. Onja watched the indentations left in the skin of her hand fade before she joined her companions.

Amar made Cybar help him carry the man down the steep steps of the butte. The other men were distressed at Amar's audacious theft from Preem.

But Amar scolded them, "We claim to be brother outlaws yet you would leave one to the judgment of the law-abiding. Whatever this man did, he is one of us now."

Delirious, the man moaned and turned his head from side to side on the ground. He was grizzled, sunburned, and filthy. His body was thin and his hands were soft. Clearly he was no laborer.

Amar said, "I think this man has some quality."

They took him to the little stream in the canyon and washed him. The cool water roused him from his burning torment, and he drank greedily, which made him retch. Amar rolled him away from the bank so that he could no longer slurp like a mad animal.

Clearly the group was not going to travel more that day, and Vame gathered firewood. While Amar nursed the man, Cybar answered questions from Kym and Vame about the sky temple. His Kez brothers often glanced warily at the quiet butte. The circling vultures were drifting away. Preem's servants would go unpaid today. A debt perhaps that would not be forgotten.

Onja sat apart from everyone, cross-legged upon a boulder at the edge of the stream. She stared toward her mountains, lost in intense thought.

Kym eventually stood over Amar and the man that had been rescued.

"Amar, the priests of Preem might notice that the vultures disappeared when they should have thickened in the sky," Kym said.

"Priests are slow. We'll move on in the morning. Do not worry, Kym," Amar said.

"Your accursed pet will not be able to travel so soon," Kym said.

Amar's dark eyes flashed up at the Kez warrior. "I do not fear Nurati priests who chain people and leave them for animals," Amar said. "This man will ride with me."

Kym shook his head because Amar puzzled him continually. "Why do you want this man? He'll certainly make no warrior for Vu. I don't think he could steal a bowl of porridge to save his life."

Amar wetted a rag and wiped the man's forehead. "He might have knowledge and rare skills. Warriors aren't everything," he said.

Kym scratched the back of his head, where his stubble was starting to grow in. "I suppose the Nurati are known for scholarship," Kym granted. He squatted next to the thin wretched man and studied him. "Yes, yes, definitely a Nurati nose. What's your name, Nurati criminal?" Kym asked.

The man's eyes were half closed. His lips moved as if he might answer, but the effort to speak seemed to be too much. Amar dribbled at little more water into his mouth and said, "I am Amar. Who are you?"

"Amar," the man whispered back and his long black lashes lifted. His crusty eyes were craters in a skull covered by tight skin. "I am Urlen."

"Urlen," Amar repeated. He liked the name. "What was your crime?"

Urlen shut his eyes as if the answer was difficult to recall. "No crime," he said. "I did what was right."

Kym chuckled. "Maybe he is a proper criminal."

Amar moved Urlen to where Vame was busy arranging kindling. Even in the balmy summer dusk, Urlen shivered and he leaned gratefully over the fire once it was burning. Amar boiled some oats and added a generous dose of salt to the gruel. Urlen ate it with trembling hands.

Amar and his companions sat in a circle, eating and watching their newest companion. As the Nurati regained a scrap of vitality, he observed his liberators. Their speech was understandable but he could not pinpoint the origin of their dialect. Upon recognizing their hair style, he realized whose company he was keeping.

"How many days were you up there?" Amar asked.

Urlen scooped another blob of gruel into his mouth with his fingers. "This was the second day," he said. "I am in your debt, and I thank you." He spoke to Amar and nodded politely to the others.

After a few more mouthfuls, Urlen made himself pause in his eating. His stomach hurt. Sighing, he said, "I was almost dead. I even dreamed a woman was there. Perhaps the blessed virgin Opeti is real after all and came to me in my need."

The men around the fire smiled as if sharing a secret joke. Amar pointed upstream. Urlen squinted and then for the first time he noticed the female figure seated on the rock.

"No," he breathed in disbelief. Then he squinted again. Something was strange. Despite being near death, he had not really believed in the presence of the virgin Goddess Opeti that women prayed to for security. But Urlen, even suffering from near sightedness, knew that not just any woman sat nearby.

"A rys," Amar explained. "She helped set you free."

"So the tales are true…" Urlen said. "Is she from the Tymelo Mountains?"

Amar nodded and then explained the proper name of the mountains. He then offered to introduce Urlen to her. With difficulty Urlen got to his feet and had to hunch over Amar's arm like an old man.

Helping him along, Amar whispered, "You will respect her."

"Yes, Amar, of course," Urlen pledged.

Onja looked over her shoulder. The hobbling Nurati was overcome by the sight of her and dropped to his knees. Onja unfolded her shapely bare legs and slid down from the boulder. Her blue body radiated feminine beauty. Her black hair tumbled around her face and neck, black as a night thick with secrets.

"I am Onja," she said. And then with a gentle smile, she added, "Amar's friend."

Amar glowed with appreciation. It was so good to be in her company.

"I am your servant," Urlen said.

She walked around Urlen, sizing him up. Looking down on his wet head, she asked him why he had been condemned to die.

Although fragile and beaten, Urlen withered even more. Some tragic weight yoked him with choking injustice.

"It makes so little sense to me that I can hardly say the words," Urlen said.

"We will not judge you," Amar said sincerely.

Urlen looked doubtfully at his savior. He supposed that heinous crimes would not shock this young but hardened outlaw, yet he feared that his crime might not be excused.

But with Onja's magical eyes bearing down on him, Urlen knew that he would speak only the truth. He coughed and then began his tale.

"I was respected and encouraged most of my life. As a boy I showed an aptitude with letters and I never grew bored among the scrolls. I would travel to every town and seek all the scholars and scribes so that I could learn more of reading and writing.

"So much knowledge I found rolled up in fabric and skin, lovingly stowed in wooden tubes. The wonder of it always made me want more. By my thirteenth year, I was making my own living copying scrolls for the aging word masters. My family was proud of me. I improved the home of my aging parents. Even my older brothers, so much taller and stronger than me, were proud of me.

"I studied hard and trained myself to letter with skill, art, and clarity. To read my script was to be a pleasure, I thought, but I also took seriously how important it was to preserve the knowledge. It seemed like a magic to me."

Urlen paused and glanced at Onja, expecting her to comment but she remained patiently silent.

In a tentative tone, Urlen said, "I read once that your kind is magic."

"What you have read is correct," Onja said. "Continue."

Urlen wished he had skin and ink now so he could interview her and record her responses. That would be a scroll of incredible value.

He licked his cracked lips and Amar kindly fetched him the water skin. Even a few words had already dried Urlen's mouth.

After a drink, Urlen said, "In time, my talent earned me a place in the court of the Nurati King. In my twenty-fifth year, I became chief scribe to my King. Such an honor for such a young man. Life at court was grand, and I was often allowed to travel to other domains in pursuit of my scholarship. In time my fame grew, and scholars came to visit me and view the library of which I was the master. Many candles burned low through many nights discussing history, nature, law, language, geography."

Urlen sighed, remembering his heyday. Such prestige would never be his again. But to cheat Preem his due was also a great achievement. Urlen would be glad to write down that event.

"I had everything," Urlen said. "But alas, no matter how I stimulated my mind, I remained a man of flesh. I came to know one of the daughters of my King. Isamahlia was her name and she was both fair and smart. But her intellect was a wicked joke of the Gods, trapped as she was in her woman's body, banned from any scholarship. Yet, her woman's body became my master."

Fascinated by his story, Onja sat down and reclined onto an elbow. Urlen shifted off his knees and got more comfortable too. Since it seemed that it was going to be a longer story, Amar sat down as well. He could well imagine at this point what at least one of Urlen's crimes had been.

From the nearby brush a crow squawked. Urlen flinched. Onja waved to the bird swaying on a flimsy perch. She told Urlen not to worry. He relaxed slightly, telling himself that he was free of the chains and the crows could bedevil him no more. With the crow now quietly among his listeners, he continued.

"It was an accident that I met Isamahlia. I suppose it is always an accident that starts such love stories. I was to be weeks away in the Domain of the Temulanka. I had been invited to lecture at a summer gathering of scholars, but my wagon broke down not long after my departure, and I came back to Telop, the Nurati capital, with my servants. My trip would be delayed only a day while I obtained another wagon."

By now the other men had settled into an attentive circle around Urlen and Onja. A tranquil dusk descended upon the land. The sunlight softened toward the horizon and cool shadows spread beneath the trees. Several small flocks of birds, which earlier in the day had been so menacing to Urlen, crossed the turquoise sky seeking their roosts. Now the birds were beautiful and serene; their flight seeming to say that all was right in the world, at least at this moment.

The wonder of surviving the ghastly torture of the sky temple briefly overwhelmed Urlen. To have lived to see the gentle loveliness of even one more sunset was the most blessed mercy he could have imagined.

"Go on," Onja prompted, impatient with his silence.

Urlen gathered his memories and said, "My breakdown was actually fortuitous for I had forgotten a scroll by Binn Bon on architecture. I wanted to take it to the gathering in order to argue that he had actually designed the amphitheater at Hespon and not Zebroh, who normally is credited as its designer. There has been some rather heated debate on this subject...." Urlen trailed off when he noted that the men looked annoyed with his tangent that was surely meaningless to them.

"Anyway, I returned unexpected to my library and found her there. Only one window was unshuttered and sunlight steamed through it. She sat in the light on the mosaic floor and held a scroll into the sunshine so that she could see it in the gloomy library that I had carefully buttoned up before leaving.

"Her tepa lay on the floor and her head was uncovered. Her black hair flowed around her shoulders with an amethyst twinkle in the golden light. I startled her and she looked up at me with guilty eyes.

"In her mad moment of being caught, she snapped the scroll behind her back, but knowing that her action was ridiculous, she brought it forth again and carefully rolled it up. Moving onto her knees, she held up the scroll to me and begged for my mercy. She pleaded for forgiveness and said that she had meant no harm. She begged me not to tell anyone, and then she could not hide her anguish, when she desperately promised me that she would not come back.

"But I was not angry. No, I kneeled before her as she begged. I took her hands along with the scroll and asked her what she was doing.

"When she saw that I was not angry, indeed that I seemed only curious, she smiled and her trap closed around me. Isamahlia told me that she only wanted to look at the scrolls. They were so beautiful and she admitted that she had been trying to figure out the symbols. It broke my heart that she could not read them. Of course a woman would have never been taught letters, but still to see someone who wanted to read, and was unable to, it hurt me in a fierce way.

"I led Isamahlia into a private room of the library where we could talk and not be noticed. I discovered that she had been sneaking into my library for over a year. Suddenly any misplaced scroll that I had puzzled over came to mind and then made sense. Enchanted by this fair daughter of my King, whose face I was never meant to see, I told her right then that she could come to the library whenever she was able and then I told her that I would teach her how to read.

"Isamahlia was more than grateful. She told me that I was the kindest best man in all of Gyhwen and that she would love no other. She kissed me. Isamahlia knew no shame or fear. She cared nothing for her maidenhead, so strictly protected for years. We loved each other among the scrolls and I learned of things that can never quite be written down correctly. At that time, I thought that our inevitable doom would be worth our joy. Today you saw how mistaken I was."

Amar asked, "How long did your affair go on?"

"Two years and three months," Urlen replied heavily. "We were so careful at first. Our fear of being caught was fresh, but as our bond grew and Isamahlia learned to read, we spent longer and longer together. Now, it was not a strange thing for me to be shut away in my library. I was not missed, but Isamahlia was. It was difficult for her to hide her absences from the women's palace. Of course, she had servants lying for her, and even some of her sisters. All making excuses and stories to explain where Isamahlia had been. I never figured out who betrayed us initially, but they all testified against her at the trial. Curse them. I don't know if it was jealousy for her happiness and intelligence that motivated them or just fear.

"We were caught together in my library that had blossomed with joy and learning. In her body I found great satisfaction for that part of me that is flesh, but there is also tremendous satisfaction in teaching an able student and to see her grateful, truly grateful, for the knowledge that I could share. And her perspective on so many things was so fresh to me. Her mind had not been infested with the crushing dogma of men that narrows so much interpretation."

Amar asked Urlen if he had been caught in the act of loving the King's daughter.

Urlen shook his head. "No. We were reading, which was perhaps worse. If I had been caught in her naked embrace, my punishment and death would have been quicker. You see, I was given over to the torture of Preem for teaching Isamahlia the letters of men, which is forbidden to women," he said.

The other men murmured in agreement, but Onja was confused. "Why is this forbidden?" she asked.

Urlen knew the official reasons well enough. They had very recently been pounded anew into his head, but he only replied miserably, "I don't know, fair and gentle rys maid."

Amar offered an explanation. "Women are the keepers of love and family. They are for children. The teachings of men are beyond them," he said.

"Is this what you think of me?" Onja demanded indignantly.

"You are not a woman," Amar answered.

No, indeed, Onja thought. "Urlen," she said. "What was done to Isamahlia? Was she put in another sky temple to die?"

Urlen stifled a sob. He wished he could answer yes and then they could go save her. "She was publicly drowned for her crime," Urlen said. His face then collapsed in his hands. They had made him watch her die. Many in the ignorant crowd had cheered. Her parents had seemed pleased that she had met a just end.

"I would rest," Urlen murmured.

"Your story was interesting. Go to your rest," Onja said. She got up and returned to her perch on the boulder and resumed her meditation.

Everyone else settled into camp and divvied up the watches through the night, nervous that the Nurati might discover what they had done. Urlen took no watch and slept fitfully. His exhaustion from his exposure and torture kept him unconscious, but his nightmares shook his slender body.

When Amar was on watch, he listened to Urlen mutter in his sleep. Amar had no doubt that Urlen would always be grateful to him for the rescue, and Amar decided that he would keep this scholar close to him. Urlen had much to offer that rogues and warriors did not.

In the morning they moved on. Urlen rode with Amar, clutching the strong back of the young warrior like a feeble baby monkey.

That day they rode well past dark, letting Onja guide them overland in the gloom. A waning half moon rose late and illuminated the land when they came out of the rugged forest onto a bare hilltop that afforded a wide view of the Temulanka Domain. For generations, the Temulanka had kept trees clear from the hill and a splendid thick turf grew atop it, crisscrossed by deer trails.

Beyond the hill, the land descended into fertile flat farmlands, broken by thick woods and blocky mesas. In the distance a few lights twinkled on a fortress on a butte.

Onja slipped off her stallion.

Kym protested, "Onja, we should not camp here. The Temulanka will see our fire from that fortress."

She said, "Camp where it pleases you, but I shall stay here." She then told Amar to come back to her in the morning.

Reluctantly he accepted that she wanted solitude. With Urlen snoring softly against his shoulder, Amar followed the others down the hill. He looked back once and saw a crow flap across the moonlit sky.

Vame located a nearby creek basin thick with old willows where they could camp unseen. Amar took the first watch. He was restless now that he had reached the Temulanka Domain, and he reflected deeply about his next steps. The others went to sleep quickly, except for Kym, who Amar knew was watching him.

At the first hint of dawn, Amar dove into his workout regimen. After his run, he found Onja in the meadow. He was sweaty and breathing hard from his workout.

Blue fire burned in Onja's eyes. "Take my hand," she commanded.

Amar complied and her grip was strong. An intense burning assaulted his palm. When she released him, his palm was amazingly not injured and he held a crystal orb. Many shades of blue streaked through the crystal and light glowed deep inside it. In awe, he gazed at it until he finally managed to ask what it was.

Onja had to consider how to explain in his language. "A warding crystal," she decided. "It is my enchantment. Carry this crystal, Amar. It will help me find you and communicate with you."

Very touched, he closed his hand around the crystal and held it to his chest. "I will guard this precious jewel with my life," he said.

"Keep it close," Onja advised. "I must leave you today."

"No," he blurted before he could help himself.

Although touched by his affection, Onja ignored his protest. "I have brought you to Wayndo. He is in that fortress," she said and gestured toward the haphazard collection of stone and wooden buildings on the butte. "I will show him to you."

Onja touched his forehead and his anxiety dissolved. At first, Amar felt trapped in a thick silent fog. Then he saw land beneath his feet and he seemed to be climbing a wide path dug into the side of a butte. Paving stones had been laid to help the road keep its shape through the seasons.

Ragged patchy grass grew alongside the path in crevices on the sides of the butte. He passed through a gate of thick timbers bound by old blue bronze. Beyond the gates was a courtyard where horses, carts, and people milled in the basic business of morning. Guard houses, towers, barns, and storehouses surrounded the courtyard.

Amar's attention was directed to the largest and newest tower constructed of cut stone. Above the tower's entrance, a sigil of a speckled senshal's face was carved into the stone. Instead of entering the tower through the door, stained freshly white, Amar felt himself fly up to a window two levels down from the roof. His stomach felt like it left his body. He hovered in front of the window and then stepped on its sill and crouched inside.

Within the chamber he spied a middle-aged man. He was lean and strong, mostly bald and what remained of his gray and black hair hung in a braid down his neck. He wore no shirt but old leather bracers covered his wrists and higher up his arms were the scars where the blades of many foes had nicked him. A loose pair of black pants sagged around his hips as he moved carefully through an upsa routine. Purposefully his hands moved away from his body and then came back together and touched his chest as he stepped through a series of slow kicks and squats.

Amar studied the movements of the man's body. Age had yet to blunt the physical abilities of this Temulanka warlord.

"Wayndo," Onja whispered in Amar's mind.

The man lingered in Amar's vision for another moment and then Onja guided his senses deeper into the tower. They explored the halls and stairs and rooms and vaults. After spying upon every space in the tower, all the images faded and Amar was back on the hill. The rys drew her hand away from his forehead. Amar blinked and stepped back, seeking his balance.

Onja said, "I heard men call him Wayndo. Do you remember his face?"

Amar told her yes. He remembered quite vividly every detail of the extraordinary journey. Amar would be able to recognize Wayndo at a glance and he knew the tower like he had grown up in it. He wanted to ask her how she had shown him such things, but he decided it was rude to constantly pester her with questions. She was magic and he should accept it without child-like curiosity.

Instead he asked her why she was leaving. The subject seemed to trouble her. She looked at the jagged blue mountains that were her homeland.

"A rys cannot stay always away from the Rysamand," she said. "The snows of winter are coming and I would go home."

Amar envied her because she still had a home to go back to. He opened his hand that held the warding crystal.

"You will contact me again?" he said, seeking reassurance.

"Someday, Amar," Onja said.

Saddened at the prospect of her absence, he dared to ask if he could go with her. Onja pondered the possibility. At last she said, "Not now, but I think that someday you will see Jingten."

"I would like that," he said, accepting the rejection that she had softened with hope.

Onja stopped gazing wistfully toward her home and regarded him seriously. "Amar, I would have you seek power. Be the prince you were born to be. I will have need of your strength, and I know I have your loyalty," Onja said.

Her statement was both ominous and exciting to Amar. He thought he knew what she wanted him to do. His own thoughts had begun to flirt with ambition, and her command gave him the courage to be more than a lousy bandit or assassin.

"Why do you help me, Onja?" he asked. "If you seek powerful allies, why don't you go to a king or warlord who already has power? You are great. No one would deny you their loyalty."

She replied, "Chance brought you to me, Amar. Sometimes that suffices to make a decision. I think that in time, these kings you speak of will lend me their strength, but they will never be my friends. Not like you."

Amar gripped his warding crystal tightly, profoundly touched by her kind words. "I will do my best," he vowed.

Onja then asked him for his iron sword. Amar gave it to her. She touched the place where the blade was recently blunted by breaking Urlen's chains. She ran her hand along both edges of the sword. Blue light sparkled between her fingers. When she returned the sword to Amar, he plucked the blade gingerly with his thumb. The edge was exceptionally sharp and perfectly restored.

"You'll not need to sharpen it again," Onja explained.

With grateful awe, he thanked her.

"I must go. Be patient. You shall see me again," Onja said. Her stallion sauntered to her side, and she bounded easily onto the animal's back.

"Good luck," he said because she seemed to be leaving with some great purpose.

Onja thanked him but knew that luck would have little to do with the future she imagined.

Amar watched her ride away, and he was bereft of comfort again. Her departure blasted a desolate hole in his heart, but he had her command to guide him. As she headed for her mountain homeland, he steered his attention to the Temulanka Domain. The path to new fortunes started here.

13. A Man That Is Feared

Gathering his courage like the dark clouds of a storm, Amar walked back to camp. He opened his palm and looked at his crystal orb. The inner light rippled suddenly as if Onja encouraged him from afar.

Urlen squinted and got up from the log he was sitting on and approached Amar. "What is that?" Urlen asked.

"A gift from Onja," Amar answered and extended his hand so Urlen could see it.

The Nurati's eyes bulged out of his thin head. He was deeply impressed. "An enchanted charm?" he breathed.

Amar nodded and then glanced sideways at Kym, Vame, and Cybar, who were looking as well.

"What does it do?" Kym asked.

"It keeps me connected to Onja," Amar said. He closed his hand around the orb and went to his pack that was lying on the ground. He pulled out scraps of leather and cord and sat down to craft a small pouch for his new treasure.

The Kez warriors exchanged concerned looks. Cybar asked where Onja was.

Amar explained that the rys was returning to her homeland. He spoke as if her absence did not bother him.

Cybar frowned, quietly unhappy about her departure.

Kym was annoyed. He stood over Amar and complained, "You said she was going to help you get Wayndo. We've been wasting time wandering around and now she's gone. What are you going to do?"

Amar finished tying a knot to secure the crude pouch around his crystal. Without looking up, he replied, "I will go to Wayndo today. You don't have to kill me, Kym."

"What will you do?" Kym demanded.

Amar placed the pouch around his neck. He stood up and met Kym's eyes. "I am going now," Amar said.

"We will go with you," Kym decided.

"It is best that I go alone," Amar contradicted. "I will not run away. I will perform my mission and prove myself to Lax Ar Fu."

Kym gave Amar a long searching look, but as usual he was confounded in his judgment of the man. Finally he grumbled that they would hunt him down and skin him if he did not return.

"If I do not return, I am dead," Amar said.

Amar put on his armor and strapped on his swords. He adjusted his leather bracers so they would be more comfortable and then he asked Kym for his haircutting blade.

Understanding that Amar wished to get rid of his Kez style haircut, Kym offered to do the cutting. "Your commitment did not last long," Kym commented as the remaining long hairs were trimmed away.

"It will grow back," Amar said. He then put his helmet on over his freshly shorn locks. Privately he contemplated that his mission might be impossible but he was excited by the challenge. He expected to gain much notoriety if he succeeded.

Going over to Urlen, Amar said, "If I don't come back, you can have my horse."

Despite the scabs around the Nurati scholar's lips, he still managed a surprised smile. He was pleased that Amar had thought of his needs at all.

Urlen said, "Thank you, Amar. May I never have cause to collect. And, if I may inquire, what do you mean to do? Just walk in there?"

"Yes. It will be easy enough," Amar answered. He looked at Kym and added that it was only a town where people came and went all the time.

"You'll get killed," Vame announced, a little anxiously.

"That is what Lax Ar Fu has in mind," Amar agreed. "But, I will do my best to avoid that."

Urlen's expression was a mixture of confusion and dismay. He feared for Amar even if he suspected that the young man was mad.

"Don't worry," Amar told the disgraced scribe and left the camp.

Amar did not look back. He was motivated anew by Onja's need for a strong friend, and the strange enchantment hanging around his neck gave him a supernatural sense of confidence.

He emerged from the wild lands onto the dirt road that wound through the countryside. At summer's end the ruts were dried and worn smooth. Amar walked along the edge where the drying weeds and grass hung over the compacted dirt. He passed a small two-wheel cart filled with split firewood pulled by a donkey. The donkey's head was bent low as it labored with its load when Amar went by. The village man walking alongside the cart looked at Amar with cautious curiosity that soon shifted to fear.

Amar did not bother making eye contact with anyone else on the road. More people passed him in both directions as he neared the fortress, but the heavier the traffic, the less people paid attention to him. He assumed he must look like any young mercenary trekking into the stronghold of Wayndo.

Amar's thighs burned as he climbed the path cut into the side of the butte. His workout that morning had been intense, but he liked pushing himself harder every day. He was still thin but his lack of body fat only accentuated the muscles bulging from his young frame.

I need to be stronger, he reminded himself. The typical body of a twenty-one-year old man would no longer suffice.

Retracing the path that Onja had already shown him through her mind felt strange. At the gate there were two Temulanka guards. They watched the regular traffic with disinterest until Amar neared the open gate. Their bronze helmets had round metal brims that shaded their brown eyes from the morning sun. One of them tapped Amar on the chest with a spear and segregated him to the side of the road like a shepherd moving a sheep.

Amar sized up the guards as they pressed close on both sides of him. They were easily ten years older than him. Hardened veterans instead of green warriors. It seemed that Wayndo did not risk his gate to untested youths.

The guards came at him with questions in quick succession. Who was he? Where did he come from? What was his business? Who was his lord?

"I am Amar. I seek to be a mercenary. I have no lord. I have heard that Lord Wayndo is wise and strong and good to serve," Amar answered.

The guards scrutinized him. Amar stared back at them calmly.

Finally, one of the guards said, "We have no need of mercenaries. There is no war."

"Then what should I do? Be a bandit?" Amar said.

"I suppose you do look hungry enough to steal," the other guard said. Then he laughed and added, "There is always need for a young strong fighter. There will be war soon enough. There always is. Go to the guard house. It's the blue building next to the stone tower. Ask for Captain Ephener. Maybe he'll take you in."

Amar eased the spear away from his face. "Thank you," he said.

As Amar passed through the gate, the first guard who spoke to him called out, "Don't expect to get paid any time soon."

Both of the guards chuckled.

Amar noted the location of the small postern gate beside the gate house when he entered the walled town. He then strolled around and perused the market stalls while examining the main stone tower. He spotted the window that he had stepped through when he traveled with Onja's mind. He wished he actually had the power to float up there with spectral ease.

He also noted the blue building where he had been told to seek the guard captain. After buying a bread roll from a vendor, he went to the communal cistern and took a cup of water. Eating leisurely he watched the men-at-arms in Wayndo's service come and go from the blue building. Some entered the tower and some came out of the tower. They all wore the helmets like the guards at the gate. They also wore the same black shirts and pants. Their other gear varied somewhat for it seemed each man had his own weapons and armor of various styles.

Amar walked by the blue building casually and studied its slate roof, especially where it connected with the tower. He then whiled away the day in the town. After buying a rope in the market, he rented a place in the loft of a tavern to nap. When he woke up, he lay on the straw mattress and stared at the wooden rafters while wondering what it would be like to assassinate someone. Amar recalled killing Patharki during his hopeless battle at the death of his tribe. But that had been in the heat of an attack when he was trying to survive. Hunting a strong target and killing him by surprise would be a different matter.

When Amar left the tavern, the setting sun glowed red upon Wayndo's tower and the street vendors were packing up their stalls. Amar went to another tavern adjacent to the blue guard house, and it had the predictable red curtains in the small upper windows.

No one questioned his presence when he entered the brothel. Downstairs men were drinking and women were dancing or sitting on laps. The music was merry but without talent. Lanterns hung on the supporting posts throughout the main room and their smoke left streaks of black up the posts and produced a dingy haze along the ceiling. The place smelled of strong drink and sweat.

As a fresh young face, Amar quickly attracted the female workers. A voluptuous woman with a bold gap-toothed grin sidled up next to him and put her arm around him. "Oh, you'd make me feel like a farm maid again," she said.

Amar said nothing. Her bad breath was far from appealing and her touch triggered no response from his body.

He gestured to another woman who had approached only because she must. Her eyes were sad and she was homely, probably the last to get chosen most nights.

Shrugging off the first whore, he took the hand of the shy sad woman. "I have coin and have been long on the road," he said.

She nodded and escorted him upstairs. The floorboards creaked on the second level that was dark except for a few oil lamps. The upstairs was divided into stalls instead of actual rooms. Old straw littered the hall that dissected the stalls along each side of the pitched roof.

From the shadows, Amar could hear the expected breathing, moaning, and grunting. With little interest in the carnal relations, he squinted in the gloom as he followed his hired mistress, and he saw what he had hoped to find. Draped over the partition of one of the cells was the black clothing of a guard. Without hesitation he snatched the garments down and the busy man behind the partition did not notice.

Amar's whore stopped at the end of the hall and meant to take him into a cell to the left, but Amar entered the cell to the right instead. She followed him across the hall and timidly said that he was not in her assigned place. Then she stared at the clothing he had stolen.

Amar ignored her and opened the shutter of the narrow window tucked beneath the eaves of the roof. He looked out into the night and examined the nearby roof of the guard house. Only a very narrow alley separated the brothel from the guard house and he judged that he could cross it.

He set aside his weapons and started quickly undressing.

"I shouldn't be in this one," the woman muttered but she untied her wrap-around shirt anyway. Reclining onto the dirty straw-stuffed mattress, she hiked up her skirt. She wore no underclothes.

Amar glanced at her, but he had no desire to entertain himself with her worn body. He quickly pulled on the black pants and shirt and put his armor and gear back on.

He dug into his coin pouch and took out twice what a sad whore like her was worth. He flicked the silver at her and it landed in the folds of her lifted skirt.

"If you can be paid to spread your legs, you can be paid to keep your mouth shut," he said.

Amar folded his clothing into a small bundle and stuffed it into his backpack. As the whore stared at him with disbelieving surprise, he ducked through the window and grabbed the eave of the roof. Holding on, he pulled his legs out and dangled over the narrow alley. For an awful second, Amar panicked as his legs flailed over nothingness, but he found his daring and pulled one foot onto the window sill. Then he was just tall enough to stretch his second leg until his foot was braced against the rough wooden planks of the guard house wall. He let go of the brothel roof and lunged for the edge of the guard house roof. Grabbing the slate tiles that stuck out over the wall, Amar took his foot from the window sill and swung it over to the guard house wall. He hung there for a moment to catch his breath. He was quite amazed with himself.

Pulling with all of his strength, he lifted himself up onto the roof. First he got his chin over the slate tiles and then an elbow and then he reached out for a new handhold. His fingers clung desperately to the tiles, and he

Rys Rising: Book I

pulled. Once he got his torso over the edge he flung a leg up. With his next pull he got his other leg onto the roof just as a slate tile snapped apart in his hands. His hand flopped desperately for a new hold and after securing himself anew, he lay still, panting from his exertion and stress.

There was no time to waste though and he quickly got onto all fours. Amar looked over his shoulder and saw the woman's dark eyes shining in the window. Her expression was inscrutable. Amar raised a finger to his lips and then turned away from her. He scrambled along the peak of the roof toward the tower.

The woman in the brothel window decided to earn her money in this most unexpected way. She had so little opportunity to rest that she went to her assigned cell and cast herself down on her miserable overworked bed and fell asleep. She did not care what deeds the handsome young stranger was about to commit.

Amar reached the tower that abutted the guard house. He ran his hands over the well-fitted blocks of stone. The window by which he had planned to enter was higher than he had judged and he could not reach it. Amar quickly scanned the yard to see if anyone had noticed him. A few torches and lanterns were lit near the cistern in the courtyard and near the entrances of buildings, but their light did not reach over the roof and he was well concealed in the darkness.

Having no choice but to climb, he sought handholds and pulled himself up. His grip between the stone blocks was frighteningly tenuous and his booted feet pressed insistently into crevices. His fingers were cramped painfully when he grabbed the stone window sill. He hauled himself into the window and was pleased that no one was in the dark room.

His luck only lasted until he got his first foot inside. Then the door opposite the window opened and two men walked in with a lantern. The light showed that they wore the garb of Wayndo's men-at-arms. Amar lurched inside and thudded heavily onto the floor when his second foot caught on the window sill.

One soldier shouted and the other lunged at Amar. Amar rolled onto his side and yanked out a sword. He thrust the blade at his attacker's neck, and hot blood spilled onto Amar's hand.

The second man with the lantern rushed forward. The light swayed up the wall and across the ceiling. Amar sprang across the room. He swiped with his sword but missed, and, when he charged again, he ran into the corner of a sturdy wooden table. The table bashed his hip and spun him aside, which actually saved Amar from the slashing blade of the soldier. Ignoring the brutal flare of pain in his hip, Amar threw himself at the soldier. They scuffled furiously before Amar cut his throat.

He shoved the dying man away from him and reeled against the wall. Panting, he listened for more men in the hall, but it was hard to hear because of the deep banging of his heart.

Amar peeked into the hall. The light from the dropped lantern inside his room spread across the floor in a golden triangle. He saw no one and moved out. He wanted to run, but it was important that he act normal. Grateful for the knowledge of the tower's layout that Onja had given him, Amar headed for the servants' stairs that rose from the kitchen at the bottom up through the tower.

When men entered the stairwell one level above him, Amar clenched with fear but he had no place so hide. Forcing himself to relax, he continued up the steps and only glanced at the three servants carrying down dirty dishes. As Amar had hoped, the servants brushed by him on the steps because he appeared to be only a typical man-at-arms.

After going up two more levels, Amar paused and tried to remember the details of the tower. The memories had a foreign feel because he had not learned them through direct experience. He left the cramped servants' stairwell and slipped into a hall. Tapers burned in wall sconces along the plastered walls. In the flickering light, the texture of the plaster was rough with shadows and the designs painted upon the walls were fractured.

Amar went to the door that led to Wayndo's private chambers. He suddenly heard voices just beyond the door and then the click of the door latch being raised. Scrambling with quiet speed, Amar darted back into the stairwell. He heard men coming his way. They were deep in conversation and oblivious to the intruder. When the three men went by the shadowy stairwell, Amar saw their backs and spotted the black and gray braid of his target. A jeweled clasp held the hair that stood out sharply against the white fabric of his shirt.

Wayndo continued with his two associates to the main stairs. He spoke loudly and with authority, probably rattling off opinions and orders but Amar was not sure what he said. His nerves were preventing his ears from unraveling the Temulanka dialect at that moment.

It did not matter. He had not come to speak with anyone.

Very carefully, Amar peeked out of the stairwell and saw a guard now at the door to Wayndo's apartment. He must have been inside with his lord until the men had come out. Amar considered killing him, but a missing guard would alert Wayndo to trouble.

Mindful of making noise, Amar padded up the stone steps to the next level. That morning he had seen that this level between the tower roof and Wayndo's living quarters was for storage and a library. Scrolls were stacked along sagging wooden shelves and dusty cobwebs draped the stacks. In the gloom that was only relieved by two oil lamps on separate tables, Amar saw tables littered with jars, bags, furs, and bundles of vegetation. Staying close to the wall to avoid the light, Amar ran his hand along the edges of some scrolls. The rolled parchment felt stiff and dry. He supposed that Urlen might very much like to see the scrolls. At random, Amar plucked out two scrolls, but his selection unbalanced the contents of the whole shelf and all the scrolls rolled forth. Amar flapped his arms comically trying to stop the flow of rolled skins. Dozens of them pattered on the floor.

Kicking the clutter aside and shoving scrolls back onto the leaning shelf, Amar cursed at himself silently. He still shoved the two scrolls, whatever they were, into his pack since he had already gone to such stupid trouble. He hoped that Urlen enjoyed them.

I hope that Urlen has a chance to enjoy them, Amar amended.

Then he heard a light thump on the spiral stairs that led up from the center of the room to the roof. Lantern light spilled down the stairs and the silhouette of a cat was cast upon the wall. The cat scooted down the steps and out of the light.

"What was that noise? Watch out, Zoodeba. Must be big mice," commented an elderly male who spoke to his pet in a tender tone.

The man came down from the roof slowly, gripping the wooden rail that wound around the stairs. Amar rushed around the edge of the room and navigated tables and shelves until he was underneath the spiral stair. The cat hissed at him.

"What's that?" the man said. He swung the lantern around various points in the room but obviously had no idea where Amar was.

Amar froze inside the shadows and tried to decide if he should kill the old scholar.

The old man was drawn to the disturbed bookshelf and bent down slowly to start setting the scrolls back in place. The cat jumped onto the top shelf and supervised his progress while he commented to the cat about how he was surprised that pile had stayed in place so long.

Amar began to think that he might be able to go about his business undetected. His presence seemed so painfully obvious though. He was surprised that the old man did not smell him. Or perhaps his body odor just seemed so strong because of the unfamiliar sweat of a stranger that permeated his stolen clothes.

While the man was on all fours collecting scrolls and the lantern was on the floor, Amar dashed up to the roof.

The wind hit him when he emerged onto the platform. It was stronger at this height and Amar had a sudden chill as his sweat cooled his skin. He was sweating more than he had realized. Thrilling fear coursed through his veins. His reckless and improvised plan to infiltrate Wayndo's inner chambers made his existence so achingly real. At this moment, Amar could savor life. In danger he could find joy.

He removed the rope from his pack and shook out its coils. He looked for a place to tie it. A sturdy timber flag pole presented itself. Wayndo's senshal banner snapped above Amar as he secured his rope.

His hands moved urgently. Between gusts of wind he could hear the old man chatting to his cat. Amar warned himself to go kill the old man, but his heart yet had some mercy in it, and Amar would gamble that the man would not discover the rope. He had already missed Amar practically walking by him.

Taking up the rope, Amar mounted the parapet above the window that he had entered mentally with Onja. A waning moon had just broken the horizon and dappled the scattered clouds with light. Stars glittered in the heavens, and the hills jutting above the dark fields were silvery and silent.

As Amar wrapped the rope about his torso and gripped it fiercely, he paused to take in the splendor of the night. It was good to see beauty and have it touch him. He needed this moment of blessing before he committed cold murder.

Amar went backwards over the edge. His arms shook as he held himself steady and his feet walked down the fitted stones. He looked down. The rope dangled unnoticed along the tower. He was not sure how close it was to the yard below. Close enough he hoped.

He continued down like a spider in search of fresh hunting grounds. Soon he came upon the window and congratulated himself on his judgment. The knowledge of the building that Onja had given him was flawless.

Inside he saw three candles burning on a mantle. He swung into the room and gathered the rope inside and coiled it neatly. Ready to hunt, he drew his iron blade that should have been an heirloom of his family. Now it was only the enchanted trinket of a killer.

A splendid and huge senshal skin covered the floor in front of the cold fireplace. In the low candle light, the empty eye sockets of the beast's head came alive again and its bared fangs gleamed with threatening hunger.

Amar crouched next to the skin and ran his hand over the fur. Even with his glove on, he could appreciate the lustrous thickness of the orange speckled fur. He looked around trying to decide where he would wait and what he would do when Wayndo returned. He would need the element of surprise, especially if Wayndo returned with the other men.

A gasp yanked Amar from his deep speculations.

A woman was gaping at him from the next room. Amar rushed her and seized her. She had just begun to scream when he clamped a hard hand over her mouth. She struggled hard. He could not recall ever feeling the strength of a woman.

As she fought frantically, Amar tried to think of what to do. He could not let her go. If she got out one good scream the guard in the hall would surely react. The ugly decision came to Amar. He pinned her against a wall and snapped her neck.

Her body went limp and he lowered her to the floor. Her body heat from her brief struggle was a gruesome affront to her swift death. Amar dragged her into the bedchamber of her lord and put her in bed. The covers were disturbed. She must have risen upon hearing him come in the window. Amar replaced the coverlet upon her and then straightened her head on the pillow to correct the bad angle of her shattered neck.

Amar was shocked by the emptiness he felt. The thrill of his own danger had suddenly ended. Killing the woman had numbed him.

I can do anything now. No one can defy me, he thought.

Strangely he was comforted by the realization of this notorious destiny. He remembered the face of his wife, or rather Gendahl's wife. In the dim moonlight, it was easy to imagine her face resting on the pillow. Amar leaned forward and kissed her lightly. Her lips were soft.

He left her side and hoped that death had come as swiftly for the fair wife of Gendahl.

Amar returned to the main room and blew out the candles. He took out his crystal orb. The milky blue light was cold. He looked into the orb. He could not wait until he was closer to the source of that power again.

He placed the orb on the window sill where his rope came in. Then he moved the senshal skin toward a corner and hid beneath it.

Beneath the timber boards of the floor he could dimly hear muffled voices and indistinct laughter. Some music started and then there was singing. Amar imagined the amusements set before the lord of the tower. He hoped that the lure of a young female in his bed drew Wayndo back soon.

As Amar waited to kill Wayndo, he thought mostly about the doddering scholar above him. He was counting on the old man going to bed instead of going back to the roof and discovering the rope. It was not too much to ask.

The grinding tedium of waiting was finally shattered by footsteps in the hall. It was just one man. Thinking of his pledge to Lax Ar Fu, Amar did not act out of honor or out of fear. He acted because he wanted to become a man that is feared. Then he would become a man that is powerful.

Amar heard the useless guard acknowledge his lord and then the door opened. Amar had positioned his head inside the senshal head and he peered through the jagged fangs. Light came in from the hall and then went black again as the door closed.

The man who entered called out a woman's name and asked why she had not left a candle burning for him. Then he stopped in the middle of the room.

"What is that?" the man whispered. He walked right by Amar toward the window where the orb glowed against the night. Just like a moth to the flame, the man went to the orb and picked it up. He stared at it with total fascination just as anyone would have done.

Too slowly he noticed the rope in the window. The enchanted light reflected on his bulging eyes. Amar struck. His sword hit his neck, and the man slumped into the window in a spray of blood. The warding crystal hit the floor but it did not shatter.

Amar pulled him back inside. The body, slick with blood, with its lolling head thunked onto the floor. Amar crouched and grabbed the crystal orb and looked quickly to the door. Still no sounds from the guard outside.

Amar held the crystal over the face of his victim and confirmed that Wayndo lay dead in front of him. In his mind he thanked Onja for his success and the living light inside the crystal orb brightened briefly. He was warmed by this sign of connection with the rys female, and the awful deaths that he had just inflicted were meaningless to him. Reverently, he returned the warding crystal to its pouch.

Moving quickly now, he finished severing the head with his sword. Striking the death blow had been far easier than this butchery, which Amar found distasteful. He recalled the command of Lax Ar Fu to bring the head and the cock of Wayndo, but Amar decided that the head would suffice. He pulled the bloody shirt off of Wayndo and used it to tightly wrap the head. He tied the sleeves into a handle for the bloody soggy bundle and tossed the rope out the window.

Descending the side of the tower was an agony of anxiety. Despite the dark he could still be noticed from the ground, and the alarm might be raised inside the tower at any moment.

The rope was not quite long enough and Amar had to jump the last distance to the ground. On his landing, his left ankle flared with pain but he did not hesitate. Limping as fast as he could, he stuck to the shadows along the other buildings and headed toward the gates.

A big lantern hung from a post outside the gate house. Amar did not see anyone outside, but presumably men were on duty. He paused to give his ankle a rest because he would have to fight and run soon. He judged that the ankle was not broken but it certainly hurt.

Carrying his grim bloody bundle as casually as possible, Amar walked up to the postern gate with confidence. He grabbed the thick wooden bar that locked it.

"What are you doing?"

Amar glanced at the gate house and saw a man-at-arms emerging from the doorway. He didn't have his helmet on nor was he holding a spear. A short sword was sheathed at his side. His demeanor was curious instead of alarmed thanks to Amar's disguise.

"Off to meet a sweet and lonely farmer's wife," Amar said and pushed on the door.

"Your speech is odd. Who are you?" the guard said, suspicious now.

The thick door scraped open stiffly. It was not often used but it served.

"Hey! You can't open that!" the guard protested. Another man came out the door now and this one had his spear ready.

Amar held onto the wooden bar that he had lifted from the door and slipped through the partially opened door. The guards protested loudly and tried to seize him. Amar jumped behind the door and pushed it shut in the guards' faces and then braced the wooden bar against the ground to hold the door shut.

Through the thick stone walls Amar heard the guards curse at him. Then a bell started ringing. He ran. The excitement of getting this far alive eased his pain and he picked up speed on the steep road down the butte. It was hazardous in the night, and he tripped three times, bashing his knees and elbows.

When he reached the level ground, he heard riders above him.

Amar left the road and ran blindly into the fields and then through the woods. In the dark he stumbled into a small creek and splashed in up to his waist. He climbed out on the next bank and continued. He planned to get his bearings in the morning and find his way back to his comrades.

He had done as Lax Ar Fu had bid him and he could truly join the Kez now. Amar had a place in the world. A place to serve…and then perhaps to rule.

14. Urgings to Defiance

The rys breed among themselves now. The second generation retains traits that we seek, yet we cannot look upon them without feeling a deep distaste. I will oversee another round of refined breeding spells with pure blood tabre. Our hopes are high that this time the Kwellstan Sect will enhance the race according to its inspired visions. ~ Daykash Fane, 1862 Kwellstan calendar

Dacian pushed away troubling concerns about his reprimand. The peace of deep meditation soothed him until a lifeforce drew his attention like sweet nectar attracting a bee. A rys was approaching Jingten from the west. He watched her with his farseeing mind while lying on his bed. Although he appeared to only be staring at the ceiling, his mind filled the Jingten Valley and went up the slopes of the mountains until he felt the aching cold of the snowy peaks in his bones.

Across this majestic landscape he watched the solitary rys female. A crow seemed to be following her.

When Dacian extracted his mind from meditation, he contemplated the mystery of where she could have been. Dacian sat up and swung his bare feet off his bed. He had begun his meditation yesterday, or perhaps…he was not sure. His body felt hungry. His meditation must have lasted longer. Even a rys needed to eat sometimes. Power did not come from nothing.

Stretching his arms, Dacian went to the open window. The morning sun was pushing back the chill that had gripped the valley all night. He selected a clean tunic from his wardrobe. He was surprised that Halor had not disturbed him from his lengthy meditation, but it was likely Daykash Breymer was keeping him busy. Dismally, Dacian supposed Halor was glad to have him out of the way since the incident with the acolytes from Kahtep.

He slipped on the tunic and cinched the waist with a leather belt. After pulling on soft suede boots he headed for the kitchen. The breakfast crowd had cleared out and the dining room was empty, but three rys workers remained in the kitchen. They were talking pleasantly among themselves until the cook sensed Dacian quietly standing between the pillars that separated the dining area from the kitchen.

"Dacian," the cook smiled and waved him into the room full of fires and kettles and rows of utensils, jars, jugs, and sacks.

"Good morning, Exaton," Dacian greeted and nodded amicably to the two other workers, Ifil and Lang, who were scrubbing dishes in a large sudsy sink.

"Ah, you are hungry," Exaton observed. "I have not seen you at a meal for three days."

"That long?" Dacian murmured.

Exaton waved a hand impatiently at his subordinates, silently commanding them to fetch a plate. Ifil and Lang reacted, but they did not take their eyes from Dacian and so they bumped into each other as they headed for a cupboard while wiping their hands.

"Come sit with me, Dacian," Exaton invited. "We were just about to have a snack." The cook ushered him to one of the work tables and pulled out a chair. As Dacian seated himself, Exaton said, "So, have you been deep in some great spell all these days?"

Dacian glanced up at the broad-faced rys in a sleeveless white shirt and clean apron. The cook was sincerely interested in what Dacian had been doing. He seemed even to think that it was important.

"Meditating," Dacian said simply.

Exaton seated himself and nodded gravely. "Yes, one such as you has much to think about. Great spells don't just make themselves up. It's not as if you are just trying to boil beans like me."

"I imagine cooking takes some care. Even boiling beans," Dacian said.

Exaton shrugged modestly, pleased by Dacian's graciousness. "It's usually easiest just to use the fires. Zapping a roast with a spell is only practical if one's pressed for time. Still, it does not come out quite the same. Some things can't be rushed," he said.

Lang set out dishes for all of them while Ifil delivered a pitcher of cold water, bread, cheese, sliced cold venison, and a bowl of spiced squash sweetened with honey.

They started eating without much more conversation. Dacian was distracted by his hunger among other things. He tried to sort out his priorities for the rest of the day. He had studies that had gone neglected. Master Halor would not ignore him forever.

Exaton, even with his average rys perception, sensed the restlessness in Dacian. The cook suggested that he accompany them to town to shop the markets. The lowland traders from Nufal would be leaving in a few days before the heavy snows came to close the pass. "A trip into town would do you good," Exaton added.

Dacian drank some water and considered the invitation. He was tempted by their companionship. The tower walls were feeling close this morning.

Instead he said, "Master Halor has bid me stay in the tower."

Exaton frowned sourly. "I know the great Dacian is not so meek. If a cook is not chained to his pot, how can it be that an acolyte is locked to his books?"

"It is not that," Dacian said. "It would be best if I did not go against the orders of my Master."

"Oh, is this still about that nonsense with those Kahtepian fools?" Exaton said. "Master Halor should get over that. You were just exercising as a strong young rys should do, Dacian. Those tabre are overreacting."

"It was more serious than that, Exaton," Dacian insisted. "I was…reckless." He recalled Bagdoa's terrible burns. At least he had healed them, but he had learned that his magic could hurt.

"You are NOT reckless," Exaton said emphatically. "You are the most thoughtful rys I have ever met. And, in my three hundred years, you are certainly smarter than any tabre I have met."

Dacian enjoyed the compliment, but he still politely declined the invitation.

"Come on, Dacian," Exaton coaxed, undeterred by two rejections. "Halor and the Daykash are all wrapped up fussing over their tabre favorites. Halor won't notice. He is busy petting his Daykash trying to make him purr."

Ifil chuckled at the derogatory observation. "Yes, come with us, Dacian," he said.

Dacian looked at Ifil and Lang, and then looked into Exaton's twinkling black eyes. They want me to go, he thought and then realized with greater clarity that they wanted him to defy Master Halor.

Their urgings to defiance were unexpectedly exciting. Dacian saw now that to his fellow rys he was not the disgraced acolyte who had caused trouble with visitors. He was the rys acolyte who had trounced a tabre in a Bozee contest, and it made them proud.

Pride is dangerous, Dacian recalled from one of his books. But pride also felt good. His strength made the other rys feel better about themselves.

Tempted as he was, Dacian would have obediently remained at the tower except that he estimated that the female rys should be arriving in Jingten any time that day. She had been somewhere in the west, and Dacian truly wanted to hear of her travels. Going to the west was forbidden of rys, and the tabre seemed disinclined.

"Very well. I shall go," Dacian said.

"Good! Good!" Exaton exclaimed. "Let's get ready."

Getting ready did not involve Exaton doing anything except trading his apron for a long vest trimmed with rabbit fur that had many pockets. The cook, however, gave numerous orders to Ifil and Lang and had them scurrying about wiping plates and tables before they left.

"They seem to mind their master well," Dacian observed wryly.

Exaton looked up from his coin purse where he had been counting his funds. "I only ask them to do their jobs, Dacian. I swept floors for a hundred years before getting head cook at the tower," he said. Then a bit defensively, he added, "And I ran off without leave from time to time." Exaton slid the coins out of his purse and muttered that he had lost his count and started over dropping the polished stone Kwellstenums into the pouch.

Dacian followed the rys workers out of the kitchen and to the stairwell. It was required of the rys servants to use the stairs.

Outside the tower the lake lapped on the gravel shore. Several boats were beached in a row and one pleasure barge was docked. The black and red painted vessel was rarely used. Dacian had been told that such vessels were common on Lake Kwellstan where tabre and humans gathered for various water events.

He helped his three companions push their row boat into the water, and then cast a quick spell that dried their boots after all of them were in the boat. Ifil and Lang thanked him profusely as they each grabbed an oar.

"I tried that once and burnt my toes," Lang said.

Dacian was not sure how to respond, but he did imagine the blackened pair of boots.

As they crossed Lake Nin, Exaton talked about the items he hoped to find in the markets. Some things he needed for the tower kitchen, but others he wanted for his home.

"My wife wants fine wool cloth from Kahtep and wine from Kwellstan," he said. "Her tastes are not cheap."

"Wife?" Dacian said. "I did not know, Exaton. Congratulations."

"Well, I am working on the wife part. She seems willing to live with me but reluctant to make promises," Exaton said.

"I have been warned that rys females are slow to commit," Dacian said.

"And quick to break off," Lang added and proceeded to describe his two failed relationships over the past fifty years.

Dacian, having never had a female companion, had no experience to share. As a Nebakarz acolyte, it would be unseemly for him to pursue the distraction of the opposite sex. Once he was an ordained Nebakarz priest, he would have more freedom to expand his personal life. For now there was great satisfaction in learning from the long tabre tradition of magic use.

They docked at Jingten's single public dock, where three other empty boats were tied. Jingten was never exactly busy. Although it was the only town Dacian had ever known, it remained a solitary colony on the fringe of the Nufalese realm. Dacian anticipated greatly the time when he could travel to Nufal and see Kahtep and then the famous Kwellstan, the crown of civilization.

Jingten was a handsome budding colonial town. The original timber buildings from the first tabre settlements some four centuries earlier were being replaced by stone buildings. The stone was quarried from the surrounding mountains, and the hard blue stone created buildings of beauty and permanence. Many of the roofs were slate, but the newer ones were sheets of copper, gleaming in the bright autumn day. The wealth of Nufal was starting now to show in Jingten, despite the misgivings many tabre had about the settlement.

Dacian took the investment in the newer buildings as a good sign that the tabre would accept the rys as cousins and the racial tensions would eventually ease. He felt encouraged toward his goal to improve tabre opinion about rys. The tabre could not ignore his talent, and once he was a Nebakarz priest of the Kwellstan Sect, he would lessen the prejudice shown his kind and perhaps even cure it.

He walked with Exaton and the others toward the town square where vendors made an open air market in the fairer seasons. Jingten was a comfortable place for Dacian. There were more rys than tabre, and he found undeniable ease among those who looked like him. The original tabre population of the settlement had dwindled over the last two centuries, and their movement back to Nufal had accelerated in recent decades. They left because their offspring had come into the world as rys blues and thereby disappointed their parents.

This fact was wounded the rys, many of whom had seen their parents abandon them. Dacian had been spared this sadness because both of his parents were rys. He was among the second generation that was entirely rys-born. Having had the benefit of both parents, Dacian and others like him tended to be sympathetic to those rys left behind by their unhappy tabre parents.

His parents resided in Jingten, as all rys did, and Dacian decided to visit them while he was in town. They never came to see him at the tower.

Once Dacian reached the market square, he told his companions that he would reunite with them later. He walked quickly across the square, only glancing at the vendors' merchandise. About half of the sellers had already left for the season, and those that remained had plenty of room to spread out their products. Dacian noted the stacks of wool cloth for which Exaton would soon be bargaining.

Many of the stalls had food to sell. The bounty of the Nufalese harvest in its lowland fields far exceeded anything that could be grown in the alpine Jingten Valley. Tomatoes beamed redly from baskets and green-skinned apples piled proudly amid sacks of wheat and rye. As Dacian walked past an open barrel of apples, the scent of the fruit danced into his nostrils, and he imagined the warm summer showers that had nurtured the fruit along with sunny days.

Two blocks beyond the square Dacian approached his ryslinghood home. His parents shared a modest timber home, tidy if aging. He meant to walk in, but it had been so long since his last visit, he felt that he should knock. As he raised his hand over the door, it opened, and his mother, Illyr, stood there. She had of course sensed her son coming down the lane. Her face brightened as she greeted him and ushered him inside.

"I did not expect to see you so soon," Illyr commented.

"I have not been here for months," Dacian said. He entered the home of his parents. The place seemed more cluttered than the last time he had been there, but he was not surprised. His father had an almost compulsive need to keep whatever trinket, tool, hat, belt, or basket that came his way no matter how worn it was or unneeded.

Dacian noted that the home had been remodeled. Fresh pine panels covered the walls. The panels were pale and polished and still smelled of the forest, which was comforting. The wooden floor had been replaced with warm red tiles. The floor was well done, but Dacian did not care for the color although he did not say so when his mother asked him if he liked it. Illyr gave him a suspicious look after he replied with polite praise.

He followed her into the kitchen. The window shutters were open and sunlight spilled between the houses and warmed the little herb gardens on the sills. Illyr gestured to a tea kettle and Dacian nodded agreeably.

As Illyr dipped the kettle in a water barrel and placed a hand on it to heat the water with her magic, Dacian heard his father coming down the stairs. Dacian greeted his father when he came into the kitchen although part of him dreaded the encounter.

Glaxon was a handsome rys, as was his son. He was tall and slender yet muscular. He worked hard in the forests, selecting trees to fell for building materials and cutting and milling the wood as needed. Glaxon wore a deerskin jerkin and matching pants. A string of crystal beads was around his neck. Making the small crystal beads with his magic was a hobby of his. Many such beads adorned Illyr's clothes, and she was admittedly proud to wear his "little charms" as she called them. A sparkling row of beads on her sleeves was one of Dacian's earliest memories.

"Should you be here?" Glaxon inquired gruffly.

"I was welcome last I knew, Father," Dacian said, unable to hide his hurt over the dismal greeting.

Glaxon frowned, a little embarrassed. "Of course, you are welcome, Dacian," he said. "Only we thought you were confined to the tower."

Dacian glanced at his mother. She took her hand from the kettle and removed its lid. Steam drifted up and she began to crumble tea herbs from a jar into the hot water. "We heard that you had needed discipline," Illyr said quietly. Sympathy showed in her black eyes.

Glaxon grabbed three ceramic cups from a cupboard and set them on the table where he sat down with his son. "You should stop mixing yourself up with those tabre. They will never approve of anything you do," he said.

Dacian fingered the lip of his cup. It had not taken any time for his father to start his old lecture. Why did I even come here? Dacian asked himself.

"Because your mother misses her son," Illyr answered.

"I miss you as well," Dacian replied and smiled as she poured him tea. "You could come to the tower to see me whenever you want." He told his parents this year after year, but they never heeded the invitation.

"And you could come live at home where you belong," Glaxon said.

Dacian had heard the admonishment many times. As he always did, he patiently explained himself. "The tabre will never respect rys if we keep to our place. Once I'm a Nebakarz, other rys will see that they can also develop their talents and pursue any position in society. We should make ourselves more a part of Nufalese society so the tabre will cease to see us as strange. In another one or two hundred years things will be better, Father. You will see," Dacian said.

"Indeed we shall see," Glaxon muttered and sipped his tea.

Dacian sighed. His mother settled into a chair at the table and they shared a moment of peace as they drank.

Leaning back in his chair, Glaxon said, "Dacian, tell me about this tabre you beat in a fight. That would please me."

Although uncomfortable with the memories, Dacian shared the story of the Bozee training that had ended so badly. He told how quickly he learned the physical moves and the spells. It had been exciting, but it was dangerous sport. He told them of getting hurt, healing himself, and then of how badly he had hurt Bagdoa before healing him.

When Dacian finished his story, the eyebrows of both his parents were arched with impressed surprise. The tabre version of the story had not credited Dacian with his deeds of magic.

Thoughtfully, Glaxon murmured, "You are powerful, my son. You would do best not to let those tabre goad you."

For once Dacian agreed with his father. "Master Halor has made that clear to me," Dacian said.

"And now he has released you from probation?" Illyr asked hopefully.

Dacian thought to lie to her, but she probably already knew that he was defying his confinement and just wanted him to admit it.

"I did not ask my Master's leave to come here," Dacian said. "But do not worry. Halor will indulge me."

"Yes, indulge you," Glaxon said. He seemed to have more to say, but he occupied his mouth with the dregs of his tea.

Dacian did not pursue the matter. He made small talk with his parents instead. Eventually, they left the kitchen and went to his father's workshop next door, and Dacian listened contentedly as Glaxon discussed the timbers he was cutting for a new building. He spoke respectfully of the trees he had cut. Dacian knew that his father took seriously the ending of each tree's life, and he was careful to select those trees that were best suited to a purpose so that he could reduce wasted wood.

The shop smelled of wood, of course, and the chippings and shavings from the timber were everywhere in curly piles. Dacian ran a hand along the mighty timber that his father was almost done squaring up with his adz. The wood was thick and strong. It would be the task of a Nebakarz priest to cast preservation spells upon the timber before it went into construction. Dacian longed to do it now and show off his skill to his parents, but enchanting the wood might only get Glaxon in trouble when he delivered it. A rys woodcutter must never presume to work the magic of a Nebakarz.

"How long can you stay?" Illyr inquired.

"I should go now," Dacian said and explained that the rys workers he had come with from the tower would be finishing their shopping soon.

"It was good to see you, Dacian. Very good," Illyr said.

He kissed her forehead. Glaxon surprised him by walking with him out into the street. Dacian bid him farewell, but his father set a hand on his shoulder to stop him. With restrained affection, Glaxon said, "It was good to see you, Dacian. But I am worried and feel I must warn you."

"Of what?" Dacian asked.

"You know that I have never approved of you becoming a Nebakarz acolyte," Glaxon said. Dacian's posture became impatient as his father continued. "This trouble you've had will not be the last time. Now that you have shown your talent instead of failing, the tabre will look for ways to keep you back. They don't want you, my son."

"Why don't you believe in me?" Dacian demanded bluntly.

"It's not that," his father quickly defended. "I suppose you just have not lived long enough to understand how much the tabre dislike our existence."

Dacian could not resign himself to his father's grim view of rys status. Indeed all rys seemed to accept the tabre-dominant status quo. I will change things. I will, Dacian vowed.

"I need to go," he said testily.

Glaxon gave his son's shoulder a squeeze and let him go. Dacian headed up the street toward the square. He did not look at the familiar homes lining the lane, and his eyes drilled through the cobbles beneath his feet without seeing them. He seethed as he always did after a visit to his parents' house. The conflict created by his need for their approval and their discouragement scratched his heart like a cat playing with a cornered mouse. It left him angry and lonely, and he welcomed the distraction when he felt the lifeforce of the wandering female. She was close, and the fire of her existence was so much brighter than ever he had noticed before. Dacian quickened his steps and hurried into the square.

Exaton waved to him. Dacian walked over to the cook but continued to scan the market. Exaton had just finished haggling with the cloth merchant and he started telling Dacian about his purchase, but Dacian only half-listened. Ifil and Lang reunited with them as well. They were carrying bundles and sharing reports on the various goods they had seen.

Exaton asked Dacian how his parents were. He answered absently, but then he saw the female and fell silent. Her entry into the market square was noticed by all. Bartering and conversations diminished as the scandalous female returned from her forbidden journey. All rys knew each other, and Onja was known to be a problem. Although being abandoned by her parents was not uncommon or particularly stigmatizing, she had always been defiant and rude to her foster parents, and gone through three different guardians before recently reaching ryshood at age one hundred and disappearing from Jingten.

She seemed to welcome the stares of the tabre vendors. A simple hooded cloak of human-made brown homespun draped her body to her ankles. The hood drooped across her forehead and a few black strands of hair hung out. A crow flapped down and landed on her shoulder.

"I wonder who will take her in this time," Ifil whispered.

Exaton said, "Unless I'm wrong, I think she is no more a rysling. She will make her own home I expect."

"I will go speak to her," Dacian announced. The symmetry of her face and the indigo gleam in her black eyes were making him truly contemplate female beauty for the first time. He liked the vulnerable thrill of the new sensation.

Exaton, who had so recently urged Dacian to break his probation, now counseled prudence. "Leave her be, Dacian. You've your own problems with the tabre right now. Mixing with her will make them worse. She is a deviant. They won't tolerate her, especially after this. Even rys are sick of her."

Dacian dared to give his elder a judgmental look. He disliked how he seemed to reject her and so suddenly accept tabre authority. It was not right. He broke off from his companions and approached her boldly.

Dacian snaked his way through the crowd. He caught her attention while still a few steps away and she stopped and looked at him. Dacian raised a hand toward her but then lowered it because his reaching seemed inappropriately eager, almost rude.

"Welcome home, Onja," he said, presuming to say her name.

Shyness made her cast down her eyes. His friendly confidence befuddled her after months away from her kind.

"I am Dacian," he added.

Her lips twitched with a little smile before she looked up. "Your name is known to all, acolyte of the Kwellstan Sect," she said.

By the way she called him acolyte, he was not sure if she was impressed or ridiculing him. Automatically, his mind sought her thoughts, but he could discern none of her feelings with any certainty. Her aura was like rowing into a thick fog on the lake. He could only be sure that there was water beneath him and he could not see the shore.

"Where have you been?" Dacian asked.

She looked among the other nearby rys. Her shyness slipped away as she announced that she had traveled to the west. A path could be found through the mountains, and many humans lived in the lowlands.

Patting her bird, she announced, "Any who would hear about the west may gather around and I will answer questions."

Her offer easily aroused curiosity and many rys decided to hear what she had to tell even if they would never dare to travel outside the valley. Dacian nodded eagerly and several rys gathered behind him. Onja looked around for a likely spot where they could sit together, but before she could proceed, the crow screamed and flew away. A score of tabre from the tower led by Daykash Breymer entered the square. The Daykash was resplendent in his red, black, and gold-lettered robes, and his acolyte and priest attendants followed him like an extension of his body.

The tabre flowed around Onja, and the Daykash stopped in front of her. They were of the same height, but her youthful face with its crisp features made his old smooth face with its high forehead look like an eroded hill.

"You will surrender yourself to the custody of the Kwellstan Sect," the Daykash announced.

Onja blinked rather innocently. Glancing at the stern tabre on all sides, she said, "It would seem that I am surrendered."

"Then come with us," Breymer said.

He started to turn, but Dacian pushed through the ranks of tabre and intercepted the esteemed Nebakarz. "Greetings, my great Daykash," Dacian said.

"What is it?" the Daykash said sharply.

"With respect, my great Daykash, why do you take this rys female into your custody?" Dacian asked.

"How dare you?" Breymer spat, and a white hot flash of anger showed in his eyes. "No one can question my actions. Be silent!"

The priestly tabre lord spun with a regal flourish and led away his party with Onja. Dacian stood still as the tabre passed by. He met Onja's eyes as she was hustled away. She seemed not to be afraid.

The tabre departed on the road around the lake to the tower. The rys and tabre in the square dispersed into murmuring cliques. The arrest of a rys was quite unprecedented, and no one knew what it might mean for the rys female who had been so suddenly interesting. Even the tabre admitted that they would have liked to have heard her reports of the west.

Exaton, Ifil and Lang came up behind Dacian, who remained standing where the Daykash had left him. With soft sympathy, Exaton said, "You see now how it is best not to mix with her, Dacian. She provokes the tabre with the liberties she takes."

Dacian said nothing. Glumly, he helped his friends with their packages back to their boat and hunkered in the boat as they rowed across Lake Nin. Along the shore, he could see Breymer marching on the road with his group and his…prisoner? The concept was ugly. Surely breaking the ban on travel out of the valley did not warrant confinement. Why can't rys go where they want? Dacian wondered.

Still glowering at the tabre on the shore, Dacian asked Exaton what they would do to her, hoping that the older rys might have some historical perspective on this incident. Exaton only shook his head.

They are not going to do anything to her, Dacian decided.

15. Many Choices

The Daykash stepped out of the levitation shaft into the observatory. Behind him two priests holding Onja rose from the shaft. Breymer grabbed Onja and hauled her onto the floor. She resisted him until she felt his paralysis spell crackle over her nerves. Daylight spilled through the skylights. Breymer noted how the light glistened like blue raindrops on Onja's sleek black hair. He shook her rigid body and his lip curled with disgust before he shoved her back to the priests who caught her arms.

They tossed her in one of the cells that lined the outer walls of the observatory. She hit the wall and slid down. The paralysis spell ended, and she lifted her head and regarded Breymer with patient hostility. He slammed the door in her face.

"Only open this door on my specific order. No food. No water. Nothing for her," the Daykash told the priests.

Breymer descended to his quarters one level below, where he found Halor waiting for him. Halor immediately sought to regain control. "Daykash, you should not have bothered yourself with that errant female. I was quite aware of her return and was planning to deal with her," Halor said.

"Something this important demanded my attention," Breymer said coolly. With a wave of his hand, the copper bound wooden doors to his suite opened soundlessly.

Halor followed him inside. The Daykash walked across the foyer and into a wide receiving room. The interior walls were lined with benches upholstered in red leather. Three windows looked out onto the lake and town with the snowy mountains in the background. Breymer took in the vista of Jingten. He had to agree with Halor that it was a fine town.

A pity the Great Divinity cursed our loins with rys for coming here, he thought. The Kwellstan Sect had been so certain that colonizing the Rysamand Mountains would add to their power, but they had not entirely predicted the outcome.

Halor stepped closer to Breymer's back. The Daykash's white hair hung just past his high collar. "There was no need to bother yourself with that female," Halor said.

The Daykash whirled. "Yes there was. I wanted all of Jingten to see that the Nebakarz are not going to tolerate the behavior of this female. My rank signifies the depth of the disapproval."

Although Halor disliked having his local authority shoved aside, he realized the futility of protesting the matter with the Daykash. What was done was done. Instead he asked Breymer what manner of punishment he should impose on the female.

Breymer brooded before answering. Halor grew more unsettled. He could feel the blame radiating from his superior. Finally the Daykash said, "How did you let that rys get so far away?"

Terribly aware of his failure, Halor meekly said that he had not immediately noticed her absence. She was just a young rys that nobody liked or paid attention to. Then she was gone.

The Daykash complained, "Who knows what she discovered about herself wandering loose among all those humans. She must be well aware of her superiority by now. We can never let her go free again. We have worked too hard to teach these rys that they are lesser because they were not born of sacred Nufal. We can't let her influence the others." The Daykash pointed toward the ceiling and continued, "She has power."

"Surely you overestimate her," Halor said. "She is untutored and I can't recall that I have ever seen her cast a spell."

"I feel it in her," the Daykash grumbled suspiciously. He glanced once more at the ceiling and white light flickered in his pupils. "But she is not the main issue here. Master Halor, did you notice that your pupil, Dacian, who is supposed to be confined, was in town?"

Oh miserable day, Halor thought. He admitted that he had noticed.

Breymer continued, "And Dacian actually questioned my seizure of the female. I think this presents me with the opportunity I have been waiting for."

"And what is that, Daykash?" Halor asked.

"Let us speak in our minds," the Daykash announced.

"As you wish," Halor responded and moved onto a bench.

The Daykash seated himself as well. Halor was disturbed that the Daykash would want to communicate with this level of security as if he feared that someone was eavesdropping.

Now settled into a mental connection, Breymer said, "I have needed a way to make Dacian overstep his bounds and give us a reason to deny him entry to the priesthood. All of this has gone on long enough."

Halor wanted to protest. He sincerely believed that Dacian deserved to be a Nebakarz priest. Dacian had the power and the talent, but rys had been deemed too volatile and alien to be welcomed into tabre society. Eighty years ago it had seemed a reasonable plan to accept Dacian as an acolyte and delay rejection. But Dacian had excelled and now expected to go to Kwellstan and complete his training.

The disappointment stung Halor, who regretted that such an able Nebakarz student had not been a proper tabre. "Daykash, I have tried to steer him from ambition and instill in him the importance of following our laws," Halor defended. "And I believe that I have succeeded. Dacian places great value on order and civilization. Perhaps you and the Grand Lumin consider him more of a threat than he is."

Breymer conceded that Halor had done a good job quelling the natural powers within Dacian. Once they had deemed it better to accept Dacian within their fold and control him instead of risking the possibility of him going wild if left adrift in rys society. But the Grand Lumin had rethought that decision since then.

"Master Halor, I know you are close to Dacian," the Daykash said. "I even see that you like him although it has not kept you from your duty to the Kwellstan Sect, and I appreciate that. Perhaps your affection for him keeps you from seeing the threat in him as I do. But I shall put a test to him and we will see how well he keeps his place."

Halor could not imagine what the test would be. "What do you propose?"

"Because this wandering female needs discipline I plan to punish her severely and judge Dacian by his reaction," Breymer answered.

"Severely?"

"Yes. And her punishment will be public. She shall endure the phlia-mel," the Daykash said.

Halor physically gasped and the magical white light in his eyes flashed sharply. He stood up and shook his head. Breaking the silence, Halor said aloud, "Daykash, you can't!"

"I must," Breymer replied.

"But it is barbarous," Halor insisted. "No one has endured such a brutish thing in a thousand years."

The light diminished from Breymer's eyes. He seemed extraordinarily calm considering that Halor had just disputed his decision.

Trying to be reasonable, Breymer said, "Halor, I know the tabre set aside such methods a long time ago, but they had their place once. In the younger days of our race, our passions were as strong as our magic. Discipline needed to be imposed so that learning and civilization could develop. Perhaps these rys need this to learn their place. The rys are a failed experiment. Their odd mutation is an embarrassment to the Sect. They must be kept under control."

Halor sputtered a few words, needing to protest more, but he failed. He knew that he could not override the authority of the Daykash.

"Do you really think anything less would teach this Onja some obedience?" Breymer said.

When Halor did not answer, the Daykash continued, "Inform the town that this female will be punished tomorrow at the gates of this tower and the rys are to come witness this."

Sadness settled into Halor's bones. Eventually he sighed and said that he would make the arrangements, but obedience brought no comfort. Great Divinity, forgive us for reviling our creation, he thought.

******

Halor was surprised that Dacian had not asked any questions. The young rys followed his Master silently as they exited the tower. Halor hoped that proximity to his Master would keep Dacian from acting up during the sick display.

Priests, acolytes, and servants were gathering outside the tower. Stray snowflakes swirled on the air. Many rys had come from the town as well. Most of them had walked but some had ridden horses, come in carts, or paddled across the lake. Small boats clogged the docks, and horses and carts were parked along the shore for a considerable distance.

The Daykash and his attendants were already presiding over the crowd. Acolytes kept a wide circle clear in front of Breymer where the accused would be presented for her punishment. Halor took his place in the front row with Dacian.

Dacian scanned the crowd of rys and was glad that his parents were not there. He would have been hurt if they had come for this sad affair after ignoring all of his pleasant invitations. Dacian looked next at the Daykash, who stood stiff and grim-faced. His hands were tucked into the sleeves of his glittering, high-collared robe.

Halor quietly told Dacian that he did not agree with what was about to happen.

Although Dacian appreciated the comment, he was too troubled to respond. Instead, he focused his mind up the tower. Nebakarz priests were removing Onja from her cell and escorting her to the levitation shaft. Dacian observed that she appeared calm, almost serene, as if her captors could not truly contain her. Dacian took some comfort from her brave demeanor.

As Onja was brought down the levitation shaft, the crowd of hundreds of rys watched the gaping doors of the tower.

She emerged with downcast eyes and a tabre priest holding each arm. The wind caught her plain brown cloak and flung it back from her perfect body and blew strands of unruly black hair across her face. She shook her hair away from her mouth because her hands were not free.

Manacles with cold white warding crystals bound her wrists. Dacian had not expected to see her clamped by a domux. Although he had never seen a domux in use, he had read about the device that was meant to contain the magic of a criminal.

"Master," he whispered. "Why the domux? She has used no spell against us."

"It is a normal procedure," Halor improvised. "Any tabre, or rys, must be so restrained when brought to judgment."

Dacian analyzed the spell in the enchanted manacles. The crystals were old, but their spell remained quite potent. Despite the strength of the ancient magic, Dacian quickly unraveled their secrets as Onja entered the circle before the Daykash.

Breymer addressed the crowd. "I have summoned you to this judgment so that you would know better the will of the Kwellstan Sect and heed the wisdom of our rule. It has always been the law that no one is to go west from these mountains. Not even I or any Nebakarz priest goes into the west. The exploration and colonization of Ektren is not to be done haphazardly. We did not rush into the Rysamand Mountains four centuries ago, and we shall not rush beyond them without careful consideration. Every part of Ektren, every region, every vale, and hill, and river and stream holds the powers of Nature that we are blessed to have a greater understanding of than any other of the Great Divinity's creatures. Today I am forced to strongly admonish this young rys female for her reckless wandering, and I thank those who have come to witness this important reminder of the need to follow our laws."

The Daykash then commanded the priests holding Onja to let her go. They released her arms and stepped back although they remained close enough to reclaim possession of her if need be.

"State your name for all to hear," Breymer said.

Now Onja raised her gaze, but not to stare defiantly at her tabre judge. She looked at Dacian. "Onja," she said, loudly and proud.

Dacian met her eyes, surprised but glad that she sought him in her time of trial. He did not dare communicate with magic in front of all the gathered Nebakarz although he had much that he wished to say to her and to ask.

"Do you understand the charge against you, Onja of Jingten?" the Daykash asked.

Onja shifted her eyes slowly toward the Daykash, as if he were a tiresome chore that she could no longer put off. "No," she replied.

Her obtuse response nettled Breymer despite all the poise and confidence that his powerful position granted him.

"Have you never once in a hundred years been informed of the rule not to leave these mountains?" he demanded, obviously not believing her.

"I have heard the rule but saw no sense in observing that which is unreasonable. You cannot charge me with any crime for traveling upon the world that I was born into. I can go where I please," Onja said.

Uncomfortable murmurs bubbled through the crowd. Both rys and tabre were quietly shocked by her unapologetic attitude.

"You are mistaken, Onja of Jingten," the Daykash said sternly. "There are bounds upon this world that you were born into. The Jingten Valley is your land, and there you are meant to stay."

Although he spoke specifically to Onja, Dacian heard the implied meaning that all rys were meant to stay in the Jingten Valley.

Onja said no more, and the Daykash ordered that the charge be officially read against her. A Nebakarz priest named Dutan stepped forward. He lifted a small wafer thin disc of stone upon which was inscribed the charge. Willful wandering the tabre legal system called it.

Then her sentence was read. She was to endure eight strokes of the phlia-mel. Although rumor had already informed all gathered what the sentence would be, discomfort still rippled through the assembled rys upon hearing the sentence.

A priest, named Angpar who was young and just advanced from being an acolyte, stepped out from behind the Daykash and held out the thin long stick that was split three times at one end where crystals were attached. The thinness of the stick gave it springiness so that its crystal-barbed splinters could deliver a whip-like sting.

Breymer said, "Long centuries ago, before tabre had fully come to master and appreciate the orderly joys of civilization, harsh methods were employed to teach us discipline. I have decided that the use of the phlia-mel has become necessary again because the rys are a young breed and, as this female has shown, have need of discipline."

No one among the hundreds of rys said anything, but Dacian could feel the collective protest caged all around him. He felt he should say something. Ask for mercy at least, but so many things held him back. Was he wrong to question his elders? Did he want to jeopardize his future as a Nebakarz? Did he have any reason to risk himself on account of this female who ignored the law?

"Begin," was all the Daykash said, and the two priests who had escorted Onja earlier swiftly grabbed her again and pushed her to her knees. Angpar walked around the trio and regarded his subject. He shook the phlia-mel once so that all could see the spring in the rod, and then he reached down and yanked off her cloak and whipped it aside. He seemed eager to have at her.

Onja's clothing was meager. She wore only a small vest and shorts and her lower back was already properly exposed. Dacian could see the muscles in her back tense in anticipation of the abuse, but she did not look over her shoulder at her punisher.

Angpar raised the phlia-mel, but his eagerness faded for a moment, and he contemplated his next action as if he suddenly realized that the world would change when he lowered his arm. Then his self righteousness returned and he swung at the rys female hard. The crystal barbs flashed with white light when they struck Onja's blue skin and her cry mixed with the meaty thwap of the rod hitting her. She lunged forward automatically but her handlers yanked her back in place.

Many rys cried out or gasped, and some turned away, and before anyone could recover from their disgust, Angpar hit her again. The Daykash fixed an emotionless gaze on Onja. Dacian could not see her face but he imagined her grimace.

Dacian looked at Halor urgently. His lips trembled with outrage. "Stop this," he begged.

"It will be over soon," Halor said woodenly. His eyes insisted on obedience.

When the third blow fell, Onja's cry was louder. Dacian heard her take a deep breath to brace herself for the next stroke. As she filled her lungs with this painful gasp, Dacian felt all his rational reasons for standing by collapse like a hillside soaked by torrential rain. He looked at the tabre priests and acolytes lined up on both sides of him. They watched the punishment raptly. Where was their compassion for her suffering?

They were all civilized creatures, but Dacian realized that their values did not entirely extend to their much-maligned rys cousins. They would watch Onja endure eight strokes from the phlia-mel and agree with the Daykash that it was necessary and proper. Civilization required order but was brutality the only path to that end?

Angpar gave Onja her fourth stroke. Her sentence was half complete.

"Stop!" Dacian shouted. He rushed forward and felt Halor grab him but he shook him off and moved toward Angpar.

He spun Angpar away from the female and then shoved his chest so that he fell on his butt. Dacian's magic erupted. The crystals of the phlia-mel disintegrated in three successive blue flashes and the old wood of the rod burst into flames. His next spell cracked the domux and it fell off Onja's wrists. Its enchanted crystals lost their power and faded to pebbles.

As the tabre holding Onja shifted to intervene with Dacian, he raised both of his hands into their faces. They were swept backwards off their feet by the hot blasting force of his attack spell.

Onja had collapsed forward and she was trying to push herself up but the pain in her back was nearly paralyzing. Purple bleeding blisters ravaged her sleek youthful back. She looked over her shoulder at Dacian. Agony twisted her tear-streaked face, but gratitude radiated from her eyes, and he could believe that she would honor him forever.

"Onja," he whispered, casting his mind toward her thoughts, her soul. He felt her lifeforce. It was hot and powerful, too powerful for her to have endured this gross mistreatment.

Distracted entirely by the sight of his downtrodden damsel, Dacian had no shield spell ready when the magic of the Daykash netted him. The spells of many tabre priests piled on next, and Dacian could not move. His legs began to wobble and the blood in his veins became hot and painful.

Dacian summoned his power and began to untangle the spells gripping his body. In this crisis, he suddenly realized that he could throw off their attacks. He was very powerful. He would teach them not to abuse a rys female for a petty infraction.

Halor was shouting for him and pushing his way through the tabre. But it was not the voice of his Master that got through to Dacian's enraged mind. It was her voice.

"Do not fight them," Onja said. "Not yet."

Dacian looked at her again. She had managed to roll onto her side, and her call to patience intrigued him. Not yet? What does she mean? Dacian thought. Even without an answer, he would do as she asked. He relaxed and the spells of the tabre bit into him vindictively. Defenseless again, Dacian crumbled in pain.

Halor put his arms around his pupil. "Enough!" he called. "Enough. Stop!" Then in a softer voice he spoke to Dacian. "Yield. Do nothing, I beg you."

Dacian nodded and was not ungrateful for the protective embrace of his Master. The tabre spells backed away although he could feel their powers still roiling around him, ready to engage again.

Halor said, "My Daykash, I ask you to be merciful. The citizens of Jingten have seen justice and know now of discipline. Call the female's sentence complete and end this."

Fiery magic blazed from Breymer's eyes but he no longer looked angry. He had gotten what he wanted. With much magnanimity, he declared to the crowd that had retreated from the upheaval that the punishment was done. The whole affair had unsettled the startled rys far more than it had shown them the wisdom of Nebakarz rule. Sensing the agitation, the Daykash decided to withdraw. He ordered that Dacian be taken into custody and that Onja remain confined as well.

Halor looked very sad when two priests yanked Dacian away from him, but Dacian spent little time considering the dismay of his Master. He looked at the rys beyond the rings of tabre. Their eyes were straining to get a glimpse of him through the press of priests, and Dacian could hear his name being repeated through their ranks. They were proud that he had acted to defend the female. Dacian could feel their approval for what he had done, and the joy of it was overwhelming. He had not realized how much he wanted approval until he felt it in such quantity. He could also sense that they wanted to help him. Many of them cared that he was being hauled into custody by those he had spent his life striving to join.

Onja was right to tell me not to fight, he realized and was glad that he was not causing the violence to escalate.

He went back into the tower without protest. The hostility of the tabre around him seared his senses. They were excited about no longer having to blunt their disdain for him with civility.

Although Dacian had naively expected to be taken to his living quarters, he was instead taken to the observatory level. Dacian had previously regarded the small rooms that adjoined the wide circular observatory platform as private meditation cells, but now they served as a different sort of cell. One of the two tabre who had escorted him to the observatory pulled open a cell door and stood aside.

Dacian looked the tabre in the eyes. He was a decade or two younger than Dacian, and his suddenly superior position to the delinquent rys made him haughty. But Dacian confronted him with equal pride, and the contemptuous expression of the tabre faltered as he realized that Dacian was choosing to submit.

Dacian entered the cell and the door closed behind him. White light flashed around the door as a tabre placed a sealing spell on it. The cell was round like a tube in a wasps' nest. Rough beige plaster coated the walls, and a spider was in residence at the center point of the little domed ceiling. Its web hung patiently in this normally unoccupied bit of the tower. The spider did not move.

Outside, Dacian heard many tabre milling around and talking excitedly. He overheard them boasting that it was their magic that had subdued the wild rys, but other tabre admonished the braggarts and said that it was the strength of the Daykash that had curtailed the rogue.

Dacian scowled. He knew that he had hardly fought against them. They sounded so smug about containing him.

Dismally Dacian started to realize that the consequences were going to be serious for him. Suddenly not knowing what to expect of his future left him with a lonely drifting feeling.

He sensed when Onja was brought up to the observatory. Her presence both excited and dismayed him. He reached out to her lifeforce with his mind. He had hoped that she would be released. The tabre placed her in a cell next to him. Dacian could feel her pain. Once the door was closed and she was alone, she sank to her knees and placed her hands on her lower back. Dacian heard her moan. Her pain was deep. With his mind's eye, he observed how she licked her lips and summoned her magic. She began to heal her own body. Her magic moved methodically through the damaged tissues, renewing flesh, clotting the bleeding, and infusing her flesh with energy needed for rapid repair.

Halor's voice tore Dacian away from his observation of Onja. Outside the cell, Halor was commanding the tabre priests and acolytes to return to their duties. The observatory was not meant for the blathering of an excited mob.

Halor was obeyed and he was the last to step into the levitation shaft and leave the observatory. Dacian watched him go down one level and enter the quarters of Daykash Breymer. Dacian intended to observe their conversation, even if they used wardings to block him. He had no desire to keep a respectful distance from the thoughts of his elders as they surely discussed his fate.

"Thank you."

His focus snapped back to Onja. She was sitting cross-legged now. Her mind was open and inviting. She wanted to converse with him.

"You will know what they decide about you soon enough," Onja said pleasantly.

"True," Dacian admitted. "I am sorry for what happened."

"You do not have to apologize for them," Onja said.

"I guess I mean that I did not expect the tabre to be so cruel. I have never seen such a thing before. They value order and civilization," Dacian lamented.

"They value order and civilization when it controls us," Onja said.

Dacian did not immediately respond. Her boldness shook the foundations of his thoughts. But he wanted to be better than a bitter brute in the face of prejudice, and he returned to his beliefs. "What do you hope to accomplish with your defiance? The tabre will not learn to respect rys if we act below the standards of society," he said.

His challenging question appeared to sadden her, and she took a moment before answering that she had not really thought about accomplishing anything. She had only wanted the dignity of her freedom.

Dacian contemplated her answer. He had never really considered that the rys were not free. Their second class status had always been such a blaring difficulty that he had not noticed the essential truth of rys life. Keeping to their places also meant that rys were not supposed to go anywhere.

But I was changing that. I was going to go to Kwellstan. Become a part of the hierarchy. Break the trail for others. What have I done? he lamented. After defending Onja how could he possibly be accepted by the Nebakarz?

Onja read his thoughts. He had such lofty goals. Awkwardly she tried to console him. "Maybe this will not be so bad for you."

He was startled by her comment because he realized that he had left his mind open to her. The intimacy felt strange. It provided an unfamiliar freedom. Dacian did not have to focus on dogma and strive for the correct answers with her.

Dacian moaned. He had not imagined that such a day as this would come. His confinement confused him, but he resolved to be patient and keep his mind away from the door and its sealing spell. Breaking free would only make things worse for him.

To Onja, he admitted, "I don't know what my life will be like now."

"Then you have never had so many choices," she said.

16. An Unexpected Taunt

Cruce's foot caught on a rock. He fell and crunched his knees into the rough mountain trail. Cruce pushed himself up as fast as he could. Breathing hard from prolonged exertion, he did not yet feel pain in his scraped leg. Two other men jogged past him. The second man, Rayden Fanlyre, looked back. His thick sandy hair flopped across his forehead as he checked on Cruce.

A precise wooden blow struck Cruce in his left buttock. Rayden faced forward and hurried on. The leyton prodded Cruce with his baton of dark walnut, worn smooth by the breaking in of many militia volunteers. Cruce muffled his groan but could not dim the flash of hatred in his eyes.

"Run, you clumsy clod!" Leyton Bevone shouted at Cruce, much louder than he needed to.

Cruce ran and soon his pants over his right knee were soaking with blood and becoming plastered with dust. Despite his hurt leg, he struggled up the trail and passed some of his comrades so as not to be the last man.

The trail grew steeper and Cruce and eleven other young men scrambled up the sharp shifting gravel. They were motivated as much by their desires to look strong for each other as the baton and rude tongue of Leyton Bevone.

After the dozen men reached a level area they slowed to a stagger. The thin air at this elevation was taking its toll, as it was supposed to, and everyone was breathing raggedly. Cruce's life at the heart of the Valley of Nufal on the shores of Lake Kwellstan had not toughened him for this. His heart pounded like it was going to burst and his vision was reddening. Gasping for air, he wiped his dripping nose.

The Leyton came up the trail behind them. Although he tried to appear casual he was winded as well and called for a break. Cruce resisted the urge to collapse on the ground. Like most of the other men, he continued a few more slow steps before hunching over with his hands on his thighs. He did not want his muscles to cramp up. Cruce had already experienced that clenching torment on yesterday's run.

Looking down the mountain as he caught his breath, he could see how far they had climbed the trail. The crude path wound with switchbacks through scraggily pines that were getting shorter and thinner as the wind grew teeth. Far below was the softer greener foothill forest where oak and maples mixed with pine. Looking small now, the city of Kahtep lounged at the entrance to the valley. It was the gateway to the heartland of Nufal, and the city marked the shift between the inner forests of the valley and the grassy plains beyond the sheltering mountains. The Inezhep rose on the western edge of town. The white stones of the square tower displayed from top to bottom relief sculptures of Nufalese lore and triumphs. The Kahtepians were especially proud of the Inezhep. They had built the tower without magical aid from the tabre.

Cruce and his fellow recruits had run higher than yesterday. Jogging these trails on Mount Elta was meant to harden the militia volunteers. They had six weeks to train before serving winter duty on the frontier, and they were told that they needed to be much stronger.

And Cruce was getting stronger. Strength training and weapons training for three weeks in Kahtep had gone well, and Cruce had been proud of his progress. But the endurance training in the mountains had been hard on him. Leyton Bevone, more than the other leytons, had seemed to revel in Cruce's difficulty.

When Cruce's breathing had steadied a little bit, he reached for his small water skin slung across his shoulders. He forced himself to drink slowly, but his dry mouth sucked the water in until his stomach felt like a cold hard lump.

"Too much water, lordling," Bevone snapped.

Cruce tensed his stomach muscles as the leyton's baton come at his torso for a rough poke.

"You be puking it up like the baby you are," Bevone said.

With a baleful look Cruce watched him walk by. The wind tugged at the graying wisps of brown hair that surrounded the leyton's bald spot, and Cruce noticed a jagged scar on the back of Bevone's neck. He envied whoever had given the original wound. Other men were drinking water faster than they should, but Bevone had chosen to single out Cruce for criticism, as usual.

Cruce plugged his water skin and sat down slowly on a boulder. He stretched his legs out and started to gingerly pull up his pant leg to inspect his wound. The knee was scrapped and bloody. Cruce flicked out the small bits of gravel stuck in his skin. The injury was not terrible, but he would have to endure the burning pain for the rest of the run.

Needing encouragement, Cruce looked across his homeland. To the west spread the Nufalese plains until they reached the Rysamand Mountains. Even at a distance the western mountains were imposing. Tall and snowy, the mountains presented a forbidding barrier at the edge of the Nufalese world. One could not look at them without contemplating their elemental presence. The plains were a dull green and gold this time of year. The heat of summer had faded the lush grasses and the first frosts of autumn were browning the land. The trees that filled the creek bottoms were still ablaze with color, as was the whole Valley of Nufal that glowed in the sunshine when he looked to the east. Surrounded by the dark peaks of the Tabren Mountains, the large oval valley was joyous with fall colors. The oaks, beeches, ashes, and maples were especially bright with red, vermillion, and gold. From these heights, Cruce could see the cities and villages populating the glorious land. Distant golden rectangles and triangles surrounded the cities where fields had been harvested. Around Kahtep the fields started on the plains and moved up terraced mountain sides next to the city.

At the center of the valley that prepared for winter with an autumnal beauty that cheerily defied cold death, Lake Kwellstan was as bright as a blue diamond in the sun. It looked cold, and Cruce recalled the cool breeze that came off the waters in the summer. He could almost smell the mossy shore at the edge of the ancient forest.

This was his land, the home of human civilization, and he was enduring this grueling training so that he could defend it from the northern savages. The wild far-ranging peoples of the northlands had always been a problem. They would raid the outer settlements of Nufal out on the plains or in the foothills. They stole food and livestock, and sometimes, to the dismay of the Nufalese, stole women and children. At least two or three times a year, the savages would waylay a small group of travelers and slaughter them gruesomely.

The attacks came in the winter months because otherwise the savages ranged far north in the warmer weather, following game to summer pastures. But attacks were becoming more frequent now because the Nufalese settlements had expanded farther from the protected heartland of the Tabren Mountains.

In response, the ad hoc militias of the past were now organized under the famous savage fighter Bellastan Carver. The established city-states of the Valley of Nufal whose lords sponsored many of the settlements now organized small formal militias to supplement the frontier fighters, although Kahtepians still supplied the majority of the effort.

The humans of Nufal desired to expand their territory despite the bloodthirsty threat from the savages. The Nufalese were enlightened, guided by the superior and spiritually blessed tabre. The howling brutal herds that seemed to comprise the rest of humanity on Ektren should not be tolerated, according to the common thinking.

Cruce believed in the professed mission of the Nufalese to expand civilization, and he wanted to defend the settlers. They were Nufalese people, and they suffered murders, rapes, thieving, and the burning of villages and farmsteads. It was right to fight the savages, and he believed he would find the strength and wisdom of manhood out on the cold dangerous plains this hungry winter.

He drew his pant leg back down over his battered knee and then tightened the laces on his boots. His feet were throbbing and his blisters were like nightmares stamped on a waking mind.

"Get up, little boys!" Leyton Bevone shouted. "We be going to the summit today and it be a long way back before sunset."

Cruce got up. He put his weight on his leg gingerly, but then glanced at the leyton and saw him eyeing him. Cruce set aside his pain and jogged to the head of the group.

An hour later, the men were plodding but the summit was near. Mount Elta was considered a friendly mountain, and in the summer ordinary albeit athletic citizens would hike to the summit for a day trip. But today the wind was biting. Cruce pulled up the soft knitted wool hood attached to his leather jacket. Some fresh snow had already fallen at this elevation, but it was only a smattering of white between the boulders and gravel.

Vegetation no longer grew along the trail, but this cold high place of dusky stone remained inspiring. Cruce was exhilarated to reach the top. His lips were chapped, his lungs hurt, and his muscles shook from exertion, but he was a lake-land boy no more.

"Seeing the world like this is worth the difficulty," Rayden commented.

"Yes," Cruce agreed. He was not accustomed to measuring his successes alongside common men from the trade or reaper classes, but he found that his joy was not lessened by the sharing of it.

Gesturing across the stunning vista, Cruce said, "We will fight for this great land." Reaching the mountain top had made him feel truly worthy of the task.

"And you will be our commander," Rayden said.

As the only estate class man among the Kwellstan recruits, Cruce knew he was bound for command rank. He resolved to do his utmost every day of training to prove himself to these young men. He wanted their true respect once he earned his command.

"I have to mentor a season under Gehr before I actually get my rank," Cruce reminded modestly.

Cruce, even at his youthful age, had figured out that his status was probably the reason for Bevone's hostility, but he still did not think it deserved. He worried that Bevone's choice to constantly single him out for ridicule would sully him in the eyes of the other men.

Cruce soothed himself with the pleasing image of returning to Kwellstan in the spring as a militia commander. Perhaps that dashing outcome would excite Ribeka. As Cruce thought about her, his fatigue faded into daydream pleasures. He looked forward to spring when he would have a chance to court her properly.

Until then, his new comrades were his companionship. They were all far from home and perhaps class differences would be lessened by regional familiarity. Studying Rayden next to him, he recalled that Rayden was from the successful trader class Fanlyre family. Rayden should have had a good position in the family business available to him. Cruce wondered if they shared a craving for adventure instead of settling into expected comforts. He asked Rayden why he had joined the militia.

Rayden frowned, looking almost angry. Cruce worried that he had offended, but then Rayden replied, "I lost my temper over a girl."

Happily interested, Cruce encouraged him to go on. Rayden rolled his eyes, embarrassed as he recalled his conduct. "I was in love," he lamented. "The girl showed interest in another man. I started a fight. I beat him good, but then there was talk of hauling me to the Judges. Gehr Bradelvo said he could get me out of Kwellstan. I'm hoping when my duty is done in five years, I can go home and it'll be forgotten."

"That sounds like a good plan," Cruce said, valuing Rayden's honesty.

"Up, you puppies!" Leyton Bevone shouted. He had given his charges little time to savor the summit because he had little interest in their aesthetic contemplations.

Conversations ended and the dozen young men slowly lined up on the trail. Bevone shouldered his way through the line with strutting contempt. "At least you boys made the mountaintop." He jabbed Cruce just below his left armpit with his baton. "Even our watery lordling not be disgracing us," the leyton added.

Cruce smothered his fiery anger and kept himself from even looking at the surly leyton. Once Bevone had passed, he rubbed the sore spot and reflected that the leyton was certainly skilled at finding the tender bits on a man.

Just as the men started back down the trail, Rayden came up close behind Cruce. He whispered, "We only have to tolerate him during endurance training."

Cruce appreciated the encouragement and expected to make a friend in Rayden.

The hike down the mountain was difficult. Descending the steep trail on sore feet and thoroughly strained muscles grew excruciating, even for young men. Leyton Bevone, who seemed to know little pain or weariness, pushed the men harder whenever they flagged.

"Run!" he commanded as soon as the trail leveled out.

The militia volunteers obeyed. Running feet often skidded on loose gravel and sometimes a man had to grab the arm or shoulder of a comrade to keep from falling.

When Rayden's hand seized Cruce's shoulder, he slowed to support him. Rayden's right leg had cramped badly. Rayden bent over and gasped as he grabbed his throbbing gluteal. Cruce stopped and the other men ran around them on the trail. Rayden collapsed.

"Keep moving," Cruce advised. "Stretch it!" He offered his hand to help him up, but Leyton Bevone swatted it away with his handy baton.

"Each man be relying on his own body," the leyton snapped as Cruce narrowly dodged the swinging wood.

For once Bevone's attention was not on Cruce. He struck Rayden on the arm and then across the back. Rayden cried out and drops of sweat flew off his wet hair as his head arched backward. He grimaced and struggled to comply, and although he was getting up, the leyton gave him no chance to succeed. He hit him in the gluteal that was cramping and Rayden went back down hard.

"The savages be having no mercy if you be down in battle. Get up or you be worse than dead," Bevone warned.

Cruce grabbed Rayden by the arms and put him on his feet. But he was only punished for giving aid. Bevone kicked Cruce in his bloody knee and chastised him with a rabid snarl. "He'll never be gaining the strength to fight out the pain if you help him!" the leyton raged. He swung his baton, but Cruce intercepted the smooth hard rod of walnut with a firm grasp. Two veins bulged on his forearm as he held back the wood with suddenly fierce strength.

Confronting the weathered face of the leyton, Cruce said, "It is right to help my comrade."

Rayden straightened as best he could and resolved to run again. "I'm all right," he announced bravely but Bevone was not listening.

The leyton narrowed his eyes at Cruce and yanked his baton away from the riled volunteer. "So you want to be showing me how full of stones you are, lordling?" he challenged.

Wanting to stay above the leyton's level, Cruce reiterated that it was only right to help a comrade. "That is basic to militia service," he added.

Bevone scoffed at the young volunteer's presumption to tell him about militia service. "Who made you the Great Divinity? Do you be thinking you're the hero to save us all? You just be wanting to show us you're better than us," Bevone accused.

Because Cruce remained ungoaded, Bevone sweetened the bait. "Or you really be here to prove your strength and make up for your broken useless father," he said.

The unexpected taunt rattled Cruce.

Bevone continued, "Oh yes, I know you be of cripple's blood. You think playing soldier be making you a man because you have no real father to show you how."

Cruce saw red. He had never known such anger was possible. He attacked the leyton with his bare hands.

Bevone had wrangled with many a militia volunteer in his time, but he had never hit a nerve so raw before. Cruce dove at his throat with both hands and grabbed the sinewy neck of his instructor. Bevone defended himself with his baton, but Cruce was oblivious to the first few blows. Cruce pushed Bevone down on his knees and continued to strangle him. Naturally desperate, Bevone whacked Cruce's arms with his baton, and the pain finally broke through Cruce's madness and made him let go.

Rayden, appalled by the eruption of violence, grabbed Cruce's shoulder and shouted for him to stop. By now the other volunteers had stopped on the trail and were looking back.

Cruce did not even hear Rayden's plea. The leyton sprang to his feet and attacked. Cruce grabbed the baton before it hit him again and they grappled fiercely, swinging punches and trying to yank each other off balance.

Several of the other men ran back to intervene. Three men grabbed Cruce from behind and two men shoved themselves in front of the leyton as Cruce was dragged away. Blood dribbled from the Leyton's split lip and his teeth were bright red from the blood in his mouth. Two pink oval marks on his neck showed where Cruce's thumbs had assaulted his windpipe.

"You'll be regretting this!" Bevone yelled hoarsely.

"I'll not let you insult my father," Cruce said. He tried to shake off the men holding him but they held him still by twisting his arms behind him.

"Get him on his knees," Bevone commanded.

"Leyton, no!" Rayden contradicted. "We won't hold down our comrade for your revenge. Let your temper cool."

Leyton Bevone was shocked. "Don't put your eggs in this bird's nest, boy," he warned and gestured at Cruce.

"Let Master Carver judge him. It is proper, Leyton Sir," Rayden insisted. His voice quivered as he realized how bold his words were.

Seeking allies, Rayden looked to the volunteers holding Cruce. He could see that they were reluctant to hold down their comrade so that their leyton could punish him. They had no doubts about how viciously the leyton would treat Cruce.

Hesitantly, one of the other volunteers said, "Leyton Sir, let Chenomet be judged by the Master. I'll bear proper witness to what happened. I swear by the Great Divinity."

Rayden moved protectively in front of Cruce. "It's my fault. He was only trying to help me, Leyton Sir."

The Leyton quelled his urge to shove Rayden aside. Although he burned to exact his revenge on Cruce while he was restrained, he suddenly doubted his vicious nature. He had driven this batch of volunteers hard. He drove each group harder than the last. Perhaps he had gone too far. These young men were comrades, and, on the mountain side with the dusk gathering, they might not tolerate the abuse that Bevone longed to deliver upon Cruce.

His shame be worse if his punishment be public, Bevone reasoned.

"He be getting no leniency from Master Carver," Bevone grumbled. Then he did push Rayden down roughly and stepped up to Cruce, who was still breathing hard from their intense struggle. With his usual skill, Bevone cracked Cruce along the jaw and knocked him senseless.

"Carry your comrade," he ordered and started down the trail without looking back.

Rayden, although still in pain from his muscle cramp, got up and draped one of Cruce's arms over his shoulders. Cruce was slack and heavy. Another man took his other arm and helped Rayden drag him down the trail.

Bevone ordered the men to resume their run with an especially surly snarl. Soon the volunteers left the two men carrying Cruce far behind. Eventually, Cruce regained his senses and was able to walk with Rayden. They reached the militia base outside Kahtep well after dark. Two militiamen were waiting for them and they promptly took Cruce into custody. They locked him in a root cellar.

Total darkness oppressed Cruce as the entrance was barred behind him. He pushed himself up from the dirt floor. His head throbbed and his body felt torn apart and put back together sloppily. He fumbled for his water skin and carefully squeezed the last drops into his mouth. Although the blow to his head had left his thoughts dull, surging anger lingered in his body. Part of him was glad that he had given Bevone a dose of his rage. If the other men had not intervened, Cruce believed that he would have trounced the veteran instructor. Bevone was wrong to call his father weak. Watching his father struggle against debilitating pain and disability had taught Cruce much about strength while growing up.

17. Exposure

Fate skulking at the edge of the firelight spawns dreams forgotten upon waking. ~ Hasen, 8th century Kwellstan poet

Morning light shot around the edges of the root cellar door and woke Cruce up. Aching terribly, he hoped that Bevone's neck still hurt.

Cruce foraged in the cellar. The raw and dirty potatoes, turnips, onions, and carrots were not appetizing, but, famished as he was, he crunched down some carrots and potatoes.

When he heard people approaching, he wiped his hands on his pants and stood up. The wooden bar scraped against the door as it was lifted away. Cruce quickly swallowed the last bite of his miserable breakfast.

He was heartened to see Gehr duck through the doorway.

"Have I recruited a hooligan?" he asked cheerfully.

The fanciful armor and white clothes that he had worn that summer in Kwellstan were gone. Gehr now wore the rougher gear of an active duty commander. A thick woolen cloak dyed brown with a hood embroidered with red spears and rams draped his shoulders. A thick leather vest studded with bronze plates encased his torso above worn deerskin pants and laced up boots. From his hip hung a sword in a beautiful copper and leather scabbard worked with semi-precious beads in the ram design that symbolized his family.

"Sorry to disappoint you," Cruce said, worried that Gehr might be besmirched by his bad behavior.

Gehr signaled for the two militiamen with him to wait outside. Then he said quietly, "The mountains won't crumble from what you've done, but you will be disciplined."

"You don't have to do anything for me, Gehr. I would not have my shame touch you," Cruce said.

"Oh, don't be so dramatic," Gehr scolded. "I will speak on your behalf to Master Carver. Bevone is a crazy bear, and gets worse every year. You're not the first recruit to go at him."

"Really?" Cruce said.

Nodding, Gehr grinned, and a few laugh lines crinkled on his tan face. "I hear that you were about to tear him apart. No one has gotten such a good strike at him. Either he is getting old or you are going to be one mad wolf fighter," he said.

Vividly Cruce recalled the feel of Bevone's hot vulnerable throat beneath his fingers. Experiencing such murderous anger troubled Cruce, who had not realized that such ugly passions lurked inside him. In the cold darkness of the night, he had accepted that he was insecure about his father's infirmity, ashamed even. It had not been easy growing up as his father slid further into invalidism.

And when his father had expected him to take over the bulk of the family's responsibilities, Cruce had abandoned him. There was guilt now too.

"What will happen to me?" Cruce asked.

"The Militia Master will judge you," Gehr said.

Cruce looked anxiously into the gray eyes of his friend and mentor. "What should I say to him?"

"Nothing," Gehr said bluntly and explained that Cruce would have no opportunity to speak. He would remain confined while the Militia Master heard the charges.

With a sigh, Cruce resigned himself to whatever grim verdict came back. Although he had only been in the militia a short time, he understood already that no one wanted to hear how Leyton Bevone had been hard on him, singled him out, and constantly goaded him with physical and verbal abuse. Cruce should not have attacked his superior. It was as simple as that.

"Can I at least go outside to piss?" he asked.

Gehr scanned the root cellar that was crowded with wholesome food. "Well, no one wants you spoiling the harvest. I'll confine you to barracks. Do I have your word not to flee?"

Cruce scowled at the notion that he would run. "Of course I will stay."

"Come on then," Gehr said and led him outside.

Cruce's first impulse was to avoid the eyes of the other militiamen, but he decided not to slink in shame. He had done what he had done. Only the judgment of the Militia Master mattered. As Cruce was escorted to his barracks, he detected no scorn or pity from the other militiamen. He supposed to them he was only a recruit that had made a mistake. A serious mistake, but still little more than gossip to a veteran.

Cruce shared a cramped barracks built of rough timbers with eleven other men. A door and two windows served the small building where Cruce had one bunk with a straw mattress and a shelf to place his possessions. His comrades had already gone to their training at dawn. Cruce imagined that Rayden would have earned himself extra attention from Leyton Bevone.

Gehr told Cruce to stay at the barracks and left with the two militiamen. Sore and tired, Cruce was glad for the rare privacy within the empty barracks. He washed and changed his clothes. He stretched out in his bunk and winced with annoyance as the prickly mattress irritated his skin. Once his training was done, he would be allowed to outfit himself better, even buy a house in Kahtep to use when he was not patrolling the frontier.

That's if I am even allowed to finish my training. I could be dismissed, he realized dismally. An ignominious return to Kwellstan had no appeal.

But immense weariness kept him from worrying at that moment. He fell asleep wondering if the Militia Master would judge him that day.

******

The insubordination of one recruit proved insufficient to overtake the calendar of the Militia Master. Cruce lounged for four days in his barracks with no news of Bellastan Carver's decision.

The confinement was more relaxing than stressful for Cruce. After weeks of grueling exercise, four days in his bunk had allowed him to recuperate. Cruce could feel how much stronger he was, and, mentally, he had healed from his rage with Bevone. Cruce vowed to himself to command his temper better.

Staying in from the deteriorating weather suited Cruce as well. The day ended with a cold north wind sweeping into Kahtep from the prairie with the sharp promise of winter. Thickening clouds stunted the sunset, and the sun escaped gratefully behind the Rysamand Mountains.

A Kwellstan recruit was rolling up a rug to stop the draft underneath the door when Gehr arrived at the barracks. The recruit stood respectfully and saluted with his right fist over his heart. The small talk among the recruits hushed as Gehr approached Cruce.

He swung his feet out of the bunk and looked at his eleven mates gathered behind Gehr. Apparently the news would not be given in private. Cruce stood and saluted Gehr, whose expression did not look encouraging.

"Am I going home?" Cruce asked.

"You can," Gehr said. "Or, you can stay with the militia and have your transgression forgotten if you accept the punishment of Master Carver."

"Which is?" Cruce prompted nervously. He glanced among his comrades and caught Rayden's worried eyes.

Gehr took a breath and answered that the sentence was three days exposure.

A few men winced.

"You could die this time of year," Rayden blurted, but another man quickly contradicted him.

Cruce also tended to believe he could survive, but he thought about how going home would make his father happy. Perhaps his sojourn into militia life had all been foolishness anyway.

"You can take tonight to think about it," Gehr said gloomily.

"I will decide now," Cruce said. He did not want to agonize about it for hours. "If I take the punishment, I can continue in the militia and still gain a command rank?" he asked for clarification.

Gehr nodded emphatically and said, "Carver will welcome you back if you accept discipline. I made sure Carver knew that you wanted to help and defend a comrade." He glanced at Rayden.

Cruce regretted being an embarrassment to his mentor, and he wanted to make things up to him. And Cruce's heart told him that returning to Kwellstan a failure would be the harsher punishment. The difficulty of obtaining the Militia Master's permission to attend Adarium meetings remained. This incident could sour the chances of Carver approving the special request, but Gehr had said that taking the punishment would forgive the transgression.

"I will take my punishment," Cruce decided.

If his fortitude pleased Gehr, he did not show it. "I'll have more food sent to you tonight. And drink as much water as you can. You will be exposed at dawn," he said.

******

All the militiamen at the Kahtep base, including trainee recruits, assembled in the main yard to witness the exposure of Cruce. Militia Master Carver presided over the punishment. He proclaimed the sentence and chastised Cruce for his insubordination.

Cruce faced his punishment bravely, but the humiliation of it stung more than he had expected. The total attention of the assembled militia pressed on Cruce. Among his comrades, he saw a smattering of respect for striking back at Bevone, but also scorn, indifference, and the worst, pity.

The Militia Master regarded Cruce curiously, perhaps a little surprised that the estate class son from soft-living Kwellstan had agreed to face an exposure. Bellastan Carver had striking green eyes that roved the landscape from his blocky face. His fur hat shook in the rising wind.

"Come forward, Cruce Chenomet," Carver commanded.

Cruce advanced. Leyton Bevone stood beside Carver. The narrow simmering eyes of Bevone drilled into Cruce. He had never seen someone look at him with malice before and it was unsettling. Beyond Bevone a tall oaken post with its single chain of thick links confronted Cruce ominously. He feared to be chained in a world in which Bevone was free.

"Are you accepting three days exposure?" the Militia Master asked.

"Yes, Master," Cruce said. "I should not have been insubordinate. I will not do it again." He hoped that it did not sound like an apology to Bevone.

"Then I be exposing you three days starting now. Great Divinity willing I'll be welcoming you back as our comrade at the finish of that time," Carver declared.

Leyton Bevone stepped forward to escort Cruce to the post. Cruce flinched. Bevone's normally grim face seemed on the verge of chuckling. Before Bevone could grab his arm, Cruce started walking to the post. He did not want to appear that he was dragged to his punishment by his accuser.

His temper rotted as the leyton started bolting the shackles on his wrists. Another man assisted Bevone in attaching the shackles to the heavy chain. He used a hammer to set the metal pins of the shackles tightly.

Bevone tested the chain and shackles to make sure they were secure and then slapped the chain painfully across Cruce's thighs.

Cruce winced but growled, "How's your neck?"

Bevone hit him across the chin and Cruce fell back hard. The pain was startling and his head felt loose.

"I hope there be a freeze every night and you die, boy," Bevone said.

Crazy bastard, Cruce thought, wondering why the militia tolerated him.

Bevone's assault seemed not to warrant notice, and Master Carver dismissed the assembly. Rayden lingered as if he might do something. Gehr left last. His parting look of encouragement helped Cruce.

With nothing else to do, Cruce sat down with his back against the pole and rubbed his sore chin. Being on display as the others went about their daily business was uncomfortable. The vendors and other visitors that came to the base looked at him curiously.

As the day wore on, thirst nagged at Cruce. He realized that the proximity of the well was an added torture. Its low stone wall was just about ten paces beyond the reach of his chain. Each time someone tossed a bucket in the well, the delicious splash warned Cruce that the next three days would be harsh. He could hope for rain, but the chill of the wet could be more dangerous than dehydration.

Hunger crept up on Cruce as well. He had eaten well the night before, but he was a young man and needed food. By the time dusk came, he sorely missed the chance for supper. Watching the other men enter and leave the gathering hall was misery, and the drifting scent of roasting beef and vegetables stabbed at Cruce's nostrils.

The trainees soon retired to their cramped barracks. Their feet dragged and Cruce knew how heavily they would fall into their bunks.

Inside the gathering hall the commanders, leytons, and veteran fighters lingered over beer and music. Cruce promised himself that he would join them as a proper militia member after the exposure was over.

Stars filled the clear night sky that promised to be cold. Cruce wrapped his cloak around himself tightly and stuck his hands in his armpits. Tired and hungry, he curled up at the base of the post and fell asleep. His sleep was shallow because of the deepening chill, and his eyes popped open when he heard approaching steps. The lamps outside buildings cast enough light to reveal the outline of a man standing over him. Smelling food, Cruce sat up quickly.

"Be quick and eat," the man said.

"Gehr?" Cruce said.

"Here's tea," Gehr said. He placed a hot ceramic mug in Cruce's hand.

Cruce clasped the mug with both hands gratefully and slurped the tea. He welcomed the blast of heat through his cold body and did not care if it was burning his mouth. Gehr had also brought him a hunk of bread. Cruce bit into it greedily.

"Isn't this risky for you?" Cruce asked between mouthfuls.

Gehr chuckled. He sounded carefree again like he had that summer in Kwellstan when he had been extolling the thrills of militia service. "Not really," he answered.

"Thank you, Gehr. I owe you," Cruce said.

"Well, I wouldn't want your fair sister to blame me if you died," Gehr said. "I'm hoping to see her again on summer leave."

Cruce automatically felt a little defensive of Dayd, even if she had covertly welcomed Gehr's advances. "She has a serious suitor you know," Cruce warned.

"And I'm not?" Gehr said.

"I don't know. Are you?" Cruce said.

"Probably not," Gehr admitted.

"I should be mad at you for toying with my sister," Cruce said.

"Dayd wants to be toyed with," Gehr said bluntly and Cruce knew it was true.

Their trivial conversation was soothing, and the bread and hot tea had made him feel much better.

"I will get you through tomorrow night too," Gehr promised. "I would rather not lose a promising fighter to exposure."

"Is this punishment really meant to kill?" Cruce asked.

"A strong man can survive three days, but you could get sick," Gehr said.

They were quiet a moment. Cruce did not want Gehr to leave, but he knew that his friend could not stay. Gehr stood up and Cruce returned the mug to him.

"Stay strong," Gehr advised and left.

The cold dark night pressed hard on Cruce, and the isolation was as unpleasant as the wind. The cheer from Gehr's brief visit faded quickly, and Cruce's only comfort was that his first day of exposure was almost done.

He curled up on the ground and struggled through fitful sleep until dawn. When he awoke, he walked out as far as his chain would allow so that he could urinate. His body was stiff and sore, and he recalled the luxury of his itchy straw mattress.

The day passed without a single person speaking to him. His hunger grew distracting. Starting to feel weak, he simply sat against his post all day, conserving his strength. The sun was a blessing in the autumn chill and he often lifted his face toward it.

By afternoon clouds gathered in the northern sky. Cruce eyed the dark mass with mixed feelings. His aching thirst craved the rain, but he dreaded the cold.

The rain was still holding back at sunset. Cruce endured watching his comrades gather for their communal meal again and tried to hide his wretched begging gaze.

As darkness came, Cruce licked his cracked lips, but that only made them hurt more. He sat like a defeated animal, listlessly staring at the lanterns hanging by the gathering hall. When he heard rain pattering on the ground, he blinked and lifted his mouth toward the sky. The rain tasted good.

Mercifully, no cold downpour came. Only light showers came in fits and starts, allowing him to wet his mouth without soaking through his cloak.

Anticipation for Gehr's visit consumed Cruce's senses as he listened to the darkness. The after dinner songs from the gathering hall seemed more boisterous tonight. He wondered what the occasion was. Perhaps it was just that it was a cold autumn night with the rain coming in and it was good to gather for song and drink.

Cruce hated the separation from the militiamen. He felt like a ghost but reminded himself that he would have a second chance at life. Even as he suffered, he refused to regret his altercation with Bevone. Discipline was important, but he was Cruce Chenomet and he was not going to suffer abuse needlessly.

Pride has its price, Cruce thought and twisted his wrists in their shackles.

When he finally heard someone coming toward him, he jumped up eagerly. "Gehr?" he whispered.

For an answer he heard something whizzing through the air just before a wooden baton slammed into his upper right arm. Awful pain erupted in his arm and he fell back against the thick post.

"I not be your mothering mentor," Bevone said and swung again.

Cruce flung himself behind the post. The baton cracked loudly against it. Cruce scrambled around the post and tried to tackle Bevone. The wily old fighter stayed on his feet and drove one end of the baton into Cruce's back. He cried out and twisted toward the arm that held the baton and grabbed it. Bevone, with his baton suddenly stymied, punched Cruce in the face and kept punching. Cruce clung desperately to Bevone's other arm that held the baton.

Cruce's recent combat training flowered in his mind and he managed to adjust his hold on Bevone's arm and twist it. Bevone yelled and tried to pull away. As Cruce was tugged forward, his feet got tangled in his chains. He went down on his knees and let go of Bevone.

Bevone made a triumphant sound and swung his baton. Because of the dark his aim was off and Cruce took a glancing blow to the head instead of a stunning crack to the skull. Fearful that Bevone meant to beat him to death, Cruce grabbed his slack chain and tackled Bevone. He looped the chain around the leyton's neck and pulled it tight. Bevone swung both arms frantically and tried to shake Cruce off, but the younger man had turned his disadvantage into a deadly weapon.

Fierce rage once again exploded from the depths of Cruce's spirit, and he twisted the chain aggressively. Bevone's choking gurgle almost encouraged Cruce to finish him off, but he escaped his violent urge before he went too far. He must not kill one of his own. As despicable as Bevone was, he was a fellow militiaman.

Cruce wrestled Bevone face down on the ground and kept the chain tight on his neck. Hissing into his ear, Cruce said, "You stay away from me. You don't even look at me again, you old son of a savage. And don't think about hurting my friends either."

Cruce then whipped the chain off and stood up. His body was shaking from exertion and anger, but his fear had been transformed into a thrilling triumph.

Gasping and cursing, Bevone lurched to his feet. Apparently tough as a tree root, he raised his baton. Cruce gathered his slack chain and prepared to swing it.

"What's going on?" It was Gehr's voice. He lifted his lantern and saw Bevone. "You vicious wretch!" Gehr exploded. Before he could hurl another curse or threat, Bevone darted into the dark.

Gehr hurried to Cruce. Cruce's bloody face sprang into the lantern light. Gehr set down the pail of food and drink and dug in a pocket for a cloth. He pressed it against Cruce's bleeding upper lip and nose.

Too excited from the fight to feel most of his pain, Cruce related the fight in a flurry of words. "I beat him, Gehr. I could've killed him but I didn't."

Gehr hushed him. "I'm going straight to Carver and requesting a guard for you. This is wrong. Bevone has gone mad," he said, and his anger violated his habitually pleasant face. Gently he helped Cruce to sit back down with his back against the post and then gave him the mug of hot beef broth and wedge of cheese. Cruce ate the food greedily, like a wolf that has worked hard to make a kill.

As the food hit Cruce's stomach, the thrilling energy of his fight dissipated and pain began to spread through his body. He had taken some bad blows but he was fairly sure that no bones were broken.

"I must go speak to Carver," Gehr said impatiently and gathered up the lantern and pail.

Cruce shook his head. "No, Gehr. If he comes back, I'll fight him. Don't ask Carver for help and make me look weak," he said.

Although Gehr was livid about Bevone, he considered Cruce's request. He understood that Cruce wanted to gain the Master's respect, but more was at stake than Cruce's pride.

He set a hand on Cruce's shoulder. "I will be watching out for you tonight," he said.

Cruce nodded gratefully and shut his eyes. With the crisis passing, he was feeling spent. As Gehr stalked away, an icy gust barreled through the garrison.

Cruce huddled against the post, trying to use it to block the increasing wind. It was better than nothing but not much. Rain pattered on the freezing ground and gradually became a stronger shower. Cruce shivered in his cloak and his cold feet hurt all the way to his thighs. When ice started to cling to the post and Cruce's cloak was crunchy with it, he got up and jogged in place. Now the exposure truly tested him.

The jogging warmed his body somewhat but the sucking cold of his wet clothes quickly sapped him of warmth. As he continued his stomping and arm waving, he noticed a line of lights on the western road moving toward the militia base. Cruce wondered who would be traveling across the prairie on such a night and how they kept their lanterns lit in the wet wind.

His dull mind eventually realized that the white lights were tabre glow crystal lamps. The impending arrival of a group of tabre roused him from his fatigue. Horses and wagons entered the main yard and pulled up by the well. Crystal lanterns hung from the corners of six wagons, casting their enchanted glow. Cruce could see the rain striking the ground and puddling in the soft white light. Tabre riders dismounted. Warding crystal brooches held shut the hooded cloaks of the priests and sparkled like stars at their throats.

From an enclosed coach a stately tabre emerged in a magnificent hooded cloak. The weave of the cloak was so tight that water beaded on it. The water droplets glimmered in the crystalline light, and two eyes glowed faintly within the deep cowl.

The fluid black stripes on the tabre's cloak surprised Cruce, who recognized the standard costume of the Daykash. Cruce could not guess why the deputy of the Grand Lumin had been in the rural west of Nufal.

Attended by a half dozen priests, the Daykash glided toward Master Carver's cabin.

Curious, Cruce walked toward the waiting group of tabre as far as his chain would allow. He hailed the nearest acolyte. The tabre did not even turn his head, but then Cruce realized that he had hardly spoken above a whisper. He was so weak and tired.

"Good Acolyte!" Cruce shouted. "What is your business tonight?"

The tabre acknowledged Cruce lazily. "Be silent, criminal," the tabre said.

Cruce bristled with offense even though he looked the part. But with little else to do he persisted in tempting the tabre toward conversation.

"Please, I am Cruce Chenomet of Kwellstan. Give me a word," Cruce said.

"The Daykash wishes to speak with Bellastan Carver. Use your eyes human child," the acolyte responded grudgingly. He turned away from Cruce to make it clear that he had no wish to be bothered.

Cruce frowned. He supposed it was obvious that the Daykash had gone to speak with the Militia Master. Stubbornly Cruce asked the acolyte where they had been.

The tabre ignored him, and no one else answered either until a voice came from a wagon. "They come from Jingten."

A figure stood up from an uncovered wagon. The crystal lanterns revealed his soggy form. The water was heavy on his hood that clung to his head with rain streaming from its edges. He swung his legs over the edge of the wagon and got down. Agitation rippled among the tabre, and a nearby horse whickered nervously. The one who had spoken to Cruce walked up to him. He pushed his hood back. With rain pelting his face, he looked Cruce up and down. His eyes were dark and they lingered on the shackles on Cruce's wrists and then followed the chain to the post.

Cruce gasped very lightly, realizing what he looked upon. The steady light from the enchanted crystals let him see the blue skin. Cruce had heard about the rys and their racial differences from the tabre, but he had never expected to see one.

Gesturing to the shackles, the rys asked, "Is this the way of Nufal?"

The question embarrassed Cruce. The rys's voice projected dissatisfaction bordering on hostility. He spoke with a strange accent.

"I made a mistake. It is punishment. I will be freed tomorrow," Cruce said, feeling intensely ashamed of being chained in front of the tabre and now this rare rys.

"What was your mistake?" the rys asked.

Cruce did not want to answer but something about this rys made it impossible for him to deny him. "I quarreled with a superior," Cruce answered.

The rys parted his lips as if to ask another question, but two tabre, full Nebakarz priests, came up behind him and intervened.

"Go back to the wagon. The Daykash's business is brief," a priest commanded.

Two sparks of blue light flashed in the rys's eyes. Cruce automatically took a step back, startled by the rise of magic within the rys.

"There is nothing interesting about this human, Dacian," the other priest declared.

An unpleasant look crossed the rys's face, but then he inclined his head toward Cruce in a cordial fashion. "It would be good to be free tomorrow," he said. For an instant the light brightened in his eyes, and Cruce felt heat rush through his body. Then the rys's eyes faded to black and the priests escorted him back to the wagon. The rys sprang gracefully into the wagon, sat down, and pulled his hood back up against the rain.

Cruce went slowly back to the post, feeling a little stunned. He contemplated the unexpected encounter with the rys. A spell had driven the cold from him and it was a blessed relief. He had never directly felt magic before, and it made him feel humble and small. He wondered if this was how his father felt after receiving a pain treatment. Cruce wondered why the rys had made the merciful gesture. Gradually he realized that the rys was in the custody of the tabre priests and had perhaps empathized with his captivity.

Puzzled by the extraordinary event, Cruce rested while the heat spell soothed his body. Unfortunately, the freezing rain storm had a strong magic of its own that sucked heat from Cruce's body. By the time the Daykash returned from his visit with Master Carver, Cruce was again alternating between exhausted huddling and jogging. The Daykash went back into the coach and his attendants mounted their horses. Master Carver came out to see them off.

The Master wore a shaggy buffalo cloak with matching hat that insulated him from the weather. He bowed to the wagon that conveyed the Daykash away. "Good travel, Divine Lords," he said, as was proper.

With the wagons moving off, only the meager light of Carver's tin lantern sputtered against the darkness. A fresh gust of wind lashed the militia base with sharp rain that glazed the rutted yard with more ice.

Master Carver checked on his exposed trainee. Cruce shook as he clenched his hand to his chest. The rain drizzled down his face and neck.

Bellastan Carver was a man weathered by the prairie winds. A square jaw and a thick brow made him look permanently stern, and his green eyes lived with the passions of tragedy and success.

"Have you gotten this lesson learned, Chenomet?" he asked.

"Yes, Master," Cruce chattered with much sincerity.

"I not be wanting you to die," Carver said. He walked away in the blustering dark but soon returned with Leyton Tulem, who had instructed Cruce in weapons. The leyton carried the tools to undo Cruce's shackles.

As the metal was pried off his raw wrists, Cruce thanked him. With liberty rushing back, Cruce felt keenly the repugnance of his captivity and burned it into his memory.

"Come with me," the Militia Master commanded.

Cruce stumbled and Tulem offered him a kind hand.

Cruce staggered inside the Militia Master's cabin. The warmth enveloped him like a hug from his mother, and Tulem led Cruce to the fireplace. Fresh wood had been recently thrown on the coals and the fire was burning brightly. Tulem helped get Cruce out of his wet cloak and shirt and then placed a thick wool blanket over his shoulders. Cruce huddled in it and drew in deep breaths of the blazing hot air radiating from the fire. His nose started to drip and his fingers and toes ached.

"Let's have a look at that face, lad," Tulem said with gruff concern.

Cruce tilted his face up. While Tulem cleaned his bloody lips and nose, Cruce looked around the cabin of his superior.

Its rustic exterior did not hint at the well-finished interior. The walls were plastered and decorated with ceramic tiles. The furnishings were nicely crafted and obviously expensive. A sun-bleached buffalo skin hung on the wall with a detailed map of Nufal painted on it. A blue painted table at the center of the main room had parchments, fabric scrolls, and tabre stone wafers piled up among a half dozen colored glass drinking goblets of tabre making.

An impressive assortment of swords, axes, maces, and shields hung on the walls along with strange artifacts, like a wooden club with crude carving and three stones lashed to it with leather cords.

Carver heaved his way out of his massive buffalo cloak and hat. He shook the cold rain from the shaggy furs and hung them on their sturdy rack in the corner where another rack held his battle armor.

Carver pulled a chair up and removed a kettle from the fire. He poured Cruce a cup of steaming tea. Cruce accepted it with shaking hands. He glanced at his superior, trying to gauge his mood. He doubted that Bellastan Carver normally took an exposed recruit into his home to nurse back to health.

"So, did Bevone bang you up?" Carver asked.

Cruce hesitated. He felt that he should not report on the leyton, yet Cruce doubted that he should lie to Carver.

After sucking some strength out of the hot tea, Cruce decided to be carefully political. "I was exposed to the elements, Master. Perhaps Bevone is included among the elements," he said.

Tulem snorted, but Carver said nothing. He only watched as the leyton finished tending Cruce's battered and wind-chapped face.

Once the dried blood was cleaned away and some salve applied, Tulem stood up. He regarded Cruce with satisfaction and said, "Well, I be judging you get pretty again in a week."

Cruce thanked him for the help and gulped more tea. Carver lifted a kettle to replenish Cruce's cup. "You may go, Leyton," the Militia Master said with a kindly tone. Tulem saluted and left the cabin.

Carver got up and strolled around his cabin looking at his weapon collection with his hands behind his back as if he were admiring it for the first time. At length, he said, "What you be knowing about me, Chenomet?"

Knowing only the basics of Carver's position and prestige, Cruce replied that Carver commanded all militias in Nufal.

Carver, intent on educating his young recruit, said, "I was the one be starting the militias proper like. It was over twenty years ago I got the Kahtep estate class to be sponsoring the first dedicated fighters. Then some you Kwellstan lords got interested in the frontier, and I be getting some fighters out of your lot. The savages don't be liking us civilizing their wild country."

"No, Master. I've heard the stories. That's why I'm here," Cruce said.

"Oh is it?" Carver said skeptically. He perused his collection again and paused to touch an old spear on the wall. "I be having a family one time," he said.

Cruce waited attentively during the painful silence before Carver continued, "I was out late hunting an old black pantura that be eating calves. With it being summer my homestead should've been safe. Never been seeing savages much in summer, at least till they started getting interested in our herds instead of hunting north like they should. Well, after a few years I be teaching them to go away again in the summer at least." He swept his hand along the wall. "Here be some of the weapons I be taking from those nasty savages. They be horrid beasts. They offend the Great Divinity to be having the same shape as us."

Although Carver's tone was mild and casual, Cruce noticed the changes on Carver's blocky face that told of hatred and violence.

"The savages killed your family," Cruce dared to surmise.

"Aye, my fine wife, two daughters, and my son," Carver said. Decades had dulled the tragedy and ample revenge had granted him the paltry comfort of justice, but it was mostly the broken heart that left him too hard for tears. "It not be just about me," he added. "More families than in my day be living and working to better Nufal. The militias be making it possible."

Cruce nodded. The importance of the militia's mission attracted him strongly.

Done speaking of the past, Carver said, "You not be just any militia volunteer."

After suffering his humiliating exposure, Cruce had to forage for his natural self confidence. He coughed before responding, "You are kind, Master."

"Kind?" Carver repeated. Such a word was rarely directed toward him, but he supposed it was not inaccurate. "Chenomet, my special eye has been watching you. That's why I didn't want to be losing you over this bad blood with Bevone," Carver said.

"Master, I'm committed to the defense of Nufal," Cruce said.

"Yes, yes, now put your ears on, young man. The savages be coming in greater numbers every year. The militia be too small. More men be needed and more food, clothing, weapons, armor, everything," Carver said and then paused as if waiting for Cruce to say something.

Under the circumstances, Cruce's wits were limping turtles, but he did not have to cross much mental distance to discover Carver's meaning. "As the Chenomet heir, you want me to finance your expansion," he said.

"Not just you -- all the Kwellstan elite. You lake-land boys outfit a few volunteers and then put it out of your big heads, knowing well that Kahtep will pay the greater part because it must, but the Kwellstan-sponsored settlements still benefit their patrons," Carver explained and Cruce had no reason to dispute him. Carver continued, "That's why I be giving you permission to serve as your father's proxy at the Adarium."

"You know about that?" Cruce said.

"Yes, Chenomet, I know. Gladly I be permitting it. I be needing you to represent the militia's needs to the Adarium," Carver said.

Cruce felt like a sparrow in the nest of a hawk. What Carver proposed seemed to put Cruce in a position where he would have to split his loyalties between his family and the militia, but then he considered an alternative view. He could think of it as a way to expand his influence with the militia and the Kwellstan estate class.

This is everything I wanted, Cruce reminded himself. "Thank you for the special consideration, Master. The Chenomet family shall seek to set a new standard among the estate class of Kwellstan regarding the importance of the militia," he said.

Carver grinned. "I knew you'd be agreeable. Pity we can't be putting our energy to a better project then killing savages, but the Great Divinity seems to be wanting it that way," he said.

Cruce contemplated the unpleasant prospect of escalating war with the savages. He believed that fair Nufal required her strongest sons to make sacrifices in her defense.

"Master," Cruce said. "I see how you value me for political purposes, but I don't want to be sheltered. I volunteered to become a warrior and serve Nufal. My wishes are sincere in that."

Carver regarded Cruce with the unabridged gaze of long experience. "You shall be a warrior, Chenomet," he promised. "You go return to your comrades now."

Cruce stood up stiffly. The places where Bevone's stick had hit him were stabbing him with bruising discomfort. Even so, he expected to sleep like a rock once he crawled into his crude bunk.

He put his damp shirt and cloak back on and was about to salute Carver when he paused. "Master, what did the Daykash want?" he asked.

His presumption noticeable irked the Militia Master, who was quite unaccustomed to such prying questions from a freshly disciplined trainee, but, as he had said, Cruce was no ordinary recruit.

The Militia Master came close to Cruce, obviously still sizing him up. "The Daykash told me to keep an eye to the west for trouble," Carver quietly confided.

"From the rys?" Cruce said. "They had one prisoner."

"Don't talk about that," Carver advised. "It'll just tie people in a worry knot. It be a tabre problem anyway."

"But the Daykash told you to watch for trouble," Cruce said.

"And we shall do as the Divine Lords say, Chenomet. Now be going," Carver commanded.

Cruce saluted and trudged through the windy slick wet to his barracks. He was glad for the favor the Militia Master had shown him, but his encounter with the rys prisoner troubled him. Cruce recalled the ominous nervousness of the tabre around the rys. Fear in tabre was not something he had seen before, and Cruce wondered if there were worse things in the world than savages.

18. Dark Future

When Dacian beheld Kwellstan in person for the first time, he clung to his dream of elevating the rys like it was a ragged possession salvaged from a burned home. He refused to believe the tabre were only hateful when he looked upon their wondrous capital. Skilled civilization had sculpted the city from the wild heart of Nufal. The giant Temple of the Mind, or Altular, penetrated the forest canopy and proclaimed the immense glory of the Kwellstan Sect. The sides of the conical building were quartered into tiers and smooth except for steep steps cut into the south facing side. Built of gray glittery granite, the Altular met the sky as a mountain conceived of pure geometry.

The Altular overlooked the famous Plaza of the Waters, and across from the temple was the ancient school of the Kwellstan Sect, the Atocha. Dacian regarded the four spiraling towers of the Atocha with a troubled heart. For decades he had never doubted that he would learn in its chambers, but his rash explosion of emotion had swept away his certainty.

Wistfully Dacian gazed at the Atocha as he entered the city in the wagon that had conveyed him like a rare animal from Jingten. Enchantments throughout the school tickled his senses, but the swelling force of magic emanating from the Altular roused his curiosity much more. The magic woven into the granite blocks of the temple reminded Dacian of the Jingten Tower, but the spells were older and tuned to the world far beyond the city. The Altular was supposedly connected to the star realm of the Great Divinity, and Dacian thought it might be true. From the distant platform at the top of the temple, Dacian felt the structure's power rising into the sky. Every four years, the Grand Lumin and his inner circle performed the Quadreni ceremony to maintain the alignment of Nufal with the Great Divinity.

Often Dacian had daydreamed that he might be the first rys to take part in that ceremony. His dreams were not so vivid anymore. Daykash Breymer had taken him to Kwellstan so that the Grand Lumin might judge him. Dacian hoped to salvage his education as a Nebakarz, but even that stubborn hope cast no light upon his dark future.

Anxiety replaced the joy he had always expected to feel upon finally reaching Kwellstan. Dacian tried to muster the will to reach out to the tabre as his kin, but it was difficult considering the tabre seemed glad that Breymer had seized custody of him.

Dacian found himself missing Halor. His old master was all that he had known, and the aloof suspicion of the Daykash was a poor replacement. As a tribute to Halor, Dacian resolved to honor his lessons about the value of an ordered society. Dacian accepted that he had behaved badly during the punishment of Onja, even if he did not agree with it, and society had a right to correct him. Two weeks ago in Jingten when the Daykash had decided that Dacian was to be taken to Kwellstan for what he called a review, Dacian had submitted himself to the Daykash and cooperated during the trip.

Although genuinely apprehensive about his meeting with the Grand Lumin, Dacian dwelled on his worry for Onja. She had been left in Jingten as the ward of Halor. Dacian suspected that she would not be receptive to the structured guidance of his old master. She was the freest spirit he had ever known.

Dacian crossed Kwellstan on a grand tree-lined avenue. Its cobbles took a meandering path because the road had been built around the original trees of the ancient forest. The elder maples, beeches, ashes, and oaks had lost most of their leaves in the freezing rain storm that had swept through the valley. Red and golden leaves littered the white paving stones and scurried back to their tree roots on little swirls of wind. A smattering of browning leaves still lingered on the branches that clattered in the cool breeze. These deciduous trees that were baring themselves for winter were eerie to Dacian compared to the evergreens of the Jingten Valley that faced the drastic alpine cold with green resolve.

The sky above the thinning forest canopy was crisp and blue. The rain had moved on and the sun still granted the afternoon some warmth. The air was heavy with the scent of moist woodland and the lake. Compared to the high alpine land that had bred Dacian, the air in Nufal was thick and soft. It caressed his skin and filled his lungs with easy vitality.

Everything here was different, especially the waters. Lake Kwellstan swelled against his perception invitingly. The icy deeps of Lake Nin were like the snarl of a hungry wolf compared to the homey purring spirit that came from Lake Kwellstan. This valley was alive with its waters that percolated up in many gushing springs that fed the lake. The strongest springs had been channeled and pooled in the Plaza of the Waters. Kwellstan was famous for its healing and revitalizing spring waters, and the plaza sparkled with fountains and pools and channels that led to the lake. Bathers, both human and tabre, came from all over Nufal to experience the natural magic of the Kwellstan waters. They were a treasure that sustained the city in many ways.

As Dacian reached the heart of the city, he could hear the gurgling pleasantness in the plaza. Flowers and shrubs lined the channels and ringed the bathing pools that descended in a series of flowing steps. The flower beds were now withered and drab, but the evergreen hedges remained merry. Tabre enjoyed the three largest pools closest to the spring source and a few humans defied the autumnal chill and bathed in the smaller satellite pools.

Close to the monumental buildings of the Nebakarz, Dacian saw Lake Kwellstan. Beyond the blue waters, there was the virgin forest of the valley. Some stubborn clusters of gold and orange leaves still brightened the forest. North of the forest rose Mount Hendrefu, and at its base spread the terraced fields and orchards that surrounded the city of Alicharat.

Although the Nufalese landscape was more subtle than the colossal grandeur of the Jingten Valley, Dacian still appreciated its beauty. This land was lush, fertile, and in harmony with the cities of tabre and humans that occupied it. There was balance. The land gave of its bounty and the Nufalese respected its wild places and let them be. Music, art, trade, schools, homes with children, and a hundred other vibrant activities cluttered the city. Dacian opened his senses to all of it. He heard humans throughout the city speaking to each other. The laughter of playing children touched his mind, and he envied their carefree joy on the sunny day. In places, the tabre mingled with the humans, but they were mostly segregated into their own neighborhoods. The tabre were more reserved than the humans who made up two-thirds of Kwellstan's population. The tabre talked less and thought more, Dacian judged. Many that he observed were meditating or working quietly on their crafts and trades, doing their work with magic as much as with their hands.

A few sharp minds were focusing back on Dacian, and he resisted the urge to slouch down in the wagon. The tabre bathing in the Plaza of the Waters stood up and watched him as the Daykash's caravan crossed the low bridge that led into the Altular. Bright droplets of water fell from their glossy dark skin that was wet with a rainbow sheen. Dacian heard many of them gasp.

Most tabre had never seen a rys, and now centuries had gone by and allowed the tabre to imagine the rys as freakishly different. I do not feel so different, Dacian lamented.

Entering the Altular was a relief. The bridge went directly between two gushing fountains filled with sculptures and into the temple. The cool dark of the hulking stone building was soothing after the bouncing random energy of the plaza. Dacian welcomed the thick enchantments of the building that insulated him from the prying minds of the tabre populace.

Dacian focused his intellect on the Altular and studied the massive enchantments that the Nebakarz had imbued into each block. For millennia magic masters had added to the spells of the temple, bringing it into nearly perfect sync with the cosmos. The Nebakarz reached for the Great Divinity and in each new moment of understanding they became more powerful.

Within the temple, great vaulted chambers loomed above Dacian as the wagons and riders stopped in the cavernous entry hall. Spheres of glowing white crystals hovered high above, bobbing gently in the air and casting their soft light. Balconies overlooked the entry hall and revealed many levels within the temple. Jewels encrusted the golden rails of the balconies and more jewels wound around the glossy black marble pillars that lined the hall. Rubies brooded like bloody eyes in the enchanted light.

As soon as the wagon stopped, Dacian sprang down to the floor. Despite his circumstances, he was excited to actually be inside the Altular.

The intoxicating power inside the temple reaffirmed his desire to be a Nebakarz priest.

I will not be denied, he thought with sudden confidence. He was worthy and the Grand Lumin would see it.

As Breymer emerged from his coach, servants poured out from several doorways along the pillared walls. Bearing cups of wine, the tabre servants clothed in simple black tunics and pants brought a drink to each of the returning Nebakarz priests and acolytes. Even Dacian was offered a cup, and he took the delicate ceramic vessel and nodded appreciatively to the servant. A deep red glaze covered the cup that had been thrown on a wheel by a tabre potter who supplemented the skill of his hands with magic. A simple little spell kept the wafer-thin walls of the cup from breaking.

Dacian sipped the wine. It was white and fruity. Much of the essence of Nufal flowed into his body as the wine passed down his throat. The sun that had ripened the grapes and the nutrients and water that the roots had drawn up and placed into the fruit were captured in the wine. Each drop upon his tongue educated him about the land of Nufal.

Dacian observed the Daykash at the head of the caravan. Along with the wine, servants had brought a basin of water and a towel so that he could cleanse his hands and face. Hurriedly, he then drank some wine but did not linger over it. Then the Daykash started toward Dacian. The rys lowered his cup but he did not lower his eyes.

Breymer's unfriendly face looked even more severe than usual. The gold lettering on his red robe was brighter inside the temple. A slight shimmer of magic glittered over each symbol.

"You will be taken to your chambers. You will stay there until summoned." Breymer spoke as if his tongue were a sharp blade chopping vegetables.

Dacian said, "As you command, my Daykash. I am honored to be housed in the Altular."

Breymer ignored the comment, but, before he turned away, Dacian asked quickly if he would see the Grand Lumin soon.

"The Grand Lumin has all of time to contemplate. He will summon you when the right moment arrives and not before," Breymer answered and then hurried away with his attendant priests.

An acolyte who had overseen most of Dacian's needs on the trip from Jingten stepped forward. "Come," he said, keeping his words to a minimum as always.

Dacian followed the acolyte across the courtyard as servants came out to stable the horses. Every pair of eyes flashed in his direction.

Levitation shafts were placed between the pillars, and Dacian followed his guide up three levels. The hall that they emerged onto was carpeted in thick red wool woven with subtle designs of clouds, all in varying shades of red. Every so often, a balcony broke through the polished granite walls and Dacian could see into the entry hall. Below, the horses were being led away, and they looked small even from just three levels up.

His acolyte keeper said nothing. Dacian thought it would have been polite if he had given him some commentary about the temple. He felt like he was at the center of all of civilized history. For the first time in a long time, Dacian felt ignorant. In Jingten he had become so familiar with everything, the land, the residents, the spells that he had almost believed that there was little else to learn.

I shall learn much here, he decided, and his taciturn guide could not prevent that. Dacian tried not to resent that he was always being watched, guarded really. Halor had taught him to obey the authority of the Nebakarz, and Dacian would have to earn the trust of his chosen brothers again.

The tabre acolyte stopped at what appeared to be a blank wall. He placed his hand on the smooth stone, and, after a white sparkle of energy snapped around his finger tips, the stone transformed into a door made from a curious alloy. Dacian touched the door lightly. The metal was a blend of iron and silver. Strong and pretty.

Dacian thanked the acolyte who did not enter the chamber with him. The tabre walked away wordlessly. The door closed on its own and even from the inside it resumed the appearance of smooth stone.

Looking around his cell, Dacian saw the meager furnishings allotted an acolyte. The room was long and narrow with a single bed, table, stool, and a cupboard. Enchanted crystals embedded in the ceiling provided an even white light. He immediately missed having a window, but then he analyzed the outer wall and smiled. Walking to the end of the room, he touched the wall and activated the spell set in the stone. A shimmering circle formed and then its milky light cleared and he could see outside. The images were a little watery but it was good to see the sun, sky and the surrounding city. And it was amazing to be seeing through stone. Dacian was not casting forth his mind and remote viewing. He was actually looking through a spell that made the thick granite clear.

After studying the spell and activating it several times, Dacian was satisfied that he knew how to recreate the effect. He hoped that he would have the chance to try it sometime. Weary after his long trip, he draped his hooded cloak over the end of the bed and then sat and removed his boots.

To rest would be logical, but his troubles pressed on his mind. He wanted to see the Grand Lumin and set things right as soon as possible.

Frowning, he walked to the hidden door. The thick carpet was soft against his bare feet.

Dacian touched the stone wall and found that the spell that operated the door was locked. Confirming this suspicion hurt, and anger stirred in his heart. Do not get angry, he commanded himself.

Dejected, he went back to the bed and stretched out. He was sick of being a prisoner, but Halor had told him that the Nebakarz would test him in this way.

Dacian tried to keep from thinking about forcing the door open. He moved his tongue across the roof of his mouth and contemplated the wine that he had drunk. Its foreign flavor was foreboding and made him intimately realize that he was not part of this land.

19. Sympathy for the Dangerous

The Drathatarlane Sect is jealous of what we seek in Jingten. The day will come when they come out of hiding to take our secrets. ~ Daykash Fane, 1951 Kwellstan calendar

Lost in thought, Alloi braided her hair and stared into the branches of an elder maple tree. It grew alongside the stone tower house she shared with her family in Kwellstan. Yellow leaves dangled on twiggy fingertips over the balcony railing. More leaves were scattered in wet golden piles on the balcony, knocked down by the recent rain. The breeze sauntering through the treetops was mild now and a pleasant surprise after the snarling chill of the storm.

Tempet leaned in the doorway. Alloi could sense his impatience. His feelings and thoughts were easy for her to read. He rarely blocked her out of his mind, and never his heart.

Alloi pinned her braided hair into a coil at the back of her head. The braided black hair was sleek and shiny like the cast iron links of a chain. She rubbed her shapely shoulders that were left exposed by her sleeveless leather dress.

She considered the challenge of maintaining diplomatic friendliness while gaining information about the rys that had just entered the city. Officially she and her brother lived in Kwellstan as ambassadors. The Kwellstan Sect outwardly welcomed Tempet and Alloi for making their summer home in Kwellstan, but no one actually believed that the hospitality was genuine.

Tempet said, "Let us enter trance and observe this rys directly. He has a strange lifeforce."

"We can't cast our minds so blatantly into the Altular. If we violate their temple, they will accuse the Drathatarlane Sect of trying to control them," Alloi said.

Tempet rolled his black eyes. "They need control. Look what they have done to Nufal. It is awash in humans. The Kwellstan think they are almost gods to these people and it has made them reckless," he said.

"I think the humans are invigorating," she confessed. Even if they lived short lives and had no magic, she still found that they were strong and clever. Their emotions and unpredictability were stimulating as well.

"You like all the animals," Tempet muttered.

Alloi frowned disapprovingly but did not make an issue of it. Walking up to Tempet and leaning close, she said, "We will go to the Altular and demand to see this rys."

"Not very subtle," Tempet remarked.

"Ask to see the rys," she corrected and smiled mischievously.

Alloi went inside and strolled to her open closet. She perused her garments. "It is a reasonable request," she continued. "A rys has never been brought here before. Of course we would want to meet him."

Tempet swaggered away from the door and draped his hard body onto a lavender and yellow couch.

Alloi slid out of her dress and selected a conservative cloth gown that covered her arms and had a high collar. The gray wool was enhanced with ultra fine silver fibers to make it sparkle. After donning the dress, she asked Tempet if he was going to change. He wore plain wool breeches and a black linen tunic that was wrinkling before her eyes.

"This will do," he said.

"No," Alloi said. She stalked into the adjoining room where Tempet slept and started looking through his closet. She returned with a long black coat trimmed in red leather that was reminiscent of Kwellstan colors. "At least put this on," she said.

Tempet got up and obediently extended his arms so she could pull the coat onto him. "It does not matter what I look like," he insisted while buttoning the coat. "The Grand Lumin will accommodate us because of you. The only beautiful tabre females are born in Drathatarlane."

Alloi enjoyed the compliment even if it was unfair. She was aware that many males found her attractive, but it was hardly true that Drathatarlane was the sole source of feminine beauty.

She brushed Tempet's bangs from his face and seemed to be satisfied with his appearance. "Let us go," she said.

They clasped hands and trotted onto the balcony. As they swung their legs over the railing, they cast levitation spells and floated to the ground in a faint sphere of white light. They ran toward the Altular like a couple of tablings playing a game.

When Tempet and Alloi reached the yawning entrance of the temple, the day was fading and the towers of the Atocha cast long shadows across the Plaza of the Waters. Alloi dipped her fingers into the nearest fountain and dabbed the cool spring water onto her warm neck. The blessed water, purified by the heart of the living world, tingled on her skin. The twins exchanged looks before entering the temple. When they passed through the invisible warding, the pleasant burble and flow of the waters outside were silenced. Tempet and Alloi walked across the vast chamber with their heads high. They asked no leave to enter, and they ignored the tabre priests, acolytes, and servants who observed them.

The twins enjoyed the respect that the Kwellstan Sect tabre grudgingly granted them. Their innate disdain born of long rivalry could not deny the truth of Tempet and Alloi's extraordinary powers. Tempet and Alloi won any contest put to them, be it physical, mental, or magical. For over one hundred years, the Drathatarlane leadership had groomed them to be the first ambassadors to Kwellstan. They had been sent to Kwellstan both as a challenge and a warning that the Drathatarlane Sect meant to reclaim the crown of respect among tabre.

Striding through the Altular, Tempet and Alloi were reminded of their great purpose to revive their Sect. Over the last two thousand years the Kwellstan Sect seemed to have flourished more. Kwellstan priests devised new spells of increasing complexity. Their buildings grew taller and stronger. Their minds saw farther across Ektren. Tempet and Alloi knew that their birth was viewed as a renewal of their Sect. The Eschalam had overseen their birth in the Pen'dalem, the great temple of the Drathatarlane Sect. All their lives Drathatarlane elders had taught the twins that they were destined to prove their Sect superior, and the twins believed it.

Opposite the temple entrance a set of golden doors confronted them. The metal was sculpted to look like a waterfall, and a spell enhanced the gold so that it shimmered like moving water. Tempet raised a hand and tugged at the doors with the force of his mind. Silently the doors opened onto a circular chamber. The twins stepped onto the disc of white crystal and floated upward. They passed twenty levels before hopping out of the shaft.

On this level red shades covered glow crystals. Red tapestries that depicted constellations draped the polished black marble walls, and thick blood red rugs muffled the footsteps of the two approaching priests. Their robes with stiff high collars, tight sleeves, and special gold lettering designated them as attendants of the Grand Lumin.

"We would speak with the Grand Lumin," Alloi said matter-of-factly.

The eyes of one of the priests glowed with his magic as he conferred mentally with his master. After a moment, he gestured for Tempet and Alloi to follow.

They passed through seven unfurnished chambers before the priests opened the Grand Lumin's audience chamber. The wizened old tabre sat upon a plain stone platform with black cushions. He wore flowing red robes, striking because of their lack of adornment. Two spheres of milky crystal hovered close to his knees. They looked like giant replicas of his blank all-white eyes that stared unblinking from his hairless head.

Over a century ago, the Grand Lumin had given up the physical sight of his eyes upon ascending to the leadership of the Kwellstan Sect. His magic alone supported his vision, and he looked upon creation without the distraction of images bombarding his eyes.

Tempet and Alloi bowed to him and the attendant priests left them alone with the Grand Lumin.

They studied each other in silence. The perception of the Grand Lumin absorbed the potent presence of Tempet and Alloi. He knew the hopes that the Drathatarlane Sect pinned on these two prodigies. He understood why their birth had aroused the ambitions of the Drathatarlane Sect that had been beaten back in the Sect War two thousand years earlier.

Despite his admiration of the twins' talents, the faith of the Grand Lumin in the superiority of his Sect remained solid. The limited philosophy of the Drathatarlane would always hold them back. They had been utterly foolish in their attempt to stomp out the Kwellstan Sect when it first broke from the shackles of Drathatarlane rule. Knowing that tabre power and intelligence would thrive through exploration, the founders of the Kwellstan Sect had expanded across the Valley of Nufal and even welcomed humans into their society to further energize their civilization.

Finally forced to accept the practicality of peace, the Drathatarlane tabre had hunkered in their mountain city and clung to their belief that they could develop tabre power by remaining rooted in the core homeland of the species. Drathatarlane was located nearest to the place where tabre had first flowered into their magic. Staying near the creative center, the Drathatarlane believed, would keep them connected to the purest magical gifts of the Great Divinity. The Grand Lumin could only snicker when he wondered how well that pursuit was going for his rivals.

The Grand Lumin was further amused to have the best of Drathatarlane before him. The twins were so special they were not even ranked as Nebakarz priests. They were a class unto themselves. Such marvelous specimens were worthy of the Grand Lumin's attention. He began his mental probing.

Alloi withdrew her mind from Tempet as she circled her mental powers to defend herself. Tempet did the same. Although he reveled in his youth, he knew when to respect an elder. The Grand Lumin would try to penetrate Tempet's thoughts like frost sinking into the cracks of a mountain.

It was always this way when they met with the Grand Lumin. Alloi knew that the Grand Lumin used his offense as a defense. By occupying her and Tempet, they were unable to peer into his thoughts. Alloi was particularly adept at mindreading. She had attempted to do it the very first time she had met with the Grand Lumin. It had been a foolish thing to do. She had not succeeded and she had revealed her capabilities.

Eventually, the Grand Lumin relented. The burning white light receded from the eyes of all three tabre, and the Grand Lumin cleared his gritty throat. His old skin stretched over his lips in his version of a smile.

"We are never to trust each other, my little lamblings," he said, using his favorite endearment for them.

Alloi could not help liking the term. She wanted to see him in a grandfatherly fashion but knew better. The bitter history of the Sect War shaped his attitude, and they would never be as kin.

Alloi said. "Some would say it is rude how you test us."

"Sister, be not so bold with our host," Tempet scolded.

"Ah, but who is to be bold if not you?" the Grand Lumin said and raised a finger and pointed blindly in their direction. "And who is to test you if not me?"

"We learn much from our encounters with you, Grand Lumin," Alloi said.

The elderly tabre nodded, seeming somewhat satisfied by her statement. "Now, I am forced to ask why have you come to me?"

"Grand Lumin, I think you could guess," Alloi teased.

Folding his arms into his voluminous sleeves, he said, "Yes, I can guess. You have come to see the rys."

"Grand Lumin," Tempet said. "We observed him being carted here like he was a prisoner. What has he done?"

"The details of that are not important," the Grand Lumin said.

"Is he powerful?" Alloi asked and tilted her head quizzically.

"He has power, yes. I thought it best to segregate him from the other rys. So as to keep order," the Grand Lumin revealed.

"Do the rys trouble you?" Tempet asked.

Alloi detected the faintest ripple within the Grand Lumin's mind when Tempet asked his question. She had to restrain herself from probing blatantly for more detail. She suspected that something important about the rys had just darted across the Grand Lumin's thoughts, and it had not been pleasant. He did not answer Tempet's question.

"Grand Lumin, We are so very curious. May we see this rys?" Alloi said, sweetening her voice as only she could.

The Grand Lumin resisted her beguiling play at innocence. He explained that he was keeping the rys isolated.

"Please, Grand Lumin," Alloi said simply.

Her immature tactic amused him. "Alloi, I have not even met with him," he said.

"Then let us see him and we will report to you what we think of him," Tempet proposed.

Clever, Alloi thought, proud of her brother.

The Grand Lumin's eyes flashed. At length, he said, "You would make a good distraction. I will observe while you meet with him."

"Of course, Grand Lumin," Alloi said and dipped her head. She surmised that the rys must be powerful indeed if the Grand Lumin needed him distracted. Alloi found that she was very excited by the prospect of meeting someone who intimidated the Grand Lumin.

The attendant priests returned and escorted Alloi and Tempet to another room. This one was furnished with two rows of black leather chairs that faced each other. Tempet and Alloi asked the priests to bring them refreshment.

"As you wish," responded one of the Nebakarz priests and he departed with his counterpart.

After a while a tabre servant delivered water and a plate of cakes. Tempet and Alloi drank and ate the cakes, which were very good. They were baked of soft wheat flour and had honey glazed walnuts in them.

"The food is better in Kwellstan," Alloi let herself say.

Tempet frowned but did not disagree. No humans were allowed in Drathatarlane, so their cooking skills were absent as well, but tabre living under the Kwellstan Sect frequently employed human cooks. Humans were gifted at creating tasty concoctions, and the tabre paid well to be provided with the best.

While wiping her mouth with a napkin, Alloi stopped abruptly. "He is coming," she whispered. The lifeforce of the rys inflamed her senses. Tempet was also startled by the approach of a being uncommonly rich with the powers of the cosmos. The rys had just ascended the levitation shaft and was being escorted to their chamber. The subtle presence of the Grand Lumin's mind settled over the room, and Alloi reminded herself to guard her thoughts well. The rys was likely not the only one the Grand Lumin wished to distract.

When the rys reached the open doorway, he stood in it with a Kwellstan acolyte at his elbow. Alloi was puzzled that one supposedly so powerful was only escorted by a single acolyte.

The rys walked slowly into the room, and Tempet and Alloi gestured for him to sit. Alloi caught the eye of the rys's escort and mentally commanded him to leave. Giving now her full attention to the rys, she noted that he was taller than her brother and slender but there was no weakness in his body. It was exceedingly strange to see one like the tabre but with the blue skin that she had heard about. Both she and Tempet stared at the rys, openly startled by his racial differences.

The rys looked back at them with a guarded expression. Alloi sensed that he was trying not to be nervous. Suddenly in a rush of sympathy, Alloi felt how very isolated he was. He had no friends here. He was away from home and did not know what to expect. She recalled how disconcerting her first time away from Drathatarlane had been. But Tempet and her parents had been with her to ease the transition. This rys had no one.

"I am Alloi and this is Tempet," she introduced.

"Perhaps you have heard of us?" Tempet said.

The rys shook his head. "I spend most of my time in study. Forgive me for not being aware of you. I am Dacian."

Awkwardly, Tempet asked Dacian what he studied.

"I study to be a Nebakarz priest," he answered with pride, knowing that the concept of a rys with such an ambition was strange.

"Why?" Tempet asked bluntly.

Dacian told himself to answer well. Every word he said was certain to be monitored. He explained that he had more power than the typical rys, and that the study of the Nebakarz way was a natural selection. "What else would I do?" he concluded.

Alloi smoothed her dress over her knees and looked down coyly. "One can be powerful without taking to the priesthood," she commented.

Dacian studied the twins anew. "Who are you?" he asked. By their clothing he could see that they were not priests, so why were they the first to speak with him at the Altular?

"We are tabre of Nufal," Tempet said, unashamed by his vague answer.

Now wondering what they had to hide, Dacian could also feel their mental skulking. There was another presence as well. The tabre wanted to know so very terribly what was on his mind. The truth was he did not know what to think. He was only trying to be contrite, as Halor had advised him.

Deciding to be open because everyone seemed to be so suspicious of him, Dacian said, "Do you want to see inside my mind, Alloi?"

She blinked, clearly startled by his question.

Dacian added, "I feel your mind probing. Why be sneaky? I will let you into my thoughts if it is your wish."

Tempet noticed how the eyes of the rys focused on his sister.

"I was only curious," Alloi said meekly.

Dacian sat back in his chair, relaxing his body as well as his mind. He deconstructed the thick walls of mental power that were the natural fortress of his mind. Growing up a rys amid tabre had long ago trained his mind to guard all thoughts. Dacian had never wanted to let his chances of success be diminished because he let an irritated thought bounce loose.

Alloi reached out to him tentatively. She meant him no harm but kept buried the dislike the Drathatarlane officially had for all works of the Kwellstan Sect, especially the rys.

Her advances warmed Dacian after his lonely uncomfortable trip from Jingten. It would have been very easy to be lulled into fully baring his thoughts and memories, but he held back. He did not want to reveal his outrage about the punishment of Onja. As Alloi connected with him, he was reminded of how Onja and he had communicated in their cells. He blocked those memories from Alloi and made sure that she knew he was stopping her.

"I'm sorry. I understand things are private," Alloi said mentally.

"What are you looking for?" Dacian asked.

"I don't know," she responded but it was only half true.

"I do not believe you, Alloi," Dacian said.

"You are clearly in some kind of trouble with the Kwellstan. If I knew what it was, maybe I could help you. I came to meet you because I could feel your power. Ones such as us are the future of Nufal. I want to know you better," Alloi said, and Dacian wanted to trust her. She was a beautiful tabre and her magic glowed forth from her lifeforce like the sun touching the green shoots of spring. Her feminine charm was very pleasing to his maturing sensibilities, and Dacian imagined that to be with her would be like having all the ugliness in the world drop away until only bliss remained.

"You are an excellent distraction," he told her as he guessed her game.

She was unaccustomed to having the hounds of her mind outfoxed. Her connection faltered, and then Dacian pushed her away. He acted so fast that he was able to fully see the mind of the other tabre that had been observing them. He had a vision of an elderly tabre with all-white staring eyes. Dacian latched onto the mind that fled from his presence like a thief discovered in the dark. Dacian's mind blasted through the heavy wardings that surrounded the inner sanctum of the Grand Lumin and he confronted the will of his supreme leader. Dacian knew his actions were brash and

Rys Rising: Book I

wrong, but he had no idea how long he would be forced to await his judgment in maddening limbo. Dacian hoped that his flagrant display of magical skill would impress the Grand Lumin who would then see the indisputable wisdom of allowing his Nebakarz education to proceed.

"I would hear your judgment, my Master," Dacian told the Grand Lumin.

Although startled by the aggressive audience that Dacian initiated, the Grand Lumin collected himself rapidly. His spirit exploded inside Dacian's head and filled his thoughts with his authoritative voice.

"Then you shall have my judgment, rys," he said.

The connection was severed. Dacian's mind and vision snapped back to the chamber where he sat facing Tempet and Alloi. The twins stared at him with shock. They knew his mind had penetrated the inner sanctum of the Altular, and they were astounded by his audacity.

Footsteps rushed toward the chamber. The two priests that attended the Grand Lumin charged through the doorway. Dacian stood, knowing that they were about to take him before the Grand Lumin as he wished.

Before leaving, Dacian spoke to his visitors. "Tempet, it was interesting to meet you. And Alloi, you are a kind spirit."

Alloi wanted to say something nice in return but her heart ached with duty. She would have to report to the Eschalam that he was dangerous. An enigma truly, but dangerous. After having been in his mind, she believed that the rys did not yet accept that he was dangerous. She wished it was not so.

"Alloi, I do not need you to pity me," Dacian said.

Startled, Alloi could not respond before Dacian left with the priests.

Once they were alone, Tempet whispered, "Extraordinary."

Alloi nodded, disturbed by the encounter with the rys in some ways that she had no wish to discuss with her twin.

Knowing that the Grand Lumin would occupy himself with Dacian, Tempet and Alloi decided to leave. The Grand Lumin could summon them later when he wished to discuss their experience with the rys.

The twins hurried from the Altular. Evening was descending on the city when they returned home. Tempet and Alloi went to their meditation chamber. Before they spoke a word, they changed the warding spells on their room. Once they were satisfied that their meditation chamber was secure, they entered trance and cast their minds homeward to Drathatarlane. The sensitive warding spells that wrapped the Pen'dalem in Drathatarlane hummed in recognition of the twins, and the high priests within the temple hurried to attend their master, the Eschalam.

The Eschalam awaited the spirit projections of Tempet and Alloi. The full body images of the twins brightened over the white crystal seeing floor in the Pen'dalem. The twins could see the Eschalam and his four highest priests, the Ubratta. They all wore white shirts and pants and black shoes that laced up their calves. Long white caps covered their skulls and hung down to their shoulders. The Eschalam had a more elaborate headdress embroidered with golden runes and set with many amethyst and blue sapphire beads. He was a younger leader than the Grand Lumin of the Kwellstan although he was a venerable one thousand and one years old. He rarely ventured out of Drathatarlane and his blood and bones were strong with the magic of his cherished and sacred home.

"What news?" the Eschalam said aloud.

"My Master, we have met with a rys brought as prisoner to Kwellstan," Tempet reported.

"He is powerful," Alloi stated bluntly and she and Tempet described how Dacian had boldly breached the inner sanctum of the Grand Lumin. The rys's magic had cut through the wardings as if they were cobwebs.

"And he pushed back my mind," Alloi concluded.

This fact fell heavily upon the Drathatarlane priests. Entering the minds of other beings was Alloi's natural genius, and for her power to be knocked aside was disturbing.

After a long silence, the Eschalam said, "Would you say that the Kwellstan have created a great warrior in this rys?"

Tempet deferred to Alloi and she was thoughtful before answering. "My Master, the Kwellstan fear the rys will hurt THEM. They do not control the rys sufficiently to make them into warriors against us. My guess is that they dare not risk it. This Dacian does not even realize how carefully they work to keep him from knowing the full extent of his talents. I think they brought him to Kwellstan because he is maturing and coming fully into his magic. The Kwellstan do not want him around the other rys. I think, my Master, that we have a far greater problem brewing in Jingten than we ever suspected."

Everyone fell silent. No one reveled in the knowledge that the Drathatarlane Sect had been right to warn the Kwellstan priests against settling beyond the Tabren Mountains. Nufal was the place for tabre, and exposing their magical lifeforces to foreign lands had done something.

When the Eschalam finally spoke, the others could tell that he had reached a decision. "Alloi, I must ask something of you that will not be easy," he said.

Trying to hide her apprehension, Alloi said, "Of course, my Master."

"I need you – and only you – to stay the winter in Kwellstan instead of coming home to Drathatarlane with your family, as would be right. You must do this so you can continue to monitor the rys," the Eschalam said.

The dismay of the twins fluttered through their translucent spirit projections.

"Do not separate us, my Master," Tempet said. "What reason could you have for this?"

The question was audacious, but the Eschalam chose to overlook the transgression. "Tempet, forgive me. I know that it must pain you to be apart from your sister, but the time has come to advance your training. Although you and your twin together are more powerful than others, this is also a weakness. Both of you will realize your fullest potential if you spend some time apart. Then you will see how you rely on each other. Trust me. This must be done, and it must be done before we urgently have need of your powers," he explained.

The snarl of displeasure was clear upon the image of Tempet in the Pen'dalem, but Alloi was able to look past her fear and hear the greater meaning of her master's words. "My Master," she said. "Do you foresee that we shall…war with the Kwellstan?"

They were awful words, and Alloi regretted for the first time that there was a rivalry between the Sects. It had always seemed so normal before, but, if it threatened the peace that they all enjoyed, then it was not so right.

"War with Kwellstan is not certain, Alloi," the Eschalam assured her. "But the Drathatarlane are committed to regaining the governance of Nufal. Obey me."

The twins were dismissed, and Tempet returned to his body seething with outrage. "I will not do it!" he declared and smacked the wall of the meditation chamber.

Alloi wrung her hands. She was upset too, but she recognized the importance of her assignment to monitor Dacian.

"Tempet, perhaps there is wisdom in his words. We do rely on each other. We could learn more about our powers if we were apart," she said.

"No!" Tempet said sharply. He cast an angry spell at the door and broke it from its hinges. He stalked from the chamber, and Alloi knew that it was useless to speak with him now.

The protests of Tempet and her parents would not change anything. They would obey the Eschalam and she would stay on alone in Kwellstan. Although she feared the separation, she recognized that the challenge excited her. Dacian's powers were alluring in a way she had never considered, and she wanted her chance to see him again, alone.

20. The Judging of Dacian

The Nebakarz priests flanking Dacian radiated disapproval in thick mental waves that even a human could have felt. Dacian knew that he had behaved badly and more than once. His esteem for law and order that his teaching master had instilled in him seemed no longer sufficient to control his behavior. Willfully he rallied his determination to salvage his education as the priests marched him into the hallowed audience chamber of the Grand Lumin.

The thin elderly tabre male in his red robes looked deceptively weak and benign, but Dacian sensed his immense power.

Dropping to his knees, Dacian said, "Great Grand Lumin, my Master, forgive me."

The attending priests went to the sides of the Grand Lumin and placed themselves near the hovering crystal orbs. Their stance was defensive, and Dacian cringed in shame.

After a painful silence, the voice of the Grand Lumin cracked out words. "After everything else, you even dare to speak first." The Grand Lumin then proceeded to harangue Dacian for his impudence and interference at the punishment of the rys female. Respect for authority was paramount in a society composed of magic beings, the Grand Lumin insisted. Dacian's crime had been doubly wrong because he had done it in public!

The Grand Lumin gave a long rattling sigh. "We gave you a chance, Dacian. The Nebakarz of the Kwellstan Sect were not blind to your potential. Often Halor spoke highly of you. All of this has been a grave disappointment," the Grand Lumin said.

Dacian did not like the direction of the Grand Lumin's speech. "May I speak in my defense?" Dacian asked.

The Grand Lumin scowled. "What defense could you have?" he demanded.

"Great Grand Lumin, my Master," Dacian said humbly. "I am more than willing to accept what penance you require to make up for my poor behavior. But please understand that I did not mean to attack your authority. I was only overcome by my emotions. The phlia-mel was so brutal and shocking. It was hurting her! Surely, the Nebakarz are well beyond such things."

"The phlia-mel was the decision of the Daykash and you should not have concerned yourself with it," the intractable Grand Lumin said firmly.

Great dejection deflated Dacian's confidence. "How can I make amends, my Master?" he said.

The thin lips of the Grand Lumin pursed thoughtfully. He pondered his options then spoke bluntly. "You cannot. This has gone on long enough. A rys will not enter the revered ranks of the Nebakarz. It is not meant to be."

Dacian gaped in disbelief. Failure beat at his dreams like an evil spouse and he felt sick. He had excelled as an acolyte. He had passed all the necessary tests. How could the Nebakarz just spurn his talent?

His goal of proving that rys were worthy of the priesthood began to wither like a plant with its roots eaten away. A mire of hateful reality sucked down his hope that rys would be included in the wider society of Nufal instead of locked away in their remote homeland like an idiot son.

Dacian scrambled for a solution, but, for all his education and training, he remained young and naive and lacked the skills to deal with a crisis. And so he slouched before the Grand Lumin, dazed by his failure instead of angered. The many predictions of his father emerged from his memories.

Suddenly Dacian wished very much to be home and see his father, his mother too. He longed for their support in this time of personal destruction. Perhaps it would be best to go meekly instead of begging the Nebakarz to absolve him and accept him back. Dacian needed time to rethink his life. If he let the situation cool down perhaps he could begin again. He would not be so easily refused. He would prove that rys were worthy and talented. He recalled that the tabre female had mentioned that there were other paths besides priesthood although Dacian was not sure what place she and her brother held in tabre society.

Dacian lowered his eyes again. "Forgive me for troubling you, Great Grand Lumin. I apologize for my earlier intrusion into your sanctum as well. I wanted only to show you my skill, but I am now ashamed of my reckless disregard for your privacy. I would return to Jingten if you will not have me," Dacian said.

"No, Dacian. You may not return to Jingten," the Grand Lumin said. Power was building around him as his lifeforce summoned his magic, and white light brightened his blind eyes. "We sentence you to stay here and serve us. You have not only grown insolent but you have grown brash. Working in the Altular as a servant will teach you humility and obedience."

"A servant?" Dacian whispered. He harbored no personal dislike for those who served. He respected them as valuable beings, but he was more than they were. That was only a fact.

"Do not question me. You were brought here to be punished and punished you shall be," the Grand Lumin said. "Only a moment ago you begged to hear your penance, so go now to your room and await duties to be assigned to you. Trouble me no more, Dacian of Jingten!"

Dacian was dumbfounded by the dismissal. Since maturity he had pursued the goal of joining the Nebakarz. It had been held out before him and Halor had encouraged him. Even when he took into account his bad behavior, this harsh rejection did not make sense. Deep inside, Dacian started to admit that he had miscalculated the prejudice the tabre bore toward the rys, but then he quashed the thought. It was too painful to confront the fact that the tabre were not going to embrace him as an equal no matter what he did.

A servant? This stinging thought rang inside his head like wind chimes in a bad storm. Accepting this sentence would not serve his goal of proving the quality of rys. It would only exacerbate the situation if he performed menial tasks in the very heartland of Nufal.

Recovering slightly from his shock, Dacian persisted, "Great Grand Lumin, I ask that I be allowed to return home. You have made it clear you don't want me. I would go home." He spoke firmly at the end, and, as he said the words, defiance built in him. He was reminded of the emotions that had flared when he defended Onja, and he was afraid of what he might do.

"You will serve us in the Altular," the Grand Lumin said. "Do not think to defy us and do not think that you will go home!" White light blazed in his eyes and the Grand Lumin tilted his head back as he concentrated mightily on his magic. The air around Dacian erupted with magical fire and terrified him with its immediate intensity.

For the first time in his life, Dacian knew mortal fear. Burning magic, irresistibly strong, tore into his chest and he felt his heart gripped by the will of the Grand Lumin. The contracting chambers pulled the scalding power of the tabre deeper into his blood. Fine needles like the hairs of mold penetrated his heart with stunning pain. Dacian had never imagined that another being could assault him so intimately and thoroughly.

A wrenching scream erupted from Dacian's throat. The Grand Lumin sagged a little after his exertion and his magic receded to a fluttering glow over his face.

Dacian collapsed forward and caught himself with his hands on the floor. His vision was blurring and he gasped for breath. Leaning back onto his knees, he fumbled with his clothes. His chest felt heavy and…wrong.

He opened his shirt and stared at his blue skin. Over his sternum an oval plate of milky white crystal was embedded in his flesh. In dismay he cried out. He had never heard or read of such a thing nor conceived of such a spell.

The Grand Lumin said, "As you see, there is much that you do not know, Dacian. You may have the power to thrust your mind into my inner sanctum like a hungry bandit, but you know nothing."

"What have you done to me?" Dacian demanded. He trembled now from fear and many other ugly feelings that were foreign invaders to his heart.

"That is a crosha. It will keep you in Kwellstan. It is linked to your body and to the land and waters here. The farther you go from the Altular, the more energy the enchantment will draw out of your body. If you go far enough, it will kill you," the Grand Lumin explained with blatant amusement. It was nice to see his uppity rys so well tethered and it had been exhilarating to cast such an obscure spell. It was worth the year it took off his life to thrust such an intricate enchantment upon a living soul.

The Grand Lumin continued, "Do not dare to think that you can disobey me. That is just one of the secret spells in my library passed down from Grand Lumin to Grand Lumin for over two thousand years."

The two attending priests came forward and grabbed Dacian by the arms. He walked backwards as they hustled him out and he stared at the Grand Lumin in miserable awe. He could feel the power of the ancient tabre clutching his body and it was the most violating experience Dacian had ever known.

The priests deposited Dacian in his cell without even looking at him. Their disregard for his feelings added to his many hurts. He crumbled onto the bunk and stared at the enchanted crystal lodged in his chest. Stroking the smooth oval, he contemplated its nature, but then a piercing headache soon distracted him. He realized that its magic was fending him off from even examining it.

Unable to bear his situation, Dacian entered trance. It was a relief to learn that the crosha did not prevent him from using his magic. His despondence impeded his concentration, but eventually he overcame his turmoil and his mind flew across the land. The delight of releasing his spirit from his body comforted him somewhat.

The dense forest of the Valley of Nufal was cold and gray with only lingering clusters of color beneath his ranging consciousness. Then he passed the city of Kahtep on the threshold of the prairie. Beyond was the Rysamand Mountains, and the sight of them renewed his trampled spirit. With greater energy, his mind dashed to Jingten.

Dacian sought Halor and when he touched the familiar lifeforce of his teacher, Dacian accosted him with urgency. His spirit projection flashed into the room where Halor had been making a journal entry.

Startled, Halor jerked back in his seat and his carving stylus left an erratic gouge on the stone wafer. "Dacian!" he exclaimed.

In a rush of mental words, Dacian told Halor of the sentence he had just been given by the Grand Lumin and the crosha.

"Master, please help me!" he begged. "You must convince the Grand Lumin that I deserve a second chance. Why has he been so harsh?"

Halor heard the poorly restrained despair of his wayward pupil. He could not blame Dacian for being upset. Halor had never heard of the crosha spell, but, now that he thought about it, inflicting one's magic upon another so vindictively had to border on illegal.

Quickly, Halor erased the thought. He was no one to judge the actions of the Grand Lumin, who was, if not above the law, right next to it.

"Dacian, Dacian," Halor responded sadly, trying to soothe. He truly had sympathy for Dacian. "I will see what I can do. I will write to the Grand Lumin on your behalf. But you must be reasonable. If you were even half as rude as you told me, you deserve to be punished."

"Master, he said this spell would kill me if I left Kwellstan," Dacian complained.

Halor physically clutched his temples trying to think of what he should say. He needed to calm Dacian down and get him to acquiesce to his situation. It was imperative that he not let Dacian's despair fester until he lashed out with dark anger. Halor resented the mess the Daykash and now the Grand Lumin had made of things. In retrospect he wished that he had made it clearer to his superiors just how very powerful Dacian was.

"Dacian, listen to me. You must be patient. You have to give me a chance to help. You angered the Grand Lumin. He had to do something to control you. This will not last forever. He will release you from the crosha if you behave properly. Do as you are told. Serve in the Altular. Show that you can be trusted," Halor advised.

Dacian was silent for a long time. The blue translucent image of his face hung over the table cluttered with Halor's stone wafers. Dacian was sullen when he responded, asking only how long Halor thought it would be before the Grand Lumin undid the crosha.

"You know I can't answer that. But I know the Grand Lumin. He will let you go, but please promise me, Dacian, that you will do as you are told and be patient. If you promise, I will do all I can to have you reinstated as an acolyte. I really disagree that your education should be stopped. You are my finest pupil ever," Halor said.

Dacian clutched the praise from his teacher like a scared child with a doll. He had known that Halor would reassure him, but he was reluctant to give his promise to serve in the Altular. There was little else he could do though, so he promised Halor that he would serve because he could think of no other way to mend the damage he had done to his future.

Rys Rising: Book I

"Good, Dacian. Try to calm down. I will do as much as I can," Halor said. "And try to be good."

Depressed but otherwise mollified, Dacian thanked Halor for the advice.

"You're welcome, and I am glad that you came to me. You know that you can always trust me…It was good to see you," Halor added. He even smiled.

Dacian's spirit projection faded but his seeing mind lingered over Jingten. The sun was sinking behind the broad shoulders of the mountains and the light dazzled silver and orange upon Lake Nin. With a nostalgic pang he appreciated the beauty of the land that had bred him. He thought to contact his parents but he decided against it. Despite longing for their soothing presence, his shame was too new and intense.

A female's voice whispered to his consciousness.

"Onja!" he answered and his sudden rush of excitement briefly shoved aside his heartbroken weariness.

Her mind guided him into the small room in the tower where she now lived. It was only down the curving hall from where Dacian had spent many years in study. She wore a simple black sack dress with a fur trimmed hood that was draped across her shoulders. The clothing was new but Dacian disliked it because the loose dress completely obscured the wondrous youthful beauty that was Onja.

"Are you well?" he asked, communing with her mind.

Onja closed her eyes and reclined onto her narrow bed. Her hood and her black hair pillowed around her head, framing her blue face with shining black mystery. She told Dacian that she was fine.

"At least you are not locked in a cell any more," Dacian observed.

"Yet I am not free," she said.

She then explained to him that she was now the ward of Halor, who had undertaken her instruction for proper citizenship. Halor had her on a probation that required that she stay within the tower so as to keep her rebellious influence separate from rys society.

"But he can't truly keep me in. My mind cannot be held in by walls or rules," she boasted with some happiness before switching the subject to his welfare. She could feel how upset he was. "What have they done to you?" she asked. Her mind spit venom when she said "they." Despite his shame, he did not hide any details from her about his terrible meeting with the Grand Lumin. She reacted with immediate anger. "Intolerable! You must fight this indignity," she raged. Her peaceful lovely face twisted with sour displeasure and her hands clenched the loose black fabric of her dress.

"Onja, I am already in such disfavor. Fighting will make it worse," he said.

"One as great as you should not have to endure THEIR judgment," she declared.

Naturally thrilled by her high opinion of him, Dacian was soothed by her admiration, but it did not change how his greatness was lost upon the tabre.

"I have already endured their judgment, just like you," he said.

Onja's temper slackened into soft regret. "This is my fault," she said.

Her guilt for his sake and the memory of her beating hardened Dacian to his fate. Everything he had worked toward was destroyed, but he could not imagine changing his actions. "Saving you from even one more brutal stroke of the phlia-mel was worth it," he said and meant it.

"Dacian," she said and smiled dreamily.

They were silent together for a while and enjoyed the twining of their minds where they both found comfort. "What will you do?" she asked him.

Dismally he said that he would serve as he had promised. It seemed the only reasonable way to get the crosha released. Onja's disappointment with the answer was palpable. She suggested that he remove it himself.

"I might die," he worried.

"Not if you unlock the power of the spell and take control of it," she said.

"True…" he admitted, reluctant but thoughtful. "But it would only mean that I would incur the anger of the Grand Lumin again."

Onja quickly rejoined that he should stop letting the Nebakarz hold him down because that is what they wanted. That was what they did to all rys and he knew it was true.

The presence of the crosha was still shockingly new, and goaded by Onja, he honestly considered the possibility of breaking loose from it. He should be capable of doing it, but he was too upset and shaken. His confidence was sucked down into a bog of failure, and experimenting with such a mighty and esoteric spell right now could be disastrous.

"I need time to think on what I might do," he told her.

Softly she agreed and apologized for her hasty words. She was upset for him and had spoken boldly because of it. "Promise to take care of yourself," she said. This promise was easy for him to give.

They lingered in each other's minds before reluctantly breaking their connections.

Once Dacian returned to his body, he realized his utter exhaustion. Never had he been so tired, and all he could do now was rest. To hold back the distress of what the Grand Lumin had done to him, he placed the image of Onja foremost in his mind and closed his eyes. He already longed to communicate with her again. Then he imagined physically being near her and his desire to return home flared painfully. His whole body suddenly ached with no possibility of relief. Onja had stirred feelings in him. Dacian understood that it was a natural part of maturity, but it did not make it any easier in the loneliness of his cell far from Jingten.

Miserably he faced the reality that he would have to serve in the Altular and serve well. He had to gain the pardon of the Grand Lumin if he was ever going to see Onja again. Along with his new longing for Onja his proud dreams of ridding the rys of oppression stubbornly lingered. The cruel disregard of the Grand Lumin proved to Dacian the importance of his cause. His battered feelings and violated body were still a small price compared to what his race had to gain if he persisted in his quest.

21. The Absolution of Halor

Halor had assigned another priest to handle Onja's civic lessons, but he could not avoid her forever. She required debriefing about her experiences in the west, and he needed to handle it personally. The Kwellstan Sect leadership was intensely curious about her firsthand observation of the region.

Although her rebellious nature unsettled Halor, he disagreed with the Daykash's suspicion that she was powerful. She seemed to be nothing except average. The only thing extraordinary about her was her flagrant disregard for rules. He supposed that her delinquency had startled the Daykash, whose tolerance for such things was undeveloped.

To prepare for his meeting with her, Halor put on his formal red and black robe. He expected the display of his rank to sufficiently impress her. Before leaving his private study, he paused at his writing desk and read again the missive he had written to the Grand Lumin. Finally satisfied that his message was sufficiently diplomatic, he cast a sealing spell upon the stone wafer so that its characters could not be altered.

Halor had asked that the Grand Lumin consider Dacian's decades of good behavior and loyalty and remove the crosha. It was a bold act to put a request to a superior in writing. Because tabre could communicate across distances, the transmission of a message in a written form was extremely formal. Of course, Halor would not dispatch a courier to Kwellstan for months. The Rysamand Mountains seemed the very source of winter, and the pass to the east was already clogged with snow. If the need was great, tabre could survive the treacherous snowscape, but the missive could wait until spring. Only a command from the Great Divinity was going to prompt the Grand Lumin to remove the crosha in less than six months anyway.

Halor tucked the disc underneath the edge of his journal and looked out the window. A howling snow storm was surging off the glaciers of the Rysamand, and a white haze absorbed the peaks around the Jingten Valley.

When the night came, it would be a biting storm. The tabre spells that supported the Jingten Tower kept it snug against the wind. No draft pushed in at the windows nor did any frost build upon the stained glass.

Halor watched snow scud over the recently frozen lake. The snow softened the peaked roofs and hard edges of Jingten in a creamy frosting. With the rising storm, the green grandeur of the alpine valley faded into an isolated blur of snow and slumping pine boughs.

Halor admitted to himself that the elemental force of the winter in this place disquieted him. Although the winters in Nufal were cold, they lacked the fierce strength of the climate in Jingten. Halor had not entirely adjusted to the climate unlike the rys who were born to it. They seemed pleased and perky during the winter and glad for the extremity of it. Halor knew that he would always be a foreigner here.

Since Daykash Breymer's visit and the trouble with Dacian and Onja, Halor had developed a case of homesickness. He had been in Jingten for hundreds of years now and his trips back to blessed Kwellstan had been infrequent. He resolved that next summer he would make a point to get back to the Nufalese lowlands.

Halor ascended to his receiving chamber on the second highest level of the tower. He settled into his high-backed chair and cast his mind toward Onja. He found her where she was supposed to be and summoned her. He was encouraged by her meek acceptance of his order. Perhaps the probation was finally convincing her of her place in society.

Too quickly, Onja appeared at the door of the receiving chamber and asked for permission to enter. Halor granted it, and, with a flicker from his mind, shut the door behind her.

Onja glanced over her shoulder as the door closed, betraying some nervousness. Her black hair hung loose and her shapeless black dress was slipping down one shoulder. Her blue skin glimmered with the energy of youth and her collar bone met her shoulder with anatomic perfection.

Halor put on a frown and looked down his long nose at her. He had never been very comfortable around females. As a Nebakarz priest there was no expectation for him to mate, and very few female tabre joined the Nebakarz. These two facts had made the priesthood a pleasantly insulated place from the mysteries and distractions of females.

"You are not supposed to use the levitation shaft," Halor scolded.

"Why?" Onja said bluntly.

"You are to address me as Master Halor," he instructed.

"Then you are my master?" she inquired.

So, she is going to be difficult, Halor realized. "Onja," he sighed. "Everyone calls me Master Halor. It is my title and I deserve it."

"Yes, Master Halor," she said.

"Now, you are to use the stairs. Is that understood?" he said, already fighting exasperation.

"I understand, Master."

"Good. I do not want you to be unhappy. If you will accept the good advice and instruction we have to offer you here, you will be able to return to rys society," Halor said and lifted his eyebrows encouragingly.

Onja was young and had little experience interacting with tabre, but her intuition told her that he was being glib. She knew that the Daykash had commanded Halor to keep her under his direct watch, and she doubted that would change.

"I have been doing as I have been told, Master Halor," she said.

"Yes, very good," Halor praised. After many years of guiding Dacian's education, he had perfected his methods for gaining someone's confidence. "Now, Onja, we have not had a proper chance to get to know each other. To begin, I want you to know that I was against what the Daykash had done to you. I do not believe in such ugly and primitive techniques for enforcing the order of society. Now that he is gone, my authority is total here, and you will not be treated badly."

Onja recognized that he expected her to respond positively to his magnanimous admission, but she remained silent.

After an unrewarded pause, Halor continued, "We have something important to discuss. Although your journey into the west was forbidden, and rightly so, your experience there remains valuable. You could make progress toward redeeming yourself if you were to describe what you saw during your travels."

Onja wanted to blurt that he was a hypocrite, but she bit back the word. Now that she was finally alone with the tabre leader of Jingten, she could act on her ambitions, but she had to be patient just a while longer.

She looked down at the stone bricks of the floor and let her mind flow outward with the spiraling design. Being as subtle as she could, she roused her magic like a tiny smoking flame that has barely taken to its tinder.

Keeping her eyes lowered, she began to recount her journey out of the mountains. At the western end of the valley there was a pass that led down to wooded foothills and then to green and fertile lowlands where streams and rivers coursed through forests of strange trees that did not grow in the mountains. In places buttes and mesas rose above the flatlands and small lakes dotted the landscape. And there were many humans. For the most part they lived in small simple communities, but there were towns and she had heard that there were cities.

"You heard?" Halor asked. "You spoke with humans."

"Yes, Master," she said.

This detail troubled Halor and he slumped thoughtfully into his green leather chair. He commanded her to tell him more.

Onja was frugal with details. She told of her meditations at the waterfalls, but did not mention the intense revelations she had had about her powers while communing with the living forces of the world. And she did not describe her rescue of Amar; instead saying only that she had met him upon the road and traveled with his group for a while before returning to Jingten.

When she completed her abridged tale, she glanced up at Halor. He did not look satisfied at all. The tendrils of her mental magic moved closer to the aura of his lifeforce. Onja was curious to use her power. She wanted to know what it would be like to challenge this tabre. He was powerful and educated. These traits were exactly why she needed Halor.

"Onja, you have not told me everything," Halor complained. "You have nothing to fear. I only want to know what you have experienced. I will not judge your actions. That has already been done and it is over."

Still projecting herself as a silly rys overburdened by his complex demands, Onja suggested that he examine her mind so that he could fully see what she knew. "I am not sure how to pick what I should tell you or how best to describe it. I am still trying to sort out my experiences, Master Halor," she confessed.

The face of the tabre priest softened with understanding. "Of course, young one. This is why you never should have traveled so far from home. You are not able to understand," Halor said, thinking that Daykash Breymer had to be paranoid to think she posed a threat.

Her naive invitation to read her mind made Halor realize that he had never actually examined the thoughts of the rys that he had governed all these years. To see the details of Onja's thoughts could be extremely informative. Insights gained from Onja might perhaps help him prevent future mischief from the rys.

Halor also considered his new responsibility with Onja. The Kwellstan Sect was not pleased with him right now, and his plea to be merciful with Dacian would hardly benefit his career. Halor needed to succeed with Onja and produce a meek and harmless rys. Proving the Daykash wrong about her would be gratifying as well.

Halor decided to cast a control spell upon Onja's mind when he processed her memories. Once she was amenable to his suggestions, he was guaranteed to succeed in curing her antisocial behavior.

He approached Onja. She watched him apprehensively. "What should I do, Master Halor?" she asked.

"Nothing, Onja," he said. Starting to tap his fingers thoughtfully, Halor had to force himself to relax. Entering the thoughts of this young female unnerved him, and he tried to focus on the intellectual nature of the task instead of the intimacy of it.

Onja cringed when his magical mind wound around her memories. The eyes of the tabre priest were glowing white and she hated the closeness of his narrow face. He was ugly to her. Alien and unworthy to call himself her superior. But Onja forced herself to submit. She had to draw Halor in. She let him absorb her memories of the west and she did not hide anything. The more he saw of her activities, the more disturbed he became, and Onja could feel his rising worry.

"What were you doing to this Amar? What do you mean you will contact him again?" Halor demanded mentally.

Onja refused to answer. All the answers were in her thoughts if Halor had the stomach to find them.

The magic of the Nebakarz priest intensified, and Onja gasped. She had not felt the full mental assault of a trained Nebakarz tabre priest before and his strength bashed across her mind like a housekeeper chasing a mouse with a broom. Flickering tendrils of energy erupted over her face and blistered across her chest. Onja wanted to see into his mind but his thoughts were expertly shielded.

Halor cried out with disgust and anger. He gnashed his teeth and spoke mentally. "You wicked foolish thing. You dare think of driving the tabre from Jingten? You'll be locked in some dark pit of stone!" he declared.

Onja decided her time had come. The tabre was off balance with surprise and disdain for her ambition. She summoned the power that she had always felt within her. Thought finally became action. Her lifeforce quickened with the living energy of the cosmos. She felt the world down to its super hot heart. The coldness of the high heavens chilled her with awesome power. Onja was untrained, untutored, and she had never before challenged another magic user, but her might overcame inexperience as her magic awoke from slumbering creation.

Onja threw up her arms and knocked Halor back. Blue fire blazed from her eyes and filled the room. The dark stone walls glittered with snapping energy as her magic reacted with the tabre spells that knit the tower's structure.

Halor stumbled, his mouth agape. He had never dreamed of being struck by such a force. His senses were in disarray and he was temporarily blind until the image of Onja loomed in his mind like the rising sun. He could not protect himself. His mind was laid bare like the covers of a bed thrown open by a ransacker.

Squeezing his mind, Onja looked at his memories. Excitement fed her power. It was so thrilling to attack this tabre and see him crumble. He had never expected her to react with such raw skill. She could not wait to do it again.

Then, amid the vengeful joy of her ascendance, she became truly angry. In Halor's mind she found a maddening detail that proved all of her natural distrust of the tabre.

"You had me beaten so Dacian would disgrace himself!" she shouted.

Halor shook his head. "It was the Daykash. I was against it. Please stop," he whimpered. He had never known such vulnerability was possible. She gripped his SOUL.

"I know who it was!" Onja snapped.

"I'm sorry. I did not want it to happen. Truly. I spoke against your beating. It was reprehensible," Halor insisted and sincerely too.

"It was painful," Onja corrected, but holding him as she did in the wet jaws of her magic, she could sense his regret. Her intellect overcame her emotion and she was inspired. Although she wanted to crush and twist this tabre that she had caught unawares and see him experience pain, it would be better to control. There were tabre enough upon whom she could later deliver the justice of the rys.

"Yes, you are sorry. I do see that. Let me offer you absolution," she whispered in his mind and started casting a spell. She poached from his mind the control spell that he had planned to work upon her. She built upon it, enhancing it with her special genius. This tabre had psychological weaknesses that she could exploit, and she extracted his regrets and reshaped them into a desire to redeem himself. Despite her excitement, Onja did not rush. Halor was powerful and educated and she would have him serve her, and serve her gladly.

When Onja finished her spellmaking, the blue light faded from the room. Halor grabbed the armrest of his chair and pulled himself up. The tabre priest plopped heavily into the seat. He looked at Onja with understanding. He no longer controlled her. He never had and he never would.

"I will do my best to make amends, Onja," he said.

"Your best will do nicely, Halor," she replied and light glinted in her eyes like two tiny shooting stars. "Take me to your library so that I might see what the tabre call wisdom."

Halor nodded wearily and rose slowly from the chair. Onja slipped a supporting arm through his arm like a good daughter helping an elderly father. She patted his arm and said, "I have seen the truth of your heart and know that you never meant me harm. I forgive you."

22. Signs from Vu

After the bold assassination of Wayndo, Amar rode day and night with his companions. Kym, Vame, and Cybar led him south toward the wintering grounds of the Kez where they expected to rejoin Lax Ar Fu. Temulanka warriors infested the countryside but only overtook the wily Kez once. The combat skills of the Kez impressed Amar. With mace, sword, or knife, they outmatched the Temulanka warriors and left none alive.

Amar was proud to have truly earned the respect of these Kez, who now fought to protect him as well as themselves. Kym, Vame, and Cybar had been awed by Amar's success when he returned with Wayndo's head. The mission that had been meant to kill him would instead catapult him to infamy. Amar intended to make the most of it.

The grueling escape had been hard on Urlen. Still recovering from his ordeal at the hands of his Nurati brethren, his stamina had been sorely tested. So they could travel faster, Amar had needed to steal Urlen a horse of his own, and the condemned scholar had flopped like a rag doll on the back of the racing steed. But Urlen had not fallen. He had clung to his mount and kept up with his fearsome criminal saviors. He knew his future was not with the forces of law and order that chased them.

Upon reaching the frontier lands between the domains of the Temulanka and the Sabar'Uto, the hunting parties disappeared. Amar assumed that his pursuers had gone home to reassess their strategy…and their leadership.

After crossing the headwaters of the Hin Lan River, they entered the foothill backcountry of the Sabar'Uto Domain and made a proper camp. Once they were settled in, Amar began an intense workout. Grabbing a sturdy tree limb, he did pull ups until he lost count. Then, while still hanging from the limb, he lifted his legs to work his thighs and abdominal muscles.

When he finally let his cramped hands release the tree limb, he crashed shaking and sweating to the ground. Amar got up and brushed himself off. He rotated his shoulders to work the burn out of his muscles. The light breeze coming from the north quickly feasted on the heat from his sweaty body. A chill set in immediately. The days were shorter and the mountains were starting to bear their fangs at the lowlands. He realized that he would not be able to let himself get so sweaty now that the weather had turned and he still lived outdoors. Amar was tired of the road. He had spent only one night inside since the Patharki had destroyed his tribe.

I am a wild animal living on the land, he thought. He knew it made him stronger, but weariness was creeping in. Even an animal needed a lair.

Amar hoped that he would find acceptance among the Kez as a whole. He would have to make sure that his meeting with Lax Ar Fu went according to his plans.

He slid off his shirt of flexible bronze plates and dropped it into a jingling heap. Working out in his armor made him stronger but he wanted the weight of it off now that he was finally going to allow himself some rest. As he stretched his arms over his head, Urlen brought him a steaming cup of tea. The handle was broken off the simple crockery mug and the tea was weak because their supplies were now scant, but Amar accepted it gratefully.

He settled in by the fire with Urlen. Thin strips of blue and purple were all that remained of the sunset, and the bold dark of the moonless night claimed the landscape.

Amar sipped the hot tea and eyed the skewered rabbit sizzling over their fire. Cybar fidgeted with the skewer, moving it often to keep the meat from burning.

"That head is starting to stink," Vame complained. "It could attract a senshal or bear. You should move it farther away."

Amar disliked their baggage as much as any of them. It hung from the same tree branch where he had been exercising. "It has to stay close. I won't risk an animal stealing it," Amar said.

Vame frowned but did not argue. Amar's amazing success within the tower of Wayndo was just one more reason not to cross the man.

"We'll be to Eferzen Springs in another day," Kym said. "Then you can deliver your prize, Amar."

Amar nodded and dwelled privately on his reunion with Lax Ar Fu. He had not liked the man. He remembered the Lord of the Kez naked and stinking of his lust with the wanton Kelsur Shamaness.

Urlen reached for the kettle to get more tea and burned his finger. He hissed and sucked on the burn.

Amar turned to his rescued scholar. "I have something for you, Urlen," he said and grabbed his backpack. During their flight he had forgotten the scrolls he had lifted from the library.

"What are they?" Urlen breathed and reached out eagerly for the two scrolls. The faint firelight flickered along the edges of the rolled parchments.

"I have no idea, but I thought you might like something to read," Amar said and explained how he had come to take them.

Urlen looked at him with grateful adoration. On top of the extreme kindness of saving his life, Amar now thoughtfully provided the only thing that could alleviate the bleak illiteracy of the primeval forest.

Vame chuckled and commented approvingly that Amar was a born Kez because while assassinating someone he had taken the time to steal something as well.

Turning the rabbit again, Cybar added, "I wish he had stolen some salt."

"Yes, that would have been better," Vame agreed. "Once you are a Kez longer you will not steal such useless things."

Urlen scowled at Vame as his hands lovingly took in the scrolls. He carefully unrolled one of them partway and leaned toward the fire, trying to see the script, but he did not dare take the brittle parchment too close to the orange flames.

The Nurati moaned with impatience and said that he would have to wait until morning.

Amar squinted at the text. The old writing was faint and the light was too weak to read by. "I should have waited until morning, Urlen. Sorry," Amar said.

"Oh, no, no! Do not apologize. This is a princely gift," Urlen insisted and stubbornly peered at the shadowy scroll. "This is definitely in the Temulanka characters."

"Will you be able to read it?" Amar asked.

Urlen nodded vigorously. "I know the characters for seven languages," he said.

Amar was impressed and said so, but the comment visibly depressed Urlen. "I have little use for any of that now. I suppose I shall have to learn how to steal my supper," he said.

"Skill such as yours will not go to waste," Amar said with certainty.

Urlen studied his serious young benefactor. He thought that he had heard some hidden meaning behind Amar's words. He set down the first scroll and opened the other. Even if he could not read the scrolls without risking setting them on fire, he still had to look.

"This might help," Amar said. He removed his warding crystal from its pouch. The blue light glowed upon his face.

Urlen accepted the crystal with a nod of thanks for being allowed to touch Amar's coveted charm, but the light faded by half in his hand.

"Here, I will hold it," Amar said. He took back the crystal orb and it brightened. He held it up to the scroll. Although he was not a scholar like Urlen, he felt stirred by the sight of the writing. It was so removed from the broad strokes of nature that composed the landscape. The characters were small and precise and artificial and they saved the thoughts of man from inevitable death. This was the magic of humans.

Urlen silently read the title and first few lines. "Interesting," he murmured, which annoyed Amar who wanted to know what it was.

"It says that it is Kali Bu's Treatise on Warfare," Urlen elaborated.

"What's a treat us?" Cybar asked.

"Treatise," Urlen corrected with a slip of snobby irritation. "It's a detailed report and analysis."

The explanation did nothing to excite Cybar, but Kym perked up with interest. "On warfare you say?" he said.

"Not really a subject I know much about," Urlen confessed. "But that's good. I will learn something."

Amar picked up the other scroll and had Urlen look at it again. Urlen announced that it was about birds.

"Birds?" Amar repeated, disappointed in the subject.

"A kinder subject than warfare," Urlen said and he continued to read the scroll until the rabbit was ready to be served.

Amar put away his crystal orb and Urlen carefully tucked the scrolls inside his tattered shirt, placated by his brief review of the material. The men ate eagerly and sucked the meat off the bones before lying back to take their rest. Vame was on the first watch and everyone else went to sleep.

The next day as they rode, Urlen barely looked past his horse's neck. He let his horse follow the others while he read in the saddle. Some passages took time to decipher without any references to help him with the Temulanka characters. Urlen missed his library sorely, but it already seemed a lifetime away. He thought of Isamahlia and how she had literally died for looking upon the knowledge stored there.

Stung by his grief, he focused harder on the scroll. To study and to think had always been his refuge from a cruel and unfair world.

By afternoon, they were navigating a steep rocky trail into a canyon. Urlen had to put away his reading and lead his horse. He tired quickly on the rough trail and sweat beaded on his high forehead. He had not had a chance to properly recover from his near death in the Sky Temple. His legs were shaking when they reached the bottom of the canyon. Amar called for a break.

While Urlen rested against his horse, Amar filled his canteen from the creek and brought a drink to Urlen.

"Did you learn anything from the scrolls?" Amar inquired.

Urlen took a deep breath and wiped his forehead. He asked Amar if he knew much of warfare. Sorrow answered silently upon Amar's young face. The light left Amar's eyes as he looked back upon ugly images.

Quietly, Amar said, "I was taught to fight. I have killed. I am a warrior."

"Yes, of course, but do you know of armies?" Urlen said. "That is what Kali Bu wrote of. Armies. How to make one and what to do with it. Or at least it was his ideas about the matter."

Amar glanced discreetly toward the Kez. The three men were spread out along the creek watering the horses. Amar lowered his voice and changed the subject. "Urlen, we will soon reach the camp of Lax Ar Fu, and I have need of a friend. I would have it be you."

Gripped by failure, shame, and grief, Urlen no longer saw value in himself. "What do you see in a weakling like me? You will be a Kez, and I will be a servant, at best."

"If I have your friendship, you will be a Kez as well," Amar said.

The concept stunned Urlen. For him to join the notorious servants of Vu was ridiculous, but it was easy to give his friendship to Amar.

"I am forever in your debt, Amar. Your friend no matter what. Truly I swear it by any God that you believe," Urlen said.

"I have no God," Amar said flippantly. "But I have a friend now." He smiled dreamily and Urlen could not guess what was on the mind of his friend.

Self conscious of his weakness, Urlen said that he was able to continue although Amar had to boost him back into the saddle. Urlen hoped that he could rest soon. To have some peace in which to let his hard unhappiness mellow into scars instead of fresh wounds was all that he craved.

They rode up the canyon, following the little creek. The water flowed on their right on its way to feed the Hin Lan River. The Rysamand Mountains loomed directly ahead of them in the east. Colossal rugged boulders crowded the canyon. They had to leave the water's edge and ride onto a narrow trail that meandered through the boulders. It was an excellent setting for an ambush and Amar expected that Kez warriors had already spotted his arrival.

When Kym halted the party, a flush of nervousness warmed Amar. Atop a boulder, a warrior hooded by a heavy black cloak rose to his full height. An arrow was nocked to his bow.

Kym hailed him in a dialect that Amar could not quite understand. They exchanged a few questions and answers and then the warrior put his arrow back into his quiver.

"Lax Ar Fu awaits you," the Kez guardian said in the dialect familiar to Amar and gestured them onward.

As they rode past the sentry, Amar's back skin prickled with the expectation of an arrow.

"Do you know what they said?" he whispered to Urlen.

The scribe shook his head.

The rough area of boulders diminished and an encampment filled the end of the canyon. Tents and rough huts of small timbers and thatch clustered against the stone walls of the canyon and ladders were propped against the cliffs to allow people to exit the canyon. Most remarkable were the steaming pools of water that broke through the land. The air was warm and moist and the largest hot pool spread back into a cave.

"Do the Kez know every cave in Gyhwen?" Amar asked Cybar.

"Vu gives us shelter so that we can live free of the city lords," Cybar replied with pride.

Amar considered how well the Kez fit into the spaces between the tribal kingdoms. With his tribe gone, he belonged here and he would commit himself wholly to succeeding in his new environment. It was Onja's command.

Kym led the party to the largest hot pool that spread out from the cave. The reflection of the cliff and cave entrance upon the dark water made the cave look like a round roaring mouth. Lazy steam curled off the top of the water, barely visible in the warm afternoon sunshine. A raft was tethered to the shore.

Kym dismounted and informed Amar that he would go into the cave and meet with Lax Ar Fu first.

Amar looked Kym in the eye. He knew that he had earned the man's respect during their journey, but he could not be certain how much, if any, of the man's loyalty he had taken.

Amar said, "You will tell him everything that has happened?" Kym nodded. "After he hears of what I have to tell, I'm sure my Lord will summon you quickly," he said.

"See that he does. I am eager to be free of this stinking head that means so much to him," Amar said.

His authoritarian tone did not seem to offend Kym, but he advised, "To be a Kez brother you must respect and obey our Overlord. Watch how you speak to him."

"I know," Amar said.

Kym delicately stepped onto the raft and the large-bodied warrior momentarily lost his lethal grace and wobbled before gaining his balance. Cybar handed him the pole from the shore, and Kym pushed the raft toward the misty cave.

Three young men came out from the settlement to take the horses from the newly arrived group. Amar untied his unpleasant package from his saddle and set in on the muddy bank. The young men looked at him with open curiosity and glanced at the head-shaped package with amazement. As they gathered the horses, they also studied Urlen and were obviously confused. One of them said something to Vame, who chuckled and shooed them away.

Vame said to Urlen that they had asked if he was a hostage.

Gesturing to his tattered garments, Urlen said, "A pitiful hostage. Do not expect any ransom for me."

"Hostage taking is an ugly chore," Vame commented, presumably from experience.

"The Kez take hostages?" Amar asked conversationally as he watched Kym disappear into the cave.

"Oh, yes. Pays very well if you know what you are doing and get the right people," Vame answered.

"They say Lord Pepum did a lot of that before the Temulanka Sabar'Uto war," Cybar said. "But that was years ago."

"What keeps the Kez busy these days?" Amar asked.

"Oh, we get mercenary work fairly regularly when some local lord doesn't want to get his hands dirty," Cybar explained. "And there is always some call for our traditional duties in the service of Vu to provide security at negotiations. Some feud always needs settling, or at least the parties want to get together to argue again and start the fight all over."

Although Amar tried not to let the memories of Gendahl surface, he wished that he had had the foresight to contract with the Kez and arrange a meeting with the Patharki. It might have intimidated Ginjor Rib, but Amar could not undo the past. He needed to apply the harsh lessons of his destroyed life to the future.

Women came out of the camp and offered food and drink to the men waiting by the hot spring. Fresh bread and cold venison with beer was gladly accepted. Amar took only water with his food.

Dusk came early to the canyon although it was still bright in the forested hills overlooking Eferzen Springs. As the air cooled, the steam thickened. Amar heard the raft moving gently over the water before he saw it.

Kym reappeared, still alone upon the raft. He poled the raft against the bank and gestured for Amar to come. He stood eagerly and tossed the wrapped head of Wayndo onto the raft.

"Come with me, Urlen," Amar said.

"Just you," Kym said.

"Urlen stays with me," Amar said and he offered his scrawny friend a hand.

Urlen did not really desire to offend anyone, but he would stick by Amar. It was the least a friend could do. He took Amar's hand and groaned to his feet. His body had been through more hardship and exertion in the past weeks than he had known his whole life. Unlike his outlaw companions, Urlen was not a physical man and he felt on the verge of falling to crippled pieces.

Kym poled them away from the shore. Amar carefully stretched forward and dipped a finger into the water and quickly pulled it out.

"Hot isn't it?" Kym said.

The hot spring amazed Amar, but he tried to hide his awe. "This must be nice in the winter," he commented.

"Oh, very. In the cave we have carved bathing pools into the rock. It's very wonderful. A luxury for kings and outlaws – not that there's much difference in the two. I can't wait to soak for a while," Kym said.

Urlen privately hoped that he would get the chance to enjoy a bath in the waters of Eferzen Springs.

When they entered the cave, torches burned in sconces along the walls. The rock ceiling rose above them, and stalactites dripped heavily from the incessant steam that wetted the rock. Inside the air was hot and the moisture was soothing to the sinuses of the men.

Sweat beaded up quickly across their faces and their hair became lank. Amar doubted that it would be acceptable to live in such an environment, but then the air cleared and the temperature dropped. They reached the inner bank of the hot spring and a slight breeze of fresh air came from above.

Kym explained that natural fissures in the rock ventilated the back of the cave and pushed the steam out so as to leave it comfortably warm but not too wet in the inner chambers of the cavern. Kym grounded the raft and the men clambered onto the stone floor of the cave that had been worn glassy smooth by centuries of occupation.

Kym and Urlen took torches off a rack and lighted them from a burning brazier. Amar picked up his nasty trophy and followed Kym into the cave.

In the enclosed area, the stink of the head overwhelmed the pleasant smells that wafted from the living chambers where incense burned and food cooked. The cozy orange glow of braziers and oil lamps spread up the striated rock walls and sparkled on flecks of quartz in the natural stone.

A dozen Kez warriors were arrayed around Lax Ar Fu where he awaited the presentation of Amar. Secure from attack, the warriors wore only loose shirts and pants. Habitual daggers were stuck in their belts but other heavier arms were laid aside. Lax Ar Fu wore the same red-dyed leather pants with fringe that Amar had seen him in at the Thievesmeet. Gold and precious stone beads filled the many necklaces that hung over his hard chest. A speckled senshal hide draped his shoulders and was tied with the leg skin and paws of the ferocious beast.

Lax Ar Fu's hair had grown in with black stubble and his eyes were set deep within his heavy black makeup. Amar scanned the cave quickly for the Kelsur Shamaness Loxane. She was not in sight. Other women were present. Their heads and faces were uncovered, and sometimes more than that. They watched from the wings of Lax Ar Fu's audience space. Some of them wore heavy eye makeup as well and crystal beads glittered in their hair.

Without any shame, they watched Amar with intense interest. Amar looked away from them and focused on Lax Ar Fu. He stepped past Kym toward the Kez Lord and dropped to one knee.

It took a moment for him to pry loose the hard knots of fabric from the head wrapping. Lax Ar Fu watched patiently and no one spoke. When Amar unwrapped the head, his memory of Wayndo's living face clashed with the grinning gruesome hunk of flesh within.

Lax Ar Fu came forward. He leaned over the head and inspected the delivery.

"Where is the cock, Amar?" the Kez Lord asked.

"I decided that I did not want to touch him there, my Lord," Amar explained.

A soft murmur moved through the audience as people commented about Amar's confident lack of concern for bringing an incomplete trophy.

"You agreed to bring his head and his cock," Lax Ar Fu reminded.

Amar said, "My Lord must agree that this head is sufficient evidence that your enemy is dead."

"You are a fool to defy me. You will not join the Kez. The deal is broken," Lax Ar Fu decided.

Amar stood up now and projected his voice. "Then Lax Ar Fu would have it said that Wayndo met his death before the revenge of the Kez could reach him."

"Amar," Kym whispered urgently, but Amar held up a hand to keep the warrior from saying more. Amar was pleased that Kym cared enough to caution him, but Amar had to assert himself now or die trying.

Lax Ar Fu's pectoral muscles flexed with agitation, but then he smiled. His teeth were white and complete. "Kym has informed me of the mountain spirit, the rys, that came to you and helped you find Wayndo," Lax Ar Fu said.

"Her name is Onja. She is great and good and I would tell you more of her if my Lord would listen," Amar said, and his passion for the rys blazed on his face.

"I would listen to one as bold as you," Lax Ar Fu announced. "Come tell me of this rys and why she has come among us." He gestured farther into the cave where his furs and mats were spread among low rocks that served as stands for oil lamps.

"Does my Lord accept me into the Brotherhood of Vu and call me a warrior of the Kez?" Amar asked.

Lax Ar Fu admired how Amar insisted on a commitment. Forgiving Amar for only bringing the head had already been difficult, but the shocking assassination of Wayndo satisfied Lax Ar Fu immensely. His spies had reported that the woman of Wayndo had been killed as well. Together they had died in his private chambers in a fortress full of men-at-arms. Already the simple folk of field and cottage spoke of the supernatural murder of the ruthless Wayndo as the vengeance of ghosts. This was exactly the type of rumor that the Kez needed to revive their notoriety among the ruling ranks of the tribes.

Kym had confirmed that the assassination of Wayndo had been the deed of Amar. Lax Ar Fu could not imagine better traits for a Kez warrior than those displayed by Amar. Such daring had great value, and his relationship with the magic creature could not be ignored. Lax Ar Fu wanted access to this strange new power.

"You shall join the Brotherhood of Vu, Amar of no tribe," Lax Ar Fu declared.

New life thudded in Amar's chest. He had expected curiosity and greed for power to lure Lax Ar Fu into accepting him. Gracious now that he had gotten his way, he said, "My Lord is generous to accept me. I will serve you and our God Vu well."

"Come, drink with your Overlord, Amar, and tell me how Wayndo died," Lax Ar Fu invited.

"Gladly, my Lord, and may my friend Urlen join us?" Amar said.

The Kez Lord swaggered over to Urlen and inspected him like he was a sick horse that might have to be put down. Lax Ar Fu's bulging strength overwhelmed Urlen's bookish slenderness. Kym had already told Lax Ar Fu about the rescue of the Nurati from the Sky Temple. Amar's defiance of the God Preem, Judger of men, further proved how bold Amar was.

"Why such fondness for your Nurati foundling? He is weak and soft. I could get you a fine boy if that is what you want," Lax Ar Fu said.

The suggestion was repulsive to Amar but he suppressed his displeasure. "Urlen has served in the household of the Nurati King. He is learned in letters and knowing of many subjects. Seven languages he reads and writes. He has much to give that cannot be provided by any others among us, my Lord," Amar said.

Lax Ar Fu shrugged and turned with a flourish of his fur cape. "Come," he ordered and headed for his living area deeper in the cave.

Amar took the lack of denial as permission and gestured for Urlen to follow him. They followed Lax Ar Fu to his lounge area, and the audience dispersed throughout the cave. The Kez Overlord reclined into a stone bench carved from the bedrock and two women came to his side and delivered drinks and apples. Amar and Urlen were obliged to find seats on the reed mats, but they were given wine and fruit as well.

Lax Ar Fun drew a dagger and sliced his apple. "Both of you, tell me of yourselves. Amar, you first." He crunched on the food and listened attentively with eager eyes.

Amar revealed that he was a survivor of the Lin Tohs massacre and that he had been adrift ever since. He described his encounter with Onja and how she had saved him. Lax Ar Fu was visibly astounded, as was Urlen. Having his legs broken should have left Amar lame, but he was sound and strong. Lax Ar Fu would not have believed it if Onja's existence had not been confirmed by Kym.

Amar concluded, "Onja said that she will come back to me someday."

"For what?" Lax Ar Fu asked.

"I do not know," Amar replied, seemingly with sincerity, although he suspected why Onja had commanded him to be strong, as a prince would be.

He drew the pouch out and removed the crystal. The gently glowing orb of milky crystal laced with blue light instantly transfixed Lax Ar Fu. He leaned forward and put out his hand. Amar reluctantly gave over the orb. As it had before in Urlen's grasp, its light dimmed when deprived of Amar's touch, which gratified him immensely. Lax Ar Fu frowned and cast a suspicious look at Amar.

"Onja made it for me, my Lord," Amar explained.

"What does it do?" Lax Ar Fu asked, letting his eyes be drawn into the magical depths of the charm.

Amar answered that it would help Onja find him and communicate with him.

Lax Ar Fu studied the crystal and even struck it against his stone seat a couple times, much to Amar's silent dismay, but it did not break or even scratch. Appearing bored with it, Lax Ar Fu tossed the crystal to Amar, who snatched it from the air.

Still wondering how best to benefit from Amar's unique relationship with the rys, Lax Ar Fu turned his attention to Urlen. The Nurati scribe related to the Kez Overlord his miserable fall from society.

"And now you ask that I take you in and let you serve?" Lax Ar Fu said.

Urlen resisted his urge to look at Amar for guidance, sensing that would somehow be inappropriate. With his soft voice, Urlen said, "My

Lord, I have been so disoriented and sick with sorrow, I have given little thought to my future. But yes, I would serve the Lord of the Kez to the best of my ability."

"There is always room for another servant," Lax Ar Fu said carelessly.

Although Urlen feared that the title servant might inflict upon him a menial life, he felt he was in no position to protest, but Amar interjected immediately. "My Lord, I believe that Urlen should be as a Kez, a true Brother of Vu."

With a rude dismissive gesture, Lax Ar Fu complained that Urlen probably could not lift a sword or know which end of a spear to use.

"Not all power is at the edge of the sword, my Lord," Amar said. "Every king must have a man of letters so that he can communicate with other kings."

Lax Ar Fu grumbled that Amar knew nothing of kings, yet he looked at Urlen anew. Emboldened by Amar's suggestion, Urlen now tried to sell himself. "My Lord, I would serve you with all that my education can offer. All kings have scribes and so should the King of the outlaws," he said.

Taking up the trappings of a king clearly appealed to Lax Ar Fu who did not mind the effect on his ego. While gnawing on his apple core, he started to talk about how the Kez needed new blood. Since the heyday of the Temulanka Sabar'Uto war, the Kez were not busy or adding to their wealth. Lax Ar Fu even admitted that he had grown lazy. At first when the war had ended, it had been nice to relax and enjoy what had been earned during the warring. But now it had become a habit. More mercenaries were operating independently of his rule. Two of his best lieutenants had been lost to fever the year before and a third died in a flash flood that spring.

Lax Ar Fu paused and looked from Amar and then to Urlen. "Perhaps Vu took my henchmen so I could start over. Both of you are indeed strange and different, and I will take these as signs from Vu that I should see how well you might serve."

The Kez Overlord continued to express his desire that the Kez needed to exert its influence again. Control of the soldier-for-hire market needed to be tightened. All mercenaries should pay homage to him. The tribal kings had forgotten who had the power between the cities. The death of Wayndo would be a reminder, but it was only a start.

"We will trouble our civilized neighbors. They will learn to respect us and share their riches," Lax Ar Fu decreed. "Tell me, Amar, do you think that the Patharki would be a good place to start?"

Hunger for vengeance sharpened Amar's appetite. "Yes," he said simply.

Lax Ar Fu tossed away his apple core and nonchalantly told Amar that he would be given men and get his chance to prove his supposed special value.

"And you," Lax Ar Fu said and wagged his dagger at Urlen. "You will write to all the kings and remind them of how they may honor our God Vu."

Amar and Urlen thanked him in unison, but Lax Ar Fu held up a hand and looked away as if offended by the sight and sound of them. "Speak not to me again until you are true Brothers of Vu. You are nothing until you survive initiation."

23. Initiation

Urlen wished that his time spent suffering in the Sky Temple of Preem could have been applied to his Kez initiation. Entering the Brotherhood of Vu was painfully reminiscent of the slow torture that had nearly killed him.

For four days Urlen had been left to fast on a cleft of rock on a cliff near Eferzen Springs. He sat there in the wind as the delirium of hunger – a now familiar sensation – gradually overtook his mind. Twice a day a jug of water was lowered to him on a rope. Urlen had learned to drink every drop quickly before the jug was pulled back up. He had thought to try to untie the burly knot that held the jug, but he worried that such an act might violate his initiation. At a minimum he suspected that stealing the water jug so that he could drink at his leisure would cause his tormentors and hopefully soon-to-be brothers to cease providing water.

Slumping into the thin slice of shade that his niche provided him, he kept his face out of the bright sun so he could doze. He recalled from the scroll about birds that his location was a suitable nesting spot for a type of hawk, but he could not remember the name of the hawk.

Urlen shifted his stiff body. No one had told him how long he was going to be stuck on the cliff. He worried that he and Amar had been exposed to slow death as a joke, but he clung to Lax Ar Fu's verbal acceptance of them, sour solace that it was. In retrospect he should have accepted Lax Ar Fu's original offer to make him a servant. He doubted that fate involved such an endurance test.

When Urlen had been placed on the cliff, he had seen them lower Amar to another nearby spot. The first day they had yelled back and forth, but that had eventually begun to wear on their drying throats. Now, they just checked in with each other in the morning.

Urlen dozed until the water jug came dangling in front of his face. He jerked awake and reached for it with greedy thirst. He guzzled the water that eased the gnawing pain in his stomach. Urlen was in no condition for a fast and his thin body struggled to squeeze life from a dwindled reserve.

When the jug was pulled up, Urlen fell back against the cliff and stared blearily at the setting sun. During the day, the cliff was bearable. The weather had been fair and the sun was warm, but the nights were cold, especially on the wind-battered cliff. Urlen was amazed that he was still alive. This was a test for strong warriors. He assumed Amar, who was in excellent physical condition, was weathering this lonely fast much better than he was.

The loveliness of the sunset distracted Urlen from his misery. The colors were especially delicate and the scattered clouds shimmered like broken rainbows. Mesmerized by the colorful display, Urlen became enraptured by the setting sun. The colors deepened and spilled onto the land like a woman letting down her hair.

Urlen wanted to touch this beautiful world that beckoned him with heartbreaking beauty. He shifted onto his knees and leaned over the edge of his rock shelf. The blossoming horizon looked so close, like he could just roll into the flowery clouds like a pile of pillows at the end of a bed.

He looked down and the canyon yawned at him with hard rocks and spiny trees. Everything had a strange angle and the landscape heaved and twisted in his vision. Terrified, Urlen pressed himself flat upon the cliff. He shut his eyes but streaking silver blurs burned inside his eyelids until he had to open them. A world impossibly vivid, especially for Urlen who walked always in the small space of his poor eyesight, clawed at his perception with rock hands bulging from the cliff dripping spider webs.

As he cowered in horror, a scrap of rational awareness warned Urlen that he had been drugged. He ran his tongue around his mouth that was suddenly pasty and bitter. His thirst had masked the taste before, but now its pungent flavor revolted him. He threw up.

Urlen had read about such potions that could make people have visions. One priest had called it "seeing with the eyes of god." Urlen had never been terribly curious about experiencing rituals with an altered mind, and he fought for control now.

The sun went down and the stars came out. The celestial lights danced in the black sky. Their streaking trailing colors wove strange patterns, and eventually monstrous distorted beasts of light and color descended from the angry vortex of the disordered heavens and rushed toward Urlen.

He cowered against the rock, struggling to resist his insane urge to flee. The potion injected him with unnatural energy. His limbs shook and he wanted to run. Wrapping his arms around his legs, Urlen hugged his unruly limbs and rocked on his butt. He repeatedly whispered to himself that none of it was real and he must not run.

The moaning wind began to wail, and Urlen shook his head as he tried to dodge the freaky visions that swooped at him from the empty darkness over the canyon. Then he realized that there were words in the wailing and in a lucid flash he recognized Amar's voice. The familiar voice helped to moor Urlen's mind, and he gripped the strand of reality.

Amar was raving. He was screaming with anger at someone called Gendahl. Into the night, he hurled wretched accusations and insults and also shouted other names that Urlen did not recognize.

As the shouting became more strident and threatening, Urlen worried that Amar might plunge off the cliff. He might actually think a vision was real and stride out into empty air to confront an imagined foe.

"Amar! It's not real! We drank a potion. Don't move. Don't move!" Urlen shouted. "It's me Urlen, your friend. Listen to me. Don't move. Just hold still!"

Amar's weird yelling stopped. The gaping silence stabbed at Urlen's ears until the breathing of the wind panted like an exhausted lover.

"Urlen?!" Amar finally yelled back.

"Yes, Amar. We're drugged. Don't believe what you see," Urlen explained.

Silence again, and Urlen imagined how Amar might be squatting in a paranoid huddle as he tried to accept that he was still exposed on a dangerous ledge, even if his eyes told him many other things. Urlen tried to think of something else to say, but he could not concentrate. The shifting darkness made him dizzy. Gripping the ledge, Urlen decided to simply contemplate his hallucinations and try to steer them toward pretty things instead of monsters, but the night seemed only to inspire fearsome shapes and snarling iridescent shadows.

A parade of a dozen demon gods passed him by before the intensity of the drug faded. The energy throbbing through his body began to dissipate. He was left shivering, dehydrated, and still barely able to blink through the rest of the night.

When the merciful dawn came, Urlen was slumped on the cold rock, staring into space. He felt utterly defeated physically and his mind was washed up on a foreign shore. Terrible aching assailed his body, like gravel had been forced into every joint.

When the water jug came, he was too thirsty to even care if it was more of the awful potion. He clutched the jug with shaking hands and drank. His mouth was too fowl for him to even taste if the water was tainted.

With his thirst slackened, he collapsed again, hoping that fatigue would take him into sleep. That was what he needed. Sleep seemed a greater need now than even food. Urlen expected neither and resigned himself to more suffering.

He could not have claimed to know how much time had passed when the rope ladder slapped down on top of him, but it was still day. Urlen fingered the thick braided hemp as if uncertain if it was real.

"Climb up!" a voice commanded from above.

Urlen looked up the cliff but black dots danced in his vision and he could not tell who was up there. Slowly he gathered the rope ladder into his hands. He doubted that he had the strength to climb.

Someone shook the rope ladder impatiently, and Urlen panicked albeit feebly. His strangling fear warned him that he needed help up, but the climb had to be part of his initiation test. If he refused to climb, he was certain that he would be left to die. Then the hawks would come to eat him and lay eggs in his empty chest cavity. That grisly thought sparked some motivation.

Do you want to live? Urlen asked himself. He did, although he was not sure why. Alone in the Sky Temple, he had begged for death more than once, but instead Amar had come. This time Amar could not save him, and Urlen realized gratefully that at least he had been thrown a rope to get out of this suffering death if he would try.

He had never been a man who needed to cultivate his courage. His life had not required it, but it did now. The Kez were outlaws, and some of them were despicable people, but all of them possessed courage.

Urlen rallied what remained of his meager body and started up the ladder. He was gasping for breath before he had even ascended three rungs. His legs shook and threatened to buckle every time he pushed up a step, but he nourished his muscles with his will. Like a woman depleted by prolonged labor he valiantly struggled on because relief would only come after supreme effort. If he kept trying, he would give birth to a new Urlen, a Brother of Vu. Although raw and bleeding from gripping the rough hemp, his hands did not fail him, and the two Kez at the top actually helped him onto the wonderfully flat and solid ground. Urlen deemed it a great act of kindness.

He lay panting, sprawled so thoroughly that he felt like he had sunk roots. When feet kept nudging him roughly in the ribs, Urlen gradually realized that he had fainted. Blearily he opened his eyes but his vision swam.

"Get up," a Kez commanded.

Then the other man said, "Get up or we'll throw you over the cliff."

To be discarded after escaping this five day trial appalled Urlen. He could not let it happen. He pushed himself up onto his hands and knees and then slowly he got his feet underneath him. Swaying badly, he staggered after his impatient tormentors.

They met with Kym and two more Kez warriors that were escorting Amar. Even Amar looked frightful after five days on the cliff. His hair was lank and his eyes were sunken. The fast had pulled his skin tight over his hard muscles. What remained was a hard, lean, and dangerous animal.

Urlen was relieved that his friend had not fallen while in a drug-induced craze. Amar did not seem to notice him. His wide pupils gave his far off stare an especially disturbing darkness.

Kym asked Amar if he recalled the vows he had been taught. At the sound of Kym's voice, Amar slowly came back to himself and then focused on the Kez. He nodded.

"Good. After the waters you shall make your pledge to Lax Ar Fu," Kym said.

The Kez then hustled the two initiates away from the cliff. Even exhausted as he was, Urlen noticed how no one had asked him if he remembered his vows.

Walking after five days confinement on a hard lip of rock proved to be a grueling painful task. Urlen hobbled along. The men gripping his arms kept him from falling, but they forced him forward at a hard pace.

The small group hiked into a pine woodland and other Kez joined them and formed a procession. Farther ahead, drumming started. The procession progressed up and down a small series of hills until they finally started down a merciful incline. Urlen doubted that he could have scrambled up one more hill.

Hundreds of Kez warriors lined the trail that they traveled. Drums throbbed from every direction and the men began to sing. Sometimes Urlen could not understand the songs, but other verses broke through to his wits and he comprehended them. The words were harsh and banging, demanding courage and sacrifice and extolling loyalty.

The singing warriors began to dance and all those who had lined the trail gathered around the procession and pressed closer. The masculine throng was shocking and oppressive after the isolation of the cliff.

Abruptly Urlen emerged from the crowd. A wide pool of water, deep greenish blue, spread out from the rocky edge before him. Two thick wet ropes came out of the water and draped the shore.

As the dancing and singing rose to a climax, Kym pulled the ropes out of the water. He hauled two circular blocks of stone onto the shore. The heavy ropes were threaded through holes drilled in the blocks and the rest of the ropes disappeared into the water.

Urlen and Amar were led forward and each placed in front of a circular stone. The dancing subsided and the singing ground down to a single chant. The surrounding Kez demanded, "Die for us, our brothers. Die for us and Vu will give you life."

The drums and voices pounded the command over and over until the deep pool rippled. Urlen trembled with fear and fatigue. He realized that he had to look like a scrawny cat recently mauled by dogs. He fought the urge to break into weeping. If this initiation was meant to break him, then he was terribly close to being smashed by its crushing force.

But a glance at Amar fortified Urlen. Amar stood with patient indifference. His eyes fixed on a far off place. Urlen reminded himself that Amar held him in high regard, and Urlen resolved to avoid shaming his friend by collapsing with abject fear.

Kym raised his hands and when he brought them down, the chanting ended. The rugged land and trees and empty sky seemed to shudder with shock at the sudden silence.

"Initiates of Vu," Kym began. "You have reached your final test to become a Kez. To be a brother you must be willing to give your life for any brother. We have no other family. We have no other home. We have each other and all that we can take from this world. In this place where the First Peoples quarried stone for their temples and strongholds are gathered the tears of Vu. Our God only cries when one of his servants dies. For all others he cares nothing. Initiates, show now your faith."

Kez warriors began to tie the circular blocks of stone to the wrists of Amar and Urlen. They triple knotted the bonds and made them tight.

With paralyzed dismay Urlen watched himself be tied to the stone. He was breathing in stuttering gasps and shaking.

"Initiates, we ask you to die for us. Cast in your stones and join the Brotherhood of Vu," Kym said.

The Kez warriors stepped away. Urlen and Amar were left with their blocks at the water's edge. Amar finally looked at Urlen.

"I'll be waiting for you," Amar said.

Then without any hesitation, he bent down and pushed his block with his bound hands. With a scrape and a splash, it yanked Amar into the water. It would not be said that Amar had hesitated at the test of the waters.

A great shout went up from the crowd. Urlen cowered beneath the noise and stared in horror at the radiating circles on the water. Amar was gone.

When Urlen did not move, the warriors began their chanting again. "Die for us and become our brother. Die for us and become our brother."

Urlen dropped to his knees and set his hands on the block. He was so weak. He was not sure if he could even shove the stone over the edge. Even the thick knots around his wrists felt heavy.

This trial sought to rip him from his most basic instinct. He was expected to publicly commit suicide, and he wavered. He saw no sign of Amar. The ripples were fading upon the waters of the ancient quarry. Urlen's mind scrambled for answers. Was Amar trying to free himself underwater? Was that even possible? The knots were well tied. And Urlen could not escape the recurring thought that all of this was an elaborate torture devised by Lax Ar Fu. Perhaps this was a false initiation meant to make them simply kill themselves.

Kym stepped closer to Urlen. The burly warrior cast a shadow over the scribe, who cringed in terror.

"You must push the stone in yourself to prove that you would give your life for us," Kym said. The chanting urgently agreed.

Urlen shifted his weight forward with his hands on the stone and got his feet underneath him again. Killing himself might have been easier if he had been given a blade to slash his arms. The thought of being dragged down into the cold water made him shudder. His human will balked from vicious primal fear.

Gazing at the water, Urlen's memories of Isamahlia's execution vividly emerged. She had thrashed as they held her head in the water. Urlen sobbed at the memory. He blamed himself for her death. Perhaps if he joined her in watery death, they would be reunited in a kinder kingdom of dead souls, but Urlen did not really believe his fanciful wish was possible.

******

Amar did not allow himself to think. The test was that he must drown himself, so he did. He would either perish or become a member of the Kez. Both options pleased him. The stone block pulled him quickly to the bottom of the quarry. The cold water shocked his body and made him want to gasp. With his precious breath still in his lungs, he sank with the block to the silty bottom. His first mad thought was to escape his bonds. Amar bent over and tried to push the ropes off his wrists with his feet, but the soggy ropes were swelling tighter. His panic mounted swiftly. Pure death confronted his body, and instinct would allow only frantic yet futile scrambling for survival.

His lungs burned at his betrayal, and Amar fought the mighty need to breathe. The physical demand to breathe would soon force him to draw the deadly water into his deprived chest.

Then the ropes around his wrists pulled him into darkness. He was moving but not up. The watery light disappeared and the cold water oppressed all his other senses. Rocky edges bashed and scraped his body, and then the inevitable gasp for life exploded from his lungs and the painful river of death flooded his strong young body.

Visions from his life raced through his mind as if his soul was determined to set its record in order before leaving his body. The varied scenes from his life were an amazing distraction from oncoming death. His first time riding a horse. His first kill on the hunt. A practical joke played on his father. His wife on their wedding night. The birth of his son…

The light returned and pain pierced his body from the inside out. Several sets of hands hauled him out of the water. Men slapped his face and his back. Back in the blessed realm of air, Amar's body lurched at the chance to breathe. Painful coughing spasms shook him as he hacked the killing water from his lungs, but he was beginning to get air back into his bedraggled body and for that he was utterly grateful. He had not feared death but he would grasp life like the greediest addict.

When he was able to lift his head, Amar saw that he was in a long narrow cave where the waters of the quarry went underground. He saw a dozen Kez warriors along the water's edge set down the long wet rope that they had used to pull him with his stone weight through an underwater tunnel. Dimly, he could hear the chanting outside and then he noticed the warriors picking up a second rope that was presumably for Urlen, but they did nothing except wait with it in their hands.

From the back of the half flooded cave emerged Lax Ar Fu attended by two warriors bearing torches. The Kez Overlord clapped his hands appreciatively and stopped in front of Amar, who tried to get to his feet. He failed, and a man had to grab his arm to keep him from toppling back into the water.

"You can stay on your knees to give your pledge," Lax Ar Fu said.

Amar was physically spent and totally vulnerable yet beginning to feel the sublime joy of receiving a second chance at life, or, in his case, a third chance.

Amar coughed wretchedly and looked at the black water with anguish. The men holding Urlen's rope still were not doing anything. Amar had to try twice before he could get words out. Worried that they intended to let his friend die, he asked for Urlen.

Lax Ar Fu shrugged. "He has not cast in his stone yet. Your runt puppy is afraid," he said.

"What if he can't do it?" Amar asked.

The Kez leader grinned. "They'll skin him alive. It offends us greatly if an initiate refuses us," he explained.

Guilt, which Amar had learned to avoid, caught him with a stinging slap. He had only saved the Nurati scribe from one torture to deliver him onto a new torture.

Amar fended off the stabbing guilt and resolved to live with what he had done. This would not be the last time he caused someone suffering, but then a lookout by the cave entrance shouted. The Kez manning the rope quickly pulled in unison. They hauled the anchor stone over the edge. Urlen was dangling from it. Two men pulled Urlen on to the shore. He was limp and blue. Amar crawled to where the Kez were trying to revive him. Amar started slapping him as well and calling his name.

After some frightful moments of banging on Urlen's slack body, water erupted from his lungs and he coughed and sputtered.

"Breathe! You're not dead. You're a Kez!" Amar cried, very glad to have his friend.

Urlen opened his eyes, and after much coughing, he started to chuckle with delirious delight.

Lax Ar Fu stood over his duo of initiates. "Yes, rejoice. You have lived where many before you have failed. Give your Overlord his pledge and become Kez," he said.

Remembering the vows as Kym had taught them was difficult after so many days of hardship, but they managed to drag the words from their aching throats.

They swore to Lax Ar Fu upon the name of Vu that they would let no woman or property come between them and their Kez brothers. No duty was higher than their obedience to their Overlord. No personal quest would come before their duties as Kez. They would obey no other gods, or lords, or kings. Their only laws would be the rules of the Kez. They would never renounce or leave the Brotherhood of Vu.

"Forever shall I serve my Overlord and brothers and bring glory to Vu," Amar said and Urlen repeated the closing pledge as well.

Lax Ar Fu reached out with his strong hands and clasped their skulls. He laughed. It was always a joy to receive the pledge of new brothers. "You are Kez!" he declared and the other warriors in the cave shouted with approval. Their voices boomed inside the cave and alerted all the others gathered outside that the initiation was complete. Joyous shouts and singing and dancing began anew around the quarry.

Women came forth with towels and thick blankets. They undressed and dried Amar and Urlen and wrapped them in blankets. The women murmured with approval and giggled pleasantly as they tended Amar. Purring seductively, they promised him their pleasures once he was rested. They were not nearly so smitten with Urlen, but they treated him tenderly and he swooned into their care.

He was now the scribe of the Kez and their outlaw exploits would soon enter history.

24. Hunting Grounds

When Amar was recovered from his initiation, Lax Ar Fu gave him fifty warriors to command. With these hardened outlaws, Amar vented his rage upon the new Patharki settlement built over the bones of the Lin Tohs Domain. Sneaking into his homeland had been easily done by her vanquished son, and Amar fell upon the Patharki on a cold quiet night when most were bundled deep in sleep. The few sentries were swiftly overrun, and even though they raised the alarm, it was of little help. The marauders torched the buildings and cut down the residents as they fled the flames. Warriors had no chance to assemble a decent defense, and many died in their burning beds.

A rare meat dawn lighted the land when the Kez were mopping up. The last of the dying and wounded were dispatched and Kez scouts ranged into the fields and woods to track down the few who had accomplished a blundering escape. The ankle deep snow revealed their scattered flights and made them easy to hunt.

Amar spared no one. Women and children died alongside their Patharki men. There was no mercy within Amar in the place where his wife and child had died. He did not pretend to call it justice. His hatred had left him as a sick predator loose in the world.

Amar toured the destroyed settlement, satisfied somewhat by the small revenge. A brisk wind carried the smoke away. The snow had melted back from the burning buildings and left soggy sad patches of ground around each hulk of fallen timbers. He knew the Patharki would start over here, which was more than he could do. That tribe was growing and its rat people were breeding into the lands of their lesser neighbors.

Kym came alongside Amar. He had volunteered to go with Amar as had Cybar and Vame. The blunt face of the veteran Kez warrior was alert after the nocturnal massacre, and his eyes bore the same wild gleam as his comrades. All of them were aglow with feral energy after the killing spree.

"We got them all, Amar," Kym reported after receiving word from the last returning scout.

Amar nodded while staring at the hand of a dead woman that lay across her chest. Her death pose was a parody of peaceful sleep. Without taking his eyes from her, Amar woodenly told Kym that they would camp nearby and leave the next day.

"Where will we go next?" Kym asked.

Some crows squawked in the bare branches of nearby trees and one bold one flew down and landed near the dead woman.

Shaking off his contemplation of the female corpse, Amar answered, "To see Ginjor Rib."

"Attack his citadel?" Kym asked with shock. It was far too big a task for fifty men, no matter how strong, cruel, and clever.

"No, Kym. Not to attack. To speak with him. He needs to retain the services of the Kez to protect his frontier settlements," Amar explained. Sweeping his hand around the still smoking ruins, he added, "The Patharki are obviously bedeviled by nomad raiders."

Kym chuckled agreeably.

In a lightly wooded hilltop across from the grazing commons of the settlement, Amar set up his camp. He had always liked this spot. It commanded a nice view of what had once been the farmlands of the Lin Tohs. To the east rose forested foothills, and looking over them like stern parents were the Rysamand Mountains. The snows were now thick upon the cold foreboding peaks. Amar sighed and thought of Onja. He wondered what her home was like within that colossal fortress of ice and stone where magic held court.

With the smell of the burning settlement on the wind, he fell asleep. The dark peace of his wearied collapse did not last with the restless spirits of his family and lost tribe so close. In a dream his wife came to him. She was warm and sweet and the smoothness of her bare skin took away all the pain. Once more he was Gendahl, young and happy and full of himself.

Then the round sweet face of his baby son smiled to him. The infant was nestled between him and his wife and they shared the tender pleasure of admiring their offspring. The clarity of the dream was bliss. Amar put out his little finger and the baby boy clasped it. He could almost believe in a kind and loving God, but nightmare forces swept in and trampled the dream into the sucking mud of nightmare.

He saw the eyes of his son go cold and dead. Blood spattered his wife. In the nightmare, Amar lurched out of the blood-soaked bedding but he could not see his enemies. To escape the biting agony, his mind banged on the doors of wakefulness.

"Amar, I'm here."

He recognized the voice and its songbird sound drove back all the misery. The images of ruin were gone, and into the peaceful void appeared Onja. Her beauty brought forgetfulness. She shimmered inside an aura of light blue. A long loose black dress obscured her body, but her charming face was radiant and her eyes glowed with the forces of the natural world.

"Let me help you." He heard her words but her lips did not move.

She had come to save him from his nightmare. She was perfect mercy. "Are you here?" he asked, speaking aloud in the dream.

"I am in Jingten, but my mind has come to you. This is no normal dream and my words are real."

Onja then asked him why he had come back to the place of his worst sorrows. Speaking inside the dream, he explained what had happened since last she saw him. As part of a larger Kez plan to intimidate many tribes, he had logically chosen to hurt the Patharki as an example.

"I have looked upon what you did to those people last night. You were cruel."

Somehow Amar knew that she was only making an observation and not judging him.

"I can help you truly have your revenge upon Ginjor Rib. Do you trust me, Amar?"

"Of course," he said.

"You will have to let me use my magic through you when the time comes."

"As you wish, Onja."

She smiled and her happiness helped Amar forget the recent trials of his nightmare. Although his loyalty and love for her were clear enough, Onja knew that giving him revenge upon Ginjor Rib would forever cement his utter devotion to her. Beholding the quickening of her creation excited her. Already Amar had done much with his opportunity, and, although rys had no magic to see the future, Onja knew that he would become a warlord whose name marched across the ages.

Onja commanded him to go to the citadel of Ginjor Rib as he had planned. She would contact him then and they would make their plan.

Quickly Amar told her that it was good to see her.

"It was good to see you too, Amar."

Her image withdrew from his mind and he opened his eyes. He had been asleep all day and a dull dusk was creeping toward night. The sky was heavy with clouds and a light snow had begun.

When he sat up, he realized that his warriors had formed a ring around him. They crouched a short distance away and gaped at him with awe.

"What is it?" he asked.

Cybar said, "She has come to you, hasn't she?"

"How did you know?" Amar asked.

Cybar answered that they had all seen a sphere of blue light move across the land and stop over his body.

Amar explained that he had spoken with Onja inside his dream. Then he ordered everyone to assemble for departure. He did not care if it was night. They needed the falling snow to cover their tracks, and he was eager to reach Ginjor Rib's citadel.

******

Amar and his band of Kez took a circuitous route through the wilds into the Patharki Domain. They approached the citadel on a southern road, appearing to come from the opposite direction of where the massacre had occurred. The cold weather deepened as winter came hard and early. The prospect of indoor warmth was welcomed by the warriors, except Amar. He had never been to Dajendarli, the capital of the Patharki Tribe, nor had he ever met Ginjor Rib, but he had plenty of other memories to make him hate the place and the man. When he looked upon the citadel of Ginjor Rib, he thought of Temdi, his loyal Infoh whose head had been taken in place of his. Had Temdi's head been tossed upon the floor of this citadel? Amar shuddered at the thought of crossing the same floor to speak with the ruler of the Patharki.

He struggled to master his boiling emotions. While still outside Dajendarli, he sent three representatives into the town to arrange an audience with the Patharki King.

The citadel of Ginjor Rib was an impressive structure. It rose above the town like a ram among lambs. The citadel was built into the outer facade of rock that formed the north rim of a canyon carved by the Tutter-Shen River. Beyond the citadel spread a broad flood plain, and the town squeezed between the river and the citadel in a jumble of wood and stone buildings. The citadel was the tallest building Amar had ever seen. Its stone block walls rose against the natural rock in a half cylinder topped by parapets and long narrow banners that slithered in the wind. A solid stone rampart surrounded the base of the citadel, and Amar estimated that it would take many men and much determination to breach the defenses of Ginjor Rib.

While waiting for the return of his representatives, Amar and his comrades camped across the newly frozen river. They did not conceal themselves, and Amar expected to be invited inside. Lax Ar Fu had by now sent all tribal leaders letters written by Urlen reminding them of the crucial services that the Brothers of Vu offered for inter-tribal relations. Of course, implied by the reminder was the threat that the Kez did not want to be ignored or circumvented in their traditional business. As secure as Ginjor Rib was, it would be unwise of him to refuse or attack the emissary of the Kez Overlord. He may have need of mercenaries some day and the Kez were capable of causing him and his tribe many minor miseries indefinitely.

Amar strolled along the riverbank. His warriors hung back, sensing his turmoil. Dead grass and reeds stuck out of the ice and snow at the river's edge like slender tombstones of seasons past. Amar dusted the snow off a squat boulder and sat down. Staring at the ice, he thought of Onja.

Amar tried to draw strength from his confidence in her, but his sadness and hatred were sabotaging his resolve.

When the biting cold let go of his body, he knew that she was coming to him. The air suddenly felt balmy against his exposed face and he closed his eyes.

"Amar, I find you upset," Onja commented.

He confessed that he did not think he could go before the destroyer of his tribe and family and calmly state his business. "My emotions are untamed," he whispered.

Onja counseled, "Savor these final hours as you stalk your victim. The senshal watches the deer for hours or days before striking for the kill. Sometimes the beast even lets chances to kill pass because it enjoys knowing that it can take its prey at any time. I have seen into the mind of the senshal and felt its perilous pleasures. Now go Amar and look upon Ginjor Rib and be joyful in the knowledge that his heart is beating its final beats. You will wipe his blood from your sword this night."

Her speech roused him from his useless misery and he asked her how this would be done. Onja told him that she had been learning new ways to use her magic. In addition to her ability to send her thoughts to him, she would cloak him with her magic so that he could move about the citadel unseen. Once Amar entered the citadel, he should listen for her to give him instructions in his mind.

"Have faith in me, Amar. We will not fail."

"You are kind to me, Onja," Amar said, but he heard no reply and the cold crashed against his flesh. She was gone.

His warriors were returning from Dajendarli. The three men on horses were spread out on the frozen river. Although it was a solid freeze, there was no reason to be reckless and encourage the ice to break by riding close together.

Amar walked back to his camp. When his returning warriors reported that Ginjor Rib invited Amar and all his company to a banquet that evening as respected guests, Amar's eyes narrowed with suspicion.

"A trap," Kym suggested readily.

Lifting his eyes toward the citadel, Amar said, "Would we not all enjoy solid walls and a warm fire?"

"Easily enough gotten at one of Dajendarli's inns," Kym replied.

"We cannot turn down the hospitality of the Patharki King," Amar said and then he turned to address all the warriors. "Do not worry about a trap from Ginjor Rib. My fair benefactress Onja has just spoken to me and luck will not serve the Patharki tonight."

Sly superior smiles broke out among the Kez. They were amazed to be a part of something new. There had never been a Kez like Amar before and they were excited to follow a man allied with a magic mountain rys.

The Kez crossed the river and entered the town. Foot traffic stepped aside from the ominous column of hardened warriors dressed mostly in black. Having no specific tribal origin, the Kez always looked foreign with their mix of traits from all regional stocks. The townspeople warily sized up the Kez, and all onlookers dwelled upon the young warrior at the fore of the group. His youth seemed inappropriate to lead such a group of veteran mercenaries.

Amar's heart thudded hard in his chest, driven by a confluence of emotions, but he armed himself with Onja's advice and relished entering his hunting grounds. His grief and jibbering weakness were buried with Gendahl. A narrow bridge across a moat conveyed them inside the outer wall of the citadel. They were vulnerable as they rode single file into the fortress, and Amar tensed for a possible attack.

Patharki warriors glowered down from the ramparts, and a squad of warriors awaited the Kez at the entrance. An extraordinarily tall man with thick long black hair stood before the warriors. A chestplate of glistening bronze inlaid with a jade image of the war God Zatooluh covered his broad chest, and he wore a heavily stitched suit of fine leather dyed a deep wine color. A sword with an impressively large ruby on its pommel stuck out from a scabbard also adorned with rubies. The tall Patharki warrior had high cheek bones and widely set eyes, and a bad scar at the corner of his mouth.

"I am Ulan, war chief of the Patharki and first man to Ginjor Rib, our great King," he introduced himself. "Who here is Amar?"

Amar dismounted and moved with casual confidence as if he had arrived at the homestead of a trusted friend. The height of Ulan was intimidating and Amar judged that the long arms of the warrior would be a formidable advantage if they had to fight.

"I am Amar, emissary of Lax Ar Fu, Lord of the Kez," Amar said and then bowed politely. This seemed to amuse Ulan who showed a toothy grin.

Ulan scanned the group of grizzled Kez on their horses and asked, "Is it the way of the Kez to put a boy in charge of men?"

Amar did not take the bait and answered cheerfully, "The Kez honor and reward ability."

Ulan knit his brow, surprised that Amar's temper could not be easily provoked. "You and your warriors will be given food and shelter. Amar, our King has words for you to return to Lax Ar Fu." Ulan spun and the warriors behind him parted. The rest of the Kez dismounted and gave over their mounts to boys who were hustling out from the stables built into the foundations of the outer rampart wall.

The squad of warriors in Ulan's company flanked Amar as he entered the citadel. They traveled a hall that took three sharp turns before opening onto a broad receiving hall that was less obviously defended. Only widely spaced narrow windows near the top of the ceiling let in cloudy daylight. Torches and braziers cast bleary orange light that bounced among the pillars like blind birds.

Ulan led his Kez guests into an adjoining hall. Serving women garbed in black from head to toe with only eye slits in the fabric were setting long tables with pitchers of wine and plates of bread and cheese. A fire roared in a great fireplace at the end of the banquet hall.

"Wait here and refresh yourselves," Ulan said.

Amar thanked him and offered the Patharki praise for their hospitality.

"We are a gracious people," Ulan said and Amar could barely keep himself from spitting at him in disgust.

The Patharki left the Kez alone. The warriors sauntered down to the fire to warm up or sat on the benches to inspect the food and drink that had been set out for them. No one immediately ate or drank. Amar shared in their suspicion that the food might be poisoned. Although he rarely took strong drink he grabbed a goblet and poured a full measure of the heavy red wine. He sipped it and then drank more. He believed that Onja would help him if he was stricken by a poison.

He felt warmth in his stomach and a creeping pleasure move up to his head, but it felt like only alcohol. When Amar seemed unhurt by the wine, the other warriors began to pour, but Amar cautioned them not to drink too much.

"We'll likely have need of our sword arms and our wits," he said.

While the others ate, Amar sat at the head of the banquet table with his back to the fire. The heat from the fireplace pressed through his cloak and armor. He folded his hands on the table and took no food. Although he had mastered his emotions, the thought of eating the food of Ginjor Rib revolted him.

His warriors often glanced at the double doors that led to the main hall and seemed to be the only way in or out. They spoke quietly about how good it was to warm up inside. Their guarded conversations receded from Amar's hearing and he welcomed the creeping presence of Onja as she slipped into his mind.

"You are performing bravely," she praised for only him to hear. "Your enemy plots to kill you and your men after a feast tonight. Then he will have decoys ride out on your horses so he can say to Lax Ar Fu that you left and he did not hurt you."

Amar tried to think his words instead of speaking aloud and discovered that he could communicate with her mentally even when awake. He asked Onja what he should do. "When the King summons you to an audience, strike when you see that my magic is with you." she said.

"What of my men?" he asked.

After a pause, Onja simply replied that they should be sent away. She then left Amar's mind. He placed a hand on his chest. The warding crystal was hot in its pouch against his skin. Beside him Kym reached for a pitcher of wine but Amar grabbed his wrist to stop him.

Quietly he said, "When I am summoned to my audience with Ginjor Rib, take all the men and go. Just walk out of here to the stables, get your horses and leave. Fight if you have to, but go quickly before they realize what is happening."

The other Kez at the table dropped their conversations and listened. Amar continued in a low voice and informed them that the Patharki planned to murder them that night.

"She has told you this," Kym said.

"She has told me," Amar confirmed.

"Then you must leave with us," Kym declared and several other warriors agreed.

"I came to have my audience with Ginjor Rib. I am the emissary of our Lord Lax Ar Fu, and I will faithfully perform my duty," Amar said. "This I can do alone. Go back across the river and await me."

His warriors frowned, unhappy with the strange orders. Clearly they would have further protested his mad plan, but the double doors swung open and Ulan filled the doorway with a squad of warriors at his heels.

"You are summoned by our King, Amar," Ulan announced.

Amar stood from the table and cast one more meaningful look at Kym to confirm that his orders would be followed.

As Amar passed through the doorway, Ulan gestured to the table and urged the Kez to relax and enjoy. "A feast is being laid out for you tonight. Let it not be said that the Patharki do not know how to reward the servants of Vu," he said.

Amar brushed by the Patharki soldiers standing in the hall. Their black cloaks and smooth round helms roused hard memories from the day his tribe died. But they were mice among big game, and Amar reminded himself to focus on his prize.

He fell into step beside Ulan and said, "Ginjor Rib honors me with so quick a reception."

"Yes, it is an honor. Our King holds court less and less," Ulan said.

Surrounded by a dozen Patharki men, Amar went with Ulan into the main hall of the citadel. The great pillar-lined hall terminated at the very heart of the citadel where the building met the wall of the canyon. When Amar reached the Patharki King, the raw natural rock loomed behind the throne. Oil lamps were artfully arranged in the crannies of the rock wall. They lighted a broad chair carved from the natural stone and polished to a glassy shine. Rich amber and green jade adorned the throne that was far finer than the wooden seat from where the lords of the Lin Tohs had once presided.

The grandeur of the throne was not embodied in Ginjor Rib. He was a thin old man, bent forward in his seat as if the fur-lined robe that draped his shoulders was a burdensome yoke. His face was long and thin and his narrow beard was white. Sunken eyes regarded Amar with a crotchety gaze.

Amar had imagined the vicious architect of his tribe's genocide as fit and dangerous. But the evident frailty of the Patharki king prompted no thoughts of mercy in Amar, who enjoyed that Ginjor Rib suffered ill health.

Ginjor Rib squinted his rheumy eyes. "Who is this boy that Lax Ar Fu sends to treat with me?" the King asked.

Amar graciously moved down to one knee and dipped his head. "A young man, Patharki King," he corrected. The spirit of Gendahl choked, but the prowling mind of Amar was pleased by his artful reply.

"I bring you Amar of the Kez, my King," Ulan said.

Ginjor Rib settled back into his throne and appeared grateful for the support of the broad chair. "Yes, the letter spoke of you, Amar. Your Lax Ar Fu suddenly seems to think himself a man of letters. Tell me what scribe have you robbed from some proper family and forced to put your demands onto writing skin?"

The tone of Ginjor Rib made it plain that he had disliked the formal requests of Lax Ar Fu. "Patharki King," Amar said, staying on one knee. "No man serves Vu by force. All of my Kez brothers are happy in their place, even the one gifted with the ink and stylus is grateful for his chance to perform his art."

"Bah!" Ginjor Rib said with a couple drops of spittle flying from his loose lips. He put out his hand and an attendant gave him a ragged scroll that he promptly threw at Amar. It bounced off Amar's shoulder, and he raised his smoldering eyes to meet those of Ginjor Rib.

The Patharki King continued, "How dare the Kez demand a retainer?! What need have we of outlaws who fancy themselves negotiators?! The Patharki need no help in any of their affairs."

"Patharki King, I ask that you reconsider. The Kez have much to offer. And with the payment of your annual retainer we would serve at your convenience. We can provide mercenaries. We can arrange secure

Rys Rising: Book I

meetings with other leaders you may wish to meet. And we are the watchers of the frontiers. We know first when danger prowls close to civilization for we live in the wilds as comfortably as owls and hawks, watching night and day. We can bring warnings of marauders at your frontiers and even offer defense," Amar said.

Suspicion deepened the lines on Ginjor Rib's face. "Yes, marauders," he hissed. "We have had word of marauders on our northeastern border."

"In the land that was recently the Domain of the Lin Tohs?" Amar asked.

The apt question startled the Patharki leader. Quietly he asked Amar what his tribe was before joining the Kez.

"I am of no tribe, Patharki King," Amar replied, but his eyes twinkled with the lie.

"I hear the accent of the Lin Tohs upon your tongue," Ginjor Rib said and the guards and Ulan perked up.

Amar, still on one knee with Ulan hovering to his left, remained calm. "My birth is my shame, Patharki King. I am bastard born. My mother was of the Lin Tohs, but she ran into the wilds and served the Kez instead of exposing me and killing herself. That is why you hear the Lin Tohs in my speech but I am not of that tribe," he said.

It seemed a reasonable explanation, and Amar heard Ulan take a breath that seemed to indicate relief. But Ginjor Rib could see the eyes of the young man before him and he was not so sure. "Ulan, what viper have you brought before me?" he demanded.

Amar felt the warding crystal around his neck become hot. Knowing that the power of Onja was with him, he sprang into action. He pulled a small dagger from his boot and stabbed Ulan in the back of a knee and jumped to his feet.

The towering war chief bellowed but still lashed out with a hard sweep of his arm. Amar dodged to the right. The guards with Ulan lowered their spears, but then they halted in confusion. Looking around as if bugs buzzed in their ears, they tried to locate Amar, but no one seemed able to see him. Then the lamps and lanterns went out and darkness grabbed the room with thick hands.

Despite the sudden dazzle and then dark, Ginjor Rib spotted the shadow coming at him. When the hard fierce grip of a strong young man took his throat, he saw clearly the face of Amar. An eerie blue light outlined his body in an enchanted halo, and Ginjor Rib's gasp turned into a gurgle as Amar squeezed his throat and flung him to the floor.

"The King!" Ulan shouted when he heard his leader's muffled cry. Ulan shifted his weight onto his good leg and yanked out his sword.

Magical fog still stymied the other guards, who clutched their spears and poked tentatively at the dark.

Amar's senses flared with enhanced sensitivity. The darkness did not impede his vision and he saw everyone in the room as detailed shapes. And he heard with greater clarity. Beyond the shouts of shock and fear, he could hear the scrape of shifting feet on the stone floor and the desperate rattling breath of the Patharki King.

With the smoke of the extinguished lamps stabbing his nostrils, Amar jumped down from the throne. Ulan confronted him with a blind sweep of his sword. The will of the mighty war chief seemed to be giving him some resistance to whatever Onja was doing to the other guards.

Amar blocked the sword and pushed the blade aside. He danced around Ulan and sliced the man's other leg. He cried out and whirled. The sword had cut deeper than the dagger, and Ulan took one hand from his sword and clamped it over the bleeding gash in his leg. Stooped and hurting, he held his weapon defensively.

"What sorcery is upon us?" he snarled.

Amar moved around him and back to Ginjor Rib. He could smell the fear sweat of the aged king and it beckoned him. Giving action to his agony, Amar plunged his sword into the vitals of Ginjor Rib. He did it three more times. The Patharki King screamed and said no and begged for help.

Amar stepped back. He heard the blood dripping onto the floor from his blade and the splat of it spurting from the old man's butchered abdomen. The fresh meaty smell was exhilarating. Amar had delivered a slow death to him. There could be no recovering from the damage done to his vitals, but death would not be immediate.

Amar had his vengeance. It set nothing right and redeemed him not from wickedness, but Amar was satisfied that the demands of sweet justice had been executed.

He ran down the length of the great hall. The fires in braziers and lamps snuffed out in his presence and darkness guided him from the heart of the citadel. From all directions he heard shouts.

Men-at-arms confronted him in the sharply turning corridor that connected the main hall to the entrance. Potent with power, he cut them all down. His mind seemed to always know where the others' weapons were striking so he could block them. And his eyes saw immediately where to cut and kill or maim.

At the last turn in the corridor, five men rushed him. Amar jumped and grabbed a metal sconce in the wall and swung his feet at his adversaries. He struck the middle man in the chest and knocked him down. Then he let go of the sconce and landed within the small group. He spun hard with his sword blade out and cut down two of them. Amar ran on and slipped through the heavy gates that had been left partway open.

Bodies littered the yard between the citadel and the outer rampart wall. The Kez warriors had just fought their way out and Patharki warriors were rushing around in disarray. They had been thrown off their purpose by the abrupt escape of the Kez who they had expected to slaughter later. Some riders had just started galloping out the gates to chase the Kez through the town.

The sun was going down. Cold blue and purple clouds streaked across red sky, and its bloody glow illuminated the high curved wall of the citadel. Amar paused to admire the beauty of the sunset on the building. With Ginjor Rib suffering at the foot of his throne, the world had been remade with twice its original beauty, and Amar beheld every detail with rapturous joy.

"They will not see you," Onja whispered in his mind.

Darting between the erratic Patharki and delighting in his enchanted stealth, Amar ran to the stable. Inside the stable there was the faint warmth of animals and the mingled odors of leather, hay, and manure. Amar found his horse munching on hay.

He saddled his horse and rode out of the stable. He actually joined a group of mounted Patharki and exited the main gate. Once they entered the town, Amar broke off onto a side lane. The narrow twisting streets of Dajendarli worked against him and he twice had to backtrack out of blind alleys before finding the edge of town and the river.

His Kez warriors were already across the frozen river. Amar saw their scattered figures gathering on the opposite river bank. Their Patharki pursuers were just leaving the town by the main road and spurring their mounts onto the ice. Amar yelled and snapped the reins. Parallel with the Patharki he raced across the river.

When he reached the middle of the river, Onja's powers turned to another task. The giant groaning rip of snapping ice smacked the river and Amar's horse faltered a few steps on the buckling ice. Shouts of dismay erupted from the Patharki. Some of the horses and men were already breaking through and being sucked into the awful rushing water below.

Amar did not look back. The cracking and screaming increased as he reached the shore and his loyal Kez warriors gathered around him. Their steaming breath caught the last of the daylight as the temperature dropped into the night. The abnormal breaking of the river ice consumed some Patharki and drove the others back to the town.

"Ginjor Rib has been punished for refusing to pay the Kez!" Amar announced and a cheer went up. The Brothers of Vu knew that their notoriety was once again on the rise with Amar to terrorize the masters of civilization.

The band of Kez warriors returned to the wilds and left the stunned town of Dajendarli behind. No more pursuers came forth from the citadel, and, as the life of Ginjor Rib ebbed, the waters of the Tutter-Shen gradually froze over again.

Amar set a leisurely pace on his way to the Domain of the Nurati Tribe. He wanted to make sure that news of his supernatural visit to the Patharki had time to travel ahead of him. As he predicted, the letter from Lax Ar Fu that demanded a retainer for the Kez was heeded by the Nurati King. Coupled with the terrifying news of the fate of Ginjor Rib, the letter was doubly impressive when the king recognized the script of his former scribe that had been left to die in the Sky Temple of Preem.

The Nurati offered the Kez no hospitality. When Amar's agents appeared at the city gates of Telop, they were met by servants of the king who bore chests of gold, silver, and iron. Excuses were made that fever afflicted the royal household and that it would be best not to have guests. Amar did not mind the lie and he departed with the Nurati's tribute. He dispatched men to hurry it back to Lax Ar Fu.

The next two tribal leaders that he called upon paid the Kez their retainers without complaint. Amar enjoyed the powerful effect he had on people. The nervous respect in their eyes fed a hunger in his soul that he had not fully realized was there until he tasted of success.

Onja, however, had been absent from his mind since the breaking of the ice. Before sleeping every night, Amar held the warding crystal in his bare hand and silently praised her and thanked her for intervening on his behalf with her power. He missed her presence, but he was confident that she would return to him. He just did not know when.

Because he could not assume her power was with him when he arrived at the royal city of the Temulanka Tribe, he did not act when the tribe barred its gate and told him and his warriors to be gone. He only ominously stated that he and Lax Ar Fu would not forget that the Temulanka had spurned their chance to retain the good will of the servants of Vu.

Their time will come, Amar told himself and decided to return to Eferzen Springs. The winter solstice had come and gone during his travels, and he required some rest and shelter from the cold before continuing south to the Domain of the Sabar'Uto Tribe.

25. The Sabar'Uto Princess

The unpunished sins of the world will beget the dro-shalum. ~ Sabar'Uto folk belief

A love song caressed the music chamber of the Sabar'Uto King's eldest daughter. The young female's voice gathered sweet energy as she imagined the ardor of some mythical perfect husband. "My devotion will bring fine sons, and forever will his strength protect me." She finished the final line and her preferred lady-in-waiting plucked the last note on her harp.

"Let's practice it again, Demeda. I want our performance to be the best," said the lady-in-waiting.

"Mallah, why be so competitive? There's no prize," Demeda said. She flopped onto a pile of cushions and ran her fingers through her lustrous black hair.

Mallah huffed. "Don't quit now. We almost have it perfect," she complained.

A gaggle of servants rushed by in the hall. Their tittering indicated some rare excitement. Sensing hot gossip afoot, Demeda sat up. "Whatever are they about, Mallah?" she wondered. "That's the third time I've heard running in the hall."

Mallah did not look up from the harp as she tightened a couple strings. "Some cook has probably cut her hand and they are rushing about to get bandages," Mallah proposed absently.

"We are no where near a kitchen," the princess protested. She got up from the pile of down-stuffed pillows.

Mallah looked up now, perturbed to see her cousin distracted.

Princess Demeda put on her slippers that had a ruby set over each toe. She casually walked about in more wealth than a whole village could produce in a year, but she thought nothing of it. The Sabar'Uto were wealthy and powerful. The tribe boasted that it set the standard for civilization and that the Gods had revealed the gifts of art, state, and agriculture to it before all others.

"You never finish anything!" Mallah complained and got up from the harp. She was plump compared to the graceful and lithe Demeda and her nose was big. Some women whispered vindictively that Demeda favored her cousin Mallah because her portly plainness enhanced the beauty of the princess, but Mallah had no reason to think ill of Demeda. The Princess had never showed herself to be anything except a true and kind friend with her only fault being a tendency to bore easily.

Demeda swung open the lightly polished wood doors of the music chamber and surprised three maids in the hallway. The young women bumped into each other as they halted and bowed to their mistress.

"What is going on?" Demeda demanded.

Mallah came up behind her and rested her chin on Demeda's shoulder.

The maids each bowed again and then by some unseen agreement one of them emerged as their representative and spoke. Her dark eyes flashed with fear, like a little child who has been told a scary story.

"My Princess, the men are all in a dither. The soldiers are moving from the palace. Word is the city gate has been barred," a maid said.

"Why?" Demeda asked and put her arm around Mallah as her friend moved beside her.

The maids all glanced at each other. They acted like a curse would be laid on them if they answered with any detail, but finally the one who spoke leaned forward and whispered, "It's the Kez, my Princess."

Although Demeda knew little of the affairs of men, she could think of no reason why the Kez should cause such a commotion in the Sabar'Uto royal palace. As far as Demeda knew, the Kez were outlaws that claimed to serve some god, which one she could not remember if she ever knew.

The maid had wit enough to see that her princess did not grasp what was happening. All servants knew that their cloistered mistresses were often the last to hear of the deeds done in the outer world.

"My Princess, there is a new warlord among the Kez. They call him Amar. People are saying that he is dro-shalum," the maid explained.

It meant curse-demon, as in a curse that has taken the physical form of an avenging beast. Demeda frowned thoughtfully. She was not some peasant to be enthralled by supernatural fears.

"Nonsense. He is just an outlaw," she scoffed.

The three maids shrank back with grave expressions as if their Princess's disregard for the dro-shalum had turned their luck bad.

"Oh, my Princess," the maid continued. "There are stories flying across the land. It is said that this new Kez warrior can sneak with the shadows. That kings wither and die in his presence."

The maid's drama finally impressed Demeda somewhat. "Then let us go see this shadow warrior," she declared with obvious glee to have something interesting going on.

Mallah poked her side and admonished her royal friend that she would get them in trouble.

"We won't get caught," Demeda said confidently because she was adept at sneaking about the palace.

"My Princess, he is not coming in the palace," the maid said. "As I said, the city gates are barred against him and will not be opened."

"Why should my father, the King, fear a lowly outlaw?" Demeda said.

The maid meant to answer, but Demeda was not interested in talking to her any more and she shooed the women away. They trotted down the hall intent on their gossip. The Princess withdrew into her chamber with her friend.

"Have you heard any of this talk?" Demeda asked.

Mallah shook her head and settled onto a square green cushion next to the harp.

"Don't you find this interesting?" Demeda said.

Mallah answered, "Yes, but I can't do anything to find out more. We are the last to hear of anything. You know this, so why don't you be patient." She strummed the harp and smiled slightly with satisfaction.

A sour look crinkled Demeda's young and delicate face. It was annoying that servants had better access to the happenings of the world than she did. She got most of her news and gossip from her brothers. She was rather crafty at teasing information out of them. But Demeda reflected that lately they had been tight-lipped, preoccupied even.

Something was going on, and Demeda was not content with the ignorant talk of servants. She tugged on Mallah's elbow and told her to come along. Her friend cast upward an affectionate look from her dark eyes and resigned herself to the Princess's desire for mischief.

They went to Demeda's dressing room and grabbed a pair of cloaks and tepas. Demeda whipped the close-fitting tepa over her head and started tying shut the face flaps with its row of small bows. Her fingers worked the strips of fabric swiftly. She had a lot of practice keeping her face covered, as was required of all females past puberty.

"We're going outside?" Mallah asked as she swung on her cloak.

"You can see very little from the women's circle," Demeda noted.

Mallah had little expectation of seeing anything no matter how far they got, but joining her royal friend on her unsanctioned outing might be fun.

The palace of the Sabar'Uto King was a massive structure that rivaled all other known constructions of man, even temples. The stone palace was built into three concentric circular buildings. The outer ring was a fortified wall with stables and barracks. The second and middle ring housed the male members of the royal family and male servants along with all the formal rooms for conducting affairs of state and the typical kitchens and workshops that were necessary. The innermost circle was for women. The wives, daughters, mothers, and sisters of the royal family lived there with female servants. Women guests were lodged here as well and the female residents rarely got to venture out, except for planned family outings to the countryside and the seasonal trek to the summer palace in the foothills.

Demeda had lived most of her life within the well-fitted stone walls of her family's palace. Most of her view was of sky, the walls of the men's circle, and the inner garden where flowers were cultivated among a ring of elderly chestnut trees. But today she would peep a little farther, and she took her friend's hand and scurried from the secluded apartment of the King's precious eldest daughter.

They did not care what servants saw them. The female workers would never tell the Princess what to do. There were men enough to do that.

Upper levels of the women's circle were connected with stone bridges to the men's circle so that it was not necessary to go down to the ground level just to cross – an arrangement that was convenient for the King to reach his wives. The upper bridges were generally unguarded. Demeda chose the bridge that went directly to the section of the men's palace where her brothers lived. With the excitement caused by the reported arrival of the mysterious dro-shalum, Demeda doubted that her brothers would be lounging about, and she was right. Mallah and she slipped unnoticed into the men's circle. Even though Demeda was only in her family's home, her heart still beat faster because she was forbidden to enter the men's circle without an invitation.

The decor revealed that they had entered the world of men. Tapestries showed broad landscapes where great and elaborate hunts for boar and stag were depicted. Sculptures of horses and men and other animals adorned the mantelpieces and weapons hung from the walls. Some were actual working weapons and others were fanciful decorative weapons.

Demeda was tempted to snoop through the personal effects of her brothers, especially her full brothers Kalzen and Ulet, but she was in a hurry. Perhaps she would have a chance on her way back.

The apartments of her brothers were eerily abandoned. The male servants must have all congregated to gossip at some other level and her brothers were likely with the King. Demeda took a back hallway that was mostly used by servants so as to avoid the main staircase of the men's circle. Mallah and she went out a door to stand on a balcony that overlooked the main courtyard between the men's circle and the outer ring of the palace. They crouched behind the stone rail and were surprised to see so many men-at-arms mustering in the yard.

Demeda observed her father's war chief, Daboh, in his full warrior regalia mounting a white horse.

"Do you think we are being attacked?" Mallah whispered.

Demeda peered over the edge a little farther. She shook her head and then announced that they needed to go higher.

"We dare not take the main stairs," Mallah said.

Demeda agreed and they rushed back inside. Eight extra stairwells ran up and down the men's circle, and the women scurried toward the nearest one. It was cramped and dark and the flap of their slippered feet racing up the steps sounded loud.

They were out of breath when they reached the top. Wind was whistling in the open door, but the fresh air was welcomed by their hungry lungs. Demeda and Mallah burst out of the stairwell and startled four men who were talking and pointing across the city. They were servants and the appearance of two women in their midst caused them to react with disapproval and shock. Demeda's red cloak over a yellow gown marked her as a royal female. Simply being near the unchaperoned females was a terrible risk for the common men.

"Go back!" shouted a cook with a rude and authoritative tone. "This is no place for women."

His male dialect sounded rough. The speech of men was always slightly foreign to female ears, but Demeda took strength from the panic on the men's faces.

"I have my father's leave to be here," she lied.

Ignoring the skeptical grimace of the cook, Demeda took Mallah's hand and marched into their midst at the edge of the roof. The wind was strong and with the spring equinox still weeks away, the claws of winter remained sharp. Demeda was grateful for the warmth and protection of the normally stifling face cover. The men backed away from the intrusive women. They were stymied as to what to do. No one dared actually touch the females to force them away.

Demeda could see over the outer wall of the palace. Most of the city of Chadenedra consisted of low wooden buildings, punctuated by stone or brick temples, and neighborhoods of nicer buildings of stone and timber. Streamers of smoke rose from chimneys. Snow blanketed roofs. Various flags and banners fluttered around the important dwellings. An impressive wall of timbers embraced the city.

"Are you up here to see this outlaw who has so many in an uproar?" Demeda asked.

Demeda knew that her high-born female dialect might be difficult for the males to understand, so she restated her question in simpler terms. Still, she got no answer, so she shaded her eyes and peered toward the city gate. As the maid had reported, it was shut, which was abnormal for the middle of the day. Beyond the town on the dark lanes marked by dirty snow she saw an ominous group of four or five dozen darkly clad warriors. She could tell little at such a distance except that they were clearly not farmers or traders.

"We should go," Mallah said. She glanced warily at the men who hung back anxiously. She was unused to being unprotected in the presence of men and all of her cultural fears of female vulnerability were barking in her mind.

Demeda squinted at the group outside the city. She longed to go out there and know their business. Who were they and why had their approach caused such an instant alarm? Although she gave into Mallah's insistent tug on her arm, Demeda resolved to find out.

She turned and snidely thanked the men for enduring their intrusion. Her delight in effectively pushing around some hapless male servants was fleeting. Her oldest brother, Ulet, emerged from the stairwell, evidently in pursuit of her. His squarely cut bangs of black hair framed an angry face – an emotion that ill-suited his seventeen-year-old face. Despite his youth, he was well grown with strong wide shoulders, lean torso, and strong fast legs. His red cape flapped from his shoulders as if applauding his disapproval.

"Sister," Ulet said. The face covering could not hide her identity from him. Ulet knew those bright defiant eyes and their long black lashes. "Come with me," he commanded in a voice that absolutely mimicked their father.

To enforce his will, four of his personal bodyguards came out of the stairwell behind him and positioned themselves around Demeda and Mallah.

Demeda refused to let her shoulders sag in defeat.

Ulet proceeded to scold her. "Why do you shame us cavorting with male servants?"

"I am not cavorting. They just happened to be here," Demeda answered without the appropriate guilt.

Exasperation rivaled Ulet's indignation. "What are you doing?" he asked.

"I was trying to see this outlaw that everyone but me seems to know about," Demeda replied and her words rushed out excitedly as she continued. "Why do we bar the city to him? He only has a few warriors. Surely he can't attack. Why do we fear him? Who is he?"

Ulet would have been irritated if the subject did not concern him so. With a flick of his fingers he indicated to his men that it was time to go. The bodyguards politely ushered the women into the stairwell and Ulet led the way down.

The close stone walls of the stairwell felt hot and confining after the open freedom of the roof. Demeda understood keenly that she was being returned to her pen like a stray heifer. She wondered who had seen her and Mallah. Due to the speed of her detection and Ulet's personal response she had to assume that one of her servants might have alerted him. The silent complicity of her servants could no longer be counted upon. Ulet obviously had spies in the women's circle.

Descending the steps, Demeda took Mallah's hand. Her trustworthy cousin silently gave her some solace.

When they exited the stairs and headed directly for the bridge to the women's circle, Demeda balked. She slipped in front of her outwardly indifferent brother. She touched his arm to try and stop him. His biceps tensed beneath his thick felt shirt.

"Ulet, tell me about this outlaw. What is going on?" she pleaded.

He shook at her grasp gently. Her interest in a strange man was unseemly.

"He's just an outlaw," he said and kept moving forward.

Demeda hung onto him. "Is Daboh going out to arrest him?" she asked.

Ulet halted and Mallah and the bodyguards stumbled to a fast stop behind him. Ulet was amazed by the thoroughness of Demeda's spying during her brief escape.

She could see that some of his anger was passing. The part of her brother that was loving kin still remained. And some juicy secret itched inside him and he wanted to scratch it, just as when they were little.

"Can we talk?" Demeda whispered invitingly. She hoped that he still wanted the safety of her confidence, where there was no male judgment.

Gruffly he told his men to deliver Mallah back to the women's circle.

Ulet and Demeda stepped into a small private dining room. The fireplace was cold but a shaft of light from the window fell on the blank table and brightened the room. Ulet looked out the second door of the room into the servants' hall to make sure no one was listening.

Demeda pulled open the drapes to let in more light. Clouds were moving in and slapping back the yellow warmth of the late winter sunshine. She then untied her face covering and let her tepa fall back. Her brother was accustomed to the lovely sight of his sister. Polished wooden combs accented with silver beads held her thick wavy black hair back from her face. Her warm caramel skin was kept abnormally light by lack of exposure to sunlight, but her pristine fairness enhanced the dripping molasses beauty of her eyes. No male outside her closely related kin had seen her uncovered since the passing of her childhood. Like all of her brothers, it was the duty of Ulet to keep it that way until she was delivered to a husband.

Ulet ran his hand along the thick stone mantel of the fireplace before picking up a bear statuette of black stone off the shelf. Turning the statue over in his hands, Ulet started to speak. "The outlaw is called Amar. The Kez have been demanding retainers from every tribe," he said.

"What's that?" Demeda asked. Her scant education had not included any terms of business.

He graciously explained that the Kez wanted regular payments of treasure and goods in exchange for securing safe relations between tribes and helping to defend outlying towns from marauding nomads. The Kez, as servants of Vu, had always sold such services, but it had been upon request. Now the Kez had turned aggressive and were trying to assume a mandatory monopoly over such activities.

Demeda listened eagerly. To hear such things was so much more stimulating than the ceaseless tedium of pregnancy, birth, and arranged marriages that dominated conversations in the women's circle.

"Are tribes paying?" she asked.

Ulet nodded but added, "The Temulanka have refused them, and we are doing the same."

"Of course," Demeda agreed. The Sabar'Uto would not want to appear weak in the eyes of their powerful rival to the north, the Temulanka Tribe. Her people had warred with the Temulanka for most of her childhood, and even Demeda was aware that the peace was tenuous. The wounds of war festered more than they healed.

She watched the statuette rolling in her brother's hands and noted how his grip tightened after each turn. She looked up to his face that was so like hers except cast in a masculine mold. A hint of little boy vulnerability hid behind the corners of his manhood.

In a lower voice, he said, "We have barred Amar from the city because there is a rumor that he has some strange power. The King of the Patharki was brutally murdered after receiving the Kez. He was pulled from his throne and butchered in the presence of his war chief and bodyguards."

Demeda gasped and thought of her father. The vision of him dead in the carefully crafted safety of his home was unsettling.

"Do you believe he is dro-shalum?" Demeda asked.

Startled, Ulet asked her where she had heard that and she told him. Ulet returned the bear statuette to the mantel. "I think maybe so," he confessed.

Demeda's skin tingled with the superstitious rustling of rising hairs. She had never experienced such a rush of foreboding and excitement.

She collected herself and quietly asked what the King would do about the Kez. Ulet said that their father would wait and see. Perhaps the Kez would do nothing. They had not communicated any specific threats. Only the shocking crimes attributed to Amar had frightened the lesser tribes into paying.

"We will see what happens in the spring when," Ulet abruptly stopped. He had let his guard down with his sister, who he had enjoyed an abnormally close relationship with because of their closeness in age. He physically withdrew from her. The indulgences he had shown Demeda over the years would have to end. It was wrong for a man to take a woman into his confidence. That lesson had been drilled into him during his upbringing, but he had always found the advice hard to follow around Demeda. He suspected that any man would find her disarming.

"What?" Demeda asked, moving so that she faced him again. She was close to getting him to reveal something even more interesting than Amar. She could feel it, and it was probably what had been keeping her brothers distant and taciturn of late.

Ulet pressed his lips shut, but Demeda saw sympathy on his face. Insatiably curious now, she grabbed his hands and kept him from moving away.

"You need to get back," Ulet insisted.

"What about the spring? Does it concern me?" she demanded, and the spirit of truth lighted his face.

Ulet softened his stance and gently held her hands. "You must not say that I told you," he murmured.

Demeda gave him her assurances as she always did when he gave up to her a secret that he longed to tell.

"A marriage has been arranged," he whispered.

Demeda went cold and her stomach became heavy with expectation. The news was not unexpected. At the age of sixteen, it was high time that she was wedded, but as the eldest Sabar'Uto princess and daughter of the King's first wife, her marriage was no trifling affair. It would be a matter of political alliance to bolster her father's power. A suitable husband would have been carefully chosen by her father.

Ulet continued, "A tutor will be sent to you soon to teach you the common dialect. It will be a diplomatic marriage."

She gasped. She would be married outside her tribe and probably never see her kin again. "Who?" she cried.

Ulet looked pained. "You don't need to know right now," he said.

Infuriated by his attempt to dodge the most important detail, Demeda pushed him hard in the stomach. "Tell me!" she yelled.

She raised her hands to push him again, but he yielded. Miserable, he said, "The Temulanka King."

His answer was so appalling that Demeda immediately clung to the hope that he jested. The concept that she would be wed to their worst enemy was ridiculous.

"Ulet, stop being cruel. Who is it?" she asked again. Fragile hope quavered in her voice.

"It's true," Ulet said. "I spoke against it. I swear, Demeda. I told our father that I would not see my sister given to our enemy. But he said that it must be done. We can't have war and this will bring peace."

The horror of it was so immense that Demeda knew that she had only begun to be outraged. The Temulanka King already had wives. She would not even be the first wife! Although she had always known that she was meant for a political marriage to serve her family and her tribe, she had never conceived of such an insult.

"I won't do it!" she declared.

"You must. You cannot defy our father. You know this," Ulet said. He was stoic now, trying to remove himself from his sister's suffering.

She narrowed her eyes. "Men start wars and then send their women to finish them," she snarled.

Her emotions were exploding like a lightning strike catching in a dry forest. The flames were racing up the tree trunks. Her grief and rage and utter helplessness consumed her with hot burning fate. Many would pity her, but none would help her.

She ran from Ulet. She ran across the bridge to the women's circle, heedless of her flapping hood and exposed face. She would cry for days, wailing in dismay until there was only the refuge of exhausted depression. Cradled in Mallah's arms, she sobbed of her terror of the Temulanka King, their blood enemy, rutting upon her.

"My own tribe is my enemy to send me to such torture," she decided.

Mallah petted her frazzled hair and whispered that it was not so. "You will do this to help your tribe, to keep us safe. I'm sure the King will explain this to you. You will see, Demeda. Perhaps this will be the end of the wars. Think of the sons you will save," Mallah said, trying to help Demeda find solace in her duty.

But Demeda only growled with discontent. "They'd spend their daughters to save their sons. I swear by all the Gods and Goddesses, they'll find no peace between my legs."

26. Predatory Will

*I do not know what I have done to drive my son into such pointless danger.
Is it the way of young men to trample good sense like a drunk in a flower
bed? ~ Journal of Zehn Chenomet, 2042 Kwellstan calendar*

When Cruce first saw the vicious work of the savages, the abuses of
Leyton Bevone became trivial. The three corpses on the prairie slapped
Cruce with horror. The eyes of the murdered shepherds had been gouged
out and their hands chopped off. Cruce had heard speculation among the
veterans that the mutilations were prompted by the savages' primitive
beliefs about the afterlife. They supposedly intended to cripple the spirits
of their enemies and make them unable to take revenge on the living. It
was ridiculous of course. The tabre taught the Nufalese that the spirit could
not be corrupted and remained intact no matter how violent the death.
Cruce's father could look forward to an afterlife unfettered by his
disabilities, and it was his only mercy. But the savages had no proper
instruction about the everlasting soul and the divine. Their wicked small
minds could only fathom superstition and cruelty.

"Off your horse, Cruce. Get those bodies covered," Gehr ordered.

Cruce shoved his mind past its shock and started to clumsily function.
Gehr and the ranger Padrek were farther down the gentle slope where the
shepherds had been left. They had dismounted at the top of the hill and
treaded carefully past the dead men as they examined the ground to get an
estimate of how many savages had committed the atrocity.

Even Cruce's untutored eyes now noticed the jagged trails trampled
into the dead grasses. Snow dusted the frozen ground and caught in tiny
drifts against clumps of grass. Many footprints were evident where the thin
snow had been stomped aside by the circling eruption of violence that had
consumed the shepherds.

Cruce guessed that at least twenty savages had done this attack, and a
chill of fear tightened his chest. Out near the foothills north of the Burlip,
the prairie sprawled to the west and north. The militiamen were exposed
and few in number. Cruce was on his first patrol with Gehr and nine other
militiamen. Five were fresh recruits, including him and Rayden, but the
others were veterans.

Cruce dismounted and glanced at his comrades to judge their distress.
The weathered face of the nearest veteran, Hance, was calm but his eyes
roved the horizon warily. Cruce approached the dead shepherds. He
swallowed his distaste and tried to appear strong. The cold had frozen them
and there was no stench of death except for a faint meaty smell. The blood-
caked eye sockets were black and unsettling. The absence of eyes seemed

to make the dead shepherds less like men. Their faces were locked into painful grimaces and Cruce focused on their bodies.

He knew that he had been told to tend the corpses because he was new. It was a way to harden him to the grim adventure ahead. He would be expected to do violence soon. He must hurt people or end up like these poor unfortunates before him. The talk was that the savages were going to be more aggressive this winter. Their attacks had been increasing for a few years now.

Cruce stooped next to the nearest dead man and tugged his cloak out from under him and started wrapping him. It was a relief to cover the mutilated face. As distasteful as the chore was, Cruce toughened himself with his sense of duty. These men, although of humble birth, were his fellow Nufalese and they deserved respect in death. His duty to defend Nufal quickened from an abstract ideal to a solid mission. His people were under attack, and his proud civilization would not be left undefended against the artless bludgeons of the savages.

Cruce finished wrapping the faces of the three shepherds with their coarse homespun cloaks. He did not see the hands of any of the men. He asked his comrades if they saw the hands anywhere, and one of the veterans grunted that the savages ate them.

"Is that true?" Rayden asked, startled to hear something even more appalling about the savages than what he had already been told.

"I don't know," the veteran laughed.

Rayden looked relieved that the other man was only having some sport with him, but Cruce silently disapproved of the joke. After touching the dead, he had temporarily lost his humor.

"Rayden, Asher!" Gehr barked. "Get down and help Cruce load those bodies."

Gehr and Padrek were stalking back up the slope. Gehr stopped next to Cruce and glanced at the wrapped bodies and appeared satisfied with the job Cruce had done. Gehr's gray eyes then met Cruce's eyes with a friendly flash of sympathy.

Cruce said, "Commander, could you tell how many there were?"

Gehr spoke so that all could hear and said about twenty five.

"Is that a lot?" Cruce whispered.

Gehr pulled up his thick brown hood stitched with red spears and rams. "Yes," he answered.

Rayden and Asher were approaching the bodies hesitantly. Before Gehr had to order them to quit being squeamish, Cruce spoke up. "This one first," he said. He bent down and grabbed the stiff lifeless shoulders. Encouraged that Cruce was actually touching the body, Asher and Rayden took up the legs.

They secured the three bodies onto horses. The animals resisted the dead cargo, but after some stern effort the bodies were strapped onto Asher and Rayden's horses. Cruce decided that his wrapping of the bodies earned him the right to keep his horse. He invited Rayden to ride double with him, and Asher joined Hance on his horse.

Gehr and Padrek had been conferring quietly while the bodies were loaded. They mounted their horses, and Gehr announced that they would take the bodies to the nearby settlement of Upella. The shepherds were likely from there, and their kin could handle the burial. Gehr and Padrek set a hard pace across the prairie. The people of Upella and the outlying farmsteads needed urgently to be warned of the band of marauding savages.

Cruce was starting to appreciate the breathtaking beauty of the open land. The Valley of Nufal was lovely with its lush and ancient forest guarded by the austere peaks of the Tabren Mountains, but the sweeping space of the grasslands unlocked Cruce's mind. Out here on the Nufalese prairie, possibilities invited him toward the future, and his privileged existence in stately Kwellstan now struck him as cloistered and limited.

Cruce was also picking up how to navigate the rolling land. He could judge his direction by the sun and remember points on maps that he had studied in Kahtep. And at night, he had been taught to look for the stars Tweena and Poler that steadfastly indicated the east and north respectively. He expected that by the end of his first tour of winter duty, he would be able to strike out across the prairie with the same confidence as Gehr or Padrek. They knew exactly where they were and how to get to Upella.

The settlement of Upella was only five timber buildings with sod roofs. The stone architecture and grace of the Nufalese cities were completely absent on this foothold of civilization. Smoke issued from the rock chimneys of three of the buildings, smudging the sky with dirty streaks that Cruce vaguely resented for besmirching the purity of the landscape. But the fires were needed for warmth and Cruce shrugged off his dark opinion. The biting wind nipped his cheeks and admonished him for mentally criticizing the only shelter available.

"Do you think we will get a hot meal?" Rayden asked from behind.

"If there's time," Cruce said hopefully.

People emerged from the squat buildings. Their keen eyes immediately noted the bodies strapped on the horses, and cries of alarm were soon carried by the wind.

A rugged man with a thick brown beard came forward to greet the militia patrol. He had not put on a cloak before rushing outside, but a huge fur hat encased his head with its dried badger face perched over his forehead. Gehr had no need to explain that the shepherds had been killed by savages. A woman exclaimed with grief when she saw the bodies. Although the dead were wrapped, she knew with certainty that one of them was her man. Two more women rushed to hold and console her in her explosion of grief and several men came to remove the dead shepherds from the horses.

The bearded man, presumably the settlement's leader, invited the militiamen inside. "All of you, please be getting out of the cold," he said courteously and gestured to his door with a courtly sweep of his hand that belied his frontier garb.

Rayden slipped off the horse so Cruce could dismount. Cruce glanced back at the dead men that were being carried into one of the buildings. He felt that he should help, but he had already done what was needed. The dead were with their kin now.

A boy hurried among the militiamen and gathered the reins of the horses. In an eager piping voice, he announced that he would water and give fodder to the mounts of the militia. Cruce yielded his horse to the boy's care and noted the borderline awe in the boy's eyes.

Cruce and his ten comrades packed into a cabin. Inside it was dark and a little smoky, but the immediate warmth embraced him and the rich scent of buffalo stew teased his hunger into a sharp pain.

The bearded man ordered a woman to put on a kettle and give the militiamen a proper mug of tea although she was already doing so.

Gehr evidently knew who the bearded man was and called him Ehlen. Cruce listened as Gehr and Ehlen discussed the situation. Ehlen's beard dipped toward his broad chest when he frowned deeply and reported that the settlers believed that a camp of savages was across the Smet River. Judging from the amount of livestock taken over the past month, he believed a large group was in the region.

Padrek leaned close to Gehr's left ear and suggested quietly that they should send to Kahtep for a tabre landscanner. The idea tempted Gehr, but requests were not to be made of the tabre frivolously. Gehr had a duty to assess the facts in his assigned patrol region as best as humanly possible before bothering the Nebakarz.

"Do you really think a full-fledged tribal pod is this far south?" Gehr asked Ehlen.

"Aye, Commander. The winter be working its way toward being harder than most. The signs be telling us a pod's out there," Ehlen concluded.

A pod was serious business, and Cruce's courage crackled with anticipation. The savages were nomadic hunter-gatherers that were supposedly adopting herding now that they were stealing livestock regularly from the Nufalese. Mostly they traveled as small family groups, but a pod was many families banded together. Livestock raided from the settlers might sustain them, but a pod also had the numbers to attack a settlement. The grains and metal tools were ample temptations.

The kettle had heated and Ehlen's wife was pouring tea. There were not mugs for everyone so Cruce and some others had to share mugs.

Cruce pulled off his gloves and gratefully pressed his red-tipped fingers against the hot ceramic. The tea was blazing hot and burned his tongue, but he drank it anyway. The hot blast filling his core pushed the cold out of his body, and he passed the mug to Rayden.

Cruce moved carefully through the crowded room so he could take a turn by the fire. A bed of coals was catching onto three new logs. The pine oil snapped in the heat and smelled good. He spread his hands toward the flames and let them cook. He hated the painful cold in his fingers more than in his feet. Seeing a spot open on the kettle rack, he draped his gloves on it so they could toast and be soothingly warm when he put them back on. Judging from the conversation Gehr and Ehlen were having, he would be riding into the wind soon.

"Those are nice," commented Ehlen's wife beneath the conversation of the men. She gestured to the gloves with her eyes because her hands were full of plates.

The gloves were carefully knit from black lambs' wool and reinforced with leather patches stitched on the palms and along both sides of the fingers.

"Thank you for noticing, Good Wife," Cruce said politely.

She smiled but said no more as she dished up the stew. Ehlen invited the militiamen to eat a hot meal, and Gehr did not turn him down.

Half the men had to eat standing, but it did not matter. Even wolfing his food, Cruce noticed that it tasted delicious. He wanted to slow down and enjoy the stew but he could not. Since his first day of training as a militia recruit, it seemed that he was always hungry.

As soon as Gehr finished his plate, he pushed back from the table and stood up. He clearly had made his decisions.

"Ehlen, send people to warn the farmsteads in the area. Encourage them to come into Upella. You will get safety in numbers," Gehr said.

Ehlen nodded gravely but warned that the farmsteaders might not all come to the settlement. "It's not easy leaving what you built up from Ektren yourself," Ehlen said knowingly.

"Do your best," Gehr said without criticizing, and then spoke to Padrek. "Go to Kahtep without delay. Tell Master Carver to send more men to Upella…and request a Nebakarz landscanner to investigate. It's warranted because we may have a pod on our hands."

Padrek left immediately. As an experienced ranger, he would be able to ride through the night and reach Kahtep late the next day.

Gehr swept his eyes among his remaining men. "The murder of the shepherds will not be allowed to pass. We are going after the raiders," he announced.

Armed with information about the last known location of the raiding gang, Gehr set out toward the Smet River, north of Upella. He declined those men among the settlers who wanted to volunteer and told them to guard the village.

The militiamen crossed the creek near Upella. It was mostly frozen except for a strip of water running down its center. The horses' hooves crunched through ice but the creek was shallow and only wetted their shaggy fetlocks.

Gehr led them along the creek bottom, using the leafless willows and cottonwoods to conceal them. The brush tamed the biting wind, and the breath of the men and horses steamed around their faces. The only sounds were the creak of cold saddle leather, the burble of flowing water, and the twiggy clatter of tree branches.

Cruce accepted that he would have to fight soon. Fear goaded his excitement into an anxious need for battle. The gouged faces of the shepherds stared into his mind and warned him of what the stakes were.

The riders came up against a massive thicket of blackberry brambles choked with wild grape vines. The thick brown dormant vines twisted like the sinews of the world laid bare, and the pitiless rows of berry bush thorns barred the way. They detoured out of the creek bottom on a narrow trail that was likely a deer path. Just before they emerged from the cover of the brush and trees, Gehr noted the scuff of a foot in the thin snow. Everyone scanned the horizon and peered into the brush behind them.

Nearby, just above the flood plain, stood two long low buildings of a farmstead. Smoke rose from the chimney. Gehr did not spare anyone to warn the farmsteaders, expecting that the men of Upella would take care of it. With only a couple hours of daylight left, Gehr had to reach the Smet River and try to find the trail of the savages. Beyond the farmstead another line of trees marked the Smet River that came roaring out of the Tabren Mountains.

The militia ducked back into the cover of the creek bottom. Cruce glanced over his shoulder at the farmstead before it disappeared into the folds of the land.

When they reached the Smet River, they turned east and moved upriver to a place called Elks' Ford. The men surveyed the open water while staying behind the branches at the river's edge. An expanse of dry rocks spread toward the half-frozen river. The militia watched and listened.

The disturbing squawk of crows warned them that something was amiss, but eventually Gehr decided they had to move into the open. It was the only way to cross the river.

The men rode out onto the rocks, and their horses stepped gingerly across the uneven river bed. Once in the open, they spotted the reason for the quarreling crows. The savages had left a grisly sign upon the fording place. A freshly butchered ram's head was hanging from its curled horns on a tree branch that jutted over the river. Very little of the carcass or hide was present but the entrails were stretched across tree branches like a gruesome spider web.

The ice at the river's edges was recently broken, and a frozen lump of sheep dung on the rocks attested to the stolen flock that had been driven across earlier.

Gehr spoke softly so his voice did not carry over the sound of the moving water. "The savages have dared to mark this ford. They need to be punished for their boldness," he said.

Cruce set his hand on his sword and sought reassurance from the hard bronze beneath the leather wrapping. His sword was new. The blade sharp but untested.

Despite the dropping temperature, the militiamen tossed their cloaks back from their shoulders to free up their arms, and they eased their hoods back from their heads. It seemed to take an intolerable amount of time to cross the Smet River. The horses were skittish and lunged reluctantly into the current.

During the crossing, Cruce cringed with the expectation of an attack. His leather vest studded with bronze discs offered more protection than trusting to luck as most of the militiamen of lesser means had to do. Before leaving Kahtep, Cruce had bought an armored vest for Rayden, and Cruce was glad that he had not let Rayden's proud protests keep him from taking the gift.

The band of fighters reached the opposite bank. The last rays of sunlight blazed gold and pink along the peaks of the Rysamand, and Cruce looked forward to the cover of the coming night.

The trail the sheep had broken through the brush was clear enough to see, but Gehr dismounted and studied the ground closely. Cruce presumed to get off his horse and look over his commander's shoulder. The savages traveled by foot because in their ignorance they ate horses instead of riding them like the Nufalese, and Cruce wanted to learn more about tracking them.

"What do you look for?" Cruce whispered.

Gehr pointed along the ground where there was a small gap in the bushes. "Here," he said. "With the snow it's nearly impossible for even the wiliest savage to hide his passing."

Cruce saw the half moon mark in the snow that exposed the frozen soil.

Gehr continued, "You look for the shape of the heel or big toe. Tracking is hardest in late summer when the ground is hard and dry, but winter is usually easy because of the snow. You see these tracks that veer off from the sheep trail? Some of the raiders broke off. They are trying to hide it, but I expected this move, so I knew what to look for. Probably a third to half the savages are taking the sheep to the pod and the rest are staying to cause more trouble. We'll strike them." Gehr looked up and scanned the tangle of brush, trees, and vines that clustered along the river. His nostrils flared "They are close," he added.

In silence they tracked the savages as the gray chill of dusk closed in. Gehr dismounted and the veteran militiamen did the same. Cruce and the other new recruits watched as their fellows removed their gloves and scraped up handfuls of dirt. They spat in their palms and mixed up some mud and started painting each other's faces. They placed stripes on their foreheads, down their noses, and across their cheeks. No one had mentioned war paint to Cruce during his training. Apparently this initiation was done in the field when the circumstances were real.

The veterans gestured for the recruits to join them, and they scrambled off their horses. Cruce looked into the eyes of Hance as the man streaked cold mud onto his face. At that moment, Cruce could not recall sharing such kinship with another man. Hance's serious blue eyes looked out from a face transformed by a few crude streaks of mud. The vaguely cat-like stripes made him a hunter of the night, and Hance's potent spirit imparted to Cruce the predatory will of a warrior.

Gehr gathered the men around them once their faces were done. Speaking very quietly he said that he expected to find the camp of the raiding savages at the edge of the river's basin where it passed higher ground and formed a natural shelter from the wind. They could expect to encounter an equal number of savages, maybe more, but their superior weapons and horses would give them the advantage. Gehr also figured they had the advantage of surprise because this was the first patrol to the Upella region this season.

"Kill any that you encounter," Gehr ordered and concluded with the standard admonishment to never leave one of their own behind.

Before breaking the circle, Gehr glanced at Cruce to check on his resolve. Cruce looked back at his commander and friend with grim certainty. The militiamen mounted their horses and moved carefully through the river bottom as night fell.

Gehr's instincts were right. They had not gone far before Cruce caught a whiff of wood smoke. They found the savages camping at the base of a crumbling bluff. Two hot orange spots were visible through the brush and acted as beacons to the Nufalese.

Cruce put the image of the mutilated shepherds into his mind and drew his sword. With his heart unlatched from the niceties of civilization, he summoned the hard violence that lurks always in men.

The howl of a sentry alerted the savages when the militiamen charged through the brush. The fires flickered as savages ran back and forth in front of them, picking up weapons and preparing to give battle.

As they were trained, the militiamen spread out around the camp so as to come at the savages from many directions and stop them when they attempted to scatter. Breaking free of the trees and brush, Cruce felt the freedom of open sky. The stars of a clear cold winter night looked down upon the human struggle.

Cruce bent low against the neck of his horse. He focused on a man half revealed by the firelight. Cruce thought nothing of the man's humanity. The savage was merely a target to be struck.

Cruce knocked into the savage with his horse. He glimpsed the savage's face. A square forehead with a mountainous horizon tattooed across it. Wide fierce eyes. A thick red beard and stringy copper hair decorated with bone and stone beads. Cruce thrust his sword at the neck. From the darkness, a thick arm shaggy with buffalo hide swung a stone club. Although an awkward glancing blow, it thudded hard against Cruce's ribs. A flash flood of mortal panic surged through Cruce's body and he hacked rapidly at the savage until he met the meaty resistance of flesh.

There was a cry of pain and the red-haired savage fell back into the dark. Cruce looked about quickly for the next man. Every orange splash of firelight highlighted details that his mind interpreted instantly. The terrible danger of the fight where life taunted death enchanted his senses with a glorious acuity. He blocked clubs and spears and struck with his sword and delivered grievous injuries that he followed up with fatal blows. His horse obeyed his unthinking directions as he charged the fur-clad men that howled and yelled.

Cruce yelled back, exulting in his mounting victory. He was good at this. His anger over anything had an outlet. The shepherds were avenged. Upella was defended. For Nufal, he pushed back the ugly savagery that skulked at the borders of his fair civilization.

And Cruce was strong. No one would look upon the Chenomet family and see wasting infirmity again.

A scream yanked Cruce from his chest-heaving moment of violent pleasure. He recognized the voice behind the scream. It was Rayden. Cruce turned in the saddle and suddenly his desperate concern made the erratic shapes shifting in the night hard to distinguish.

"Rayden!" he shouted and rushed in what he guessed to be the right direction.

Cruce swiped at a savage, but the man ran off. Suddenly quiet replaced the shouting rage that had engulfed the camp. Whether the assault had lasted a minute or an hour, Cruce could not begin to know. His blood sprinted through his flesh with frightening force, and the cold could not reach his hot body.

"I'm bleeding!" Rayden cried. The panic in his voice warned of death.

Cruce jumped off his horse and blundered toward the voice. He bumped into the brown lathered shoulder of Rayden's mount and grabbed the horse's bridle. Rayden slid from the saddle and thudded into a heap at Cruce's feet. His hyper-alert senses caught the fresh smell of blood.

Just as Cruce was about to bend down to help his friend, Gehr's voice slapped him with orders. "On your horse!" His voice was urgent and stone hard. Then, to all his fighters, he called them to unite and form a circle.

Woodenly Cruce obeyed and stumbled back to his horse. His training demanded that he reassemble with the others to guard their wounded, but letting go of Rayden felt to Cruce like bitter betrayal. Truly now the fierce meaning of comradeship impressed itself onto his soul. His instinct told him to hold onto his friend, but Gehr was right. Cruce served Rayden best by doing his duty.

Gehr stayed on the ground with his fallen man and the militiamen gathered around them. The thick press of horses and the jingle of gear and weapons kept back the dark hostile wilds. Many savages had been killed but others had scattered and they might counterattack.

Rayden shouted again, and his shock and hysteria might have overtaken him if Gehr had not clamped a hand over the wounded man's mouth and ordered him to silence. Rayden gasped and struggled to master his pain. Gehr lifted him back to his feet, and in the darkness, tried to judge how severely his man was hurt.

"Back on your horse, man," Gehr hissed. He grabbed the reins of Rayden's horse and pulled the animal close. It took all of Gehr's strength to boost Rayden back into the saddle. The young man slumped precariously and clung feebly to the thick mane of the horse. "Use a hand to push hard where it hurts to slow the bleeding," Gehr advised.

Then, the commander sprang quickly onto his horse and ordered that they withdraw. The militiamen rode away from the spray of bodies around the dwindling fires. Cruce moved alongside Rayden to monitor his friend.

They moved as fast as they could in the darkness. Branches scratched at their arms and faces as if the ghosts of the newly dead savages chased them and sought to mutilate them.

Before they reached the banks of the Smet River, Cruce heard a thud and a moan when Rayden plopped to the ground. Cruce stifled his alarm and called softly for the others to wait. With help from two men, Cruce pulled Rayden into the saddle with him so that he could hold his friend up. Rayden's head lolled back onto Cruce's shoulder. Riding double with a slack body in his arms was difficult, but Cruce struggled on, knowing that he would not let Rayden fall again.

Worried that his friend might be bleeding to death, Cruce hurried into the river with his comrades. The splashing of hooves through the cold rushing waters seemed exceptionally loud, and Cruce realized that his heart was still banging against his chest. He had never felt more completely alive, and he hoped that the explosion of vitality within him would envelope Rayden and protect him from death.

Gehr led his men to the farmstead they had passed earlier. Despite the late hour, the windows were lit, and the humble cabin seemed in that moment a beacon of civilization as great as any tabre temple.

"We have reached help, Rayden. You will be fine," Cruce told his friend.

The cabin door burst open and a burly form hefting an axe darkened the doorway. He shouted a challenge, but Gehr's appropriate reply and request for help immediately relaxed the farmsteader. The silhouette of his axe lowered in the warm glow of his threshold.

"Wife," he barked. "A wounded man they've got. He be needing your attentions."

27. A Magic House

Every oil lamp in the cabin burned brightly, and Cruce was startled when he finally saw Rayden's state. Drying red-brown blood smeared into the mud paint on the left side of his face.

The woman of the house hastily spread a thick gray felt blanket in front of the crackling fireplace. Cruce hovered anxiously as Hance and Gehr laid Rayden down.

"My wife be fixing up your man," the barrel-chested farmsteader declared confidently. He hung his axe over the door and slammed it shut.

Gehr looked earnestly at the woman who knelt beside Rayden. While tying up her loose sandy hair, she sought to reassure him. "I be from a long line of fleshmenders," she said.

"Who was your mother?" Gehr asked.

"Nalene of Ufessa," the woman replied. "I am Ajel."

Gehr nodded with recognition. He knew most fleshmender women on the frontier, including now its newest daughter grown to womanhood. "Well met, Good Wife," Gehr said. "I fear that the militia shall often be in your debt."

They shared an instant of grim agreement and then Ajel turned to the defender of her land fallen upon her hearth. Gehr stood up and the master of the household was waiting to greet him properly.

"I am Duvek," he said in his deep voice. "I see that the savages have had a go at you."

"We struck them," Gehr corrected. His satisfaction at taking blood was obvious. "Just after nightfall across the river."

Respect brightened Duvek's face.

Gehr now noted three other men standing around the table. He recognized one of them from Upella. "I see you have been brought warning of the savages," Gehr commented.

A sinister gleam lit the dark eyes of Duvek. "Aye," he said. "We be plotting our own strike on those miserable animals."

Gehr stepped past Cruce to address the civilian men more directly. Knowing to be diplomatic with his advice, Gehr reminded the men that he recommended that they guard the village instead of hunting the savages.

"Commander, we knowing your advice to be good," Duvek said. "But this time, I'll be having my blood before the sun sets again. That I swear by the Great Divinity. My kin was among those three butchered shepherds. A nephew." Duvek stopped. He seemed about to say more but a tender grief shut his throat and his blunt bearded face revealed his struggle against emotion.

Gehr did not argue the point. The duty of the militia was to defend the frontiers of Nufalese civilization. Usually that meant placing themselves between the citizens and the savages, but Gehr knew when not to get in the way of people. "What's your plan, Duvek?" Gehr asked.

Duvek gestured for Gehr to join them at the table. "I'd be glad of hearing your advice on this," he said. Gehr took a seat and the other men settled onto the benches as well. Duvek started to lay out his plan to ambush the raiders next time they crossed the river.

Cruce noticed that Ajel had paused in her examination of Rayden to eavesdrop on her husband, and he gently asked her about his friend's condition.

She murmured an apology and returned her attention to the semi-conscious young man. She dabbed a wet cloth at the clotting blood that stuck Rayden's helmet to his hair. She gently pushed back the helmet. After wiping away more mud and blood, she tenderly parted his hair and exposed an ugly cut that started at the base of his skull and cut into his left ear. The cut stopped where the weapon had met the edge of the bronze helmet, but the scalp was bruised and swelling from the blunt force.

Ajel hurriedly folded some absorbent cloths and pressed them against the cut because it was still bleeding. "Be holding these firm for me," she said. Cruce moved around behind Rayden's head and sat on the warm flagstones of the hearth. He took off his gloves and pressed on the wound as she directed. Ajel examined the rest of Rayden's body. Carefully she removed Rayden's gear and clothing. Cruce had to raise Rayden a little so she could get off his cloak, armored vest, and shirt.

"This is nice armor," she commented as she set it aside.

"We just got it. This was our first battle," Cruce said. His spirit still seemed to be shaking like a small flag in a high wind.

Ajel glanced up at him. Her brown eyes contrasted strikingly with her blonde hair and fair face, speckled by a few freckles. She studied Cruce a moment and then assured him that his friend would be all right.

The door opened as the two men who had been tending the horses came inside. The fire snapped irritably at the rush of cold air, and the door was quickly shut. They looked with concern at Rayden but did not bother the fleshmender with questions.

Ajel unfolded a large cloth kit on the floor and removed a few sprigs of dried plants and crushed them into a nearby kettle to boil. As the strange aroma rose from the brewing herb, she continued undressing Rayden. Once he was down to his underclothes, she located another small wound on his thigh. She cleaned it quickly and bandaged it. Next, Ajel wrapped him in a soft felt blanket trimmed on one side with lambs' fleeces.

Sometimes Rayden would try to speak, but she hushed him with an authoritative tone that seemed beyond her youth. Cruce supposed that her commanding presence came from her fleshmender training.

Ajel poured a cup from the kettle and blew on the pale green tea. A simple gesture from her told Cruce to sit Rayden up for a drink.

"For the pain," Ajel murmured, tender as the best mother, and held the cup to his lips.

After Rayden was settled back into his blankets, he became drowsy and no longer squirmed feebly beneath the bloody cloth Cruce pressed against his head.

Ajel strung thick black thread onto a glistening sharp metal needle.

"What metal is that?" Cruce asked. It did not look as bright as silver, but it seemed precious.

"It be of tabre making. They call it loter. They not be sharing its crafting with humans, but we fleshmenders have a relationship with the

Nebakarz in Kahtep, and they make these fine instruments for us," Ajel explained.

"Do you think Rayden will need a tabre healer?" Cruce asked.

Ajel shook her head confidently. She traded places with Cruce and brought an oil lamp close to Rayden's bloody head. She eased away the bloody cloths that Cruce had been pressing against the cut. The bleeding had slowed to a weary oozing of red.

As she began stitching, perfect concentration drew her face into a scowl. Her fingers worked precisely without any sign of squeamishness. With so many people in the house, it grew hot and stuffy and sweat shone on her forehead. Cruce obligingly obeyed her terse commands to cut a thread or move the light.

When she was done, she finished cleaning the blood from Rayden's face and hair. Although sleeping fitfully, he appeared restored to life except for the angry cut swelling against the perfect black stitches. The cleaver of butcher Death had been put away this time.

After wrapping Rayden's head in clean cloth, Ajel sat back and the serious mask of a fleshmender slipped away and she was a young woman again. Tired and a little frazzled, she rubbed her eyes and looked wearily upon militiamen hunkered on the floor.

"I'll get you a drink," Cruce offered, glancing around for the water jug.

"Kind of you," Ajel murmured and pointed to the work table tucked beneath shelves of pans, dishes, ceramic jars, and racks of cooking utensils.

Cruce spotted the water jug and rose stiffly from the floor to get her a drink. It was the least he could do after she had applied such amazing skill to his friend. He found a drinking gourd and placed it under the spigot. When he gave her the water, she drank it done with obvious thirst.

She thanked him but Cruce shook his head. "No, Good Wife, thank you. I was very worried for Rayden. But I'm not any more," he said.

A lovely and well-practiced veil of modesty slipped over Ajel's face. "You be welcome, warrior of Nufal. Your efforts to be protecting us settlers are appreciated," she said.

Sudden and sick concern for her twisted in Cruce's gut. Her small home upon the plains jutting into the domain of brutal savagery was so vulnerable. "You will go to the village in the morning, right?" he asked.

The subject seemed to disgruntle her. Instead of answering, she glanced at Duvek without any wifely tenderness.

"Don't be worrying about me," Ajel reassured him and got to her feet. She announced that Rayden had been tended and should heal in due time and then asked if anyone else had been hurt. Two men responded. As Ajel beckoned them to her, she turned to Cruce and asked him if he would show his comrades the water jug so they could all get a drink.

"Of course, Good Wife," he replied and noticed an appreciative twinkle in her brown eyes before she turned from him.

After Cruce distributed all the mugs and cups that he could find, he sat next to Rayden. Only a little blood had seeped into the bandaging, and he seemed to be resting comfortably. Cruce tucked the blanket around Rayden's shoulders and then allowed himself to relax against the thick cabin wall. Along his neck he could feel a cold draft coming through the logs. He took off his helmet and pulled up his hood.

The cutting excitement of battle was beginning to dull, and a tremendous weariness consumed his body as if he had drunk some of Ajel's herbal painkiller. His brain was still processing his violent episode with the savages and finding new details from the encounter. He had killed. He was sure of it, but he felt no moral revulsion. The savages were awful, and he felt proud of defending Nufal. Glad to have survived his first test, he succumbed to fatigue and his chin dropped onto his chest.

Rayden's voice roused him in the morning. "Get off me," he croaked.

Cruce opened his heavy eyes. He was cuddled up to his wounded friend and stealing half of his blanket. The cabin was empty. Although wondering where everyone was, he was happy to see Rayden awake and asked him how he felt.

"My head hurts and I'm about to piss myself," Rayden complained.

Stiffly Cruce stood up and searched for a chamber pot. He felt bad about it, but he had to go into the bedchamber of his host and hostess to find one. He called for Duvek or Ajel before drawing back the curtain but no one answered.

Coming back to Rayden with the pot, he helped his friend up so he could relieve himself.

Rayden sighed, pleased that he had not suffered the indignity of wetting himself. "Where are we?" he asked.

Cruce explained as he headed to the door to look for the others. Just when he reached the door, Ajel opened it from outside. Behind her, fresh snow was falling gently.

"Good morning," she said and smiled, which was pleasant to see.

"Good morning, Good Wife. Where is everybody?" Cruce asked as he moved out of her way.

"They be hunting savages with Duvek," she replied.

Startled, Cruce felt like he had just overslept on his wedding day. He meant to rush outside as if to catch his comrades before they left, but Ajel set a hand on his chest. Shutting the door behind her, she explained that his commander had decided that he should stay with Rayden until she deemed him fit to travel. Then Cruce was to escort her and Rayden to Upella and await his company's return.

Cruce was shocked and apprehensive about being left on the isolated farmstead.

"Why didn't your husband take you to Upella this morning?" Cruce said.

"He has his kin to avenge," she said dismissively. "And your friend be needing me here in case he took a bad turn, but I see that he be livelier already." She peeked around Cruce and smiled to Rayden.

Cruce felt an unhappy feeling of abandonment. There were savages to kill and his desire to fight stirred like his sudden hunger for breakfast.

"I'll get some water heating so you can wash up, warrior of Nufal," Ajel said.

Realizing that his mud face paint was still on him, Cruce was embarrassed by Ajel's comment about his griminess.

He went outside and fed his horse and Rayden's horse with fodder from Duvek's barn. By the time he was done, Ajel had a warm basin of water waiting for him and breakfast. While he washed himself clean and noticed the light stubble of his beard on his chin, Ajel opened her baking pan on the fireplace and removed golden biscuits that she then set afloat in a boat of gravy and venison sausage.

When she gave him his bowl she told him brightly that he looked much better. "Thank you, Good Wife," he said a little shyly.

"What's your name?" she asked.

"Cruce Chenomet from Kwellstan," he replied and then sat at the table and dove into the breakfast with eager purpose. As he chewed, he watched Ajel tend Rayden and feed him the same breakfast. He did not eat as much as Cruce because now that he was sitting up the head injury made him a little queasy. Ajel tucked him back beneath the blankets and told him to rest.

With her charge well tended, she filled a plate for herself and joined Cruce at her table. She ate quietly although she often looked thoughtfully across the table at Cruce when she dipped her spoon into her bowl.

"Are you worried?" he asked.

"About the savages?" she said and he nodded.

For a moment her youth and femininity allowed her to look vulnerable before her confidence took back over. "They say the savages be afraid to enter a proper house," she said and gestured with her spoon to the sturdy roof. "They fear our magic."

Cruce considered that and then said, "They have no houses?"

Ajel shook her head. "They camp upon the land in tents or nothing the year round. It be true," she explained.

As she had, Cruce now regarded the roof. It seemed not enough magic to keep back the bloodthirsty.

"When can Rayden travel?" Cruce whispered.

Ajel said that she expected him to be well enough to move the next day. Cruce was not sure if he should be glad that he only had to be their single guard for one day or if he should dread the prospect of the three of them venturing out on the open land the next day.

"Perhaps your husband will return tonight," he said hopefully.

Ajel gave that possibility careful thought but then rejected it. "He and your commander settled on plans to cross the Smet and be hunting out savage raiding parties between here and the hills. Duvek told me he would be swinging back to Upella to meet us. That'll take them two or three days for certain," she explained.

Cruce resigned himself to the situation and popped the last of his breakfast into his mouth. In his opinion, Duvek should not have left his wife in such a vulnerable situation, but Cruce decided against saying anything. It was not his place to criticize her husband. Gehr had been right to leave someone with her and Rayden, and Cruce decided to attend to the responsibility as best that he could.

He cleaned and sharpened his sword and knife and often went outside to observe the horizon. The snow continued to fall. To the east, the Tabren Mountains glowed in the fresh layer of whiteness. To the southeast the craggy hills of the Burlip blocked his view of where the prairie met the Valley of Nufal. He thought of his home and family. He imagined them warm at home, admiring the snow. He wondered if the lake had frozen over yet.

Cruce also wondered if his family was thinking of him. Before going on frontier duty, he had received a letter from Dayd and one from his mother. According to them, life was fine at home, but the absence of a letter from his father had been a stinging omission.

Before going back in the cabin to warm up, he shook off the distraction of home and carefully examined the trees along the nearby creek. He saw nothing and went inside.

Ajel was checking Rayden's stitches and applying a fresh dressing. His head still hurt and she prepared another herbal tea for him.

"Any savages?" she asked cheerfully.

"No," Cruce said a little uncomfortable with her carefree humor.

"When I be done with your friend, play me a game of dotty tiles," she said.

"Thank you, but I need to keep watch," Cruce said.

"You're going to make a fine militiaman," she remarked.

Still sipping his tea, Rayden said, "Cruce is going to be a commander."

"Yes, I be seeing he's estate class," Ajel said. "Now play some tiles with me. Bar the door. When the savages get here, you can fight them."

Her cavalier attitude astonished him.

"Relax. If this be our last day on Ektren, let us be enjoying it," Ajel declared.

There seemed to be no defying her, and Cruce privately admitted she made some good points. Besides it was cold out.

He joined her at the table and played dotty tiles all afternoon. Rayden even joined them in a few games, until his head hurt too much. Ajel brewed him a stronger cup of painkiller and bade him to rest.

As Cruce studied the lines and dots on the tiles looking for his best move, the threat of the savages receded. He did relax and even enjoyed himself. Ajel was pleasant company. She made a challenging opponent and an attractive one although he was trying not to notice.

After a string of losses, Cruce finally beat her two games in a row. Ajel sighed and declared that he had worn her down.

"My chores need doing," she said.

Reaching for his helmet and cloak, Cruce told her that he would tend the animals for her. He wanted another good look around outside before the dark came. She smiled appreciatively and set about preparing dinner.

Candles were lit throughout the cabin when Cruce returned and the fireplace snapped with a big hot fire.

"Bring in more wood," Ajel said quickly before he shut the door. Cruce went back out and gathered as much wood as he could carry from the pile of split logs. As he unloaded them by the fireplace, Ajel added that she could feel that this night was going to be colder than the last.

Cruce thought of his comrades out upon the open land. When they were not on the move or fighting, they would be huddled with their animals in a hollow. Although he did not envy their exposure, he still wished that he was with them, serving in the fight as he should.

Ajel had another hot meal prepared. Beef stew with winter vegetables and rye bread managed to sate Cruce's young appetite. He sighed when he was finished and remembered to thank his hostess for her attentive care.

"My pleasure," she said and cleared the dishes.

Cruce sat on the floor next to Rayden, who was tucked in comfortably next to the banked fire. Since the other militiamen had left, he could have all the spare blankets so he was warm and well padded now.

"I won't mind sharing a blanket tonight," Rayden said.

"Thanks," Cruce said. He spread his hands toward the fire to warm them. The domestic quiet and coziness were relaxing. His life had been so intense and lacking in luxury since he had gone through militia training and then started his frontier duty. Two nights out in Kahtep had been all the leisure he had known since leaving home. It was nice to pause and sit still in a real home. Looking at Rayden's bandaged head, Cruce only regretted the cause of this respite.

Ajel kneeled before the fireplace and crushed herbs into a steaming kettle. The fire glowed warmly on her skin, like a spring dawn on a white rose. She contemplated the brewing tea as if meditating. When she deemed the moment right, she retrieved the kettle from the fire and poured a cup for Rayden. She blew on it before handing it to him.

"This is a strong cup. It'll keep the pain back so you can sleep well tonight," she explained.

After thanking her, Rayden sipped diligently. Ajel rose and serenely blew out half the candles. With one candle in her hand, she then slipped away to the other room. Cruce got up to check that the door was properly barred and that the windows were tightly shuttered. Frightening thoughts of savages swarming over the cabin and breaking in to butcher them all besieged him. He wondered how he would get any sleep this night. When Cruce tried to console himself with Ajel's opinion that the savages feared to enter buildings, he only imagined the savages starting the cabin on fire and bringing hideous death.

I'd go out to fight them, Cruce told himself and meant it.

Although he was not prone to prayer, he silently asked the Great Divinity to spare them such awfulness this night.

"Cruce?"

He turned and saw that Ajel had come out of her bedroom. Her hair was freshly brushed and the golden tresses were spreading carelessly over her flowing linen nightgown.

"Would you be liking to stay in my room?" she asked.

Fear, uncertainty, confusion, excitement, and joy slammed together in Cruce's core. The chill of winter that infiltrated the room was driven back from his suddenly flushed body. Deciding that he must have misunderstood her, Cruce said that he would stay where he was. He then looked over to Rayden urgently, but his friend had slipped away into blissful sleep.

Ajel walked up to Cruce and put a hand on his shoulder. He was wearing his heavy shirt and armored vest, but the light pressure of her hand on his body was intensely stimulating. He could not stop looking into her playful brown eyes.

"You ever been with a woman?" she asked.

Her questions made his mind reel with forbidden possibilities. He swallowed and then managed to whisper, "Not entirely."

She came closer and he tentatively set his hands on her hips. Her sweet face and parted lips reached up toward his face that was compelled to lean closer to her. The reality of her body against his finger tips invited him to appease his natural lust.

But she was married. That fact traveled through his body like the shock of quaking land. Adultery. It was a crime declared by the Great Divinity. Adultery made disorder and it led man astray from civilization. Duvek could even kill him, and rightly so. And part of Cruce just wanted to be truly honorable and rebuff the advances of another man's wife on principle. Cruce would not commit such offense on a fellow man. Surely not.

Of course Cruce rejected all moral arguments in an instant. To escape what was happening was impossible and certainly not desirable. Ajel was desirable. She was all that was possible at that moment.

They kissed tentatively. Ajel pressed closer into his embrace that tightened happily. Her nightgown was thin beneath his hands and he could feel her hot flesh beneath.

Cruce liked kissing her. The intensifying pleasure of it drove the ugly demons of fear from his mind. Each hungry suck of their lips against each other made Cruce bolder. He kissed her face and her neck. He grabbed her left breast. She gasped, and that sound aroused him fully.

"Come," she urged breathlessly drawing him into her bedroom. They shuffled through the curtains to her private chamber.

Once inside the colder bedroom where candles burned in sconces along the walls, Ajel made Cruce let go of her and she began to undo his armor and clothing.

He stood still as she stripped him, more than a little amazed to suddenly find this lovely woman taking off his clothes. Excited as he was, the cold air did not cause him to shiver. It only enhanced the sensitivity of his skin. Naked before her, he was not embarrassed. He felt fully proud of his unleashed masculinity. Such vitality had never rushed through his veins before, and he felt like the most powerful man in the world.

"Let me see you," he dared to say and reached for her nightgown.

Ajel allowed him to lift it away. As her naked body was revealed to him, he told her she was beautiful. Her full breasts with hard dark nipples and smooth curving hips and light curling pubic hair called him to take his final step into manhood.

With nothing to restrain him, Cruce grabbed her. His hands went everywhere on her body. He kissed her breasts and her stomach before picking her up and falling with her into her bed. Ajel's legs parted with a willingness he had certainly dreamed about, and his inexperience as a man went away with only a bit of guidance from her.

As a young and eager man, he climaxed soon.

"I be hoping to get more from you than that," Ajel told him as she lay within his grateful arms. Cruce was more than committed to obliging her in any manner.

"I can teach you about loving a woman, Cruce," she said.

Through the night they made love. Ajel showed him pleasures that he had never known and she showed him how to please her as well. He gladly learned of her womanly mysteries, and took much satisfaction from pleasing her. Each time they joined in carnal totality, her cries of ecstasy came louder. Her musical outcries thrilled him and encouraged him. Animals knew the lusting rut, but humans knew passion, and he was so happy to bask in its energy.

Never had woman known such freedom in her marriage bed, and her male companion indulged in her wanton bliss with unjudging enthusiasm.

Just before the dawn came, Cruce twirled her tousled hair around his fingers. Only a couple of the candles remained burning. The others had gone to puddles of tallow as they had worked their bodies in the flickering light. Her face was satisfied and happy.

"I love you, Ajel," he whispered.

She smiled. "No, Cruce. You cannot," she whispered back without opening her eyes. Then the fact of their adultery dropped back into his mind like bird dung on the wind. Cruce snuggled up against her thoughtfully.

At length he said, "You could leave him. Be mine. I am a man of means. You would give up nothing. You would gain from it, I promise."

Ajel opened her eyes now. She kissed him but then grew serious. "Cruce, I know you be meaning what you say, but in time you be knowing that your offer be foolish. Duvek not be deserving such humiliation and my place be here. I am a fleshmender and serve my people happily. This night was for pleasure. If you love me, be accepting my gifts as they are."

Cruce did not reply. Perhaps, as he had accepted her other lessons this night, he should take this advice as well.

Knowing that an inevitable confusion was descending upon him, Ajel sought to dispel the unpleasantness. She rolled on top of him and slipped her sweet thighs over his loins for another sporting romp before they finally took some sleep.

Cruce woke after the sun was up. Ajel was gone, and, alone in her bed, he felt the slap of guilt finally strike. But it left no mark. Tired but suffused with contentment after so much release, he could not really summon any regret.

After putting on his pants and boots, he gathered the rest of his things and went out in the front room. Ajel was not there. Presumably she was at the barn doing chores, but Rayden was propped up on his bedding eating breakfast.

He grinned broadly at Cruce. "How was all night guard duty?" he joked.

Cruce felt his face turn red. "I thought you were drugged," he said.

"Not that drugged," Rayden laughed. "You showed her a good time."

Putting on his shirt, Cruce said, "Rayden, you can't tell anyone."

Growing serious, Rayden said that of course he would keep the secret. Adultery was no light matter in addition to defiling the hospitality of Duvek's house.

Changing the subject, Rayden told Cruce that Ajel had left breakfast for him in a pan by the fire. Cruce dished it up. He was truly ravenous. While scooping food into his mouth, he asked Rayden how he was feeling.

"Much better," he replied and did sound like himself more than the day before.

Cruce was glad and said so, but as he heard Ajel banging around the wood pile outside the door, he reached a decision quickly.

"Rayden, could you have a relapse? It would be a pity if we could not stay here another night," Cruce suggested.

Flashing with playful resentment, Rayden declared, "I'm who she should be nursing so carefully."

"Are you feeling dizzy?" Cruce said.

Rayden rolled his eyes and slumped dutifully onto the blankets. "You owe me, Cruce," he said as Ajel came through the door.

28. A Spell Upon Flesh

Onja discreetly controlled Halor and avoided arousing the suspicion of the other tabre. She kept to her quarters and wore the black sack dress that she disliked. The Nebakarz only glanced at her when they passed in the halls. She always stood aside and lowered her eyes while sensing their smug satisfaction for her punishment.

In the month since claiming Halor, she had secretly studied many of the written works available in the tower. The philosophies and spells of the tabre had been stimulating, but she could tell that the reference collection in Jingten was incomplete. Some texts hinted at greater possibilities or flirted with darker notions, but they never elaborated. Clearly the tabre had not wanted to risk exposing their greatest knowledge to the despised rys.

Even so, this cursory Nebakarz education improved her mental discipline. Her enormous capacity to see so much of the relationship between matter and energy tended to drag her inspirations toward chaos, but basic Nebakarz techniques were helping her gain a better command of her vast vision.

With her confidence rising, Onja reasoned that she would only discover the most profound expressions of her magic through experimentation. Unable to discuss her thoughts with any of the tabre or rys available to her, Onja had been pleased to discover that her crow, Clatta, was a remarkable being with which to converse. His mind was sharp. He understood both kindness and evil and when each was appropriate.

Clatta visited her chamber daily. He was currently strutting along the stone window sill as Onja reclined on her narrow bed. The window was open and a light breeze was scooting a dusting of snow into the room. Clatta's feathers were fluffed up against the cold, and he would pause in his strutting to preen himself every few steps.

Onja was lost in her examination of how the sunlight reflected off his black feathers with an iridescent sheen. The beauty of it was a magic in itself. His coloring shifted subtly as he moved, and Onja admired how his blackness could yield every color of light.

Clatta hopped to the floor. Onja reached down and he climbed up her arm with his wings open and then alighted onto her bed.

Onja opened her mind to his thoughts. On the mental level, Clatta had picked up on language quite easily although his rough throat was capable of only scratching out a few barely recognizable words, and Onja had asked him to stop trying. Clatta's thoughts would suffice now that she had tuned her mind to hear them.

"You want to help Dacian," she heard Clatta think.

Onja sighed. She longed to cleanse Jingten of the hateful tabre and then go all the way to Kwellstan and help Dacian escape, but her next steps could not falter. She plotted against the full might of an ancient and powerful civilization. A child did not replace its parents in a day. The success of her bold assault on Halor encouraged her, but she was still debating how to expand upon this initial victory.

She could not delay action much longer. The other tabre would not remain oblivious to Halor's altered state forever. Once her aggression was discovered, the other tabre would attack her. Onja expected that she could defend herself against a combined assault of tabre magic users, but she needed to be mindful of how she might kill them. Her hate and contempt for her oppressors certainly justified violence, but she wanted to make sure that the other rys perceived her correctly. She wanted them to see her as the bringer of their justice and not just a rogue. She would have to engineer the circumstances of her takeover of Jingten carefully.

Clatta squawked and then shared his thoughts. "Kill the tabre and I will eat of their flesh and become magic too," he said.

Onja laughed lightly. "I do not think that will work," she said.

"What would make me magic, Onja?" Clatta asked, and his seriousness surprised her.

"Is that why you have stayed near me? You think I can give you powers like mine?" she asked.

"Ever since I saw you and realized what you were, I wanted to be like you. I can fly, but you can do everything else," Clatta said and his envy was easy to feel.

"Flying is a power to be proud of," Onja said. She could control many things and create and destroy. She even possessed the ability to levitate, but to physically take off across the sky was beyond her, and she suddenly envied Clatta his one power.

"I will give thought on how to make you magic," Onja decided as possibilities germinated in her mind. Some ambitious experimentation with a willing Clatta might allow her to attain even greater power. Perhaps undertaking something bold would hone her skills before devoting all her energy to freeing Jingten of the tabre.

"Make me magic!" Clatta declared happily.

Onja enjoyed having Clatta as a confidant, but now that he had revealed his secret ambition to her, she had to wonder how trustworthy he really was.

"Clatta, if I can make you magic, you'll have to swear to serve me and only me always," she said.

Clatta scrutinized her with his intelligent black eyes. "I will think on it," he said now that he realized his dream of greatness would require a high price.

For the next two days Onja sequestered herself in her quarters. Clatta's request stimulated her mind more than she had expected. The crow's desire was an enormously intriguing problem. Onja even considered returning to the tower library and attempting to research the question, but she did not want to risk arousing suspicion.

Sometimes she paced her small chamber as ideas rushed through her mind like bats pouring from a cave at dusk. Other times she remained still, sitting on her bed and staring at the wall lost in thought.

Clatta would come and go through the window as he pleased. Upon each return, he would ask about her progress. Onja would smile and tell her pet that he must be patient.

After yet another inquiry she stood at the window and watched him fly away. Clatta certainly wants the power, she observed.

Clatta sought out some favored perch in the forest, and his dark flapping form withdrew in the distance. Onja allowed herself to reach a conclusion that she had been avoiding. She simply could not make Clatta magic. She could do many things to his form and even his mind, but rys, or tabre for that matter, did not know what made them so powerful. They were born with gifts, just as a bird was hatched with wings.

Yet this conclusion did not mean that Onja was defeated. Options remained. The results might not be entirely what Clatta envisioned, but Onja knew that she could suit her purposes.

Onja sensed that the weather would turn soon. The docile winds would give way to the blizzard she felt gathering in the north mountains. But right now icicles dripped in the sunshine as the heavenly light of the inferno sun touched the cold snow. She wished she could be outside. Inspiration was filling her mind and she wanted to be free upon the open land and set it loose when the storm struck.

But the tabre knew that she was confined to the tower as Halor's ward, and her departure would be noticed. She did not want Halor bothered with questions. Onja encouraged Halor to stay in his study, which was not really that unusual for him, but she still knew that her silent coup could be noticed at any time. She needed a way to leave seemingly with Halor's blessing.

Pondering this problem, Onja decided that her game with Halor was growing wearisome. He needed to serve a new purpose. Quickened by a sudden decision, Onja grabbed her plain brown cloak and swung it around her shoulders. When she left her quarters she could barely conceal the surging confidence inside her. She was envisioning a great spell unlike anything a rys had done before, and the excitement of it was the sweetest pleasure she had known so far in her life. She could not wait for the full experience. She wanted to swagger through the tower like she owned the place because soon she would, but the time for stealth had not expired. With her eyes lowered, she forced her feet to keep the cautious pace of a shy outcast. On her way to the levitation shaft, she passed two tabre acolytes and one priest. They did not speak to her, but Onja felt how their eyes flickered toward her body because they could not resist. They might think her low, but deep down they acknowledged her fine rys body. They'll soon see more than that, Onja told herself and reveled privately in her careful planning.

She entered Halor's study without knocking and barred the door behind her. She reinforced the lock with a spell. As her magic reacted with the deep tabre spells that had gone into the construction of the tower, she enjoyed how their foreign power yielded beneath her native touch.

Halor looked up from the wafer he was reading. For a second, he appeared confused by her entry, but then his mind snapped into the place where she had trained it to go.

"What do you need, Onja?" he asked. Halor started to get to his feet, but Onja gestured generously for him to stay in his chair. She sat down on his desk, seductively close.

"Have you heard from Dacian?" she asked.

Genuine sadness seeped across Halor's expression. He shook his head and reported that Dacian had not contacted him since the Grand Lumin had judged him.

"Now that I think about it, Onja. No one from Kwellstan has contacted me. That is a bit unusual," Halor said.

"It's probably for the best," Onja said and rewarded him with a soothing smile. She was glad that he had not been mentally contacted via a spirit projection from a powerful Nebakarz in Kwellstan. During such a magical communication, a smart tabre might have noticed how she had spun Halor's mixed emotions into a net of servitude.

"I think you should contact Kwellstan," Onja suggested.

"You do?" Halor said, surprised.

"Yes, and in person. But first you must leave a note for your colleagues here explaining your departure," Onja said and moved his writing stylus and a blank stone wafer across his desk and parked the instruments under his nose.

"You want me to travel to Kwellstan in the winter," Halor said, clearly resisting the notion.

"You've been coddled as a priest too long. Cold and snow are nothing for us to fear," Onja said. "Now start your letter and explain that you urgently had to take me to Kwellstan. I was becoming rebellious and needed firm control, like Dacian. You deemed it necessary to get me away from Jingten immediately before I polluted the peace that you work so hard to maintain."

Halor was fidgeting with his pinkies by the time she finished explaining what he was to write. Radiating true sympathy, he sought to counsel Onja because it was his natural way of interacting with rys. He said, "Onja, if you are thinking that we can rescue Dacian, I don't think you understand just how many tabre there are and what they are capable of."

"Don't tell me what I understand," she snapped. Tabre arrogance knew no bounds even when it was trapped in her cage.

Halor persisted but with a weaker tone, "We can't just dash off to Kwellstan and make the Grand Lumin release him."

"We will do as I say. Do not concern yourself with the details. Now write," she commanded. She got off his desk and stood over his shoulder as he dutifully etched into the stone disc why he would be leaving with Onja.

Onja took it from him once he was done and read it over carefully. "Good. Now get your cloak. We shall go quietly," Onja said.

"Right now?" Halor said, but her sharp look told him to get moving. He marveled at how she could switch from beautiful to terrifying as if the states were actually no different.

Halor left the note on his desk and went to an adjoining room. When he returned with a black cloak, he said, "It would not make sense that I would leave for such a trip and not pack or take an entourage."

"It does not have to make sense," Onja said tersely and pulled up her hood.

If Halor was thinking of resisting her, the blue flash of her eyes within the dark cowl made him abandon the possibility. He knew he could not resist her. She had bested him once and he knew she could do it again. It was better to serve in defeat than let her shove his face in the cesspool of his guilt where he could only surrender.

When they left Halor's study, no one was in the hall. Dinner was being served in the dining hall and the lifeforces of those who occupied the tower were concentrated there. Halor and Onja descended the levitation shaft together.

The circular receiving chamber of the tower was empty. Its cavernous heights reached to the observatory and crystals glowed along the walls in every direction.

Halor cast the spell that opened the main doors. He suspected that Onja was hustling him outside so abruptly because she wanted him as a hostage during her escape. He supposed it was the least he could do for her. The ignominy of being controlled by a rys and then kidnapped would ruin his career, but he did not even mind that outcome. After so many years of responsibility over the accursed rys, he was ready to be free of it. He could even describe his time under Onja's dominion as a relief. She left him mostly to do what he preferred. To study and reflect in peace without having to think about how to execute the bidding of his Kwellstan Sect masters. His lifelong loyalty to the Nebakarz had become remote under Onja's influence, and the freedom from it was not unpleasant.

Outside, the rising wind came out of the glacial peaks like a nightmare of meat cleavers. The snow rode the brittle gusts like tiny unstoppable marauders. Onja took Halor's hand and led him into the stormy darkness along the lake shore.

The raw blast of the elements invigorated Onja and she drew energy from the cutting storm. More would change during this blizzard than just the depth of the snow.

Onja looked back. The window lights of the tower could still be seen. Clatta flew a jagged line in the rough wind and landed on her shoulder. His talons gripped her thick cloak and the crow tucked his head into her hood beneath her chin.

Onja had known that Clatta would not be late to meet his destiny.

"Will you swear to serve me always?" she whispered.

He squawked his agreement.

Onja swerved away from Lake Nin and hiked north into the forest. Among the pines the wind was somewhat lessened, but the treetops groaned in the wind and the branches clattered and creaked, like protesting prisoners rattling their cages.

All through the night they hiked. The valley floor began its inexorably incline into the mighty mountains. The snows deepened and swirled around their bodies, but Onja had her rys senses to guide her so she did not falter from her course. She began to cast a cloaking spell around herself and Halor to block any tabre who might now be scanning the land in search of them.

Concealed by her spell, Onja led Halor toward the rocky heights. Gradually the trees became shorter and bent and the elemental force of the blizzard hit them full in their faces as it charged hungrily down the face of the mountain.

Just as they passed the tree line, Onja found the place that she had located beforehand. A wind-sculpted snow bank concealed a cave. The flash of her magic briefly illuminated her surroundings, and the snowflakes on the wind sparkled like a misty rainbow. A chunk of snow blew outward from the cave and crumbled at her feet. She led Halor through the shattered pieces of hard packed snow into the dark hole in the mountain.

They were protected now from the vindictive wind that howled outside. Already snow was drifting over the entrance in an angry scramble to repair what had been broken. Onja counted on it covering the cave again by morning.

"Halor, make us crystals for light," Onja commanded.

The tabre coughed. The physical exertion of struggling across the land in the snow storm had battered his body that was not hardened for such activity.

"Why are we here?" he demanded, a little testily.

"To sort out your future," Onja snapped, and by her tone, Halor knew that he best attend to the task that she had just given him.

It was a trifle for a Nebakarz priest to produce glow crystals. Promptly he produced three crystals and set them along the back of the cave. Minerals sparkled in the stone walls and a slender vein of silver shone from the rock.

Along the back of the cave, Onja saw some crude drawings, probably done with charcoal from a fire long gone cold. She examined them with interest. A male figure with the antlers of a deer or elk danced over a female figure giving birth. A sun radiated from the belly of the infant that was springing forth from the squatting loins of the female.

Onja knew that the images had been made by humans as they attempted to grapple with the forces of creation that besieged their puny minds.

Clatta let go of her shoulder and flapped around the cave before settling down. Onja heard his thoughts. He wanted to know if she would make him magic now.

"Soon, sweet one," she said, and Halor looked at her suspiciously.

Tired, Halor hunkered against the wall beneath the human drawings of which he took no note. "Onja, do you really think that you can hide in this cave?" he asked.

"Do you really think you can keep me locked up in your tower?" she spat back. She cast a warding spell throughout the cave to block the minds of prying tabre.

Halor folded his arms. He was cold. He disliked being in the open weather. He greatly preferred the cozy and magically sealed tower. Although Onja controlled him, he still persisted in his habitual course of keeping the peace.

"Onja, let me go. I'll say you escaped," Halor proposed. "But know that the Kwellstan Nebakarz will hunt you down. I know that you want us gone from Jingten, but how will kidnapping me help you? It will only draw more tabre to Jingten to punish you."

Onja was standing over him now and looking down on him. "Enough of your useless prattle. It's time for you to give me your best," she said.

Clatta crowed excitedly and flew up to her shoulder.

"What do you mean? What can I do?" Halor wondered. "If you want me dead, do it. I won't fight you. Strike me down. You have just cause."

Onja bent down and grabbed him by his cloak and pulled him to his feet. With her lips almost touching his, she whispered, "It's not your death I want. It's your life."

Her deft hands untied his cloak and let it fall to the ground. Then she began to undo his robe. Halor trembled. Her eyes had disappeared within blazing blue light as her fierce mind stoked her magic.

She took off his outer clothes and the cold air pressed against his dark skin like the hands of a strangler. Onja bade him to remove the rest of his clothes and his shoes. Despite his fear, Halor complied. Naked before her, he understood true vulnerability. The last of his free will screamed a warning. She had brought him here to commit some awful deed. Her magic was coming from a dark place of disorder and malice. The trumpets of war were sounding from the gates of some netherworld of the damned, and he was caught in its crushing maw.

Halor began to fight. He was a scholar, a teacher, a priest, and an administrator. He was not a warrior, trained in the Bozee or fighting magics, but he had magic and he used it now.

Onja absorbed his attack as if he had only thrown a raindrop at a thunderstorm. Her magic consumed him utterly until she could see the minute workings of every cell of his body, but she went deeper. She seized Halor's very soul and dragged his essence toward her own. He felt his lifeforce ripped from its foundation and sucked into her voracious will like the scent of a rose traveling into nostrils.

"Give it to me," she commanded mentally. Halor resisted. She had no right to devour his immortal soul.

She continued, "Give yourself to me and you'll know no worry or care. You'll know only freedom even as you accept my commands. Live in peace and give up your soiled existence as my corrupt oppressor."

Halor never actually consented. Her demand was too dear to him, but she preyed on his weakness. He was guilty of oppressing her and the rys and he felt bad about it. His secret wish to be free of such shameful deeds made him vulnerable and denied him the strength to retain his soul. Halor, in his last moment of awareness as himself, felt his will evaporate into Onja's will.

Onja reached up to Clatta and seized the bird by his neck. With Halor subdued and crumbled against the stone wall, she absorbed the crow's lifeforce with her magic as she had done to Halor. Clatta did not resist her. He gave up his soul to his powerful mistress along with his pledge to serve.

"Your mind shall be the one to endure," Onja promised and thrust Clatta's beak against Halor's neck. "Take of his flesh," she commanded, and the crow pecked greedily into the tabre's skin and ripped a piece of flesh away. As the crow swallowed the meat, Onja cast her spell.

The blue light of her unleashed powers swirled brightly within the cave. The crystals that Halor had made cracked into fine dust. Onja took the flesh and the souls in her possession and recast them according to her vision.

When it was done, Onja collapsed. She was shaking and she could feel that her body was thinner. With spots dancing across her vision, Onja looked upon the creature that the world had not birthed.

Halor and Clatta had been replaced by another thing. The size of Halor had been maintained and now a splendid pair of giant wings was folded along his back. His feet were transformed to bird feet but his hands remained, except with claws. Clatta's fine bird head had replaced the tabre head and glorious blue-black feathers covered the creature's whole body. Its eyes were closed and a sublime unthinking peace clung to its face as if it still slumbered in the egg.

Gray cool light was coming through the snow drifted over the cave. Dawn had come, but the storm still blew and scraped upon the land without any mercy. The scouring snow outside reshaped the drifts and bent the trees and ground away at the very peaks.

Onja felt as heavy as the mountain. She could not lift her head. An inescapable weariness assailed her. She had suspected that this spell in which her thoughts conceived upon the flesh of others would leave her spent. Afflicted by crushing oppressive exhaustion, she had been wise to select this hidden location because she would need time to rest. Her creation apparently required time to sleep as well. Onja was not sure how long that she would need to recuperate but she was content to let the snow build up and bury her.

29. Dark Art in the Dungeon

Dacian dumped a measure of oats into the feed trough. The horse munched contentedly, and Dacian stroked its face. The animal was indifferent to him, but that was soothing companionship compared to the snickering tabre servants who had laughed while he mucked out the stalls of the temple's stable. As he petted the horse, he envied the beast. The animal maintained its spirit while still submitting to its harness. Dacian wished he could obtain such peace with his circumstances.

Sighing, Dacian put the grain scoop back in its bin and left the stable. Dejection dragged at his shoulders. Each step took special effort because he wanted to collapse in despair.

Dacian emerged into the entry hall of the Altular. He could not bring himself to look up at its grand interior. For too long he had dreamed of serving the Great Divinity from within this temple, and the drudgery that the tabre inflicted on him was a wretched punishment. Such duties wasted his talent, and the humiliation galled him. The Grand Lumin had said that his menial duties were meant to teach him humility, but Dacian knew the humiliation was not just about him. The tabre believed all rys belonged at the bottom of the society, quiet and obedient.

For weeks, Dacian had kept quiet and obedient. Every day he worked at such things as cleaning floors or tending horses, and every night he retired meekly to his small room. But resentment smoldered inside him until finally his restraint was reduced to ash.

As Dacian approached his room, his apathy snapped. His blood flow quickened, and the flare of rebellion brightened his spirit.

After entering his room, he slapped his hands against the metal door as it faded into the appearance of smooth stone. His sharp mind unraveled the magic that governed the shifting materials of the door and put them back together with a new spell, his spell.

When the work was done, Dacian stepped back and felt his first flush of satisfaction in a long time. No one was entering his room unless he wished it. Extracting what pleasure he could from the tiny triumph, Dacian stretched out on his small bed and enjoyed some decent sleep.

When the prying spells of tabre came scratching at the door, Dacian's subconscious perception prodded him awake. With his seeing mind, he knew that the sun was halfway through its morning route. His failure to report for his ridiculous duties had finally prompted his tabre handlers to look for him. Their vexation radiated through the sealed door. Dacian relaxed with his hands behind his head and smiled smugly at their efforts to undo his spell. Whenever they came close to opening the door, Dacian cast another spell and thwarted them anew.

All day a procession of acolytes made failed attempts to open the door. Dacian surmised that they were hoping to avoid telling their superiors about his rebellion. Eventually a trio of full Nebakarz priests arrived, and Dacian vied with them into the evening. Driven to indignation, one of the frustrated priests cast his spirit projection into Dacian's room and scolded him to his face. Dacian easily outclassed the priest and dissolved his image with a lazy flick of magic. Having already suffered severe punishment from the Grand Lumin, Dacian had no patience for the threats of a middling priest.

Touching the crosha on his chest, Dacian was sobered by the enormity of his problems. Toying with the acolytes and priests had been an amusing rebellion, but Dacian could not waste his attention on a virtual shoving match with the Grand Lumin's underlings. He needed to contemplate the crosha even if it hurt.

Dacian opened the door. His sudden appearance startled three priests and a crowd of acolytes and servants. Dacian regarded them with disdain.

"You can make me your prisoner, but you will not bother me with your pointless labors," he announced.

The half circle of gaping tabre actually amused Dacian. He swung his gaze over the nervous tabre, expecting them to disperse. At length, a senior priest said, "Very well." At his direction the tabre departed.

Dacian went back into his room and sealed the door again. He crumpled on to his bed and clasped his face. The petty entertainment of his rebellion was over, and he wondered what the next move of his captors would be.

To his surprise, he was left in peace for four days. No one brought him food or water and he did not seek any. Knowing that he could survive indefinitely without sustenance if necessary, Dacian focused his precious unmolested time on the crosha. Applying his mind to the crystal that had fine filaments reaching into his heart caused him pain, but he clung tenaciously to his task despite the needling discomfort.

Eventually failure mauled his intellect into surrender. He could devise no way to undo the insidious enchantment that gripped his life. Exhausted and truly dispirited, Dacian collapsed, knowing that his enemies would surely come for him.

An intense blast of magic roused him. Dacian opened his eyes and saw his door glowing orange and then turn to vapor. Daykash Breymer burst through the super heated smoke. Dacian flung out his hands and cast a shield spell, but the Daykash did not attack him with magic. Aided by two priests, they pounced on Dacian and seized his arms. When he saw a small hollow needle in Breymer's hand, Dacian cringed with panic, but firm hands drew him upright. The needle jabbed into his neck. Dacian cried out at the sharp pain, but his resistance crumbled immediately. A foreign substance permeated his neck tissues and kept spreading. His muscles stopped reacting to his will, and his magic receded from the reach of his mind. Paralyzed and bereft of his natural powers, Dacian sagged in the grip of his enemies.

The Daykash pulled the needle out. Sinister satisfaction spread over his narrow face as he stepped back and admired the fully subdued rys.

"You did not know we could do that to you, did you rys?" Breymer said. "You'll beg your masters for mercy before long," he predicted and whirled into the hall.

The two priests hauled Dacian up by his arms and dragged his dead weight for a few steps before applying a levitation spell to him. Dacian felt his paralyzed body lighten, and the helpless floating made his terrified mind reel with disorientation. Watching the carpet slide past beneath him, Dacian naturally sought to feel his surroundings with his advanced perception, but the toxin polluting his flesh left only yawning emptiness in his head.

Dacian was hauled past the foundations of the Altular. Outside, the wondrous temple lorded over the great forest and inspired the citizens of Nufal with its ultimate grandeur, but few of them ever considered its dark fearsome depths. Kwellstan Sect builders had delved deeply into Ektren's stone body. Below common storage basements lurked secret chambers accessed by only the Grand Lumin and his closest priests. From the cellars, a narrow stair led to an even lower room carved from the cold stone where a wide, circular pit gaped from the darkness like the birth canal of an unholy beast. This secret levitation shaft opened onto a deep natural cave that the Nebakarz kept mostly free of water with their enchantments. Even so, the constant drip of the relentless waters that blessed Kwellstan above rained in slow motion within the cave, leaving stalagmites and stalactites and other strange sculptures of glistening minerals to beautify the humid hole.

Here Dacian was brought and thrown face down inside a circle of jagged glowing crystals. Daykash Breymer laughed. Dacian had never heard him do that before, and the mirth of the Daykash scourged Dacian with hopelessness. The tabre left him paralyzed upon the damp heartless rock. Dacian did not know how long he lay in that timeless pit, but mercifully he felt the poison dissipate. Grateful to feel his body respond again, he moved his limbs. The white light pulsing languidly within the crystals brightened and magic pressed on his body. An enchantment akin to the tumor-like crosha radiated from the ring of crystals.

Slowly he became aware of a Nebakarz priest beyond the ring of enchanted crystals. As the poison continued to slip from Dacian's nerves, he moved again, and the priest leaned forward from the darkness and put a tube to his dark lips. After a spurt of air, a dart pricked Dacian and replenished the poison. His agony was allowed only the feeble outlet of groaning. He continued in this poisoned limbo through darting after darting.

He was not sure how many days passed in this misery. With his mind impaired, he could not look at the world above and count the risings and settings of the sun. Sprawled against the slick stone of the dungeon floor, Dacian kept still the next time he felt his control return. Moving would only summon another dart from the watchful shadows.

As his mind cleared, he sensed the approaching lifeforce of the Grand Lumin. Dacian turned his head and let his other cheek slap onto the floor so that he could look at the levitation shaft coming out of the cave's arching ceiling. The glow of the Grand Lumin's magic swelled out of the tunnel like a mockery of moonlight.

The Grand Lumin settled softly onto the floor and his floating orbs bobbed alongside him. Illuminated by the orbs' soft light amid deep shadow, his red robe looked like fresh blood. The heavy fabric seemed to weigh heavily on his thin elderly body as he shuffled toward Dacian with blind-yet-seeing steps. One priest came down the shaft to attend him.

"He is watching us," the Grand Lumin whispered and his attendant slipped a fresh dart into his blow tube.

"Wait," the Grand Lumin said and entered the ring of crystals alone.

Standing over the rys prisoner, the Grand Lumin said, "Are you willing to serve me now, Dacian?"

"No," Dacian replied. His defiance was his sole possession in life. A satisfying wave of fury came off the Grand Lumin. The powerful so disliked the audacity of rebellion. It reminded them that courage came from a place that could never truly be owned or controlled.

"I could leave you here," the Grand Lumin warned.

"Why not just kill me?" Dacian demanded.

"Why not indeed?" the Grand Lumin said. His floating orbs blazed hotly and swooped down. They crashed into Dacian's head and exerted a levitating force that dragged him to his feet. Pressed against his ears, the orbs held him up straight in front of the Grand Lumin while a piercing sound snarled at Dacian's sanity.

"You are powerful, Dacian," the Grand Lumin said. "Powerful enough to warrant study."

Dacian unclenched his teeth. "Are you saying that I am superior to tabre?" he asked.

The Grand Lumin's thin lips pulled back from his teeth. As when he created the crosha, his spellcasting erupted like birds flushed from bushes. His magic tore violently into the rys. Pain screeched along Dacian's nerves like a splinter of wood jamming jaggedly under fingernails.

Dacian screamed. His shield spells banged around the cave like drunken lightning.

The Grand Lumin probed beyond Dacian's thoughts. Dacian felt the gates of his lifeforce weaken, but he must never let this powerful tabre touch him in the reservoir of his soul. Dacian fought. Even impaired and weakened, he marshaled strength from deep in his being. He raised his hands and clutched the orbs pressed against his ears and pulled them away from his head.

Pain and determination twisted his face into a wretched grimace. In his mind, he saw the cold blind eyes of the Grand Lumin trying to peer into his soul, but Dacian would never let him see the essence of his power.

Dark rage threatened to overtake Dacian's emotions, but he feared the ugliness that this treatment was conceiving within him. He did not want to hurt anyone. He did not want to be cruel. Was the Grand Lumin trying to corrupt him toward violence so that he could then claim that rys were dangerous? To what would that lead? Dacian feared that he would become an excuse for the tabre to unleash some horrible campaign of oppression against the rys that was far worse than what they already did.

Trembling, Dacian held the Grand Lumin back from seizing his soul, but he resisted setting free the rabid dogs of injustice that howled and frothed next to his wounded heart.

When the Grand Lumin seemed disgusted with the stalemate, Dacian assumed that he had avoided the tabre leader's trap. The horrible noise that pierced Dacian's skull rose in intensity, and the Grand Lumin cast a spell that incinerated Dacian's shirt. Then the Grand Lumin lashed out with one thin arm through the ash and smoke. His scrawny fingers with their hard dry nails scratched Dacian's stomach, and, aided by precise attack spells, the physically weak hand became the claw of a pitiless predator and tore his flesh. Split muscle revealed the loosening bulge of Dacian's viscera and purple blood spilled from the ragged wound in a grotesque satire of a waterfall.

An awful cry of despair issued from Dacian's gaping mouth. Fighting for his life, his shocked metabolism boiled the poison from his body. Dacian let go of the orbs and pushed his guts in with his hands. The orbs slammed back into his head, but their power could not stop his healing spell that blazed around his torso.

The Grand Lumin observed how Dacian reconnected tissues and rapidly regrew flesh. It was a tremendous display of genius power. Truly the Nebakarz had wrought something great in Jingten, but the Grand Lumin doubted that the rys could be properly controlled. Dacian and his kind were too dangerous to risk acceptance. The Grand Lumin had sensed this for years now. What remained to be determined was if the power of the rys could be harvested.

With his body whole again, Dacian felt some of his fury slip free. After what the Grand Lumin had just done, Dacian lost one of his moral handholds. Again he pushed the orbs away from his head and this time flung them back at the Grand Lumin. Justified anger enflamed Dacian's magic as he prepared to attack.

"He's free!" the Grand Lumin gasped, and his priest waiting behind him fired a dart.

Dacian's mind shot the poisoned dart with a super-hot thought, and it disappeared in a spray of sparks.

The Grand Lumin thrust a dart that had been up his sleeve into Dacian's bare chest.

"No!" Dacian shouted despairingly. He could not even lift a hand to take out the poisoned needle. The sting of the Grand Lumin was savagely stronger than the poison Dacian had heretofore experienced. Its toxic bite rampaged through his body, causing both mental disorientation and a violent physical reaction.

Lurching in a seizure, Dacian toppled to the floor, slamming painfully into the rock. Convulsions wracked him until paralysis gradually quieted his jerking body. Then the Grand Lumin stooped slowly beside him and retrieved his dart.

The Grand Lumin's orbs were hovering behind his head, and Dacian could only see his tormentor in silhouette.

The Grand Lumin said, "Now that I have you worn out, Dacian, I don't think you will be resisting me much longer."

Dacian wanted to shut his eyes, but the paralysis forced him to stare while the damp air cooled his eyeballs. He was tired after so long without food or proper rest, but he was Dacian and he was powerful and he would fight this awful battle for a thousand years if he had to.

Dacian let go of his anger and rallied his magic around his soul. Let the Grand Lumin drill with his malicious mind. He would never take what was not his.

A priest came down the levitation shaft. He approached the arena where the Grand Lumin practiced his dark art.

"What is it?" the Grand Lumin asked testily.

"Alloi is here, Grand Lumin. She asks to speak with you," the priest said.

The Grand Lumin scowled and his blind white eyes flashed. He was annoyed with himself for not noticing that Alloi had entered the Altular.

Meddlesome Drathatarlane, he thought. I best send off their pretty spy before I continue here.

Stiffly the Grand Lumin straightened and shuffled away from Dacian.

Dacian had overheard the message and he found the thought of Alloi comforting. She had not been like the other tabre, and he was admittedly grateful for her serendipitous interruption.

"Enjoy this respite," the Grand Lumin said over his shoulder. "You obviously need more time to think about your future. I expect to find you more cooperative when I return." Then to the priest who would stay below, the Grand Lumin said, "Drown him. That ought to weaken him enough."

Dacian was not sprawled at an angle that allowed him to see the Grand Lumin leaving, but the cave grew a little darker once the cruel tabre leader ascended with his glowing orbs. The future was too painful for Dacian to think about. Perhaps there was no such thing as a future in this timeless pit of torment.

The priest who remained in the cave cast a spell. The confining enchantment now felt like boulders pressing on Dacian's skeleton. The light increased in the cave. The crystal formations that penned Dacian grew from the hard stone and transformed his pen into a circular cell. Then the crystal walls bent inward to encase him in a dome with only a small opening at the top. Water started to drizzle and then pour through the hole, and Dacian realized that the priest had loosened the spell that kept the groundwater out of the chamber.

Now the Grand Lumin's last words embraced comprehension in Dacian's mind. He was actually going to be drowned. Already the paralysis hindered his ability to breathe, but at least a little air was drifting into his lungs. The water was pooling on the floor and starting to seep into Dacian's slack mouth. He had to do something to prepare his body for this ordeal. A rys could enter a state in which breathing was not necessary, but he needed his magic. With the sickening poison polluting his mind, he felt like a fish flopping on a riverbank, its gills fluttering in futility.

Desperately Dacian sought to enter a trance. He had to destroy the poison in his body. He squeezed all the strength he could from his desire to survive.

Water continued pouring into the cell and covered his head. Dacian transformed his fear into peace. He imagined the floating calm of the womb where once he had developed inside the true magic of his mother's creative force. In that place he had been pure and protected.

Thinking of his mother boosted his desire to overcome this attack. He would not submit to the intolerable shame of perishing in the bowels of his oppressors' stronghold. Glaxon and Illyr had made a son meant for a greater fate than that.

Dacian reached his magic that had retreated deeply within his spirit. When he clutched this precious reservoir, it was as if the Great Divinity had blessed him again with the gifts of his race. He grasped this thin line of power that fluttered like the loose thread of a tattered garment. He told himself to focus only on the poison. The water seeping into his lungs mattered for nothing. He could wait to breathe.

Focused entirely on his physiology, Dacian began to segregate the wicked poison and expel it from his body. It sweated out his pores, and lavender swirls of his purple blood floated away from his eyes and nose, and then he was free of the poison. Dacian surged back to his true power. Before the glorious rush of triumph overcame his good sense, Dacian told himself not to be guided by only his anger. He would gain his freedom, but he must show himself to be better than the tabre. Despite his sick fury that howled for justice, he would show that rys were civilized, good, and worthy of respect.

The crystal cell exploded into a million shards. The water washed the Nebakarz priest away until a stalagmite snagged him by his robe like driftwood in a flood.

Dacian stood up. He renewed his body with a subtle heat spell that drove the water from his skin and ragged clothing. With steam curling over his skin, he stepped away from the patch of bedrock where the tabre had shown themselves for what they truly were.

He sloshed by the priest, who was scrambling to loosen his robe from the spiny stone. The tabre was frantic with fear. He had never expected Dacian to shrug off the Grand Lumin's poison and obliterate the holding cell. The nearly witless priest tore his soggy garment free and stumbled away from Dacian.

Dacian headed to the levitation shaft and reached out to the shaft's line of energy, but a mortal pain stabbed his chest, like his heart muscle was cramping. Dacian released his connection. Gasping, he realized the crosha had hurt him. The chamber was still filling with water and it was up to Dacian's thighs now. The other tabre priest waded up to him. His eyes were wide and glowing with his power, but he did not dare attack. The priest connected with the levitation line and instantly flew upward.

Dacian watched him go, knowing that the tabre would soon be alerted to his partial escape. After studying the dark tunnel, he resigned himself to having to make his way out the old fashioned way. Dacian undid the rest of the spells that held back groundwater from the chamber and accelerated its flooding so he could float to where he could reach the sides of the tunnel.

******

The Grand Lumin settled onto his cushions and prepared himself mentally for his encounter with Alloi. His experience with Dacian had made him feel his age, and he had not liked that. But the Grand Lumin set his turmoil aside. He would never want a Drathatarlane to sense his distraction.

When he was ready, he telepathically informed his attendants to show her in. Alloi was lovelier than ever. The absence of her twin brother allowed her splendorous appearance to shine more brightly without being shaded by Tempet's masculine grandeur. Alloi's black hair was pulled back smoothly from her face and held in place with jade clips. A black tunic with a wolf fur collar and loose pants draped her statuesque figure. A single silver pendant adorned her neck, showing off the symbol of the Drathatarlane Sect, a squat gnarled tree within a streaking comet.

The Grand Lumin was soothed to look upon her in his mind. She even made him briefly wish for his forsaken physical vision, but he knew too much of power to truly be tempted by flesh.

"Alloi, I am pleased to be graced by your company," the Grand Lumin said.

She bowed politely and thanked him for receiving her.

"What wisdom would you learn from me today?" he asked.

Alloi tried to control her disgust. She noted that the Grand Lumin did not seem to be trying to probe her thoughts. His sick games with Dacian had probably taxed him too much.

"I would see Dacian again," Alloi announced bluntly.

"Why?"

"I found him interesting," she said, and it was the truth.

"Dacian is not available," he said.

Alloi's ingrained dislike for the Kwellstan Sect swelled inside her. The Sect was insufferably arrogant just as she had been taught. And the Grand Lumin was an unprincipled slime who knew nothing of the glories of the Great Divinity.

"I know what you are doing to him," she said.

The words hung uncomfortably between them as the Grand Lumin pondered the possibility that she might actually have the power to see down into his most secret den.

"You know nothing, young lambling," he said.

His grandfatherly endearment infuriated her. "I saw you take him to your nasty dungeon," she said. "Why are you treating him so?"

The floating orbs near the Grand Lumin spun like agitated bumble bees and then stopped.

"Why would I tell my business to a Drathatarlane spy?" he asked.

"How dare you?" she shot back indignantly. "I am an ambassador!"

The Grand Lumin scoffed at her semantics. "You are a sneaky little spy. You Drathatarlane criticize us Kwellstan for going forth in the world to learn, and then your lazy masters send you to steal all that we know."

"I have never stolen anything," Alloi declared.

"Only because I'm not foolish enough to allow you to see anything that is useful," the Grand Lumin said.

Returning to her original purpose, she asked again to see Dacian.

"It is impossible," the Grand Lumin said.

"You are hurting him. I can feel it," she said and her sympathy colored her voice. "He needs discipline. We are his masters and he needs to accept that," the Grand Lumin said. "Now go, Alloi. This does not concern you."

Alloi refused the dismissal. "I am an elite citizen of our shared realm and I will not stand by while you torture someone. It is wrong," she said.

"Wrong!" the Grand Lumin almost laughed. "I'll not listen to moral lectures from a Drathatarlane spy. Go ask your masters about their secrets. See how much they care about the pain of others when they want something."

Alloi hoped that she did not show how much his words bothered her. She was young and did not know all the ways and secrets of her Sect. They probably did hide things from her.

But that was not what mattered at the moment. The Grand Lumin was doing something awful to Dacian. She had to find out what it was because it was her duty and because Dacian could not possibly deserve it.

She sheathed herself in a potent shielding spell that was far stronger than any she had ever used in a Bozee bout. Dancing white fire radiated from her body as she flaunted her strength.

"Show me Dacian so that I might see that he is well treated. No tabre can be hurt without a trial witnessed by his peers," she declared.

"Bah! He is no tabre," the Grand Lumin spat.

"Where is it written that rys are not tabre?" she demanded.

"We all know it to be true. And I've heard enough complaints from your Drathatarlane masters since our colonization of the Rysamand about the abomination of the rys. Forget your puny argument. Dacian has no tabre rights. Now, little Drathatarlane spy, stop your tantrum and leave me," the Grand Lumin commanded.

Alloi hesitated. She knew that the Grand Lumin was hiding a terrible secret. Dacian was powerful, and she suspected that the Grand Lumin was working some dark art in his dungeon. For the sake of her Sect, she needed to find out what it was, and, personally, she wanted to save Dacian from whatever torment he suffered. Clearly the Kwellstan Sect thought of Dacian as merely an experimental animal, but she intuitively saw the error in that attitude. The Grand Lumin was provoking Dacian and he had to be stopped before something horrible happened that neither the Kwellstan nor the Drathatarlane could control.

"Let me see him!" Alloi shouted. She brazenly cast her magic toward the mighty will of the Grand Lumin, surprising even herself with her audacity. But she was Alloi, the most powerful of her generation, and it was time that she embraced her role. The nasty Kwellstan Sect would feel her righteous disapproval.

The Grand Lumin met her challenge with supreme confidence. He deflected her magic and physically knocked her back against the doors to his inner sanctum. His white-hot mind plunged into Alloi's awareness as if she did not shield herself at all. He was thrilled to best her so swiftly, and he held her tiny mouse mind down mentally with the paw of his power.

Alloi quailed as his magic encased her physically and mentally. She had overstepped herself, and done so brashly in the lair of her enemy. Perhaps this was the lesson that she had been meant to learn when her brother was not at her side to save her. Determined to regain control, she shoved back with her magic. Fueled by her pride, her power flared fiercely from her lifeforce. She expelled the Grand Lumin's leering awareness and cast an attack spell that was meant to physically remind him that he had no authority over her.

He fended her off with a shield spell, but her impudence enraged him. The Grand Lumin lifted off his seat and flew across the room at her. His floating orbs shot out ahead of him, and Alloi caught them in her hands before they crashed into her face.

Burning power seared her flesh, but she kept him at bay.

"Would you start a war?!" the Grand Lumin thundered. "Would you cast away two thousand years of peace and progress because I denied you one request? Are you going to be the one to do it? You, all by yourself without the leave of your Drathatarlane masters, would be the one to challenge the Kwellstan Sect?"

"You tempt me!" she snarled, but she was shaking from exertion. Sparring magically with the highest among the Kwellstan Sect was unsanctioned folly.

The Grand Lumin floated back and recalled his orbs.

Alloi eased her power down to just a precautionary shield spell.

"That is better, lambling. You don't want to start a war. We Kwellstan could tear down your mountain towers if it suited us," he boasted.

"Is that what you hope to do once you twist Dacian's power to your will?" she asked, putting the fears of her masters to her lips.

She sensed how her accusation summoned a suspicious discomfort within the Grand Lumin. Whether she had spoken the truth or not, he at least harbored a deep desire to settle the ancient rivalry between the Sects once and for all.

"You will go now," the Grand Lumin said.

The doors behind Alloi opened and bumped her in the back. Despite the intense confrontation, the Grand Lumin's mind seemed suddenly to be elsewhere. Two attendant priests rushed into the inner sanctum. They brushed by Alloi, obviously concerned with some other urgent business.

One priest shooed Alloi out while the other kneeled before the Grand Lumin.

As the door was forced shut in her face, Alloi actually detected the mental command of the Grand Lumin. He had not bothered to carefully shield his thoughts. A lapse she had never expected to enjoy.

"Send the Daykash to take care of it," she overheard the Grand Lumin command his priest.

Tangible alarm radiated through the Altular. Waves of energy from a great work of magic were seeping upward from the temple foundations. Alloi had to find out what was happening. Had they remade Dacian into some enthralled uber warrior? Or was he rampaging toward escape?

Alloi cast a cloaking spell over herself. The attendants of the Grand Lumin burst out of the inner sanctum. She ducked behind a statue to supplement her cloaking spell. The priests ran by her, their feet and robes flapping in undignified urgency.

Keeping her lifeforce masked, she followed them. They met up with Breymer who carried a slender spear, and then they hurried into the dark underbelly of their temple. Alloi pursued them cautiously. Through the storage cellars she trotted down dark stairs with her whispering steps until she reached the grim place where the levitation shaft waited like a gallows.

Many priests were already gathered. Glow crystals cast their shadows upon the rocky cavern walls, making a distorted shadow forest of heads, arms, and long bodies. Alloi found a natural crevice in the stone and ducked inside it. She kept her cloaking spell active.

She could smell water. The wondrous waters of Kwellstan that she had come to appreciate gave off a pure aroma this far below ground. Filtered through the rock, the waters were clean yet enriched by their prolonged contact with the potent body of the world.

Tentatively she peeked with her awareness over the heads of the priests and looked into the levitation shaft. It was filling with water and some of it shot up along the levitation line like an ornamental fountain.

The Daykash held his spear poised over the water. Alloi detected the poison called sho loaded into the hollow tip of the spear. It was a very concentrated formula of sho, and Alloi shuddered when she considered what it would feel like to have that fearsome paralysis drug clogging her veins.

Dacian's hands reached out of the water. His strong fingers gripped the rock wall of the levitation shaft. His head emerged from the water and he took a great breath. Blue light glowed in his eyes and he reached for the lip of the shaft.

The Daykash thrust the spear into Dacian's left shoulder. He cried out in defiance more than pain. Instead of splashing back into the frothing water, he grabbed the spear and twisted it from Breymer's hand. Dacian hurled the light spear over the edge and the priests scrambled out of its path. The enchanted wood clattered on the slick rock floor as Dacian swung out of the water. A stout shield spell glowed around his body, and the sho darts of other priests hissed and bounced off the shell of his power. His bare chest was heaving, and the milky oval of the crosha had taken on an amethyst tinge.

Daykash Breymer ordered his priests to stop shooting, and he stepped in front of Dacian. "You cannot escape. The crosha will kill you," he announced.

Dacian felt the horrible enchantment drilling into his chest. He still did not know how to get it out of his body. "Why do you hate me?" he demanded. "I have never sought to be anything except your faithful brother!" Bewildered pain marked his voice, and it made Alloi's heart ache.

"We will fight you. All of us," Breymer said.

"Why?!" Dacian cried. He could not understand them. "Remove the crosha and let me go in peace."

"Do you think we are foolish?" the Daykash asked. He believed utterly that without the crosha to contain Dacian, he would go back to his rys and rouse them to rebellion.

"Let me go. I do not want to fight you," Dacian said.

After an unspoken command from the Daykash, all the priests hit Dacian with their attack spells. He actually dipped to one knee beneath the combined fury of the assault, but like a weight lifter, he rallied his strength and returned to his feet. Despite so much provocation, he did not counterattack. He was not ready to accept the chaos of vengeance. His patient suffering might get through to his tabre cousins yet. How long could they pummel him with hatred before they saw his goodness and the goodness of his kind?

Protected within his shield spell, he walked toward the narrow stair. He looked forward most to seeing the sun again. Being locked away in the deep dark world of solid stone had been hard on him. Bred in the highest mountains of the world, he needed to return to the balcony of the heavens.

The Daykash halted the attack. Dacian's passive resistance puzzled him and he clearly suspected that Dacian plotted some trick. Those priests who still blocked Dacian's way stepped aside, unable to conceal their fear and awe.

The entrance to the stairs beckoned Dacian but he hesitated when the white glow of two floating orbs illuminated the steps. The Grand Lumin made his way slowly to the bottom step. His long red robe slipped down the last few steps before settling again around his feet.

He held his gnarled hands open in a welcoming gesture. "I am impressed, Dacian. Truly," the Grand Lumin said. "It is a high art of our Sect to repel the sho potion. Honestly, I am amazed."

The unexpected praise rattled Dacian more than any crude attack could have done.

"You will not keep me in this dungeon," Dacian said softly.

"I can see that," the Grand Lumin agreed. "Forgive this treatment, Dacian. I have tested you harshly. But as the first rys to seek to join us, we had to know your mettle. The Kwellstan Sect is the elite of Ektren. We can never examine a candidate too deeply, especially one with your…aptitude."

Confusion crept into Dacian's mind like moss growing on a tree stump. What the Grand Lumin said did not seem right, but Dacian suddenly felt unable to think critically. Had all his suffering been an elaborate test? Was the Grand Lumin about to give him everything he had always wanted? It did not seem possible, but neither did the misuse he had suffered since coming to Kwellstan. Maybe the Kwellstan Sect had been testing his loyalty. Perhaps Halor had been forbidden to warn him about this grim initiation.

Alloi listened in shock to the Grand Lumin's words, but she had no dreams of joining the Nebakarz to skew her thinking. She recognized the sly magic of the Grand Lumin. Not all magic was easy to notice, and sibilant little spells sang inside his words, delicately pollinating Dacian's mind with thoughts of submission. Dacian's fatigue was obvious, and, despite his power, she knew that he was not invulnerable.

Alloi revealed herself. To actually see the Grand Lumin and Daykash Breymer startled was supremely satisfying.

"Dacian, it is me, Alloi. I've come to help you. The Grand Lumin is tricking you," she warned.

Her unexpected entry jolted Dacian out of the mental trap, but her offer to help him was just as confusing as the Grand Lumin's sudden acceptance of his talent.

The Grand Lumin hissed with rage when he saw Alloi. "Vile Drathatarlane!" he gasped, truly furious.

Daykash Breymer seized Alloi by the wrists. "How did you get here?" he demanded.

"By the stairs," she said snidely.

More priests grabbed Alloi from all sides.

"Not a spy?" the Grand Lumin criticized, shuffling up to her.

Alloi was the winner of many Bozee bouts and she used an attack spell to force the priests to release her. As soon as the grip of her rivals gave way, she slipped by the Daykash so she could face Dacian.

With only a fleeting moment of freedom, Alloi said, "Dacian, I'll give you sanctuary. Come to my house and I'll contact my Sect and tell them to help you. I'll ask for our best Nebakarz to come and help you free yourself of this…" She reached out to his crosha, but before her sensitive fingers could brush the smooth enchanted stone, the Grand Lumin shouted, "Enough!"

Daykash Breymer's hands closed around Alloi's upper arms and yanked her back against his chest. He steered her toward the stairs.

"Dacian," she called urgently, wanting his answer.

He looked at her painfully. Alloi was lovely and seemingly kind. She was powerful too, which he respected, and among so much hostility, her offer of help should have been irresistible.

But, despite everything, Dacian was of the Kwellstan Sect. He had spent decades studying as a Kwellstan acolyte and he was born of a Kwellstan colony. To side with a Drathatarlane felt unthinkable.

Dacian shook his head. He saw her amazed disappointment as Daykash Breymer hustled her to the stairs.

The Grand Lumin approached Dacian, waving away the two priests that moved to buffer him from Dacian.

"Only the maker of a crosha can undo it. Dacian is not going to harm me," he said.

His orbs started circling Dacian's body and sparking against his shield spell.

Dacian said, "Grand Lumin…Master, please remove the crosha and let me go."

The Grand Lumin said, "In time, Dacian. Once you have shown that you can be obedient and perform the tasks I set for you."

Dacian assumed that meant more humility training with menial tasks. On behalf of the rys, he could not accept it. "I am leaving," Dacian announced and walked by the Grand Lumin. No priests moved to stop him.

"You cannot leave Kwellstan," the Grand Lumin reminded.

Without stopping, Dacian said, "As you have tested me, I shall test you."

The Grand Lumin watched Dacian in his mind as the rys climbed the steps. Mentally he told his followers that Dacian would be back. "Place him in his quarters upon his return," the Grand Lumin commanded.

Dacian rushed up the steps. His eagerness to go outside motivated him more than fear of those behind them.

When he reached the ground level of the Altular, he kept his attention fixed on the exit to the Plaza of the Waters. Dacian ignored the startled tabre who looked at him in wonder and fear. He knew he made an unpleasant sight. What remained of his clothes was ragged and dirty. His body was thin from exertion and the crosha branded him as a criminal.

When he left the Altular, only a dreary winter day presented itself as freedom. Dacian was still glad for the cloudy cold daylight, and the half frozen waters in the streams and bathing pools possessed a clean loveliness.

The obscured sun was ducking out of the short day as quickly as it could. Dacian thought of Jingten far to the west and started to run. The leafless treetops surrounding the city loomed above rooftops and Dacian hurried toward the forest. He ignored the rising pain in his chest.

By the time he reached the last building along the westerly road, he was staggering. Determined and delirious, he pressed on beneath the old trees, but the city could still be seen through the trunks when he collapsed. Dacian clutched a smooth-barked beach tree and gasped as he fought to master the pain. He looked down at the crosha. Its color had deepened to a misty purple. Countless fine needles pierced his heart.

Still gripping the tree, he struggled to find the fortitude to continue. He sobbed once in weary despair before lapsing into pitiful silence. He could not decide what to do. Returning to the Grand Lumin was a sickening thought, but forcing himself to take another step away from Kwellstan might be suicide.

Alloi came to him. She placed her hand on his chest and cast magic to block the pain from his mind.

"Does that help?" she asked.

"Yes. Thank you," he said and looked at her gratefully.

She studied the crosha and its sinister character quickly appalled her.

Still blocking much of his pain, Alloi helped Dacian to his feet. He kept an arm around her shoulders and her hand remained on his chest. "What was your crime?" she whispered.

Dacian remembered the phlia-mel striking Onja. He wanted to answer Alloi's question but it did not seem right to speak to her of Onja. Or perhaps it was not right to think of Onja with Alloi so close. He was not sure which.

He only shook his head. Alloi took him to her house. Humans stepped aside in shock as the tabre and rys made their way slowly down the street. And tabre watched with wary disapproval.

"You should not associate with me," Dacian whispered. He had no idea what Alloi's agenda toward him might be, but he feared that her kindness would only lead her to misfortune.

"I can take care of myself," she said, and was surprised by the sudden confidence of her statement. She had never really thought of herself as an individual force. Tempet had always been entwined with her existence. Even as she recognized how her autonomous identity strengthened her, she missed Tempet. At this moment, his assistance would be welcome.

Alloi brought Dacian inside her home. She lowered him onto a couch. He shut his eyes. Sitting next to his head, she started to stroke his hair and study his face. His rys appearance was intriguing. She was not sure if it was attractive, but she did not find him ugly.

Being alone with him granted her a thrill that she had never before known.

Gradually she ended her pain-blocking spell, but then Dacian shifted uncomfortably. She resumed her spell and apologized, saying that she had only wanted to see if he was still in pain now that he was back in Kwellstan.

"The pain is only absent in the Altular," he said. He rubbed his temple. He had a terrible headache.

"Stay here and rest," Alloi said. "I will give you sanctuary and contact my Sect and find out if anyone knows how to get this horrible enchantment off of you."

"You are kind," he murmured.

Dacian appeared to fall asleep. Alloi felt his body slacken beneath her finger tips. She could feel his immense weariness. Freeing himself of the Grand Lumin's dungeon had cost a great toll.

The dusk deepened and the glow crystals throughout Alloi's house brightened in response. She felt pity for Dacian. He and all his kind were an abomination, yet he seemed a noble being. Perhaps he was even better than all the tabre for not lashing out with violence after so much provocation.

Filling with affection, Alloi bent down and brushed his forehead with a tender kiss. Dacian's eyes opened and she withdrew, embarrassed.

Dacian sat up and moved away from her. He groaned as the pain from the crosha returned but he waved her away.

"I must go back to the Altular," he said.

"Dacian, no!" Alloi cried.

"It is the only way," he said bitterly. "I can't think with this pain eating my mind. I must rest and then find a way to get this off me." He dug his fingernails into the skin around the crystal as if he might physically rip it from his flesh.

"Dacian, I will help you, I swear," she insisted.

Embattled and alone, he was sorely tempted by her offer, but there was nothing to gain by accepting help from a Drathatarlane. Miserably, he explained, "Alloi, you have been kind, but I cannot accept your help. Jingten is controlled by the Kwellstan Sect. If I side with Drathatarlane, the Kwellstan might punish all rys."

He stood up to leave. Alloi jumped up to prevent him. "Please, Dacian, I can help you!" she pleaded.

"Are you sure?" he demanded bitterly. "Are you sure the Drathatarlane will help a rys?"

Alloi hesitated. "I will convince them to aid the rys," she said.

"You can try," he said and headed for the door.

Reluctantly she let him go. Outside a gentle snow was falling, and the moist cold flakes were soothing on his bare skin. He trudged through quiet streets and returned to the Altular like a chastened runaway. To have the pain from the crosha go away was worth crawling back into this cell. At least he was out of the dungeon.

He flopped onto his narrow bed, knowing that he would not rise for days. Although lacking the strength to cast his mind to Jingten, he fell asleep thinking of Onja. Her help he would accept.

Onja, I need you, he thought.

30. A Weighty Vengeance

When we Kez demanded retainers to honor Vu, we expected the bigger tribes to scoff at us. What those tribes did not expect or had forgotten was how those who serve Vu and control the wild places can make them suffer in their great halls high on their city hills. ~ Urlen, Kez chronicler

The bloom of spring renewed Demeda not at all. Her male relatives ignored her bitter protests about her arranged marriage to the Temulanka King. Her female relatives, although sympathetic, only tried to spin her misery into a shroud of duty.

Demeda hated them all. For all her life her blood kin had been everything to her. She had been proud of her royal heritage, but now she saw the value of her breeding as only an accursed hoax. How could she have value if her own family would send her to lie with their enemy?

A tutor was sent to Demeda to coach her in the common dialect so that she could communicate better in the Temulanka household. Filled with spite, Demeda refused her lessons. She fought her mother, and her sisters, and even Mallah as they all tried to make her attend her language lessons. But she shut her eyes and plugged her ears whenever the tutor began his lesson. In another attempt to thwart him she continually pulled off her tepa so as to reveal her face to the tutor, who lowered his eyes appropriately and left the room until Demeda's relatives and servants covered her again.

Her battle against her language lessons raged for a whole week until her father intervened. Upon finally seeing her father, who had refused to give her audience, Demeda cast herself wailing at his feet. She begged him to call off the marriage and pity her as his flesh and blood. All manner of pleadings and arguments she blathered at him through dripping desperate sobs, but her father pried her off the floor and stood her up. With two regal fingers under her chin, he tilted her head up so she could look him in the eyes. Demeda saw his handsome kingly face that resisted the lines of worry and age. She saw sadness in his dark eyes but not pity as he explained that the treaty marriage was necessary to protect their tribe. The land and the people were not fully recuperated from long years of war, and the Sabar'Uto needed time to renew their strength. The last war had proven that the Temulanka and the Sabar'Uto were evenly matched. War had brought neither of them decisive victory. It was Demeda's duty to serve her tribe in this way. The marriage treaty would mellow old bitterness and give peace and prosperity a chance to flourish again.

Duty to her tribe consoled Demeda not at all. She resented having to be the one to cure the problems made by other people, like her father. Angry and wanting to hurt him, Demeda asked him why he did not go get in bed with the Temulanka King if peace meant so much to his tribe.

Then the Sabar'Uto King beat her. Demeda fought him even without the hope of defending herself, and the hands of her father fell on her hard until she was cowering and crying in a corner. Furniture was knocked over and ceramics broken. Her clothes were torn and her lips bloody.

The King said that it was best that she had thrown her tantrum now because such actions would shame her and her tribe if she behaved so at the Temulanka court.

He bade her to do her duty as a royal princess and turned to leave. Demeda heaved herself up and spat a bloody glob of spittle at his feet. He heard the noise and looked back, shocked to his core by her unspeakable action. For a daughter to scorn a father in such a way was unbelievable. For a woman to scorn a king…it was unthinkable. Fury cracked across his face and Demeda expected him to beat her again, but he did not. His eyes misted up a little, but Demeda knew that it was not for her. The King of the Sabar'Uto did not hold back tears for the daughter that he would soon lose. He was upset because he was weak. He had to send a woman to buy his peace that he could not win as a man.

Drugs followed her father's attempt to beat her into submission. Something began to sweeten her drinks in an evil fashion that flushed her mind of thoughts and pain. Demeda welcomed the feeling after weeks of turmoil. To escape the awful pain and helplessness of her situation was a relief. Meek and quiet, she sat through her language lessons, speaking softly, and politely thanking her tutor each day.

Demeda felt the dose increasing as her departure drew close. With detached eyes she watched servants pack her clothing and jewelry. Listlessly she listened when her mother came to her and explained about being married to a man. Holding her hands, her mother told her about when she had first been married and how afraid she had been. But then things had gotten better. She told Demeda how she would make new friends and find a place for herself in a new household, and life would continue for her much as it did now. Then her mother hugged her and started sobbing because she had to say goodbye to her eldest daughter. Demeda's heart briefly softened for her mother's sake, and she hugged her back and declared her love. She would miss her mother because all people miss their mothers. After many tears, her mother brought her a cup of milk and told her to drink. Demeda drank it down, knowing that it would guide her to an uncaring place of calm waters.

Demeda was three days out from Chadenedra now and Mallah was holding a silver cup adorned with leaves and berries to her lips. Mallah extolled the virtues of the fresh milk and said that it had honey in it too. Demeda was deeply tempted, but she was done hiding in her drugged haze. They were approaching the Temulanka Domain and she had no desire to present herself as a sleepy and pliant offering. Her spite was a more alluring toxin than the brew meant to make her a soft and lovely tool of her tribe. Because her father felt duty was so important, then she decided that it should be her duty to look upon the Temulanka King with eyes that conveyed the undying hatred of her tribe. How would the mothers of those sons that fell during the war look upon him she wondered? She imagined how the Temulanka King would gloat over his prize of a Sabar'Uto princess. She would represent a victory for him and that made Demeda shudder. She did not want to be his trophy, and she did not want to be the bringer of peace. Perhaps if her tribe had asked her to pay this price, she would have proudly gone forth, but instead she had been rudely commanded, like a whip thoughtlessly striking a mule. Demeda renewed her commitment to spoiling the treaty. She would find a way to make the Temulanka King regret the bargain he had struck with her father. Everyone, both her tribe's enemies and her kin, would pay for mistreating her. They all said that what she did mattered for everything but they treated her like nothing. Demeda wanted to correct them all.

"I'm not thirsty," Demeda whispered and pushed the cup back.

"Demeda, you must have a little," Mallah insisted sweetly. "I made it for you myself."

"Then you drink it," Demeda snapped.

Mallah blinked and looked very hurt. "It will make you feel better," she persisted.

Demeda caught her tongue. She did not want to hurt Mallah with her viperfish ill humor. She was glad that her dear cousin had been allowed to accompany her on this trip. To be able to see the familiar face of her best friend until the very end was a tiny comfort.

Demeda reached out and held aside a curtain from her covered coach. Outside she saw Sabar'Uto warriors. Most of them were off their horses as they took a midday meal. The men had shining bronze helmets and bronze plates strapped over their arms and chests. Their mustard yellow tunics and black breeches reminded her of bumble bees. Demeda rubbed her eyes and took a deep breath, still trying to clear her head. Whatever she had been drinking often made her mind wonder among strange images. Demeda opened her eyes and leaned a little closer to the open air. Beyond the warriors that ringed her caravan, she saw trees aglow in the splendid greens of new spring foliage. A gentle cool rain pattered pleasantly on the leaves. The forest looked to be pressing thickly against the roadway. She guessed that they were near the frontier lands between the domains of the Sabar'Uto and the Temulanka.

"Don't let them see you," Mallah fretted and tugged at the curtain.

Demeda slumped back against her cushions and let Mallah fix the curtain. "Can I not look upon the world on my one journey through it?" she said.

Mallah patted her knee. "Demeda, I hate to see you so miserable. You must stop tormenting yourself," she said.

Demeda ground her teeth. She could not recall being more bothered than at that moment. How could Mallah say that she was tormenting herself? But lashing out at Mallah served no purpose. Her dear friend was not the source of her suffering, only its handmaiden.

Mallah cozied up next to her and offered the drink again. Demeda accepted the cup this time.

"That's so much better," Mallah said, clearly happy that Demeda had ceased being difficult.

But Demeda quickly sat up, stuck the cup through the curtains, and poured it out. She wanted to toss the cup on the ground but that would only bring attention to her defiance. Handing the cup back to Mallah, she said that Mallah must report that she drank it.

Aghast, Mallah shook her head. "Demeda, you must not make me lie. You must drink it," she said fearfully.

Suddenly Demeda realized that threats had probably been used to elicit Mallah's cooperation with the constant drugging.

"Just lie for me, please Mallah," Demeda said and crumbled back into her cushions.

Mallah fidgeted with the cup nervously. "It's best if you drink," she whispered. "All the ladies say so, even your mother. In time, they say you won't need it, but for now, it's best. Will you drink at dinner?"

"No," Demeda said flatly. She was done with the walking death that the world offered her. She felt almost on the threshold of sobriety now, and she wanted to stay there no matter how painful.

The coach started moving and Mallah put her arms around Demeda. She started crying quietly and told Demeda how much she would miss her.

"You drink it for me tonight," Demeda suggested. Mallah deserved the relief.

They held each other as the coach bounced and rocked along the road. Demeda was so sick of the motion. She wished that she could ride a horse, but her father had denied that request. Demeda suspected that he guessed her heart. If she were on a horse now, she would ride as fast as she could and not look back ever.

Demeda tried to imagine the wind in her hair as she raced away from her many masters, but her dull and downtrodden mind had trouble summoning a sensation that she had not felt since she was a young girl. Since maturing to womanhood, she had been allowed no outdoor activities with her hair or face exposed to the open air.

A brooding gloom settled heavily over her face, whose features were too young to bear such weight. She stared at the green and brown curtains that surrounded her and hated always being shoved into a fabric box.

Denied a view, she simply shut her eyes and tried to doze, but with the calming potion finally wearing off she felt increasingly awake. Mallah shifted beside her and started to talk, trying to cheer her as always.

In a soft voice, Mallah whispered with taboo delight, "Perhaps the Temulanka King will be handsome and fall helplessly in love with you. He will grant you many favors and your life will be far more pleasant than you can imagine."

"I'm not interested in silly fantasies," Demeda said.

"It could happen," Mallah insisted. "You are very fair."

Demeda touched her face. She supposed she was nice looking although she truly had no idea what effect her appearance would have on men. Demeda supposed she would soon find out.

Mallah continued to spin out possible scenarios in which Demeda found love and happiness at the Temulanka court. Demeda wanted to verbally stomp on her cousin's nonsense, but she let her prattle on. Mallah was trying to be kind, and Demeda did not bother to remind her of the sickening facts. She would not be the first wife of the King. As the new wife, she would likely be the target of jealous intrigues from the other wives. Demeda had seen such unpleasantness often enough growing up at the Sabar'Uto court. Above all that, the fact that the Temulanka King had been her tribe's blood enemy for many years rotted all hope from her heart.

The afternoon passed with excruciating slowness for Demeda who was surprised at how accustomed she had grown to the mindless floating of the drug. Mallah ended up taking a nap beside her, but Demeda could not sleep. A deep grasping terror had consumed her soul like the roots of a plant left in its pot far too long.

When her caravan halted for the evening, Demeda considered the ability to leave her coach to be a scrap of mercy. Mallah and she put on their tepas, and her brother Ulet came to escort them to their tent. Her brother was decked out in his full royal warrior regalia and looked especially handsome and strong. His thick dark eyelashes accentuated his large brown eyes. Thousands of gold beads adorned his dark blue clothes and threads of silver inlaid on his bronze armor sparkled like frost. A fine dagger with a handle covered in rubies hung from his waist and a newly forged sword made from iron was on his other hip.

Despite his magnificence, Demeda noted his troubled expression. On this trip, he had not bothered to converse with her. Both of them had been content to travel in silence. Their inevitable sharp words were not worth the energy.

The rain had stopped and the western sky was clearing for a lovely sunset. Forested hills surrounded the muddy road, and the air was fresh and sweet to breathe. Spirited birdsong sang from every direction as birds emerged from their leafy shelters to rejoice in the glistening clean forest.

Demeda slipped her hand through the arm Ulet offered and walked with him to where serving men were putting up tents for the women and Ulet and his honor guard. Mallah fell into place behind Demeda and her other serving women got out of the other coaches and followed.

Through her tepa, Demeda peeked at Ulet. The hard line of his tense lips and drawn brow indicated that he pondered bad news.

"Is something wrong?" she whispered.

Ulet glanced at her suspiciously. His impulse was to brush her concern aside, but ultimately he chose to answer her because this would be one of his last chances to talk to his sister before he saw her safely delivered to the Temulanka.

"A Temulanka envoy was supposed to meet us here at Jatuh Creek and escort us into their domain, but no one is here. I suppose they are only late," he said.

Demeda suddenly tingled with the hope that the Temulanka were backing out of the treaty. Perhaps the envoy had not come because the Temulanka King had decided to reject her. But she refused to let herself cling to the hope that was as attractive as the tempting drink that Mallah would soon be preparing.

Ulet continued, "And with this rain the creek is high. My scouts say the fording might be difficult. We might have to wait a couple days for the water to go down a bit."

Demeda knew nothing about fording creeks but she was skilled at knowing her brother's mood. "Do you fear a Temulanka trap?" she asked.

He frowned with disapproval and wondered why her wits had suddenly resurfaced. He supposed her calming drink had worn off since lunch.

"There are many reasons an envoy could be delayed," he said. "Tomorrow I'll send scouts across the creek to look for them."

Demeda grabbed his arm. Urgently she said, "Ulet, withdraw. It's a Temulanka trap to get members of the royal family. Take me home."

"Demeda, I can't do that," he said.

"Why? You're in command. You see bad signs. Don't ignore them," she urged.

Despicable pity softened his face. "You are not going to trick me into letting you have your way this time. I'm sorry," he said. He removed her hand from his arm and pointed to her tent.

Demeda wanted to argue, but she had spent so many weeks pleading and begging that she knew it was hopeless. She smacked aside the tent flap and ducked inside her fabric box. Angry tears overflowed. She hoped they were falling into a Temulanka trap and were about to be murdered in the night, but even that raging wish did not comfort her. She wanted to live, just not like this.

******

Amar sensed the excitement of the twenty warriors gathered around him. The mission against the Sabar'Uto camp was a risky one, and they needed faith that they would succeed. He drew out his crystal orb and held it up so that they could see its enchanted glow.

"Go in silence through the dark and begin the revenge upon those who scoff at our value," he said. "The kings of civilization are not the sole source of justice. I have proven that myself, striking as the unseen hand against Ginjor Rib. As the power of the rys was with me then, know that it is with you now," Amar declared.

The warriors saluted him, and Amar liked their respect and awe. As the Lord of the Lin Tohs he had been given his due by his subjects, but, as Amar of the Kez, he received a deeper respect that had been earned…and was feared.

The twenty Kez around him were thieves and assassins who were good at skulking in the dark and killing quietly. Amar had been rapidly learning how to draw upon the various rogue talents within the ranks of the Kez, and these men would serve as the first wave and quietly overtake the Sabar'Uto sentries. They wore little clothing and no armor because they would be donning the clothes of the sentries that they killed.

Amar waited for full darkness to claim the forest before sending them. The leaves were still dripping after the rainy day and the soft sound would help mask the stealthy approach of his sentry hunters. Amar would lead the second assault himself, penetrate the Sabar'Uto camp, and then rendezvous with Kym once they had their hostages.

Amar believed that he had manipulated the situation perfectly. The advance scouts of the Temulanka reception party had already been killed, which had caused the rest of the Temulanka to pause inside their border, fearing some Sabar'Uto treachery. As for the Sabar'Uto, Kez spies had confirmed that Prince Ulet was leading the caravan. He would make a splendid hostage as would the Sabar'Uto princess. Her capture would jeopardize the treaty between the tribes. Fracturing the fragile peace between the war-weary tribes would give the Kez a weighty revenge upon the two tribes that had refused to honor Vu with retainer payments. The delicate diplomatic errand of the delivery of the Sabar'Uto princess to the Temulanka King should have been escorted by the Kez. Their neutral presence would have assured both sides of safety in the transaction of the treaty marriage, but now both would suffer the consequences of failing to pay Lax Ar Fu.

Amar put away his crystal orb and darkness covered his face. Alongside him remained Kym and Urlen, who was sniffling unpleasantly with a cold. Although Urlen had little to offer during the fight to abduct hostages, his writing talents would be needed to communicate the demands of the Kez to both tribes.

Urlen foresaw that all tribal kings would come to dread messages in his handwriting. He had even been adding a distinctive flair to his script so that it would be more easily recognizable. Like all scholars, he wished for recognition.

Urlen smothered a sneeze with a small linen cloth. Urlen supposed that infamy as the secretary of Vu might not be all bad. He was trying to adapt to his new situation. Despite always feeling small and foppish around the gang of killers he now called brothers, he was glad to be on this mission with Amar. He preferred the company of his friend greatly to that of Lax Ar Fu who often repulsed him with his licentious appetites and cruelties. Urlen's time that winter at Eferzen Springs had been a taxing horror.

Urlen folded his handkerchief and slipped it into his pouch. He noted how Amar was increasingly mentioning Onja when he wanted to encourage his warriors. Urlen had also noticed that Amar did not do it so blatantly when Lax Ar Fu was present although Urlen had no doubt that the Overlord was aware of the power game that Amar was playing. For both their sakes, Urlen hoped that he played it well.

With the first wave of twenty Kez dispatched, flickers of light shifted among the nearby trees as the remaining Kez lit lanterns and covered them. At the end of the coming battle, some men would uncover their lights and reveal themselves to lead their enemies on a false trail while the hostages were taken in another direction.

To Kym, Amar said, "We'll come straight up the road to the creek. I will try to slip out with our prizes while the battle still rages in the camp."

"I will be ready," Kym promised. At first Kym had been offended that Amar had not assigned him to the main assault, but then he realized that

Amar honored him with commanding the escape. Nothing mattered if the escape did not succeed.

Kym asked, "How will you find the princess? The women will be covered and you can't grab them all."

"The tent of the princess should be easy to identify," Amar said. "Her tattoos will mark her as royalty, and I believe that the prince will rush to defend his sister. I will look for him and hopefully take them together."

"Get him at least. He'll be the most valuable," Kym advised.

"I know, but he might also be harder to take alive," Amar said.

"He'll surrender," Kym predicted with a derisive tone. "A royal will know we want ransom. He won't fight to the death."

"I will soon find out," Amar said.

Kym chuckled. "And the two strongest tribes will soon find out that they should not disrespect the Kez."

Amar could tell that Kym relished what they were doing. He was not the only Kez warrior that Amar had noticed to be renewed with enthusiasm and pride for their brotherhood. In a short time, he had reawakened the slumbering power of the Kez and sent fresh terror among the people of many tribes. With a little help from Onja on top of his own daring, Amar had reinvented the Kez into something more frightening than what they had been before. And the credit for this was clearly given to him. Lax Ar Fu was the Overlord, but all Kez knew that Amar was their new inspiration.

Amar was pleased that he was succeeding at becoming powerful, as Onja had bade him. Kym, who had begun as Lax Ar Fu's watchdog, was now his man. Cybar and Vame continued to show genuine loyalty. They would fight beside him tonight.

Before leaving with Kym, Urlen said, "Fight well my friend." He touched Amar's biceps as he passed. The muscle was hard beneath Urlen's soft fingers.

"I will," Amar said, and his anticipation for the fight thrilled through his body like a man who has caught the sight of his lover after long absence.

Amar gathered his warriors. Forty men fingered their weapons, and their eyes revealed a criminal gleam. They were ready to take on the one hundred warriors that spies reported were with Prince Ulet. Amar counted on the element of surprise and the disarray that his advance warriors would cause once they disguised themselves as Sabar'Uto sentries. And he expected that the rising notoriety of the Kez would inflict extra fear upon their targets. The Sabar'Uto were probably expecting an attack from the Temulanka, but once they saw that Kez warriors were among them, they would have to think about the dro-shalum. Amar knew the name that people had given him, and he liked it.

Amar advised his warriors to stay close to him when they descended on the camp. They would act as a spear being driven into flesh. By remaining in a compact unit, the numerous Sabar'Uto warriors would be unable to reach them all at once. Plus, the Kez brothers in disguise as sentries would raise false alarms around the camp and draw warriors off the main assault.

After reviewing the technical details, Amar roused the bloodlust of his men with stronger words. "Cut them. Kill them. Punish their arrogance. Show them what waits for them in the shadows and the wild lands while they sit in their palaces and suck up the wealth of Gyhwen that they deserve no more than any other," Amar said.

He unsheathed the iron blade that would have been the heirloom of his lost tribe and the bronze one that he had stolen from a Patharki warrior. Lifting the blades and turning within the circle of men, Amar felt like the whole universe smiled on him. Above the trees, stars twinkled through the thinning clouds and their faint light reflected off the edges of his comrades' weapons and helmets. He could feel the men's energy, waiting for him to release it. They looked forward to the violence. Together they would fall upon the Sabar'Uto with feral confidence that would shatter the other men.

Cybar spoke. "We fight for Vu! We fight for Amar!"

For the sake of quiet the other Kez repeated Cybar's declaration with sinister whispers.

Amar took a deep breath and exhaled, enjoying the moment of clarity that descended upon his corrupted soul. He was the lord of these men.

Expecting that his sentry hunters were by now plucking the Sabar'Uto watchmen from their posts, Amar led his warriors into the trees. They walked slowly and quietly, picking their way carefully around trees in the dark and ducking low beneath brush and vines. The frontier lands between the domains of the Temulanka and the Sabar'Uto were unsettled and not frequently traveled. The undergrowth of the forest crept close to the road and provided good cover.

When Amar could discern the torches and watch fires of the Sabar'Uto through the trees, he was pleased to hear only the quiet sounds of a camp in repose. His sentry hunters must have been successful.

One of his men signaled with the familiar call of a night bird with one note added. The return signal came immediately. The forty Kez plus Amar moved like a herd of deer from the woods onto the road where fires were burning low and warriors were snoring on the ground. Amar recognized the face of the sentry beneath the bronze helmet. He quickly flashed a few hands signals to Amar to indicate that they had achieved total success.

Rys Rising: Book I

The royal tents were easy to spot across the road inside a protective ring of warriors and watch fires. Amar's new sentries had weakened their watch fires, and the inner circle of Sabar'Uto warriors on guard duty now looked out on a darker scene. Gloom obscured the quiet entry of over forty intruders. Amar quickened his pace as did his companions. Despite their stealth, Sabar'Uto warriors were roused from their sleep by the passing of so many strange feet. Whenever a head popped up, a spear or sword lashed out from a Kez like a scorpion's tail and killed each chance for the alarm to be raised. This harsh strategy allowed the Kez to gain several crucial seconds of undetected freedom before an outcry finally arose. Guards shouted and rang their bells. With a charge of Kez warriors erupting from within the camp, none of the Sabar'Uto had a chance to wonder how the outer sentries had failed. There was only time to fight.

Amar shouted his command and his comrades flung throwing stars, knives, and spears at the Sabar'Uto. The slicing missiles hurt nine or ten warriors, but some archers fired back. Two arrows flew by Amar, and one nicked his arm. He heard a familiar voice cry out. An arrow had hit one of his men, but Amar did not turn to look. He had instructed each of his warriors to choose two partners to help them escape if wounded. If possible, no one – dead, wounded, or alive – was to be left behind. It would increase the mystique of the Kez if the traces of their coming and going were kept faint.

The sentries were now shouting about attacks from all sides and causing great confusion. The first warrior who opposed Amar only got his sword halfway out of its sheath before Amar's iron blade inflicted mortal pain. Amar leaped over the falling body and tackled the next warrior. When Amar hit the ground, he rolled and came up running. He actually laughed. He could feel how much stronger he was than a year or even six months ago. His rigorous workouts were transforming him into a man superior to most.

Two Sabar'Uto came at him with spears. Amar blocked one spear with a sword and dodged the other spear while he struck the man holding it with his second sword. The warrior's armor saved him but he stumbled back from the blow. With another slash of his iron sword, Amar broke one of the spears and spun around to strike the second warrior across the back of his neck. He fell forward, dying quickly.

Sabar'Uto warriors pressed thickly around the Kez. Amar fought hard. His swords slashed and spun as his body dodged weapons and bullied its way through struggling bodies. He was close to the tents. The royal emblems were clear to see, and Amar saw the young man who had to be Prince Ulet burst out of a tent. The flapping fabric fluttered behind him as he took in the chaotic scene. The glittering golden beads on his blue clothes and his splendid armor marked him as the heir of the Sabar'Uto dynasty. His captain ran to his side to report.

Filled with a sick zeal for victory, Amar promptly killed two more warriors. Strength, growing skill, and an unrelenting desire for power drove Amar. His opponents in contrast were bumbling in surprise. Amar sheathed a sword and seized a spear from one of his fallen enemies. He threw the spear and pierced the captain in the throat. The prince stepped back, aghast by the red gushing sight of his murdered captain. With the best of his honor guard crumpling to the ground, the prince drew his sword. As Amar had predicted, the prince fled into the next tent where the princess likely was.

Amar drew his second sword again, rallied his men, and raced for the tent. The Sabar'Uto honor guard fought back, but the Kez were well inside their position, like flooding waters overtopping a levee. Amar burst into the tent chasing the prince. Squealing female cries and frantic disarray greeted him. Glowing embers from a central fire pit and a single oil lamp provided meager light that revealed a half dozen women, their heads uncovered and dark hair flying loose. The soft scents of perfume and incense filled the air with the beckoning aroma of female treasure. Amar saw the prince grabbing a young woman, dressed only in a white nightgown. A handmaiden was trying to slip a robe onto the young woman along with a tepa.

Amar overhead the prince saying "I'll get you out."

The women noticed Amar's entry and screamed. One threw a plate at him and he blocked it with a sword. Another woman threw a heavy crockery bowl and it caught him on the chin. Shocked by the blow, he reeled away, slashing blindly with his swords to protect himself. The prince cursed and charged the intruder. Amar forced himself above the stunning pain in this chin and reconnected with the throbbing joy that he derived from combat. He blocked two strikes from the prince before more Kez barged into the tent.

Cybar kicked the prince in the small of his back and then hit him with his sword handle on the back of his bare head. The prince fell forward onto his knees. Amar then kicked him in the face and the prince toppled onto his side.

The young woman who now had on a blue robe and a tepa flopping open over her face dove over the prince.

"Don't hurt him!" she shrieked.

Amar did not even glance at her exposed face. Sheathing his swords, he grabbed her arms and looked at her hands. The royal Sabar'Uto designs were tattooed onto her hands as surely as they were stitched onto the flags outside the tents.

"I have her!" he shouted and crossed her wrists so that he could bind them.

She gasped but Amar was surprised by her lack of resistance. She trembled with fear but was otherwise cooperative as he lashed her hands tightly with braided leather cords.

"Why do you want me?" she asked in her household dialect, forgetting her education in the worldly tongue at that moment.

Even if Amar had caught her meaning, he would not have bothered to answer. She cried out as he tossed her roughly over his shoulder.

"Demeda!" a woman screamed.

"Mallah, save yourself," commanded Amar's captive.

Amar yelled to his warriors to get the prince up. They finished binding his hands and hoisted him to his feet. Ulet was only vaguely conscious, but with two Kez dragging him, he could stumble along.

Amar grabbed the oil lamp and threw it at a trio of crying women. They ducked and the oil and flames splashed onto the tent. Amar took out a sword and slashed an escape hole.

With the princess over his shoulder and his warriors dragging the prince, they emerged into the cool night air. Vame caught up to Amar outside and saw that the prizes had been taken. He quickly put a horn to his lips and blasted the signal. Half the Kez in the camp rallied to the sound of the horn to cover Amar's escape while the others led the Sabar'Uto fighters on a decoy chase.

Amar ran as his fighters cut down anyone who tried to block his path. The excitement of the abduction masked the searing exertion of running with the woman over his shoulder. Although she was only a slender young woman, her weight presented a sufficient burden when running for his life.

He raced by the edge of the camp. In the light of the nearest watch fire, he saw some of his sentries in disguise aim their bows at the Sabar'Uto warriors who pursued them. Amar knew that his men would fire a few shots and then scatter into the forest.

Desperate and unthinking, the Sabar'Uto fired arrows down the road at the disappearing Kez. Amar laughed at their stupidity. The princess over his back would protect him from their arrows.

A sharp cry made Amar turn because he did not recognize the voice. He figured that the prince had been struck.

"Keep him coming!" Amar shouted and resumed his run. He could hear the rushing water of the swollen creek and knew that escape was only a few more strides away.

Kym came forward to assist his comrades into the canoes that he had brought downstream to carry them swiftly beyond the reach of the Sabar'Uto.

Breathing hard, Amar transferred the princess to Kym.

"Did you get them both?" Kym asked urgently.

"Yes," Amar panted. He bent over a moment to catch his wind. Sweat dripped steadily off his forehead and ran in small rivers down his chest and back.

Cybar and his companion arrived at the creek with the prince, who was trying to shout for help. Cybar clamped a hand over his mouth but Ulet bit his thumb. Cybar yelped and punched him painfully in the ear. The prince slumped to his hands and knees. Another Kez kicked him in the ribs and told him to get up.

Amar took charge. "He's not going to do what you say," he snapped. He grabbed the prince by his hair and yanked him up. Amar noticed how the prince was trying to keep weight off his right leg. He bent down and ran his hands over the prince's body. He plucked a dagger from his belt and handed it to Cybar, and then he found an arrow sticking out of the prince's right buttock. Amar grabbed the shaft and wiggled it. The prince cried out, sounding more boy than man.

"Get ready," Amar said, thoroughly enjoying himself. He pulled the arrow out of the man's muscle. The prince wailed and then gasped in shock once it was over. Amar tossed the bloody arrow away and shoved the prince toward the muddy bank of the creek. Three Kez warriors scrambled to grab the prince and load him into a canoe. Amar waded into the flowing water and grabbed the edge of a canoe and got in. The canoe rocked again as Kym got in behind him. At the front of the canoe sat Urlen, who sneezed and then welcomed his friend.

"Glad to have you back, Amar. I've found that I can actually paddle a canoe," Urlen said, pleased that he had found a physical activity that he could perform competently.

"Then start paddling," Amar said.

Eight more warriors loaded up into the remaining canoes and the rest ran off into the night. Kym confirmed that the prince and princess were secured in canoes, and they all paddled into the brawny current. The swift creek would take them beyond the reach of the Sabar'Uto. The plan had employed the landscape and been executed perfectly. Amar was proud of his cleverness and daring. He had done this without the power of Onja to aid him, yet he had done it for her.

Resting in the canoe while Urlen and Kym paddled, Amar touched the pouch around his neck. Until her call came, he would amuse himself with his fine catch of a prince and princess. They would surely bring much sport and treasure for the brotherhood. And all of it born of his deeds and not those of Lax Ar Fu.

31. Wild Disregard

Terror and helplessness jangled over Demeda's nerves like dueling tom cats.

She sat in the canoe with her hands bound, flowing through the darkness. Warriors sat in front of her and behind her. The landscape was only a rocking black netherworld where water gurgled against unseen banks and men shouted, increasingly in the distance.

Demeda was pretty sure that Ulet was in one of the other canoes. She called out to him and received his reply.

"Not a sound from you!" hissed the man behind her. He prodded her menacingly in the back of her head with his paddle.

Demeda did not call out to Ulet again. It was enough to know that he was there. Terrible fear made her tremble like she had just been pulled from a freezing lake. She and Ulet were hostages. Her best guess was that they had been kidnapped by the Temulanka.

Lifting her bound hands, she started to tie shut the face flaps of her tepa. As she knotted the last tie, she realized the utter futility of the act. The covering was meant to protect her femininity from undeserving eyes, but what possible protection could her cloth sack offer now? Demeda hated the headdress anyway, but she left it tied out of habit.

The shouting voices from the bank faded. The rushing waters carried her and her brother away from help in a matter of moments. After weeks of being drugged, the extreme reality and peril of her situation flung her mind into a startling wakefulness.

The canoe hit rocks or a submerged log. The man in front of Demeda let slip one curse word. Demeda wanted to grab the edges of the canoe for stability, but with her hands tied she flopped to one side and caused the canoe to rock even more precariously. The abductor behind her leaned forward and grabbed her. He pulled her back and her head landed in his lap. With her body centered in the canoe again, he paddled furiously. Water sprayed onto her face as his paddle went from one side of the canoe to the other.

She awkwardly wiped her face with her bound hands and looked at the man, but it was too dark to discern his face. He continued to struggle with the current and gave her no more regard than a sack of summer squash.

Still quaking with shock and fear, Demeda accepted that she was abducted. She had been stolen from the camp and was already beyond reach of rescue. Naturally she worried that the strange men meant to rape her, but, as a female hostage, she would be completely worthless if ravished. If they raped her she would be considered dead and no ransom would be paid.

Freshly educated in how much compassion her father had for her, Demeda suddenly worried that he would assume she was raped and refuse to ransom her. Then she would be consumed by the strange men for certain. Grasping for a way to survive, she told herself that she would have to make sure that she kept her abductors entirely aware that her maidenhead was truly golden.

Ulet, however, had no such protection from abuse. His danger could be dire, and Demeda resolved to try to help him if she had the chance. Their captors, especially if they were Temulanka, might put Ulet to many tortures. She recalled some servants' gossip from years earlier about the eyeball of a hostage being sent to his family.

Demeda feared for Ulet. Already they had been harsher with him than her. She recalled the man who had caught her and tied her. In retrospect she wondered why she had not resisted, but now that she thought about it she knew why. What difference did it make if she was being abducted or delivered to the Temulanka King? Either way she was a captive. And if these strange men raped her, what difference would it be from suffering the lust of her enemy's leader? That brave thought floundered as she grimly imagined being raped by many men. All the fears of male aggression that had been built into her mind her whole life erupted like a winter plague in a damp town. Her tepa was a useless protection.

She hoped that her father would pay her ransom on the chance that she remained unmolested because she was with Ulet and important to the Temulanka treaty. But ransom would not buy her freedom. No freedom of any kind existed for her. Unexpectedly this dismal realization summoned her courage. A brave bit of ambition germinated inside her. The abduction represented her only chance to experience something outside the strict task of being a treaty bed prize. Because she could not stand her paralyzing fear, Demeda decided to find a way through this crisis. Her abductors would only expect withering fear from her, and she would see if she could do better.

She heard voices from another canoe and sat up. Her canoe was moving toward a light on the shore. All the canoes jostled together along the bank. Splashes and sloshes indicated that men were going ashore. Then the two men with Demeda got out, and one of them hauled her over his shoulder and waded onto the bank. Her heart hammered against his strong back.

As soon as her slippered feet were set on the cool mud, short leather straps were tied around each of her arms. One man pulled her by a strap while the other held the second strap from behind.

Demeda called out to Ulet again. She heard a muffled reply. Then a man tersely gave an order and another man stuffed her tepa in her mouth and tied the loose fabric behind her neck.

She was hustled up a steep bank. Her feet often slipped on the wet and rocky trail, but her handlers lifted her by the straps. Her tender body was soon throbbing with exertion to which it was unaccustomed, and her breathing became ragged. Demeda soon lost track of even her fear as she simply struggled to keep moving. Her chest and her legs flamed with pain and she wanted to collapse.

Finally, they reached the top of a ridge. The moon had risen and its wedge of light showed her the curving ribbon of the creek far below. She could barely believe that she had hiked to such a height so quickly.

Demeda decided to give into her shaking legs. There was no reason that she should not inconvenience her captors. When they tried to lift her back up, she let her legs remain slack. The straps dug into her arms like vengeful tourniquets as they dragged her.

After a short distance, the big man behind her grumbled something and picked her up. Demeda was grateful to be carried. After a few moments of rest, she reached around the man's waist and grabbed the handle of his sword. With her wrists lashed together, pulling the sword free proved difficult. The man turned in a circle comically as he reacted to her attempt to take his weapon. He rolled her off his shoulder and she yanked the blade free. Demeda hit the ground swinging.

"Ow!" he cried as he belayed his attempt to take back the sword.

Another man on the trail behind them opened his lantern. He laughed when he saw the teenage girl scrambling across the ground with his comrade's sword.

Demeda radiated the vicious energy of a cornered animal, and the men regarded her carefully. Another man came forward with a spear and poked at her hands and tried to make her drop the sword.

She hacked at the spear but she was unskilled, and the man used his spear to trip her. Demeda fell sideways and crashed into a bush that gave way beneath her and sent her skidding down the steep slope.

She screamed beneath her gag before a small tree caught her across her stomach and stopped her fall. Sitting up, she pressed her face against its rough bark, fearful that she was about to fall down a cliff.

Someone grabbed her ankles and pulled her back up on the trail. Stones and pine needles poked her body, and her robe and flimsy gown were pulled up to her waist. She felt the chill night breeze on her exposed bottom and finally cracked into hysterics.

Thrashing and crying she fought at anyone who touched her while shoving her clothing back in place. A crowd of men had gathered and they were laughing at her embarrassment.

"Where's my sword?" demanded the man who had been carrying her and the other men roared with more laughter.

The noisy mirth drew their leader into the lantern light. Demeda recognized the man who stalked back down the trail as the one who had bound her hands. He had a young face set in hard lines, and the laughter hushed upon his appearance.

He took in the scene quickly and Demeda succeeded in finally righting her clothing. While she was at it, she loosened her gag before someone yanked on one of her straps and she dropped her hands.

The leader confronted the man who had been carrying Demeda. "You can't carry a girl?" he asked.

The man dropped to one knee. "Forgive me, Amar," he said.

Demeda became perfectly still as she realized that she was looking upon the dro-shalum. Amar of the Kez had taken her and Ulet. She had naturally imagined him as older. Demeda thought that it was strange that his youth should command such solemn authority over these men. Her brother was young and shown respect and obeyed, but not like this. The men around her feared this Amar not because of his station but because he was the curse demon. Kings withered in his presence, and now he possessed her.

Disgust flitted across Amar's face. He waved dismissively at the man who knelt before him and approached Demeda. She quailed back a step. He grabbed both straps on her arms and yanked her toward him. She fell against his chest. His net-like armor of small bronze plates poked through her thin clothing. Demeda looked up into his eyes and glimpsed a wild disregard for all of society that opened a gateway to a world unimagined.

Amar turned away and pulled her along like a surly farmer that has caught an errant donkey. She scrambled along behind him to the head of the line. A few more warriors carried lanterns and in the light she saw Ulet. Their eyes met briefly as she passed him. Blood smeared his chin and one of his eyelids was puffy, but at least he was on his feet.

Demeda trudged behind Amar. The trail started descending the other side of the ridge, and the trees blotted out most of the moonlight. Several times she had to reach out and touch Amar to catch her footing in the dark.

The moonlight returned like a smile when they entered a meadow. Here many saddled horses awaited the Kez. Amar lifted Demeda easily onto a horse. His strength impressed her. When he had been running with her over his shoulder she had been too terrified to think about it, but now that she was set on the course of an unknown fate, she could notice details better.

Amar started tying her hands to the saddle. Rubbing her chin against her shoulder, Demeda managed to loosen her gag enough to speak. She dragged her unwanted knowledge of the civil dialect out of her head, and said, "Do not tie me. I'll ride where you say."

His fingers did not pause in the knotting and he did not respond. But, once his knot was complete, she felt his finger moving along her left hand. She realized that he was tracing her tattoo, checking again to see that she was a princess.

Then he got on another horse and started quietly giving orders. Demeda was assailed by the wish that he was still touching her hand. The pressure of his finger still lingered on her skin. She had never known such a sensation, and the undertow of pleasure that swept through her body confused her utterly.

Her ride through the darkness passed like a feverish blur. She was sweaty and thirsty, and her mind swung between terror and excitement. Her very limited world had been smashed like a mold being broken away after the poured bronze has cooled. Demeda felt utterly exposed, but her fear flirted with the concept of liberation. After long weeks of rage about the diplomatic marriage, Demeda regarded the cords digging into her wrists as threads of freedom, unless her father ransomed her, her virginity was confirmed, and the marriage proceeded as planned. Demeda pondered the dismal irony that her only hope was the ransom, which she dreaded just as much if not more than unknown alternatives.

Demeda did not bother calling out for Ulet again. She believed that he had to be on one of the horses in the line of Kez riding the trail. They rode at a steady pace, apparently knowing where they were going. She would glimpse some lantern light ahead of her and behind her as the riders made sure they were on whatever secret trail they were using. Men on foot occasionally ran by her horse going to the head of the line and then to the back, presumably relaying messages.

The trail began to steadily incline. Demeda noted that the lanterns dimmed and then they emerged onto an exposed ledge cut into a high hillside. A light wind fluttered against Demeda's tepa and robe and was cool around her ankles. The moon had set and only starlight streaked the wispy dark veils of trailing clouds. The trail curved around the hill, taking them higher, and then she saw lights on the hilltop. Two torches blazed like captured meteors at the base of a jagged dark bulk that dominated the hill like a set of horns on an old bull. The torches marked the entrance to a ruined stone building whose origin Demeda could not guess. If she were still in Sabar'Uto land or had passed into the Temulanka Domain she did not know, but clearly this place had known no master except Nature or outlaws for a long time. Warriors stepped out of the shadowy ruins. Demeda heard a few soft words exchanged as her horse was led inside the crumbling courtyard. Against the starry sky she saw pillars that no longer had a roof to hold up and broken walls. More torches burned within the old structure, revealing vine-covered stone friezes with strange designs that she did not recognize. Swirls in many conflicting directions were carved into the pillars and walls along with grotesque beasts and naked people. Demeda had never imagined that artisans would put their hands toward making such lewd and bestial imagery. With her eyes so wide that they hurt, she considered anew what her possible fate might be.

A man came to her and cut her free from the saddle but left her wrists bound. He pulled her to the ground. He was not Amar, which disappointed her. She wanted a chance to speak with him. Although Demeda had no idea what she should say, she decided that she had to try and assert herself with the infamous Amar if she was going to influence her situation at all. Her whole life had always been dictated by others and it was audacious for her to dream that it should be otherwise, but with her situation so desperate, she had to try. Perhaps she could even find a way to help Ulet.

The Kez hauled Demeda into the ruins. The roof had long ago fallen in and the ground was rough with debris upon which she often stumbled. She was tossed into a small chamber. She put out her bound hands to stop her fall and was relieved to crash into Ulet who had jumped up to get her. A single torch burned in the corner of the chamber and two Kez remained on guard outside the entrance.

"Demeda," Ulet breathed. He held her face tenderly with his bound hands and caressed the fabric of her tepa as a toddler touches a favored blanket.

Demeda pressed against him and sobbed a little. For a moment it was relief enough that they were reunited.

"Have they hurt you?" he asked urgently.

"Not really," she said and heard him sigh shakily. He was possibly more worried about her virginity than she was.

Then Demeda noticed that Ulet was leaning against her and favoring one leg. She asked if he was hurt. He sank back to the floor and told her about the arrow.

Ulet lay on his left side as he allowed Demeda to tend him. After opening her headdress so she could see better, she brought the torch close and saw the bleeding hole in his flesh through the torn clothing. Because her hands were tied, she had Ulet help her tear the sleeves off her robe to make bandages.

"Water!" she demanded of the guards outside. When they did not respond, she went to the doorway and demanded water again and adamantly stomped a slippered foot as if she had been telling men what to do her whole life and was accustomed to being obeyed.

"I must tend Prince Ulet's wound. If he bleeds to death you'll get no ransom," she added, and this reasoning prodded one of the guards to comply. He left and came back with a wooden bowl of clean water.

Demeda took the bowl and narrowed her eyes at him to silently chastise him for the slow service. Before washing Ulet's wound, she and her brother drank. Exertion and stress had parched them.

Ulet reminded her to tie her tepa back up.

"What does it matter?" she said bitterly.

"Demeda, do as I say," he insisted.

His bossiness perturbed her. She was the one helping him, but she had no wish to quarrel over his stupid enforcement of social norms. Demeda secured her face flaps and started washing the wound. She had never done such a thing before. She had to get past her natural squeamishness about the blood. She supposed that her life was going to be very much raw and real from this point forward.

Keeping her voice low, she told Ulet how she had learned that they had been taken by Amar, the dro-shalum.

Ulet groaned. "Maybe the Temulanka paid the Kez to attack us," he worried.

"Why would they do that?" Demeda wondered. She had no knowledge upon which to base any speculation about such affairs.

"To torment us. To provoke war or make father pay to avoid it," Ulet answered.

"Do you think Father will pay our ransom?" Demeda asked.

"Of course," Ulet answered quickly, but then he realized that he had been thinking of himself. He glanced at Demeda worriedly, realizing for the first time the ominous possibility that their father might write her off as loss. He had other daughters. Ulet grabbed her arm. "I won't leave without you," he promised passionately.

Beneath her tepa Demeda smiled. She could feel his many apologies for being so cold to her about the marriage. Patting his hand, she thanked him but added, "You take your chance to get home when it comes, Ulet. You're more important to our people than me. I...I will take care of myself." When she spoke those words, they summoned confidence within her along with an actual desire to take care of herself. With the sudden potency of revelation, she understood that determining her own course was all that she had ever desired.

Ulet looked aghast. "You don't know what you're saying," he said.

His dismissive attitude annoyed her and she focused on his wound. Demeda cleaned it and bandaged it and then helped him pull his pants back up.

She then considered the edge of his fine plate of body armor and started rubbing the cords that bound her hands against the blunt metal edge. Ulet found his own edge to begin working at his bounds. The going was slow but not hopeless. They would have broken the leather cords except that they were interrupted.

Accompanied by a half dozen outlaws, Amar entered the chamber of his captives. The Kez flowed around the sides of the room and surrounded Ulet and Demeda. The men stuck two more torches into cracks in the old walls. Ulet sat up tenderly and slid an arm around Demeda.

The hot torchlight cast blunt shadows at many angles, and each Kez bore the same hungry expression. The shaved sides of their heads and tightly braided hair made them look like a pack of well-matched marsh hounds.

But Amar did not match them entirely. Although his hair was shaven along the sides, his remaining black hair was shorter and unbraided, and he regarded his captives like a farmer about to bring in a good crop after a season of hard work.

Another man entered the room and stood beside Amar. He was smaller and thinner, conspicuously lacking the brawn and swagger of the warrior outlaws. A tall widow's peak in his dark hair made his face appear long and thin. The effect was made worse by the shaved sides of his head. He squinted at the young man and woman on the floor.

"I have come to explain to you why you are here," Amar announced.

"Doing the Temulanka's bidding no doubt," Ulet dared to say in a fit of princely arrogance.

Amar looked at the man standing closest to Ulet. He understood the unspoken command and kicked Ulet swiftly in the thigh and then smacked him on the side of the head.

"Stop!" Demeda shouted and started to get to her feet, but Ulet pulled her back down.

"Foolish prince," Amar scolded. He knew well how stupid young princes could be. "I am just as displeased with the Temulanka as the Sabar'Uto."

Ulet eyed his captor earnestly, intending now to listen.

Amar looked up to the stars as if seeking the strength to be patient with a difficult child. "Prince Ulet, do you not recall the insult your tribe spat at Vu and his servants this winter?"

"You can't expect us to give mercenaries money for nothing," Ulet said.

"I think you'll find that peace and security are made quite valuable when absent," Amar said.

"What do you want?" The words were ground out of Ulet by the heavy mill of defeat.

"The same thing my Lord, Lax Ar Fu, asked of you this winter. Your respect for us and an annual retainer to honor Vu. If you had done so, the Kez would have provided security during the delivery of your princess to her marriage. A matter of importance to your tribe that is now endangered because of your disregard for us," Amar explained.

"No matter what you say it's extortion," Ulet complained.

"Extortion," Amar repeated, speaking each syllable with emphasis. "A fancy word from a fancy mouth."

A couple of the Kez in the chamber chuckled ominously at the reference to the prince's mouth, and Ulet shifted nervously.

Pleased by his captive's discomfort, Amar added that in addition to a retainer, the Kez now needed a ransom for him and his sister.

Ulet tightened his arm around Demeda. "You must not harm her. You'll get no ransom if you defile her," he said.

"I know," Amar said. "And I want to waste no time arranging the ransom. My scribe has come to write the demands of our Lord and send them out to your royal family. Of course I have to prove that I possess you. Normally, we'd take your little fingers as evidence, but my scribe has offered to allow you to write to your king and father yourself to prove your captivity."

Urlen stepped up. "There is no reason to be unnecessarily brutal. Do you know how to write Prince Ulet?" Urlen asked.

Ulet nodded. He had rarely needed to make letters himself, but he was literate.

Because the princess had no way to communicate her status, Urlen said, "You will attest to your sister's captivity I am sure?" He looked at Demeda and met her eyes that stared out from her tepa, hardly blinking. The sight of Demeda, captive and cowering, summoned wrenching memories of his lost Isamahlia's last days.

Urlen shifted off his shoulder his leather bag that contained his new set of writing supplies, but Amar put a hand to his chest.

"A moment, my friend. The Sabar'Uto are in debt to Vu and their prince must begin to pay as soon as possible," Amar explained, and the other Kez in the room swiftly descended upon the captives.

Demeda was snatched away by one warrior and held in a corner while the rest of the Kez grabbed Ulet by all four limbs. Wounded and outnumbered, he could hardly resist. His armor and boots and jewelry were stripped away and then he was beaten swiftly into a drooling bloody mess that was dumped back on the floor.

The Kez passed his finely crafted boots among themselves and the man on whom they fit the best got to keep them. They did the same with the two jeweled rings pulled from the royal fingers. The valuable rings of the Sabar'Uto prince were soon decorating the hands of two Kez who slept on dirt more often than not.

As this was done to Ulet, a second Kez aided the man holding Demeda and they pried the rubies off her favorite slippers. They ran their hands over her body, searching for more jewels, but she had just taken all her jewelry off to prepare for sleep when she had been abducted. The bold hands of the outlaws slipped playfully around all her curves. Demeda tensed her body as hard as wood in terror of the startling sensations.

Amar inspected the armor taken from Ulet. The chestplate was of solid bronze adorned with silver tracery and padded on the inside with suede leather. He held it up to his body.

"Looks to be a good fit," Urlen commented.

A rare grin alighted Amar's face. He was immensely pleased to claim this treasure.

Amar began to pull off his old armor of strung together bronze plates and Urlen helped him. Amar offered the old armor to Urlen, who shook his head modestly, but Amar then insisted in a cajoling way. Urlen reconsidered and wiggled into the clinking vest that hung loose over his shoulders. Although he never fancied himself a fighter, Urlen admitted to himself that the bronze platelets were reassuring as he ran his hands over them. The subdued brown shine of the bronze looked good over his simple black wool garments. He thanked Amar for the gift.

Amar then lifted the chestplate to his body and Urlen adjusted and tied the laces around the back. No one paid any attention to Demeda's pleas or curses.

Happy in his thievery, Amar thumped his chest. A thick metallic thud attested to the quality of the armor.

"Lax Ar Fu will be jealous of this," Urlen whispered.

"He can have the ransom," Amar said without a hint of worry.

Demeda was let loose and she plunged to her brother's side. She sobbed a few sympathetic comments to him and then hurled insults at the outlaws who had beaten him. She surprised herself with her verbal viciousness, but she mispronounced a couple curse words and the Kez laughed.

Amar informed Urlen that he could now proceed with his letter writing. One Kez stayed in the chamber with Urlen and the rest withdrew with Amar. Two men remained on guard beyond the doorway.

Demeda helped Ulet to sit up against a wall while Urlen opened his writing kit. He unrolled a small rectangle of good parchment selected for this occasion and poured ink into a small bowl and then tightly stoppered the ceramic ink bottle again. He presented Ulet with a choice of three styluses. The prince blearily regarded them before making a selection. With his hands bound, he held the stylus awkwardly. After wiping a sleeve across his bleeding nose and mouth, he slowly started to write. Urlen oversaw the work. Sometimes Ulet would glance at Urlen, who stared at him with a reproachful gaze that warned him not to think Urlen was bluffing about his literacy. He knew what Ulet was writing, and could read it easily even when looking at it upside down.

Demeda watched her brother write their ransom note. She had never been privileged to see the actual act of writing. It was knowledge forbidden to women because writing was for the larger world of men. She was ambivalent about whether her brother was making a good case for her to be ransomed. She assumed that he was attesting to her intact virtue, but she still found no hope in the concept of ransom. It would only take her back to another miserable world. The tortures there were more delicate, but still never ending.

"You didn't have to beat my brother," she commented to Urlen as she cleaned blood from Ulet's swelling face with yet another strip of fabric ripped from her dwindling robe.

At one time, Urlen would have been appalled by the standard methods of the Kez, but his trial and tortuous execution at the Sky Temple of Preem had hardened him. Likewise with his Kez initiation. Very little kindness existed in this world, and he doubted that the Sabar'Uto prince would have treated a captive any better.

"We won't have to worry about him being able to escape for a little while after a good beating," Urlen explained dispassionately.

Demeda frowned and returned her full attention to Ulet. She pitied him. Even in all her rages over the arranged marriage, she had never wished such a misery on him.

"Done," Ulet muttered with terrible exhaustion and dropped the stylus on the cracked stone floor.

Urlen grabbed the parchment and read it over quickly. Satisfied, he thanked Ulet with habitual politeness and gathered his writing kit.

"This message and the formal demands of the Kez will go forth in the morning," Urlen said as he stood up.

Ulet did not respond. He slid down the wall and curled painfully into a fetal position. He was sure a few ribs were cracked and each breath hurt him worse than his pummeled pride.

Urlen and the other warrior in the chamber departed. They took all but one of the torches with them. The remaining torch was almost burned out. In its wavering light, Demeda could barely recognize her battered brother. Ulet, so handsome only a few hours ago, had been reduced to a battered wretch. He had already slumped into a troubled sleep, but Demeda could not rest, not even as her body tightened painfully with fatigue and overexertion. She might never have another chance to act to help Ulet or explore the unknown possibilities of this new situation. Moving slowly so as to stay quiet, she checked on the guards outside the chamber. They were sitting against pillars with their heads resting on arms folded across their knees, obviously asleep.

She slipped over to the sputtering torch. Pulling her wrists apart as much as she could, she held them to the flame. There was no way to avoid burning herself and she clenched her teeth against the intense pain. The burning leather gave off a dirty smell, but the bonds did not last long against the tiny flame, and she soon broke free.

The leather cords had gouged her soft skin, and the burns stung but she forced herself to ignore them. Actually freeing herself gave her an exhilarating rush of excited satisfaction. Her free hands seemed like the greatest accomplishment in her whole life.

Demeda went to the doorway. She hugged the stone walls and wished that she was a spider that could walk along the wall unnoticed. The old stone pressing against her cheek was craggy and still wet from the recent rains that had soaked into the mossy crevices. The odor of decay crept up her nostrils.

Demeda eyed the sleeping guards for a long spell. One of them snored a few times before shifting his head and quieting. Behind her, Ulet moaned and muttered but neither of the guards reacted.

Convinced that they were soundly asleep, Demeda took a tentative step outside the chamber. She felt like a mouse that knows an owl patrols the sky. Holding her breath, she put her foot down slowly with each step. As she silently snuck past the first Kez, nervous terror coupled with potent excitement threatened to make her cry out, but she forced herself to focus on moving slowly, carefully, and as quietly as possible.

After passing the first guard, she wanted to dart away, but her instincts advised her to remain slow. Her slow creep across the ruined temple would not stir the senses of the sleeping Kez, but a rushing female flitting through the dark would.

And it was dark. As she passed the second guard, she could not see where to go. She reached out blindly until she felt the cool round stone of a column. Shifting herself carefully around the column, she reached out and found a wall. Demeda moved along the wall until she found the gap of another doorway. She stuck her head through it. Torches revealed the inside of the temple's main chamber. A few dwindling campfires glowed on the floor with men sleeping around them. Apparently the Kez felt very safe and secure in this location. Demeda noted no one awake. They were all very tired after their daring attack on the Sabar'Uto diplomatic caravan.

She studied the scene for quite a while, but observed no movement among the men, except for the normal shifting of sleep. She did not spot Amar, but she supposed that he slept in a separate area as befitted a leader.

Demeda saw another large gaping doorway on the other side of the room and some firelight was coming from that chamber. She started across the main chamber. Staying low and near the walls, she skirted the clumps of sleeping men until she reached the next doorway. Clothed only in flimsy sleeping garments and tattered slippers, she padded as stealthily as a cat. Demeda slipped through the doorway. Crouching with her back to the wall, she looked around.

This had once been the inner sanctum of a temple. Now open to the sky, half of its columns had fallen down. Two statues were crashed against each other before an oval stone altar where a bright fire burned within a stone dish. Long centuries of weather had blurred the stone faces of the statues, and vandals had long ago stripped the place of any valuable materials. One alabaster eye still stared out from a statue, and it startled her. She regretted her sharp intake of breath, and hoped that the sound had not been louder than the soft snap of the fire.

Demeda crept across the room. When she reached the leaning statues, she pressed her body against one. Perhaps the stone figure had once represented a god, but now it only hid her in its cold embrace.

Slowly, she looked around the statue. Along the back wall overlooking the altar relief carvings of every phase of the moon arched across the cracked and vine-covered stone wall. Stone carvings of naked women danced beneath the moons. Time had broken off some of the full breasts and nipples, but the women's curving hips and uplifted arms still waved at the moons.

Beneath this ancient scene of mysterious worship lay Amar beyond the altar where once ancient rites were performed. Demeda was sure that it was Amar because she recognized his hair and the familiar straps of her brother's stolen armor across his back.

Apparently, even the dro-shalum allowed himself the vulnerability of sleep. For a moment, Demeda questioned herself. To approach this rogue was foolish. She might startle him awake and cause him to plunge a blade through her heart. She would have to keep a bit of distance. Still moving carefully and quietly, she ducked beneath the statue and slipped toward the altar. Despite her fear, this might be her only chance to speak with the Kez leader on her brother's behalf. Her daring confrontation seemed far more desirable than slinking back to her holding cell.

Demeda touched the altar. She imagined grisly sacrifices made on the thick stone slab. Her flesh rose into goose pimples as a profound realization swept through her. Now that the pure terror of the abduction had peaked and plateaued, she understood that her life would never be as it had originally been meant to be. Demeda was about to do something radical of her own free will and she did not know what the consequences or results would be.

She stepped forward, studying the man on the floor. His body was lean yet well-muscled with the threatening potential of a senshal. And like that predatory cat, he was stronger than the larger prey that he stalked and brought down. Amar was death in the night and yet as alluring as soft speckled orange fur that begged fingers to caress it.

She paused, remembering the reach of his sword. She wished that she could see his face. What did this young Kez look like in sleep? Was his face soft and carefree?

Amar sprang to his feet and spun to meet her. He was pure animal in that moment, defensive as a baited bear. But his wild eyes registered who had entered his chamber and his sword stopped halfway from its sheath across his back. The sight of any other person would have surely drawn the blade the rest of the way out and into flesh.

Demeda fell to her knees. She would show him submission, even as she slaughtered her fear with newly found courage conjured from all her past rages and desires. It was time to find a new way in the world or perish in the quest.

She was proud of her steady hands as she untied her tepa. She exposed her face and drew the headdress back onto her shoulders while shaking free the long glistening black tresses of her hair. Never before had she exposed her mature female face to a man outside her immediate family. The night air was cool on her hot face that burned with defiance of all that a highly ordered society had stamped on her mind.

"Amar, I would speak with you," she said.

32. The Whip of Temptation

Living among dangerous men had sharpened Amar's senses. A gentle noise out of place was enough to rouse him from sleep.

He opened his eyes and watched the firelight bounce on the females carved into the stone wall. Faint steps tickled his ears. The footfalls were very light, as if from small feet on a small body. Amar was always expecting Lax Ar Fu to send a man to kill him. Amar was surprised that it had already taken so long. He was sure that he was not overhearing Urlen who had retired to a small adjoining room. Urlen would not be creeping about his chamber in this suspicious manner.

The person came closer and then paused. Amar pictured first in his mind how he would move his body and then he acted with maximum swiftness. He estimated where to strike so as to cut flesh but not give an immediately mortal wound. He intended to talk to this intruder.

Pushing himself up and spinning around, Amar expected to see one of his fellow Kez, but the sight of the princess shocked him. How had she eluded her guards and every warrior in the ruined temple? Was he dreaming?

Then she removed her headdress. What madness could prompt this wanton display?

And she was lovely. Unprepared for the sight of the female, Amar found himself vulnerable to her forbidden appearance. Her dark eyes and high cheekbones radiated a striking confidence. Her tender youth aglow with ripe feminine allure struck his unguarded spirit. Amar had thought himself permanently hardened against such a thing, but a tremor of temptation rippled through his body. Amar fought back the surge of feelings. He did not want them.

Uncovered and consciously aware of how she was snagging him with her beauty, she told him that she would speak with him. It was not a request for an audience, but an announcement of what she expected.

Amar returned his sword fully to its sheath. Casually, he looked around the chamber for other threats. Perhaps this female was a distraction for another assassin, but they seemed to be alone.

"How did you get loose?" Amar asked. His men had been slovenly in their guard duty. Then with a nip of panic, he wondered if the prince was still captive, but he did not rush to check. Ulet was wounded and beaten. He could not get far, and Amar was too intrigued by the princess kneeling before him to remove his attention from her. What man could ignore this extraordinary visitor? This princess was meant to placate the war hunger of the Temulanka King, and she had come to him.

Demeda ignored his question. She spread her hands in a friendly gesture, and Amar noted quickly the little burns on her wrists that explained how her bonds had been removed. She was crafty and unafraid of a little pain.

"I have come to ask for my brother's release," she said.

Amar was glad to know that the prince was still in his custody. He said, "I admire your loyalty to your brother, Princess, but do not trouble yourself. Your father will pay the ransom and he will go free."

"But he is hurt. Let him go. I offer myself as his ransom," Demeda said, and even though she was determined to be brave, she quivered inside with fear of the unknown. She had done it. She had offered herself to this dangerous rogue. She expected him to promptly seize her and do what a man could do.

Having been raised to believe that her body was coveted by all men and therefore must always be guarded, she was surprised when he only stared at her with confusion.

"Has the prince told you to do this?" Amar asked. He could not imagine that it was her idea and perhaps her brother was despicable enough to offer his sister's maidenhead to outlaws.

Demeda shook her head. "No, Ulet knows nothing of this. I offer myself to you if you will return my brother to his people."

Amar smirked with contempt. "Foolish girl. How could you expect to enforce such a bargain?"

Demeda had to think for a moment. She wanted to answer intelligently, which was difficult because she was making things up as she went.

"I can hope that I can please you enough that you will grant my request," she explained.

Still quite disbelieving, Amar walked around her and examined her thoughtfully. Demeda's fear spiked when he stopped behind her. She wondered what this killer might do.

She stood up and faced him. His mesmerizing dark eyes were waiting for her. Demeda felt a startling attraction to him. She realized that she had been attracted to the very thought of him since he had first approached Chadenedra. He was the notorious dro-shalum, and he looked like pure freedom.

Suspicion clouded his face. "You have come to me for some reason besides your brother," Amar determined.

Demeda's brash facade faded because he had guessed her heart. She supposed that she should tell him. Regaining her courage, she said, "Amar, I wish to be free. That is why I offer myself to you. Without my virginity I won't be accepted back."

He simply stared at her, amazed and not really understanding.

Demeda continued, "I don't want to marry the Temulanka King. His tribe is the enemy of my tribe and the thought of it makes me sick. I won't do it. When you took me tonight, you saved me." She reached out to him, but he withdrew a hasty step as if her touch would strike him dead.

"Princess…"

"Demeda. My name is Demeda," she interjected.

Amar scowled, upset with himself for allowing his female captive to unsettle him. He should call for his men and have her put back in her cell, but he did not do it.

"You must be mad," he decided. "I'm not going to touch you nor let any other man touch you. Lax Ar Fu wants your ransom. I'm not going to throw away that gold just for the pleasure of breaking you in."

"I know you aren't going to let any other man touch me," Demeda agreed with purring pleasantness. She did not understand how he was resisting her. Perhaps a virgin was not as appealing as she had always been led to believe. Maybe if she was an experienced woman she would know how to properly seduce him. Still, it was an amazing thrill to try. It made her feel powerful. She had never in the most liberal daydream imagined that she would fling herself at a notorious outlaw. She liked it.

Demeda continued, "Amar, no one will know if my honor is intact before paying my ransom. You risk nothing. I will even help you make twice as much on my ransom. Tell your scribe to write on my behalf to the Temulanka King. I will personally ask him to ransom me because I am officially his. If he calls himself a man and a king, he must save me or otherwise my tribe will blame him for letting me be taken by outlaws on the border of his domain. It is his duty to pay the ransom if he truly wants the peace treaty. It's the only way to prove that he was not behind this abduction."

Amar raised his eyebrows, impressed by her devious cleverness.

Demeda continued, "My demands of my future husband will resound through our lands. He will be shamed and the treaty doubly threatened. He will pay just to save face."

Amar considered her idea. It might actually produce a double ransom, or at least increase the chances of receiving a ransom for her at all. But the greatest appeal of her proposal was that it would increase the tension between the Sabar'Uto and Temulanka even more, which was precisely what Amar wanted.

"I like your idea. I will have Urlen write it in the morning," Amar said.

Demeda smiled. She was beginning to be less a victim and more a conspirator in her abduction, but she needed more. She grabbed his hands. He tensed and a cold emotionless wall descended over him like a falling portcullis, which actually encouraged her. He was trying very hard to ignore the closeness of her body.

"You must promise me that no matter who ransoms me or if no one does that you will not turn me over to either tribe. I don't want to go home or go live with the Temulanka. You have shown me a third path and I will follow it!" she declared.

Her bizarre passion intrigued Amar. Why would a woman, especially of her privileged birth, want this? Other lawless women lived outside society and even among the Kez, but they were of low birth. He supposed she could become like them, but she could not possibly know what that life would be like.

Her fingers traced the edge of his leather bracers. Amar touched her hands lightly, and the contact made him tingle. He had thought that he had put aside such feelings. They were only weakness and he needed to be strong, but Demeda had awakened him with a sharp crack from the whip of temptation. Amar tentatively reached for her body. His lust had been dormant, not dead, and, as a bulb must swell and flower in the spring rains, he allowed himself to feel desire. He touched her shoulders and then ran his hands up her neck. She shuddered and Amar saw fear flash in her eyes. This was truly something of which Lax Ar Fu could be jealous. This sweet cup of triumph could only be sipped from once, and perhaps it was fitting for Amar to indulge in one more spoil from his successful raid on the Sabar'Uto caravan.

"No bargains. No promises," Amar said. And then he said her name, speaking it purposefully as if casting a spell. "Demeda, if you would be with me, then do it because you want me and nothing else."

Demeda knew she must not throw away her one rare treasure without gaining his promise – whatever it might be worth, but she had gone too far. She was not in control. The power she had been playing with consumed her in its fire. His hands were on her, and the hot harness of youthful instinct yoked her body. Demeda nodded weakly. She would be with him just because she wanted him.

Amar touched her breasts. Gently he found the nipples beneath the fabric and rubbed them until they popped up like mushrooms after a rain. He bent in for a kiss. They brushed their lips together. Their movements were hesitant and slow. When their tongues met, he pulled her clothing off her shoulders and shoved her loose tepa onto the floor.

Demeda gasped as his movements grew stronger. His passion drank deeply of her body. She had imagined what this would be like many times, but her fantasies had not prepared her for the intensity of the experience. A hungry pleasure flowed through her body and she could only let the feast proceed. She was not sure what to do, but Amar steered her steadily toward their coupling. His hands massaged her breasts and moved down to her hips. He pulled all of her clothing off. Cool air breezed through her legs and she shivered despite the heat blushing her skin.

"Touch me," he commanded with his face in her neck.

Demeda obeyed. Amar was muscle and metal. Her own brother's armor separated them, but she forced that weird coincidence from her thoughts. She located the waistband of his pants and slid her small hands into his clothing. His erection startled her. Amar chuckled at her virginal reaction and slid a hand between her legs. Warm, wet, willing, she could not help but press against his caressing fingers that sought out her most sensitive places. She moaned and her breath came in stuttering wisps of air and then she cried out.

Amar grabbed her by the buttocks and swung her around onto the altar. He mounted her and abandoned himself to the pleasures that they were sharing. Her soft female body encased his hardness, and he descended into a thoughtless place. It was like the bliss of battle or being near Onja, but it was hotter and kinder. The sensations were almost alien to him at first. This had been the world of Gendahl. A thing that other men indulged in, but not Amar. Yet, he was taking her and letting himself revel in the possession and passion.

After climaxing, he pulled Demeda into a sitting position on the altar and hugged her. Petting her tousled hair, he nuzzled her face with kisses and murmured her name.

She was sweaty and tears streaked her face. The fierce strength of Amar's embrace had been both frightening and wonderful. A feeling of inescapable submission had consumed her, but now it was passing. She suspected she might never fully understand how that moment of helpless craving could make her feel good.

Amar looked over her shoulder, and Demeda felt him tense. She turned to look as well. The doorway to the temple's inner sanctum was crowded with Kez warriors, all of whom looked rather bemused.

She realized that her cries must have roused them, and they had rushed to investigate. She had to wonder how long they had watched, and then she cringed with embarrassment. She buried her face against Amar's armor.

His hand massaged her neck, reassuring her. "Go check the prince. See that he is well guarded," he said

"Yes, Amar," someone said and the men left.

Amar returned his attention to Demeda. He carried her off the altar and lowered her onto the single blanket that he had been sleeping on earlier. Taking off his armor and the rest of his clothing, he descended upon her fully naked now.

She touched his face and ran a hand along the shaved side of his head. "Amar," she said and kissed him.

Amar began to kiss all over her body, prowling inexorably lower with his lips. Demeda noticed the pink dawn strike the tops of the ruined columns and walls as she lay back with him between her legs. Then pleasure tipped her toward oblivion, a marvelous oblivion that had never experienced before. Arching her back, she cried out, not caring if every man in the area heard her. She knew they were all thinking about her anyway, so let them hear. She was with Amar and none of them could touch her. The world could not touch her. She had escaped her fate.

******

Amar raised himself onto an elbow so he could look down on Demeda. The midmorning sun had driven the dramatic mystery from the temple's crumbling inner sanctum. The ruins appeared like the sleepy half-memory of a dream as the daylight brightened the foliage vining among the old stonework.

He ran a hand along Demeda's body, cupping her breast and then toying with her belly button. She was soft and a little thin. A woman whose bloom had just opened its first petals.

Amar felt sated, but he was not quite sure if he liked the feeling. He derived more energy from wanting and craving. But he did not regret his indulgence. Demeda had shown herself to be extraordinary in many ways. Although he considered her strange, he admired her daring, and he had to admit that she had impressed him by slipping past all his Kez warriors in the night, which reminded him that some reprimands were in order.

"Get your clothes," he told her while reaching for his own.

Demeda watched him dress. The sight of his hard young body intoxicated her. She could not imagine giving up her virginity to a finer man. She hoped that she would never forget the tenderness that she had extracted from his fierce flesh.

"Urlen," Amar hollered as he put back on his new armor.

Expecting company, Demeda finally snatched at her flimsy gown and the remnants of her robe. She wished that she could have been abducted before she had undressed for the night.

Urlen hustled into the sanctum with a water jug. He handed it to Amar and said that it had just been drawn from the spring at the base of the hill. Amar quaffed a big drink, rinsed his teeth, spat, and then drank.

Demeda thought he was the most delightful picture of an outlaw as he spat on the floor of a place that had once been sacred. She then forced herself to meet Urlen's curious gaze.

Urlen removed a piece of dried fish from his pack and offered it to Amar, who gladly started chomping on the chewy flesh. Between mouthfuls, he told Urlen about the message that Demeda wanted to send to the Temulanka King. Urlen smiled at her audacity.

With the fish quickly eaten, Amar grabbed his belts and slapped his blades back into their proper places. He scooped up the water jug and handed it to Demeda. Briefly, he looked into her eyes as if he might say something, but, without another word, he walked away.

Demeda resisted her urge to run after him. She clearly was not invited, but she did not know what to do with herself.

Urlen helped her past that awkward moment when she began to wonder what destroying her life might mean for her. He cleared his throat in a bureaucratic manner and slipped closer to her.

"Welcome to our club," he said.

His amused attitude allowed her to smile back. Such a strange thing to smile at this man who could see her face. Kicking aside an unwelcome wave of shyness, Demeda asked if her brother was all right.

Urlen nodded but did not mention the round of torment Ulet had suffered that morning as the other Kez had teased him about what his sister was doing with Amar.

Urlen opened his bag and rummaged out a stale chunk of bread for her. "Not exactly royal fare," he apologized.

She accepted the torn loaf that clearly had forsaken freshness. She was very hungry. As she ate, Urlen turned to business and reviewed with her what she wanted to say to the Temulanka King. He offered a few suggestions to embellish the shame she was trying to inflict on the man who should have been her husband.

Urlen added, "We'll also need to send a few copies to others besides the King. The Temulanka council of war chiefs will need to hear of this and I think the high priest of Jayshem's temple in the Temulanka capital should be notified. Oh! I know, you will appeal to them for help because you're such a good and pious virgin."

Demeda's eyes widened with shock. She was not used to any of this. She was chatting with a man about manipulating the political players of the Temulanka Tribe. Urlen's criminal nonchalance was a marvel to behold.

Rubbing his hands together, Urlen invited her to join him while he wrote. He had found a nice spot outside the temple that provided an excellent view.

Demeda hesitated. "Where is Amar?"

"Well," Urlen stalled. He felt like he should advise their lovely captive in some way, but what could he say? Tell her not to get too attached to the murderous villain she had been fornicating with all morning? He chose to say only that Amar was a busy man.

Demeda looked down at her tepa that was still on the floor. The discarded lump of fabric summed up how trampled she felt. She reminded herself to be brave. She still had her chance to make a new life whatever it might be. As the stale bread she had just eaten indicated, not everything on this course would be as pleasant as Amar's embrace.

"I should check on my brother. He is hurt," she said.

Urlen plainly saw her dread for that unpleasant reunion. "Would you like me to go with you?" he said.

The offer brightened Demeda, and she decided that she liked Urlen.

Demeda took the water jug with her. Outside the chamber where Ulet was kept, she noted two Kez attentively on guard. Their cut lips dripped blood, and she realized that Amar had just punished them for failing to guard her properly the night before. Demeda imagined Amar striking his underlings, and fear of him fluttered against her heart.

I must never let him see me afraid of him, she decided.

Ulet looked terrible. The gold beads on his clothes had proved too tempting for his captors, and he had been stripped to his under garments. Demeda pitied his swollen face, but his ugly scowl showed that he already considered her as good as dead.

Despite his obvious scorn, Demeda resolved to show herself to be the better person. "I've come to clean your wounds, Brother," she said.

Ulet cringed. "Don't touch me, whore," he snarled.

The coarse word stabbed her, but she hid her hurt. Demeda kneeled beside him and bent over his face. "Shame on you, Ulet. Don't judge me. You were taking me to whore with your enemy so you could have peace. If you can't be nice, don't talk to me," she scolded him and started to ease the crude dressing off his buttock.

The damning truth of her cold words blunted his sharp tongue. Ulet would never admit it, but he knew that he had done far worse by her than she had by him.

After a few tense moments with Urlen looking on, Ulet finally attempted conversation again. "You'll get no ransom now," he said.

Demeda wiped his wound and applied a fresh scrap of bandage over it. "That does not concern you any more," she said.

With a growl, Ulet accused her of tricking him. "You made me write that ransom note on your behalf and then threw yourself at that outlaw."

"I did not trick you," Demeda said.

"They'll all rape you," Ulet spat.

Demeda murmured that she doubted it, and her quiet disregard for her disgrace stymied her brother.

As Demeda finished tending Ulet, she asked Urlen if her brother could have food. Urlen said that he would see to it. Demeda stood up, glad that the strained meeting was about to conclude.

Allowing herself a final triumph, she said, "You should have listened to me when I told you to go back. Because of your mistake, I am free of you. And when you get back to your father, tell him I am free of him now too."

Feeling like the queen of all Gyhwen, she spun around and walked out of the chamber. The guards shifted uneasily as she passed them with Urlen in tow, but they did not stop her. Apparently, their reprimand from Amar had not included any new orders to restrict her.

The Kez remained at the temple hideout for another two days. A couple times a day, Kez scouts came and went after speaking with Amar. Demeda mostly kept to herself or chatted with Urlen. She saw Amar very little. He kept a strict physical regimen of running, other exercises, and weapons practice with his closest warriors. But at night when she went to sleep in the inner sanctum of the ruins, he would come to her. Demeda loved having him to herself. This mysterious man whose name was fear among many tribes took her in his hard unyielding arms and poured his passion into her. Sometimes he was fierce and other times he was gentle, savoring every line and curve of her body. On their third night together, he led her down to the spring at the base of the hill. They bathed and made love beside the cool waters, and Demeda felt like they were the only people in the world. The moon glowed above the hilly forest that sang wild songs. A lantern set on the rocky edge of the spring cast its yellow rippling glow across the pure waters. Demeda arched her head back into the water to wet her hair and slick it back from her face. She then floated her breasts so that the nipples just barely poked out of the water. Amar swam over to her, slipped beneath the water and came up between her breasts. He rose to his feet and his shoulders and hard chest passed before her eyes as he wrapped his arms around her. They kissed and Demeda ran her hands along his splendid chest until she clasped the small pouch around his neck. His hand instantly intervened and he stopped kissing her.

Demeda apologized. "I won't take it," she said.

Amar loosened the pouch. He took out the crystal orb and Demeda gasped lightly when she saw its blue radiance glowing upon his palm. The light inside the smooth orb moved lazily. Amar lowered it below the surface of the water and it illuminated the water down to the pebbly bottom and cast shifting blue light over their naked bodies.

"What jewel is this?" Demeda asked.

"Not a jewel. Onja made this crystal with her hand," Amar explained.

"Onja? She is the rys that Urlen told me about?" Demeda said.

Amar nodded. Demeda asked if she could touch the crystal and Amar gave it to her. When its light dimmed in her hand, she realized that its power was especially attuned to Amar.

"What does it do?" she asked.

"It helps Onja contact me," he explained.

"Does she do it often?" Demeda said.

"Not of late. Onja has gone back to her people, but she will come back. She has a purpose for me," he said, and Demeda noted his dreamy expression when he spoke about Onja. Jealousy flashed in Demeda, but she forced it away. She was with Amar now and his rys patron was far away.

Handing the crystal back to him, she thanked him for showing it to her. As he returned the orb to its pouch, Demeda tried to keep this rare spurt of conversation going.

"Urlen told me your tribe was destroyed? Which tribe?" she said.

When he told her that he had been born to the Lin Tohs Tribe, she said that she had never heard of it.

"And you never will," he said.

Demeda suddenly started to grasp what it was to be an outlaw. It was to be without a tribe, and in Amar's case, he had no tribe to go back to. Demeda had no tribe to return to either. She started kissing him again and they returned to the blanket spread beside the spring where their bodies joined late into the night.

After they dressed and were hiking the trail back up to the temple, Demeda pulled him to a stop. With her hand still in his, she noted the moment, hoping she would remember it always. Even in their short time together, she had learned that his leadership position among the Kez meant a great deal to him and left little time for her.

"Amar, are you really dro-shalum?" she asked.

"Yes," he answered readily and tugged her up the trail.

His chilling candor startled Demeda, yet she smiled. Her life had never been interesting before. Now it was dangerously unpredictable and it made her feel alive.

They next morning, they left the temple hideout. Demeda rode behind Amar and enjoyed the act of traveling with her head uncovered. She noted the curiosity, interest, and sometimes lust in the eyes of the other Kez, but no one spoke to her rudely or touched her. She supposed that her association with Amar accounted for their restraint.

Ulet was in the middle of the line of warriors, and she was glad for the distance between them. Riding was painful for him because of his wound, but the Sabar'Uto prince suffered his captivity bravely. He refused Demeda's help and looked after his hurts himself now.

Demeda could feel the great wedge of disgrace that she had jammed between them. She also understood that Ulet was incapable of grasping her reasons for what she had done. How could he fathom that she might want to make a decision for herself? Demeda refused to believe that she was causing any harm in discarding her supposed duty. The tribes would inevitably war. Her marriage might have delayed a war, but not prevented it forever.

The Kez traveled their secret trails through the hilly forests between the domains of the Sabar'Uto and the Temulanka. Wary of warriors from either tribe, they frequently sent scouts in various directions. After their first night of camping in the forest, Demeda noted how carefully the Kez broke their camp. Ashes from campfires and horse apples were scattered, and everybody took care to limit signs of their passing.

On the second night, they did not light any fires. Scouts had reported a Sabar'Uto search party at the mouth of a nearby canyon. Amar had Ulet gagged in case he might decide to start yelling.

Without any fires, the evening shadows gathered ominously. An instinctive fear of the dark assailed Demeda. She had never been so exposed to Nature with the cold ground beneath her and the inhuman presence of the trees around her. The spirit of Gyhwen was strong in the night, and she was but a single small creature cowering upon the face of a powerful world.

Loneliness oppressed Demeda as well. Since leaving the temple, Amar had not lain with her or barely spoken to her. She worried that he was done with her, and that thought was terrible. She needed his protection.

At least Amar had given her a deer skin, and she wrapped herself in it now. The night air was growing chilly and a drizzling rain started. She pulled the skin over her head to create a crude tent over her body. Demeda clung to her courage. She could not go back to her old life and she did not want to. Despite her brave resolve, quiet tears flowed with the raindrops on her face.

Nearby Amar and Urlen were chatting softly, but she could not catch what they were saying. She envied their quiet conversation. They sounded like friends. Thinking of Mallah, the pang of friendship lost strummed the strings of her soul. With nothing else to do in the wet dark, she slumped to the ground and yielded to fitful sleep.

It was still dark and raining harder when Demeda recognized the touch of Amar's hand on her face. For a delighted instant she hoped that he was going to lay with her and keep her warm, but he commanded her instead to get up.

"What's wrong?" she whispered.

"I want to move on while it's still dark. A Sabar'Uto war party is close. The rain will help cover our tracks," Amar explained.

Demeda was glad that he was taking such care to avoid her possible liberation by her tribe. Part of her then thought of Ulet, who was suffering, but his freedom would be bought in due time.

The Kez rode all night and pressed on into the next day until Demeda was nearly delirious in the saddle. Her body had been through more in less than a week than it had experienced in her whole life. She could feel herself getting stronger, which never would have happened in her former life.

Demeda catnapped during the few breaks the Kez took that day. She never bothered to ask where they were headed. She would not have recognized any destination anyway.

After taking a particularly rough trail up a ridge, the group stopped and Amar dismounted. As he walked back to Demeda's horse, he signaled discreetly to Kym.

Amar helped Demeda off her horse and led her over the crest of the ridge. The rest of the Kez stayed behind. The land was steep and she relied on Amar's help to keep from stumbling. Her tattered slippers offered scant protection from stones. Finally they skidded to a stop along the edge of a ravine.

Holding her hand as he usually did, Amar tugged her along at a quick pace until they reached a rope bridge across the ravine. The thick but weathered ropes and sticks that comprised the bridge blended with the dusky granite of the ravine. It would be easy not to notice the bridge, especially how it was positioned in the shade of two large trees overhanging the ravine.

Amar tested the bridge with his weight and then scampered across it. He turned and beckoned Demeda, who eyed the bridge doubtfully. The stream in the ravine below splashed around boulders, and Demeda hesitated.

Don't let Amar see you afraid, she told herself and hurried across the bridge. Amar continued along a narrow trail. A trio of goats crossed the path and Demeda guessed that someone lived nearby.

The dusk was gathering when they reached a grass and moss covered stone cottage built into the base of a rocky hill. A woman stood in front of the cottage and she waved. Her dark hair was held back by a green headband, and a leather tunic that only went halfway down her thighs was all that she wore except for sandals.

After days among only men, Demeda brightened at the prospect of female company. She was used to almost exclusively being with women and their absence had created a jarring emptiness. When another woman wearing a green cloth dress came out of the cottage, Demeda was even more excited. She needed some female companionship and she hoped that she might at least be able to get some more clothing.

By the time Amar and Demeda reached the cottage, a third woman approached, apparently returning from foraging in the forest. Her basket bulged with fresh spring herbs and greens. She was older with streaks of gray through her hair and lines on her brown face. Bright confident eyes twinkled from her broad face that commanded a big curvy body.

The women assembled to greet Amar. They bowed to him while eyeing Demeda with strong interest.

"I need a favor," Amar said.

The older woman responded saucily, "I lay awake at night hoping to hear those words from you, Amar."

He ignored her flirtation and introduced Demeda. Then he bade the other two women to take Demeda into the cottage so that he could speak alone with the older woman.

The two younger women beckoned Demeda warmly and ushered her into the modest cottage. She looked back questioningly but followed politely.

Inside the cottage was dark, but it smelled fresh, spicy even. Low beds made of small split logs piled with furs and brightly dyed wool blankets ran along two sides of the single room, and a large hearth, table, and benches filled up the rest of the cottage that was stuffed with jars, baskets, bags, and all manner of clutter, familiar and strange.

The two women introduced themselves. Their accents were difficult for Demeda but she managed to learn that the woman with the green headband was Mei and the one in the green dress was Luci, who was missing a front tooth, but had a happy smile all the same.

They brought Demeda a cup of water, which she accepted gratefully. Mei and Luci were eager for conversation, but the low voices outside distracted Demeda. Her intuition flashed with warning. Putting down the drinking cup, she rushed out.

Amar and the woman appeared to have just finished speaking. The older woman took Demeda's arm as if to put her back in the cottage, but Demeda shook her off with a willful yank and confronted Amar.

"Are you leaving me here?" she demanded.

He looked uncomfortable. He glanced at the sunset that was a yellowish pink hot spot through the trees.

"I think you will be safest here," he said.

"I am safest with you," she countered.

Amar frowned thoughtfully. Demeda wondered how the man, who could hold her so passionately, at times even tenderly, could be so reluctant to speak with her.

Amar seemed to accept that Demeda was not a woman that he could drop off without an explanation. Based on her behavior so far, he judged that she would come after him if he could not convince her to stay. But explaining his actions annoyed him.

"Demeda, I go to Lax Ar Fu, Overlord of the Kez, to present my captive and await his and perhaps your ransom," he said.

"Why can't I come?" she said.

Glancing again at the sunset, Amar said, "Word has reached me that Lax Ar Fu is unhappy with what I have done…with what we have done."

Demeda softened her stance. She had not even conceived that her actions could trouble him. He was the dro-shalum.

Amar continued, "My Lord thinks I have overstepped myself by deflowering a female captive of such importance. And I suspect he is jealous. I leave you here so he is not tempted to hurt you to spite me." Amar reached out and touched her hair. "I think it best that Lax Ar Fu not to see what he has missed. Bringing you to him will complicate matters for me. I can show no weakness to Lax Ar Fu."

Demeda laid her head on his chest. She was the weakness of the dro-shalum. Amar wanted to make sure the Kez Overlord did not seize her. She was grateful for the sign that Amar actually possessed some true feeling for her. Demeda also considered that she must strive not to be a source of problems for Amar.

"I understand," she whispered.

Amar allowed himself a sniff of her hair and then detached himself from her, without even a kiss. He told her that within two or three weeks, he might know if a ransom was coming for her, and he would send for her then.

Outrage drove off Demeda's fatigue. "I will not be ransomed! You won't give me back!" she declared.

Amar was not used to someone speaking to him like that, but he did not lift a hand to punish her. Dispassionately, he said, "The ransom is important and you will be presented for it. Whether you go with them remains to be seen."

"I won't!" Demeda sounded like a petulant child.

"Perhaps in a few weeks you will reconsider," he said gently.

Demeda shook her head. Maybe Amar was being kind to give her a second chance. This life she had cast herself into certainly had its hardships. "Amar, I would be expected to kill myself if I went home," she said and imagined with wrenching distaste how her own relatives would bring her a cup of poison.

"Still, I will send for you," Amar said. "This is about the ransom and flexing our muscles with your tribe and the Temulanka. I must attend to that." He turned.

Demeda took a step after him, but then crushed the pathetic clinging display that she was about to make. Amar was not attracted to weakness and she sternly told herself not to blubber after him. Everything he had said was spinning through her mind. He was leaving her here for safety's sake. She was in danger.

"Amar, wait," she called. "When you send for me, how will I know that it is you and not Lax Ar Fu?"

He stopped and looked back. Surprise highlighted his face. "A good point," he admitted. After a moment's thought, he reached into a small pouch and brought out a silver chain with an amulet of a hawk carved from amber. He had Demeda examine it so that she could recognize it again. "If I can't come myself, the men I send will bear this token," he said.

Demeda nodded and handed it back to him. "What if no ransom comes?" she whispered fearfully. "Will I ever see you again?"

If Amar worried about the continuation or discontinuation of their relationship, his face gave no hint of it. Gesturing to the cottage, he said the women frequently camped with the Kez and wintered with them. "Stay with them and learn from them," he said. "And our paths will cross again."

With that he jogged into the forest, rushing to rejoin his Kez warriors. Demeda slumped to her hands and knees and started to cry. She tore at her hair and the weeds and grass. The older woman came out to her with a light blanket, wrapped it around her shoulders, and took her inside. She introduced herself as Bo Tah and murmured many sympathies to the distraught teenage girl now in her care.

Eventually, Demeda's sobbing subsided. She had cried for more than just Amar's departure. She had cried for everything. For her lost family. For Ulet, who still suffered captivity, and for all her fears of an unknown future.

Bo Tah, Mei, and Luci were very kind to her. They heated water so that she could bathe and they gave her fresh clothing. The homespun cloth felt foreign against Demeda's royal flesh, but she was grateful to have something more substantial to wear.

The women fed her a good meal of rabbit stew. They stayed up late into the evening questioning their guest and Demeda did likewise as she developed an ear for their accent. She had never even guessed that women lived outside the total control of male society. Mei and Luci had sad stories of escaping abusive husbands after being married off very young. Mei had been forced to leave behind a baby boy that she had not seen for five years, but fleeing had been the only way to save her life.

Bo Tah had a different history. She had never been married she said. At the age of twelve she had left her village and gone to live in the forest with an older woman, now dead, who had taught her everything she knew.

All three women cavorted with the Kez and other outlaws. Sometimes they even took lovers. Their relationships seemed to come and go. The Kez warriors, Bo Tah explained, were not supposed to permanently tie

Tracy Falbe

357

themselves to women. They had lovers, children too, but the relationships never came before service to Vu.

Bo Tah noted Demeda's disappointment when she said this, so to make her guest feel special she commented how Amar had never been interested in a woman before Demeda's appearance. With Mei and Luci confirming, Demeda learned that Amar, since coming to the Kez the year before, had shunned women. None seemed to interest him in that way, despite an active interest from almost all women who encountered him. The news did make Demeda feel special. She had seduced Amar when others had failed, but it was not exactly reassuring to know that Amar's affections were constantly tempted.

At last Demeda fell asleep in a bed. She slept soundly, and for the next week she went to bed early and slept late each day. She was astoundingly tired. Since the abduction she had barely slept at all. She needed to renew herself after the radical transformation that had claimed her life.

During this time, her blood came to her, and she was glad to be in the company of the women and have access to rags and clean water. Amar had been right to leave her in this place instead of continuing to drag her cross country in a night gown.

The coming of her blood proved that she was not pregnant, and Demeda was utterly grateful for that fact. In her times of passion with Amar she had thought little about pregnancy, but she could not be so foolish in the future. Demeda did not want to have a child. Not after she had escaped the bitter confines of her arranged marriage and begun to truly know the world.

One morning while Mei and Luci were out milking the goats, Demeda asked Bo Tah if any way existed to avoid pregnancy.

Bo Tah looked up from the bread dough that she was patting into loaves beside the hearth and chuckled. "All us wild women know about that," she said.

"Then it can be done?" Demeda pressed excitedly.

"More or less," Bo Tah said and started patting another small loaf. "We will teach you."

Over the next week, Bo Tah, Mei, and Luci instructed Demeda about her body. They explained how to count the days between her blood so she would have a good chance of knowing when she was fertile or not fertile. Demeda was amazed by the information. She had never heard of such things. Her ignorance then angered her. She had lived among many women her whole life and no one had ever told her.

Bo Tah became uncharacteristically grave and said that civilization broke off women from their natural knowledge. "Some of us still know, but we'd be killed quick if we went to town and started telling every farmer's daughter and wife what she needs to know. In the world of men with their plows and smithies and wars, our best use is havin' babies," Bo Tah said.

Demeda was shocked and troubled. This was a great deal to think about and she was sure to contemplate Bo Tah's statement for a long time. Although excited about what she had learned, the other women had emphasized that tracking one's fertility could be imprecise. Nature did not like her system to be gamed, and women were meant to have babies. Demeda also realized that she might not always be in a position to refuse sex. She could not imagine refusing Amar, and the grim fact remained that any man could force himself on her.

Timidly, she inquired about this problem and Bo Tah explained that a brew of special herbs made the blood come and reverse a possible pregnancy.

"It's best to keep those herbs on hand. We'll show you how to gather them in the forest. The main ingredient is just blooming this time of year and we'll be gathering it through high summer."

Demeda repeatedly thanked the women for the knowledge that they shared with her. The knowledge would help her navigate the rest of her life. The women were glad to help her. Bo Tah told her that no woman should be refused this knowledge, but then she cautioned Demeda to be careful in its sharing if she ever rejoined civilization. Such women were often killed.

Demeda settled into a routine with her new companions. Burying her royal snobbery, she did the chores assigned to her. As Amar had recommended, she was learning from the women. Demeda eagerly studied with her sisterly tutors while awaiting Amar's return. Despite her fear of the ransom, she was impatient to move past this simple existence in the forest. She had come to know high excitement at Amar's side and she wanted more.

33. Demons of Revenge and Justice

Great Divinity spin for us the magic circle of life. Bring forth life from death. Renew the faithful as You renew all-giving Ektren. ~ Kwellstan Sect prayer of Poteny

Alloi expected that the Grand Lumin would expel her from the city after their shocking confrontation. When the order never came, she assumed that the Kwellstan Sect did not want to appear threatened by her presence.

Through the winter, she monitored the Altular but did not detect any more torture. Dacian seemed to be in a stalemate with his captors. The Grand Lumin continued to offer promises to remove the crosha if Dacian would become compliant. Alloi doubted the Grand Lumin spoke in good faith, and, based on her sly observations of Dacian, he also seemed unmoved by the Grand Lumin's proposal.

When Alloi spied on Dacian, she felt his patient dejection. Her natural instinct was to soothe someone in distress, but she could do nothing. Dacian had already flatly refused her help.

Alloi wondered why Dacian could not free himself of the crosha. She had witnessed his great power, but apparently the crosha was far more potent than anything she had ever known. When she had reported to the Eschalam about it, her master had been truly disturbed. He had divulged to her that such an enchantment was baytolo, which meant forbidden.

Assailed by a foreign loneliness, Alloi passed the winter learning to cope with her twin's absence. She recognized the many-layered lesson that the Eschalam had imposed on her, and she learned to depend more fully on her own mental fortitude.

Her rigorous solitude ended in spring when her brother and parents finally returned. Alloi ached with anticipation as her family approached Kwellstan. She hired a carriage to take her out of the city so that she could greet them sooner.

Tempet met her in her mind before they physically saw each other. Sitting in the carriage, she started to quietly weep with joy as Tempet wrapped his loving thoughts around her rising emotions. The human driver looked over his shoulder at her. Alloi waved to him pleasantly to let him know that she was fine.

She reunited with her family on the road amid the stately trees of the Valley of Nufal. Birds sang sweetly with springtime optimism as they built their nests, and the sun fell like a golden ribbon upon the road snaking through the shady forest.

Tempet jumped off his horse and ran to embrace Alloi as she alighted from the carriage. The firm physical presence of Tempet's arms and chest renewed Alloi. The relentless tension caused by his absence dissolved and she felt as carefree as a tabling. The twins laughed and cried until they finally let their hug diminish to handholding.

Alloi's parents waited in a wagon with their baggage. Pride for their offspring glowed in their dark eyes. Their father, Havax, waved to Alloi enthusiastically. Although a quiet tabre, he had once been a famous Bozee champion. Now he was content to spend his days with his mate, Deda, and chaperone their revered twins on their diplomatic missions. Deda was a very respected tabre in Drathatarlane. She had done an incredible thing in conceiving twins and bearing them. Havax and Deda had been audacious to experiment with the forces of reproduction, but the results had been impressive. Tempet and Alloi were exceedingly powerful. Yet Deda had paid a price for her creation. She had poured her vital power into the development of her twins and the act of bearing them had aged her prematurely. Her hair was all white and the fine sharp features of youth had given way to the softer face of an elder. Deda retained her powers but her creations had shortened her life. Tempet and Alloi were gratefully indebted to their mother and felt the most absolute devotion to her.

When the family returned to their tower house in Kwellstan, Alloi was relieved to feel merry again. To celebrate, she had hired human cooks to prepare and serve a fine meal, and the four tabre delighted in conversing about pleasant subjects. Havax, Deda, and Tempet caught Alloi up on the gossip in Drathatarlane, and Alloi did likewise about Kwellstan.

When the evening grew late, Havax and Deda announced that they would go to the Plaza of the Waters and refresh themselves. Being among the very few Drathatarlane tabre who ever ventured out of their mountain city, they had become very fond of Kwellstan's famous waters. Although they would never speak openly about it, they understood how the fabulous springs of Kwellstan had tempted the tabre out of the mountains thousands of years ago and thus begun the spiritual schism within their race.

Tempet and Alloi retired to their chambers. They had too much to express to fumble with words. Sitting side-by-side, they conversed in their minds.

Tempet gushed with feelings for Alloi, and she soaked up his pure love like a plant that has been saved by water just in time to survive a pitiless drought. She revived Tempet in the same way. They felt whole again, but their separation had strengthened them. Tempet described how he felt harder inside after a few months without Alloi's gentle influence. And Alloi reflected on how she had become more aggressive without the sharp edge of Tempet's potent power to rely upon. Tempet could now admit that the Eschalam had been wise to put them through this ordeal, but they both wished fervently that they would never suffer a separation again.

Tempet then pressed her for details about her confrontation with the Grand Lumin. Alloi shared her memories of the brief struggle, and Tempet was deeply impressed and proud of his sister.

He broke off their mental connection and spoke. "If I had been with you, we would have beaten him."

Opening her eyes, Alloi whispered, "You should not speak of such a thing, especially here."

Tempet stood up and stretched his arms above his head. "An idle boast," he announced to the ceiling as if addressing the Grand Lumin who might be spying on them that very moment.

The birds and clouds painted on the plaster ceiling did not respond. Walking over to a counter, Tempet poured himself a cup of water from a gold-plated pitcher.

"I was surprised you took such a risk over that rys," he commented before taking a drink.

His disapproval tickled Alloi's senses. She told him that she would defend anyone being treated in such a beastly fashion.

"Really, Sister?" Tempet asked.

"Of course," Alloi said. "You know I would."

For an instant Tempet tried to be mollified by his sister's answer. He knew her to have the kindest heart, but he could not let go of the anger rotting inside him. He had hidden it from her so far. In the glow of their joyous reunion, Alloi had missed the ugly animal that had crawled onto the bank out of the waters of his love for her.

"I saw you with him," he said.

"Who? The Grand Lumin?"

"The rys," he hissed. "I saw you bring him to our own house. I saw the kiss."

Alloi at first meant to argue. She had not kissed Dacian, but then she recalled her brief brush of the lips on his forehead when she was moved by pity. Tempet was jealous she realized.

"I don't know why I did it," she confessed. "He was in so much pain. I wanted to make him feel better."

A sick looked crossed Tempet's face before he bottled his rage again. He could not abide the thought of any male attracting his sister. He knew it was not right, but it was true.

"You have affection for him," he said.

Alloi shook her head. "Compassion, Tempet, compassion. There's a difference," she insisted.

"I suggest you rid yourself of both," he declared and slammed his cup on the counter.

Alloi gaped at his harsh command. Tempet stalked onto the balcony and Alloi hurried after him. The air was cool and fresh with the scent of fresh foliage. A group of human males walked by on the street below. They were laughing at one of their mate's crude jokes.

Alloi set a hand on her brother's shoulder. He was leaning over the railing and watching the humans as they strolled toward the lake. Through gaps in the trees, a few lighted boats tinkling with music could be seen on the water now that the weather was mild.

"Are you going to start giving me orders?" Alloi asked.

When Tempet shut his eyes, she felt his distress radiating from him like heat from a fire. His thoughts and feelings were a tangle and he was pulling the knot tighter.

He apologized to her and then embraced her. With his lips next to her ear, he cast a warding spell. Alloi relaxed inside the bubble of his protective energy and added her own power to it.

Once they were certain that not even the Grand Lumin could overhear them, Tempet whispered, "Dacian is dangerous. You must cease to pity him."

Reluctantly, Alloi said, "I know he is dangerous…but he does not want to be."

Do not tell her, Tempet reminded himself. The Eschalam said I must not tell her.

Keeping a secret from her was uncomfortably difficult. Tempet hoped that revealing his jealousy over her so-called compassion for Dacian had masked his deeper turmoil.

He said, "Alloi, the rys is a Kwellstan abomination. Reserve your compassion for your own kind."

Then he broke off his warding spell so they could not pursue the delicate subject further.

Alloi noticed him clenching his right hand into a fist. He had closed part of himself away from her. This shadow within his thoughts puzzled her as much as it hurt her. Perhaps it was their long separation that had spawned this sudden zone of privacy. Trying to be respectful, she resisted confronting him and asked instead about the new black ring he wore on his right forefinger.

Tempet slipped it off. "It's a new charm our Sect wishes for me to test," he explained. He then applied his magic to the ring. White energy glittered around it and then it swelled into the shape of a ball. Just as Alloi exclaimed with delight, Tempet changed the shape to a butterfly with flapping wings. She laughed and Tempet let the charm return to its original ring shape and handed it to her. Alloi amused herself with the charm, making it into a bracelet and then a cup. She was glad for the diversion that had steered their conversation to a pleasant place.

Returning the charm to a ring shape, she slipped it back on her brother's finger. Quietly she said, "Do not be jealous, Tempet."

He nodded with an apologetic light in his eyes.

Alloi retired to her bed. The happy glow from reuniting with her family had faded into troubled thoughts, and she snuggled a soft rabbit fur blanket to her face. The spring breeze came in the open windows and fluttered against the gossamer curtains hanging around her bed.

Tempet entered the room and slid into the bed with her. They hugged each other in mutual fetal positions. Contritely, he apologized for speaking to her in anger.

"Rest, my Sister," he whispered, and Alloi fell asleep in his arms and slept blissfully well.

******

The Altular had been abuzz for days as the priests prepared for Poteny. On the high holiday that marked the beginning of planting season the mighty Nebakarz beckoned the blessings of the Great Divinity to invigorate the land and the people. Music, dancing, sports, theatric performances, and art burst from every street in thriving Kwellstan during the celebration.

Poteny was always a beautiful holiday, hectic with optimism and joy at the passing of dreary winter. Even if clouds or rain blocked the view of the horned moon, the festive atmosphere was not diminished.

Dacian suspected that he cast the only gloom upon the upcoming Poteny. He stood on the balcony near his modest room and watched tabre putting the finishing touches on the Grand Lumin's carriage in the great hall below. Delicate spells of preservation were being applied to the flowers as they were attached to the carriage so that not a single petal would fade.

On Poteny, the Grand Lumin left the Altular and paraded through the city in his flower-covered open carriage. He started in the morning and went to Dedenep Square in the heart of the human district. There, the Grand Lumin would perform acts of healing upon the sick and injured. Poteny was the only day humans could hope for freely given Nebakarz healing magic, so needy supplicants from throughout Nufal would pack the square. The powerful theatrics of the event renewed the emotional devotion of the humans.

Then the Grand Lumin would proceed to the Plaza of the Waters where gathered many tabre from throughout Nufal, except for Drathatarlane. Upon reaching maturity, tabre made a pilgrimage to Kwellstan to receive the blessing of the Grand Lumin. This important rite of passage swelled the city with enthusiastic young tabre and maturing tablings and added to the festive atmosphere.

The Grand Lumin would perform blessings upon tabre at the Plaza of the Waters until sundown when the sliver of the first quarter moon was revealed just above the mountains.

As Dacian contemplated the festival preparations, he could hardly tolerate memories from his earlier and stupidly naive life. He had once imagined being the first rys to join the Poteny procession and thereby lifting the status of all rys. Stewing in hostility, Dacian ridiculed all his foolish fantasies.

Despair over those crushed dreams had impaired Dacian during the lonely disgraceful months since he had escaped the torments of the pit. His misery made it difficult to concentrate. And when he had tried to contact Onja, he had been unable to find her or Halor.

Only the mental discipline that he had honed over the decades saved him from spiraling into a total listless stupor. Even unable to grasp the concept of hope, he had repaired his mind enough to grapple with his main problem, the crosha. Struggling through the pain, he had meditated and studied its sinister enchantment at length. He was discouraged by what he had discovered, which explained why the Grand Lumin had not interrupted Dacian's examination of the crosha. It drew energy from the pump and flow of his living body. He had discovered that he could weaken the crosha by slowing his body. When he approached a hibernative state, its deadly grip on his heart loosened a little, but Dacian believed that he would have to enter a prolonged hibernation to ultimately free himself. He would be utterly vulnerable if he entered full hibernation, and the Grand Lumin or almost any tabre could kill him or worse during that time.

Embittered by harsh treatment, Dacian had begun to consider strategies more foul. He could forsake his moral high ground and unleash his hostility. A pile of dead tabre might induce the Grand Lumin to set him free. It would certainly prompt a confrontation in which Dacian would either escape or die. He welcomed either outcome if it meant an end to this depressing stalemate.

In his desperation Dacian had thought to call upon the Great Divinity. He wanted the help of his creator, but his prayers were buried in the grave of his heart. He dismally figured that his accursed existence proved that the rys were not the favored race.

Although unwilling to call upon the divine, Dacian still longed for help. He wished that he had been able to contact Onja. He suspected that she had fled into the human lands of the west again and perhaps Halor had gone after her. Dacian had only looked for them in Jingten. He considered going back to his room and entering a trance and sending his mind farther west, but how would that help him? Even if he found Onja, she would be too far away to aid him. Accepting that he was utterly alone, Dacian decided that Poteny was his chance to act.

******

Music awoke Dacian on Poteny. From his narrow bed he could feel the sunny day outside. The Plaza of the Waters brimmed with tabre and humans. Inside the Altular, Nebakarz musicians were tuning their instruments and warming up their voices. They cast spells upon the wood, bone, strings, and metal parts of their various instruments to enhance the sound. All instruments always played more beautifully in the hands of a tabre artist.

Dacian listened to the music and even allowed himself to enjoy it. The Nebakarz sang their holy praises of the Great Divinity, and the faith evident in their glorious voices stirred even Dacian's cynical soul.

He tracked the Grand Lumin as his immense presence came down the main levitation shaft to the ground floor. Dacian subdued his ugly hatred and tried to observe casually the movement of the elder tabre as he made his way into the carriage. Dacian did not want to attract any attention to himself with powerful emotions. His neutral disregard for the holiday seemed to suit his captors, who appeared content to leave their dirty laundry inside on this high holy day.

The Grand Lumin stepped into his carriage. It had no wheels, but his magic raised it off the floor so that it could gracefully levitate while being gently pulled by an impeccably groomed white horse. Flower petals of every possible hue had been applied to the carriage in a careful progression of colors from light to dark. Meticulously blended petals created subtle shifts between each color so that the whole carriage looked like a rainbow cast upon a cloud. It was a work of art truly worthy of the Great Divinity.

As the Grand Lumin exited the Altular and greeted the roaring crowds, Dacian noted that Daykash Breymer remained in the Altular with a few select priests.

So I won't go unguarded after all, Dacian thought. It did not matter. He was going to act today, and he almost did not care what the results would be. Taking action was what mattered. The stalemate had to end. Upon reflection, his whole life seemed to be a stalemate. The uneasy relationship with his parents and plodding tutelage of Halor were glaring examples. Dacian believed now that he had never really done anything until he had stopped Onja's beating with the phlia-mel.

Dacian waited while the Grand Lumin wended his way toward Dedenep Square. Daykash Breymer returned to his chambers. The Altular had never felt so still. Barely twenty five tabre were left inside the enormous building. The others were occupied with duties around the city or were out enjoying themselves.

Dacian stood up. He was ready. During his meditations over the last two days, he had not focused on how to remove the crosha. He would never have the safe privacy to do so inside the Altular. Instead he had braced himself to endure its pain and hopefully slow its lethal effect.

Dacian cast a cloaking spell around his body like he had observed the Kahtep acolytes do the summer before. When he left his chamber, the hall was silent and empty. He walked to the balcony and casually peered down. The scent of flowers drifted up. The delicate and clean smell summoned the true meaning of Poteny, and Dacian inhaled deeply. Poteny hailed the coming bounty of the planting and growing seasons, and Dacian would allow the foul seeds of his fate to grow and bear fruit within him.

Dacian hurried toward the main levitation shaft and shot upward, passing through the Grand Lumin's private level and stopping at the highest level. He had no delusions about his cloaking spell actually masking his movement from Breymer, but he was trying to get attention right now.

The uppermost level of the Altular held meditation chambers reserved for the highest ranking priests. Here they experimented with spells and contemplated the heavens that arched above the sacred altar mounted on the pinnacle of the temple.

Dacian entered a chamber that had an hour-glass shaped window that faced east. Instead of glass in the window, a permanent spell kept the elements out. Dacian brushed his fingers against the magic and it flickered redly around his finger as if living tissue had been irritated by an allergen.

He sauntered over to the vision crystal mounted at the center of the room. It was a perfect sphere, milky white, and swirling with enchanted light. Crystals such as these were linked to crystals in the other temples in Kahtep and Hedenar. Dacian doubted that anyone was watching him through a crystal in another town. The Nebakarz priests would be overseeing their smaller Poteny festivities throughout Nufal. Dacian knocked the sphere from its stand and it rolled along the tile floor before stopping against a rug. The light within the sphere flashed furiously. Dacian smiled with mischievous satisfaction and then cast a much more thorough cloaking spell.

Rushing back to the levitation shaft, he jumped into the vertical tunnel but purposefully did not take hold of the focused force. He free fell down the length of the Altular. The mortal thrill of it made Dacian feel more alive than he had thought possible.

At the last moment, he cast a levitation spell to halt his fall and he dove through a doorway. He hoped that his diversion in the upper chambers would misdirect Breymer. With his cloaking spell still blurring his lifeforce, Dacian trotted to a small service stairway that connected to the Grand Lumin's private level.

He stepped lightly, barely making any sound as he raced up almost twenty levels. He sensed the Daykash and his comrades using the levitation shaft. As Dacian expected, they were now looking for him on the top level.

Adjusting his cloaking spell again, Dacian stepped out of the narrow stairwell. A thick red curtain covered its entrance and he moved it aside only a little to look with his eyes before proceeding. A permanent hush dwelled within the sprawling chambers of the Grand Lumin's level. Blood red carpet and lovely tapestries that mapped the stars furnished the many empty rooms. Dacian could feel tabre rushing around the level above. His ruse would not last long.

Dacian headed directly for the audience chamber of the Grand Lumin. A spell sealed the doors. With a fierce sense of superiority, he cracked the sealing spell with a single pulse of his magic and entered the seat of Kwellstan Sect power.

The room was not nearly so intimidating without the Grand Lumin perched upon his black cushions. But Dacian was not particularly interested in this room. The rooms beyond were certain to hold more interesting things. Dacian cracked the sealing spell on the next set of doors. He found himself in a work shop and supply room. Swiftly he tuned his mind for the sho poison and scanned the cupboards. He located only three small bottles. Bitterly he assumed that the Grand Lumin's supply had run low. Dacian shoved the bottles into his pocket and then he found the darts and blow guns, but he only took the darts. Many other interesting potions occupied the shelves, but he could spare no time to ponder them. Dacian felt the lifeforces of Breymer and the other priests flare within the levitation shaft as they jumped down a level.

With the force of his mind, Dacian yanked the doors to the audience chamber shut and put a sealing spell of his own on them. He did the same to the doors of the workshop and rushed deeper into the private rooms of the Grand Lumin.

He sought the library. The running feet of the Daykash and the priests echoed in Dacian's sensitive mind as they rushed through the empty rooms. Dacian found the library and barged in, but even in his terrible haste he skidded to a halt as he beheld the heart of Nebakarz knowledge. Scrolls and bound books filled narrow rows of shelves from floor to ceiling. Some of the preservation spells were so strong on the oldest documents that they gave off a faint glow. Tens of thousands of wafer thin stone discs lightly carved in Nebakarz characters were stacked like dishes in dozens of cupboards mounted on the end caps of the bookshelves. He had often dreamed of learning of the wonders so carefully recorded here.

The floor vibrated angrily beneath his feet. The Daykash had just blasted through the first set of doors. Dacian ran down a row. He looked up and down, truly bewildered. His task was hopeless. He had wanted to find the spell for the crosha but he had no time. Without knowing the filing system – if there was a system – Dacian would need weeks maybe months to find the information.

A powerful force attracted his attention. In the far back of the library, he found a massive stone door bolted in place with enchanted crystals. A sealing spell of perilous complexity barred this door, and upon it Dacian recognized the seal of the Grand Lumin. The angular script of the ancient Nebakarz was engraved within a circle that represented Ektren. The door was surely the vault of the Kwellstan Sect's most important treasures and records. If the spell for the crosha had ever been written down, then it was reasonable to look for it in that vault. Dacian examined the spell locking the door and hesitated. This was no normal enchantment. It might kill him if he triggered it incorrectly.

He heard the doors on the workshop bang open and knew that he would never get his chance to see inside the vault of supreme secrets.

Frowning with regret, he ducked down another row of books. The tabre were nearly upon him. He opened a bottle of sho and dipped three darts into the bottle. Tabre priests rushed into the library. Dacian cast an attack spell at the shelves closest to the priests. The shelves and scrolls exploded. Hot splinters of wood struck one tabre who cried out. Dacian blew up another shelf and it crashed into the next shelf, which started a chain reaction throughout the library. Dacian raced to the end of the row and avoided the tumbling shelves. He then cast a heat spell upon the debris, and flames instantly took hold. Decay that had been thwarted for so long took hot bright revenge upon the ancient texts.

The tabre priests cried out with alarm to see the swift destruction of their sacred library. One even started to frantically slap at the fires, completely distracted from his original purpose.

Dacian rushed for the door. Three tabre barred his escape. Dacian summoned a shield spell and tossed the three darts. Driven by his mind, the darts spread out and each struck a tabre. It had been easy to guide the darts with his powerful will. Easy.

Attack spells struck Dacian but withered as the tabre slumped against the wall. The middle tabre fell backward through the door. Dacian jumped over him and noted the tabre's amazed expression. All tabre felt threatened by his power yet their prejudice caused them to always underestimate him.

Dacian ran back the way he had come. He sensed the trap waiting for him in the audience chamber but he entered anyway. As soon as he came through the doors, six tabre priests assaulted him with combined attack spells. Dacian lurched and twisted as the biting energy thrust and tugged painfully on his body. His flesh felt about to rip off his bones. He bowed to one knee not far from the black cushions of the Grand Lumin. The crosha pained Dacian as well. Clutching the evil charm embedded in his chest, he rallied his mental discipline and blocked the pain. When he looked up,

Breymer was standing in the doorway. His eyes glowed with white light and his narrow face leered with gloating glee.

"I knew you would do this today," Breymer said.

Dacian looked up at his tormentor as the other tabre priests pressed closer in a tightening circle. Their spells were intensifying.

"Your library burns," Dacian hissed and rage quaked across Breymer's face. Such audacious desecration deserved infinite horrors, but Breymer was not going to linger over the punishment. He would put this rys beast down.

"All your kind will die," Breymer promised. "Their souls will be stripped of their magical essence to increase our power and then they will burn." The Daykash cast his attack spell, aiming for the crosha so as to build upon the Grand Lumin's magic that already sabotaged Dacian.

Dacian gave up his long fight against his raging demons of revenge and justice. The ordered world of civilization that the Nebakarz had created had no place for him. Dacian burned the leeches of restraint from his good heart and allowed the bitter rotting anger of his whole life to consume him. His attack spell exploded from the inner fire of his magical soul. His power thrust the six tabre priests back against the walls and pinned them there, and the Daykash's attack spell passed harmlessly over Dacian's body.

The Daykash took an involuntary step back, truly afraid. Dacian did not cast another attack spell. While still pinning the other priests against the walls, he stalked up to Breymer until his chest heaved against the chest of the second most powerful Kwellstan Nebakarz.

Breymer reached for a poisoned dagger and Dacian reached for his neck. The rys was faster than the lifting blade. "This is for Onja," he said and grabbed Breymer and snapped his head loose from the spine in one swift expression of merciless physical violence.

Dacian twisted the head until only loose flesh connected it to the body. The light faded from Breymer's eyes, and Dacian cast a heat spell that cooked the brain. Breymer, Daykash of the Kwellstan Sect, died. His soul slipped away from his slack body. Dacian let the dead weight of the tabre tumble from his hands. It slapped against the floor and the loose head rolled like a ball on a string.

A final wave of Breymer's malice lashed at Dacian as the dead tabre's soul swirled around its killer, but Breymer could do the rys no harm. The inexorable pull of the next world beckoned the soul toward forgetfulness and freedom.

Dacian took a deep breath. His body shook from serious pleasure. He was not disgusted with himself. Breymer deserved what he had gotten. Dacian was only defending himself, but that was not the only source of his satisfaction. He had killed for Onja and that felt good. He knew that he would defend her always because she was all that was beautiful and powerful and free in rys.

He turned and released the other six tabre from his spell. They regained their footing but did not advance. They gaped at Dacian, too overcome by his awesome power to do anything.

Dacian swept his blazing eyes around the room, meeting the gaze of each tabre.

"I never wanted this. This is YOUR fault," he declared and stalked away.

Dacian was not immediately followed. The surviving priests scurried to save their library and mentally raise the alarm among the other priests.

Dacian descended the levitation shaft and met no resistance in the main hall. When he exited the levitation shaft, he looked over his shoulder thoughtfully and then gathered his magic to cast another spell. His power exploded within the magically constructed shaft and splintered stone. Dacian repeated the spell and blasted more rock away from the sides of the shaft until a heavy cascade of rubble crashed down and filled up the entrance to the levitation shaft. Satisfied, he shut the golden doors.

Let the Grand Lumin take the stairs, Dacian thought.

Heading for the golden sublime sunshine that glowed through the entrance of the Altular, Dacian meant to continue his celebration of Poteny.

34. On the Temple Steps

Humans respectfully gave way for Tempet and Alloi despite the pressure from the thick Poteny crowd. They moved through the crowd behind the Grand Lumin's procession to Dedenep Square, named after the legendary man who had first accepted the Nebakarz as bringers of civilization.

As Tempet and Alloi advanced down the street, humans exclaimed with delight to see the tabre twins so close up. Alloi enjoyed the attention and waved and smiled to her many admirers. Tempet had surprised her when he invited her to experience the festivities at street level, and she was enjoying herself.

When they entered the square, the crowd was too thick for them to proceed toward the stage unless they pressed the issue. Tempet and Alloi found a spot at the base of a Dedenep's statue that was laden with children, who squealed to see the important tabre. The square was packed and hot although the weather itself was perfect. People hung out of doors and windows on every building surrounding the square and the rooftops were thronging with people as well. The estate class of Kwellstan gathered on the roof of the Adarium Hall. Their sun umbrellas and colorful banners rippled in the strong breeze off the lake.

The Grand Lumin had begun giving audience to the sick and injured. Every few minutes an eruption of applause and cheering swept through the crowd, and people shouted praise for the Grand Lumin and thanked the Great Divinity.

Tempet and Alloi observed the Grand Lumin beyond the tangle of people. The red and black robes of his priests controlled the crowd around the stage as they determined which supplicants would be allowed to go forth and receive healing.

"What amazing energy!" Alloi remarked. She had never been in the midst of such a large crowd. Although Bozee bouts drew thousands of spectators, she had never been so close to them. Here the lifeforces and excitement of the gathered thousands bombarded her senses. The raw energy bursting with faith and excitement was thrilling and something that she could never have experienced in Drathatarlane where humans were forbidden. Alloi suspected that the Grand Lumin knew how to draw sustenance from this gathering, and she imagined the possibilities.

Tempet folded his arms and leaned against the statue's base. "Look how he has these humans groveling," he complained. The Grand Lumin had just healed a small boy and fervent gratitude was spreading from the center of the crowd with weeping joy and proclamations of miracles. Tempet added, "I'd swear these humans would act like this if he just juggled soup bowls."

Alloi warned her brother mentally that he should not criticize the humans right in front of them. Tempet shrugged. The humans were not listening to him. Alloi tried to make him focus on the positive. "It was a good idea to come here. We should learn more about this energy from the human audience," Alloi said.

Tempet nodded, albeit reluctantly. He was restless and not interested in learning about the Kwellstan Sect's Poteny traditions. He had known that the crowd would distract Alloi, and he needed a break from constantly guarding his thoughts from his sister. He had only kept the secret from his sister thus far because Alloi had not been trying to discover why he was preoccupied. Since returning to Kwellstan, she had been notably willing to give him privacy. Tempet also suspected that Alloi was also preoccupied, probably about Dacian. Jealousy tightened Tempet's chest, but he smashed the feeling. He did not want to arouse her attention.

Tempet mentally suggested to Alloi that they start healing people to annoy the Grand Lumin. Alloi giggled.

"Let's go to the Plaza of the Waters," Tempet said.

Alloi sensed that he was already bored, but she was immersed in watching the different people and dissecting the sensations of all the swirling emotions. She envied how the Grand Lumin was at the center of this energy, soaking it up. She guessed how divine that must feel.

"Not yet," she whispered and took Tempet's hand. Her gentle touch would keep him from pestering her for a little while.

Alloi was so enthralled by the crowd that Tempet was the first to notice a tremor of discord among the priests surrounding the Grand Lumin. Tempet straightened to his full height and cast his mind over the crowd. He saw that the Grand Lumin had halted his examination of a laborer's broken hand. The Grand Lumin scowled and his floating orbs drew closer to his head as if they were urgently whispering secrets. At the same time, two priests rushed to the Grand Lumin's side while the rest of the priests returned to the stage. A Nebakarz acolyte escorted the injured man back to the queue of waiting supplicants. Confusion replaced enthusiasm among the spectators as the Grand Lumin shuffled toward his carriage. He was leaving much too soon, and shrieking disappointment arose quickly from the gathering of needy people.

"Alloi," Tempet said. "See what is happening at the Altular."

The aura of anxious expectation around Tempet was unmistakable now that Alloi looked for it. In a flash of insight, she realized that today would be a perfect day for Dacian to try something. Had he learned to overcome the crosha? With haste, she cast her mind across the city to the Altular. Tabre filled the Plaza of the Waters and their bright clothing and laughter contrasted sharply with the startling chaos within the temple.

Magical light faded from Alloi's eyes as she returned to her body. She could barely even put into words what she had seen. "Dacian has killed the Daykash," she whispered.

Her report made Tempet feel that everything he had been told by the Eschalam had been confirmed. The rys had shown himself to be deadly dangerous.

"Go home and wait for me," Tempet said. "You'll be safe there."

He turned away from Alloi and ran from the square. Alloi was astounded that he would abandon her. How could he even dream that she would simply go home when he rushed into peril?

And if Dacian was about to rampage, Alloi thought that she might be the only one capable of saving him and others. Alloi believed completely that the Kwellstan Sect had driven him to kill and she hoped to stop the violence.

She ran after Tempet.

******

Dacian walked into the sunlight and lifted his arms as if greeting a welcoming crowd that wished to cheer him. The wrath storming forth from his lifeforce quickly drew the attention of the tabre holiday makers dancing and mingling among the bathing pools and canals. Fear jolted the tabre, and the songs and laughter faded. The humans present noticed quickly the changed mood of the tabre and they started to notice the rys – the subject of gossip for months – at the entrance of the Altular.

Dacian walked to the nearest pool where a fountain sprayed sparkling streams of water from the mouths and hands of charming tabre statues. Dacian cupped his hand into the water and brought a drink to his lips. Sweet and refreshing, the waters of Kwellstan deserved their fame, but Dacian knew suddenly that the pure glacial melt of the Rysamand Mountains would suit him better. He longed for home.

Still close to the Altular, the crosha warned him with only a mild sting, but Dacian braced himself mentally for greater pain.

From behind he sensed priests approaching. Dacian looked back and saw two tabre duck out of sight behind columns near the temple entrance. He smiled at their fear. He knew that the tabre were communicating the alarm mentally throughout the city. Already murmurs of shock and panic were rising among the tabre in the plaza. Out of the crowd a bold tabre acolyte stalked up to Dacian. By the disdainful look of determination on the tabre's dark face, Dacian could tell that the acolyte thought this would be his chance to prove himself by detaining the unruly rys.

Dacian raised a hand and cast an attack spell at the acolyte. He blasted apart his rib cage and sent a fountain of boiling blood through the young tabre's body, killing him swiftly. The acolyte toppled backward with a gruesome splash of steaming blood.

Screams of unprecedented horror burst from hundreds of tabre and people. Groups scattered in all directions and the waters were whipped into a froth as tabre and people jostled to get out of the pools.

Dacian was astonished by his lack of regret for the tabre he had just killed. The terror he was inflicting was too satisfying to be blunted by morality.

He hopped onto the edge of the fountain pool and walked along it, waiting for more priests or acolytes to come forth and give him battle. Dacian watched excitedly in his mind as the Grand Lumin rushed back from the human district to attend to the emergency.

Dacian was ready to fight until the end. Flush with the extreme thrill of dealing out mortal blows, Dacian resolved to heap bodies at his feet until the Grand Lumin released the crosha. Dacian was no longer afraid to execute such a cruel plan and he did not fear dying. He was even buoyed

Rys Rising: Book I

by the hope that his probable death would outrage his fellow rys to the point of rebellion.

None of this was what Dacian had wanted. He had worked so hard to break another path, one that would have led the rys into the blessings of Nufalese civilization. But even choked by his tragic failure, Dacian would allow himself to revel in the vengeful battle that was about to begin. Today he would become a legend.

As the Plaza of the Waters rapidly emptied, Nebakarz priests and acolytes rushed in, summoned by their master to the fight. They gathered into groups at the edges of the plaza, awaiting guidance from the Grand Lumin.

Dacian eyed the milling groups of Nebakarz and stoked his appetite for killing. Suddenly the air grew hot. He cast a stout shield spell and was thrown across the fountain by an attack spell. The waters near him exploded into steam and Dacian fell against the outer wall of the Altular. He fortified his shield spell as another attack spell battered him with a crushing blast of energy.

Dacian rolled off the wall and ran toward the steps built into the outside of the temple. He scrambled up a dozen of the sacred steps that were only to be used to mount the Altular for the Quadreni ceremony. Standing tall, Dacian turned his blazing eyes upon the plaza. The lifeforces of the tabre below shone like burning flowers within his perception and his magic quickened with fierce dislike. He would blacken the foul meadow of their pride.

He thrust his potent mind at the Grand Lumin who had almost reached the plaza in his carriage. Dacian unleashed an attack spell at his tormentor. The Grand Lumin defended himself with a shield spell, but his carriage crashed to the roadway; its flowers reduced to drifting ashes. The single horse panicked and reared in its harness and dragged the carriage a little way before priests stopped the animal.

Dacian attacked the Grand Lumin again but the shielding magic of the old master of the Kwellstan Sect did not buckle. The Nebakarz in the plaza rushed at Dacian, leaping over canals and pools and shouting. Their combined magic roiled with sparking energy like clouds swelling into a fierce storm. Dacian ran farther up the steps and recast his shield spell. His mind tapped into the enchantments that reinforced the Altular. He had spent long days in his bed analyzing the magic of the temple and now he called upon it to protect him. A massive wave of attack spells surrounded Dacian and the world blurred into blinding whiteness. Dacian had to shut his eyes but his flesh remained unhurt. As the first attack faded, Dacian opened his eyes and laughed at the Nebakarz. It was marvelous to use the power of their impregnable temple against them. The priests and acolytes below did not mount the steps, observing their taboo.

Arcing white lines of energy lifted off the Altular and connected with Dacian's hands.

"Bring the Grand Lumin!" he shouted. "Bring him!"

Dacian attacked again. The tabre below despite their power and skill were unschooled in real life-and-death combat. A full fifty of them died in a scorching blast of Dacian's enchanted rage.

The Grand Lumin had left the wreckage of his ceremonial carriage and was floating along the street, carried by his levitation magic. His pair of crystal orbs spun around his head in furious orbits. His heightened power transformed his elderly face into an ageless mask of sublime knowledge. The tabre in the plaza fell back around their arriving master and cast a thousand layers of shielding magic around him.

Dacian tore open his shirt to reveal the cancerous crystal attached to his chest. Purple veins sickened its smooth milky white surface.

"Grand Lumin, free me!" Dacian demanded. "I give you this chance for peace. Free me so I can go home."

The Grand Lumin unleashed his attack spell through the stone fabric of the Altular. The surge of energy coursed through the enchantments that Dacian already tapped. He screamed as withering pain streaked up his limbs. He broke off his connection before the attack reached his vitals. With his arms and legs split, burnt, and bleeding, he collapsed onto the steps. The Grand Lumin had put an end to him using the power of the Nebakarz against them.

******

Amid the rising chaos, Tempet entered the plaza. The Kwellstan Nebakarz were too engaged by Dacian to notice Tempet.

He gasped in awe when he beheld Dacian killing dozens of tabre with one great stroke of magic. The potent thrill of witnessing such wanton and lethal use of magic opened a door in Tempet's mind. The tabre had left so many levels of power unrealized as they lounged in luxury and schemed over petty politics. Tempet no longer worried that he would falter in a true struggle for his life. He was meant for real combat, and the meaning of his life became clear to him for the first time.

Tempet slipped the black ring off his finger and awoke its enchantment. Golden lines brightened the surface of the ring that started to expand in his hand. Tempet trotted around the edge of the Kwellstan priests. They were focused on shielding the Grand Lumin and still did not notice him. He mounted a small bridge that spanned a canal. The bridge elevated Tempet so that he would have a clear shot over the heads of the other tabre.

He watched Dacian buckle after the Grand Lumin attacked. With Dacian hurt and stunned upon the steps, Tempet took his shot. He focused his spell into the expanding ring and it rapidly reshaped itself into a sharp-edged disc. Tempet threw the disc. He guided it with his mind and refined the spell as it whirred through the air. A thousand fine spines erupted from the disc when it hit Dacian's neck.

Tempet heard the rys scream as the small enchanted weapon dug into his flesh, probing and piercing with its miniscule needles that did not stop until they rooted deeply inside nerves. Dacian clutched his neck and thrashed wildly. His shield spell flickered and then failed. Dacian was undone. Ready to kill the rys as the Eschalam had commanded, Tempet gathered his power to cast an attack spell. It would be good to rid Ektren of the rys who had summoned soft feelings from Alloi.

"Tempet, no!"

His sister rushed toward him. Other priests started pummeling Dacian with attack spells now. Wounds opened on Dacian's body and he rolled down a few steps.

"Why?" Alloi demanded when she ran onto the bridge and grabbed Tempet's arm.

Relief swept over Tempet. He no longer needed to keep the secret from her. "The Eschalam said I had to make sure that Dacian died. There was too much risk that the Kwellstan could twist his power to their agenda," Tempet explained in a rush of words.

Alloi looked up at Dacian. The agony of his suffering throes pierced her in an empathetic rush, and she started to cast a spell to help him.

"No!" Tempet said harshly and grabbed her by the wrists and yanked her face close to his. "It has to be this way," he insisted. The Eschalam had been right about Alloi lacking the strength to bear this ugliness, but Tempet knew that she would side with him eventually. She beat against his chest and tried to break free. Tears spurted from her glossy black eyes, but Tempet held her firmly. It would be over soon. The priests had stopped their attack on the rys, and the Grand Lumin had mounted the steps with the intention of seizing Dacian at the moment of death.

Then Tempet realized that he must not let the Grand Lumin make the killing blow. The Eschalam had warned him about this although he had not fully explained his reasons. Releasing Alloi, Tempet focused his mind to send an attack spell to shatter Dacian's defenseless body, but an unnatural shriek crashed in his ears and a wide black shadow crossed the plaza.

All the tabre cringed and looked up. Pure astonishment transfixed the tabre, even the Grand Lumin in his blindness. A huge bird-like beast swooped down onto the steps of the Altular. Its bird claws scraped the stone. Iridescent black feathers covered the monster, but it was not wholly a bird. Arms hung beneath the wings and they held a rys female. It set her down next to Dacian and then turned its grotesque parody of a bird head toward the tabre and squawked like the angry demigod of ravens that it was.

A hazy aura of blue illuminated the rys female, who regarded the tabre with palpable rage. She stepped away from her bird monster and cast an attack spell upon the crowd. Her long black hair lifted and rippled in the waves of energy emanating from her body.

Alloi reacted with her famous speed and shielded herself and Tempet from the danger, but other tabre near them bent and fell in pain and sometimes death. Appalled, Alloi expanded her shield spell and started to protect those nearby, even if they were Kwellstan Sect.

The Grand Lumin gaped in true shock. He had been on the verge of turning a very public debacle into a triumph, but now he was confronted by the unexpected. He shielded himself as the female rys cast another attack spell.

With the tabre temporarily cowed, the female dragged Dacian to his feet. With her shoulder under his arm, she raced up the temple steps. Her bird companion flapped ahead of her. It reached the top and waited for her on the highest and most holy altar of the Kwellstan Sect.

35. Time of Bliss

Onja lowered Dacian onto the narrow temple roof. The wind whipped their hair and clothing against their bodies. Dacian slid his hand along her shoulder. "You came for me," he said with utter gratefulness.

Despair cracked across Onja's face. She had not prepared herself to see him in such bad condition.

"Dacian," she said and smoothed his hair away from his face. She wanted to embrace him and heal him and express all her feelings but they needed to escape.

Onja touched the crosha upon his chest. She gasped in wonder upon finally examining the harsh enchantment. Such wicked genius, she thought and regretted that she did not have time to ponder its intricacies. "Do you know how to get it off?" she asked and looked down the temple.

Dacian explained quickly his hypothesis that a prolonged state of hibernation would loosen it.

"I'll help you with that as soon as we get away from here," Onja said and pulled him upright, but he resisted her.

"Onja, it will kill me if I go far from here. You'll have to leave me," Dacian said. He tried to push her away. The joy of her unexpected rescue had turned to misery because he was endangering her.

Resolute, Onja shook her head. "I'll get it off now," she said.

"No time," Dacian argued. Despite his battered state, he cast a shield spell to protect them as the tabre attacked again.

Onja's bird beast flapped away from the hot explosion of magic and took to the air.

With the Grand Lumin starting up the temple steps, Onja glanced around her foreign surroundings desperately. "Help me," she whispered and slipped her mind into Dacian's thoughts so that they could communicate more quickly.

They directed their magic at the Atocha across the plaza. By combining their magic, they swiftly increased the magnitude of their power. One of the four towers on the school started to shake and then its foundation split with a thunderous explosion and the tower that had stood for a thousand years teetered and started sliding down to grinding ruin.

The tabre in the square scattered. The Grand Lumin turned around and cast a spell to prop up the tower, but he was too late. Its stone bulk crashed across the Plaza of the Waters, crushing ten priests and acolytes. The Grand Lumin directed his surviving followers into the Altular.

As dust and death settled over the plaza, Onja and Dacian eased their minds apart. The destruction was breathtaking and their joining had been a thrill.

Dacian looked into Onja's eyes and envisioned a future that had been unimaginable until that moment. But he forced away the new and wonderful emotions.

"They will attack us from inside the Altular," he warned. "You must go."

Onja touched the crosha again. Concentration twisted her lovely face as she focused intently on the crystal. "Let's get it out right now," she decided.

Her bird beast returned and landed on the altar, impatiently waiting.

Dacian was about to protest, but Onja grabbed his face. "You must believe I can help you," she commanded. "Stop your heart. Die so it will let you go."

Dacian stared back at her in horror. She was proposing that he somehow commit suicide by sheer act of will so that the enchantment would release his dead flesh.

Onja tried to order her thoughts so that she could explain. Inspiration was flashing through her mind, but it was difficult to explain. "Dacian, I'll hold your soul close so you can return to your body as soon as I pull the crystal off. We have to try. Trust me," she pleaded. Her grip on his face changed to a caress. "I won't leave you," she whispered.

Dacian accepted that her idea might work, but he did not know if he could actually kill himself. That was radically different from slowing his body to the point of death through an ordered descent into hibernation, and he told her so.

The bird beast squawked and Onja looked away. Tabre archers were taking aim from the windows of the Atocha. And in the plaza below, more Nebakarz were coming back out of the Altular, armed with bows and spears.

Fearing the sho poison, Dacian pulled Onja down. "Don't let their weapons hit you," he warned and cast a fresh shield spell.

With a renewed assault imminent, Onja threaded her way through her panic. She had to do something. Cowering against Dacian, she forced her fear of the coming arrows out of her mind and focused on what had to be done.

Dacian lurched when her spell struck him in the chest. She took him completely by surprise. Her magical mind seized his heart and stopped the power of his lifeforce from contracting the living muscle. Dacian thrashed briefly in her arms. "Die," Onja whispered. "Just let yourself die. I have you."

His body slackened as the arrows clattered on the Altular or whizzed by close to her head. Onja cried out as one hit her in the thigh, but luckily it was not poisoned. She dragged Dacian to the other side of the altar so that they could have some shelter.

Onja focused her powerful mind on Dacian's soul. The essence of his lifeforce was laid bare to her and she tenderly eased it away from the moorings of his flesh. Possessing him in such an intimate way made her shake with ecstasy. His power was profound. A rare slice of the cosmos had been born inside him and now the cosmos wanted it back. Onja fought the automatic pull of the next world, the source and keeper of all souls. She would not let go of her precious Dacian.

Strained as she was to keep his soul under her control, Onja still had to focus on the crosha. Dacian had been correct. With his flesh now free of pulsing life, the enchantment within the crystal was fading. Onja grabbed the smooth oval embedded in his chest and started to wrench it off. Blood seeped around the crosha and wetted her fingers. She pulled and the crosha began to jaggedly tear away from his flesh. Once she had it about halfway removed from his chest, the crystal simply turned to vapor and disappeared. All that remained was an ugly wound upon his chest that oozed purple blood. Onja slammed her hand over the wound. "Live!" she cried. "Live!" The heart that she had so artlessly halted only a moment earlier, she now slapped back to life with her magic.

Tabre were running up the Altular. Their spears lifted and terrible fury blazed in their eyes. Onja's bird beast grabbed both her and Dacian in its arms and jumped off the Altular. Doubly burdened, the bird beast glided down the face of the Altular, flapping its great wings and trying to gain momentum and seize the air.

It achieved true flight just as it came perilously close to the ground. Then, with powerful flaps of its elegant wings, it gained height and flew over Kwellstan toward the lake.

Onja kept her hand clutched over Dacian's chest. Now that his heart was beating again, blood poured from the wound. He needed to be healed.

With a thought she commanded her crow to land, and it stopped on one of the tiny rock islets that dotted the lake. A stiff spring wind had roused a few white caps upon the water that lapped noisily against the rocky pillar.

The bird beast looked on as Onja lowered Dacian to the mossy rock. His eyes opened, but he said nothing. His experiences of the past moments had shown him the horizon of death, and he remained focused on that place.

Onja attended to his wounds. She stopped the bleeding on his chest first and then began to heal the long and blistered cuts on his arms and legs. Taking out the spiny disc lodged in his neck was a delicate task. Some of its hair-like needles broke off inside the flesh and she had to draw them out one by one. As she healed his neck she noticed that the enchanted disc had retracted into a ring. Onja reached for the ring, but it skidded across the rock away from her hand and tumbled into the water.

She wondered if the enchantment within the ring itself had made it retreat from her touch or if the mind of another had yanked it away.

Onja had witnessed many clever uses of magic already during her brief foray into Nufal. She reminded herself not to let her hatred of the tabre tempt her into underestimating them. They had powers and ancient crafts of which she was ignorant.

Upon Dacian's legs she cast regenerative spells. As she did this, Dacian lifted his head and looked at his chest. Seeing that the crosha was truly gone, he dropped his head and moaned gratefully. "Thank you," he said.

Onja moved up by his head. "I'm so sorry," she declared while touching him tenderly.

"What are you sorry for?" he asked, truly baffled.

"I didn't warn you. I killed you without asking…" she frowned tearfully with regret for her callous recklessness.

Dacian felt the trauma in his chest. Each beat of his heart ached, but the discomfort would pass. Onja's lethal attack had violated him horribly, but she had cradled his soul with care. She had touched the key to his inner power, but Dacian forgave her.

"You did what was right. I would have fought for my life if I knew what you were going to do. You saved me," Dacian explained.

Onja nodded and brushed a tear from her cheek. Her struggle for composure after enduring so much risk endeared her to Dacian. Such bravery on his account banished the chronic loneliness that had marked his life to this point.

Dacian was quickly feeling better. The relief of being free of the crosha renewed him. He sat up and told Onja that they had to keep moving. The Grand Lumin and the other Nebakarz would attack with their magic soon. Dacian did not know what their range was, but sitting on a rock in the middle of Lake Kwellstan was not far enough away.

After removing the arrow from Onja's thigh and tending it with a quick healing spell, they flew on. The strong wind over the water allowed the bird beast to get back in the air even with two rys to carry. They flew by the towers and walls of Alicharat nestled among its terraced fields and orchards on the mountainside overlooking the lake.

For a time, the trio flew in silence. Dacian's sudden liberation overwhelmed him, and he did not want to think about what had happened to him or consider the future. The pleasure of being released from confinement and subjugation was worth dwelling on.

Onja's close physical presence, however, tempted him to focus beyond the fact of his escape. They faced each other as they held onto the strong arms of the weird feathered creature conveying them. Dacian admired her beautiful eyes and the perfect lines and angles of her exquisite face. The terror and despair that he had suffered over the past months dissolved into happiness – an emotion that was almost unthinkably strange.

Dacian could sense her happiness as well. They were together and that was how it should be. This was a truth of the world as surely as the rising and setting of the sun. Onja would always be the horizon awaiting his sun, and he accepted totally this absolute connection.

Although embraced by relief and joy, Dacian eventually noticed that the ground was creeping closer. He and Onja posed a great burden for the flying beast, and they would not be aloft much longer.

Onja selected a canyon amid the rolling foothills of the Tabren Mountains. They were still inside the valley, but they hoped that the spot would be sufficiently remote. Here only a single road snaked along the ridges surrounding the forest, and Kwellstan, Alicharat, and Kahtep were roughly equal distances away. No human settlements were in the vicinity because the tabre limited human habitation within the Valley of Nufal.

When the flying creature landed, it folded its great wings and slunk beneath a nearby stand of fir trees. Onja went with the creature while Dacian waited in the open glen. She praised her pet and cast gentle spells to ease its fatigue and left it to rest.

When Onja returned to Dacian, she said, "The Tatatook needs rest before he can fly us again."

"The Tatatook?" Dacian said. During the scramble to escape, he had not questioned the strange creature's existence but now he wanted to know about it.

"That is what it is called," Onja said and slipped a hand into Dacian's hand.

"Where did the Tatatook come from?" he asked.

"I made it," Onja answered and sounded a little amazed by herself.

Dacian squeezed her hand. He was privileged to grip such power. Onja was a natural talent, and Dacian realized he had not truly guessed her abilities. She was easily his equal, and he was excited by the prospect of having a companion worthy of him. But her creation unsettled him. "How did you make it?" he said.

"We should not stand in the open," Onja said and guided him under the deep shade of the fir trees. The moist and piney smell refreshed Dacian, and despite the foreign land he was dimly reminded of the Jingten Valley.

Onja was right about keeping under cover. Although the tabre might be able to detect their lifeforces, staying out of plain sight would allow them to elude cursory landscanning. Hidden among the trees, Dacian looked across the land. He could still see Kwellstan in the distance. In the setting sun, the mountains cast long shadows that almost reached the Altular jutting through the canopy of the great primeval forest. They were still in the heartland of Nufal. Dacian hoped that the Tatatook did not need to rest for long.

"You did not answer my question," Dacian reminded Onja gently.

A wave of discomfort flashed through her. Onja knew that she had given herself away, and she could think of no effective way to lie. "You will be unhappy with me," she warned.

Dacian studied her guilty yet contrite look. Only a moment ago he had felt like he had known her forever, and now she seemed a stranger. He waited for her to explain. Reluctantly, she told him of the making of the Tatatook. Her success had been total, but the cost had been great. She had needed to hibernate for months to recover. Dacian was duly impressed. Indeed, it was a masterwork of magic, and she was barely mature.

Still sensing that she had held something back, Dacian considered her story. He admitted that he was uncomfortable with the fact that she had used a tabre to create her Tatatook, and then suspicion clouded his face.

"What tabre did you sacrifice for this spell?" he demanded.

Obviously bracing herself for unpleasantness, Onja confessed that it had been Halor.

"Halor!" Dacian cried, too loudly. He looked into the trees. The Tatatook had its head tucked under a wing, sleeping bird fashion. "You killed Halor!"

Onja shook her head. "No, no. I changed him," she said.

"But Halor is gone," Dacian argued.

"Yes, but he was willing. Dacian, I swear he was willing. He felt terrible about what was being done to you in Kwellstan. He agreed to help me when I forced the issue. But what could I do? What could we do? I had no way to get to Kwellstan, or get you out. That's when I thought that if I had a flying creature I could get you." When Onja finished her speech, she was eye-to-eye with Dacian and glistening with earnestness. Quietly she added, "This was how Halor could help. He was willing. It is the truth, Dacian. I would never lie to you."

Dacian felt sick and moved away from her. He had spent many years as Halor's disciple. And, in his way, Halor had been kind to him. Dacian could not help but feel appalled that his former master was now a creature of Onja's making. Severed from normal creation and locked within the vision of another mortal seemed worse than death.

There was no undoing what had been done. Slowly he walked over to the Tatatook and studied it up close. It slept peacefully, apparently without any cares. Dacian doubted that Halor would have wanted the Atocha damaged and many of his fellow tabre killed, but the Tatatook appeared oblivious to the destruction. Halor was gone. Onja might call it changed, but Dacian knew dead when he saw it.

Onja eased her way back to Dacian's side. With sympathy, she said, "Dacian, I know you were close to Halor, but he was a tabre."

Onja did not need to say more. Dacian had been force fed the truth that there would be no joining between rys and tabre. The tabre meant to dominate and likely destroy the rys, strangling the unwanted birthings of their experiments. Dacian had to bury his dreams of integration and respect for rys. It hurt. It all hurt as terribly as the tortures the Grand Lumin had put to him.

Onja took Dacian's hand and rested her head on his shoulder. Her warm skin against him did not hurt.

******

For half that night they rested, casting cloaking spells to hopefully avoid detection.

When the Tatatook awoke, they took to the air again. They passed out of the valley, flying over Kahtep. Its streetlights and watch fires glittered upon the landscape like a jewelry box of civilization spilled upon a dark untamed world.

The young moon had set earlier, but in the starlight Dacian saw the distant peaks of the Rysamand Mountains, and he wept. The tears were cold on his face as they traveled through the high frigid sky. He could not wait to touch the mountains of his birthland.

The Tatatook reached the mountains with the dawn. It landed clumsily on the outer slopes of the nearest mountain because of its great weariness. After it let go of Dacian and Onja, the Tatatook collapsed with its wings still open, like a bird beaten down by a wind storm. Onja soothed her pet with praise and healing spells. She helped the Tatatook to fold its wings and settle down comfortably. She bade it to fly back to Jingten when it was able. She and Dacian could walk from here.

After helping the Tatatook, Onja joined Dacian, who stood on a rocky ledge overlooking the prairie. The rising folds of land were just switching to forested slopes and, high above, the snowy peaks loomed like the icy shoulders of a watchful god.

With the Rysamand Mountains at his back, Dacian looked upon Nufal. After this day he would never consider Jingten nor its mountains as part of Nufal again.

Totally liberated from his youthful dreams, Dacian did not know what to do next. Onja put an arm around him and gazed at the sun rising over the Tabren Mountains. Nufal's dark mountains glowered at the rys, who even at this distance sensed the fury rising from Kwellstan.

Dacian turned away from Nufal to embrace Onja. His battered spirit needed to be immersed in her loveliness. With a finger he traced her lips and cast a tiny spell meant to stimulate the tender skin in a pleasing way. Onja quivered and pressed closer. Dacian had never given much thought to physical pleasure with a female. He had always directed his energy to more important subjects, but suddenly that seemed to be an ignorant mistake. He cast another pleasure spell upon her lips and while that one was still sparking upon her mouth, he started to stroke her fine eyebrows and then her earlobes, igniting the skin with tingling energy as he went.

Onja's face slackened as she relaxed into his magical massage. She raised her hands and touched his chest. His flesh was still pale lavender where she had healed it. Where once so much pain had drilled through his body, she now awoke pleasure beneath her fingers.

Slowly and patiently they gently touched each other, awakening physical passions from their powerful bodies. And as each stimulated the other's flesh, they joined a little more in their minds and spirits. Their magic blended as they stirred their bodies with rising pleasures.

Onja murmured, "I've been so alone."

"No more, my love, no more," Dacian vowed. "You came for me. You saved me and we shall never be parted."

"Never!" Onja agreed and kissed him, taking their intimacy to the level of physical joining.

They pulled away their clothing. Their bodies could not bear any barrier between them. Their spells escalated in intensity as they aroused each other to greater ecstasies, and they fell together to the ground.

With the mountain beneath them, they became wholly locked in a spell of mutual desire that sought oneness. Sometimes Onja was atop Dacian and sometimes Dacian was atop Onja as they tossed their powerful bodies. Connected to each other, their connection to the mountains beneath them deepened. They connected with the sacred power of Ektren emanating from its churning core and they realized together that they would not use the word the tabre had given to the world any more. They would call their world Rystavalla, and in their joyous coupling they touched the true power of this ancient child of the cosmos.

Their lovemaking continued and the burgeoning magic within them beckoned the elements. The sky to the south darkened over the prairie with the first thunderstorm of the season. Sable thunderheads roiled with purple and blue and released their rampaging armies of wind, lightning and rain. Trees bent in the tempest and the prairie grasses rippled furiously in the blowing and pelting rain. White-streaked vermilion lightning raged between the clouds as if the Great Divinity had been split in two and now argued bitterly with Itself. And thunderbolts hit the land and struck near Dacian and Onja.

Gripped by their voracious pleasure, the rys lovers understood the colossal energy of the world more than ever before and soaked up the powers exploding around them. When the storm passed over them heading north, the passions of Dacian and Onja ebbed. With the rain pattering gently upon their naked bodies, they finally eased away from each other. Neither spoke for a long time. They stared thoughtfully at the complete rainbow arching over the prairie. Transformed by their shared experience, they relaxed as they had never relaxed before. Total comfort and intimacy erased their insecurities and welcomed them to a new state of consciousness.

Dacian wondered how he had ever tolerated his ignorance of the other half of his kind now that he had joined with a female. Likewise, Onja marveled at her experience of joining with a male. So close to Dacian she had found relief for a longing she had never truly understood.

Gradually the sun came out and dried their naked bodies. Side by side, they said nothing and only smiled at each other. This was their time of bliss. Even the tabre were briefly forgotten, including all the woe that had been and all that was sure to come.

Eventually Onja stood up. Two white butterflies breezed by her breasts in the golden light of the rainbow-cleansed sun. "There are tabre in Jingten," she said, concluding the potent perfection they had enjoyed.

Dacian sat up. He wished they could have lingered in their happiness, but they were not safe. Taking so much time for their lovemaking had been reckless although not regrettable.

While dressing himself, he was amazed at how aware and alive he felt. He had crossed over into a new understanding of his power and how it could be elevated through connection with another rys.

Onja put her clothing back on and she ran her fingers through her long glistening black hair. Dacian stood behind her and smoothed her dark tresses over her shoulders. He struggled to grasp the meaning of his love for her. The love was so different from the love he had for his parents, which was sometimes antagonistic, grudging even, but always automatic. This love for Onja was more intense, new, and unpredictable like red molten rock erupting from the slumbering depths of Rystavalla. Dacian liked his new feelings even without understanding them.

Analyzing the subtleties of his personal life could wait. Matters of far greater importance demanded his attention. Dacian was powerful, perhaps even supremely powerful, as was Onja, and they had to assume responsibility for the defense of the rys. The vengeance of the tabre would be quick to arrive. Quite possibly the tabre in Jingten had already begun to persecute the rys for his so-called crimes.

"We must go to Jingten," he decided. "And remove the Nebakarz from power. Make a place ruled by rys for rys."

Onja faced him with a devilishly happy smile on her face. She said, "We will cast the tabre from their tower and take it for ourselves. All tabre will be expelled from Jingten and those that oppose us will die."

Agreement shone in Dacian's black eyes. His moral distress about hurting tabre had diminished considerably.

"Let us go quickly," Onja said, taking his hand.

But Dacian did not move. He could sense Onja's eagerness to purge Jingten of their tabre masters, but he was thinking beyond that glorious task.

"Onja," he said. "After we cleanse Jingten, the tabre will not stay away. They will be mad for revenge and their wounded pride will drive them with great malice. The tabre have greater numbers than us and many of them have advanced magic training whereas rys are mostly ignorant. The tabre also have thousands of humans, many of which are armed. We must consider how to face the armies of Nufal. We need an army," Dacian concluded and the difficulty of their daunting need troubled him.

Onja's smile broadened. "I can get an army," she said. "When I was in the west, I cultivated an alliance with mercenary warriors there. I will call the humans of the west to our service. We will prevail and beat back Nufal until they whimper for mercy."

The staggering realization that Onja had planned to oppose the tabre for a long time finally hit Dacian. He marveled at the audacity and planning in one so young. He suddenly envied her free existence on the fringe of rys society. Her deviant nature had protected her from the slave collar of society that had snagged him with dreams of inclusion and normal prestige.

Onja understood that Dacian was seeing her secrets for the first time, and she tried to explain herself. "I admit that I have envisioned this conflict," she said. "But what other course could I have chosen? I knew as a rysling that I was powerful, and I saw plainly that the tabre had no good use for me."

Her blunt words pained Dacian. Where she had been practical he had been a pathetic supplicant to the ruling order. What folly!

"Why do you think rys are forbidden to go into the west?" Onja asked. Dacian, to his shame, had never much pondered the prohibition, but the reasons dawned on him as Onja explained, "The tabre know that if we were among humans outside the control of the Kwellstan Sect that we could draw power from them. And we can! They will serve us, Dacian, and give us the strength and numbers to face Nufal."

A wave of cynicism hit Dacian. "You are kind to include me in your plans," he murmured. He was disgusted with his own blindness and with the decades wasted studying to be a Nebakarz priest while Onja had followed the true path to liberty.

Pained by Dacian's self-loathing, Onja shook her head vigorously. "Oh, Dacian, I am nothing without you. The rys love you. I have focused too much on my bitterness and have spurned the kindness of other rys. But all rys admire you and you shall return to Jingten in triumph. They will greet you as their king for none are higher than you."

"A king?" Dacian asked, and when Onja explained the word of the western humans, he was intrigued. The secular title seemed peculiar. Religion bestowed authority among the tabre, but Dacian realized that he was still thinking in the old way of his unwanted masters.

"A king," Onja pledged.

With Onja close and the memory of their shared pleasures still tingling upon his spirit, Dacian brushed aside his anger with himself. His strength would expand now that he was free. Onja had broken for him a new path of confidence instead of conciliation. Dacian could still guide the rys into the better world of acceptance and respect that they deserved. But he would not do it alone.

"What is the word for she that rules at the king's side?" he said.

"A queen," she answered, claiming the title.

"Then you shall be queen," he said.

They hiked into the mountains, moving with the tireless speed of rys. As they climbed higher into the alpine forest, patches of snow appeared in the shadier places. Spring made its way slowly up the slopes. They hiked cross country until they reached the road into the only pass to the Jingten Valley. Walking in reverent silence, they passed the tree line. In the sunnier places, the snow was gone from the highland meadows and brave little flowers bloomed blue, yellow, pink, and red alongside sparkling banks of snow.

Dacian and Onja followed the road into the pass and paused as they beheld the Jingten Valley together. The town and tower beside the lake looked as it always had except that it would soon be theirs.

Between them and the town, the Tatatook flew across the sky, ominously large upon the sumptuous landscape.

The air flowing through the pass overwhelmed Dacian with its sweet scent of home. He dropped to his knees. This vision of green pines, pure water, and awesome blue stone peaks sheathed in ice had walked the gauntlet of despair with him during his trials in Kwellstan.

Onja waited for him patiently. She knew what it felt like to come home after long absence, and she had not suffered as Dacian had.

With the omnipresent chill of the mountains touching his skin, Dacian was healed by his homeland. He recovered fully inside and his hurts were banished. He was alive with vigor and grand plans, but his mind slowed to a perfect place of clarity and he contemplated his future. A choice confronted him. He could fight the tabre to a standstill and then make peace. Or, he could go farther and let vengeance have its long season of harvest upon Nufal, as it deserved. Dacian saw what the right choice was because in his heart he respected civilization, but he also understood that he was part of a greater power. He was meant to deliver upon the tabre the destiny that they had wrought.

******

Rys Rising continues in Savage Storm: Rys Rising Book II.

Please support my fiction and get the novel at www.braveluck.com.

Thank you for taking the time to read my novel.

Sincerely, Tracy Falbe

Excerpt from Savage Storm: Rys Rising Book II

"Amar. Dro-shalum. Amar. Dro-shalum."

The voices of the Kez shouted each syllable precisely as their feet pounded around the bonfire. The chanting and stomping matched the commanding pulse of the booming drums. Amar wove among the circles, taking turns in each line so that all the Kez warriors could see him and praise him. They bowed to him and extended their arms toward him without touching him while continuing in their hectic shuffling dancing lines.

Amar felt himself dissolve into the larger entity of the gathered men. All of them were together now, moving as one, feeling the drums and bound by the intoxicating joy of lawless success and the promise of more.

Witnessing the magic light that had enveloped Amar had utterly convinced the men of their warlord's greatness. None of them were mere outlaws anymore. They were now part of something extraordinary. The hardships of their lives were rendered meaningless. The amazing attention of Onja erased the shame of their crimes. The magic rys, daughter of the highest mountains, had chosen one of them as her most favored. She had not chosen a king or a priest. She would raise an outlaw above all others, and with him would be his followers.

Amar reveled in their mutual bliss. The caressing presence of Onja had renewed him physically and spiritually. He was filled with raw potent confidence. His time was at hand. As he had remade himself he would remake the world because Onja asked it.

She had praised him for the progress he had made among the Kez, but she needed more from him. Many enemies she had provoked, and she would have her human friend be as powerful as he could be.

Amar was ready to oblige. Already these warriors who had been riding with him for months were entirely his. Even those who had begun as Lax Ar Fu's spies and minions had become enamored of Amar – more of them everyday.

Amar worked his way to the bonfire. The conflagration was reaching its peak. Bright orange and yellow light illuminated Amar in his princely armor, and the heat shimmered behind him in a hot radiating halo. He turned his back to the fire and raised his arms. He shouted down the chanting, calling for his fighters to listen. His black silhouette against the glorious fire made him look like a dark demon rising from an eternally flaming pit.

"My Kez! My Kez!" he shouted until they ground to an attentive halt. The drumming quieted to a respectful yet ominous rumbling. "My Kez, you saw tonight that the rys Onja came to me," Amar said.

Everyone shouted.

"She is pleased with how we have taught the tribal kings to respect us. She is pleased, but we have more to do. Much more. The world is bigger than you know. The world is richer than you know. The day will come when Onja will show us riches and glories that will make old legends fade. What was before us will be forgotten. We will be the elite men who serve the highest power. We will be the agents of the greatest will upon Gyhwen."

******

To read Savage Storm: Rys Rising Book II please go to www.braveluck.com and support my fantasy fiction.

Sincerely, Tracy Falbe

About the Author

I've always written stories. When I was a kid I wrote stories and drew pictures for them and stapled them together to make books. My mother recently showed me one of these little books apparently based on my older brother's Dungeons & Dragons gaming.

When I was 14 I wrote a sci fi novel. When I was 15 I wrote a fantasy novel. I set them aside and never looked at them again. Then I grew up and had some adventures and became disillusioned about most everything except my dream of being a novelist. In 1997 at the age of 25 I started writing again. Now it's 2011 and I am working on my eighth novel. No publisher was ever interested in me. I stopped beating my head on that door in 2004. But rejection from people who could never care about my dream only emboldened me. I began self publishing my fantasy fiction in 2005. That was before being an indie author was cool. Despite relentless obscurity and general disrespect, I was always encouraged by a steady trickle of sales and the occasional kind comment from a reader.

To be honest, being a novelist is always a struggle. I get criticized in public and don't get called by any movie producers, but also every day someone somewhere buys my novels and that amazes me. I'm humbled by my readers. I will always do my best to craft stories worthy of them. I love the stories I write, and sometimes other people like them too. I'm having a good dream.